THE COMPLETE
ARROWS TRILOGY

MERCEDES LACKEY

THE COMPLETE
ARROWS
TRILOGY

ARROWS OF THE QUEEN

ARROW'S FLIGHT

ARROW'S FALL

DAW BOOKS, INC.
DONALD A. WOLLHEIM, FOUNDER
375 Hudson Street, New York, NY 10014

ELIZABETH R. WOLLHEIM
SHEILA E. GILBERT
PUBLISHERS
www.dawbooks.com

INTRODUCTION

I'VE BEEN AT THIS for thirty years, professionally.
Hard to believe. But there it is; I made my first professional sale in 1985, to Marion Zimmer Bradley, although my first *published* story was a Tarma and Kethry story for *Fantasy Book* magazine. What an interesting journey it has been . . . although just how old you are is really driven home to you when people who were named after your characters present their children to you.

I sold short stories while working as a computer programmer by day and writing in every bit of my free time. With the help of C. J. Cherryh, I got the manuscripts of my first books whipped into shape fit to be seen by a publisher at the same time. I went through roughly fourteen or fifteen drafts of what would become the *Arrows* trilogy before sending it to DAW. I waited nervously for the response. I expected something by mail, but instead, I got the response in person.

I was walking with C. J., Elizabeth Wollheim and her husband, and a couple of other people between hotels at the North American Science Fiction Convention in Austin, Texas. We were on our way to see the famous bat flight at sunset, and Elizabeth—Betsy—dropped back to have a word with me. "We like your books and want to buy them, but they need some work," she said, tentatively, probably waiting to see if I was going to be a diva about it or not. "Betsy," I said, trying not to run screaming in circles for joy, "if you'd told me that when I was still working on a typewriter, I'd probably slit my wrists . . . but I'm on a computer now, I'll do as many revisions as you like!"

Larry has always said that publishers are not looking for a person who can write one great book. They are looking for a person who can write a *lot* of *good* books and is easy to work with. I think that story pretty much proves him right.

So, several more revisions later, the first two books came out in 1987 and the last in 1988. It was pretty exhilarating. Don Wollheim was starting to hand off the editorial work to Betsy, and I think I was one of the first authors who she got to work with from the very beginning. Another first is that Jody Lee, who has done all my DAW covers but one ever since, got *her* first cover assignment for DAW with *Arrows of the Queen*. I was just stunned by her beautiful work, and I was even more blown away when I got to see it in person. It was all colored pencil! And it's *huge*. I think it's five feet by three feet, or thereabouts. I don't think I've ever gotten better covers than Jody's.

With those three books began a thirty year span in which I have never published less than one book a year with DAW, and generally two. This year will probably see the publication of my hundredth book, which is kind of exhilarating and kind of daunting at the same time.

Here's looking forward to another hundred!

—Mercedes Lackey
Claremore, Oklahoma

Arrows of the Queen

Dedicated
to Marion Zimmer Bradley
and Lisa Waters
who kept *telling* me I
could do this . . .

CHAPTER 1

A GENTLE BREEZE rustled the leaves of the tree, but the young girl seated beneath it did not seem to notice. An adolescent of thirteen or thereabouts, she was, by her plain costume, a member of one of the solemn and straight-laced Hold families that lived in this Borderland of Valdemar—come there to settle a bare two generations ago. She was dressed (as any young Holdgirl would be) in plain brown breeches and a long, sleeved tunic. Her unruly brown curls had been cut short in an unsuccessful attempt to tame them to conform to Hold standards. She would have presented a strange sight to anyone familiar with Holderfolk; for while she sat and carded the undyed wool she had earlier cleaned, she was reading. Few Hold girls could read, and none did so for pleasure. That was a privilege normally reserved, by long-standing tradition, for the men and boys of the Holdings. A female's place was not to be learned; a girl reading—even if she *was* doing a womanly task at the same time—was as out of place as a scarlet jay among crows.

If anyone could have seen her thoughts at that moment, they would have known her to be even more of a misfit than her reading implied.

Vanyel was a dim shape in the darkness beside her; there was no moon, and only the dim light of the stars penetrated the boughs of the hemlock bushes they hid beneath. She only knew he was there by the faint sound of his breathing, though they lay so closely together that had she moved her hand a fraction of an inch, she'd have touched him. Training and discipline held her quiet, though under other circumstances she'd have been shivering so hard her teeth would have rattled. The starlight reflected on the snow beneath them was enough to see by—enough to see the deadly danger to Valdemar that moved below them.

Beneath their ledge, in the narrow pass between Dellcrag and Mount Thurlos, the army of the Dark Servants was passing. They were nearly as silent as the two who watched them; only a creak of snow, the occasional crack of a broken branch, or the faint jingling of armor or harness betrayed them. She marveled at the discipline their silent passage revealed; marveled, and feared. How could the tiny outpost of the Border Guard that lay to the south of them ever hope to make a stand against these warriors who were also magicians? Bad enough that they were outnumbered a hundred to one—these were no simple barbarians coming against the forces of Valdemar this time, who could be defeated by their own refusal to acknowledge any one of their own as overall leader. No, these fighters bowed to an iron-willed leader the equal of any in Valdemar, and their ranks held only the trained and seasoned.

She started as Vanyel's hand lightly touched the back of her neck, and came out of her half-trance. He tugged slightly at her sleeve; she backed carefully out of the thicket, obedient to his signal.

"Now what?" she whispered, when they were safely around the ledge with the bulk of a stone outcropping between them and the Dark Servants.

"One of us has to alert the King, while the other holds them off at the other end of the pass—"

"With what army?" she asked, fear making her voice sharp with sarcasm.

"You forget, little sister—I need no army—" the sudden flare of light from Vanyel's outstretched hand illuminated his ironic smile, and bathed his white uniform in an eerie blue wash for one moment. She shuddered; his saturnine features had always looked faintly sinister to her, and in the blue light his face had looked demonic. Vanyel held a morbid fascination for her—dangerous, the man was; not like his gentle lifemate, Bard Stefen. Possibly the last—and some said the best—of the Herald-mages. The Servants of Darkness had destroyed the others, one by one. Only Vanyel had been strong enough to withstand their united powers. She who had little magic in her soul could almost feel the strength of his even when he wasn't exerting it.

"Between us, my Companion and I are a match for any thousand of their witch-masters," he continued arrogantly. "Besides—at the far end of the pass there isn't room for more than three to walk side by side. We can hold them there easily. And I want Stefen well out of this; Yfandes couldn't carry us double, but you're light enough that Evalie could easily manage both of you."

She bowed her head, yielding to his reasoning. "I can't like it—"

"I know, little sister—but you have precious little magic, while Evalie does have speed. The sooner you go, the sooner you'll have help here for me."

"Vanyel—" she touched his gloved hand with one fur mitten. "Be—be safe—" She suddenly feared more for him than for herself. He had looked so fey when the King had placed this mission in their hands—like a man who has seen his own death.

"As safe as may be, little sister. I swear to you, I will risk nothing I am not forced to."

A heartbeat later she was firmly in the saddle, Evalie galloping beneath her like a blizzard wind in horse-shape. Behind her she could feel Bard Stefen clinging to her waist, and was conscious of a moment of pity for him—to him, Evalie was strange, he could not move with her, only cling awkwardly; while she felt almost as one with the Companion, touched with a magic only another Herald could share.

Their speed was reckless; breakneck. Skeletal tree limbs reached hungrily for them, trying to seize them as they passed and pull them from Evalie's back. Always the Companion avoided them, writhing away from the clawlike branches like a ferret.

"The Dark Servants—" Stefen shouted in her ear "—they must know someone's gone for help. They're animating the trees against us!"

She realized, as Evalie escaped yet another trap set for them, that Stefen was right—the trees were indeed moving with a will of their own, and not just randomly waving in the wind. They reached out, hungrily, angrily; she felt the hot breath of dark magic on the back of her neck, like the noisome breath of a carrion-eater. Evalie's eyes were wide with more than fear; she knew the Companion felt the dark power, too.

She urged Evalie on; the Companion responded with new speed, sweat breaking out on her neck and flanks to freeze almost immediately. The trees seemed to thrash with anger and frustration as they eluded the last of them and broke out on the bank above the road.

The road to the capital lay straight and open before them now, and Evalie leaped over a fallen forest giant to gain the surface of it with a neigh of triumph. . . .

Talia blinked, emerging abruptly from the spell her book had laid on her. She had been lost in the daydream her tale had conjured for her, but the dream was now lost beyond recall. Someone was calling her name in the distance. She looked up quickly, with a toss of her head that threw her unmanageable hair out of her eyes. Near the door of the family house she could make out the angular figure of Keldar First-wife, dark-clad and rigid, like a stiff fire iron propped against the building. Keldar's fists were on her hips; her stern carriage suggested that she was waiting Talia's response with very little patience.

Talia sighed regretfully, put up her wool and the wire brushes, and closed the worn little cloth-bound volume, laying aside the rocks she'd used to hold down the pages as she'd worked. Though she'd carefully marked the place, she knew that even without the precious scrap of ribbon she used to mark it she'd have no trouble finding it again. Keldar couldn't have picked a worse time; Herald Vanyel was alone, surrounded by the Servants of Darkness, and no one knew his peril but his Companion and Bard Stefen. Knowing Keldar, it would be hours before she could return to the tale—perhaps not even until tomorrow. Keldar was adept at finding ways to keep Talia from even the little reading she was grudgingly allowed.

Nevertheless, Keldar was Firstwife; her voice ruled the Steading, to be obeyed in all things, or suffer punishment for disobedience. Talia responded to the summons as dutifully as she could. She put the little book carefully away in the covered basket that held carded and uncarded wool and her spindle. The peddler who had given it to her last week had assured her many times that it was worthless to *him*, but it was still precious to her as one of the three books she owned and (more importantly) the only one she'd never read before. For an hour this afternoon she'd been transported to the outside world of Heralds and Companions, of high adventure and magic. Returning to the ordinary world of chores and Keldar's sour face was a distinct letdown. She schooled her expression with care, hoping none of her discontent showed, and trudged dully up the path that led to the Steading, carrying her basket in one hand.

But she had the sinking feeling as she watched the Firstwife's hardening expression that her best efforts were not enough to mislead Keldar.

Keldar noted the signs of rebellion Talia displayed despite her obvious effort to hide them. The signs were plain enough for anyone with the Firstwife's experience in dealing with littles; the slightly dragging feet, the sullen eyes. Her mouth tightened imperceptibly. Thirteen years old, and *still* fighting the yoke the gods had decreed for her shoulders! Well, that would change—and soon. Soon enough there would be no more time for foolish tales and wasted time.

"Stop scowling, child!" Keldar snapped, her thin lips taut with scorn, "You're not being summoned for a beating!"

Not that she hadn't warranted a beating to correct her attitude in the past. Those beatings had done precious little good, and had drawn the feeble protests of her Husband's Mother—but it was the will of the gods that children *obey*, and if it took beating to drive them into obedience, then one would beat them with as heavy a hand as required, and pray that *this* time the lesson was learned.

It was possible that she, Keldar, had not possessed a hand heavy enough. Well, if that were indeed the case, *that* situation would be corrected soon as well.

She watched the child trudge unwillingly up the path, her feet kicking up little puffs of dust. Keldar was well aware that her attitude where Talia was concerned was of a harshness that bordered on the unfair. Still, the child drove her out of all patience. Who would ever have imagined that so placid and bovine a creature as Bessa could have produced a little scrap of mischief like this? The child was like a wild thing sometimes, intractable, and untamable—how *could* Bessa have dared to birth such a misfit? And who would have thought that she'd have had the poor taste to die of the birthing and leave the rearing of her little to the rest of the Wives?

Talia was so unlike her birth-mother that Keldar was perforce reminded of the stories of changelings. And the child *had* been born on Midsummer's Eve, a time long noted for arcane connections—she as little resembled the strong, tall, blond man who was her father as her plump, fair, deceased mother—

But no. That was superstition, and superstition had no place in the lives of Holderkin. It was only that she had double the usual share of stubbornness. Even the most stubborn of saplings could be bent. Or broken.

And if Keldar lacked the necessary tools to accomplish the breaking and bending, there were others among the Holderkin who suffered no such lack.

"Get *along*, child!" she added, when Talia didn't respond immediately, "Or do you think I need hurry your steps with a switch?"

"Yes ma'am. I mean, no ma'am!" Talia replied in as neutral a voice as she could manage. She tried to smooth her expression into one more pleasing to her elder, even as she smoothed the front of her tunic with a sweaty, nervous palm.

What am I being summoned for? she wondered apprehensively. In her experience summonings had rarely meant anything good.

"Well, go in, go in! Don't keep me standing here in the doorway all afternoon!" Keldar's cold face gave no clue as to what was in store. Everything about Keldar, from her tightly wrapped and braided hair to the exact set of her apron, gave an impression of one in total control.

She was everything a Firstwife should be—and frequently pointed this out. Talia was always intimidated by her presence, and always felt she looked hoydenish and disheveled, no matter how carefully she'd prepared herself for confrontations.

In her haste to edge past the authoritative figure of the Firstwife in the doorway, Talia stumbled a little on the lintel. Keldar made a derogatory noise in the back of her throat, and Talia felt herself flush. Somehow there was that about Keldar that never failed to put her at her faultiest and clumsiest. She regathered what little composure she had and slipped inside and into the hall. The windowless entryway was very dark; she would have paused to let her eyes adjust except for the forbidding presence of Keldar hard on her heels. She felt her way down the worn, wooden floor hoping not to trip again. Then, as she entered the common-room and could see again in the light that came from its three windows, her mouth suddenly dried with fear; for *all* of her Father's Wives were waiting there, assembled around the rough-hewn wooden table that served them all at meals. And all of them were staring at her. Eight pairs of blue and brown eyes held her transfixed like a bird surrounded by hungry cats. Eight flat, expressionless faces had turned to point in her direction.

She thought at once of all her failings of the last month or so, from her failure to remember her kitchen duties yesterday to the disaster with the little she was supposed to have been watching who'd gotten into the goat pen. There were half a hundred things they might call her to account for, but none of them were bad enough to call for an assemblage of *all* the Wives; at least, she didn't *think* they were!

Unless—she started guiltily at the thought—unless they'd somehow found out she'd been sneaking into Father's library to read when there was a full moon—light enough to read without a betraying candle. Father's books were mostly religious, but she'd found an old history or two that proved to be almost as good as her tales, and the temptation had been too much to resist. If they'd found that out—

It might mean a beating every day for a week and a month of "exile"—being locked in a closet at night, and isolated by day, with no one allowed to speak to her or acknowledge her presence in any way, except Keldar, who would assign her chores. That had happened twice already this year. Talia began to tremble. She wasn't sure she could bear a third time.

Keldar took her place at the head of the table, and her next words drove all thought of that out of Talia's head. "Well, child," she said, scowling, "You're thirteen today."

Talia felt almost giddy with relief. Just her Birthing Day? Was *that* all it was? She took an easier breath, and stood before the assemblage of nine Wives, much calmer now. She kept her hands clasped properly before her, eyes cast down. She studied the basket at her sturdily-shod feet, prepared to listen with all due respect to the lecture about her growing responsibilities that they'd delivered to her every Birthing Day she could remember. After they were sure that she'd absorbed all their collective wisdom on the subject, they'd let her get back to her wool (and not so incidentally, her tale).

But what Keldar had to say next scattered every speck of calm she'd regained to the four winds.

"Yes, thirteen," Keldar repeated significantly, "and that is time to think of Marriage."

Talia blanched, feeling as if her heart had stopped. Marriage? Oh, sweet Goddess *no!*

Keldar seemingly paid no heed to Talia's reaction; a flicker of her eyes betrayed that she'd seen it, but she went callously on with her planned speech. "You're not ready for it, of course, but no girl is. Your courses have been regular for more than a year now, you're healthy and strong. There's no reason why you couldn't be a mother before the year is out. It's more than time you were in a Household as a Wife. Your Honored Father is dowering you with three *whole fields,* so your portion is quite respectable."

Keldar's faintly sour expression seemed to indicate that she felt Talia's dower to be excessive. The hands clasping the edge of the table before her tightened as the other Wives murmured appreciation of their Husband's generosity.

"Several Elders have already bespoken your Father about you, either as a Firstwife for one of their sons or as an Underwife for themselves. In spite of your unwomanly habits of reading and writing, we've trained you well. You can cook and clean, sew, weave and spin, and you're trustworthy with the littlest littles. You're not up to managing a Household yet, but you won't be called to do that for several years. Even if you go to a young man as his Firstwife, you'll be living in your Husband's Father's Household. So you're prepared enough to do your duty."

Keldar seemed to feel that she'd said all she needed to, and sat down, hands folded beneath her apron, back ramrod straight. Underwife Isrel waited for her nod of delegation, then took up the thread of the lecture on a daughter's options.

Isrel was easily dominated by Keldar, and Talia had always consid-

ered her to be more than a little silly. The Underwife looked to Keldar
with calf-like brown eyes for approval of everything she said—nor did
she fail to do so now. She glanced at Keldar after every other word she
spoke.

"There's advantages to both, you know; being a Firstwife and being
an Underwife, I mean. If you're Firstwife, eventually your Husband
will start his own Steading and Household, and you'll be First in it. But
if you're an Underwife, you won't have to ever make any decisions.
And you'll be in an established Household and Steading—you won't
have to scrimp and scant, there won't be any hardships. You won't have
to worry about anything except the tasks you're set and bearing your
littles. We don't want you to be *unhappy*, Talia. We want to give you
the choice of the life you think you're best suited for. Not the *man* of
course," she giggled nervously. "That would be unseemly, and besides
you probably don't know any of them anyway."

"Isrel!" Keldar snapped, and Isrel shrank into herself a little. "That last
remark was unseemly, and not suited to a girl's ears! Now, child, which
shall it be?"

Goddess! Talia wanted to die, to turn into a bird, to sink into the
floor—anything but this! Trapped; she was trapped. They'd Marry her
off and she'd end up like Nada, beaten every night so that she had to
wear high-necked tunics to hide the bruises. Or she'd die like her own
mother, worn out with too many babies too quickly. Or even if the impossible happened, and her Husband was kind or too stupid to be a danger, her *real* life, the tales that were all that made living worthwhile,
would all but disappear, for there would be no time for them in the
never-ending round of pregnancy and a Wife's duties—

Before she could stop herself, Talia blurted out, "I don't want to be
Married at all!"

The little rustlings and stirrings of a group of bored women suddenly ceased, and they became as still as a row of fenceposts, all with
disbelief on their faces. Nine identical expressions of shock and dismay
stared at Talia from the sides of the table. The silence closed down
around her like the hand of doom.

"Talia, dear," a soft voice spoke behind her, breaking the terrible
silence, and Talia turned with relief to face Father's Mother, who had
been sitting unnoticed in the corner. She was one of the few people in
Talia's life who never seemed to think that everything she did was
wrong. Her kind, faded blue eyes were the only ones in the room not
full of accusation. The old woman smoothed one braid of cloud-white
hair with age-spotted hands in unconscious habit, as she continued.

"May the Mother forgive us, but we never thought to ask you. Have you a vocation? Has the Goddess Called you to her service?"

Talia had been hoping for a reprieve, but that, if anything, was worse. Talia thought with horror of the one glimpse she'd had of the Temple Cloisters, of the women there who spent their lives in prayer for the souls of the Holderkin. The utterly silent women, who went muffled from head to toe, forbidden to leave, forbidden to speak, forbidden—life!—had horrified her. It was a worse trap than Marriage; the very memory of the Cloisters made her feel as if she was being smothered.

She shook her head frantically, unable to talk around the lump in her throat.

Keldar rose from her place with the scrape of a stool on the rough wooden floor and advanced on the terrified child, who was as unable to move as a mouse between the paws of a cat. Keldar took her shoulders with a grip that bruised as it made escape impossible and shook her till her teeth rattled. "What's *wrong* with you, girl?" she said angrily, "You don't want an Honorable Marriage, you don't want the Peace of the Goddess, what *do* you want?"

All I want is to be left alone, Talia thought with quiet desperation, *I don't want anything to change*—but her traitorous mouth opened again and let the dream spill.

"I want to be a Herald," she heard herself say.

Keldar released her shoulders quickly, with a look of near-horror as if she'd discovered she'd been holding something vile, something that had crawled out of the midden.

"You—you—" For once, the controlled Keldar was at a loss for words. Then—"*Now* you see what comes of coddling a brat!" she said, turning on Father's Mother in default of anyone else to use as a scapegoat. "*This* is what happens when you let a girl rise above her place. Reading! Figuring! No girl needs to know more than she requires to label her preserves and count her stores or keep the peddlers from cheating her! I told you this would happen, you and your precious Andrean, letting her fill her head with foolish tales!" She turned back to face Talia. "*Now*, girl—when I finish with you—"

But Talia was gone.

She had taken advantage of the distraction of Keldar's momentary tirade to escape. Scampering quickly out the door before any of the Wives realized she was missing, she fled the Steading as fast as she could run. Sobbing hysterically, she had no thought except to get away. With the wind in her face, and sweating with fear, she ran past the barns and the stockade, pure terror giving her feet extra speed. She fled through the fields as the waist-high hay and grain beat against her, and up into the woodlot and through it, following a tangled path through the uncut underbrush. She was seeking the shelter of the hiding place she'd found, the place that no one else knew of.

There was a steep bluff where the woodlot ended high above the Road. Two years ago, Talia had found a place where something had carved out a kind of shallow cave beneath the protruding roots of a tree that grew at the very edge of the bluff. She'd lined it with filched straw and old rugs meant for the rag-bag; she kept her other two books hidden there. She had spent many hours stolen from her chores there, daydreaming, invisible from above or below so long as she stayed quiet and still. She sought this sanctuary now, and scrambling over the edge of the bluff, crept into it. She buried herself in the rugs, crying hysterically, limp with exhaustion, nerves practically afire, ears stretched for the tiniest sound above her.

For no matter how deep her misery, she knew she must keep alert for the sounds of searchers. Before very long, she heard the sound of some of the servants calling her name. When they drew too near, she stifled her sobs in the rugs while her tears fell silently, listening in fear for some sign telling her she'd been discovered. She thought a dozen times that they'd found some sign of her passage, but they seemed to have lost her track. Eventually they went away, and she was free to cry as she would.

Wrapped in pure misery, she hugged her knees to her chest and rocked back and forth, weeping until her eyes were too dry and sore to shed another tear. She felt numb all over, too numb to think properly. Any choice she made seemed worse than the one before it. Should she return and apologize, any punishment she'd ever had before would seem a pleasure to the penance Keldar was likely to devise for her unseemly and insubordinate behavior. It would be Keldar's choice, and her Father's, what would befall her then. Any Husband Keldar would choose now would be—horrid. She'd either be shackled to some drooling old dotard, to be pawed over by night and to be a nursemaid by day—or she'd be given to some brutal, younger man, a cruel one, with instructions to break her to seemly behavior. Keldar would likely pick one as sadistic as Justus, her older brother—she shuddered, as the unbidden memory came to her, of him standing over her with the hot poker in his hand and the look on his face of fierce pleasure—

She forced the memory away, quickly.

But even that fate would be a pleasurable experience compared to what would happen if they decided to offer her as a Temple Servant.

The Goddess's Servants had even less freedom and more duties than Her Handmaidens. They lived and died never going beyond the cloister corridor to which they were assigned. And in any case, no matter what future they picked for her, her reading, her escape, would be over. Keldar would see to it that she never saw another book again.

For one moment, she contemplated running away, truly fleeing the Steading and the Holderkin. Then she recalled the faces of the wandering laborers she'd seen at Hiring Fairs; pinched, hungry, desperate for anyone to take them into a Holding. And she'd never seen a woman among them. The "foolish tales" she'd read made one thing very clear, the life of a wanderer was dangerous and sometimes fatal for the unprepared, the defenseless. What preparation had she? She had the clothing she stood up in, the ragged rugs, and nothing else. How could she defend herself? She'd never even been taught how to use a knife. She'd be ready prey.

If only this were a tale—

An unfamiliar voice called her name—a voice full of calm authority, and she found herself answering it, climbing out of her hiding place almost against her will. And there before her, waiting at the top of the bluff—

A Herald; resplendent and proud in her Whites, her Companion a snowy apparition beside her, mane and tail lifting in the gentle breeze like the finest silk. Sunlight haloed and hallowed both of them, making them seem more than mortal. She looked to Talia like the statue of the Lady come to life—only proud, strong and proud, not meek and submissive. Behind the Herald, looking cowed and ashamed, were Keldar and her Father.

"You are Talia?" the Herald asked, and she nodded affirmatively.

She broke out in a smile that dazzled her—it was like a sudden appearance of the sun after rain.

"Blessed is the Lady who led us here!" she exclaimed. "Many the weary months we have searched for you, and always in vain. We had nothing to go on except your name—"

"Led you to me?" she asked, exalted, "But, why?"

"To make you one of us, little sister," she replied, as Keldar shrank into herself and her Father seemed bent on studying the tops of his shoes. "You are to be a Herald, Talia—the gods themselves have decreed it. Look—yonder comes your Companion—"

She looked where the Herald pointed, and saw a graceful white mare with a high, arched neck and a knowing eye pacing deliberately toward her. The Companion was caparisoned all in blue and silver, tiny bells hanging from her reins and bridle. Behind the Companion, at a respectful distance, came all her sibs, the rest of the Wives, and all the servants of the Holding.

With a glad cry, she ran to meet the mare and the Herald helped her to
mount up on the Companion's back, while the Hold servants cheered, her sibs
stared in sullen respect, and Keldar and her Father stared at her in plain fear,
obviously thinking of all the punishments they'd meted out to HER and expect-
ing the same now that she was the one in power—

The sound of hoofbeats on the Road broke into her desperate daydream. For one panicked moment she thought it was another searcher,
but then she realized that her Father's horses sounded nothing like this.
These hoofbeats had a chime like bells on the hard surface. As the
sound drew nearer, it was joined by another; the sound of real bells, of
bridle bells. Only one kind of horse wore bridle bells every day, and
not just on Festival Days—the magical steed of legend, a Herald's
Companion.

Talia had never seen a real Herald, though she'd daydreamed about
them constantly. The realization that she was finally going to see one
of her dreams in actual fact startled her out of her fantasy and her tears
completely. The distraction was too tempting to resist. For just this one
moment she would forget her troubles, her hopeless position, and
snatch a tiny bit of magic for herself, to treasure all her days. She leaned
out of her cave, stretching as far out as she could, thinking of nothing
except to catch a glimpse—and leaned out too far.

She lost her balance, and her flailing hands caught nothing but air.
She tumbled end over end down the bluff, banging painfully into roots
and rocks. The wind was knocked out of her before she was halfway
down, and nothing she collided with seemed to slow her descent any.
She was totally unable to stop her headlong tumble until she landed on
the hard surface of the Road itself, with a force that set sparks to dancing in front of her eyes and left her half-stunned.

When the grayness cleared away from her vision and she could get a
breath again, she found herself sprawled face downward on the Road.
Her hands were scraped, her sides bruised, her knees full of gravel, and
her eyes full of dirt. When she turned her head to the side, blinking
tears away, she found she was gazing at four silver hooves.

She gave a strangled gasp and scrambled painfully to her feet. Regarding her with a gentle curiosity was a—well, a Herald's Companion
was hardly what one would call a "horse." They transcended horses in
the way that panthers transcend alleycats, or angels transcend men.
Talia had read and heard plenty of descriptions of the Companions
before, but she was still totally unprepared for the close-hand reality.

The riderless Companion was in full formal array, his trappings silver and sky-blue, his reins hung with silver bridle bells. No horse in

Talia's experience had that slender, yet muscular grace or could match the way he seemed to fly without taking a single step. He was white—Companions were always white—but nothing on earth could possibly match that glowing, living, radiant white. And his eyes—

When Talia finally had the courage to look into those sapphire eyes, she lost track of the world—

She was lost in blue more vast than a sea and darker than sky and full of welcome so heart-filling it left no room for doubt.

Yes—at last—you. I Choose you. Out of all the world, out of all the seeking, I have found you, young sister of my heart! You are mine and I am yours—and never again will there be loneliness—

It was a feeling more than words; a shock and a delight. A breathless joy so deep it was almost pain; a joining. A losing and a finding; a loosing and a binding. Flight and freedom. And love and acceptance past all words to tell of the wonder of it—and she answered that love with all her soul.

Now forget, little one. Forget until you are ready to remember again.

Blinking, she came back to herself, with a feeling that something tremendous had happened, though she didn't know quite what. She shook her head—there had been—it was—but whatever had happened had receded just out of memory, though she had the odd feeling it might come back when she least expected it to. But for now there was a soft nose nudging her chest, and the Companion was whickering gently at her.

It was as though someone were putting loving arms about her, and urging her to cry all her unhappiness out. She flung both her arms around his neck and wept unrestrainedly into his silky mane. The feeling of being held and comforted intensified as soon as she touched him, and she lost herself in the unfamiliar but welcome sensation. Unlike her lone crying in her cave, this session of tears brought peace in its wake, and before too long she was able to dry her eyes on a corner of her tunic and take heed of her surroundings again.

She let go of his neck with reluctance, and took another long look at him. For one wild moment, she was tempted to leap into his empty saddle. She had a vision of herself riding away, far away; *anywhere*, so long as it was away from here and she was with him. The temptation was so great it left her shaking. Then practicality reasserted itself. Where could she go? And besides—

"You've run away from someone, haven't you?" she said quietly to the Companion, who only blew into her jerkin in answer. "I can't have you, you could only belong to a Herald. I'll—" she gulped. There was a huge lump in her throat and tears threatened again at the idea of parting with him. Never, ever in her short life had she wanted anything as much as the way she wanted to—to—be his, and he hers! "I'll have to take you back to whoever you belong to."

A new thought occurred to her, and for the first time that afternoon, hope brightened her for a moment as she saw a way out of her dilemma. "Maybe—maybe they'll be grateful. Maybe they'll let me work for them. They must need *someone* to do their cooking and sewing and things. I'd do anything for Heralds." The soft blue eyes seemed to agree that this was a good idea. "They're bound to be nicer than Keldar—they're so kind and wise in all the tales. I bet they'd let me read when I wasn't working. I'd get to see Heralds all the time—" Tears lumped her throat again, "—maybe they'd let me see you, once in a while."

The Companion only whickered again, and stretching his neck out, nudged her with his velvet nose toward his saddle, maneuvering for her to mount.

"Me?" she squeaked. "I couldn't—" Suddenly, the reality of what *he* was and what *she* was came home to her. All very well to dream of leaping on his back; but in cold, sober reflection the very idea that she, grubby and ordinary, should sit in the saddle of a Companion shocked her.

The enormous, vivid blue eyes looked back at her with a trace of impatience. One hoof stamped with a certain imperiousness, and he shook his mane at her. His whole manner said as clearly as speech that he thought her scruples were ridiculous. After all, who was going to see her? And now that she thought about it, it was quite possible that he had come from a goodly distance away; if she insisted on walking, it was likely to take forever to return him.

"Are you sure you don't mind? That it's all right?" She spoke in a timid voice, unmindful of the incongruity of asking a horse for advice.

He tossed his head impatiently, and the bridle bells rang. There was little doubt that he felt she was being excessively silly.

"You're right," she said in sudden decision, and mounted.

Talia was no stranger to riding. She'd done so every chance she could, often sneaking rides when no one was looking. She'd ridden every horse of an age to bear her weight, broken or not, saddled or bareback. She was the oldest of the littles on the Holding, and hence the only one considered responsible enough to be sent to other Elders with messages or to the village on errands. She was usually a-horseback at least once a week legitimately. She was generally found sneaking rides at least three or four times that often.

But riding a Companion was nothing like any riding she'd ever done. His pace was so smooth a true little could have stayed in his saddle without falling, and if she'd closed her eyes she'd never have guessed he was more than ambling along. Her Father's beasts had to be goaded constantly to maintain more than a walk; of his own volition the Companion had moved into a canter, and it was faster than the fastest gallop she'd ever coaxed out of any of *them*. The sweet air flowed past her like the water of the river, and it blew her hair back out of her face. The intoxication of it drove all thought of anything else clean out of her mind. It was as if the wind rushing past them had swept all her unhappiness right out of her and left it behind in an untidy heap in the center of the Road.

If this was a daydream, she hoped she'd die in the middle of it and never have to wake to the dreary world again.

CHAPTER 2

◄———◄◄ ►►———►

WITHIN A SINGLE candlemark they were farther from her Father's Holding than Talia had ever been before. The Road here ran parallel to the River; on one side of it was the steep bluff crowned with trees and brush, on the other was a gentler drop-off down to the River. The River here was wide and very slow; Talia could see glimpses of the farther bank through the trees that grew at her edge of it. These trees were huge willows that made a living screen with their drooping branches. There was no sign of any human habitation. All she could hear was birdsong and the sounds of insects in the branches overhead and to either side. All she could see were the trees and the occasional glimpse of the River, and the Road stretching on ahead. Although she couldn't be entirely sure, Talia had a notion that the lands of the Holderkin were now all behind her.

The sun was still relatively high, and its warmth was very pleasant, not harsh as it would be later in the summer. The Road's surface was of some material she had never seen before, since she had never actually dared to venture down to the Road itself even once in her life, and there was little or no dust. The scent of green growing things on the breeze was like wine to her, and she drank in every bit of her experience greedily. At any moment now she might come upon the Herald this Companion rightfully belonged to; her adventure would be over, and it wasn't likely she'd ever get to ride a Companion again. Every moment was precious and must be stored away in her memory against the future.

As candlemarks passed and no Herald—in fact, nothing more than a squirrel or two—came into view, Talia began to fall into a kind of trance; the steady pace of the Companion and the Road stretching ahead of her was hypnotic. Something comforting just at the edge of her awareness lulled her into tranquility. She was lost in this trance for some time, and only came back to herself when the setting sun struck her full in the eyes. Her anxieties and fears had somehow disappeared while she'd ridden unmindful of her surroundings. Now there was only a calm, and a feeling of rightness about this journey—and a tentative feeling of excitement. But night was coming on fast, and she and the Companion were still alone together on the Road.

The shape of the landscape had changed while she rode unaware. The double drop-off had leveled off, very gradually, so gradually that she hadn't noticed it. Now the woods and fields to her right were level with the surface of the Road, and the Road itself was only a foot or two above the lapping surface of the water. The River was a scant two horse-lengths away from the verge of the Road. The land had flattened out so much that Talia knew for certain she was no longer even close to the lands belonging to the Holderfolk that lay on the Border of the Kingdom.

"Are we going to travel all night?" she asked the Companion, who cocked his ears back to catch her words. He whuffed, shook his head, and slowed to a walk. Now she could hear the sounds that birds make only when they're preparing to roost; quiet, sleepy little chirrups and half-calls. The Companion seemed to be looking for something on the woodward side of the Road; at least that was the impression Talia got. Just as the setting sun began to dye his white coat a bright scarlet, he seemed to spot what he was looking for. With no warning, he sped up and trotted right off the Road and down a path into the woods.

"Where are you going?" she cried.

He just shook his head and kept to the path. The trees were far too thick on either side for her to even think of trying to jump off. The underbrush was thick and full of shadows that made her fears reawaken. She had no idea what might be lurking in the growth beneath the trees. There could be thorns there, or stenchbeetles, or worse. Biting her lip in vexation and worry, she could only cling to the saddle and wait.

The path abruptly widened into a clearing, and in the center of the clearing was a small building; only a single room, and windowless, but with a chimney. It was very clearly well-maintained, and just as clearly vacant. With a surge of relief, Talia recognized it from her reading as a Herald's Waystation.

"I'm sorry," she said contritely to the ears that were swiveled back to catch her words, "You *did* know what you were doing, didn't you?"

The Companion only slowed to a stop, pivoted neatly before the door of the Waystation, shook his forelock out of his eyes and waited for her to dismount.

The tales she'd read were a great help here; Talia knew exactly what she'd find and approximately where to find it. She swung her leg carefully over the Companion's back and slid slowly to the ground. Moving quickly (she discovered with a touch of dismay) wasn't possible. She'd never spent this much time in a saddle before, and her legs were feeling very stiff, and a little sore and shaky.

She knew that her first duty was to see to the needs of the Companion. She unsaddled him quickly, and noticed with a start of surprise as she removed the bridle that it had no bit, being little more than an elaborate hackamore. There was no way that it could "control" him, not unless his Herald had the strength of arm to wrench his head around by main force. It was a most peculiar piece of tack—and what it implied was even more peculiar.

She stacked the tack carefully by the door of the Waystation, then lifted the latch and peered around inside. There was just enough daylight left for her to locate what she was looking for; a tinderbox on a shelf just inside the door.

She laid tinder and cautiously lit a very small fire in the fireplace; just enough to give light to see. With the interior of the Waystation illuminated, Talia was able to locate her second requirement; rags to clean the tack, and a currycomb to groom the Companion.

He stood far more placidly than any of her Father's horses while she groomed every last speck of sweat and dust from his coat. When she'd clearly finished with him he cantered to the center of the clearing for a brisk roll in the grass. She giggled to see him drop his dignity and act so very horselike, particularly after the way he'd been acting up until this point—almost as if it was *he* that was taking *her* to someone. She cleaned the tack just as carefully as she'd cleaned him, with a sensuous enjoyment of the leathery scent. She put it just inside the door where the dew wouldn't reach it. There had been two buckets next to the pile of rags; in the blue dusk she hurried down to the river with them while she could still see. The Companion came with her, weeds whisking his legs and hers, following her like a puppy, and drank his fill while she filled the buckets.

The delightful feel of the cool water around her feet reminded her how grubby and sticky she was. There had been first her run through the woods, followed by the fall down the bank, then the long ride to ensure that she needed a bath. And part of the regime of any Holdchild was an almost painful devotion to cleanliness. Talia was more used to feeling scoured than dirty, and fastidiously preferred the former sensation.

"You may be a Companion," she told the watching stallion, "but you still smell like a horse, and now so do I. Do you think it would be safe to bathe here?"

The Companion whickered, then took a few steps away from her and pawed with his hoof at the edge of the water, nodding his head as if to be certain she caught his meaning. She went to where he was standing, and peered through the gathering darkness down into the waterweeds.

"Oh!" she cried delightedly, "Soaproot! It must be all right then; Heralds wouldn't plant soaproot where it wasn't safe to bathe."

Without another thought, she stripped down to the bare skin. She started to pile her clothing on the bank, but changed her mind, and took it into the water with her. It would probably dry wrinkled, but wrinkles were better than dirt.

The water was sun-warmed, like silk against her bare skin, and the bottom here was sandy rather than muddy. She splashed and swam like a young otter, enjoying the sensation of being able to skinswim like a little without wondering what Keldar would do if she caught her. It occurred to Talia that her bridges were all burned now, for certain sure. No female of marriageable age gone overnight without leave would ever be accepted back into the Holding as anything but a drudge, and that only if the Husband and Firstwife were feeling magnanimous. For one moment Talia felt frightened by the idea, for after her performance of this afternoon no one at the Holding was likely to feel generosity on her behalf—but then her eyes fell on the luminous white form of the Companion waiting for her on the bank, and she decided that she should make up her mind not to care, not even a little bit.

When she'd scrubbed herself and her clothing with clean sand and soaproot and the air was beginning to feel chilly, she decided she'd had enough. The Companion continued to follow her all the way back to the shelter, and once they'd reached their goal, he nudged her toward the door with his nose and whickered in entreaty. There was no doubt in Talia's mind as to what he wanted, and it no longer seemed odd to be taking her direction from him.

"Greedy!" she chuckled, "Want your supper, do you? *That* should teach you not to run away, Rolan!"

She paused then, and frowned a little in concentration. "Now where did I get that name?" she wondered aloud. She gazed at the moonlight-dappled Companion, who stood easily, ears cocked forward, watching her. "From you? Is that your name? Rolan?"

For a moment she felt disoriented, as if seeing through someone else's eyes. It almost seemed as if she and something else were briefly joined as one—it was uncanny, and yet not at all frightening. Then the moment passed.

"Well, I suppose I have to call you *something*, no matter where the name came from. Just let me put my things up to dry and go back for the buckets, Rolan. Then I'll get supper for both of us."

She poured a generous measure of grain for him, then took a fire-blackened pot she'd seen earlier to make a grain-and-fruit porridge for herself. Rolan finished his own portion before her porridge was done and moved closer to lie in the grass an arm's length off from her with every sign of content. Insects sang in the woods all around them, and leaves rustled slightly. The firelight shone on Rolan's coat as she leaned up against the Waystation wall, feeling oddly happy.

"What I don't understand," she said to him, "is why you ran away. Companions aren't supposed to do that sort of thing, are they?"

Rolan simply opened his eyes wide at her and looked wise.

"I hope you know where we're going because I certainly don't. Still, we're bound to meet a Herald sometime, and I'm sure he'll know what to do with you."

The porridge looked and smelled done; she pulled the pot out of the fire with a branch and began to eat it with her fingers as soon as it had cooled enough.

"It really is strange, you coming along when you did," she told him. "I expect I'd have been found before dark or gotten resigned to the situation and gone back to the Holding myself." She regarded him with speculative eyes. "I don't suppose—you didn't come to *rescue* me, did you? No, that's ridiculous. I'm not a Herald, I'm just Holderkin; just strange Talia. Why would you want to rescue me? Besides, if you'd meant to rescue me, you would have brought your Herald along, wouldn't you?" She sighed, a little sadly. "I wish *I* was your Herald. I'd like to live like this always."

Rolan's eyes were closed, and his head nodded. Now that her stomach was comfortably full, Talia found her own head beginning to nod. The woods were very dark, the ground beneath her was very hard, and the interior of the Waystation looked very inviting to a girl who'd seldom spent a night out under the sky, and never alone.

"Well, if you're going to go to sleep, I'd better do the same."

She banked the fire, covering the pot of porridge with the coals and ashes to keep the rest of it warm for breakfast, then pulled up armfuls of the long grass to use to fill the bedbox. It didn't take very long; once she'd settled, Rolan moved to lie across the door, almost like a guard dog. It seemed to her that she'd no sooner tumbled into it, than she was fast asleep.

She woke to the sound of birdsong with Rolan standing in the Waystation beside the bedbox nudging her shoulder. For one moment she couldn't remember exactly where she was, confused with sleep; then with full awareness it all came back with a rush. She jumped out of her nest of sweet-smelling grasses to hug Rolan's neck, overwhelmed with thankfulness that it hadn't all been a dream.

She ate her breakfast quickly, then cleaned herself and the shelter to the best of her ability. She buried the ashes of the dead fire with a little twinge of guilt; she knew that etiquette demanded that she replace the wood she'd used, but without an axe, that simply wasn't possible. She'd have felt a lot guiltier had it been Midwinter instead of Midsummer, and she'd really used very little of what seemed to be a plentiful supply. Once all was in as good order as she'd found it, she saddled Rolan and they trotted back to the Road.

The morning passed swiftly. Not only was every moment with Rolan a delight and a treasure, but now there was more to see as well. The dense woods began to give way to cultivated fields; in the distance she saw stock grazing, and once or twice a cottage, shaded by trees and cooled by ivy. Then, just after the sun crossed overhead, the Road curved and dove down into a village, set in a small valley.

Talia couldn't help but stare about her with amazed eyes; this village was very different from the one she'd lived near all her life. The Holderfolk wore nothing but somber colors, nothing gayer than a dull saffron; but here it seemed that everyone had a touch of bird-bright color about them. Even the shabbiest had at least a scarf or hair ribbon of scarlet or blue. Some (the look of them showing they were prosperous folk who needn't worry about soiling their clothing with work) were dressed entirely in colors. Even the houses were festive with bright designs on their whitewashed walls, and the shutters were painted to match. Those houses looked extremely odd to Talia—why, they couldn't have held more than one man, his Firstwife, and a few littles! There was obviously no room at all for Underwives and *their* littles. Talia wondered if each Wife had her own house, then giggled at the unseemly (but amusing) notion of the Husband running from house to house in the night, intent on doing his duty with each of his Wives.

The village itself, besides looking prosperous and well-cared-for, was also unenclosed; a startling sight to one who was used to seeing walls and stockades around inhabited places.

She reined in Rolan at the sight of a man standing beside a small hut positioned just at the verge of the Road where it first entered the village proper. He looked as if he must be some sort of guard or official; he was dressed in garments of a bright blue that matched, from boots to hat. He had a quiver of short arrows on his back, and Talia saw a crossbow leaning beside him against the wall of the hut.

The sight of him alarmed her no small amount—in her experience, men (especially men in obvious positions of authority) were creatures to be feared. They held the power of life and death over the members of their families; they decreed the rewards of the obedient and the punishments of the rebellious. How many times had the Elders or her Father deemed it necessary that she be beaten or sent into isolation for far, far less than she'd done in the past two days? Too many times to count easily, for certain sure. There was no indication that this stranger might not order the same punishments for her now; or worse, send her back to the Holding. Yet she was going to have to speak to *someone*; she'd been searching for nearly a day now and hadn't found any clue to where this Companion belonged. He seemed to have a friendly, open face, and she took her courage in hand to address him.

"P-pray excuse me, sir," she said politely, stuttering a little, "but have you seen a Herald who's lost his Companion?"

Her question seemed to startle him, and he approached the two of them slowly, as if trying not to frighten her (leaving his crossbow behind, Talia noted with relief).

"No indeed, young miss," he replied. "Why ask you?"

"I found this Companion alone on the Road yesterday," she answered hesitantly, still not sure she hadn't done wrong despite the fact that it didn't seem he was going to take her into custody or hail her before a Council of Elders just yet. "And it seemed to me I should take him back to whoever he belongs with."

He measured her with his eyes; she found his scrutiny unnerving. "Where are you from, child?" he asked at last.

"Sensholding, near Cordor. Back that way." She waved vaguely back down the Road in the direction she'd come.

"Ah, Holderfolk," he said, as if that explained something to him. Well, young miss, there's only one thing you can do if you find a lone Companion. You have to return him to the Herald's Collegium yourself."

"*Me?*" Her voice broke with alarm. "The Collegium? By myself?"

He nodded, and she gulped. "Is it very far?" she asked in a near-whisper.

"By ordinary horse, three weeks or more, depending on the weather. You're riding a Companion, though, and a little thing like you would be hardly more than a feather to him. You should get there in eight or nine days, perhaps a bit more."

"Eight—or nine—days?" she faltered, looking self-consciously down at her wrinkled, travel-stained clothing. In eight or nine days, she'd look like a tramp. They'd probably shoot her on sight, for thieving Rolan away!

His eyes crinkled at the corners as he smiled, seeming to read her thoughts. "Now, don't you worry, young miss. The Queen makes provisions for circumstances like these. Just wait right here."

She didn't have much choice; Rolan seemed to be rooted to the ground. The man returned in short order with a pair of saddlebags, a brown wool cloak draped over one arm, and a small piece of metal in his hand. "Goodwife Hardaxe has a girl a bit older than you; there's a couple of changes of clothing she's outgrown in the lefthand bag."

She attempted to voice a protest but he interrupted her. "No argument, young miss. I told you the Queen herself makes provisions for this sort of thing. We help you, and we get half taxes next year, the whole village. The righthand bag's got some odds 'n ends in it; fire-starter, comb and brush, things you'll need if your Companion can't find a Waystation. Don't be afraid to use what's in the Waystations either; that's what they're there for."

He tossed the bags over Rolan's back, fastening them securely to the back of the saddle. "This cloak's good oiled wool; it should keep the rain off you, and this time of year it ought to be enough to keep you warm if the weather turns nasty. It's more than a bit big, but that's all to the good. Means less of you will hang outside it. Ah, here comes the Innmaster."

A pleasant-faced, plump man came puffing up. He had a waterskin, a small pouch, and a dun-colored frieze bag with him. The wonderful meaty odors rising from the bag made Talia's mouth water, and her

stomach reminded her forcibly that it had been a long time since breakfast.

"I saw you didn't have a belt-pouch, so I left word with Daro that
you might be needing one," the first man said. "People are always
leaving things behind at the Inn."

"I just filled this bag with good spring water," the plump Innmaster
said, slinging it on one of the many snaffles adorning the saddle before
she could say anything, "And there's an eating knife and a spoon in the
pouch. Put it on now, there's a good girl; I've got more left-behind
eating tools than you could ever imagine! And these pasties ought to
stay sound for longer than it'll take you to eat 'em, if I know the appetite of a growing child!" He handed her the bag, and wiped his hands
on his apron, smiling. "Now you make sure you tell people how good
our baking is! I have to get back to my custom." And he puffed off
before she could thank him.

"See this?" the first man said, holding up a little scrap of engraved
brass. "When you get to the Collegium, give this chit to the person
who asks you for it. This tells them that we helped you along the way."
He handed it to her, and she placed it carefully in her new belt pouch.
"If you need anything, just ask people dressed the way I am, and they'll
be sure to help you. We're part of the Army, the Roadguards."

Talia was all but incoherent with surprise at her good fortune. Not
only had she not been punished or even scolded for her actions, not
only had she not been sent back home, but it seemed that she was actually being rewarded with the opportunity to go where she'd never
dared to dream she'd be allowed! "Th-th-ank you! B-b-bright Lady, it
just doesn't seem like enough just to *say* thank you—"

The guard chuckled, his eyes disappearing in the smile-crinkles.
"Young miss, it's *us* who'll remember you with thanks, come tax-time!
Anything else you need?"

Rolan seemed to think it was time they were on their way again,
and began moving impatiently off. "No, nothing," she called over her
shoulder as he waved a casual farewell.

Rolan quickly resumed his normal pace and the village fell rapidly
behind them, so quickly that Talia had only just realized that she didn't
even know the name of the place or her benefactor when it was gone
from view.

"Oh, well," she said to Rolan as she bit hungrily into a lightly spiced
meat pie. "I'm not likely to forget the baking of Darowife. Even Isrel
never made anything that tasted like *this*, not even for feastdays!"

She looked with curiosity at the brass "chit." It bore a number, and the word "Sweetsprings."

"Sweetsprings?" she mused. "That must be the town. I wish I knew what was going on! I've never read or heard anything about Companions running away before, but he acted like it happens all the time."

She passed through another village near to suppertime. This one was much smaller than Sweetsprings had been, mostly a collection of houses and huts around a blacksmith's forge. It was apparently too small to warrant one of the blue-clad Guards, but the people seemed just as friendly. They waved at her as she cantered past, bridle bells ringing, and didn't seem to find anything at all disturbing in the sight of a slightly grubby girl atop a Herald's Companion. Talia could not help contrasting their friendliness with the reaction she'd have gotten from Holderfolk. At best, her own people would have stared, then coldly turned their backs on such unseemly behavior from a girl-child. At worst, they'd have tried to stop her; tried to pull her from Rolan's back to incarcerate as a thief.

Once again, as night was about to fall, Rolan found a Waystation. The Road and the River had parted company not long since, but this shelter boasted a well, so they didn't lack water. Talia discovered among the odds and ends the guard had assembled for her a little box of soft, homemade soap and a washcloth, as well as a currycomb and brush for Rolan. When the moon rose, both of them were much cleaner.

She decided (somewhat reluctantly) to save the pies for her midday meals and manage with porridge for the rest. Once again she fed the two of them, and fell soundly asleep in spite of the relative discomfort of the primitive Waystation.

On the third day of the journey, Talia was sufficiently used to the novelty of riding Companion-back that she found her mind drifting to other things. The position of the sun would remind her that at home she'd have been at some particular task, and she found herself wondering what the Holding was making of her disappearance. There wasn't anyone in her extended family she was really close to anymore, not since Andrean had been killed in a raid and they'd sent Vrisa as Underwife to old man Fletcher. Of all her kin, only those two had ever seemed to really love her—even Father's Mother hadn't cared enough for her to stand up for her when she'd done something that truly enraged Keldar. Only those two had dared to brave the Firstwife's anger. Vris acted covertly, smuggling forbidden meals when punishment included doing without dinner. Andrean had been more open, demanding she be allowed to do something or coaxing Father to forgive her sooner. It had been at Andrean's insistence that she was allowed to continue her reading, for as Second son, his words had carried weight. And she and Vrisa had been closer than sibs; almost like twins in spite of the difference in their ages.

Tears stung her eyes at the thought of Andrean—so gentle with her, protective; always with a smile and a joke to share. He had been with her such a short time—he'd been killed when she was only nine. She could still remember him clearly, looming over her like a sheltering giant. He'd been so kind and patient—so ready to teach her anything she wanted to learn. He was everyone's favorite—except for Keldar. Truly the Goddess must have wanted him with Her, to take him so young—but Talia had needed him, too. They'd scolded her for crying at his wake, but it had been herself she had been crying for.

And poor Vris; she'd been terrified at the prospect of Marriage to old Fletcher, and it seemed she had been right to be so fearful. The few times Talia had seen her at Gatherings, she'd been pale and taut-looking, and as silent as one of the Lady's Handmaidens. All the sparkle had been snuffed out of her, and nothing was left but the ashes.

Talia shuddered—Vris' fate could so easily have been her own. The Companion's timely arrival seemed little less than miraculous in that light.

As she rode, she found her hands itching for something to do. Never since she could remember had there ever been a time when her hands hadn't been filled with some task. Even her reading was only allowed so long as she was occupied with some necessary job at the same time. To have empty hands seemed unnatural.

She filled her time with trying to take in as much of the changing landscape around her as she could, attempting to make some kind of mental map. Small villages appeared with greater frequency the farther she went toward the capital. The apparent lack of concern people showed over her appearance had her baffled. One could almost suppose that the sight of a strange adolescent riding a Herald's Companion was relatively commonplace. The only answer seemed to be as the Guard had hinted, that this sort of thing happened all the time. But why hadn't her tales made any mention of this? Companions were clearly of a high order of intelligence; look at the way he'd been caring for both of them all along this journey. Her first thought, that he'd run away like a common farmbeast, was obviously incorrect. At this point there wasn't much doubt in her mind as to which of the two of them was truly in charge. The tales were all true, then—Companions *were* creatures of an intellect at the least equaling that of their Heralds. She weighed the little she knew of Companions against her experiences of the past three days. It wasn't enough to help her. The Holderkin held themselves aloof from the Heralds, forbidding the littles to speak of them, and dealing with them only when they must. Only the Elders had any contact with them. And the little illicit gossip she'd heard had concerned only the Heralds and their rumored licentiousness, not the Companions.

But if you had to draw conclusions—Rolan must have chosen to have her accompany him, for there was no question that he could have returned to the Collegium perfectly well on his own. And if that was the case—could he have purposefully selected her for some reason? Perhaps even arrived at the Holding with the express *intention* of acquiring her and escorting her off to the capital? That was almost *too* like a fable. Talia simply couldn't believe that something like that was possible. Not for her—for some mage-gifted youth like Vanyel perhaps, but for a plain little girl of Holderkin? No one in his right mind would even consider such a possibility.

Yet—the questions remained. Why had he appeared when he had; why had he inveigled her into his saddle, and why, of all whys, was he carrying her off to the one place she wanted to go more than anywhere else on the earth or all five Heavens? The puzzle was almost enough to make her forget her idle hands.

When the sixth day of her journey arrived, she'd finished the last of the meat pies, and had decided to make a test of the instructions the guard had given her. Perhaps she would learn more from the next Guard, now that she knew that there was far more going on than she had any hope of puzzling out for herself.

The next village—perhaps—would hold the answers.

CHAPTER 3

$$\longleftarrow\!\!\!\!-\!\!\!\!-\!\!\!\!\ll \gg\!\!\!\!-\!\!\!\!-\!\!\!\!\longrightarrow$$

TOWARD NOONING SHE found they were approaching the outskirts of a very good-sized village. It lay in a little valley, well-watered and green with trees. Like the others Talia had seen, the shops and houses were colorfully painted with bold trim and shutters in blues, reds, and yellows. The bright colors contrasted cheerfully with the white plaster of the walls and the gold of fresh thatching. The scene was so unlike a faded gray Holding that it might well be in another land altogether. In the distance Talia could clearly see another guard-shelter; it appeared diminutive in contrast to the two- and three-storied buildings that stood near it. This was the first such shelter she had seen since early morning—it appeared that as she drew closer to the center of Valdemar, the overt presence of the Roadguard decreased. It seemed that this was the logical place for her to attempt to learn what this mystery was about and to reprovision herself at the same time.

The guard-shelter was placed in the deep shade of an enormous tree that completely overshadowed the road. Of all the buildings around, it alone was not brightly painted; rather, it was of plain wood, stained a dark brown. As they neared, Talia saw movement in the shadows, but the bright sun prevented her from seeing the Guard clearly at first. Her mouth fell open in amazement when she saw that the Guard who emerged from the shade was a woman—and one who wore a uniform identical in every respect to the first Guard's. For one bewildered moment she thought that she must *surely* be mistaken—certainly the idea was preposterous. She shook her head to clear her eyes of sun-dazzle, and looked again. The Guard *was* a woman. Impossible as it seemed, there was no mistaking the fact that *women* seemed to be part of the Army as well as men.

Before she could collect herself, the Guard had walked briskly to where they had halted and was standing at Rolan's head.

"Welladay!" she exclaimed before Talia could think what to say. "This *is* Rolan, isn't it?" She patted his neck as he nuzzled her graying black hair; she laughed, and slapped his nose lightly, then bent to examine some marks that Talia had noticed earlier on the saddle. "It certainly is! You've been a long time out, milord," she continued, clearly speaking to the horse. "I certainly hope it's been worth it."

Rolan lipped her sleeve playfully, and she laughed again.

"Now." The Guard turned her attention to Talia, squinting a little in the noon sun. "What can I do for you, young miss?"

Talia's confusion was doubled; however could she have guessed this Companion's name? And "Rolan" was hardly common—to have thought of it purely by accident all on her own—it seemed to hint at a great deal more than coincidence. "His name really *is* Rolan?" she blurted—then hung her head, blushing furiously at her own rudeness. "I'm sorry," she said to the pommel of the saddle. "I don't understand what's been happening to me. The—the Guard in Sweetsprings said other Guards could help me—"

"Sweetsprings!" the woman was plainly surprised. "You're a long way from home, childing!"

"I—guess I am," Talia replied faintly, watching the Guard out of the corner of her eye.

The Guard studied Talia as well, and the girl thought she must be appraising what she saw. Talia was wearing her original clothing, after doing her best to wash the worst of the travel stains from it, and keep it from drying with too many wrinkles in it. The loaned outfits had been of a heavier weight than was comfortable, riding all day in the sun—and at any rate, she hadn't felt quite at ease in them. Once everything had been worn once, it had seemed better to try and clean her own gear and return to it. Now she was glad she had; the Guard seemed to recognize exactly what she was just by the cut of it.

"Holderfolk, aren't you?" There was ready sympathy in her voice. "Huh. I've heard a bit about them—I'll bet you *are* confused, you poor thing. You must feel all adrift. Well, you'll find out what this is all about soon enough—trust me, they'll set you right at the Collegium. I'd try and explain, but it's against the rules for *me* to tell you if you don't already know, which is probably just as well—you'd probably end up more confused than ever. As to how I knew this was Rolan, well everybody on Roadguard duty knew he'd gone out; all his tack's marked with his sigil, just like every Companion—see?" She pointed to the marks she'd looked at, carved into the leather of the saddle skirting. Now that Talia knew what those marks meant, she could see they were a contracted version of Rolan's name. "Now, how can I serve you?"

"I'm afraid I need some provisioning," Talia said apologetically, half expecting a reproof. "They gave me some lovely meat pies—I did try to make them last, but—"

"How long ago was that?" the woman interrupted.

"Four days—" Talia replied, shrinking away a little.

"Four *days*? Hellfire! You mean you've been stretching your food for that long? What've you been eating, that dried horsecrap they keep in the Waystations?"

Talia's expression must have said plainly that that was exactly what she'd been doing, as the Guard's mouth twisted a little, and she tightened her lips in annoyance.

"Rolan," she said sternly, a no-nonsense tone in her voice. "You are letting this poor childing off your back for an hour, you hear me? You know damn well you can make up the time, and she needs a decent meal inside her before she comes down with flux, or something worse! *Then* where would you be?"

Rolan snorted and laid his ears back, but he didn't move off when the woman reached up to hand Talia out of the saddle. Talia slid down, feeling awkward under the eyes of the Guard, gawky and untidy—and once off Rolan, uneasy. Rolan followed close on their heels as the Guard led Talia by the hand to the Inn at the center of the village.

"I suppose the Guard back at Sweetsprings was a male, hm?" she asked wryly, and the woman nodded a bit at Talia's shy assent. "Just like a man! Never once thinks you might be more frightened by all this than excited, never once thinks you might not know the rules. Totally forgets that you may be Chosen but you're also just a child. And you're no better, Rolan!" she added over her shoulder. "Men!"

The Companion only tossed his head and made a sound that sounded suspiciously like a chuckle.

The inn was a prosperous place, with tables placed outside in the shade of a huge goldenoak that grew in the very center of its courtyard. There were a fair number of folk eating and drinking at those tables already. The Guard sat Talia down at one of these tables that was still unoccupied, and bullied the serving maid into bringing an enormous meal. She ordered Talia in tones that brooked no disagreement to "tuck into that food." Talia did so, suddenly realizing how hungry she'd been the past few days, while the Guard vanished somewhere.

She returned just as Talia finished the last crumb, carrying the saddlebags that had been fastened to Rolan's saddle and which now fairly bulged at the seams.

She sat down beside Talia, straddling the bench, and laid the bags between them. "I've replaced your clothing. It's Holderfolk style and colors; some of the younglings around here wear that sort of thing for heavy work. I know you'll feel more comfortable in that kind of outfit, and this way people will know when they look at you that you're not used to being out in the big world; hopefully, they'll realize that you're going to be confused."

Talia started to protest that this wasn't necessary, but the stern look the guard gave her made her fall silent again.

"There are enough changes there to get you to the Collegium without you having to wash it yourself. Innkeeper's bringing you some wayfood. I told him no wine; that right?" At Talia's affirmative nod she continued, "Don't stint yourself; you're still a-growing and you don't want to be falling ill. Don't eat that crap they keep at the Waystations. That's supposed to be for the Companions and dire emergencies, no matter what that lazy lout at Sweetsprings told you. I'll tell you, the emergency would have to be pretty *damn* dire before *I'd* stomach that stuff! You stop every day for a hot nooning, unless there're no towns. That's an order! Here's your townchit," she said, handing another scrap of brass to Talia, who put it safely in her pouch. "Frankly, if it weren't for the damn rules, I'd keep you here overnight so's I'd know you'd gotten a hot bath and a proper bed, but—never mind. You'll have to stop once more for wayfood. Try Kettlesmith. The Dayguard there's an old friend of mine; she knows about Holderfolk and she knows children; she'll make sure you're all right. Ready to go?"

Talia nodded dumbly. This woman had all the brisk efficiency of Keldar with none of Keldar's coldness—she had taken charge of everything so quickly that Talia's head spun. And it seemed, at least, that she was concerned that Talia was all alone on the Road. Having someone concerned for her well-being was a strange sensation. Talia might almost have suspected an ulterior motive except that the Guard was so open and honest. If there was anything to be wary of in her manner, Talia couldn't read it.

"Good enough; off you get." She gave Talia a gentle shove toward the edge of the court where Rolan was waiting, surrounded by children. They were all vying for the chance to pet him or feed him a choice tidbit, and he seemed to Talia's eyes to be wearing a very smug, self-satisfied expression.

The Guardswoman gave Talia a boost into the saddle, refastened the saddlebags to the cantle and the bags brought by the Innkeeper to the snaffles at the front skirting, and gave Rolan a genial smack on the rump to send them on their way.

It wasn't until they were far down the Road that Talia realized that she hadn't yet had a single one of her questions answered.

At least—not directly. Indirectly though—now that she thought about it, there had been some information there. The Guardswoman had mentioned "rules" about journeys like this; that implied that they were commonplace. And she'd spoken to Rolan as she would have to a person—that implied that Rolan *was* as remarkable as legends claimed, and that his actions involving Talia were planned and intentional.

So—that meant that there was something that the Companion intended for her to be doing. But *what*?

To have only bits of information was as maddening as having only half a book! But some of that information was beginning to make a pattern.

All right; it was time to try putting more of this together. The three books Talia owned always (now that she thought about it) referred to Companions as having some kind of magical abilities; a mystical bond with their Heralds. There had been an implication, especially in Vanyel's tale, that Companions could communicate sensibly with their Heralds and vice versa. The Guard had spoken to Rolan as if he were a person—actually as if he had taken charge of Talia. That bore out the feeling that Talia had had ever since the first day—that it was Rolan who knew where they should be going and what they should be doing.

Rolan had given every evidence of understanding what the Guard had said to him. For that matter, he seemed to react to everything Talia said in the same way. *He* was the one who found the Waystations every night; *he* was the one who plainly guarded her. He was the one who knew the way back to the Collegium—the Guard had said as much.

It followed that he'd really had a purpose in being where she had encountered him—the Guard had said he'd been out a long time—and that purpose involved her. There was no getting around it. The question was—why?

Was it—dared she think—he might have been looking for someone to be tested as a Herald-candidate?

She had no notion of how Heralds actually *became* Heralds—except that they had to undergo strenuous training at the Collegium. Only Vanyel's tale had mentioned early on that he nearly hadn't had the courage to take up the task—the tale had made no mention of how he'd been picked. And all she knew of Heralds from Hold gossip was that they were supposedly monsters of moral depravity; wanton and loose, indulging in sensuous, luxurious, orgiastic behavior. She had suspected most of this was spite and sheer envy, especially since Heralds gave short shrift to Hold ideas of a woman's inferiority and proper place in life, and they answered to no authority but that of the Monarch and each other. That there were women in the Guard had come as a surprise, but since her first book had been the quest of Sun and Shadow, Talia had long been aware that there were women as Heralds who held equal position with the men. That freedom was one of the reasons she'd longed to become one.

Did she dare to dream that might happen now?

Just when Talia thought she might be getting used to the surprises of her journey, she was taken unawares again. The guard at Kettlesmith was not only another woman, but was one bearing obvious battlescars, with a peg of wood replacing one leg from the knee down. She told Talia, quite offhandedly, that she'd lost the rest of the leg to a wound she'd taken in the last war. The idea of a woman being in battle was so foreign to Talia's experience that she was in a half daze all through her meal and until she reached the outskirts of town afterward. It was only meeting with the Herald that shocked her out of it.

The Road led down into a wooded valley, still and cool. The trees were mostly pines, and Rolan's hooves crushed the needles that had collected on the Road's surface so that they traveled in a cloud of crisp scent. They were well inside the wood itself and out of sight of habitation within a few moments. Finally, in the heart of the wood the Road they'd been on met with another—there was a crossroads there. Talia didn't even notice that there was someone approaching on the other road under the shadows of the trees until an exclamation of startlement jarred her out of her trance.

She looked up, starting out of her daze. Facing her she saw, not more than four or five paces away and his astonishment written plain on his face, a white-clad man on a cloud-white mare. It was a Herald, a real Herald, mounted on *his* Companion.

Talia bit her lip, suddenly feeling a chill of fear. Even after all she'd been told, she still wasn't entirely sure she was doing right. *Now* she was for it; there was no disguising that Rolan was a Companion and that she wasn't any kind of a Herald. If she was to find herself in trouble, this encounter would bring it. She was conscious of an odd little disappointment, though, under all her apprehension; somehow it didn't seem quite proper for a Herald to be so—homely.

For the young man now approaching was just that. Carrying himself with all the authority of his office, poised, collected, yes. Obviously sure of himself, and every inch the Herald, but still—almost ugly. He certainly was nothing like the beautiful Vanyel or the angelic Sunsinger of the tales.

His voice made up for it, though.

"By the Hand of the Lady! Rolan, as sure as I stand here!" The words were melodious and unexpectedly deep. "By all the gods, you've finally Chosen!"

"Th-they told me to take him back to the Collegium, m'lord," Talia stuttered with nervousness, keeping her eyes down as was proper for a girl speaking to a man of rank, and waiting for the axe to fall. "I didn't know what else to do, and they all seemed so sure—"

"Whoa! You're doing the right thing, exactly right," he cut her torrent of explanation short. "You mean you don't know? No, of course you don't, or you wouldn't be acting like I'd caught you with your hand in my beltpouch."

Talia looked up for a second, bewildered by his words. He didn't speak anything like the Heralds in her tales, either. He had almost sounded like Andrean for a moment.

She longed to see if his eyes looked like Andrean's, too, but glanced hastily back down to the pommel when he tried to meet her gaze.

He chuckled, and out of the corner of her eye she could see that his expression was of gentle good humor. "It's quite all right. You're doing exactly as you should. Keep straight on the road you're on, and you'll be at the capital before dinner; anyone there can direct you to the Collegium. Hellfire, Rolan knows the way better than anyone else—you won't get lost. I wish I could tell you what's going on, but it's against the rules. You have to be told the whole of it at the Collegium—otherwise you'd be getting all kinds of stories about what all this means, and you'd be taking days to get straightened out afterward."

"But—" She was longing for someone, anyone, to explain this whole mess to her. It was like being caught in some kind of enormous game, only she was the only one that didn't know the rules and was stumbling from square to square without knowing why or where she was going. If *anyone* knew the whole truth, it would obviously be a

Herald. And the kindness in his eyes made her long to throw the whole tangle in his hands. How anyone so homely could put her in mind of Andrean, she had no idea—but he did, and she found herself drawn to him as she'd not been to any male since her brother's death.

"No buts! You'll find out everything you need to know at the Collegium! Off with you!" With that, he rode close enough to reach out and smack Rolan's rump heartily, surprising the Companion enough that he jumped and broke into a canter, leaving the Herald far behind. Talia was so busy regaining her balance that she didn't notice the Herald and his own Companion galloping off into the trees, on a course that would eventually bring them back onto the road considerably ahead of Talia.

By the time she'd gotten over her startlement, the road was becoming crowded with other wayfarers, both going in her direction and in the opposite; other riders, walkers, carts drawn by various beasts, pack animals. But although she craned her neck in every direction, there was no sign of other Heralds.

The crowd on the road was not quite like any other crowd Talia had ever found herself among. For one thing, it was loud. Holderfolk kept their voices restrained at all times; even the Harvest Fair gatherings at the height of bidding excitement hardly generated more than a buzz. For another, all these people wore their emotions, their personalities, plain to be seen on their faces. The faces of well-schooled Holderfolk were closed, giving nothing away, and unlikely to display anything that would reveal their true feelings to one of their fellow creatures.

The other travelers took little special notice of her for the most part. Rolan threaded his way among them with delicate precision, making far better time than most of their fellow wayfarers, although keeping a good pace didn't really seem to be a prime consideration for most of them. Talia was so involved in people-watching that she forgot to watch for the city.

Then they topped a rise, and there it was.

It was so enormous that Talia froze in fright at the sight of it. Once again it was just as well that it was Rolan who plainly had charge of their journeying, or Talia would have turned him back along the way they'd come, bolting back to the familiarity of the Hold.

It sat in a river valley below them, and the view was excellent from the hilltop they'd just mounted. From here it could be seen that it had originally been a walled city, much as the Hold villages were but on a much bigger scale. With the passage of time and increased security, however, the city had been allowed to spread beyond the walls, spilling over them like water from the basin of a fountain. And like water, the spillage had followed certain channels; in this case, the roads.

Within the walls, houses crowded together so thickly that all Talia could see were roofs. Within the first wall there seemed to be a second wall, enclosing a few large buildings and a great deal of green, open space with trees in it. Outside the walls were more buildings, from single-storied huts to massive windowless places that could have held every structure at Sensholding within their walls. These clustered all around the first wall, then trailed out in long arms that followed the paths of the roads and the river. Talia's eyes were drawn irresistibly back to that inner space of green and trees and a stone edifice that towered over all the rest. This—this surely was the Palace and the Collegium—but before Talia could be certain that this was indeed the case, Rolan's steady pace had brought them down past the point where the view was so clear.

As they came closer to the area where the city dwellings began, Talia found herself assaulted on all sides by sound and noise. Hawkers were everywhere, crying their wares; shopkeepers had people stationed by the doors, screaming at the tops of their lungs, extolling the virtues of the goods within the shops. Children played noisily in and around the crowd, often skirting perilously close to the hooves of the horses, donkeys, and oxen that crowded the street. Neighbors screeched gossip to each other over the noise of the crowd; from the vicinity of inns came voices loud in argument or song. Talia's head reeled, her ears rang, and her fear grew.

And the smells! She was assaulted by odor as she was by sound. Meat cooking, bread baking, smoke, dung, spices, sweat of man and beast, hot metal, spilled beer—her poor, country-bred nose was as overwhelmed as her ears.

They came to the gate in the first wall; there were guards there, but they didn't hinder her passage though they looked at her with expressions she couldn't quite read; curiosity, and something else. The wall they passed under frightened her even more; it was as tall as the rooftop of the Temple back home. She felt terribly small and insignificant, and the weight of it crushed her spirit entirely.

The noise and tumult, if anything, were worse inside. Here the houses were multi-storied, and crowded so closely together that their eaves touched. Everything began to blur into a confused muddle of sound, sight, and scent. Talia huddled in Rolan's saddle, unaware that she was drawing pitying looks from the passersby, with her eyes so wide with fear in her pinched, white face. It was just as well that Rolan knew exactly where to go, for she was so frightened that she would never have been able to ask directions even of a child.

It seemed an age before Rolan paused before a gate in the second, inner wall. The gate was small, only large enough to admit a single rider, and closed, and the guard here looked her over curiously. Unlike the lighter uniform of the others, this man was clad in midnight blue with silver trimmings. He opened the gate and came forward as soon as he saw them, and Rolan waited for his approach. He smiled encouragingly at Talia, then drew close enough to read the little marks on Rolan's saddle, and gave an exclamation of glee.

"Rolan!" he cried with delight, seeming to forget momentarily about Talia's existence. "Finally! We were beginning to think you'd never find someone! There was even a bet on that you'd jumped the Border! The Collegium's been in a fine pother since you left—"

He finally seemed to see Talia, nerves strung bowstring-taut and white-faced.

"Your ordeal is almost over, childing," he said with real sympathy even as she shrank away from him. "Come down now, and I'll see that you get to where you need to go."

He aided her down out of the saddle as if she'd been a princess; no sooner had she set her feet on the ground than another uniformed person came to lead Rolan away. Talia watched them vanish with an aching heart, wondering if she'd ever see him again. She wished with sudden violence that she'd followed her first impulse and ridden him far away. Whatever was to happen to her? How could she have dreamed that she'd be of any significance to folk who lived in a place like *this*?

The guard led her into the gray stone, multi-storied building at the end of the path they walked. It was totally unlike any structure Talia was familiar with. Her heart was in her shoes as they entered a pair of massive, brass-inlaid wooden doors. Never had she seen anything to equal the work in those doors, and that was just the beginning of the wonders. She was feeling worse by the minute as she took in the grandness of her surroundings. The furnishings alone in just one of the many rooms they passed would have exceeded the combined wealth of the entire Holding. Not even the Temple High Sanctuary was this impressive. She would have bolted given a moment to herself, except that after the first few minutes she was well and truly lost.

At last he brought her to a room much smaller than many of the ones they'd passed; about the size of a large pantry, though no less rich than the rest of the building.

"Someone will be with you in just a few moments, youngling," he said kindly, relieving her of her townchits. "You're among friends here, never doubt it. We've been waiting for you, you know! You and Rolan were a welcome sight to these eyes." When she didn't respond, he patted her carefully on the head. "Don't worry, no one is going to harm you—why, I have little ones nearly your age myself! Make yourself comfortable while I let the proper people know you're here."

Make herself comfortable? How, in a room like this?

She finally chose a leather-padded chair as the one she was least likely to damage and sat on it gingerly. In the silence of the unoccupied room, she began to lose her fear, but her discomfort grew as the fear faded. Surrounded by all this luxury, she was acutely aware of the fact that she was sticky, damp with nervousness, smelt faintly of horse, and was dressed in the kind of fabrics they probably made grain bags out of here. She was also painfully aware that she was only thirteen years old. When she'd been with Rolan, none of that had seemed to matter, but now—oh, *now* she was all too aware of her shortcomings. How had she ever dared to dream she might become a Herald? Never—never—only people born and bred to surroundings like these could aspire to such a position. The Guard had probably gone for some underservant to give her a bit of silver and send her on her way—if she was lucky, it would be someone she could talk into giving her a job.

A miniature whirlwind burst into the room, interrupting her thought.

"Oh!" said the girl, a little of about seven with chestnut hair, blue eyes, and a rather disagreeable expression on an otherwise pretty face. "What are *you* doing here?"

For the first time since she'd seen the city, Talia felt back on secure ground. Littles were one thing she *could* handle!

"I'm waiting, like I was told," she replied.

"Aren't you going to kneel?" the child asked imperiously.

Talia hid a smile. It was amazing how so simple a thing as having to deal with an obviously spoiled child made her feel so very much more confident.

"Kneel?" she asked with mock-astonishment. "Why should I kneel?"

The child was becoming red-faced with temper. "You're in the Presence of the Heir to the Throne!" she replied haughtily, the capital letters audible, her nose in the air and her expression disdainful.

"Really? Where?" Talia looked around her with an innocent face that covered inner mischief newly aroused by the child's pretensions. This little was about to receive the treatment her bad manners deserved. If she *was* the Heir—well, someone was obviously not doing his job in training her. And if she wasn't, she deserved it for lying. "I don't see anyone like that."

"Me! Me!" the girl shouted, stamping her foot, frustrated and angry. "*I'm* the Heir!"

"Oh, I don't think so," Talia said, thoroughly enjoying herself. "You're nothing but a little having a temper tantrum; one that fibs a lot. I've read all about the Heirs. The Heir is always polite and gracious, and treats the lowest scullery maid like she was the Queen's own self. You act like you'd treat the Queen like the lowest scullery maid. You can't possibly be the Heir. Maybe I should call a guard and tell him there's an imposter in here."

The child's mouth opened and closed wordlessly with frustration and rage.

"Maybe you're a fish," Talia added ingenuously. "You certainly look like one."

The girl shrieked in anger, and drew back one balled-up fist.

"I wouldn't," Talia said warningly. "I hit back."

The child's eyes widened in surprise, then her face grew even redder with rage. "I—how—oh!"

"You said that already."

At that the girl gave an ear-piercing squeal, pushed over a small table that stood nearby, and ran out of the room before it hit the ground. Talia had expected her to do something of the kind and had sprung to the table's rescue, catching it before it was damaged and righting it with a sigh of exasperation.

A dry chuckle came from behind Talia, who turned to see a curtain pushed aside, and a tall, handsome woman in Herald's Whites step into the room. Though she wore a long skirt with the thigh-length tunic instead of breeches, and the materials were clearly fine velvet and silk, she was no different in appearance from other Heralds Talia had seen or heard about. Her face was triangular and strong rather than pretty; her hair was bound in a knot at the nape of her neck and was the same golden color as raival leaves in the fall. She had very penetrating, intelligent blue eyes the same intense sapphire blue as a Companion's.

Talia started to scramble to her feet, but the woman gestured that she should remain seated.

"Stay where you are, youngling," she said, as Talia resumed her place and continued to watch her shyly. "You've had a long and tiring ride—you deserve to sit on something that isn't moving for a while!"

The woman studied the child seated obediently before her and liked what she saw. There had been competence in the way that she had handled the Heir's rudeness and temper; there had been enough mischief there to suggest a lively sense of humor, but at the same time this child had been clever without being cruel. That boded very well indeed for her future success.

"Well, so you're Talia. I hope you don't mind the fact that I was eavesdropping, but I wanted to see how you'd handle her," she said, with a hint of apology.

"With a hairbrush to her behind, if I had charge of her," Talia replied, almost automatically. The incident and the woman's obvious approval had put some of her fears to rest, and if Keldar exuded an air that always made Talia feel nervous and incompetent, this woman had the very opposite effect on her.

"She's had precious little of that," the woman sighed, "and I fear she's overdue for a good share of it."

She examined Talia more closely and was even more encouraged by what she read in the child's face and manner. There was intelligence and curiosity in her large brown eyes, and her expression was that of a child blessed with an unfailingly sweet and patient nature. The woman guessed that she was probably a bit older than she appeared to be; perhaps around thirteen or fourteen. The heart-shaped face crowned by tousled brown curls was very appealing. The sturdily built, well-muscled body showed that this child was no stranger to hard work. With every observation it seemed as if Rolan had supplied the Collegium with the precise answer to all of their hopes and prayers.

"Well, that's tomorrow's problem," she replied. "I am told you're the one Rolan brought back—is that correct? Has anyone told you anything yet?"

Talia was encouraged by the understanding in the woman's face. The encouragement she found there, and the unfeigned interest, and most of all the reassurance, caused words to boil up out of her without her even thinking about them.

"No! Everybody seems to know what's going on but me!" she blurted. "And nobody wants to *explain* anything!"

The woman seated herself with a careless grace. "Well, now someone will. Why don't you tell me about what's happened to you—from the beginning. I'll try to help you understand."

Talia found herself pouring out the whole tale, from the time Keldar called her into the house till this very moment. Before she'd finished, she was fighting back tears. All the doubts that had occurred to her were coming back—she had nothing to count on except the dubious possibility of their gratitude. And she fully realized just what kind of a hopeless situation she was in if the Heralds chose to turn her out.

"Please—you must know someone—someone—"

"In charge?"

"Yes. Can't you please find me something to do here?" Talia begged shamelessly. "I'll do anything—mend, wash, scrub floors—" She stopped, afraid the tears would come if she went on. How had she *ever* dared to dream she might join these magical people? They were as much above her as the stars.

"Dirk was right. You haven't a clue to what's happened to you, have you?" the woman said, half to herself. Then she looked up, and Talia averted her own eyes from the intensity of her gaze. "Did you really mean what you said to the Firstwife, that you wanted to be a Herald?"

"Yes. Oh yes!" Talia was studying the hands clenched in her lap. "More than anything—I know it's not possible, but—I didn't know any better, then. No one ever told me what this place was like, and I don't think—I don't think I could have pictured it anyway. Sensholding isn't anything like this. I never could have guessed what I was asking. Please—please forgive me—I didn't mean any disrespect."

"Forgive?" the woman was astonished. "Child, forgive *what*? It's no disrespect to dream of becoming a Herald—though it's not like the tales, you know. It's work that is both dull and dangerous; if not one, then the other. Half the Heralds never live to reach old age. And it's a life where you find you have very little time for yourself. It's a wonder that anyone *wants* the job, much less dreams of it as her heart's desire. A Herald has to always consider her duty above all else, even her own well-being."

"That doesn't matter!" Talia cried, looking up.

"Why not? What does matter?"

"I'm not sure." She groped for the words to express what until now she'd only felt. "It's that Heralds *do* things instead of complaining about them, things that put peoples' lives back together, even if it's only settling a quarrel about a cow. And—" she faltered, "there's the Companion—"

Tears began to flow despite her resolution as she remembered with bright vividness the days on the road, and how, for once in her life, she hadn't been lonely. It might have been imagination, and yet—it had seemed, at least, that Rolan had cared for her. Dared she think—loved her? There was no doubt in her mind that she had loved him. And now he was gone, no doubt taken to the Herald he *truly* belonged with.

"Oh my poor child," the woman reached out instinctively and gathered Talia to her, to let her sob on her shoulder.

Talia tried to pull away, fighting back the tears, even though she longed to relax on that comforting shoulder. "I'm all over dirt," she sobbed, "and you're in Whites. I'll get you all grubby."

"There are more important things in life than dirt," the woman replied, holding her firmly, exactly as Vris had done more than once. There was something almost as comforting about her as there had been about Rolan—or Vris, or Andrean. Talia's reticence evaporated, and she cried herself out.

When Talia was again in control of herself, the woman gave her a handkerchief to repair the damages with, and said, "It's fairly obvious that, for some reason, you were never told of how Heralds are chosen."

"Aren't they just born into it, like being Eldest Son? I mean—all this—"

"'All this' means nothing—if you haven't the right makings. It is true that Heralds are born to the job, since no one can *learn* to be a Herald, but blood doesn't matter. No, the Companions Choose them."

And it all came flooding back—that bright, joyful moment when she'd first looked into Rolan's eyes. "I Choose you," he'd said in her mind. She remembered it all now. . . .

The woman smiled at Talia's gasp, as all the little bits of the mystery suddenly assumed their rightful pattern. "It usually happens that they don't have to go very far. It's a rather odd thing, but for various reasons anyone who is of the proper material to be a Herald finds his or her way to the city, the Court, or the Collegium more often than not. Sometimes, though, the Companions have to go seeking their Heralds themselves. There's one Companion that *always* does this; tell me, in the tales you read, did you ever come across the title 'The Monarch's Own Herald'?"

"Ye-es," Talia replied doubtfully, still a little dazed with the revelation and the newly awakened memories, "but I couldn't make out what it meant."

"It's a position of very special trust. It takes a very extraordinary person to fill it. Everyone needs someone to trust utterly, someone who would never offer false counsel, someone who could be a true friend in all senses of the word. The Monarch needs such a person more than anyone else because she is so surrounded by those who have nothing but their own interests at heart. This is what the 'Queen's Own' really is; the very fact of the Queen's Own's existence is one of the reasons this Kingdom has had so little internal strife over the years. When a ruler knows that there is at least one person who can be utterly trusted and yet will always tell her the truth, it tends to make her more confident, more honest with herself, less selfish—and altogether a better ruler. The position of Queen's Own is a lifetime one, and the person to fill that position is always Chosen by the Companion of the last Herald to hold it. When that Herald dies, the Companion leaves the Collegium to search the Kingdom for a successor. In the past reigns that hasn't taken more than a day or two, and quite often he Chooses someone who is already a Herald or nearly ready to be made one. This time, though, it was different. When Herald Talamir died, his Companion was gone for nearly two months, something that hasn't happened in a very long time."

Talia was so wrapped up in the story the woman was telling that she forgot her apprehensions. "Why?" she asked simply.

The woman pondered Talia's simple question for a long time before answering it. The child deserved the best answer she could give, and an honest one.

"Well, we think it has something to do with the current situation," she replied after long thought. "The Heir has been badly spoiled—that's partly the Queen's fault: she allowed too much of her time to be taken up with politics and things that seemed important at the time, but in the long run, were not. The child's nursemaid is from outKingdom and has given the girl a very exaggerated idea of her own importance. It's not going to be an easy task to make the brat into the kind of woman that deserves to sit on the Throne. Talamir's Companion had to roam far to find someone equal to it."

"He *did* find someone, didn't he?" Talia asked anxiously.

"He certainly did. He brought her to us today."

She watched Talia's reaction carefully, knowing it would tell her a great deal about the girl.

The child was completely incredulous. "*Me?* But—but—I don't know *anything*—I'm just a low-born farmgirl—I don't fit—I can't talk right—I don't look right—I'm not anything you'd want—"

"You know how to handle a spoiled child. Talia, I will admit I was hoping for someone a little older, but—well, the Companions don't make mistakes. You'll be close enough to Elspeth in age that you can be her *real* friend, once you've tamed the brat. As for not fitting in—she's been too much cosseted by courtiers as it is; she could use a good dose of farm sense. Yes, and a good dose of country spanking if it comes to that! And for the future—if I'd had someone that I'd have felt easy in confiding in—gossiping with—I expect I'd never have wedded her father." She sighed.

"You—her father—you're the *Queen?*" Talia jumped to her feet, her eyes horrified, and the Queen did her best to stifle a smile at the look of utter dismay she wore. "I've been getting the *Queen* all grubby?" She would have fallen to her knees, except that the Queen prevented it, insisting that she return to her seat beside her.

"Talia, dear, the Queen is only the Queen in the Throne Room," she replied. "Anywhere else, I'm just another Herald. And I'm a mother who needs your help very badly. I've bungled somewhere, and I haven't the skill to put things right. I think from what I've seen just in the past hour that you have, despite your tender years."

She hoped that the child could read the entreaty in her eyes.

"No one can force you to this. If you honestly don't feel equal to the task of being Queen's Own to a woman old enough to have mothered you and to a spoiled little monster, we'll find someplace else here where you can be happy. I'll admit to you that this is a job *I* wouldn't want under any circumstances. You can say no, and we'll send Rolan out again. But—I think his judgment was right when he Chose you. Will you be a Herald, Talia, and Queen's Own?"

Talia gulped nervously, still not certain that she wasn't victim of a terrible mistake. She opened her mouth intending to say no, but once again her heart betrayed her.

"Yes!" she heard herself saying. "Oh, yes!"

The Queen sighed as though a heavy burden had been lifted from her shoulders. "Thank you, Talia. Trust me, you won't have to bear this alone for a long, long time. You have too much you need to learn, so there will be many willing and able to help you. The most important thing is that you become Elspeth's friend, so that you can start to guide her. I may set my Heralds hard tasks, but I try not to make them impossible." She smiled, a smile bright with relief. "Is there anything else I can tell you?"

"Could I—" she swallowed a lump in her throat. "Could I see Rolan? Once in a while?"

"See him? Bright Havens, child, he's *your* Companion now; if you really wanted to, you could sleep in his stall!"

"I can? He is? It's really all real?"

It was too much like a tale. At any moment now, Talia expected to find herself waking in her bed back in the attic of the Steading. This couldn't be real. It had to be that she was dreaming. Yet, would a dream have included the feeling of being slightly grubby, and the hard edge of the chair that was digging just the tiniest bit into her leg?

She was forced to conclude that this was no dream. Suddenly she felt dizzy and half-drunk with compounded relief and elation. She was going to be a Herald—she really was going to be a Herald, like Vanyel and Shadowdancer and all the others of her tales and legends! And not just any Herald at that, but the highest ranking Herald in the entire Kingdom.

Best not to think about that for a moment. It was too much to really comprehend completely.

She raised her eyes to meet the Queen's, dropping her Holderkin reserve and letting her happiness show plainly.

"Yes, Talia. It's quite real." The Queen's eyes softened with amusement at the naked joy on the child's face. This girl was so self-possessed that it was quite easy to forget that she was only thirteen—until she herself reminded you. Like now, when she was all ecstatic child. It would not be hard to care for this Talia in the least. Especially not at moments like this.

Then she made the switch again, back to miniature adult. "Where do I start? What do I need to do?"

"You start now," the Queen pulled a bellrope behind her to call the Dean of the Collegium, who had been impatiently awaiting the results of this interview. "As soon as Dean Elcarth gets here. He'll get you settled at the Collegium. As for what you need to do; you learn, Talia. And please—" Her eyes were very sober. "Learn as quickly as you can. I—*we*—need you more than you can guess."

CHAPTER 4

⊸——◄ ►·——➤

THE QUEEN'S SUMMONS was answered immediately. Talia hadn't the faintest notion of what to expect, but her first glimpse of the diminutive man in Herald's Whites that the Queen introduced as the Dean of Herald's Collegium gave her a feeling of intense relief. Dean Elcarth was a brisk, birdlike, elderly man, scarcely taller than Talia. The wary unease she usually felt around men evaporated when she saw him; he was so like a snow-wren (complete with the gray cap of hair to match a wren's gray crown) that it was impossible to be afraid of him.

"So," he said, surveying Talia with his head tilted slightly to one side, his round, black eyes bright with intellect. "This is our new Herald-in-training. I think you'll do well here, child, and I'll be the first to tell you that I'm never wrong." He chuckled and Talia responded with a tentative smile.

He nodded slightly to the Queen. "Well, with your permission, Selenay—"

"I leave her in your capable hands," the Queen replied.

"Excellent. Come along with me, youngling. I'll show you about; perhaps find someone to help get you settled in among us."

He led her out the door and down the wood-paneled hall. Talia obediently fell in beside him; she was glad that he was nearly as small as she was, otherwise she'd never have been able to keep up with him. The pace he set forced her to take two steps for every one of his just to match him.

She watched him carefully, despite her earlier judgment. She had had too many nasty surprises in her life to wish another, especially not here, alone among strangers.

He saw her wary, covert gaze and made note of it. Elcarth had been Dean of Herald's Collegium for decades. He had had plenty of practice in that time in assessing the newly-Chosen, and he hadn't missed a single nuance of Talia's behavior. The way she'd shrunk into herself before she'd gotten a good look at him told him more than she could possibly have guessed. The way she had blindly obeyed him told him even more. He mentally shook his head. She was obviously unaccustomed to taking the initiative. Something would have to be done about that. And this wild-animal shyness spoke of abuse; mental and emotional, and perhaps physical abuse as well. Fortunately, she may have had her spirit bent but it wasn't broken; Rolan would never have Chosen her otherwise. He made another internal note; to discuss the Holderfolk with the Queen. That this child had been left in ignorance of Companion's Choice was criminal. And young Dirk had been right— the child was so withdrawn and reticent it was scarcely to be believed. Women did not seem to evoke the reaction nearly so strongly as men— it almost seemed as if she expected blows and abuse from a man as a matter of course. It would take a very long time indeed before a strange man could win her trust. He made swift revision of his original plans; until she was comfortable with what life here meant, it would be best for her mentors to be mostly female. Only Herald Teren was likely to be unthreatening enough that she'd lose her apprehension in his presence.

Elcarth questioned Talia closely as they walked, keeping his tone carefully light and projecting a calming aura at her as he did so. The answers he got were highly satisfactory; he'd feared the child would be at best functionally illiterate. In reading and writing, at least, she was at a comparable level with most of the youngsters Chosen at her age, and she had an incredible thirst for knowledge. So far as academics went, he was confident that all that would be needed would be to give her access to information and teaching, and she would do the rest without external prodding.

In only one area was she frighteningly deficient; she seemed to know little or nothing of self-defense and weaponry. This was more than simply unfortunate; she'd have to learn to protect herself, and quickly. There were many in the Heraldic Circle who doubted that Talamir's death had been happenstance; he shared those doubts. A child, alone, knowing nothing of self-defense—against those who had been able to make the death of an experienced Herald seem due to simple old age, she was no opponent at all. She was so vulnerable—so very vulnerable; such a fragile creature to carry all their hopes. Weaponsmaster Alberich was the *only* instructor capable of teaching her at any speed, and Alberich was likely to frighten her on appearance alone! He made yet another mental note to speak with the Weaponsmaster as soon as he'd left her in good hands. Alberich was no fool; warned how shy she was, he would know how to treat her.

Meanwhile—Elcarth continued his questions, even more alert to nuances of behavior than he had been before. There was no reaction she made that escaped him.

Talia for her part was more than a little puzzled at Dean Elcarth's questioning, for it seemed to follow no pattern that she could see. He flitted from subject to subject so rapidly that she had no time to think about her answers, and certainly was unable to anticipate his questions. Yet the answers she gave him seemed to please him; once or twice he'd seemed *very* satisfied by what she told him.

They traversed long wood-paneled, tapestried corridors; only the few that had exterior windows and gave Talia a glimpse of sun and trees allowed her any clue even of what direction they were taking. They passed at length through a pair of massive double doors. "We're in the Collegium Wing now; Herald's Collegium, that is," Elcarth said. "There are two other Collegia here associated with the Palace— Bardic Collegium and Healer's Collegium. Ours is the largest, but that is in part because most of the academic classrooms are here, and we save space that way. Healer's has its own separate building; so does Bardic. The House of Healing is part of Healer's Collegium; you may have heard of it. Now, down this corridor are the classrooms; the first floor is entirely classrooms. The door at the far end leads to the court in front of the stables, and the training grounds beyond that. Behind us, on the other side of the doors we just passed through, are the private quarters of the Kingdom's Heralds."

"Are *all* of them here?" Talia asked, overwhelmed by the thought of all those Heralds in one place.

"Well, no. Most of them are out on their circuits. But all of them have at least one room here, some shared, some not, and those on duty permanently at the palace or the Collegium have several, as do those who have retired from active duty if they decide to stay here with us. There's a staircase behind this door here; there's another in the middle of the building and a third next to the door at the end. We'll go upstairs now, to the students' quarters."

The wood-paneled staircase wasn't as narrow as the ones at the Holding, and a little window halfway up lit the stairs clearly. There was a door on the second landing, and the Dean opened it for her.

"This is the dormitory section," he said. Like the hall below them, it was paneled in some kind of dark wood, sanded smooth, but not polished. The doors here were much closer together than they had been in the hall below, and the hall itself seemed oddly foreshortened.

"As you can see, this hall is a bit less than half the size of the one downstairs, since on the other side of that wall is the common room where all meals are served, and on the other side of that is the boys' section. We're standing in the girls' side now. The third floor is one room, the Library and study area. The Library is entirely for the use of students and Heralds; you can go there any time you don't have classes or other tasks to do." Elcarth smiled encouragingly as Talia's eyes lit. "Just try to see that you spend a *little* time in eating and sleeping!"

Just then a small boy, wearing a uniform much like the Guard had worn, but in light blue instead of midnight blue, came running up to Elcarth. He was trailed at a distance by a richly dressed but harried-looking middle-aged man. This was the first person *not* wearing some kind of uniform that Talia had seen since she'd arrived.

"Havens, what is it *now*?" Elcarth muttered under his breath as the boy pounded up to them.

"Dean Elcarth, sir, it's the Provost-Marshal, sir," the boy said in a breathless treble.

"I can see that, Levand. What's happened this time? Fire, flood, or rioting in the streets?"

"Some of all three, m'lord Herald." The Provost-Marshal had plodded within hearing distance and spoke for himself, as Talia tried to make herself invisible back against the wall. "You know the Lady-fountain in Tailor's Court? The one that used to vent down a culvert to Breakneedle Street?"

"Your choice of words fills me with foreboding, m'lord," Elcarth replied with a sigh. " 'Used to'?"

"Someone chose to divert it, m'lord Herald. Into the cellar gathering-room of Jon Hapkin's Virgin and Stars Tavern. Which is, as you know—"

"The third-year Bardic students' favored place of illicit recreation; yes, I know. This rather smacks of the Unaffiliates, doesn't it? The plumb-line and compass set—"

"Partly, m'lord."

"You fill me with dread. Say on."

"The Bardic students took exception to gettin' their feet wet, m'lord Herald, and took exception very strongly."

"And went hunting the perpetrators, no doubt?"

"Aye, m'lord. I'm told that drum-beaters make fine cudgels, and there's a few among 'em that lately fancy walking about with carved staffs."

"Well, that covers the flood and the rioting in the streets. What about the fire?"

"Set by the Bardic students, m'lord. In the alley off Fivepenny. Seems the ones they blamed for the water had holed up in the Griffin's Egg and wouldn't come out, and someone gave them the notion to smoke 'em out. They lit a trash-fire and fed the smoke in through the back door."

"Lord—" Elcarth passed his hand over his eyes, looking to Talia as if he had a headache coming on. "Why take this up with me, my lord? So far you need to speak to the parents and patrons of the Unaffiliates involved, and the Dean of Bardic."

"The which I've done, m'lord Herald. *That's* been taken care of."

"There's more? Lady save me—"

"When all the hue and cry was over, and the gentlemen and ladies separated from one another, it was discovered that they'd had their purses lifted, one and all. The purses were found, intact, hanging from the trees in the Cloister gardens; the Lady's priestesses never saw anyone put them there, of course, but several of the combatants remembered someone in the thick of all the pummeling that had been wearing Heraldic student Grays."

"Needless to say—"

"Aye, m'lord Herald. Only one student you've got that's able to pull that prank."

"Lord-Dark and Lady-Bright," Elcarth muttered, rubbing one temple. "Hold on a moment, my lord Provost-Marshal. I have another bit of business I'll have to delegate, and I'll be right with you."

Elcarth looked around, and spied Talia shrunk as inconspicuously as possible in the corner. "Child, this is unbearably rude of me, but I'll have to find you another guide for the moment," he said, putting his hand gently behind her shoulders and propelling her forward a little. The door to the common room opened, and a small group of young women, all dressed identically in gray, stepped into the hall.

"And there," Elcarth said with satisfaction, "is just the person I was needing. Sherrill!"

One of the young women, a tall, slender brunette with a narrow face and hazel eyes, turned at the sound of her name being called, smiled, and made her way toward them.

"Sir?" she said, then looked curiously at Talia.

"This is the young lady Rolan brought in," Elcarth replied. "She's from one of those Border settlements that might just as well be out-Kingdom, and she's very confused. She'll need lots of help in adjusting. Unfortunately, the Provost-Marshal has some other business I need to handle. Would you—"

"Take her off your hands? Surely! Is she as badly off as *I* was?" The young woman's smile was infectious, and Talia returned it tentatively.

"Seriously, yes—worse, in some ways," the Dean replied.

"Bright Havens, that bad? Poor baby!" The young woman gave Talia another encouraging smile. "Well, we'll see what we can do for her. Uh, sir—is the 'business' Skif again?"

"It looks that way."

"Oh, Havens. Doesn't he ever learn?"

"He does. He never does the same trick twice," Elcarth replied, fighting down a chuckle. "It isn't too bad this time. He's not the main perpetrator, apparently; he's more of a loose end. I think I can get him off easily."

"Well, I hope so; I like the little monkey."

"Don't we all? Except possibly Lord Orthallen. You will take good care of young Talia, won't you? I'm counting on you, since the Provost-Marshall is beginning to look impatient."

"Yes, sir." She grinned. As she turned toward Talia, the grin became sympathetic. "The Dean knows I was in the same predicament as you are now when I first came. My people are fisherfolk on Lake Evendim, and all I knew was fish. You should have seen the saddlesores I came in with—and I couldn't even read and write!"

"I can read—and write and figure, too," Talia said shyly.

"See? You're three better than I was to start with! Dean—" She recaptured Elcarth's attention from wherever it had been wandering, "Basic Orientation with Teren tomorrow, sir?"

"Naturally; we've been holding the class until Rolan returned. I'll arrange a schedule for her and leave it with Teren. And tomorrow I want you to take her over to the training grounds and let Alberich decide what he wants to do with her."

Sherrill looked from Talia to the Dean, a little surprised that the girl was being put into Alberich's class so quickly, and caught Elcarth's silent signal that he wished to talk more with her later. She nodded briefly and Elcarth bid them both farewell, hurrying off with the harried Provost-Marshal.

She took a good look at the latest (and most important) of the Chosen. The poor little thing seemed exhausted, shy, and rather worried, and was most certainly bewildered by all that had been happening to her. Sherrill was surprised by a sudden surge of maternal feelings toward the child.

"Well, Talia, the first thing we need to do is find you a room and get you your uniforms and supplies," she said, hoping her casual tone would put the girl at ease. "How old are you, anyway?"

"Thirteen," Talia replied softly, so softly Sherrill could hardly hear her.

"That old? You don't look it," she said, leading the way. "I'll tell you what, though, it's not so bad being small; there aren't that many Chosen that are your size, and at least you can count on getting uniforms that aren't half patches!"

"Uniforms?"

"Like my outfit—take a good look. It's identical to a Herald's except that it's silvery gray instead of Herald's White, and the materials are a bit different. You see, wearing uniforms puts us all on an equal footing, and it makes us easy to identify as Heralds-in-training. Bardic and Healer's Collegia do the same; full Bards wear scarlet, and the trainees wear red-brown; Healers have their Healer's Green, and the Healers-in-training wear pale green. We wear gray until we've earned our Whites. There are some students that don't belong to any of the Collegia; they wear uniforms too, but they're pale blue. Officially they're called the Unaffiliates; we call 'em the Blues. There's all kinds—people learning to be something more than just simple clerks, ones that have talents for building things, highborns whose parents think they ought to have something to do besides choose new horses and clothing."

She frowned for a moment in sudden thought, wondering how much to tell the girl about the Blues. Should she frighten the child, perhaps needlessly, or should she leave her in ignorance of the intrigues going on all around her? It was hard to judge when the girl seemed determined to show an impassive face to the world. Sherrill knew she hadn't the ability of Elcarth to "read" someone, and this Talia might just as well have been a rock for all that *she* could judge of what might be going on behind those big eyes.

She decided on a middle course. "You might want to watch out for them," she warned. "Both Bardic and Healer's Collegia are pretty careful about who they accept for training, and anyone in Grays has been Chosen by a Companion, but the unaffiliated students have no selection criteria applied to them. All that's required is that they keep passing the courses they choose. A good half of the ones from the Court circles are no better than well-born bullies, and there's one or two of them that are *really* nasty-minded. In your place, I'd try and stick close to other Grays in public places." She stopped, and opened one of the doors at the very end of the hall. "Now, this will be your room."

The little room revealed had scarcely enough space for the furniture—bed, desk, chair, bookcase, and wardrobe. It was obvious that to Talia, however, it seemed palatial. No doubt she'd shared at least a bed with other girls and very possibly had never had even a corner of a room to call her own before this. Sherrill slipped a card with Talia's name printed on it into a holder on the door, and smiled at her expression. She sympathized completely; before she'd been carried off to the Collegium by her own Companion, she'd spent most of her life packed together with the rest of her family like salt-fish in a barrel. Her summers had been spent on the boat, with nowhere to go for any kind of privacy, the winters were spent in a one-room longhouse with not only her own family but the families of both her uncles as well. She sometimes wondered now how anyone managed to ignore the press of people long enough to ensure that the family name was carried on!

"Do you like it?" she asked, trying to elicit some response from the child.

Talia was overwhelmed. She'd slept all her life in a bed shared with two of her sisters in the barracks-like attic of the Housestead. This room—now all her own!—seemed incredibly luxurious in comparison. Sherrill seemed to understand, and let her contemplate this wealth of privacy for a long moment.

"Oh, yes!" she replied at last. "It's—wonderful!"

It was more than wonderful; it was a long-wished-for haven, a place she could retreat to where no one else could go. Talia hadn't missed the fact that there was a bolt on the inside of the door. If she wanted to, she could lock the whole world out.

"Good! Now we go see the Housekeeper," Sherrill said, interrupting Talia's reverie before she had a chance to really get used to the idea of having her own room. "She'll get your supplies and put you down on the duty roster."

"What's that?"

"A question at last! I was beginning to wonder what had happened to your tongue!" Sherrill teased gently, and Talia flushed a little. "It's the tradition of the three Collegia that everyone share the work, so there are no servants anywhere around here. In fact, the only people in the Collegia that aren't students and teachers are the Cook and the House-keeper. We all take turns doing something every day. The chores never take that long to do, and it really drives home to the 'gently-born' that we're all equals here. If you're sick, you're excused, of course. I suspect they'd even have us doing all the cooking if they weren't sure that we'd probably poison each other by accident!"

Sherrill chuckled; Talia laughed hesitantly, then offered, "I can cook. Some."

"Good. Make sure to tell Housekeeper. She'll probably put you down as Cook's helper most of the time, since most of us don't know one end of a chicken from the other."

She chuckled again as she recalled something. "There's a Herald that just got his Whites a month or so ago, his name is Kris, who was one of the 'gently-born' and pretty well sheltered when he first came here. First time he was Cook's helper, Cook gave him a chicken and told him to dress and stuff it. He hadn't been the kind that does any hunting (scholarly, you know) so Cook had to tell him how to slit the chicken for cleaning. He did it, then looked inside and said 'I don't need to stuff it, it's already full!' He *still* hasn't lived that one down!"

By this time they'd descended the stairs past the landing on the first floor and had reached the bottom of the staircase. Sherrill knocked twice at the door there, then opened it and entered. Behind the door was a narrow, whitewashed room lit by a window up near the ceiling; Talia reckoned that the window must have been level with the ground outside. This room contained only a desk, behind which sat a ma-tronly, middle-aged woman who smiled at them as they entered.

"Here's the new one, Housekeeper," Sherrill said cheerfully.

The woman measured Talia carefully by eye. "Just about a seven, I'd say. We don't get many Chosen as small as you. Did you bring any-thing with you, dear?"

Talia shook her head shyly, and Sherrill answered for her. "Just like me, Housekeeper Gaytha; the clothes she stood up in. You're going to have to have a word with Queen Selenay about that—the Companions never give the Chosen any time to pack!"

The Housekeeper smiled and shook her head, then left the room by a door in the wall behind her desk. She returned shortly with a pile of neatly folded clothing and a lumpy bag.

"Collegium rules are that you wash before every meal and have a hot bath every night," she said, handing half the pile to Talia and half to Sherrill. "Dirty clothing goes down the laundry chute in the bathroom; Sherrill will show you where that is. You change the sheets on your bed once a week; you'll get them with the rest of the girls, and the old ones go in the laundry. If you've been working with your Companion or at arms practice, change your clothing before you eat. There's no shortage of soap and hot water here, and staying clean is very important. Heralds have to be trusted on sight, and who'd trust a slovenly Herald? You can get clean uniforms from me whenever you need them. I know this may not be what you're used to—"

"I had trouble with it," Sherrill put in. "Where I come from you don't wash in the winter since there's no way to heat enough water, and you'd probably get pneumonia from the drafts. I never visit home in the winter anymore—my nose has gotten a lot more sensitive since I left!"

Talia thought of Keldar's thrice-daily inspections, and the cold-water scrubbing with a floor-brush that followed any discovery of a trace of dirt. "I think I'll be all right," she answered softly.

"Good. Now as Sherrill has told you—or should have—you all have small chores to see to every day. What can you do?"

"Anything," Talia replied promptly.

The Housekeeper looked skeptical. "Forgive me, my dear, but that doesn't seem very likely for someone your age."

"She's older than she looks," Sherrill said. "Thirteen."

Talia nodded. "They were going to make me get married, so I ran away. That's when Rolan found me. Keldar said I was ready."

The Housekeeper was plainly shocked. "Married? At *thirteen*?"

"It's pretty common to marry that young on the Borders," Sherrill replied. "They don't wait much longer than that back home. Borderers treat themselves and their children just like they do their stock; breed 'em early and often to get the maximum number of useful offspring. There's no one true way, Housekeeper. Life is hard on the Border; if Borderers were to hold by inKingdom custom, they'd never be able to hold their lands."

"It still seems—barbaric," the Housekeeper said with faint distaste.

"It may well be—but they have to survive. And this kind of upbringing is what produced us a Herald that has a chance of turning the Brat back into a proper Heir. You'll take notice that Rolan didn't pick any of *us*." Sherrill smiled down at Talia, who was trying not to show her discomfort. "Sorry about talking about you as if you weren't there. Don't let us bother you, little friend. Not all of us have had the benefits of what Housekeeper calls a 'civilized upbringing.' Remember what I told you about not washing in winter? Housekeeper had to hold me down in a tub of hot water and scrub me near raw when I first got here—I was a *real* little barbarian!"

Talia couldn't imagine the immaculate and self-assured Sherrill being held down and scrubbed by anyone—still less could she imagine Sherrill *needing* that kind of treatment.

"Talia, can you cook or sew? Anything of that nature?"

"I can cook, if it's plain stuff," Talia said doubtfully. "Only the Wives did feasts; they were too important to be left to us. My embroidery isn't any good at all, but I can mend and sew clothing and knit. And weave and spin. And I know how to clean just about anything."

The Housekeeper suppressed a chuckle at the exasperated tone of the last sentence. That tone convinced her that Talia probably was capable of what she claimed.

"It's so unusual that our students have as much experience in homely tasks as you do, that I think I'll alternate you as cook's helper and in the sewing room. There's never any lack of tears and worn spots to be mended, and there's generally a dearth of hands able to mend them. And Mero will be overjoyed to have me send someone capable of dealing with food for a change." She handed Talia a sheet of paper after consulting one of the books on her desk and writing in it. "Here's your schedule; come see me if it's too hard to fit in among your classes and we'll change it."

Sherrill led the way back up the stairs to Talia's new room. Talia examined her new clothing with a great deal of interest. There were loose linen shirts, meant to be worn with thigh-length tunics of a heavier material, something like canvas in weight, but much softer, and long breeches or skirts of the same fabric. There were some heavier, woolen versions of the same garments, obviously meant for winter wear, a wool cloak, and plenty of knitted hose, undergarments, and nightgowns.

"You'll have to make do with your own boots for a bit, until we have a chance to get you fitted properly," Sherrill said apologetically, as she helped Talia put the clothing away. "That won't be for another week at least. It's too bad—but there's nothing worse than badly fitted boots; they're worse than none at all, and Keren will have your hide if you dare try riding without boots. Unless it's bareback, of course."

They'd only just finished making up the bed when a bell sounded in the hall outside.

"That's the warning bell for supper," Sherrill explained. "Get one of your uniforms, and we'll go get cleaned up and you can change."

The bathing room was terribly crowded. Sherrill showed her where everything was located; the laundry chute, the supplies for moon-days, towels and soap—and despite the press of bodies managed to find both of them basins and enough hot water to give them at least a sketchy wash. Talia felt much more like herself with the grit of riding and the last trace of tears scrubbed away. Sherrill hurried her into her new clothing and off they went to the common room.

Supper proved to be a noisy, cheerful affair. Everyone sat at long communal tables, students and adults alike, and helped themselves from the bowls and plates being brought from a kind of cupboard in the wall. It seemed much too small to have held all that Talia saw emerging from it; Sherrill saw her puzzled look and explained over the noise.

"That's a hoist from the kitchen; the kitchen is down in the basement where Housekeeper's office and the storerooms are. And don't feel *too* sorry for the servers. They get to eat before we do and Mero always saves them a treat!"

Talia saw several figures in Herald's White interspersed among the student gray.

"The Heralds—are they *all* teachers?" she whispered to Sherrill.

"Only about half of them. The rest—well, there's Heralds just in from the field, a few retired from duty who choose to live here and don't care to eat with the Court, and a couple of ex-students that have just gotten their Whites that haven't been given their internship assignment yet. There's also three Heralds on permanent assignment to the Palace; to the Queen—that's Dean Elcarth; to the Lord Marshal—that's Hedric, and we don't see him much; and the Seneschal—that's Kyril, and he teaches, sometimes. They almost always *have* to eat with the Court. There ordinarily would be a fourth, too, the Queen's Own, but—" She stopped abruptly, glancing at Talia out of the corner of her eye.

"How—what happened to him?" Talia asked in a small voice, sure that she wasn't going to like the answer, but wanting badly to know anyway. The Queen had said—as had her tales—that being a Herald was dangerous, and there had been something about the way people had spoken about the former Queen's Own that made her think that Talamir had probably encountered one of the dangers.

"Nobody seems to be sure. It *could* have been an illness, but—" Sherrill was visibly torn between continuing and keeping quiet.

"But? Sherrill, I *need* to know," she said, staring entreatingly at her mentor.

Her urgency impressed Sherrill, who decided it was better that she be warned. "Well, a lot of us suspect he was poisoned. He was old and frail, and it wouldn't have taken much to kill him." Sherrill was grim. "If that's true, it didn't gain the murderers anything. We think the reason he was eliminated was because he was about to convince Selenay to send the Brat out to fosterage with some family that wasn't likely to give in to her tantrums. I guess you don't know—the law is that the Heir also has to be a Herald; if the Brat isn't Chosen by a Companion, the Queen will either have to marry again in the hope that another child will prove out or choose an Heir from those in the blood who *are* Chosen. Either way, there would be an awful lot of people maneuvering for power. Poor Selenay! Any of the rest of us could just choose a partner and go ahead and *have* as many children as needful, without bringing a possible consort and political repercussions into it—but there it is, she's the Queen, and it has to be marriage or nothing. It's not a nice situation." Sherrill regarded the tiny, frail-seeming girl at her side with sober eyes. She was beginning to have a good idea why Elcarth wanted Talia weapons-trained so early.

Talia thought Sherrill had a talent for understatement. Her revelations concerning the former Queen's Own frightened Talia enough that the rest of her speech—which rather bore out the Holderkin assertions of the immorality of Heralds—passed almost without notice. "What about the—the people who poisoned Herald T-T-Talamir?" she stuttered a little from nervousness. "Would they—am I—would they try to—hurt me?" As she looked into Sherrill's eyes, watching for the signs that would tell her if the older girl was speaking the truth, she could feel her hands trembling a little.

Sherrill was a little surprised at Talia's instant grasping of the situation—and hastened to reassure her. Those big brown eyes were widened with a fear even Sherrill could read. "They won't dare try that *particular* trick again, not with the suspicions that have been raised. What they probably *will* try and do is to make life unpleasant enough for you that you give up and leave. That's one reason why I warned you about the Blues. They might get orders from their parents to harass you. You should be safe enough with us, and I'm fairly sure you'll be safe with the Bardic and Healer students, too." Sherrill smiled down at Talia, who returned the smile, though a bit uncertainly. "Talia, if *anyone* bothers you and you think you can't handle them, tell me. My friends and I have taken the scales off the Blues a time or two before this."

Maybe. Talia wanted to trust her—desperately wanted to fit in here, but even of her kin only two had ever proved willing to back her against others. Why should a stranger do so? She ate in silence for a while, then decided to change the subject. "How many students are there?"

"About sixty in Healer's, forty in Bardic, and with you, exactly fifty-three in Herald's Collegium. The number of Blues varies; there's never less than twenty, not often more than fifty. I couldn't tell you the exact number right now, you'd have to ask Teren. He's Elcarth's assistant, and you'll have him as your first instructor tomorrow."

"How long does it take to become a Herald?"

"It varies; around five years. Usually we arrive here when we're about your age, most of us get our Whites at eighteen; I'll probably earn mine next year. I've seen younger Chosen, though, and Elcarth wasn't Chosen till he was nearly twenty! And Havens! Elcarth made up for being Chosen so late by being made full Herald in three years! After you get your Whites, there's a year or year and a half internship in the field, partnered by a senior Herald. After that, you're usually assigned out on your own."

Talia thought about this for a while, then asked worriedly, "Sherrill, what—how do I learn what I need to do?"

Talia was so earnest that Sherrill laughed sympathetically. "You'll learn, don't worry. You'll have Orientation class first. We've had four more Chosen in the past month, and they were only waiting for Rolan to come back before starting it. For the rest—you'll be placed in your classes according to where the Dean feels you fit in, which means you may be taking some classes with me, and some with beginners."

Talia smiled suddenly. "In other words, you throw the baby into the River and see if she learns to swim quickly!"

Sherrill laughed again, "We aren't quite that extreme! Are you finished?"

Talia nodded, and they carried their implements to the hoist inside the cupboard. "I've got dishwashing tonight, so I'll have to leave you on your own," Sherrill continued. "Will you be all right alone, or would you like me to find someone to keep you company?"

"I—I'll be all right. I would like awfully to see the Library if you don't think anyone would mind."

"Help yourself, that's what it's there for. Just remember not to wait too long before you take your bath, or all the hot water will be gone. I'll come by for you in the morning."

Sherrill clattered down the stairs and Talia climbed cautiously upward.

*　　*　　*

Sherrill was grateful that dishwashing took so little time, and equally grateful that Mero let her off early when she told him that the Dean needed to speak with her. Elcarth would not have given her the signal he had—in fact, he would have said what he intended to openly, in front of the child—had he not felt that there were things he needed to discuss with Sherrill that he would rather Talia were not privy to.

As she had pretty much expected, Sherrill found him waiting for her in the cluttered little room attached to his suite that served him as an office of sorts. It was hardly bigger than a closet, and piled high with everything under the sun, but he would never move to anything more spacious, claiming the clutter would "breed" to fill the space if he did so.

"Any problems getting away?" he asked, removing a pile of books and papers from one of the chairs, a comfortable, padded relic as old as Elcarth.

"I had dishwashing—it made a convenient excuse. Right now Talia's probably having raptures over the Library," Sherrill replied with a half-smile, taking her seat as Elcarth perched himself behind a desk heaped with yet more books and papers.

"Good; can I take it as given that you don't mind being her mentor? She needs one rather badly, and you're the only student with the kind of background that's close to her own."

"Poor little thing—no, Dean, I don't mind at all. Although I don't think my background is all that close." Sherrill frowned slightly, thinking about the little that Talia had allowed her to learn. "You know Evendim clans, we're all noise and push, and we're almost incestuously close. I got the feeling she's been sat on so much that now she's afraid of being punished for breathing—*and* I got the feeling nobody's ever bothered to give the poor thing a little love. She holds everything inside; it's hard to read her, and I don't recall much about Holderkin from class."

"There you've hit it. The fact of the matter is that we just don't *know* that much about Holderfolk. They're very secretive; they keep almost totally to themselves and they don't encourage long visits or curiosity from strangers. Until we heard Talia's story, we didn't even know that they don't tell their children about Companion's Choice!"

"They *what?*" Sherrill was shocked.

"It's quite true; she hadn't the vaguest idea of what it meant when Rolan Chose her. I'm fairly certain she still isn't entirely aware of what his true nature is. This is what I need to talk to you about. You're going to be dealing with a child who seems to have had a very alien upbringing. I can make some educated guesses; she seems to be afraid of men, so I can assume she tends to expect punishment from them. That would fit in with what I do know about Holderfolk; their familial life is patriarchal and authoritarian. She seems to be constantly repressing her emotions, and again, that would fit in with what I know of her people. They frown on any sort of demonstrative behavior. At the same time, she always seems to be—almost at war with herself—"

"Holding herself back, sir?" Sherrill offered. "As if she wanted to make overtures, but didn't quite dare? She seems to be wary all the time, that much I can tell you. I doubt that she trusts anyone at this point, except maybe Rolan."

"Exactly. The first moves are always going to have to be yours, and I think she'll continue to tend to keep her feelings very much to herself," Elcarth replied. "It's going to be up to you to discover if there's anything bothering her because she'll never tell you on her own."

"Gods." Sherrill shook her head. "Just the opposite of my people. I don't know, sir; I'm more used to dealing with folk who shout their minds and hearts to the world. I'm not sure I'm good enough to read the signs of trouble, assuming she'll give me anything to read."

"Do your best, that's all I ask. At least you both came from Border Sectors; that will be a bond."

"Why are you turning her over to Alberich so early?" Sherrill asked curiously. "I realize why she'd best learn self-defense as soon as possible, but I should think, with the kinds of insecurities she seems to have, that he would be the *last* person you'd want to expose her to. I mean, Jeri would be a much less threatening figure to deal with."

"I wish there were some other way, but she knows absolutely *nothing* about self-defense; I know that Jeri is very good, but she isn't the kind of experienced teacher Alberich is. He's the only one likely to be able to teach her with the speed that's necessary. If a mob of troublemakers should corner her—or, Bright Lady forbid it, someone should decide that a knife in the dark solves the problem of the new Queen's Own turning up . . ."

He let the sentence trail into silence.

"And I can't be with her all the time. Well, I hope he gentles his usual routine with her, or she may drop dead of fright on the practice field and save an assassin the trouble." Sherrill's tone was jocular, but her eyes held no amusement.

"I've already spoken with him, and he's not as unsympathetic as you might think. He was my year-mate, you know. I have reason to believe he'll be quite soft-handed with her."

"Alberich, soft-handed? Really? Tell my bruises that some time, sir."

"Better bruises now than a fatal wound later, no?" Elcarth grinned crookedly. "I could wish one of Talia's year-mates was another girl; I could wish we had someone more likely to understand what she won't let us see. You're the closest I could come. Well, that's all I have to tell you. It isn't much—"

"But it's a start. Take heart, Dean. Companions don't Choose badly, and look how long it took Rolan to find her. She'll manage. And I'll manage. Heralds always do."

At the head of the staircase Talia opened a door that led into a single enormous room filled with bookshelves. There were cubicles containing desks and chairs at the ends of the rows of shelves along the walls. She had been expecting perhaps twice or three times the number of books in her Father's library—twenty—but nothing prepared her for this. There were hundreds of books here; more than she ever dreamed existed, all colors, and all sizes. It was more than a dream come true— it was a vision of heaven.

Dusk had fallen while they'd been eating, and lanterns had been lit at intervals along the walls. Talia peeked into the nearest cubicle and saw that there were candles on the desk, and a permanent holder affixed to one side of it.

She heard footsteps approaching from the farther end of the library, and she turned to see who it could be, hoping for someone she knew.

"Hello!" said a cheerful tenor. "You're new here, aren't you? I'm Kris."

The young man who stepped into the circle of light cast by the lantern was in Whites and as incredibly beautiful as the Herald Talia had met outside the city had been homely. His features were so perfect they didn't seem to be real, every raven hair was neatly in place, and his sky-blue eyes would have been the envy of any Court beauty. Talia immediately felt as awkward and ungainly as a young calf—and more than a little afraid as well. Dealing with her older sib Justus had taught her that beauty could hide an evil nature. Only the fact that he was a Herald—and there simply *wasn't* any such thing as an evil Herald— kept her from bolting outright.

"Yes," she replied softly, blushing a little and staring at her boot-tops. "I'm Talia."

"Have you been up here before?"

She shook her head, beginning to relax a little.

"Well," he said, "the rules are very simple. You can read anything you want, but you can't take the book out of the Library, and you have to put it back exactly where you found it when you're done. That's pretty easy, isn't it?"

Talia could tell by his patronizing tone of voice that he was feeling just slightly superior. Yet he seemed to be friendly enough, and there hadn't been anything in his manner to indicate that he was ill-tempered. The patronization annoyed her, and she decided it was safe to get a little of her own back.

"Y-yes," she said softly. "As simple as stuffing a chicken."

"Ouch!" he laughed, clapping one hand to his forehead. "Stung! Isn't there *anybody* that hasn't heard that story? I deserved that—I shouldn't have talked down to you. Well, enjoy yourself, Talia. You'll like it here, I hope."

He turned with a parting grin and exited through the door she'd just used, and she heard his footsteps descending the staircase.

She wandered through the forest of bookcases, losing all track of time, too overwhelmed by the sheer numbers to even begin to make a choice. Gradually, however, she began to notice that the books were arranged by category, and within each category, by title. Once she'd made that identification, she began perusing the bookcases with more purpose, trying to identify what groups there were, and where they were, and marking the locations of particular books that sounded interesting. By the time she had it all clear in her mind, she found herself yawning.

She made her way to her own room, found one of her new bed-gowns, and sought the bathing-room. Sensholding had possessed the relatively new indoor latrines, so those hadn't surprised her any when Sherrill had shown them to her. However, all hot water for bathing back at the Holding had needed to be carried in pots from the kitchen. Here at the Collegium there were several charcoal-fired copper vessels for heating water, each at least the size of one of the tubs, with pipes at the bottom to take the hot water to the tubs and a pump to refill them with cold water from the top. This arrangement positively enchanted her; being neither little nor adult, she'd rarely ever gotten a really hot bath. The littlest littles were always bathed first, and the adults waited until later when all the kettles of water had been filled and heated a second time. Those who were too old to be bathed but too young to stay up late and bathe with the adults had to make do with whatever was left after cleaning the babies—which wasn't often much, or very warm.

There were several girls and young women there already, and all the bathtubs were in use. Talia took her turn at the pump, after being hailed by "you must be the new one" and shyly giving her own name.

"I'm glad you turned out to be a girl," one of the ones near her own age said, pumping water vigorously. "The boys outnumber us by too many as it is. Every single one of the other new ones has been a boy! That's why our side's smaller."

"Well, my sister's at Healer's, and it's the opposite there," a voice replied out of the steam.

"Besides, it's quality that counts, not quantity," the second bather's voice was half covered by vigorous splashing. "And it's quite obvious that we women have the quality."

The rest giggled, and Talia smiled tentatively.

"Sherrill told me there were fifty-three of us," she replied after a moment, reveling in the fact that she was one of the fifty-three. "How many of each are there?"

"Thirty-five colts and eighteen fillies," replied the girl at the pump. "And I'm referring to the human foals, not the Companions. It wasn't quite so bad until those four new boys came in, but now they outnumber us by almost two to one."

"Jeri, you're betraying your youth," said the young woman who was climbing out of the nearest tub. "You may not be old enough to appreciate odds like that, but Nerissa and I *are*. In my part of the Kingdom, women slightly outnumber the men, and I like it much better the other way 'round. I'd much rather be the one being courted than the one doing the courting. Whoever's next, I'm done."

"Is it like that where you're from, Talia?" Jeri asked, looking at her curiously as she claimed the now-vacant tub.

"I—I suppose it must be," she said, momentarily distracted from her shyness, mentally trying to count the distribution of the sexes in the Holdings she knew. "I'm Holderkin."

"Where's that?" the young woman called Nerissa asked, folding a towel around her wet hair.

"East—on the Border," Talia replied, still thinking. "I know it's rather dangerous off the Holdings themselves. More men die every year than women; there are lots of wild animals, and raiders come every winter. I think there's nearly twice as many women as men, at least on the farthest Holdings."

"Havens! You must be knee-deep in old maids."

"Oh, no—if you don't go to the Goddess, you *have* to get married. My father had eleven wives, and nine are still living."

"You can have my tub, Talia," Nerissa emerged from the steam. "Why do females *have* to get married?"

"W-why women can't Hold a Steading, or speak in Council or—anything important. It wouldn't be seemly," Talia said in astonishment.

"So-ho! That must be why they never send female Heralds to the lower Eastern Border. They wouldn't be listened to. Talia, it's very different here. It's going to take a lot of getting used to, and it's going to seem strange for a long while. We reckon a person's importance by what they are, not by what sex they are," Nerissa told her. "There's no such thing as 'seemly' or 'unseemly.' Just doing the job you're given."

Talia nodded thoughtfully, immersed in her tub. "I-it's hard to think this way. It j-just doesn't seem natural. I-I-I think *I* like it. Most of my Father's wives would hate it, though. Keldar for sure, and Isrel would be miserable without someone to give her orders."

"Nessa, the child doesn't need a lecture at this time of night!" the first woman called from the doorway. "Honestly, they should make you a teacher when you go into Whites, I've never heard anyone make so many speeches! Come *on*, or you'll be here all night!"

"All right, all right!" Nerissa replied, laughing a little. "Pleasant dreams, little one."

Talia finished her bath and found her room, feeling drained to the point of numbness. It seemed very odd to be climbing into a bed that had no one in it but herself. Her mind whirled in circles—this entire adventure hardly seemed real. In less than two weeks she'd gone from being the scorned scapegrace of Sensholding to a Herald-in-training; it seemed impossible. She kept returning to the astonishing moment when she'd realized what all that had occurred to her truly meant, holding the memory as wonderingly and gently as a new kitten, until sleep began to overpower her.

But her very last thoughts as she drifted off to sleep were of Nerissa's words, and the sudden decision that she *did* like it here.

Now if only all this was half as wonderful as it appeared on the surface—and if only they would let her fit in.

CHAPTER 5

S HE WOKE TO Sherrill's light tap on the wall and pulled on her unfamiliar uniform before opening her door.

"It's about time, sleepy!" Sherrill said genially, looking altogether *too* awake for sunrise. "The waking-bell rang ages ago, didn't you hear it? If we don't hurry, there won't be anything left but cold porridge." Without looking to see if Talia was following, she turned and headed for the door of the common-room.

Sherrill had exaggerated the "danger," as Talia found when they entered the double-doors. There was still plenty left to eat—an almost bewildering variety for Talia, who expected little besides the afore-mentioned porridge, bread and milk, and perhaps a little fruit. And there were plenty of other students who trailed in after them, rubbing sleepy eyes or complaining cheerfully to one another.

After breakfast, a somewhat more subdued meal than supper had been, and punctuated more by yawns than conversation, Sherrill led her to the first floor and out the door at the far end of the corridor. Talia recalled that the Dean had told her this door led to a court and the stables beyond it. They crossed a wide, paved courtyard that lay between the two build-ings, with the sun casting long shadows on the bedewed paving-stones before them, and Talia lingered a little, hoping wistfully to see Rolan.

"Talia, come catch up!" Sherrill called back over her shoulder, squinting against the sunlight. "Or don't you want to see your Com-panion this morning?"

Startled, she ran to overtake Sherrill. "Aren't the Companions in the stables?" she asked breathlessly.

"In the stables? With the regular horses? Bright Havens, they'd disown us! The Companions have their own place—we call it Companion's Field—and an open building so they can come and go as they like. On a beautiful morning like this, they're all probably out in their Field."

They'd come to a tall wooden fence surrounding a park-like area full of trees, and Talia thought that this must have been the green place she'd seen within the walls when she'd first caught sight of the capital. Sherrill climbed up on the fence, as agile as any of Talia's brothers, put her fingers in her mouth, and whistled shrilly like a boy. When Talia joined her, she could see tiny white shapes moving off in the distance, under the trees. Two of these detached themselves from the rest and began trotting toward them.

"I don't mindcall at all well—not unless I'm scared stiff," Sherrill said, a little shamefacedly. "Ylsa says I'm blocked—so I have to whistle for Silkswift. She doesn't seem to mind any."

Talia had no difficulty in recognizing which of the two Companions approaching was Rolan, and her joy at seeing him again was such that she didn't once wonder what Sherrill had meant by "mindcalling" and "being blocked." With a cry of happiness she jumped off the fence to land beside Rolan and spent several jubilant minutes caressing him and whispering joyous nonsense into his ear. He was even more of a magical creature than she remembered him being. Someone had tended him well last night, for he had been groomed until he nearly glowed. His coat and mane were softer than the finest fabric she'd ever touched, and he was as beautiful as one of the Moon-steeds that drew the Lady's chariot. He nuzzled her with something she no longer doubted was love, whuffing softly at her, and the feeling of total well-being and confidence she'd had when with him on the road returned. While she was with him, she feared nothing, doubted nothing. . . .

"I hate to say this, but we *do* have an appointment with Master Alberich," Sherrill said at last, reluctantly. "Talia, it's part of your training to spend a lot of time with your Companion—you'll see him again this afternoon. You have to—from now on tending him and grooming him will be all up to you. They may be incredible darlings, but they don't have hands; they need us as much as we need them. So you'll get back to him before supper—and we really do have to be going."

Rolan nudged her toward the fence, then shook his forelock as if in admonishment. When she continued to hesitate, he gave her a good shove with his nose and snorted at her.

"All right," she replied, "I'll be good and go. But I'm coming back, classes or not!"

Sherrill took her to a long, low building just beyond the stables; inside it was all but bare—smooth, worn wooden floors and a few benches, with storage cabinets built into the walls. Between the cabinets were a few full-length mirrors, and the place was lit from windows that were high up on the walls, near the ceiling. There they found the man Sherrill introduced as Alberich, the Weaponsmaster. He alone of all the instructors was not wearing Whites; rather, he was dressed in old, supple leather; part armor, part clothing, and of a dark gray color like old ashes, darker than Student Grays.

"I thought all the instructors were Heralds," Talia whispered to her guide as they approached him.

"All but one—but Alberich is a Herald; he's just a law unto himself. He never wears Whites unless he's being official."

The Weaponsmaster frightened Talia into near speechlessness when he turned to face them. He was tall, lean, and dark; his face was seamed with scars, and he looked as though he never smiled. Thick streaks of white ran through his abundant black hair, and his eyes were an agate gray and very penetrating. As his sober stare held her pinned in place, Talia decided that now she knew how a mouse felt in the gaze of a hawk.

"So," he said at last. "You are how old? Thirteen? What physical training have you, child? Know you any weaponry? Tactics? Eh?"

She hardly knew how to answer—she really couldn't make out what he was asking of her. Physical training? Did playing games count? Was the sling she'd used to keep wolves off the sheep a weapon?

At last he gave her a wooden practice knife, and stood with his arms crossed, still looking fierce and hawklike.

"Come you, then. Come at me—"

She still hadn't the faintest notion what he wanted of her, and stood stonelike, arms stiffly at her sides, feeling clumsy and ridiculous.

"What ails you? I told you to attack me! Is it that women do not fight among your people?" he asked, his speech heavily accented, his brows drawing together into an intimidating frown. "Have you no weapons skill at all?"

"I can shoot a bow, a little," she said in a small and shamed voice. "One of my brothers showed me. He wasn't supposed to, but I begged him so hard—and I guess I'm all right with a sling."

She thought with misery that she seemed to have gotten into the wrong again. It seemed that nothing she'd ever learned was appropriate here—except, perhaps her housekeeping skills. And she'd never once read a tale that praised a Herald's ability at peeling roots!

She waited, cringing, for him to dismiss her back to the building in disgust. He did nothing of the sort.

"At least you have sense not to pretend to what you have not," he replied thoughtfully. "I think it is too late to teach you the sword. Fortunately, you are not likely to need to use one. Bow, of necessity, and knife, and hand-to-hand. That should suffice your needs. Return one hour after the nooning." Then he did dismiss her, after staring at her long and broodingly.

Talia was very subdued and discouraged by this encounter; Sherrill managed to see this even though she tried to mask it. "Don't feel badly," she said, and Talia could clearly hear the encouragement in her voice. "You actually got off pretty easily. When he first saw me, he threw his hands up in the air and growled, 'Hopeless! Hopeless! Let her throw nets and dead fish to defend herself!' At least he thinks you're worth working with. He left me to one of his assistants for months!"

"But—why d-d-did he say that ab-b-bout the f-fish?" Oh, that hateful stutter! No matter how confident she tried to appear, it always gave her away!

"Because I spent half my life on a boat and the other half in very crowded conditions; the last thing you want to do on a slippery deck or a floor thick with babies is run! I had to learn how to move freely, something you've always known."

"It d-d-didn't seem as if he th-thought I was worth anything."

"He didn't scream at you—that's a wonder in itself. He didn't tell you to get yourself back home and raise babies, either. I think maybe you won him a little by being honest about how little you know—an awful lot of new students try to pretend they're more expert than they are, and he generally does his best to make fools of them in front of everybody by way of punishment."

By now they'd reached the Collegium building again. Sherrill held the door open for Talia and stopped outside the first classroom door on the right. "Here's where the rest of the new ones are. I'll meet you for lunch." With that, Sherrill vanished down the hall, leaving Talia to face the next ordeal alone.

She tugged the door open and tried to slip inside unobtrusively, but felt more like creeping inside than anything else when she felt everyone's eyes on her. There seemed to be at least a dozen people there.

There were no other girls. The boys were mostly her own age, and though they made her feel rather shy, didn't arouse her unease; but the one who stood at the head of the classroom was one of those fearful creatures of ultimate authority, an adult male. As such, he made her wary immediately. She had to keep reminding herself that he was a Herald—and no Herald would ever do anything to harm anyone except an enemy of the Queen and Kingdom.

"Be welcome, youngling," he said, perching casually on the front edge of his desk. "Boys, this is your fifth year-mate; her name is Talia. Talia, the red-haired fellow is Davan, the tall one is Griffon, the twins are Drake and Edric—and I can't tell them apart yet." He winked at them, and the twin boys grinned back, obviously very much at ease with him. "Maybe I should ask Alberich to give one of you a black eye—then at least I'd know which of you was which until it faded."

Talia slipped shyly into an unoccupied seat and took a closer look at her teacher. Like Alberich, he was lean, but his brownish hair was only beginning to gray, and he had none of the Weaponsmaster's hawkishness about him. He put her more in mind of a hunting hound, all eagerness, good nature, and energy. His eyes were hound-brown, and just as friendly. And there was something about him—once again she was reminded of Andrean; she wanted to trust him—something within her was prompting her to do so, and she was a little surprised at herself.

"Well, now that you're here, I think we're ready to start. First, let me explain what this class is all about. I'm here to help you understand what being a Herald really means; not the hero tales, nor the horror stories, nor the wild rumors of drunken debauchery—" he wriggled his eyebrows, and the twins giggled. "But rather what our job really involves. Davan is probably the only one of you who knows—or thinks he knows—what being a Herald is all about. That's because both of his parents are Heralds themselves. So I'll start Davan with the question I'm going to ask each of you: Davan, what exactly does a Herald do?"

Davan's brow wrinkled in thought. "They dispense the Queen's justice," he finally replied.

"Good enough answer, as far as it goes, but *how* do they do that?"

"Uh, they ride circuit in their assigned areas, going through all the towns and villages, they deliver the new laws of the Kingdom and report on the acts of the Council and Queen. They see that the people understand the laws and act as judges, and sometimes lawgivers when something comes up that isn't covered in Kingdom law or by local custom."

"Bright Havens! You mean those poor people have to wait a year or more to get anything settled?" Teren asked in mock dismay.

"No, no! There's regular judges, too."

"So why not use them?"

Davan couldn't seem to think of a good answer, but one of the twins was waving his hand over his head. "Herald Teren?"

"Go ahead, whichever you are."

"Drake. Our village was too small to have a judge."

"That's a fair reason. But there's another; sometimes it happens that the feelings of the local people—and that includes the judge—are too worked up for a case to be adjudicated fairly. There's one reason for you. Davan, you have another?"

"Heralds can do the Truth Spell; regular judges have no way of knowing who's lying."

"Good! But that works *only* if someone involved in the case knows what really happened, remember that. All right, Heralds are judges and lawgivers. What else, Drake?"

"They report on what they see on their circuits to the Queen and the Council."

"Why should they do that?"

"So that the Queen knows the true condition of her Kingdom. Sometimes the mayors and head-men don't always tell the whole truth in their Domesday Book reports. Heralds know what's been reported, and how to look for things that don't match."

"Quite true. Edric, your turn."

"They serve as ambassadors to other Kingdoms. While they're there, they can see if there's something wrong the Queen should know about, like maybe an army that's awfully big for a country supposed to be peaceful. Since Heralds can't be bribed, she can always trust what they say."

"That's correct," said Herald Teren, "and there's more; the kind of training a Herald receives here makes it possible for him to note little things that others might miss—things that tell him that there may be more going on than he's being told. Griffon?"

"Heralds are the Queen's messengers. There's no faster, safer way to get a message across the Kingdom than to give it to a Herald, 'cause Companions run faster and for longer than any horse ever born. That's why Heralds are called 'the Arrows of the Queen.' And they act as warleaders in an emergency, until the regular Army can arrive. That's another reason for the name."

"Very good. Talia, your turn."

She had thought hard while the others were giving their answers. "They—make the Kingdom safe," she said softly. "Sometimes they're just what the rest said, and sometimes other things—spies, scouts, sometimes thieves—they do whatever needs doing so that the Queen knows what she needs to know to guard us all. They risk everything for that, for the safety of the Kingdom, and for her."

"And that is why," Teren said slowly, holding each of their eyes in turn, "about half of us don't live to see an honorable old age. Being a Herald is important—the Queen has said that we're the 'glue that holds everything together'—and it can be exciting. For the most part we are very much honored in this Kingdom; but being a Herald can also be a fatal occupation. Hero tales aside, younglings, songs don't help you much when you're looking death in the face and you're all alone. And being alone is another thing you are when you're a Herald. There aren't enough of us, and we get spread very thin. That puts you in the front line in a lot of very dangerous situations."

His eyes clouded a moment. "The danger is in direct proportion to the importance of the job at hand and your own ability to see it through. It's a sad fact that the better a Herald you are, the more likely it is that the Queen will set you risky tasks. I'm sure each of you has had a lazy fit now and again, sloughed some job off; but by the time you've earned your Whites, you will be totally unable to give anything less than your best to whatever is set before you. And when you're in the front line—well, that white uniform makes a pretty obvious target. I'm telling you all this now because this is your last chance to leave the Collegium. No one will think any the less of you for it. Well? Anyone want out?"

Talia cleared her throat.

"Yes, Talia?"

"I never got to finish the tale of Herald Vanyel, sir. The tale said at the beginning that he nearly didn't become a Herald at all because he was afraid—but he decided it was something he had to do anyway, that the job needed doing and he was the one chosen to do it. The last I read he was trapped by the Dark Servants, like he'd seen happening in a vision years before. What happened to him?"

"He died. The Dark Servants hacked him to pieces before help could arrive—yet he held them back long enough that his King was able to bring up an army in time to repel their invasion. But he still died, alone, and all the songs in the world won't change that. Now I want you to think about that for a moment—really think hard. Does that frighten you? Any of you could be asked to pay Vanyel's price. The Queen will weep that she had to send you, but that won't stop her from doing it. Want to leave?"

"No, sir." Talia's voice was very small, her eyes very large.

"Doesn't the idea frighten you?"

"Yes, sir," she said, softly, biting her lip. "Only somebody awfully stupid wouldn't be—" She stopped, groping for words.

Griffon found the words for her. "We've all heard the tales, sir—the ones with the bad, nasty endings right along with the ones that end with the hero's welcomes and celebrations. And I got here right after Talamir was buried; you think we didn't hear the talk then about poison? My own brother said right out he thought I was crazy to want to be a Herald. When we hear the bad tales, you best bet we get scared! But it's still something we *got* to do, just like Vanyel. Maybe you can't be made a Herald, maybe you got to be born one, and all this teaching you give us does is show us how to do better 'n easier the things we know we got to do anyway. Whatever. It's like bein' likker-cravin' or something. You still got to do it, no choice; couldn't stop, don't want to." He sat down with a thump, only then realizing he'd risen to his feet making his speech.

Herald Teren's tense expression eased. "I take it that you all agree with Griffon?"

They nodded, very much sobered.

"Then I can only say that once again, as always, the Companions seem to have Chosen aright. Griffon, you have unexpected depths of eloquence in you. I think you ought to consider seriously taking Logic and Oration—you could be very useful as a diplomat."

Griffon blushed, and looked down at his hands, murmuring a disclaimer.

"Now, having obliquely touched on the subject—you all know that it is the Companions that choose new Heralds, but do any of you know *how* they do it?"

They looked at one another in puzzled silence. Teren chuckled. "Nor do I. Nor does anyone. A few—the most sensitive to the bond that forms between a Herald and his Companion—have described that first encounter as 'a feeling that I was being measured.' But *what* it is that they measure, no one knows. All that we do know is that after a Companion has Chosen, there exists a kind of mind-to-mind link between him and his Herald that is similar, but not identical, to the kind of mind-link that exists between twins," he said, sharing a grin with Drake and Edric. "You'll learn more about that bond later, and how to use it. For now, it's enough for you to know that it *does* exist—so if you feel something between you and your Companion, you know that you're not imagining it or going mad. As you get older, you may develop one of the Gifts—what outsiders call 'Herald's magic.' You'll learn more about those later as well—but if you *thought* your Companion spoke to you when he Chose you, you were right. He did. No matter if you never have more than a touch of a Gift, your Companion will always speak to you in your heart at that moment—even if he never does so again. It wasn't something you dreamed. And if you have the right Gift, one day you'll learn to speak back."

Talia breathed an unconscious sigh of relief, not noticing that all the others except Davan were doing the same.

"And there's another thing about them that you should know," Teren continued. "Never, ever, for one moment doubt that they are something considerably more than animals. Any tale you've ever heard is no more than a pale reflection of their reality. Now, to elaborate on that, do any of you know where the Companions first came from?"

Davan nodded. "My parents told me, sir."

"Then tell the rest of us, if you would."

"It goes right back to before this Kingdom ever existed," Davan began. Talia gave him every bit of her attention, for this tale was all new to her. "It happened there was a good man who was living in a land with a bad King, way off to the East, right past any of our neighbors. His name was Baron Valdemar; he lived on his own Kingdom's western border. His King was the kind who took what he wanted and never paid any attention when his lands and people suffered, and most of his nobles were like minded. For a while Baron Valdemar was able to at least protect his own people from the King; that was because he was a wizard as well as a Baron, and his lady was a sorceress—old magic, the kind that's gone now, not Herald's magic. But the day finally came when there wasn't any way of stopping him short of outright rebellion. Baron Valdemar knew, though, that rebellion wasn't the answer either; he couldn't hold out against all the might the King could bring against him for very long at all. There were plenty of his neighbors who would be only too pleased to help the King destroy him for a share in his lands and goods after. So he did the only thing he could do; he fled away into the West, taking with him every last one of his people as were minded to follow. He led them on until he was sure there wasn't anybody following; then right here where we're sitting he stopped, and founded a whole new Kingdom, and those who'd come with him made him the King of it." Davan paused for a moment to think. "There was a whole lot about all the hardships they went through, and I can't remember that part too good."

"You're doing fine, Davan. You'll all get more detail later in your History classes; just go on with what you do remember."

"Well, 'ventually they got this city built; they all started to have a pretty good life by the time King Valdemar was an old man. Right then is when he took the time to notice how old he was getting, and to think about the future. He hadn't exactly had much time for thinking before this, 'cause there was too much to do, if you take my meaning. Anyway, what he thought was, 'I know *I'm* a good ruler, and a good man; I'm pretty sure my son will be the same—but what about my son's children, and theirs? How can I make certain that whoever takes this throne will be good for the people who support it?'"

"A good question. So what did he do?"

"Well, he waited till Midsummer's Day; he went out into the grove that stands in the middle of what we call Companion's Field now, and he asked every god he'd ever heard of to help him. An' Mama told me in the version she'd read, it said he cast a special spell, too, 'cause remember, he was a magician—a *real* magician, not just Gifted. She says there used to be lots of real magicians down where he came from, and that there used to be lots here, too, but that Vanyel was the last Herald-mage."

"That's the tradition; go on."

"Well, he started out at dawn; it wasn't till sunset that he got an answer. Everything went kind of light all over, like when you get too much sun on snow, and all he could hear was the sound of hoofbeats—hoofbeats that sounded just like bells. When the light cleared away, there were three horses standing in front of him; horses with coats the color of moonshine and eyes like pieces of the sky. Old Valdemar hadn't ever seen anything like them before in his life. And when he came up close to them, one of them looked him straight into the eyes—well, that's all there was to it. Ardatha told him her name in his mind and bound them together—"

"And the first Companion had Chosen."

"Right then his chief Herald—and a Herald was just a sort of mouthpiece for the King back then, didn't do a tenth of what Heralds do today—came looking for him. The second Companion—Kyrith—Chose *him*. The King's son, the Heir that was, he'd come along, and Steladar Chose him. When they all were in a mind to be thinking again, 'twas the King decided that the title of Herald should be made to mean more than it did, since only one person can be King or Heir, but there could be lots of Heralds."

"And King Valdemar, Prince Restil, and Herald Beltran began the work of making the Heralds into what they are now, starting with decreeing that the Heir must also be a Herald. The work wasn't easy, and it took the lifelong toil of several Kings and Queens, but it was with those three that it first began. By the time Valdemar died, there were twenty-one Heralds, including himself, his Heir, and his Heir's second son. You have a good memory, Davan, thank you," Teren concluded.

"Where did all those Companions come from?" Edrik wanted to know.

"At first they all came from the Grove in the middle of what we now call Companion's Field, like the first three; other than that, no one knew. After a while, though, the mares began foaling, and now all Companions with a single exception are born right here at the Collegium. That exception is the Companion to the Monarch's Own Herald," his glance flickered from Edrik to Talia and back again, so quickly she couldn't be certain she'd seen his eyes move. "*That* Companion appears from the Grove just as the originals did. He is always a stallion, and he never seems to age. He always gives his name to his Herald; the others may or may not do so, and may allow their Heralds to pick a name for them. If he is killed—and many have been—another appears from the Grove to take his place. If the Monarch's Own Herald is still living, that is the Herald he Chooses; if not, he stays only long enough to be caparisoned and goes out to seek the next in line. It is usually someone already a Herald or about to receive Whites that he Chooses, but that is not always the case."

"Talamir was Queen's Own, wasn't he, sir?"

"Yes, he was. His Companion was Rolan," Teren replied, nodding.

"Then that makes Talia Queen's Own, doesn't it?"

"Yes, it does. It's an important position. Are any of you jealous of her?"

Drake shook his head vehemently. "Ha!" he said. "We've seen the Br—, I mean the Princess. I wouldn't want any part of the job!" The rest nodded agreement.

Teren half smiled. "Watch your tongues carefully, younglings. We can call Elspeth the Brat among ourselves—the Queen calls her that, in fact—but make sure nobody from the Court overhears you. Some people would be only too happy to use that to make trouble. You're right; Talia is going to have a tough job. She'll need our help with it, all of us, because there are people at Court who would like very much to see her fail. Only Talia can do her job—but the rest of us can help her by making certain that no one makes it more difficult for her than it is already. Right, gentlemen?"

The boys nodded agreement; but Talia, determined not to be any kind of a burden on the Collegium or those in it, and still not quite ready to believe in the trustworthiness of strangers, pledged silently to manage on her own, no matter what.

A bell rang twice in the corridor outside. "Which of you is Cook's helper today?" Teren asked.

Talia raised her hand a little.

"For future reference, all of you, that's the signal for the helpers; the servers go on three rings, and the meal is served on four. Off with you, youngling. Gentlemen, if you left your rooms in a mess, you'd better rectify the situation; there's inspection after lunch. I'll see you here tomorrow morning."

Teren directed Talia to use the door and staircase near the door leading out to the courtyard. Instead of letting out into the Housekeeper's office, this one led her to a huge kitchen—and much to her surprise, the cook was a balding, moon-faced man. She was too surprised to find a man in charge of the kitchen to even think to be afraid of him, and his easy, gentle manner kept her from being alarmed, despite his sex.

He ignored what seemed to be chaos swirling around him to question her as to her abilities, his smile broadening with each of her answers.

"Finally!" he said, round face beaming. "Someone who knows what to do with food besides eat it!" He gave her charge over the vegetables.

While she peeled and chopped them, she peered about her, curiously. This place didn't seem all that different from the kitchen of a Hold house; even the ovens were in the same place. That was at first—then she began to notice small things; pumps to bring water to the huge sinks, another one of the copper boilers to heat the water, pipes leading from the sinks to carry the waste away. There was an almost fanatical precision about the placement of pots and pans and tools and the scrupulous cleanliness of the place—Keldar would surely have approved. She was surprised to see that all the ovens were in use; there wasn't much noticeable heat coming from them. They must have been insulated with far better care than the ones in the Holding. Or perhaps—as she considered it, it occurred to her that they actually extended out beyond the outer wall. Perhaps that had something to do with it.

She soon saw that what had seemed like chaos was in fact as carefully orchestrated as any general's field maneuvers. No one was allowed to stand idle for more than a moment or two, and yet the Cook

had gauged his helpers' abilities and stamina perfectly. They usually
tired just as their tasks were completed, and one by one were sent to
rest at a trestle table. Then, just as tired hands had recovered and tired
legs were ready to move again, the dishes began coming out of the
cupboard and the pots off the stove and out of the oven, and they
began transporting the filled dishes to the hoist. When the last of them
had vanished upward, they turned to find their table laid ready with
tableware and food.

Talia edged over onto a corner, and discovered her seatmate was
Jeri. "I *like* this job," Jeri said, filling her bowl and Talia's with stew.
"Mero always saves the best for us."

The cook grinned broadly; even his eyes smiled. "How else to in-
sure that you work and not shirk?" he asked, passing hot bread and
butter. "Besides, doesn't the Book of One say 'Do not keep the ox who
threshes your grain from filling his belly as he works'?"

"What's the 'Book of One'?" Talia whispered.

"Mero's from Three Rivers—there's a group up there that believes
there's only one god," Jeri replied. "I know it sounds strange, but they
must be all right, 'cause Mero's awfully nice."

It seemed more than very strange to Talia, and she knew what the
Elders would have said. Yet there was no denying the warmth and
kindness of this man; he went out of his way to coax Talia into helping
herself when she seemed too shy to dive in the way the others were.
What Nerissa had said last night was beginning to be something more
than words.

But before she could begin to grasp this more than dimly, the Cook
produced a hot berry pie from the oven with a flourish worthy of a
conjurer, and all other thoughts were banished. Abstract thought takes
a poor second place to berry pies when you're only thirteen.

They were just finishing when the dishwashing crew arrived, and
the Cook banished them all back upstairs. Remembering what Herald
Teren had said about room inspections, Talia made haste to straighten
hers before anyone could see the state she'd left it in that morning. She
changed quickly into one of her older and more worn outfits for working with the Armsmaster before hurrying out to the practice yard.

By now the sun was high; the trees that ringed the practice yard
gave very welcome shade. The "yard" itself was nothing more than a
square of scuffed, yellowed grass, with benches along two sides of it,
and a small well behind the benches. Just beyond the trees was a cleared
area with archery targets at one end; there were racks of bows and arrows at the other end. As Talia watched, two of the students picked up

several bows in succession, trying them till they found one to their liking; apparently no one had his own special weapon. She moved hesitantly to the practice yard itself, where the Armsmaster was currently holding forth; he seemed to be dividing his time equally between those who were shooting and the ones practicing hand-to-hand fighting.

She had been filled with dread at the thought of re-encountering the fearsome Alberich, but she discovered that afternoon that having served as the butt of her older brother Justus' cruelty had been useful after all. Alberich actually looked mildly pleased when she demonstrated that she knew how to fall without hurting herself and how to use a bow without ruining forearm, fingers, or fletching. So far as proficiency with the bow went, she thought she wasn't much worse than the other students her own age and began to feel a tiny bit more confident. There were a lot more of them than she thought there would be, for mixed among the gray of her own Collegium were uniforms of the pale green of Healer's and the rust-brown of Bardic. It did seem a bit odd, though, that she was the youngest to be receiving training with edged weapons. Most of the students her age were being put to stave-work or hacking away at dummies with clubs that only vaguely resembled practice-blades.

Once again Jeri was there; a familiar face was comforting, and Talia sat next to her when her turn at the targets was over. "Why aren't there any Blues?" she asked curiously.

"Them?" Jeri gave a very unladylike snort. "Most of *them* have their own private arms tutors—at least the ones that aren't learning to be scholars or artificers. The scholars don't need weapons-work—the courtiers wouldn't want to soil themselves among us common folk. Besides, Alberich won't coddle them, and they know it. King or beggar, if you don't lunge right, he's going to smack you good and hard. Oh-oh," she groaned, as Alberich dismissed the boy he'd been working with and nodded at her. "Looks like it's my turn to get smacked."

She bounced to her feet to take her stance opposite Alberich with her practice blade in hand. Talia watched her enviously, wishing *she* could move like Jeri did.

"Don't let Jer fool you, young 'un," chuckled an older boy, who Talia judged to be about sixteen. "Her blood's as blue as the Queen's is. If she hadn't been Chosen, she'd be a Countess now. She's had a good share of the benefit given by one of those private tutors she was demeaning just now; that's why she's so incredible at her age."

"And why Alberich treats her rougher than the rest of us," put in another, a short, slim boy near Talia's own age, with dark brown hair, bushy eyebrows and nearly black eyes, and a narrow, impish face. He had just finished a bout with another student, and dropped down next to Talia, mopping his sweating face with a towel. He winced as Alberich corrected Jeri's footwork by swatting the offending leg with the flat of his blade.

"He doesn't approve of private tutors?" Talia hazarded. "He doesn't like nobles?"

"Starseekers! No!" the second boy exclaimed. "He just expects more out of her, so he rides her harder. I think he may have ideas about making her Armsmistress when he steps down—if she survives his training and her internship!"

"Believe me, with swordwork that good, by the time she gets her Whites the only way to take Jeri down will be with an army," the first replied.

"Well, Coroc, if anyone would know, you would," the second admitted, watching him step forward to replace Jeri. "His father's the Lord Marshal, so he's been seeing the best swordwork in the Kingdom since he was born," he told Talia.

Talia's eyes widened. "The Lord Marshal's son?"

Her compatriot grinned, hanging his towel around his neck. "Whole new world in here, isn't it? On your right, the Lord Marshal's son, on your left, a Countess—and here we sit, a former thief and beggar"—he bowed mockingly—"that's yours truly, of course—and—a—what are you, anyway?"

"Holderkin."

"Farmgirl, then. Hard to believe, isn't it? Like one of those mad tales we used to listen to. You're Talia, right?"

She nodded, wondering how he knew.

"I'm Skif—if you were with the Dean when the Provost-Marshal came by, you probably heard plenty about me! It's not fair, I know; we all know who you are just because you're the only female face we don't recognize, but you have fifty-two names and faces to learn! And as if that wasn't bad enough, everything you've been seeing probably runs against all you've been taught at home, and you're all in a muddle most of the time." He reached out too quickly for her to flinch away and tousled her hair with a grin of sympathy. "As they kept telling me all during *my* first year, 'this, too, shall pass.' We're all glad you're with us, and we all most fervently wish you luck with the Royal Brat. Now it's *my* turn to get whacked on by Master Alberich—with luck I'll get a set of bruises to match the last batch he gave me. Take heart," he ended, rising. "You follow me."

Despite his own words, Skif seemed to give a good accounting of himself with the Armsmaster. Talia, in spite of her lack of experience in weaponry, saw that Alberich was drilling him in a style radically different to the styles Coroc and Jeri had used. Skif's weapon was a short, heavy blade, as opposed to Jeri's lighter rapier or Coroc's long-sword. His bout seemed to include as much gymnastics as bladework, and seemed to depend on avoiding his opponent's weapon rather than countering it in any way. He bounced about with the agility of a squirrel—nevertheless, Armsmaster Alberich eventually "killed" him.

Skif "died" dramatically, eliciting a round of applause at his theatrics; then rose, grinning, to present Alberich with his own gloves—which Skif had filched from Alberich's belt some time during the practice bout. Alberich received them with a sigh that said wordlessly that this was not the first time Skif had pulled this trick, then turned to motion Talia to take his place. She came forward with a great deal of trepidation.

"You were watching Skif closely?" Alberich asked. "Good. This is the style I wish you to learn. It has nothing of grace, but much of cunning, and I think it will do you more good to know the ways of avoiding the blade of the assassin in the arras than the duelist on the field of honor. So. We begin."

He tutored her with far more patience than she had expected, having witnessed his outbursts of temper over some of his pupils' mistakes. He favored her with none of the sarcastic comments he had heaped on the others, nor did he administer any corrective slaps with the flat of his practice blade. Perhaps it was her imagination, but he almost seemed to be treating her with a kind of rough sympathy—certainty he paid far more attention to the level of her spirits and energy than he had any of the others—for just when she was quite sure she could no longer keep her rubbery knees from giving way with exhaustion, he smiled briefly at her (an unexpected sight that left her dumb) and said, "Enough. You do well, better than I had expected. Rest for a moment, then go to work with your Companion when you are cool."

She rested just long enough to cool down without stiffening up, then ran to Companion's Field with an eagerness that matched the reluctance with which she had gone to arms practice.

As she approached the fence, she saw that Rolan had anticipated her arrival; she scrambled up the rough boards and swung from the top of the fence to his back without bothering to saddle him, and they set off across the field at a full gallop. It was intoxicating beyond belief; though she'd urged the farmbeasts to an illicit gallop many times, there was no comparison to Rolan's speed or smooth pace.

The Field proved to be far more than that—almost a park, full of trees and dells and with streams running all through it. It was so large that when they were most of the way across it, the people near the fence on the Collegium side looked hardly bigger than bugs. At the far edge of the Field they wheeled and returned at top speed to the fence. She leaned into his neck, feeling so at one with him that it seemed as if it were her own feet flying below them. She gripped a double handful of the mane whipping about her face and whispered, "Don't stop, loverling! We can take it! Jump!"

She felt him gather himself beneath her as the fence loomed immediately in front of them—she shifted her weight without thinking—and they were airborne, the fence flashing underneath his tucked-up hooves. It was over in a heartbeat, as he landed as easily as a bird, his hooves chiming on the paved court on the other side.

As she combed her own hair out of her eyes with her fingers, she heard a hearty laugh. "And I thought I'd have to coax you into the saddle with a ladder!" a rough voice said behind her. "Looks like you might be able to teach me a trick or two, my young centaur!"

Rolan pivoted without Talia's prompting so that they could face the owner of the voice; a tall, thin woman of indeterminate age, with short, graying brown hair and intelligent gray eyes, who was clad entirely in white leather.

The woman chuckled and strode toward them, then walked around them with her hands clasped behind her back, surveying them from all sides. "No doubt about it, you have a very pretty seat, young Talia. You're a natural. Well, you've shown me what you can do bareback, so let's see what you can do in the saddle, shall we?"

Herald Keren (who proved to be Teren's twin sister—which explained the grins he'd traded with Drake and Edric) was openly pleased at having so adept a pupil. She told Talia after the first hour that she intended Talia to learn everything she herself knew before very long. What Keren could do with a horse was incredible and what she could do with her Companion was nothing short of phenomenal.

"Before you've got your Whites, m'dear," she told Talia on parting, "you'll be able to duplicate anything you can do afoot on the back of your Companion. You're going to be a credit to both of us; I feel it in my bones. When I'm done with you, the only way anyone will be able to get you off Rolan's back unwilling will be dead."

Talia, much to her own surprise, felt the same instinctive liking for Keren as she had for her twin. It was disturbing; almost frightening. Her instincts were all telling her to trust these people—but everything she'd ever learned urged her to keep her distance until she could truly be *sure* of them. After all, she'd been hurt and betrayed time and time again by her own blood-kin. How could she expect better treatment from strangers? And yet, and yet—something deep inside kept telling her that her fears were needless. She wished she knew which inner prompting to trust.

Keren called a halt to the drilling when the sun was westering, insisting that both she and Rolan were tired—or should have been. "Just go out into the Field together for a while. Ride if you like, walk if you prefer, but be together—the bond that's to build between you has a good start, but it needs nurturing. Don't *try* to do anything, just enjoy each other's company. That'll be enough."

Talia obeyed happily; she climbed over the fence and walked dreamily beside Rolan, thoughts drifting. There was no explaining why, but at this moment she could feel none of the tenseness and anxiety that had been a part of her for as long as she could remember. For now, at least, she was held securely in a place where she *belonged*; and with that certain knowledge came another trickle of confidence. Being with the Companion erased all her doubts and stilled all her fears. She didn't come to herself until she heard the double bell for the Cook's helpers sound across the field.

She swung up on his bare back and they trotted to the enormous tack shed near the middle of the Field. Keren showed her where to find Rolan's gear; she groomed him hurriedly, but still with care, and flew back to her room, having scarcely time to wash and change before sliding into a vacant place at dinner.

She'd thought she would be too excited to sleep, but to her own surprise found herself nodding over her plate. She had barely enough energy to take the prescribed bath—and was grateful that there was little competition for the tubs this early in the evening, for if she'd had to wait in the steamy room for long, she'd have fallen asleep on her feet.

This time she had no thoughts at all, for she was asleep when her head touched the pillow.

CHAPTER 6

E VERY DAY FOR the next week Talia followed the same schedule; she woke just after sunrise to the sound of the waking bell—
which she'd somehow slept through her first morning. She would
either bundle herself hastily into her uniform and run downstairs to
help with breakfast, or spend a more leisurely hour in getting both herself and her room ready before the meal. After breakfast came the Orientation class, and other classes were added every other day as the time
spent there was shortened. Her afternoons were given over to Master
Alberich in self-defense class, equitation with Herald Keren, and, of
course, in building her bond with Rolan. On the days she wasn't helping with breakfast or lunch she spent long hours with several others
mending a seemingly endless pile of gray uniforms.

At the end of the week Herald Teren dismissed them for the last
time, but asked Talia to remain behind as the others filed out. She
tensed without realizing it, her outward relaxation draining away as
she waited, biting nervously at a hangnail, to hear the reason why he
wanted to speak to her.

She watched him covertly as he leaned a little on his desk, not meeting his eyes except by accident. He looked worried and slightly unhappy, and in her experience that sort of expression on an adult face
meant trouble for her.

Teren was uncomfortable with the situation he found himself in now; this poor, confused child was having more than enough problems in trying to come to terms with the Collegium and her new role, without having to cope with trouble from her family as well. He mentally cursed their cruelty; who could send a message so coldly calculated to destroy what little stability the child had gained?

"Talia—" he began, then hesitated, seeing her start from raw nervousness. "Childing, there's nothing for you to be afraid of—I've just got some rather unpleasant news for you that I thought you would rather receive alone. It's word from your family."

"My family?" she repeated, her expression surprised and puzzled.

"We sent a messenger to them, just as we do with every child Chosen, telling them what had happened to you. Now usually no matter how angry they are, the honor of being Chosen seems to make every parent forgive whatever disobedience had occurred, and we thought that would happen for you, too."

Now at last she was looking directly at him, instead of from underneath downcast lashes. He was uneasy beneath her stare, and oddly at a loss for words. "Talia, I wish things had gone as we'd expected; I can't tell you how sorry I am—this is all the reply they gave us."

He fumbled in his tunic pocket and pulled out a much-folded bit of paper and handed it to her.

She opened it, smoothing out the creases unthinkingly, while Teren waited in apprehensive anticipation for her reaction to what it held.

Sensholding has no daughter Talia, it read. The half-literate scrawl bore her Father's mark.

She didn't realize that she was weeping until a single hot tear splashed on the paper, blurring the ink. She regained control of herself immediately, swallowing down the tears. She hadn't realized until this moment just how much she'd hoped that the Family would accept her because of her newly-won status. She hadn't thought, though, that the Heralds would have told them—she'd expected that it would be she herself that would break the news; perhaps by riding one day into the Holding in the full formal array of Herald's Whites. It was when she had first realized that she really *was* a Herald that she had begun to hope that the achievement would mean forgiveness—even, perhaps, a hint of approval. Holderkin did not condemn *everything* Heralds did and stood for, and even the most critical of them generally admitted that Heralds served an important function. Certainly the Holderkin welcomed their intrusion into their midst when the raiders came over the Border, or a feud needed settling! Perhaps, she'd hoped, her kin would realize now why she'd done things that were a bit unseemly—they'd realize she was only following her own nature. Surely *now* they'd understand. Perhaps they'd welcome her back, and let her have a place to belong.

It was odd, but when she'd chosen to run away, their certain excommunication hadn't seemed so great a price to pay for freedom; but somehow now, after all her hopes for forgiveness had been raised only to be destroyed by this one note—

Never mind; once again she was on her own—and Herald Teren would hardly approve of her sniveling over the situation. "It's all right," she said, handing back the note to the Herald. "I should have expected it." She was proud that her voice trembled only a little, and that she was able to meet his eyes squarely.

Teren was startled and slightly alarmed; not at her reaction to the note, but by her immediate iron-willed suppression of it. This was not a healthy response. She should have allowed herself the weakness of tears; any child her age would have. Instead, she was holding back, turning further into herself. He tried, tentatively, to call those tears back to the surface where they belonged. Such suppression of natural feelings could only mean deep emotional turmoil later—and would only serve as one more brick in the wall the child had placed between herself and others around her.

"I wish there was something I could do to help." Teren was exceedingly distressed and tried to show that he was as much distressed at the child's denial of her own grief as with the situation itself. "I can't understand why they should have replied like this."

If he could just at least get her to admit that the situation made her unhappy, he would have an opening wedge in getting her to trust him.

"Perhaps if we sent another envoy to them, later—" he offered, trying to hold her gaze.

Talia dropped her eyes and shook her head; there was no return for her, at least not as the triumphal Holderkin Herald. To even her closest kin she would be a total stranger, and "Talia Sensdaughter" had never lived. She had violated the Holy Writ that a girlchild be totally obedient in all things; she was outcast, and they would *never* change their minds.

"But—"

"I'm going to be late—" Talia winced away from his outheld hand and ran, wishing that Teren had been less sympathetic. He'd brought her tears perilously close to the surface again. She'd wanted, above all other things, to break down and cry on his shoulder. But—no. She didn't dare. When kith and kin could deny her so completely, what might not strangers do, especially if she exposed her weaknesses? And

Heralds were supposed to be self-sufficient, self-reliant. She would *not* show that she was unworthy and weak.

Fortunately, the next class—History, which as far as Talia was concerned was no less than one never-ending tale—was engrossing enough that she was able to concentrate on it and ignore her unhappiness. Like many of the classes it was structured cyclically, so that a student could drop into it at any point, completing it when the point at which he'd entered came around again. An elderly woman—Herald Werda—taught this class. Today the lecture and the discussion that followed were fascinating; enough to make her forget for a while.

And Geography was nearly as enthralling. All Heralds at the Collegium for more than a few days taught it in turn, covering their own home areas as they came under study. Teren's conclusion of the Orientation class brought him to lead this one for a time, since it was covering the Lake Evendim area.

This class was not just the study of maps, but a study of everything that made up the environment of the area, from the topography and vegetation to the weather. These things were then related to the people who lived there, and how their lives had been shaped; how changes in these factors might affect them. This too was engrossing enough to hold her attention away from her rejection.

Teren made a tentative gesture in her direction when the class was dismissed—Talia pretended not to see it and hurried on to the next, part of the crowd, and yet apart from it.

Following this class was Mathematics; Talia had never been overly fond of figures, but Herald Sylvan seemed to love the precision and intricacies of her subject so much that some of that enthusiasm was bound to be contagious.

Talia's newest class, just before lunch, was something called "Courtly Graces"; she was feeling very uneasy about it. She was certain that she'd look as out of place at Court as a goat. Most especially did she dread it now, when she was so knotted up inside and out of balance. She almost feared meeting the instructor, picturing some stiff-necked, gilded aristo, and anticipating ridicule.

She crept in, and hid herself behind several of her taller classmates before the instructor entered. She slumped into her seat as the buzz of conversation ended, hoping to remain unnoticed.

"Isn't Talia here? I thought she was joining us today," the puzzled voice was very familiar and startled Talia into raising her head.

"Bright Havens, child," Housekeeper Gaytha smiled, "we ought to put stilts on the bottoms of your boots—you're almost too tiny to see!"

"You're not—" Talia blurted, then blushed.

"I'm not a courtier, as such, and I'm not a Herald either—but before I accepted this position I was Governess to House Ravenscroft; that's why I teach this class," Gaytha explained patiently. "A Governess sees the court from a unique viewpoint; within it, yet invisible. For this reason I can teach you all the manners that smooth the way, and the means of seeing the poison fangs hid by the velvet tongues. Make no mistake about it, if you retain the habit of speaking before thinking, the fangs will be felt!"

The tiny, gentle smile she wore softened the rebuke.

Perhaps Courtly Graces wasn't going to be as horrid as Talia had thought.

In fact, it was rather fascinating; a convoluted, intricate dance of manners—though Talia had cause to wonder more than once if she'd ever truly understand it all, much less feel comfortable treading the measures of it.

A free reading hour spent in the Library followed lunch and that class, and it would have taken drawn daggers to keep her out of that room of wonders. Remembering Davan's tale of the beginnings of the Kingdom, she chose a book from the very front of the section on History.

Today she wasn't Cook's helper, so following her reading hour was an hour spent in the sewing room, a cramped but well-lit room, crowded with tables holding baskets of uniforms in various stages of disrepair. It was here, with her hands full but her mind unoccupied, that she found she could no longer keep her loneliness at bay—especially not with the other students laughing and chattering away about things and people she had no acquaintance with whatsoever. She found a corner partially in shadow and screened by a mound of things to be mended, and took her basket of work there. The misery had to come out sooner or later, and this was a good time and place; one where she wouldn't be noticed. The torn hose acquired a certain salty dampness before the hour was over.

At least today she wasn't forced to deal with the demonic Alberich—he had delegated the ex-thief Skif as her tutor instead. She had found herself warming shyly to the boy during the past week. Skif seemed to sympathize with her awkwardness, and was endlessly patient with her. Without rebuke, he helped her position her rebellious limbs and slowed his own movements down enough that she could see exactly what she was supposed to be doing. When she looked downhearted, he cheered her with ridiculous stories about the preposterous things he'd supposedly done back in his days as a street-child, beggar, and pickpocket. She responded tentatively to his open friendliness, and he seemed to know when to reach out to her and when to back down.

From there she went to archery practice, and then to Rolan.

Once in her Companion's presence the ache of loneliness vanished. They worked over the obstacle course until they were both tired, then went off to a far corner of the Field to cool off together and to be alone. Again, simply being with him worked some kind of alchemy on her spirits. When she thought about how lonely she'd been even with her two closest kin—and how fulfilled she felt when she was with Rolan— the price she had paid for coming here no longer seemed so high. By the time Rolan was brushed and curried, Talia had very nearly re-gained her cheer. Whenever she was with him, she knew without doubt that she was loved and that *he* would never leave her friendless.

Either she was growing used to the pace or her endurance was in-creasing; she was not tired enough to stay indoors after supper, so she decided to explore the gardens that abutted the Collegium grounds.

It was there that she learned why Sherrill had warned her not to confront the unaffiliated students alone.

She was walking the graveled paths between the mathematically-laid-out flowerbeds, as the sun set and the coming dusk seemed to thicken the air and turn it blue. The scent of the roses mingled with that of the nightblooming flowers that were only just beginning to open. She was half daydreaming and didn't notice that there was any-one about until someone spoke.

"Do I smell manure?" a male voice behind her sniffed superciliously. "I really believe that I do!"

"Perhaps the gardeners have manured the flowerbeds?" It was a girl's voice this time, and one with a nasty edge to it.

"Oh, I think not," the first replied. "This smell is most decidedly fresh, and altogether goat-like."

Talia turned, startled; there were four or five adolescents in blue uniforms lounging in the shadow of a hedge.

"Why, what have we here?" the first speaker feigned surprise at see-ing her. "I do believe that I've found the source of the odor!"

"No doubt of it," the girl at his side replied, "since it's that wench from the Border. What a pity—they'll allow *anything* into the Colle-gium these days. Still, you'd think they'd bathe it before letting it roam civilized surroundings."

They watched her with expressions of sly anticipation. Talia had first thought to give them word for word, but thought better of the idea at once. There were five of them, and she was alone—and from what Sherrill had said, they weren't likely to stop with insults, nor to fight fairly.

"My Lady, these creatures are steeped in filth; a hundred baths couldn't wash the smell away," the boy continued maliciously. "Which isn't surprising, considering that they are also steeped in ignorance. I'm given to understand that this one tried to give its Companion back to the Collegium—that it hadn't the faintest idea what it meant to be Chosen."

Talia's ears burned with shame and anger.

"Is it as stupid as it is smelly?" a third asked.

"It must be, since it apparently doesn't realize that we're talking about it."

Tears sprang up, and were as quickly suppressed. There was no way that she would let *this* lot know how their insults had hurt—that would only encourage them. Talia shut her smarting eyes and began to walk away; they moved up on her so quickly that she didn't realize that she was surrounded until a calculated shove sent her sprawling headfirst into a well-watered flowerbed. She wasn't ready for the tumble, and landed hard, getting a face full of dirt and dead leaves.

As laughter faded into the distance, Talia extricated herself. She'd had the breath knocked out of her; the bed had been planted with rose-vines and none of the thorns seemed to be less than an inch long. By the time she got out, her uniform was ruined, and she was scratched and bloody as well as filthy.

Hot, angry tears slipped over her cheeks; she scrubbed them away with the back of a gritty hand and sprinted for the safety of the Collegium, grateful for the cover of gathering darkness.

It was early enough that there was no one in the bathing room; she hastily shoved the ruined clothing down the chute. A long soak changed the angry scratches into cuts she could have picked up in practice and the sound of the running water covered her sniffles as she sobbed, half in anger, half in hurt.

She had no intention of asking Sherrill for help; she couldn't spend all her time in the older girl's company, and the minute she was alone she'd be a target again. Besides, despite what Sherrill had told her, Talia had strong misgivings about her real willingness to tolerate the constant presence of a child at her side, day in, day out.

And Talia had had plenty of experience with bullies before this; she knew what to expect. Once they'd started, they wouldn't leave her alone until they'd become bored with the game.

And there was another facet to be considered as well. She pushed her wet hair out of her eyes and regarded the coin-sized scar on the palm of her left hand soberly. How old had she been when Justus had burned that into her hand with a red-hot poker? Nine? Ten? No matter. When the thing had happened, the adults had believed him and not her, when he'd said she'd done it to herself.

So why should anyone here believe her—she was new, unknown; they were obviously children of ranking courtiers. Given the circumstances, who'd be thought the liar? Better to remain silent. They'd had their fun; perhaps they'd become bored soon if she didn't react, and leave her alone.

Her hope was in vain.

The very next day she discovered that someone had purloined her History notes; the day following, a shove from behind sent her blundering to her knees, bruising both knees and elbows on the floor of the corridor. When she collected her books and her wits, there was no one to be seen that could have shoved her—although she could faintly hear giggles from somewhere in the crowd about her.

Two days later she was pelted with stones by unseen assailants as she was running to weapons class alone. The day after that, she discovered that someone had upended a full bottle of ink over her books, and there was no sign that anyone had been near them but herself. That had been a nearly unbearable humiliation—to be thought to have been so careless with a *book*.

She began to acquire a certain reputation for awkwardness, as she was shoved or tripped at least once a week; more often than that if she dared to go anywhere outside the Collegium.

And there was persecution of a nonphysical nature as well.

She began receiving anonymous notes; notes that appeared mysteriously in her pockets or books, notes that picked her shaky self-confidence to tiny pieces. It got to the point where the mere sight of one would bring her to the edge of tears, and she couldn't show them to anyone because the words faded within moments after she'd read them, leaving only common bits of unmarked paper.

And she didn't dare to confide in anyone else—for there was no evidence to her mind that the perpetrators were confined to the Blues. Granted, if things were as they seemed, it was wildly unlikely that any of her fellow trainees was part of the group tormenting her—but Justus had hidden his sadism behind an angelic expression and a smiling face. Things were not always as they seemed. No, it was better to bear things alone—at least there was always Rolan.

But Keren had seen that *something* was wrong. She'd already had her twin's report on the note Talia had received from her family; a session with Elcarth had convinced her that *she* might be just the person to get the child to emerge from her shell of isolation. *She* had seen no evidences of clumsiness when she'd worked with Talia, and the reports of constant accidents sat ill with the evidence of her own eyes. There was something amiss, badly amiss.

As a child Keren had schooled herself to develop incredible patience—had been known to sit for hours with a handful of breadcrumbs, scarcely moving an eyelash, until the birds fed from her hand. She used that same kind of patient stalking with Talia now; dropping a word here, a subtle encouragement there. If there was someone persecuting the child, soon or late Keren would find out about it.

There were times she cursed the protocol of those Gifted with thought-sensing; if not for those constraints, she could have read plainly what was bothering the child—or if she couldn't, there were others who could have penetrated *any* shield. But the protocols were there to protect; one simply didn't ruthlessly strip away the inner thoughts of anyone, no matter how well-meaning one's intentions were. If the child had accidentally let something slip, it would be another case entirely. Unfortunately, she was entirely too well walled off. Nor was there any likelihood that someone more talented than Keren would "hear" something; Talia's reticence was being interpreted as a desire for privacy, and was being respected as such. Those who can hear thoughts tend to be fanatical about privacy, whether their own or others; a good thing under most circumstances but a distinct handicap for Keren in this case.

Although Talia hadn't consciously noted Keren's solicitude, the attention was making itself felt. She was on the verge of telling the riding-instructor about the notes, at least, when she began receiving another set—

Do go and tell someone about this, bumpkin, these notes said, *it will be so entertaining to watch you try and explain why you haven't got anything but blank scraps of paper. They'll think you're mad. They might be right, you know. . . .*

That frightened her—the specter of madness had haunted her ever since she'd gotten the first of the letters. After all, how could letters vanish from off the paper after they were read? And if they only *thought* she were mad—they might turn her out of the Collegium, and then where could she go? It wasn't worth the risk. She confided in no one and wept in private.

Then, just as her nerves were at the breaking point, the three months of Midwinter revelry began at Court and the persecution ceased abruptly.

When several days passed without even a note, Talia began to hope; when a week went by, she dared to relax her guard a little. By the end of the first month free of pursuit, she decided that they'd grown tired of her non-reaction and found some other game.

She threw herself into her life at the Collegium then with such unrestrained enthusiasm that before Midwinter Festival she began to feel as if she'd come to belong there. Her Family's rejection no longer ached with the same intensity.

The Collegium suspended classes for the two weeks of the Festival; those students that didn't return to their own homes for the holiday generally visited with friends or relatives near the capital. It was only Talia who had nowhere to go; she had kept so much to herself that no one realized this in the rush of preparations.

The first day of the holiday found her wandering the empty halls, listening to her footsteps echo, feeling very small and lonely, and wondering if even the Library would be able to fill the empty hours.

As she listened to the sound of her own passing echo eerily in the hallways, another, fainter sound came to her ears—the sound of a harp being played somewhere beyond the doors that closed off the Heralds' private quarters from the rest of the Collegium.

Curiosity and loneliness moved her to follow the sound to its source. She pushed open one of the double doors with a faint creak, and let the harp-notes lead her down long corridors to the very end of the Herald's wing, and a corner overlooking the Palace Temple. It was quiet here. Most of the rooms were singles, occupied by Heralds currently out on Field duty. The place was easily as empty as the Collegium wing. The harp sounded sweet and a little lonely amid all the silence. Talia stood, just out of sight of a half-open door on the ground floor, and lost all track of time in the enchantment of the music.

She sighed when the harp-song ended.

"Come in please, whoever you are," a soft, age-roughened voice called from within the room. "There's no need for you to stand about in a dreary hall when I could do with some company."

The invitation sounded quite genuine; Talia mastered her reluctance and shyly pushed the door open a bit farther.

Sunlight poured in the windows of the tiny room on the other side, reflecting from paneled walls the color of honey and a few pieces of furniture of wood and fabric only a shade or so darker. A brightly burning fire on the hearth gave off the scent of applewood and added to the atmosphere of light and warmth. Seated beside the fire was an elderly man—older than anyone Talia had ever met before, surely, for his silver hair matched the white of his tunic. But his gentle, still-handsome face and gray eyes held only welcome, and the creases that wreathed his mouth and eyes were those that came of much smiling rather than frowning. His brow was broad, his mouth firm, his chin cleft rather appealingly, and his whole demeanor was kind. He held a harp braced against one leg. Talia's eyes widened to see that the other, like that of the village guard she had met, was missing from the knee down.

He followed her gaze and smiled.

"I am more fortunate than a good many," he said, "for it was only a leg I lost to the Tedrel mercenaries and the King's service, and not my life. What keeps a youngling like you here in these gloomy halls at Festival time?"

Perhaps it was his superficial resemblance to her Father's Mother; perhaps it was simply that he was so openly welcoming of her; perhaps it was just that she was so desperately lonely—he made Talia trust him with all her heart, and she spoke to him as candidly as she would have to Rolan.

"I haven't anywhere to go, sir," she said in a near-whisper.

"Have you no friends willing to share holiday and hearth with you?" he frowned. "That seems most unHeraldlike."

"I—I didn't tell anyone that I was staying. I really don't know anybody very well; my family doesn't want me anymore, and—and—"

"And you didn't want anyone to know; perhaps ask you to come with them not because they wanted you, but because they felt sorry for you?" he guessed shrewdly.

She nodded, hanging her head a trifle.

"You look to be about thirteen; this must be your first Midwinter here or the entire Collegium would know you had nowhere to spend it. There's only one newly-Chosen that fits that description, so you must be Talia. Am I right?"

She nodded shyly.

"Well, there's no loss without a little gain," he replied. "I, too, have nowhere to spend my Festival. I could spend it with the Court, but the crowding is not to my taste. My kith and kin have long since vanished into time—my friends are either gone or busy elsewhere. Shall we keep the holiday together? I am called Jadus."

"I—would like that, sir. Very much." She raised her eyes and smiled back at him.

"Excellent! Then come and make yourself comfortable; there's room next to the fire—chair, cushion, whichever you prefer."

A keen sensitivity alerted him to the depths of Talia's shyness, and he made a show of tuning his harp as she hesitantly placed a fat pillow of amber velvet on the hearth and curled up on it like a kitten. His Gift was thought-sensing, and while he would never even dream of prying into her mind, there were nuances and shadings to her thoughts and behavior that told him he would have to tread carefully with her. He was by nature a gentle man, but with Talia he knew he would have to be at his gentlest, for the least ill-nature on his part would frighten her out of all proportion to reality.

"I'm glad that my playing lured you to my door, Talia."

"It was so very beautiful—" she said wistfully. "I've never heard music like that before."

He chuckled. "My overweening pride thanks you, youngling, but the hard truth is that any Master Bard would make me sound the half-amateur that I truly am. Still—honesty forces me to admit that I have at least *some* Talent, else they'd never have admitted me to Bardic Collegium in the first place."

"*Bardic* Collegium, sir?" Talia said, confused.

"Yes, I know. *Now* I am a Herald, complete with Companion, who is even now sunning her old bones and watching the silly foals frolic in the snow—but when I first arrived here, it was to be admitted to Bardic Collegium. I had been there for three years, with two more to go; I was sitting in the garden, attempting to compose a set-theme piece for an assignment, when something drew me down to Companion's Field. And *she* came, and proceeded to merrily turn my life inside out. I was even resentful at the time, but now I wouldn't exchange a moment of my life for the coronet of the Laureate."

Talia watched the strong, supple fingers that caressed the silken wood of the harp almost absently.

"You didn't give up the music, though."

"Oh, no—one doesn't forsake *that* sweet mistress lightly after one has tasted of her charms." He smiled. "And perhaps Fortunea did me a favor; I've never needed to please a fickle crowd or ungrateful master, I've sung and played for the entertainment of only myself and my friends. Music has served me as a disguise as well, since Bards are welcome nearly everywhere, in Kingdom or out. And even now, when my voice has long since gone the way of my leg, I can charm a tune from My Lady to keep me company. Or to lure company to my door."

He wrinkled his nose at her, and she returned his smile with growing confidence.

He looked at her appraisingly, taken with a sudden thought. "Talia, youngling, can *you* sing?"

"I don't know, sir," she confessed, "I'm—I *was*—Holderkin. They don't hold with music; only hymns, mostly, and then just the priests and Handmaidens."

"Holderkin, Holderkin—" he muttered, obviously trying to remember something. "Ah! Surely you know the little sheep-calming song, the one that goes, 'Silly sheep, go to sleep'?"

He plucked a simple melody.

She nodded. "Yes sir—but *that* isn't music, though, is it?"

"Even a speech can be music in the right hands. Would you sing it for me, please?"

She began very hesitantly, singing so softly as to be barely audible above the voice of the harp, but she began to gain confidence and volume before long. The harp in counterpoint behind the melody fascinated her; soon she was so engrossed in the patterns the music made that she lost all trace of self-consciousness.

"I thought so," Jadus said with self-satisfaction as she finished. "I thought you had a touch of Talent when I listened to you speak. You'll never give a major Bard competition, little one, but you definitely have—or will have, rather—a quite good singing voice. Would you be willing to give an old man a great deal of pleasure by consenting to yet another set of lessons?"

"You mean—music lessons? Teach *me*? But—"

"It would be a shame to waste your Talent; and you do have it, youngling." He smiled, with just a hint of wistfulness. "It would truly be something that I would enjoy sharing with you."

That decided her. "If you think it's worth wasting your time on me—"

He put a finger under her chin, tilting her head up so that she had nowhere to look but his earnest, kindly eyes. "Time spent with you, my dear, will never be wasted. Believe it."

She blushed a brilliant crimson, and he released her.

"Would you be willing to begin now?" he continued, allowing her to regain her composure. "We have all the afternoon before us—and we could begin with the song you just sang."

"If you don't mind—I don't have anything I was going to do."

"Mind? Youngling, if you knew how long my hours are, you would never have made that statement."

Jadus felt a bond growing between the two of them—felt without really thinking about it that it was his own "helpless" condition that allowed Talia to feel he wasn't any sort of a threat. He had been allowing himself to drift in a hermit-like half-dream for several years now, allowing the world outside his door to move off without him. It just hadn't seemed worth the effort to try and call it back—until now—

Until now, when another heart as lonely as his had strayed to his door, and brought the world back with her. And as he watched the child at his feet, he knew that this time—for her sake—he would not permit it to drift away again.

Talia learned quickly, as her teachers already knew; music was a whole unknown world for her, and in one way this was all to the good as she had nothing to unlearn. She was so enthralled that she never even noticed how late it was getting until a servant arrived to light candles and inquire as to whether Jadus preferred dinner in his room.

When she would have absented herself, he insisted that she share dinner with him, saying that he had had his fill of solitary meals. When the servant returned, he sent him on another errand, to search out some songbooks he'd had stored away. These he presented to Talia over her protests.

"I've not missed them in all the time they've been stored," he said firmly. "The music and the memories are safe enough in here"—he tapped his forehead—"so I have no need of the books themselves. A Midwinter Gifting, if you like, so that you can learn fast enough to please your tyrannical teacher."

She departed only when her singing was punctuated by yawns. She felt almost as if she'd known the old Herald for as long as she'd been alive, and that they'd been friends for all of that time. She felt comfortable and welcome with him, and could hardly bear to wait for the new dawn and another day with him.

She rose nearly with the sun. But she feared to intrude too early and disturb the aged Herald, so she gulped down a hasty breakfast of bread and milk from the stores in the Collegium kitchen and took her energy out to Rolan.

She and he played like the silliest of children, she tossing snowballs at him and he avoiding them adroitly or trying to catch them in his teeth. She felt quite lightheaded with happiness; happier than she ever remembered being before. Finally he curvetted coaxingly toward her, in a plain invitation to mount and ride. They galloped together until the sun was quite high, fairly flying over the Field. This was enough to loosen her taut nerves and spend some of her energy without losing any

of her enthusiasm. She tapped on Jadus' door at midmorning with sparkling eyes and flushed cheeks.

By the end of this, the second day of her lessons, the servants had
gotten wind of what was going on and could be seen lurking in the
vicinity of the Herald's room. Though untrained, Talia's voice was
good and her pitch was true; the servants were finding the lessons to be
rare entertainment indeed. Now that Midwinter Festival was at its
height there was scarcely enough room in the Great Hall for all the
nobles come to Court, much less an off-duty servant—but here in this
little corner of Herald's Hall there was entertainment in plenty. Before
long, had anyone chanced by, they would have seen folk perched quietly like a flock of sparrows in every available nook and cranny. Talia
was unaware that they were there, oblivious as she was to everything
but her lessoning. Jadus knew, though, his ear long sensitized to the
unusual sound of anyone in his out-of-the-way corridor; and he tacitly
welcomed their presence. He had spent enough lonely holidays to
know how cheering a bit of music could be—and he was showman
enough to appreciate having an audience. Besides, knowing they were
there made him put a bit more polish on his own performances, and
that was all to the good where his new pupil was concerned.

Midwinter Eve itself came before Talia was aware that it was upon
them.

That afternoon Jadus had been telling her tales drawn from his own
experiences as a young Herald, when there was a hesitant knock on the
half-open door.

"Come," he answered, one eyebrow rising quizzically.

It was the young servant who habitually tended to Jadus' needs.
"Your pardon, Herald," he said diffidently. "We—the rest of us, that
is—couldn't help but listen to yourself and young Talia all this past
week, and we wondered—well, to put it shortly, sir, it's this. You two
haven't anywhere to go this Midwinter Eve and you're plainly not
wanting to spend it at Court either, or you'd be there now. Would you
be caring to share *our* celebration? And, if you could be bothered to
sing or play a bit for us, we'd be beholden to you. We entertain ourselves, you see; 'tisn't masterly, but it's fun, and it's homelike."

Jadus broke into a wide smile. "Medren, I do believe that's one of
the handsomest offers I've had since I was Chosen! Talia, what think
you?"

She nodded speechlessly, amazed that *anyone* would come seeking
her company.

"Right gladly do we accept—and right gladly will we do our best to help amuse and please you."

Medren's sturdy brown face was wreathed in smiles. "*Many* thanks, m'lord Jadus. We'd have asked you aforetime, but that we thought you wished to be alone. But then when you and the child began the lessoning, well, we bethought maybe we were wrong."

Jadus rested his hand fondly on Talia's head. "I have lived overly much in my memories, I think. It was time someone woke me to the present. Welladay, will you send someone to fetch us when the time comes?"

Medren nodded. "Second hour after sundown, Herald, and I'll come myself. Do you wish your carry-chair?"

"Oh, I think not. I'll do well enough with my cane and my friends," he replied and smiled at Talia with affection.

Medren was prompt; enthusiastic cries of greeting met them at the door of the Servant's Hall as they entered. The room was approximately three times the size of the Collegium common room, with a fireplace at either end, oil lamps along the walls, and one door leading into the hallway in the middle of one of the longer walls, and another leading to the Palace kitchen in the middle of the other. There were many trestle tables set up in the middle of it, all crowded with off-duty servants. Jadus entered through the hall-door slowly, managing very well with his cane and one hand resting lightly on Talia's shoulder for balance. She held his harp in both arms with great care, feeling honored that he trusted it to her. Tucked into her belt was the little shepherd's pipe he'd given her a few days previous. Jadus' eyes widened and lit from within at the sounds of welcome; he seemed even to stand a bit straighter. The greetings they received were warm and unrestrained, for although she hadn't known it, Talia had long ago won the sympathy of the servants with her stalwart refusal to give in to self-pity out of loneliness. Jadus was another favorite—partially because he never demanded any favors though he'd long since earned the right to demand special treatment, and partially because he had never stood on protocol with anyone, servant or noble.

First there was a feast, prepared at the same time as that being served in the Great Hall; everyone able took his or her turn at waiting on the others. Following the food came the entertainment. As Medren had said, it was not "masterly," but the enjoyment was perhaps more genuine. While several amateur musicians played simple country-dances, the rest sent their feet through their paces. Tiny Talia often ended up being swept completely off the floor by some of her more energetic partners. There were some attempts at juggling and sleight-of-hand, all the more hilarious because the outcomes were so uncertain.

When at last everyone's energy was drained to the point where they were willing to turn their attention to something quieter, Talia and Jadus took their turn.

Jadus first played alone; his skillful fingers wove a spell of silence over the assemblage. There wasn't a sound to be heard as he played but the crackling of the fire on the hearth. The silence that endured for several long moments when he'd finished was a poignant tribute to his abilities.

Before the silence ended, Jadus nudged his young protégé, and Talia joined him on her pipe, playing the melodies she'd learned taking her turn on watch during the long, cold nights of lambing season. The tunes themselves were simple enough, but with Jadus' harp behind them, they took on new complexity and an entirely new voice. There was another eloquent silence when they'd done, followed by wildly enthusiastic applause. Talia's heart was filled with joy at the sight of the new life and light in Jadus' face. She was fiercely glad then that they'd come.

Then Jadus played while Talia sang something he'd picked out of an old book—a comic ballad he remembered from many years agone called "It Was A Dark and Stormy Night." The spontaneous laughter that followed the last line about the lute was so hearty that Talia was soon blushing with pleasure. Now she, too, knew how heady a drink acclaim could be.

The two of them then performed as many requests as they knew, until it grew so late that Talia found herself beginning to nod, and Jadus confessed that his fingers were growing tired. Talia helped him back to his room; she scarcely knew how she found her own bed. She thought before sleep claimed her that without a doubt it was the finest Midwinter Festival she'd ever had.

CHAPTER 7

AFTER MIDWINTER'S EVENING there could have been no firmer friends in all the Collegium and Circle than Talia and the old Herald Jadus. Even after classes began again, she always found the time for music lessons and practice sessions with him every evening. He seemed to take as much joy in her company as she did in his—and not even the fact that her unknown tormentors resumed their games soon after the end of the holidays served to take that happiness out of her heart. It sometimes occurred to her that if it hadn't been for Jadus and Rolan, she'd have thought more than once about giving it all up and running away—though where she'd go, she had no idea. Without those two stalwarts to turn to, her misery would have been deeper than it had been at the Holding at the worst of times.

The signal that "they" were still at her came in the form of another of the anonymous notes. It appeared among her books just before one of her music lessons, and she was hard put to make herself seemly after the spate of tears it caused.

It would have been impossible to hide the fact that she was troubled and upset from Jadus; her red-rimmed eyes gave her away immediately. He insisted, gently but firmly, that she tell him something of what was wrong.

"You know I would never say or do anything against your will, little one—" His voice was soft but held a note of command. The hesitant, wary child that had replaced the cheerful Talia that he had come to know and love was not at all to his liking, "But you aren't happy, and if you're not happy, than neither am I. I wish you would tell me why—and who or what is the cause. You know by now you can trust me, surely?"

She nodded slowly, hands clenched in her lap.

"Then tell me what your problem is. It may even be I can help."

She was reluctant to confide in him, but found herself unable to resist the kindness of his eyes. "Y-y-you have to promise something, please? That you won't tell anyone else?"

He promised that he would not, rather than lose the trust she had given to no one else. The promise was given with great reluctance. "If that is the only way you'll tell me—yes. I promise."

"I-It's like this—" she began, telling him eventually only of the shovings, the destructive tricks, and not of the notes. She feared *those* were too wildly unlikely even for Jadus to believe.

He sensed that there was more to these pranks than she was telling him, and it worried him.

Bound by his promise, though, there was little he could do for her but offer an emotional shelter and proffer some advice. He hoped that that would be enough.

"Don't go anywhere alone—well, you know that already. But try to stay only with people you know; Sherrill, or Skif, or Jeri. None of those three would ever hurt you. And—here's a thought—try to always be within sight of one of your teachers. I doubt that even the cleverest would dare try anything under the eyes of a Herald. And little one—" He touched her cheek with a gentle hand, eliciting a wan smile. "—*I* am always here for you. No one would dare try anything against you here, and any time you want someone to cry with—well, I have a plenitude of handkerchiefs!"

That actually earned him a tiny chuckle, and Jadus felt amply rewarded as they began the lesson.

"Make friends, child," he urged her before she left him. "The other Herald-students won't bite you. They won't try to hurt you, either, and the more friends you have, the better protected you'll be. Now think— have you ever seen or heard *any* of them do or say anything intended to be cruel?"

"No," she had to admit.

"I know your life wasn't easy at the Hold; I know people often hurt you deliberately. Things are different in the Collegium. You trust me—now I tell you to trust them as well. If nothing else, once you are part of a group, you'll be less of an available target for tricks."

Jadus was proved right—she *was* a less conspicuous target. The pranks began to decrease in frequency immediately.

There was more—though he was bound by his promise to say nothing, Jadus was aided by the fact that some of the teachers and older students, Keren, Teren, and Sherrill among them, had decided that there was something odd and unpleasant afoot and had begun making a habit of keeping an ostentatious eye on her. Keren especially had long since made that decision, and when Talia had begun to show signs of unhappiness again had taken to lurking in the child's vicinity, looking as conspicuous as possible. The perpetrators of her misery soon found it nearly impossible even to slip those mysterious notes among her things without being seen—and being seen was no part of their scheme. Before a month was out they seemed to have given up; Talia's cheerfulness was restored, and Jadus heaved a profound mental sigh of relief.

None of them guessed that there was more afoot than petty harassment.

Collegium and Circle alike had incorrectly assumed that the suspicions surrounding the death of Talamir had frightened the anti-Herald faction off of any serious attempt to rid the Kingdom of the new Queen's Own. The case was otherwise. The harassment had been at the instigation of the parents of some of the nobly-born "unaffiliated" students; courtiers who had everything to lose should Elspeth be salvaged and made Heir in fact as well as presumptive.

These older conspirators had long ago made their decision regarding Talia. If it did not prove possible to induce her to leave the Collegium, she was to be gotten rid of—by any means that came to hand.

Since she had now proven impossible to drive away, the next step was to turn to more permanent measures.

They were only waiting for Talia to make the mistake of being alone to put their new plan into motion—and their chance came on the coldest day of the year.

The sky was overcast; a dull, leaden gray. The snow was creaky underfoot, and the cold ate its way up from the ground to Talia's feet even through sheepskin boots and three pairs of woolen stockings. The wind was strong and bitter, and Talia had decided to take the longer way from classroom to training salle, past the stables, where there was some relief from the wind's bite.

As she rounded a corner with her thoughts miles away, she suddenly found herself surrounded by Blues. Their faces were far from friendly.

Before she could think to flee, they grabbed for her, trying to pinion her arms and legs.

She was befuddled for only a scant second; she fought back with all the skill she had so far managed to acquire at Alberich's hands. He had taught her a "no holds barred" discipline; she kicked, pulled hair, and bit without compunction—and muffled cries of pain attested to the fact that she was scoring on them, even though they were fairly well protected by bulky winter garments. Oddly enough, it seemed almost as if they had no real intentions of hurting her; as if their intentions were rather to immobilize her for some unknown reason.

She took advantage of this apparent reticence on their part to bolt through a gap between two of them, leaving her cloak behind in the hands of a third.

She almost managed a clean escape—then a flying tackle from behind sent her headfirst into the stable muckpit. The contents were fresh, well-watered, and soft. She was covered from head to toe with the stinking mess, and flailed about, helpless with retching.

"Oh, poor little bumpkin—it's made a mess," cooed one of the girls in a sugary voice. "How awful for it!"

"Perhaps it thought it was home," replied a boy, as Talia tried to scrape filth off her face and away from her eyes. "We'd better get it clean—it certainly doesn't know how to clean itself."

They pulled her out and seized her before she could flounder free, knocked her down, and stuffed a piece of rag into her mouth before she could scream for help. They took turns rubbing handfuls of muck into her face and hair, as if in retaliation for the injuries she'd managed to inflict on *them*, then some of them pinioned her arms and others her legs. They hauled her outside where the stuff froze stiff in the icy wind and she couldn't get her eyes open to see. She was still trying to catch her breath after the blow that had knocked her down, and couldn't seem to get any air into her lungs. Right now, full lungs seemed the most important thing in the world—

She was half-carried, half-dragged, acquiring numerous scrapes and bruises from the cobblestones. She couldn't seem to think further than trying to breathe—couldn't guess what they planned next as they dragged her along. They seemed to be hauling her halfway to the Border!

Then, as she felt the road begin to climb, a vague idea of what they planned came to her, and she began to thrash in panic.

"Into your bath, goatling!" the hateful male voice sang out.

She tried to wriggle loose and kicked as hard as she could, but it was all to no avail. They were bigger and stronger than she, and far outnumbered her. She only succeeded in causing their grip to slip a little so that the back of her head cracked against the stone paving, stunning her briefly. That gave them the relief they needed; she felt herself tossed up into the air, landing in the icy waters of the river with a shock that drove what little breath she had from her lungs.

The water closed over her head; she fought for the surface, pulling the rag out of her mouth as she did so, only to have her throat fill with water as she tried to breathe inches too soon. As she reached the air and choked and gasped in the icy wind, she heard someone call out, voice receding into the distance, "Farewell, bumpkin. Give our greetings to Talamir."

Only last week a careless would-be daredevil had died here, trying to cross on the ice instead of the bridge. Talia began to thrash hysterically, remembering that he hadn't lasted more than a few moments in the frigid river. What ice she could reach that didn't break when she grabbed it was too slippery to get a grip on—there was nothing to hold to, and no way she could haul herself up on it. Her sodden clothing, especially those heavy, water-logged sheepskin boots, was pulling her down, the current was tugging her inexorably farther from shore, and she could feel her limbs growing numb and unresponsive.

She couldn't keep her mouth above water for long; she couldn't get enough breath to cry for help. Her mind shrieked in incoherent fear.

Then, like a gift from the gods, a trumpeting neigh split the air and something huge and heavy plunged in beside her. Strong teeth seized her collar and pulled her to within reach of a broad warm, white back that rose beside her like magic.

"Rolan!" she gasped; she tried to make her fingers work enough to grab mane or tail while he maneuvered himself to support as much of her as he could.

For a moment it almost seemed as if it would work.

Then her fingers loosed themselves and she began sliding away from him, dragged by the punishing weight of her clothing and the strong pull of the current. Her mind went numb, as cold as the water. She lost her last tentative hold on his back, and darkness closed over her mind as the water closed over her head. Her lungs filled with water again, but she was beyond caring.

Something jerked at her collar; her head broke the surface and a stubborn spark of life made her cough and gag once again in the painfully icy air.

Then she was being hauled roughly across the ice, and many hands reached to pull her up on the bank where she was pounded and pummeled until she'd coughed all the water out of her lungs. A babble of angry, frightened voices filled her ears as she was wrapped in something heavy and made to drink a fiery liquid that brought tears to her eyes and made her choke. Her vision cleared of the dancing sparks that had taken the place of the darkness when they'd started pounding on her, and she saw she was surrounded by the anxious faces of her teachers and fellow students.

Safe. She fainted.

She half-roused as someone lifted her up to a rider's arms and they galloped to the very doors of the Collegium. The rider vaulted from the saddle still carrying her, and sprinted effortlessly with her up the stairs to the dormitory floor.

She was passed into more hands on the other side of a steamy portal, and those hands stripped her of her soaked, filthy garments quickly and efficiently. Once again she found herself up to her neck in water, but this time it was blessedly hot.

That brought her fully awake again; that, and the fact that she was being scrubbed with strong soap by three other people.

"Wha—" she coughed, her throat raw. "What happened?"

"That's what *we'd* like to know," said Jeri, soaping her hair vigorously. "Ugh—your hair is *full* of this muck! Rolan heard your mindcall for help; he alerted the rest of the Companions, and they roused their Heralds. Then he went after you himself. Lord of Lights! You should have seen the Collegium—it looked like a nest of angry wasps! People came boiling out of everywhere! Most of us got to the riverbank just in time to see you slip off Rolan's back and go under. Keren was just a fraction ahead of everyone else, and she dove right off the saddle after you; Sherrill was right behind her. They managed to pull you out— when I knew you were alive, I came back here to get Housekeeper and start what we'd need to warm you up again. Once they'd gotten the water out of you, Teren brought you here. This tub's filthy. We're going to change. No," she warned as Talia started to move, "don't try to do anything—let us do the work for you. You've got an awful bump on your head and you might get dizzy and fall."

They lifted her over to a second tub; she still seemed chilled to the bone.

"Are they—all right?" Talia managed to get out.

"Who? Sherrill and Keren? They're fine. Don't you remember? They're from Lake Evendim. This isn't the first ice-rescue they've done. And there were two more riders waiting to bring them here, too. They're both soaking in hot tubs, the same as you."

"They are?" Talia raised her head, as the room spun before her eyes, and tried to look around. The bathing room seemed oddly turned backward, reversed in mirror-image.

"What ha'n'd to th' room?" Her tongue didn't seem to quite want to behave.

"You're on the boys' side, silly," Jeri giggled, "It was closer. Take a good look—you might not get a second chance."

"Hush," Housekeeper Gaytha scolded affectionately. "Talia, I think we've gotten the last of the filth off you. How are you feeling?"

"Still c-cold." There seemed to be an icy core that the heat didn't touch. They drained some of the water and ran in more that was fresh and hotter than before. She finally felt herself stop shivering and began to relax. Then a sudden thought made her struggle to sit up.

"Rolan!"

"He's perfectly all right." Jeri and Housekeeper Gaytha held her firmly in place. "It'll take more than a cold ducking to stop him!"

"The worst was heaving him up onto the bank; he wasn't even chilled, and he's inordinately proud of himself," said the third member of the group, silent until now. "I suppose he has every right to be, since your bond isn't supposed to be strong enough at this stage for you to call one another, even in panic. You're very lucky that wasn't the case for the two of you."

Her sight seemed to be blurring, but Talia finally got a good look at this third person as she moved to within Talia's range of vision to speak to her. The woman was a square-jawed ash-blond, and she wore full Heraldic traveling leathers with the silver arrow of a special messenger on one sleeve.

"I'm sorry we weren't properly introduced, Talia," she smiled. "I'm Herald Ylsa. Keren may have mentioned me?"

Talia nodded, and was immediately sorry. Her head began pounding, and her vision blurred still more. "Keren—was going—t' be waitin' f'r you—" she said with difficulty.

Ylsa saw the glazed look, the fixed pupils of Talia's eyes, and said sharply, "Problems, kitten?"

"I can't—see too well. And m' head hurts."

"Can you tell what's wrong?" Gaytha asked the Herald in an undertone.

The woman frowned a little. "Well, I'm no Healer, but I know the technique. Hold still, kitten," she addressed Talia. "This isn't going to hurt, but it may make your head feel a little odd." She caught Talia's blurring gaze and looked deeply into her eyes—and Talia felt something like a light touch inside her head. It *was* a very odd sensation.

Ylsa placed one hand on Talia's forehead in the lightest of featherlike touches once she'd caught Talia's attention, beginning her probe.

She continued to speak in a casual voice, knowing commonplaces would keep Talia from becoming too alarmed if she sensed anything. "I'd only just come through the gate when the alarm went up. Keren's got the tightest bond with that stallion of hers that I've ever witnessed. The two of them were headed for the river before Felara had managed to do more than tell me that there was bad trouble. We took off after them, but we couldn't even manage to keep up. Her mindlink with her brother is almost as strong, and she must have told him what was needed before we even hit the riverbank because he came pounding up with blankets and ropes right after she went in. I knew that she and Dantris were good, but I have *never* seen anyone move like they did—I never even knew you *could* slingshot into a dive from the back of a Companion in full gallop!"

While she spoke, she "read" the child as the Healers she had worked with did. Since she was not formally Healer-trained, she took longer at it—and inadvertently made more contact than she'd intended to.

Talia's head wasn't exactly feeling odd, but the sensation of internal touch was stronger than ever, and she was seeing the strangest things. They came in flashes, confusing and disorienting, as if she were seeing things through someone else's eyes—and what she was seeing concerned Keren and this stranger—intimately. And it was very heavily laden with overtones of complex emotions—

She blushed an embarrassed crimson. Ylsa and Keren—long-time lovers? She didn't even *know* this woman; why should her mind be producing a fantasy like that? She looked up at Ylsa in startled confusion.

Ylsa hastily broke the contact between them when she realized what the child was sensing, and stared at her with wide-eyed respect. First the mindcall to her Companion, and now this! Ylsa *knew* she had one of the strongest shields in the Circle, yet this untrained child had picked out something it might have taken a master to extract. Granted, Ylsa's shields were probably lowered a trifle because of the reading she was doing, but it should have taken someone fully trained to have taken advantage of the fact. This child was certainly far more than her appearance led you to believe.

"Concussion," she said to the others, "and if she had some kind of cold before she went in, it's getting worse by the moment. I think we'd best get her into a warm bed and have a real Healer take her in hand."

And I'd better have a word with Keren as soon as I can! she thought to herself. *If this poor child begins a fever, there's no telling what she's likely to pick up. Anybody that watches her had better have excellent shields—for her sake.*

The three of them helped Talia out with care, dried her off, and put her into her warmest bedgown. She wasn't allowed to walk at all; they gave her over to Teren who carried her to her room and tucked her into her bed. It had been warmed, and she was glad of it, for once out of the steam-filled bathing room the air had been very cold and she was shivering by the time they reached her room.

She was having trouble holding to reality. It only seemed that she'd gotten the blankets tucked around her when there was a stranger standing beside her, come out of nowhere, appearing at her bedside as if he'd been conjured. It was a cherubic-faced man whose beardlessness made him seem absurdly young; he was dressed in Healer's Green. He held one hand just fractions of an inch from her forehead and frowned in concentration.

Talia's head was truly beginning to hurt now; it felt like someone was pressing daggers into her skull just behind her eyes. The rest of her was starting to ache, too; her chest rasped when she breathed and she wanted badly to cough, but knew it would only set off an explosion in her head if she did so.

The young Healer took his hand away and said to someone just outside the door, "Concussion for certain, though the skull doesn't seem to be broken. And I'm sure you noticed the fever—pneumonia is a real likelihood."

There was a murmur in answer, and the Healer leaned down so that his face was at Talia's eye level. "You're going to be a very sick young lady for a while, youngling," he told her quietly. "It isn't anything that we can't cure with time and patience, but it isn't going to be very pleasant. Can I count on you to cooperate?"

She made a wry face, and whispered, "You wan' me t' drink p-potions, right? Willowbark tea?"

The Healer chuckled. "I'm afraid that will be the least of the nasty things we'll ask you to drink. Can you manage your first dose now?"

She nodded just the tiniest fraction; carefully, so as not to send her head pounding. The Healer busied himself at her fireplace for several long moments, and returned with something green and foul-looking.

With his aid she drank it as quickly as she could, trying not to taste it. Whatever it was, it was a great deal stronger than Keldar's willowbark tea, for she found the pain in her head beginning to recede, and her alertness as well. With her alertness went her awareness. Before long, she was soundly asleep.

She woke to fire and candle-light. There was someone sitting in the shadows beside her bed; soft harp-notes told her who it was.

"Herald Jadus?" she whispered, her throat too raw and swollen to produce real sound.

"So formal, little friend?" he asked, laying down his harp and leaning forward to place one hand on her hot forehead. "How do you feel?"

"Tired. Cold. Head hurts. Everything hurts!"

"Hungry?"

"Thirsty," she rasped. "Why'r'you here?"

"Thirsty can be remedied if you're willing to take another one of Devan's evil brews first. As to why I'm here, that's easy enough. You need someone to help you while you're ill, and I have plenty of time for my friend Talia." He handed her a mug of the same green potion she'd drunk before, nodding in approval as she downed it as fast as she could, then handed her another mug of broth. "We're taking it in turn to keep an eye on you, so don't concern yourself over me, and don't be surprised to see Ylsa or Keren. Ah, Devan—as you predicted, she's awake."

The same Healer moved into view on silent feet, smiling down at her. "You're a tough little thing, aren't you? Sometimes being a Border brat like we both are has its positive aspects."

Talia blinked owlishly at him over the rim of her mug. "How long—sick?" she croaked.

"A few weeks; perhaps more. And you'll feel worse before you feel better. Comforting, aren't I?"

She managed a weak grin. "Truth better."

"I thought you'd probably prefer it. You may start seeing things when you get more fevered. There will always be someone with you, so don't worry. Beginning to feel sleepy?"

"Mm," she assented.

"Finish that, then get more rest. I'll leave you in Herald Jadus' competent hands." He departed as silently as he'd come.

"Is there anything else you'd like, youngling?" Jadus asked, relief evident in his voice.

Talia surmised vaguely that the Healer's confidence had allayed some worry he'd had. He took the now-empty mug from Talia's heavy fingers.

"Play for me?" she whispered.

"You have only to ask," he replied, sounding inordinately pleased and surprised at the request. She drifted off to sleep followed by harpsong.

Ugly dreams and pain half-woke her; someone—it might have been

Ylsa—calmed her panic, and coaxed her to drink more broth and medicine.

She half-woke countless more times, obediently drinking what was put to her lips, letting herself be steered to and from the bathing room and the privy. She was otherwise unaware of her surroundings. She alternately froze and burned, and lived in a dream where people from Hold and Collegium mingled and did the most absurd things.

When her dreams turned evil, they were always chased away by harpsong or comforting hands.

Finally she woke completely to see sunlight streaming in her window. Her head ached abominably; she felt at the back of it, and winced as her fingers encountered a lump.

"Hurts, doesn't it?" the rough voice from the chair beside the bed was sympathetic. Turning her head carefully, Talia saw that Keren had assumed the position she'd last seen occupied by Jadus. She was lounging carelessly in Talia's chair with her feet up on the desk that stood beside it.

She also had her sword resting unsheathed in her lap.

"You're all right!" Talia croaked with relief.

Keren cocked an eyebrow at her. "You forget, little centaur; *I* went in of my own will. My entry was a bit more controlled than yours was. You're damned lucky to be here, you know. You slipped right under the ice when you lost your hold on Rolan's back. I almost couldn't reach you. One fingerlength more and we'd not have found you till Spring thaw."

Once again, Talia seemed to be seeing things through other eyes— and feeling things as well. She felt a dreadful fear not her own—and saw herself being pulled under the thick sheet of ice that covered most of the river. And she saw what had followed. She spoke before she thought. "You went under the ice after me—" she said in awe "—you could have died!"

Keren nearly choked. "Nets of the Lady, Ylsa was right! I'd best watch what I think around you, youngling. We might share more than either of us want to! To change the subject—yes, since you know already, it was a damned close thing. Good thing for both of us that it was Sherrill that was behind me. Once I'd hooked you, she was able to pull both of us out from under, the more 'specially as I'd had the wit to grab one of Ylsa's spare lead-ropes from her saddle and clip it to my belt on the way to the river. When Sherrill saw *that* trailing out behind me, she grabbed it. Good thing she's been on ice-rescues herself."

"She's all right, too?"

"Oh, she's not as tough an old snake as I am; she caught a cold. Don't feel sorry for her—since we'd put you out of reach, the rest of the trainees made a great fuss over her. She's their heroine; they packed her into bed and waited on her hand and foot till she hadn't so much as a sniffle."

"What do you mean, put me out of reach? Why? And why have you got your sword out? What aren't you telling me?"

Keren shook her head ruefully. "You look so naive—innocent, helpless—but even half-dead with concussion and pneumonia you don't miss much, do you? Ah, little one, there's no use trying to keep it from you. We're guarding you. The ones that threw you in the river were caught; you've got friends in Servant's Hall who spotted them coming in mucky. They swore it was just a 'joke'—some joke!—and all the Queen could legally do was banish them from Court and Collegium. On the surface of it, since there weren't any witnesses to contradict them, she had no choice. Well, I would have had their heads"—Talia could feel the anger that Keren's bland expression concealed—"or rather, their hides; but I'm not the Queen, and there's only so much she could do by the law. Since you managed to survive their little 'joke,' she couldn't even call Truth Spell on them."

"One of them told me to give their greetings to Talamir—that was before Rolan came," Talia said quietly.

Keren whistled, and Talia could feel her anger mount. "Damn! I wish we'd been able to tell the Council *that* when that lot came up on charges! Well, nobody really believed them, so Ylsa, Jadus, and I have been taking it in turn to guard you; Mero's been making all your meals himself and Teren brings 'em straight from his hands."

"Jadus?" Talia looked at Keren's sword doubtfully.

"Don't make the mistake of thinking he's helpless because he's short a leg, lovey. There's been a loaded crossbow within reach the whole time he's been up here, and that cane of his has a swordblade in it. Anybody trying to take him would have had one hell of a surprise."

"Is all this really necessary?" Talia asked, beginning to feel more than a bit frightened.

"The danger's real enough to warrant a few simple precautions. We lose enough of the Circle as it is—we're not about to lose you through carelessness," Keren paused, and then added, (half in anger, half in hurt), "—and next time, youngling, *tell* somebody when there's something wrong! We could have avoided all this—maybe caught whoever was chewing your tail! Heralds *always* stick together, dammit! Did you think we wouldn't believe you?"

"I—yes—" Talia said, and was horrified that her mouth had once again betrayed her. To her further horror, slow tears began to fall, and she was helpless to stop them.

Keren was out of her chair and at her side in a moment, holding her against a firm shoulder, anger turned immediately to concern and a touch of guilt. "Lovey, lovey, I didn't mean to upset you. We want you, we need you—it'd half kill us to lose you. You've got to learn to trust us. We're your family. No, we're more than that. And we'll never, ever desert you. No matter what happens."

"I'm—sorry—" Talia sobbed, trying to bring herself back under control and pulling away from Keren.

"No, you don't. It's time you let some of that out," Keren ordered. "Cry all you want. If my twin's right—and he usually is—you've got a lot of crying to catch up on."

Her care—her sincerity was too much to stand against. Talia yielded with speechless gratitude, as the barriers within her that had been weakened by her friendship with Jadus came crumbling down. Keren held her as if she were her own child, letting her sob herself into dry-eyed exhaustion.

"Feel better?" Keren asked, when the last of the tears were gone.

Talia smiled weakly. "Sort of."

"Except that now your head aches and your eyes are sore. Next time, don't let things build up for so long. That's one of the things friends are for—to help you with troubles. Now—about that 'new' thought-sensing ability of yours—"

"It's real? Then I *am* feeling what you're feeling? And you and Ylsa—" She broke off in confusion. "But where did I get it from? I couldn't do that before!"

"You're still picking up from me? Oh hell!" Keren frowned a little in concentration, and abruptly Talia was no longer awash with confusing emotions. "That better? Good. Oh, this thought-sensing is real, all right, and disconcertingly accurate. Only the Circle knows about Ylsa and me; we couldn't have kept it from them with all the Gifted about, even if we'd wanted to. We're lifebonded; I don't suppose you've heard of that, have you?"

"Like Vanyel and Stefen? Or Sunsinger and Shadowdancer?" Keren's amazed glance flicked over Talia like a spray of cold water, but given Talia's penchant for tales it wasn't overly surprising that she *had* heard of lifebonding. Rare among Heralds, rarer still in the general population, a lifebond was a very special tie, going far beyond the physical.

"Not so dramatic, but yes, like Vanyel and Stefen. Well, I'd guess that either the blow to your head woke your Gift early, or overwhelming fear did. It happens sometimes. Now if you *weren't* Queen's Own, we wouldn't even think about training you to use it for another few years, but you're by definition a special case. Do *you* want it trained?"

"Please—not another set of lessons—" Talia said pathetically.

Keren chuckled. "All right then, lovey, we'll leave things as they are. Maybe when your head heals, it'll go away; I've seen that happen before. But if it starts to get bothersome, you tell one of us, all right?" She paused, and eyed Talia speculatively. "It doesn't disturb you—about Ylsa and me?"

"No," Talia replied, a trifle surprised. "Should it? I mean—there's lots of—um—" she blushed again "—'special friends' on the Holdings."

"Are there?" Keren raised an eyebrow. "I never figured on that, old rocks that they are. Makes sense, I guess—all those Underwives, and damn few of 'em wed for affection." She relaxed visibly. "I won't deny that I'm glad to hear that from you. You've got an old head in a lot of ways, lovey; I'm beginning to think of you as much as my friend as my student, and I'd hate to see anything get in the way of that friendship."

"Me? Your friend?" Talia was visibly startled.

"Surprised? Jadus thinks of you as a friend, too, and he hasn't opened up to anyone in years. There's something about you that I can't pinpoint—you're so much older than your years, sometimes. Maybe it comes of being Queen's Own. Lady knows *I'm* not old enough to have known Talamir as a lad. You seem like someone I've known and trusted for years. Like a little sister. As close, maybe, as my twin—which is damned odd, considering that I've got a niece and nephew nearly your age. I'm not the only one to feel that way. There's Jadus, like I said—and Sherrill, and Skif, and probably more."

Talia digested this with wonder.

Keren shook her head, "Enough of this—how's the skull feel?"

"Awful."

She stood up and examined the lump with gentle, skillful fingers.

"Lovey, luck was all on your side in this. An inch or two lower, or on the temple instead, and you'd have been unconscious or paralyzed when you hit the water. You'd have gone under without a ripple, and we'd never have known what happened to you. Think you can stomach more of that vile green brew? It'll take the ache out, anyway."

Talia nodded slowly, and Keren brought her a mug of the concoction, then returned to her former perch on the chair; feet propped up and sword on her lap.

"How much of my classes have I missed?"

"Not a thing that can't be made up quickly, 'specially since you're excused from chores and Alberich's tender mercies till you're well again. If your eyes play tricks on you, we'll read to you, and everybody in the Collegium wants to loan you their notes. Fair enough?"

Talia was about to answer when a deep, somber-toned bell—one she'd never heard before—began tolling somewhere nearby.

Keren stiffened as her head snapped up on the first peal. "Damn," she said softly, but with venom. "Oh, *damn*."

"What's the matter?" Talia did not like the tense bitterness on Keren's face. "What's happened?"

"That's the Death Bell." Keren stared sightlessly out the window, tears trickling unheeded down her cheeks. "It rings when a Herald dies. It means that the bastards got another one of us. And one of the best. Ah, gods, why did it have to be poor Beltren?"

CHAPTER 8

$\longleftarrow\ \cdot\ \longmapsto\!\!\longmapsto\ \cdot\ \longrightarrow$

MINUTES AFTER THE bell began its somber tolling, someone tapped on Talia's door; before Keren could answer, Skif stuck his head inside.

Keren lowered the blade she had aimed reflexively at the entrance.

"Keren," Skif said hesitantly, "your brother sent me. He thought you might want to be with the others. I can watch Talia."

Keren pulled herself together with an obvious effort. "You sure? I know you *think* you're good, youngling—"

Talia didn't even notice Skif's hand moving, but suddenly there was a knife quivering in the wall not an inch from Keren's nose. Both of them stared at it in surprise.

"Huh!" was all the reply Keren made.

"If there had been a fly on your beak, I could have nipped it off without touching you," Skif said soberly, with none of his usual boastfulness. "I know I've got a long way to go in everything else, but not even Alberich can best me with these."

He held up his right hand, with a dagger that matched the first in it. "Anybody who tries forcing their way in here is going to have to get around six inches of steel in his throat."

"I'll take your word for it." Keren rose and sheathed her sword. "You may regret this—because I'll probably arrange for you to share Talia-watch from now on."

"So? I volunteered, but Ylsa wouldn't take me seriously."

"Well, I will." She passed him, waving him into the room. "And youngling? Thanks. You've got a good heart."

Skif just shrugged and pulled his knife out of the wall.

"What's going on?" Talia whispered hoarsely. "What's the Death Bell?"

Skif perched himself cross-legged on the top of her desk; his expression was unwontedly serious. "What do you want answered first?"

"The Bell."

"All right—since I don't know what you know, I'll take it from the beginning. There used to be a little temple in the Grove in Companion's Field; King Valdemar had it put up. It had a bell-tower, but not until just before he died was there a bell in it. The bell was actually installed the day before he died, but the rope to ring it hadn't been hung, and it didn't have a clapper. So you can imagine that when a strange bell was heard tolling before dawn the next morning, people were pretty startled. When they went out to look, they saw what you'd see now if you were to go out to the Field—every Companion here gathered around the tower and staring at it. When they got back to the Palace they learned what the Heralds had already known—that Valdemar was dead. The temple's long gone, but the tower is still there—and every time a Herald dies, the Death Bell tolls."

"And Keren?"

"Every Herald knows when another one dies, and whether or not it was from natural causes. You sort of start to get the sensing of it around about your third year—sooner if your Gift is strong; I haven't got it yet. It hurts, they tell me, like something of yourself has died—the ones with the strongest Gifts may know details of what happened. You always know who, if you're a full Herald, and a little of how, as soon as the Bell begins to ring. Most of 'em find it easier to be together for a while, especially if it was someone they knew really well. That's why Herald Teren sent me—Beltren was one of Keren's year-mates."

There wasn't much Talia could say in reply. She and Skif stared gloomily out the windows for a long time, listening to the Bell; the tolling that sounded like the cold iron was sobbing.

Word on what had actually befallen Beltren did not reach the Collegium for several days. When news came, it was not good. Someone or something had ambushed him, and sent both Beltren and his Companion over the edge of a cliff. There were no clues as to who the murderer was—and if the Queen knew why it had happened, she kept her own council.

The atmosphere became more desolate and oppressive, with every passing day. Talia's newly-awakened sensitivity left her painfully aware of it, and the weakness she was prey to as she recovered did not make bearing the brunt of this easy.

Skif (who, true to Keren's threat, was now sharing guard-duty with the three adults) did his best to cheer her with Collegium gossip and more of his absurd stories, but even he could not completely counteract the effect of the mourning of all those around her.

Finally the Queen gave orders—and the Heralds flew like the arrows they were named for to obey. Talia never did hear details, but the murderer was caught—though not even the news that he had been found and condemned by Queen and Council did anything to ease the atmosphere of pain, for Beltren had been universally held in high regard by the members of the Circle.

The entirety of the Collegium as well as those of the Circle at Court assembled for the memorial service several weeks later. As was all too often the case, there was no body to bury, and the service was held at the single pillar that held the names of all those Heralds who had sacrificed themselves for Monarch and Kingdom.

Talia had only just been allowed to leave her bed, but something impelled her to beg the Healer, Devan, to permit her to attend the memorial. Impressed by the urgency she was obviously feeling, he overrode his own better judgment and agreed that she should be allowed to go. She had not confided how strongly she was being affected by the mourning about her to anyone yet; she had been hoping that Keren had been right and it would go away. And having been accused of having an overactive imagination more than once, she couldn't be entirely sure how much of this she might be conjuring out of her own mind.

Nothing of the ceremony was any too clear in her mind; everything seemed to be washed away in a flood of sadness and loss. She stood through it in a fog of pain, sure only now that she was in no way inflicting any of this on herself. When those assembled had begun dispersing, a locus of agony sharpened and defined.

It was the Queen.

Talia had not been this close to Selenay since her first day at the Collegium; she would not have dared to disturb her except that the Queen's emotional turmoil drew on her with an irresistible attraction. She approached shyly, as quietly as she could.

"Your Majesty?" she said hesitantly. "It's Talia."

"*I* sent him to his death," Selenay replied as if in answer to some internal question. "I knew what I was sending him into, and I sent him anyway. I murdered him, just as surely as if it had been my hand that pushed him to his death."

The pain and self-accusation of the Queen's words triggered something within Talia, something that impelled her to reply. "Why are you trying to convince yourself that he didn't know the kind of danger he was in?" she said, knowing that her own words were nothing less than the stark truth, but not knowing *how* she knew. "He was fully aware, and he went despite that knowledge. He wasn't *expecting* to die, but he knew it was a possibility. Majesty, we *all* know it can happen, and at any time. You had no choice either—wasn't it absolutely imperative that someone be sent?"

"Yes." The word came reluctantly.

"And wasn't he the best—perhaps the only—Herald for the task?"

"He was the only Herald with any hope of convincing the people of the area to part with the information I needed. He worked as my agent there for three years, and they knew and trusted him."

"And did he not succeed in sending you that information? Was there any substitute for it?"

"What he sent to me will save us a war." Selenay sighed. "Even among rulers blackmail sometimes works wonders, and I'll blackmail Relnethar with a cheerful heart if it will keep him off our borders and within his own. Lady knows I'd tried every other way to get it—"

"Then you had no choice at all; you acted for the good of *all* our people. It's the kind of decision that you and only you can make. Majesty, in Orientation class they told me in good plain terms that it is quite likely that a Herald will perish, perhaps horribly, before he ever has to think of retiring because of age. They tell everyone that—but it's never stopped anyone from becoming a Herald. It's something we *have* to do—just as making hard choices is something you have to do. And behind all of it, I think, is that we all have to choose to do what we *know* to be right; you as Queen, the rest of us as your Heralds. I *know* if Beltren could be standing here right at this moment, he'd tell you that the choice you made was the only one you could have made."

The Queen stared at Talia, her eyes bright with unshed tears, but Talia could feel the agony within her easing. "Child," she said slowly, "you very nearly perished yourself because of my actions—or lack of them. Can you stand there and tell me you would have been glad to die?"

"No," Talia said frankly. "I was awfully afraid—I didn't want to die, and I still don't, but if it happens, it happens. I made the choice to become a Herald, and if I knew I was going to die tomorrow, I still wouldn't choose otherwise."

"Oh, Talia—child—" the Queen sat abruptly on the side of the memorial, and Talia hesitantly touched her, then sat beside her and put one arm around her shoulders, feeling odd and a little awkward, and yet impelled to do so nevertheless. It was apparently the correct action, as Selenay suddenly relaxed long enough to shed a few, bitter tears, allowing herself the brief luxury of leaning on a strength outside her own.

"How have you become so wise, so young?" she said at last, composing herself. "Not yet even a year at the Collegium—yet, truly Queen's Own. Talamir would approve of you, I think. . . ." She rose gracefully, her face once again a serene mask. Talia sensed that while she still mourned, the burden of guilt had been lifted from her shoulders. "But you are not yet well, little one—and I see your keepers looking for you. And I must face the Ambassador of Karse, and dance in diplomatic circles about him until he knows with absolute certainty that I have the proof of his lord's double dealings. Thank you, Queen's Own."

She turned and walked swiftly back to the Palace, as Keren and Teren approached.

"When you didn't come back with the rest, we began to worry," Teren half-scolded. "Healer Devan wants you back in bed."

"You look like someone forced you through a sieve, lovey," Keren observed. "What's wrong?"

"The Queen—she was so guilty-feeling, so unhappy. I could feel it and I *had* to do something about it—"

"So you went to talk to her." Keren nodded with satisfaction at her twin. "All the right words just seemed to flow from you, right?"

"How did you guess?"

"Lovey, that's what makes *you* Queen's Own, and the rest of us ordinary Heralds. Grandfather used to claim he never knew what he was going to say to the King beforehand, yet it was always exactly the right thing. Trust those instincts."

"Grandfather?" Talia asked in a daze.

"Talamir was our grandfather," Teren explained. "I think he secretly hoped one of us would succeed him."

"Well, I didn't," Keren replied firmly. "After seeing the kind of hell he went through, I wouldn't have the job under any circumstances. I don't envy you, Talia, not at all."

"I agree." Teren nodded. "Talia, you still look a bit wobbly. Will you be all right now?"

"I . . . think so," she said slowly, beginning to feel a bit better now that the overwhelming burden of the sorrows of the rest of the Heralds was dissipating.

"Let's get you back to your room then, and I'll have a little talk with Dean Elcarth. If nothing else, we should show you how to shield yourself so you don't take on more of other people's feelings than you can handle. If your Gift hasn't faded by now, it's not going to," Keren said as her twin nodded his agreement.

Keren stayed with her until Elcarth arrived, then left the two of them alone. Talia sat carefully on the edge of her chair, concentrating on what Elcarth had to say, afraid she might miss something vital. She was beginning to think she couldn't bear much more of this business of carrying other people's emotions and thoughts around inside of her. If there was a way to stop it from happening, she most devoutly wanted to learn it!

But this "shielding" was a simple trick to learn—for which Talia was very grateful.

"Think of a wall," Elcarth told her. "A wall all around you and between you and everyone else. See it and *feel* it—and believe that nothing and no one can reach you through it."

Talia concentrated with all her strength, and for the first time in days, she felt a blessed sense of relief from the pressure of minds around her. With its lessening her own confidence in the "shield" grew—and the shield grew stronger in response. At last Elcarth was satisfied that nothing could penetrate what she had built, and left her to her own devices.

"Don't ever hesitate to drop it, though," the Dean urged her. "Especially if you suspect danger—your Gift may give you the best warning you're likely to get."

Talia made a thoughtful gesture of acquiescence, thinking how, if she'd been able to detect the maliciousness of her tormentors, she'd have been warned enough to have gotten help with them long before things had come to so nearly fatal a conclusion.

A few days later the Healer pronounced her fit, and she returned to her normal round of classes. Outwardly her life seemed little different— yet there were some profound changes.

The first thing that had changed was her bond with Rolan; it was so much stronger now than it had been before the river incident that there was no comparison.

She discovered this not long after she had learned how to shield out the emotions of others.

She was sitting in a quiet corner of the Library; she had just finished her book and had closed it with a feeling of satisfaction, as it was one of the histories that concluded on a positive note. There wasn't enough time for her to start a new book before the next class, so she was simply sitting for a moment with her eyes closed, letting her mind wander where it would. Almost inevitably it wandered toward Rolan.

Suddenly she was seeing a corner of Companion's Field, but her view was curiously flat and distorted. There seemed to be a blind spot straight ahead of her, her peripheral vision was doubled, and she seemed to be several inches higher than she actually stood. There was that feeling of slight disorientation that she had come to associate with seeing through the eyes and memories of others—

Then a start of surprise, followed by an out-pouring of love and welcome. It was then that she realized that she was sharing Rolan's thoughts.

From that moment on she had only to think briefly of him to know exactly where he was and what he was doing, and if she closed her eyes she could even see what he was seeing. Thoughts and images—though never words—flowed between them constantly. An emotion so profound it transcended every meaning Talia had ever heard attached to the word "love" tied them together now, and she understood how it was that Heralds and their Companions so seldom survived one another when death broke that bond that held them together.

It was shortly after this that her relationship with the Queen underwent a similarly abrupt change.

Selenay had sought the sanctuary of the barren gardens—a place where, with the last of winter still upon them, it was unlikely that she would be disturbed. Talia had found herself pulled inexorably to those same gardens; on seeing the Queen pacing the paths, she understood why.

"Majesty?" she called out softly. Selenay shaded her eyes against the weak afternoon sunlight and smiled when she saw who it was that had called her.

"Another lover of desolation? I thought *I* was the only person who found dead gardens attractive."

"But the potential is here for more. You only have to look ahead to what will be in the spring," Talia pointed out, falling into step beside the Queen. "It's not so much desolate and dead here as it is dormant. It's just a matter of seeing the possibilities."

"Seeing the possibilities—long-term instead of immediacy." Selenay became very thoughtful, then began to brighten visibly. "Yes! That's it *exactly*! Little one, you've done it again—and I have to get back to the Council. Thank you—"

She strode rapidly away, leaving Talia to wonder just what it was that she'd done.

But as time passed, such incidents became more and more commonplace. And as winter became spring, it was less often the case that Talia sought the Queen's company as it was the other way around. Selenay actively hunted her out at irregular intervals; they would talk together, sometimes for hours, sometimes only for a moment or two. Talia would find the words to express the things she knew, somehow, that the Queen needed to hear, and Selenay would take her leave, comforted or energized. Talia often thought of herself, with no little bewilderment, as two people; one, the ordinary, everyday Talia, no more wise than the next half-grown adolescent, the other, some incredibly knowledgeable and ancient being who only manifested herself in Selenay's presence.

With this assumption of her duty as Queen's Own, Talia was reminded of yet another. The apparent reason that Rolan had Chosen her, after all, was because she was supposedly the one person who could civilize the Brat—yet in all this time she had seen Elspeth only once and that when she had first arrived. It was true that until now she had been too busy adjusting herself to the Collegium to have any time or emotional energy to spare for dealing with the child. Still, that wasn't the case anymore. It was definitely time to do something about the Heir-presumptive.

"Glory! What a long face!" Skif exclaimed, plopping himself down in the chair next to Talia in the Library, and earning himself a black look or two for disturbing the silence from the trainees sitting nearby. "What's the matter, or should I not ask?" he continued with less volume.

"It's the Brat. I'm supposed to be doing something about her, but I can't get anywhere near her!" Talia replied with gloom and self-disgust.

"Oh, so? And what's keeping you away?"

"Her nurse—I think. The foreigner, Hulda—I haven't once seen the old one. I can't prove anything, though. She seems very conscientious; the very model of respect and cooperation, yet somehow whenever I try to get anywhere near the child, *she's* there, too, with something Elspeth absolutely *has* to be doing right that very moment. And it's all very logical, all quite correct. It's just that it's happened too many times now."

"'Once is chance, twice is coincidence,'" Skif quoted. "'But three times is conspiracy.' Has it gotten to the conspiracy stage yet?"

"It got to that point a long time ago. But I can't see how I can prove it, or where everything fits in—"

He bounded to his feet and tapped her nose with an outstretched finger. "You just leave the proving it to good old Sneaky Skif. And as for figuring out how everything fits together, I should think Herald Jadus would be the best source for information. He's been stuck here at the Collegium since the Tedrel Wars were over; the servants tell him *everything*, and he's got the thought-sensing Gift to boot. If anyone would know the pieces of the puzzle that go back forever, he would. So ask him—you see him every night."

"I never thought of Jadus," Talia replied, beginning to smile. "But Skif—is this likely to get you into trouble?"

"Only if I get caught—in which case I'll have a good story ready. And you'd better be ready to back me up!"

"But—"

"Never you mind, but! Life's been too quiet around here. Nothing to get my blood stirred up. Besides, I don't intend to do this for nothing, you know. You owe me, lady-o."

"Skif," she replied unthinkingly, "if you can help me prove what I suspect, you can name your reward!"

"Thank you," he grinned, waggling his bushy eyebrows in what he obviously *thought* was a lascivious fashion, but which fell a lot closer to absurdity. "I'll do just that!"

Talia succeeded in sparing his feelings by smothering her laughter as he bounced jauntily out.

"Elspeth's nurse?" Jadus was so startled by Talia's question that he actually set My Lady down. "Talia, why in the name of the Nine would old Melidy want to keep you away from Elspeth?"

"It's not Melidy that's doing it, it's the other one," Talia replied. "Hulda. Melidy really doesn't seem to do very much, actually; she mostly just knits and nods. Hulda seems to be the one giving all the orders."

"That puts another complexion on things entirely," Jadus mused. "Youngling, how much do you know about the current situation—the background, I should say?"

"Not one thing—well, almost nothing. Selenay told me that her marriage with Elspeth's father wasn't a good one, and that she felt that a lot of Elspeth's Bratliness is due to her own neglect. And since nobody mentions him, I supposed her husband was either dead or vanished—or banished. That's about all."

"Hm. In that case, I'd better tell you starting from the Tedrel War. That was when Selenay's father was killed."

"That was at least fifteen years ago, wasn't it?"

"Just about. All right; Karse intended to overrun us without actually declaring war. They hired the entire nation of Tedrel Mercenaries to do their dirty work for them. The King was killed just as the last battle was won—and if I'd just been a little more agile he'd still be alive—" he sighed, and guilt washed briefly over his features. "Well, I wasn't. Selenay had only just completed her internship when the war broke out; she was duly crowned, completed the work of mopping up the last of the Tedrel, and settled down to rule. As was to be expected, anyone of rank with a younger son to dispose of sent him to the Court. One of those visiting sons was Prince Karathanelan."

"With a name like that, he could only have been from Rethwellan."

Jadus smiled, "They *are* rather fond of mouth-filling nominatives, aren't they? He was, indeed. He was also almost impossibly handsome, cultured, intelligent—Selenay was instantly infatuated, and there was nothing any-one could say that would make her change her mind about him. They were wedded less than a month after he'd first arrived. The trouble began soon after that."

"Why should there have been trouble?"

"Because he wanted something Selenay could never, by law, give him—the throne. Had he been Chosen, he could have reigned as equal consort, but no Companion would have anything to do with him. Selenay's Caryo even kicked him once, as I recall. He had brought a number of landless, titled friends with him, and the Lord knows we have unclaimed territory enough, so Selenay had granted them estates. He didn't see why she couldn't just as easily give him rank at least equal with hers."

"But why didn't he understand? I mean, everyone knows the law is the law for everybody."

"Except that outKingdom the monarch's word frequently is the law; he wouldn't or couldn't accept that such is not the case here. When he couldn't get what he wanted by gift, he began scheming to take it by force, under the mistaken assumption that it was his right to do so."

Talia shook her head in disbelief.

"At any rate, he and his friends, and even some of our own people, began plotting a way to remove Selenay and set him in her place. And to allay any suspicions, he reconciled with Selenay and had his own nurse travel here to help Melidy with Elspeth. I don't think that *his* intention was to kill Selenay—I really do believe he only intended to hold her until she agreed to abdicate in his favor or Elspeth's with him as Regent. I do know for a fact that his friends were far more ruthless. Their intention was assassination, and they planned it for when Selenay was alone, exercising Caryo. It might have worked, too—except for Alberich's Gift."

"Alberich has a Gift? I never guessed. . . ."

Jadus nodded; "It's hard to think of Alberich as a Herald, isn't it?"

"It is," Talia confessed. "He doesn't wear Whites. I scarcely ever *see* Kantor, with or without him. And that accent and the way he acts; he's so strange—where is he from, anyway? Nobody ever told me."

"Karse," Jadus said, to her surprise. "Which is why you'll never hear a Herald use that old saying 'The only things that come out of Karse are bad weather and brigands.' He was a captain in their army—the youngest ever to hold that rank, or so I'm told. Unfortunately for him—though not for us—his Gift, when it works, is very powerful. It caused him to slip a time or two too often, to seem to know far more than he should have, especially about the future. His own people—his own company of the army—were hunting him as a witch because of that. They had him cornered in a burning barn when Kantor galloped through the flames to save him. Well, that's another story and you should ask him to tell it to you some time; the pertinent thing to this story is that Alberich's Gift is Foresight. Without telling Selenay why, he insisted on accompanying her, along with a dozen of his best pupils. Every one of the ambushers was killed; among them was the Prince. The official story is that he was killed in a hunting accident along with his friends."

"I suppose that's marginally true. They *were* hunting Selenay."

Jadus grimaced. "Child, you have a macabre sense of humor."

"But didn't his own people have anything to say about such a flimsy tale?"

"They might have, except that circumstances had changed. As it happened, their King had since died and the Prince's brother was reigning, and there had been no love lost between the two of them. The new King knew what his power-hungry sibling was like and was just as pleased that the scandal was shoved beneath the rug so neatly. Well, after that Selenay was kept very busy in attempting to ferret out those conspirators who hadn't actually been among the ambushers— and to tell you the truth, I still don't think she's found all of them. I'll tell you now what I've suspected for some time—Talamir *was* murdered because he was about to propose to the Council that Elspeth be fostered out to some of his remote relations. They were isolated folk of very minor noble rank. They weren't going to put up with any nonsense from a child, and they were isolated enough that there was no chance Elspeth would be able to run away. But they are stubborn folk and Talamir was the only one likely to be able to persuade them to take the Brat on, and when he died, the plan was given up. But that all came later—after Selenay had been so busy that she had very little time to spare for Elspeth. Up until two years ago none of us had any inkling of trouble—we just turned around one day, and the sweet, tractable child had become the Royal Brat."

"What's all this got to do with Hulda?"

"That is something I can't tell you; I'd been under the impression that it was Melidy who was in charge of the nursery, but from what you've observed that doesn't seem to be the case. That's exceedingly disturbing since I would have bet any amount of money that Melidy was the equal of anyone, up to and including Alberich! I can't picture her just handing everything over to a foreigner."

"Something's changed drastically, then," Talia mused. "And it looks like it's up to me to find out what."

"I fear so, youngling," Jadus sighed, seeing the determination in her eyes. "I fear so."

Another change in Talia's life was in the way the other students treated her. Hitherto they had assumed Talia's reticence was due to a wish for privacy and had honored that wish. Now that they knew it was simply due to shyness, they went out of their way to include her in their gossip and pranks.

Sessions in the sewing room were no longer a time for Talia to hide behind a mound of mending. The change was signaled one afternoon when there were no boys sharing the task.

Nerissa was the current target of teasing about her most recent amorous conquest. She was being quite good-humored about it, but the jibes were getting a little tiresome. She looked around for a possible victim to switch the attention to, and her eye lighted on Talia.

"Ridiculous! And old news as well," she replied to the most recent sally. "Besides, there's somebody here who's managed to captivate a lad who's a *lot* harder to catch than Baern is."

A chorus of "Who?" greeted the revelation.

"What?" Nerissa's eyes glinted with mischief. "You mean none of you noticed *anything*? Bright Havens, you must be denser than I thought. I would have figured that *someone* else would have seen that our Skif's attentions to Talia are a great deal warmer than brotherly of late."

"Oh, *really*?" Sheri turned to look at Talia, who was blushing hotly. "I thought you were my friend, Talia! You might have told *me*!"

Talia blushed even redder and stammered out a disclaimer.

"Oh, my—" Sheri teased. "So vehement! Sounds to me a little too vehement."

After a while, Talia managed to stop blushing and to give as good as she got. From then on, her relationships with her fellow students were a great deal easier.

Meals were another time when she could forget the problems with getting closer to Elspeth. There had always been a certain amount of pranking about in the kitchen; Mero saw to it that their hands were always too full for them to get into mischief, but he put no such rein on their mouths. Mero himself was a favored target, and Talia, with her innocent face, was now the one generally picked to try and fool him.

"Haven't you forgotten something, Mero?"

"I? *I*? Talia, you are surely mistaken."

"I don't know, Mero," one of the others chimed in. "It seems to me that the salt cellar is missing—"

"By the Book! It is! What could I have done with the cursed thing?" He searched for it with feigned panic, watching out of the corner of his eye while they passed it from hand to hand, grinning hugely. At last Talia got it back again and placed it prominently on the table while his back was turned.

"Ha!" he shouted, pouncing on it. "Now I *know* I looked there before—" He stared directly at Talia, who shrugged guilelessly.

"Kobolds," he muttered, while they smothered giggles. "There must be kobolds in my kitchen. What's this place coming to?"

Five minutes later he got his revenge.

"Would you say, young Talia, that you are a fairly good hand in the kitchen?" he asked, as the hoist went up with the precious salt-cellar on it.

"I—guess so."

"And would you say that you know how to prepare just about any common dish of your Hold people?" he persisted.

"Definitely," she replied injudiciously.

"Ah, good! Then certainly you can show me what to do with *this*." He dropped an enormous gnarled and knobbly root in front of her.

Talia, who had never seen anything like it in her life, coughed and tried to temporize, while Mero's grin got wider and the rest of the kitchen helpers giggled.

Finally (since it was evident that he wasn't going to feed them unless she admitted her ignorance or told him how to prepare it) she confessed to being defeated.

Mero chuckled hugely and took the thing away, replacing it with their lunch. "What is it, anyway?" Griffon asked.

"A briar burl," Mero laughed. "I doubt Talia could have done anything with it that would please a human palate—but she might have managed a gourmet meal for a termite-ant!"

Meals themselves were high points of the day. She had a permanent seat now at the second table, sandwiched between Sherrill and Jeri, across from Skif, Griffon, and Keren. To the eternal amusement of the girls and their teacher, both Griffon and Skif insisted on cosseting her, Griffon with the air of a big brother, Skif's intentions obviously otherwise although he attempted to counterfeit Griffon's. Griffon wasn't fooled by Skif in the least.

"Watch yourself, you—" he growled under his breath. "You treat my Talia right, or I'll feed you to the river with your best clothes on!"

Sherrill and the others overheard this "subtle" threat, and their faces puckered with the effort not to laugh.

Skif retaliated by picking Griffon's pockets bare even of lint without the larger boy even being aware of the fact.

"More greens, brother?" he asked innocently, passing Griffon a plate containing his possessions.

Talia had to be saved from choking to death as she attempted to keep from giggling at the dumbfounded look on Griffon's face.

That night Talia was on the receiving end of unmerciful teasing when they all got their baths at the end of the day.

"Oh, Talia—" Jeri piled her hair on the top of her head and simpered at her in imitation of Skif. "Would you like a—mushroom? Take two! Take a hundred!"

"Oh, thank you, no, dear, *dear* Skif—" Sherrill batted her eyelashes coyly at "Skif." "I'd much rather have a—pickle."

"I'll just bet you would, wouldn't you?" "Skif" replied, with a leer.

About this time the real Talia was torn between hilarity and outraged embarrassment. "I don't know where you get your filthy minds," she said, attacking both of them with a bar of soap and a sponge. "But they plainly need a good scrubbing!"

The episode degenerated at that point into a ducking and splashing match that soaked every towel in the room and brought down the wrath of the Housekeeper on all three of them.

"Hist!" someone hissed at Talia from behind the bushes next to the entrance to the gardens. She jumped, remembering all too well the misery of the months previous—then relaxed as she realized the whisperer was Skif.

"What on earth are you doing in there?" she asked, getting down on hands and knees, and seeing him in a kind of tunnel between two planted rows of hedges.

"What I told you I'd do—spying on the Brat. There's something I want to show you. Squeeze on in here and follow me!"

She looked at him a bit doubtfully, then saw that he was completely serious, and did as he asked. They crawled through the prickly tunnel for some time before Skif stopped and Talia all but bumped into him. He signed at her to be quiet, and parted the twigs on one side, just enough for both of them to peer through.

Elspeth and her two nurses, Hulda and Melidy, were no more than a few feet away. They had no problem listening in on their conversation.

"Oh, no, dear," Hulda was saying gently. "It's quite out of the question. Your rank is *much* too high for you to be associating with Lord Delphor's children. You *are* the Heir to the Throne, after all."

Talia bit her lip angrily as Elspeth's face fell. Old Melidy seemed to wake up a little from her half-doze. Her wrinkled face was creased with a faint frown as she seemed to be struggling to remember something.

"Hulda, that . . ." she began slowly, " . . . that just doesn't seem *right* somehow. . . ."

"What doesn't seem right, dear?" Hulda asked with artificial sweetness.

"Elspeth isn't . . . she can't . . ."

"Be expected to know these things, I know. Now don't you worry about a thing. Just drink your medicine like a dear love, and I'll take care of everything." Hulda poured a tiny glass of something red and sticky-looking and all but forced it into Melidy's hand. The old woman gave up the struggle for thought and obediently drank it down. Not long afterward she fell asleep again.

Skif motioned that they should leave, and they backed out of the hedgerow on all fours.

"That's what I wanted you to see," he said, as they exited the hedge in a distant part of the garden. "Hold still, you've got twigs in your hair." He began picking them out carefully.

"So've you. And leaves. She must be drugging Melidy, and keeping her drugged. Witch! But how did the old woman get into a state where she *allowed* herself to be drugged in the first place?"

"You've got me; *I* can't hazard a guess. Ask Jadus, maybe he knows. Want me to keep watching?"

"If you don't mind. I want to know if she's doing this on her own or at someone else's direction. And I want to know what else she's telling the child."

"Oh, I don't mind; this is fun! It's like being back on the streets again, except that now I'm not in danger of losing a hand or being hungry all the time." He grinned.

"Oh, Skif—" She stopped, unsure of what to say next. Then, greatly daring, she leaned forward on an impulse and kissed his cheek lightly, blushed, and scampered away.

Skif stared after her in surprise, one hand raised to touch the spot she'd kissed.

Jadus didn't know anything about the state of Melidy's health, but he directed her to one of the Healers who would.

"Melidy *was* ill about two years ago," she said thoughtfully. "Do you know what a 'brainstorm' is?"

"Isn't that where an old person suddenly can't move or talk—maybe even falls unconscious for a long time—and then gets better, slowly?"

The Healer nodded. "That's what happened to Melidy. She *seemed* to have recovered completely, at least to me. I might have been wrong, though. Lady knows we aren't infallible."

"Maybe you weren't wrong—or maybe she was affected in some way that you wouldn't have noticed," Talia replied, sounding much more adult than she appeared, and making the Healer's eyes widen in surprise. "Keldar's mother had a brainstorm after she brought her to live at our Hold. She seemed completely all right—except that you had to be very careful what you said to her because she'd believe *anything* you told her, no matter how absurd it was. That might have been what happened to Melidy."

And if it was, she thought grimly, *she'd have been easy prey for Hulda.*

"As for that medicine you saw Hulda giving her, I never prescribed anything like that for her, but it might be a folk remedy, or one of the other Healers might have ordered it for her. I can check if you'd like. . . ."

Talia belatedly realized that this might not be a wise idea. She didn't want Hulda alerted if the woman *was* up to something—and she didn't want her embarrassed if she wasn't.

"No, that's all right, thank you. It probably is just a folk remedy. In fact, now that I think of it, it looked a lot like a syrup Keldar used to give her mother for aching joints."

The Healer smiled, with obvious relief. "Melidy does have arthritis, and unfortunately there isn't much we can do for her other than try and ease the pain. The potion might very well be one of ours. I'm glad the other nurse seems to be taking care of her, then. Is there anything else I can do for you?"

"No—thank you," Talia replied. "You've answered everything I needed to ask."

But, she thought as she walked slowly back to her room, *you raised a lot more questions than you answered.*

CHAPTER 9

"IF ONLY I could go back in time. . . ."

"If only you could *what?*" Skif asked, looking up from the book he'd been studying. Talia was perched in his open window, staring out at the moonlit trees, her own mind plainly not on study.

"I said, 'if only I could go back in time,'" she repeated. "I'd give half an arm to know if there was anyone besides Elspeth's father involved in bringing Hulda here—especially since she arrived after he was dead. But the only way I could find that out is to go back in time."

"Not—quite—"

Skif's expression was speculative, and Talia waited for him to finish the thought.

"There's the immigration records—everything about anyone who comes in from outKingdom is in them. If Hulda had any other sponsors, they'd be in there. And it seems to me there's something in the laws about immigrants having to have three sponsors to live here permanently. One would have been the Prince, and one Selenay—but the third might prove very interesting. . . ."

"Where are these records kept? Can anybody get at them?" Talia's voice was full of eagerness.

"They're kept right here at the palace, in the Provost-Marshal's office. Keeping those records is one of his duties. But as for getting at them"—Skif made a face—"we can't, not openly. Well, *you* could, but you'd have to invoke authority as Queen's Own, and Hulda would be sure to hear of it."

"Not a good idea," Talia agreed. "So we can't get at them openly—but?"

"But I could get at them. It's no big deal, just—"

"Just that The Book is there, too," Talia finished for him. "Well, you haven't had any misdemeanors down in The Book for nearly a year, have you?"

"Hell, no! You've been keeping me too busy!" He grinned, then the grin faded. "Still, if I got caught, they'd figure I was in there to alter The Book. Orthallen doesn't like me at all; I'm like a burr under his saddle. I don't grant him proper respect, I don't act like a sober Heraldic Trainee. He'd love the chance to really slap me down." He looked at Talia's troubled face, then his grin revived. "Oh, hell, what can he do to me, anyway? Confine me to the Collegium grounds? I haven't been off 'em since I met you, almost! I'll do it, by the gods!"

There was something wrong—there was something very wrong. Skif wasn't late—not yet—but Talia suddenly had the feeling that he was in a lot of trouble, and more than he could handle. And tonight was the night he was supposed to be getting into those immigration records. . . .

Although she had no clear idea of what she was going to do, Talia found herself running through the halls of the Collegium—then the halls of the Palace itself. It was only when she neared Selenay's quarters that she paused her headlong flight, waited until she had her breath back, and then approached the door of the Queen's private chambers shyly. The guard there knew her well; he winked at her, and entered through the door to announce her. She could hear the vague murmur of voices, then he opened the door again and waved her inside.

She drew in a trembling breath and prayed that *something* would guide her, and went in. The door closed quietly behind her.

Selenay was sitting at the worktable, flushed and disturbed-looking. Elcarth, Keren, and the Seneschal's Herald, Kyril, were standing like a screen between Talia and something behind them. Standing between Selenay and the Heralds was Lord Orthallen. Talia's heart sank. It *was* Skif, then. She had to save him. He'd been caught, and it must have been much worse than he thought. But how was she going to be able to get him off?

"Majesty—" she heard herself saying, "I—I've got something to confess."

Selenay looked confused, and Talia continued, "I—I asked Skif to do something for me. It wasn't—quite—legal."

As Selenay waited, Talia continued in a rush, "I wanted him to get the Holderkin records for me."

"The Holderkin records?" Selenay repeated, puzzled. "But why?"

Talia had no notion where these ideas were coming from, but apparently they were good ones. She *hated* the notion of lying, but she daren't tell the truth, either. "I—I wanted to make sure I wasn't in them anymore." To her own surprise, she felt hot, angry tears starting to make her eyes smart. "They didn't want me—well, I don't want them, not any of them, not ever! Skif told me Sensholding could claim Privilege Tax when I earn my Whites, and I don't want them to have it!"

Now she was really crying with anger, flushed, and believing every word she'd told them herself. Selenay was smiling a smile bright with relief; Elcarth looked bemused, Keren vindicated, Kyril slightly amused, and Orthallen—Talia was startled by his expression. Orthallen looked for one brief instant like a man who has been cheated out of something he thought surely in his grasp. Then he resumed his normal expression—a cool, impassive mask, and try as she might, Talia couldn't get past it.

"You see, Orthallen, I told you there'd be a simple explanation," Elcarth was saying then, as the Heralds moved apart, and Talia could see who it was that they had been screening from her view. She wasn't surprised to see Skif, white and tense, sitting in a chair as if he'd been glued there.

"Then why wouldn't the boy tell us himself?" Orthallen asked coldly.

"Because I didn't want Talia in trouble, too!" Skif said in a surly tone of voice. "I *told* you I wasn't after The Book, so what business was it of yours what I did want? *You* aren't the Provost-Marshal!"

"Skif," Kyril said mildly, "He may not be the Provost-Marshal, but Lord Orthallen is entitled to a certain amount of respect from you."

"Yes, sir," Skif mumbled and looked steadfastly at his feet.

"Well, now that this matter seems to have cleared itself up, shall we let the miscreants go?" Selenay smiled slightly. "Talia, the next time you want something in the records, just ask Kyril or myself. And we'll make sure you aren't listed in the Census as Holderkin anymore, if that's what you want. But—well, I still don't quite understand why you didn't come to me in the first place."

Talia knew from the tightness of the skin of her face that she had gone from red to white. "I—it was selfish. UnHeraldlike. I didn't want anybody else to know. . . ."

Elcarth had crossed the space between them and placed an arm around her shoulders. "You're only human, little one—and your kin don't deserve any kindness from you after the way they've disowned you. Skif—" He held out his hand to the boy, who stood slowly, and came to stand beside Talia, taking one of her hands and staring at Orthallen defiantly. "You and Talia go back to your rooms, why don't you? You've had a long night. Don't do this again, younglings, but—well, we understand. Now get along."

Skif all but dragged Talia from the room.

"Good gods—how the *hell* did you think of that? You were great! *I* started to believe you! And how did you know I was up to my ears in trouble?"

"I don't know—it just sort of came," Talia replied, "and I just knew you were in for it. What happened? How did you get caught?"

"Sheer bad luck," Skif said ruefully, slowing their headlong rush down the hall. "Selenay needed some of the Census reports and Orthallen came after them. He saw my light in the Provost-Marshal's office, and caught me red-handed. Gods, gods, was I stupid! It wouldn't have happened if I'd been paying any attention at all to the sounds from the corridor."

"What was he going to do to you?"

"He was trying to get me suspended. He couldn't get me expelled unless Cymry repudiated me, but—well, he was trying to get me sent off to clean stables for the Army for the next four years—'until I learned what honest work means,' he said."

"Could—could he have done that?"

"Unfortunately, he could. I've got one too many marks in The Book. There's an obscure Collegium rule covering that, and he found out about it, somehow. If I didn't know better, I'd say he's been *looking* for a way to get me."

"You'd better stop helping me, then. . . ."

By now they were outside Talia's door.

"Be damned if I will! This is so frustrating—I'd just found Hulda's records, too! Well, we'll just have to give up on those, and stick with what we've been doing. But there's no way I'm going to let this stop me!"

He stopped, and gave her a quick hug, then pushed her toward her door. "Go on, get some sleep. You look like you could use it, and I feel like somebody's been using me for pells!"

Talia was studying alone in her room one night, when there was a light tapping on her door. She opened it—to find a black, demonic-looking creature on the other side.

A hand clamped over her mouth before she could shriek, and the thing dragged her back inside, kicking the door closed behind it.

"Shh! Don't yell—it's me, Skif!" the thing admonished her in a hoarse whisper.

He took his hand away from her mouth gingerly, ready to clamp it down again if she screamed.

She didn't; just stared at him with huge, round eyes. "Skif—what are you trying to *do* to me?" she said finally. "I nearly died of fright! Why are you rigged out like that?"

"Why do you think? You don't go climbing around in the restricted parts of the Palace dressed in Grays—and I'm a bit too young to look convincing in Whites. Get your breath back and calm yourself down because tonight you're coming with me."

"Me? But—"

"Don't argue, just get into these." He handed her a tight-fitting shirt and breeches of dusty black. "Good thing you're my size, or nearly. And don't ask me where I got them, or why, 'cause I can't tell you." He waited patiently while she laced herself into the garments, then handed her a box of greasy black soot. "Rub this anywhere there's skin showing, and don't miss anything—not even the back of your neck."

He went to her window, opened it to its widest extent, and looked down. "Good. We won't even have to go down to the ground from here."

He produced a rope and tied it around Talia's waist. "Now follow me—and do exactly what I do."

The scramble that followed was something Talia preferred not to remember in later years. Skif had them climbing from window to window across the entire length of the Collegium wing, and from there along the face of the Palace itself. Talia was profoundly grateful for the narrow ledge that ran most of the way, for she doubted she could have managed without it. At length he brought them to a halt just outside a darkened window. Talia clung with all her might to the wall, trying not to think of the drop behind her, as he peered cautiously in through the cracks in the shutter.

He seemed satisfied with what he found, for he took something out of a pouch at his belt and began working away at the chink between the two halves of the shutter. Before too long, they swung open. Skif climbed inside, and Talia followed him.

The room disclosed was bare of furniture and seemingly unused. Skif led her to the closet set into one wall, opened it, and felt along the back wall. Talia heard the scrape of wood on wood, and a pair of peepholes was revealed.

Light shone through them from the other side. Talia quickly put her eye to one, and as she did so, Skif handed her a common drinking glass. He pantomimed placing it to the wall and putting her ear against it. She did, and realized she could hear every word spoken in the other room, faintly, but clearly.

"—so at this rate, the child is unlikely ever to be Chosen, much less made Heir. You're dong quite well, quite well indeed," an unctuous baritone said with satisfaction. "Needless to say, we're quite well pleased with you."

"My lord is most gracious." Talia could see the second speaker, Hulda, but was unable to see the first, and his voice was too distorted by the glass for her to recognize it. "Shall I continue as I have gone?"

"Has the child-Herald made any further attempts at Elspeth?"

"No, my lord. She seems to have become discouraged."

"Still," the first speaker paused in thought, "we cannot take the chance. I suggest you continue your practice of telling 'bedtime tales'— you know the ones I mean."

"If my lord refers to those featuring Companions who carry off unwary children to a terrible fate, my lord can rest assured that I will do so."

"Excellent. Here is another supply of the drug for the nurse and your usual stipend."

Talia heard the chink of coins in one of the two pouches Hulda accepted.

"You will come out of this a wealthy woman, Hulda," the first speaker said as footsteps marked his retreat.

"Oh, I intend it so, my lord," Hulda said with venom to the closed door. Then she, too, turned and left the room by a second door.

Talia was too busy thinking about what she'd witnessed to worry about the return trip.

When they reached her room, Talia seized a towel and began ruthlessly scrubbing the soot away. "Is that the first time you've watched that?" she asked as she scrubbed.

"The third. The first time was by accident; I'd been following the witch and had to duck into that other room to hide from her; I found the cracks behind a patch in the closet. The second time I took a guess that the first was a regular meeting. I was right. You know something else—no, that's too far-fetched."

"What is?"

"Well, a couple of times Melidy started to refuse that drug the witch has been feeding her, and—well, she *did* something, I dunno what, but it made her drink it anyway. If I didn't know better, I'd have sworn she was using *real* magic, you know, old magic, like in the legends, to hold power over Melidy's mind."

"She's probably got some touch of a Gift."

"Yeah—yeah, I guess you're right."

"Here, get into these. They're too big for me, so they might fit you." Talia handed Skif a set of clothing.

"Why?" he asked, astonished.

"Because as soon as you're dressed, we're going to Jadus."

Jadus was asleep when they reached his room. Under ordinary circumstances Talia would never have dared disturb him, but she felt the occasion warranted her waking him. Skif opened his door silently, and both of them slipped inside.

He roused before Talia and Skif could reach his side, staring at them with a dagger suddenly in his hand.

The elderly Herald had been sleeping uneasily for several nights running and had taken to sleeping as he had in his younger days; with a knife beneath his pillow. He woke with wary immediacy and sat up with the knife in one hand before they were halfway across his bedroom. He blinked in surprise to see the two soot-streaked trainees frozen in midstep.

"Talia!" He was shocked at *her* presence—Skif, with his penchant for pranks, he might have expected. "Why—"

"Please, sir, I'm sorry, but it's an emergency."

Jadus shook the last sleep from his head, sat up, and gathered a blanket around his shoulders. "Very well, then—I know you better than to think you'd be exaggerating. Blow up the fire, light some candles, and tell me about it."

He heard them out, Talia prompting Skif to tell his part. Before they'd told him more than a quarter of their tale, he knew that it definitely warranted the classification of "emergency." By the time they'd finished it, he was chilled.

"If I didn't know you both, I'd have sworn you were making up tales," he said finally. "And I almost wish you were."

"Sir?" Talia asked after a lengthy silence, her face drawn with exhaustion. "What should I do?"

"You, youngling? Nothing." He reached out to both of them, gathering one in each arm and hugging them, grateful for their intelligence and courage. "Talia, Skif, both of you have done far more than any of your elders have managed; I'm pleased and proud of both of you. But now you'll have to trust me to take care of the rest. There are those who need to be told who will listen to an adult, but not to the same words from the mouth of a child. I hope you'll let me speak for you?"

Skif sighed explosively. "*Let* you? Holy stars, I was afraid you were going to make me tell all this to Kyril or Selenay myself! And after getting caught going after those records, I'm afraid my credit isn't any too high with them right now. Oh, no, Herald, I'd much rather that *I* was not the bearer of the bad news. If you don't mind, I'd rather go find my bath and my bed."

"And you, Talia?"

"Please—if you would." She looked up at him with eyes full of exhaustion and entreaty. "I wouldn't know what to say. There's too many questions we can't answer. We don't know who 'my lord' is, for one thing, and if Lord Orthallen starts shouting at me, I—I—think I might cry."

"Then go, both of you. You can leave everything to me."

The two rose and padded out, and he sat in deep thought for a moment before ringing for his servant.

"Medren, I need you to have Selenay wakened; ask her to come to my room and tell her that it's quite urgent that she do so. Then do the same for the Seneschal, Herald Kyril, and Herald Elcarth. Build the fire up, and bring wine and food." He stared thoughtfully into the distance for a moment. "I have the feeling that it is going to be a very long night."

Talia heard no more about Hulda the next day—nor, in fact, did she really care to. She was content to leave the matter in the hands of the adults. The sweet smell of spring blossoms tempted her out into the garden that evening at dusk; since the banishment of the troublemakers there was no danger in roaming the grounds at any hour anymore. She was breathing in the heady scent of hicanth flowers, when she heard strangled sobs emanating from one of the garden grottoes that were so popular with couples after dark.

At first Talia thought that it must be a jilted lover or some other poor unfortunate of the same ilk that was weeping, but the sobs sounded child-like as they increased in strength. She began to feel the same compulsion to investigate them that had prompted her to the Queen's side the winter before.

She remembered what she'd been told about trusting her instincts, and acted on the impulse. She approached the grotto as noiselessly as she could, and peered inside. Lying face-down on the moss, weeping as if her heart were broken, was the Heir.

She entered and sat down beside the child. "You don't look much like a fish anymore," she said lightly, but putting as much sympathy as she could muster into her words. "You look more like a waterfall. What's wrong?"

"Th-th-they s-s-sent Hulda aw-w-way," the child wept.

"Who are 'they,' and why did they send her away?" Talia asked, not yet knowing the results of Jadus' conference.

"M-m-my mother, and that nasty Kyril, and I don't know why— she was my only, only friend, and nobody else likes me!"

"I'm sorry for you—it's awful to be lonely and alone. I know; when I was your age, they sent my best friend away to be married to a ghastly old man, and I never saw her again."

The tears stopped. "Did you cry?" the child asked with artless interest.

"I did when I was alone, but I didn't dare around other people. My elders told me that it was sinful to cry over something so unimportant. I think that that was very wrong of them because sometimes crying can make you feel better. Are you feeling a little better now?"

"Some," the child admitted. "What's your name?"

"Talia. What's yours?"

The girl's chin lifted arrogantly. "You should call me Highness."

"Not yet, I shouldn't. You're not *really* the Heir until you have a Companion and prove you can be a Herald first."

"I'm not? But—that's not what Hulda said!"

"It's true though, ask anybody. Perhaps she didn't know—or perhaps she lied to you."

"Why would she lie to me?" the child was bewildered.

"Well, I can think of at least one reason. Because she didn't want you to make friends with other children, so that she could be the only friend you had. So she made you think that you were more important than you are—and you've made other people so annoyed with you that they've left you all alone."

"How do I know that *you* aren't lying?" the girl asked belligerently.

"I'm a Herald—or I will be in a few years, and Heralds aren't allowed to lie."

The child digested this—and looked as if she found it very unpalatable indeed. "She—probably lied to me all the time then. She probably even lied to me about being my friend!" Her lip quivered, and it looked as if the weeping was about to break out anew. "Then—that means I don't have *any* friends!"

The threatened tears came, and Talia instinctively gathered the unresisting child to her. She stroked her soothingly while she cried herself to exhaustion again and produced a handkerchief to dry the sore eyes and nose when the weeping bout was over.

"You haven't any friends now, but that doesn't mean that you can't *make* friends," Talia told her. "I'll be your friend, if you'd like, but you have to make me one promise."

"Tell me what I have to promise first," the child said with a hint of suspicion—which told Talia more about "nurse Hulda's" treatment of the girl than a thousand reports could have.

"The promise is very simple, but it's going to be awfully hard to keep. I'm not sure you'll be able to . . ." Talia allowed doubt to creep into her voice.

"I can do it! I know I can! Just tell me!"

"It's in two parts. The first part is—no matter what I say to you, you won't get mad at me until you've gone away and thought about what I said. The second part is—you still won't get mad at me unless what I said wasn't true, and you can prove it."

"I promise! I promise!" she said recklessly.

"Since you're my friend now, won't you tell me your name?"

The child flushed with embarrassment. "Promise you won't laugh?"

"I promise—but I wouldn't laugh anyway."

"Hulda laughed. She said it was a stupid name." The child stared at her lap. "It's Elspeth."

"There was no reason for Hulda to laugh; you have a very nice name. It's nicer than Talia."

"Hulda said only peasants are named Elspeth."

Talia had a suspicion that she was going to grow very weary of the words "Hulda said" before too long. "That's not true; I know that for sure. There were three Queens of this Kingdom named Elspeth; Elspeth the Peacemaker, Elspeth the Wise, and Elspeth Clever-handed. You'll have a hard time living up to the name of Elspeth. Especially if you want to become the kind of person that could win a Companion and be the Heir."

Elspeth looked frightened and worried. "I—I don't know how—" she said in small voice. "And Companions—they—I'm afraid of them. Can you—help me? Please?" The last was spoken in a whisper.

"Well, first you could start by treating people nicer than you do now—and I mean *everybody,* highborn or low. If you do that, you'll start having more friends, too, and they'll be real friends who like being with you, not people who only act friendly because they think you can get them something."

"I treat people nicely!" Elspeth objected.

"Oh, really?" Talia screwed her face into an ugly scowl, and proceeded to do an imitation of the Brat at her worst. "If that's treating people nicely, I'd hate to have you mad at me! Do you really think that anyone would want to be a friend of someone like that?"

"N-no," Elspeth said in a shamed voice.

"If you want to change, you have to start by thinking about everything you say or do before you say or do it. Think about how you'd feel if someone acted like that to you." Talia reached out impulsively and hugged the forlorn child. "I can see that there's a very nice person named Elspeth sitting here, but there's an awful lot of people who can't see past the Brat. That's what they call you, you know."

"Can't my mother *make* me the Heir? Hulda said she could."

"The law is that the Heir must also be a Herald, and not even the Queen is above the law. If you're not careful, Jeri may get the title. She's got blood as good as yours, and she's already been Chosen."

The vulnerable child that looked out of Elspeth's eyes won Talia's heart completely. "You really will help me?"

"I already promised I would. I'm your friend, remember? That's what friends are for—to help each other."

Lord of Lights, what have I gotten myself in for? Talia frequently asked herself throughout the next few weeks. She found herself running from classes or chores to the Royal Nursery and back again on at least a thrice-daily basis. She had breakfast with Elspeth now, rather than with the Collegium. After supper (which was served at the Collegium at a much earlier hour than at Court) she would return. Then in the evening after supper she would spend the time until Elspeth returned to her rooms with Jadus; when Elspeth got back, they would walk in the gardens before the child's bedtime.

Hulda had vanished from her rooms before Selenay could have her taken into custody for questioning. Someone—presumably someone on the Council—had warned her in time for her to flee. Talia had little time to spare to wonder what had happened to the woman; she was too busy trying to unmake the Brat.

It was an uphill battle all the way.

Elspeth pulled temper tantrums over the smallest of things; her milk was too cold, her bath was too hot, her pillow was too soft, she didn't like the color of the clothing chosen for her. Talia put up with the first two of these displays of temper, hoping if she ignored them, Elspeth would stop. Unfortunately, this trick didn't work.

The third of Elspeth's tantrums brought Talia's first attempt at correcting her; it began when one of her maids pulled her hair while brushing it out. The child grabbed the brush and slapped the woman with it without thinking.

Talia took the brush away and handed it to the startled maid. "Hit her back," she ordered.

"But—miss, I can't—" the maid stuttered.

"I'll take the responsibility. Hit her back. As hard as she hit you."

To Elspeth's open amazement, the maid gave her a sturdy smack on the rear with the offending brush.

Elspeth opened her mouth to shriek, indulging in a full-scale fit, the kind that had always cowed others into doing things her way before.

Talia calmly picked up a glass of water and threw it in her face.

"Now," Talia said, as the child sputtered. "These are the *new* rules around here; anything you do to someone else, you'll get right back. If you can't learn to think before you act, you'll have to take what's coming to you. She didn't pull your hair on purpose, after all." She turned to the maid. "I'm sure you have other things to do than wait on an unruly little beast."

The maid recognized a dismissal when she heard one; her eyes gleamed with amusement. She could hardly wait to spread the word about the new ordering of things! "Yes, milady," she said and vanished.

"Now, since you can't be trusted not to abuse the privilege of having a servant do it, you'll just have to brush your own hair—and tend to everything else as well." Talia handed the brush back to Elspeth, who gaped in astonishment as she left.

So Elspeth struggled along without the aid of servants.

She looked like a rag-bag and knew it and hated it. The servants, on the Queen's orders, were not bothering to conceal their own enjoyment of the new state of things, nor were they backward in making it obvious that they thought Elspeth was only getting what was due her. The courtiers were worse; they smiled and acted as if nothing were wrong, but Elspeth could tell that they were inwardly laughing at her. Talia continued to spend time with her and would help her with hair or clothing—but only if she asked politely. It was an altogether unexpected and unsatisfactory state of affairs.

Elspeth's reaction was to prove she didn't care, by wrecking her nursery. She spent one very satisfying morning overturning furniture, tearing the bedclothes off the bed and heaping them in the middle of the room, breaking toys and flinging the bits about. She was sitting in the middle of the wreckage, slightly out of breath and quite satisfied, when Talia arrived.

Talia surveyed the ruins with a calm eye. "Well," she said, "I suppose you realize the nursery is going to stay this way until you clean it up."

Elspeth gaped at her; she'd expected Talia to be angry. Then the implications began to dawn on her. "B-b-but where am I going to sleep?"

"Either in the middle of the floor or on the bare mattress, it's up to you. Either one is a better bed than Skif ever had in the street or I had on sheep-watch. For that matter, it's a better bed than I get now when I've got foal-watch."

Elspeth began to cry; Talia watched her impassively. When the tears didn't bring capitulation, Elspeth picked up a wooden block and threw it angrily at Talia's head.

That brought a response all right—but it wasn't the one Elspeth wanted. Talia dodged the missile with ease and advanced on the child with compressed lips. Before Elspeth realized what was happening, Talia had picked her up and administered three good, stinging swats to the girl's rear, then set her down again.

"Next time," Talia warned, before the real howls of outrage could begin and drown her out, "it'll be six swats."

Then she left the room (although, unknown to Elspeth, she stayed close by the door) and shut the door behind her. Elspeth cried herself nearly sick, missed dinner, and fell asleep in the tangle of blankets in the middle of the room.

Talia knew very well that one missed meal was hardly going to hurt the child, but made a point of appearing the next day with a very hearty breakfast on a tray, acting as if nothing was wrong. She helped the much-subdued youngster to bathe and dress, and got her hair untangled for the first time in three days. All was well until lunch—when Elspeth demanded to know when someone was going to clean up her room.

"It will get cleaned when you do it—not before," was Talia's adamant reply.

This elicited another tantrum, another hurled toy, and the promised six swats. And Talia left for afternoon classes, with Elspeth still crying in a corner.

After three days of this, Talia arrived at the nursery after dinner to find Elspeth struggling to untangle the heavy blankets. She had already gotten what furniture she could lift back in the upright position, and more-or-less back in place. Wordlessly Talia helped her with the rest, gathered the broken toys with her, and put them back on the shelves. That night Elspeth slept in her bed for the first time in a week, falling asleep with Talia holding her hand and singing to her.

* * *

The next battles were over the broken toys.

When the toys she'd smashed weren't "magically" replaced as they'd always been in the past, Elspeth wanted to know why.

"You obviously didn't care about them, so you won't get any more," Talia told her. "If you want toys to play with, you'll have to fix the broken ones yourself."

This occasioned a near-repeat of the previous week—though *this* time Elspeth had more sense than to throw anything at Talia. She cried herself sick again, though; and by the end of the fifth day Talia was heartily tired of this tactic. She figured it was about time to put a stop to it—so she picked the girl up, dumped her in the tub in her bathing-room, and doused her with cold water.

"You were making yourself sick," she said as gently as she could while Elspeth sputtered. "Since you wouldn't stop, I figured I'd better stop you."

Elspeth took care never to cry herself sick again, though this time she held out for a full two weeks more. At the end of that time, Talia found her with a glue-brush in one hand and a broken wagon in the other. She had bits of paper sticking to her hair and face and arms and glue all over her, and was wearing a totally pathetic expression.

One slow, genuine tear crept down her cheek as she looked up at Talia. "I-I don't know how to fix it," she said quietly. "I tried—I really, really tried—but it just stays broken!"

Talia took the toy and the brush from her hands, and hugged and kissed her, oblivious to the glue. "Then I'll help you. All you ever had to do was ask."

It took the better part of a month to fix all the broken toys, and some were smashed beyond redemption. Talia did not offer to have these replaced; Elspeth had a tantrum or two over this, but compared to her earlier performances, they were half-hearted at worst. She was beginning to get the notion that Talia was a much better companion when Elspeth wasn't making fur fly. Then Talia judged that it was about time for the girl's schooling to start.

After the first day of screaming fits—only screaming, no attacks and no destruction, Elspeth had learned that much at least—Talia arranged to miss a week of her own morning classes. By the end of that week she felt as if she'd been breaking horses, but Elspeth had bowed beneath the yoke of learning, and was even (grudgingly) beginning to like it.

Gradually, Elspeth's good days began to outnumber her bad ones; as they did so, more and more amenities came back into her life. Her servants returned (she treated them like glass—apparently afraid they'd vanish again if she so much as raised her voice); first the toys that had been totally destroyed were replaced, one by one, and without a word being said, then the ones that had been broken and inexpertly mended. All except for one doll—one that had been torn limb-from-limb, and which Talia had repaired. When Elspeth saw that the broken toys were being replaced, she took to keeping that one with her and sleeping with it at night. Talia smiled to herself, touched—and the doll remained.

Progress was being made.

Now there was a second problem to deal with. The child really had a horror of Companions; she had nightmares about them and couldn't be persuaded to go anywhere near the Field.

Talia began trying to undo the effects of Hulda's horror stories with Collegium gossip, which included as many tales about Companions as about the trainees. As soon as she thought it feasible, she started taking Elspeth on walks before bedtime, and those walks took them closer and closer to Companion's Field. Finally she took Elspeth right inside, having Rolan follow at a discreet distance. As days passed and the child became accustomed to his presence, Talia had him move in closer. Then came the triumphant day when she placed Elspeth on his back. The quick ride they shared cured the child of the last of her nightmares and hysterics and gave Talia a handy reward to offer for good behavior, for Elspeth had become as infatuated with Companions as she had been terrified before.

There were wonderful days after that—days when Elspeth was sweet and even-tempered, when being around her was a pleasure. And then there were the occasional miserable days, when she back-slid into the Brat again.

On the bad days she had temper-tantrums, insulted the servants (though she never again laid a hand on one), called Talia names, and wrecked her nursery just for the sheer pleasure of destroying things. Talia would bear with this up to a point, then give her three warnings. If the third wasn't heeded, the Royal Brat got a Royal spanking and was left to her own devices for a time until she sought Talia out herself to apologize.

Gradually the good days came to outnumber the bad by a marked percentage, and it soon became possible to get the child to toe the line simply by reminding her of the fact that she was approaching "Bratly" behavior.

Talia was exhausted, but feeling well-rewarded. As a concession to the incredible amounts of time she was putting in with the girl, she was first excused from her chores for a time, then from foal-watch duty. As the Brat became more and more Elspeth, she began to take those tasks up again. As Elspeth became more interested in Companions and less afraid of them, she became enthralled with the notion of foal-watch (which, in summer, was a far from onerous duty, though it could be—and often was—pure misery in the winter).

Companion mares did not foal with the ease of horses; those who had Chosen, of course, had their Heralds or trainees to stay by them when the time came, but those who had not Chosen had no one. If there were complications, minutes could often mean the life of mare or foal. Keren did what she could, of course, but she couldn't be everywhere, and she needed a certain amount of sleep herself. So one of the duties of the trainees was to spend the nights when an unpartnered Companion mare was nearly ready to foal constantly by her side. Talia had one such stint just after Midsummer, and Elspeth begged so hard to share it with her that Talia relented and gave in.

She hadn't expected anything to come of it—nor, from what she could pick up from Rolan, was the mare herself expecting to drop for at least a week. But much to everyone's surprise, just before midnight the mare awakened Talia and her charge with urgent nudges, labor well under way.

It was Elspeth who ran to fetch Keren when it was evident to Talia's experienced eye that the foal was breech; Elspeth petted the mare's head and cooed to her (the creature a few months ago from which she would have fled in terror) while Keren and Talia got the foal turned. And it was Elspeth who helped the shaking little colt to his feet afterward and helped rub him down with coarse toweling. The mare imparted a message to Keren as the little one first began to suckle; Keren grinned, and carefully pulled a few hairs from her tail, and a sleepy but overjoyed Elspeth was presented with a ring and bracelet braided on the spot, as a "thank-you present from his mum." She put them on immediately and refused to take them off—and thereafter, when Talia was sometimes expecting a temperamental outburst, she would often see the child stroke the bracelet, gulp hard, and exert control over herself. That night signaled the real turning-point.

At last, well past Midsummer, Elspeth approached her mother, and asked permission (so politely that Selenay's mouth fell open) to watch Talia at her afternoon classes.

"Have you asked Talia if she minds an audience?" the Queen asked her transformed offspring.

"Yes, lady-mother. She said it was all right to come to the morning ones, too, but I've got different lessons from her then, so I didn't think that would be a very good idea. I'm supposed to be watching the fighters training in the afternoon though, and riding, so that's the same if I'm doing it with the Collegium students, isn't it? And—I'm tired of doing it alone. Please?"

The Queen gave her permission, and turned to Talia (who had accompanied Elspeth but had not spoken during the interview) as the child left the room.

"I can't believe my eyes and ears!" she exclaimed. "Is that the same child who terrorized her servants this winter? You've worked miracles!"

"*Elspeth's* worked miracles," Talia corrected. "I just had to give her reasons to change. I think we're all fortunate that this Hulda creature only had a really free hand with her for less than two years. If she'd had Elspeth at any earlier age, I don't think there would have been much anyone could have done to change her back."

"Then I thank all the gods that you discovered it was Hulda that was behind the change. All I knew for certain was that Elspeth gradually began to become a problem. I couldn't even take her on rides with me anymore; she had hysterics when Caryo came near—hysterics only Hulda could calm," Selenay said thoughtfully. "I can't believe how clever Hulda was about all this. The worst we thought she was doing was giving the child some inflated notions about her own importance. She claimed it was only a phase Elspeth was going through. And I was having some problems of my own in dealing with her. She was growing to look more and more like her father every day, and it was sometimes very hard for me to deal with her because of that. I could never be sure if I was making a rational judgment about her behavior or one based on dislike of the man she resembled. Talamir proposed fostering her; it's common enough to cause no comment. Poor old man, he simply didn't feel that he was capable of handling so young a child. Then, when we thought we had a solution, he was murdered."

Talia bit her lip. "So you know it for a fact now?"

"We found a vial of a rather strong heart medicine among the things she left behind. A little of it is beneficial—but too much, and the heart gives out in strain—exactly as Talamir's did. Poor Talamir, we always seemed to be stretching out to each other across a vast gulf of years—

and never quite meeting. I *know* he did his very best for me, but he was too embarrassed by the situation to ever feel comfortable about being my confidant. And he was too much of a gentleman to give me a good set-down when I obviously needed it; not even verbally."

"Well, *I* certainly can't spank *you*!" Talia retorted, with a touch of exasperation at the self-pitying mood the Queen had fallen into.

"Oh, no?" Selenay laughed. "That sounded like a well-placed verbal spank to me!"

Talia reddened. "I-I apologize. I have no right to speak to you like that."

"Quite the contrary. You have *every* right to do so; the same right that Talamir had and didn't exercise." Selenay regarded the girl with her head cocked slightly to one side. "You know, the tales all claim that the wisdom of the Queen's Own knows no age barrier, and I'm beginning to believe the tales don't say everything. You're just as much my Herald as if you had twice your years, as well as being Elspeth's. And believe me, little one, I intend never to have to do without you!"

CHAPTER 10

SEVERAL DAYS LATER, the same topics came up again in con-versation between Talia and the Queen.

"Bad enough that Hulda vanished," Selenay said, more than annoyed—angered, in fact—at herself for letting the woman escape almost literally out of her own hand. "I meant to have someone question her under the Truth Spell about 'my lord'; even though I don't think she would have been able to tell us much. But Kyril has discovered that the immigration records on her have vanished as well."

"Bright Havens! Then we may *never* learn who she was working with. According to Skif, the man she spoke with was always hooded and masked, and he doubts she even knew who he was." Talia was troubled; more troubled than she was willing to admit. "But is she likely to give us further problems?"

"I doubt it. What could she do, after all? Even Melidy is recovering—as much as she can."

"That's *very* good to hear." Talia sighed with relief. "Then whatever that drug was, it isn't going to have any lasting effects?"

"The Healers say not. And I can't tell you how grateful I am to hear that you seem to have cured Elspeth's fear of Companions."

"It's rather remarkable how it vanished when Hulda did," Talia re-marked dryly. "It didn't take more than a few visits to Rolan and the others to cure it. She adores them now."

"I'd noticed," Selenay replied with a wry twist of her mouth. "Especially after Elspeth suddenly decided she wanted to share my afternoon rides with Caryo again. That gives me a thought. I know you're busy, more so than ever before, but could you spare me an hour or so a week?"

Talia sighed. "I'll make the time, somehow. Why?"

"I'd like you to take Talamir's place at Council."

Talia choked. "*What?* Now? Why?"

"Why not? You'll have to take it sooner or later. I'd like you to get used to the machinations going on, and I'd like the Councilors to get used to seeing you there. You needn't say anything during the sessions at all, but you just might see something that I wouldn't, that would be useful to know."

"What could *I* possibly see?"

"Perhaps nothing—but perhaps a great deal. Besides, this will give you a certain amount of protection. Having you at my Council table will make it very clear that I will *not* ignore attempts to harm you just because you're not a 'real' Herald yet."

"May I make a condition?"

"Certainly."

"I'd like Elspeth with me; that way she won't feel left out, and it will show her more clearly than anything I could tell her that the job of reigning is *work*."

"I agree—and I would never have thought of that."

"That's not true," Talia protested.

"It is, and you know it. And since you're acting as Queen's Own, you might as well call me by my given name. I'm getting tired of being 'highnessed' and 'majestied.' To you, I am just Selenay."

"Yes, maj—Selenay," Talia replied, returning the Queen's smile.

"The next Council meeting is just after the noon meal, two days from now. Till then?"

Elspeth had arrived promptly for Talia's arms-lesson with Alberich, and thereafter never missed one. The child seemed to be fascinated by the different styles the Armsmaster was training them in. The rest of the trainees, warned in advance that Elspeth would be watching, went about their normal activities with only a hint of stiltedness. After a few moments, they began pausing now and again for a nod or a friendly word with the child, attempting to act as if she were just another trainee.

Before very long, they no longer had to act. It seemed natural to accept her as one of them.

Elspeth was a silent observer for a week or two when Alberich evidently decided he had an idea he wished to try. And in a fashion typical to Alberich, he did so without telling Talia about it beforehand.

When he'd finished with Talia, his eye lighted on Elspeth, seemingly by accident—though Talia was well aware that where lessons were concerned *nothing* Alberich did was by accident. "You—child!" he barked. "Come here!"

Talia saw Elspeth's chin begin to tighten and her nose to tilt up—a sure sign that she was about to revert to her old behavior. She managed to catch the girl's eye and made what Elspeth had taken to calling the "Royal Awful" face. Elspeth giggled and fingered her bracelet, all haughtiness evaporated, and she obeyed Alberich with commendable docility.

"Look, all of you," he said, giving a short practice blade to her. "At this age, she has learned no bad habits so there is nothing for her to unlearn. She has more flexibility than an acrobat, and she'll learn more quickly than any three of you put together. Name, child?"

"Elspeth, sir."

He demonstrated one of the primary exercises for her. "Can you do that?"

A tiny frown between her brows, Elspeth did her best to imitate his movements. He made some minor corrections, then ran her through the exercise several more times, the last at full speed.

"There, you see? *This* is what you are striving to imitate—the agile and receptive mind and body of the young child. And watch—"

He suddenly attacked her in such a way that the natural counter for her to make was the exercise he'd just taught her. She performed so flawlessly that she drew impromptu applause from the other students.

"At this stage, once learned, never forgotten. Try to emulate her."

At Alberich's command, they returned to sparring with one another. He beckoned to Talia. "You have charge of this one?" he asked, as though he had no idea of Elspeth's identity.

"Yes, sir," she replied respectfully.

"I should like to include her in the lessons. This can be arranged?"

"Easily, sir. Would you like to learn weapons-work, instead of just watching, Elspeth?"

"Oh, yes!" the child responded eagerly, her eyes shining. "Only—"

"Yes?" Alberich prompted.

"You won't hit me *too* hard, please, sir? Not like you hit Griffon."

Alberich laughed, something Talia hadn't seen him do very often. "I gauge my punishments by the thickness of my students' skulls, child. Griffon has a *very* thick skull."

Griffon, who was close enough to hear every word, grinned and winked at the girl.

"I think," Alberich continued, "That you have not so thick a skull, so I shall only beat you a little. Now, we might as well begin with what I just taught you."

Talia realized as she watched them that Alberich had helped to deliver the death-blow to the Brat.

Now there was only Elspeth.

After that, though there were occasional brief lapses, the child was able to maintain her good behavior with very little effort. Throughout the hot days of that summer, she rapidly became the pet of the Collegium, although she was never in any danger of being spoiled as everyone remembered only too well what the Brat had been like.

Rather than simply watching things, she began volunteering to help. At archery practice she brought water and arrows to replace those broken, at weapons practice, chalk and dry towels. She did her best to help groom Companions and clean tack, and not just Rolan and his gear, but turning a hand to help anyone who happened to be there. When it was Talia's turn at chores during "their" afternoons, Elspeth even insisted on doing her share; Mero the Cook soon began looking forward to having her in the kitchen and always had a special treat for his helpers on the days that she and Talia shared the work. Elspeth even had a certain fascination for the mending chores, never having known before how it was that torn clothing came to be repaired. She was not very good at it though, not having the patience for tedious work, and preferred to do something active, like sorting the clothing into piles of "still good enough," "wear only to work out," and "hopeless"—her own terms, quickly adopted by the rest. "Hopeless" was a particular favorite—the mender in question enacting mourning scenes over the offending garment. It got to be a regular game, one all of them enjoyed to the hilt.

By the time the leaves were turning, no one could imagine the Collegium without Elspeth running about with the trainees.

One chilly afternoon, with the last desiccated leaves blowing against Talia's window, there was a quiet knock on her door. When Talia opened it, Sherrill was standing there—in Whites.

Talia was speechless for a moment—then hugged her friend as hard as she could, exclaiming breathlessly, "You did it! You did it!"

Sherrill hugged back, one happy tear escaping from her eyes. "I guess I did," she said when Talia finally let her go. "You're the first to know, except for Elcarth."

"I am? Oh, Sherri—I don't know what to say—it's wonderful! I'm so glad for you! When are you leaving on your assignment?"

"Next week," she said, seeming to feel more than a little awkward suddenly, "and I had another reason for coming here—seeing as I'm sort of your mentor—well—there's something I have to tell you about before I leave."

"Go on," Talia replied, wondering why her friend was so ill-at-ease.

"Well—what do you think of—boys?"

"I never really thought about it, much," she replied.

"I mean, do you like them? You seem to—like Skif a lot."

"I'm not like Keren, if that's what you mean."

"No, it isn't." Sherrill squirmed in frustration. "You know—about babies and all that, right?"

"I should hope so, seeing as they'd planned on marrying me off before I came here!" Talia replied with some amusement. "And I think I've helped Keren with more foals than you ever have in just one year on foal-watch! I think they wait for me!"

"Well, do you know how *not* to have them? I mean, you must have noticed that you don't often see a pregnant Herald, and we're hardly a celibate bunch. . . ."

"Yes in answer to your second question," Talia said, thinking wryly of the nocturnal activities of her next-door neighbor Destria. "But no to your first!"

"We've got something the Healers make up for us," Sherrill said, obviously relieved that she wasn't going to have to explain the facts of life to her young friend. "It's a powder—you take some every day, except when you're having moon-days. It doesn't even taste bad, which is truly amazing considering the way most of their potions taste. You can also use it to adjust your cycles if you have to, if you know you're going to be in a situation where having your moon-days would be really awkward, for instance. You just stop taking it earlier, or keep on longer. I figured I'd better tell you about it, or it was possible no one would. I know you haven't needed it yet—but you might want it soon if the gleam I've been seeing in Skif's eyes means anything."

"You remembered to tell me this on the day you got your Whites?" Talia asked incredulously, ignoring the comment about Skif. "Oh, Sherri, whatever did I do to deserve a friend like you?"

The powder worked just as well as the little sponges Sherrill had shown her how to use in place of the rag-clouts for moon-days, and

Talia was more than grateful to Sherrill for telling her about it. Being able to adjust her cycles was wonderful in and of itself—which was just as well, since she never really got a chance to test the efficacy of the other application.

She and Skif were so often thrown together that Talia had lost any self-consciousness around him, and had certainly long since unconsciously relegated him to the category of "safe" males, especially after the help he'd been with the Hulda affair. It helped that they were much of an age and size and that the normally rowdy Skif muted his voice and actions around her, as if being aware how easily she could be startled or frightened by a male. They had started out being quite good friends—but now he was being attracted to her in another way, as his mealtime behavior had so ardently demonstrated. So what occurred next between them was hardly surprising.

After Talia had so nearly died in the icy water of the river, Alberich had assigned Sherrill to give her the same kind of swimming lessons a child of the Lake would have. Sherrill's last act before going out on her internship was to surprise Talia on the bridge and toss her into the same spot she'd been thrown before. The water was almost as cold, though the ice was scarcely more than a thin skin among the reeds. Sherri stood ready to haul her out if she had to, but Talia "passed" this impromptu exam with flying colors and chattering teeth.

Skif met her coming back to her room, laughing, shaking with cold, barefoot and dripping and wrapped in a horseblanket.

"Holy stars!" he exclaimed in shock. "What happened to you?"

"Sherri pushed me in the river—no, wait," she forestalled his rushing off to mete out the same treatment to the innocent Sherrill. "It was on Alberich's orders. She's been teaching me what she knows, and she wanted a foolproof way of testing whether I'd learned or not."

"Some test," Skif grumbled, then to Talia's surprise, picked her up and carried her to her room.

"They don't *ever* let up on you, do they?" he complained, helping her out of her sodden clothing and building up the tiny fire in her room. "Holy stars, you do *twice* the work of the rest of us, and you *never* get a break, and then they turn around and do things like this to you. . . ."

She turned unexpectedly and stumbled. He caught her, and she found herself staring into his brown eyes at a meager distance of an inch or two. He froze, then seized his opportunity and kissed her.

They broke apart in confusion a long moment later.

"Uh, Talia . . ." he mumbled.

"I like you, Skif," she said softly. "I like you a lot."

"You do?" he flushed. "I—you know I like you."

"And you know who my next-door neighbor is. Nobody'd notice if we—you know."

"You mean—" Skif could hardly believe his ears. Or his luck. "But you've got your good uniform on—you're going somewhere. Tonight maybe?"

"I've got a Council meeting, but after that . . ."

Alas for poor Skif—the Council meeting was long and boring, and Talia was a good deal more tired from Sherri's "trial by water" than she realized. She arrived at her room a little before him and sat down on her bed to rest. By the time he got there, much to Skif's chagrin, she was fast asleep.

He bit his lip in annoyance; then his expression softened. He covered her carefully with a blanket and gave her a chaste kiss on one cheek; she was so weary she didn't even stir.

"No matter, lady-o," he whispered. "We can try again another time."

"Bright Havens, little one!" Jadus exclaimed, seeing Talia's strained expression as she arrived for her nightly visit. "What ails you?"

"I—I'm not sure," she replied hesitantly. "But everyone's so *angry*— I thought I could keep it out, but it won't stay out—"

"You should have said something sooner," he scolded gently, using his own Gift to reinforce her shielding. "Elcarth could have helped you."

"Elcarth was busy, and everybody else was too angry to get near. Jadus, what's wrong with everyone? I thought Heralds didn't get angry—I've never felt anything like this before!"

"That's because you weren't in any shape to sense the mood of the Collegium last winter, dear heart."

"You're changing the subject," Talia said, a bit tartly. "And if this affects Selenay or Elspeth, I need to know what it's all about."

Jadus hesitated, then sighed and concluded that she was right. "It's not a pretty tale," he said. "There's a young Herald named Dirk who became infatuated with one of the Court beauties. That's not too uncommon, especially the first time a Herald is assigned to the Court or Collegium, but she apparently played on it, built it into something a great deal more serious on his part. And all the time she was simply toying with him—intended using him for the rather base end of getting at a friend of his. When she was found out, she said some very cruel things—deliberately came very close to destroying his fairly fragile ego. She totally shattered his self-esteem; she's got him convinced he's worth less than a mongrel dog. He's been sent back to his home for a while; hopefully in the company of his family and friends, he'll recover. I pray so; Dirk is a good lad, and a valuable Herald, and worth fifty of her. I knew his father at Bardic, and the lad did me the service of visiting me now and again to pay his respects. The anger you feel is largely due to the fact that we are legally and ethically unable to mete out to that—woman—the punishment she richly deserves. And child, we *do* get angry; we're only human—and it hurts to know we are helpless to avenge what has been done to one dear to us because *we* obey the spirit *and* the letter of the law."

Talia left Jadus deep in thought, wondering if *she'd* ever truly be worthy of that kind of caring.

Skif slipped Talia a note at breakfast. "My room, tonight?"

She smiled and nodded very slightly.

He arrived at his room, Talia and the proposed rendezvous temporarily forgotten. He was battered, bruised, and sore from his head to his heels, and all he was really thinking about was whether or not he could coax Drake or Edric into bringing him something from the kitchen so that he wouldn't have to drag his weary body to the commonroom.

He blinked in surprise to see food and hot tea waiting on his desk. He blinked again to see Talia sitting on his bed.

"Oh, Lord of Lights—Talia, I forgot!"

"I heard," she said simply. "But I thought you could use food and a friend—and we'll see if we can't get you in shape for other things with those two."

"He's a sadist, that Alberich," he moaned, lowering himself, wincing, into the chair, and reaching for the tea. " 'Time you had some responsibility,' he said. 'You're going to be my assistant,' he said. 'It'll give you less time for picking of pockets and evil habits.' He *didn't* say he'd be giving me extra lessons. He *didn't* say that he was going to make me the sparring partner for hulking brutes who've already *gotten* their Whites. He *didn't* tell me I was going to be teaching three giants who never saw anything more sophisticated than a club. Holy stars, Talia, you should *see* those three! They were farmers, or so they tell me. Farmers! Talia, if you asked directions from one of them, he'd probably pick up the plow, ox and all, to point the way!"

Talia murmured sympathetically, and massaged his shoulders.

"I hurt in places I didn't know I had," he complained, eating his dinner with what, for him, was unnatural slowness.

"I might be able to help with that," Talia smiled, continuing to massage his aches.

It was a short two steps to his bed; she got most of the clothing off him—and not so incidentally off herself. She had gotten hold of some kellwood-oil and warmed it to skin temperature, using it to help get the knots out of his bruised and battered muscles. Under her gentle ministrations he was even beginning to feel somewhat revived; then he made the mistake of closing his eyes.

Talia realized it was hopeless when she heard his gentle snores.

She sighed, eased herself out of his bed, tucked him in like a child, and returned to her own room.

This Midwinter, she stayed at the Collegium quite gladly, enjoying the unusual freedom to read until all hours of the night if she chose, and greatly enjoying Jadus' company. She discovered that this year Mero and Gaytha were remaining over the holiday, along with Keren and Ylsa, and the six of them often met in Jadus' room for long discussions over hot cider.

Keren and Ylsa took her out with them on long rides into the countryside outside the capital. They even managed to persuade Jadus to accompany them on more than one of these expeditions—the first time he'd been off Collegium grounds for years. The three of them had found a pond that had frozen with a black-ice surface as smooth as the finest mirror. While Ylsa and Jadus stayed by the fire they built on the shore, laughing at the other two and keeping a careful eye on the rabbit and roots they were roasting for a snow-picnic, Keren taught Talia how to skate. With runners made of polished steel fastened to her boots, Keren glided on the surface of the pond with the grace of a falcon in flight.

Talia fell down a lot—at least at first.

"You're just trying to get back at me," she accused. "I never got a sore rear from riding, so you're trying some other way to make it hard for me to sit down!"

Keren just chuckled, helped her up again, and resumed towing her around the pond.

Eventually she acquired the knack of balancing, then of moving. By the time they quit to return home, she was thoroughly enjoying herself, even if she looked, as she said, "more like a goose than a falcon!"

They repeated this trip nearly every other day, until by Midwinter itself Talia was proficient enough to be able to skate—shakily—backwards.

Once again they shared the revelry in the Servant's Hall, this time with the other four as additions to the group. It was altogether a most satisfactory Midwinter holiday.

When classes resumed, she added one in law and jurisprudence and another in languages and lost the free hour in the library. Often it seemed as if there simply weren't enough hours in the day to do everything, but somehow she managed.

Her bond with Rolan, if anything, continued to deepen; now it seemed as if he was always present at the back of her mind. She knew by now that *he* was the source of some of the wisdom that she'd had spring unbidden into her mind when the Queen needed it, and that it had been Rolan who had guided her when she'd needed to bail Skif out of Orthallen's ill graces. Rolan, after all, had the benefit of living in the mind of a man of great ability—the former King's Own, Talamir—for much of Talamir's life as a Herald, and made all of that wisdom available to his new Herald. Yet some of it, at least, was all Talia's own; the instinctive judgment that only the Monarch's Own Herald possessed.

Before she realized how much time had passed, the trees were budding again. There was a new crop of trainees, and Talia was amazed at how *young* these children looked. Sometimes she was just as surprised, when looking in a mirror, at how young *she* still looked—for she felt as if she must appear at least a hundred years old by now.

Spring did bring one respite; Keren had taught her all she knew. There would be no more equitation classes, as such. From time to time she would help Keren with the younger students who needed individual help, but it was not the steady, draining demand that the class had been.

Now that Keren was no longer Talia's teacher, their relationship ripened into an incredibly close friendship, closer even than the relationship Talia had had with her sister Vris. For all of the difference in their ages—Keren was slightly more than twice Talia's age—they discovered that the difference was negligible once they really began to talk with one another. The closeness they had begun over the Midwinter holiday began to deepen and strengthen. Talia found that Keren was the one person in the entire Collegium with whom she felt free to unburden herself—perhaps because Keren was strongly sympathetic to the weight of responsibility on the shoulders of the Queen's Own, having had that burden in her own family. Being able to say exactly what she pleased to *somebody* made life a great deal easier for Talia.

As for Keren—Talia was one of the few people she'd ever met, even in the Heraldic circle, who was willing to accept her, her relationship with Ylsa, and all that this implied, without judgment. Once Talia's loyalty was given, it was unswerving and unshakable. Most Heralds liked and admired Keren, but many were uneasy about getting too close to her, as if her preferences were some kind of stain that might rub off on them. Talia was one of the few who gave her heart freely and openly to one she considered to be her best friend. And with Ylsa so often away, life up until now had been rather lonely—a loneliness Talia did much to alleviate, simply by being there.

Talia learned something new about her friend, something that few guessed. The outward strength and capability of the riding instructor masked the internal fragility of a snowflake. Her emotional stability rested on a tripod of three bonds—the one with Teren, the one with Dantris, her Companion, and the one with Ylsa. It was partially because of that that the Circle had assigned the twins to teaching full-time at the Collegium when the advance of middle years made it time to think of taking them from field duty (although the primary reasons were that they were experts in their areas—Keren with equitation and Teren for his talents in dealing with children and true gift for teaching). There was very little chance that anything untoward would occur to either Dantris or her brother here. Ylsa had been given her own assignment as Special Messenger because of the unusual endurance of Felara, second only to Rolan's—though it was true that the duty of special messenger was not as hazardous as many of the others, which had again been a minor consideration. Still, Talia often thought with a vague dread that if anything ever happened to Ylsa, Keren might well follow.

The night was warm; it was too early for insects, the moon was full. It was an altogether idyllic setting. There was even a lovely soft bed of young ferns to spread their cloaks on. Talia had met Skif quite by accident when she was coming back from walking with Elspeth in Companion's Field. With unspoken accord they had retraced their steps, and found this ideal trysting place. . . .

"Comfortable?"

"Mm-hm. And the stars—"

"They're gorgeous. I could watch them forever."

"I thought," Talia teased, "that you had something else in mind!"

"Oh I did—"

But *he* had just spent his afternoon dodging Alberich, and *she* had been up since well before dawn.

Talia returned his hesitant, but gentle caresses. She was both excited and a little apprehensive about this, but from the way Skif was acting she evidently wasn't being *too* awkward. She began to relax for the first time since early that morning, and she could feel the tension in his shoulders begin to go out—

—and they fell asleep simultaneously.

They woke with dew soaking them and birds overhead, and the sun just beginning to rise.

"I hate to say this," Skif began with a sigh.

"I know. This isn't going to work, is it?"

"I guess not. It's either the gods, fate, or the imp of the perverse."

"Or all three. I guess we're stuck just being good friends. Well, you can't say we didn't try!"

To Skif's delight, their classmates seemed totally unaware of the fact that their trysts had been abortive. Talia was thought of as being very hard to get; Skif was amazed to discover that his reputation had been made as a consequence, and proceeded immediately to try to live up to it. Coincident with this, Alberich dropped him as assistant, and appointed Jeri, so he never again had the problem that had plagued his "romance" with Talia. Talia simply smiled and held her peace when teased about Skif, so their secret remained a secret.

The Death Bell tolled four times that year; Talia found herself in a new role—one that she hadn't expected.

She'd attended the funeral of the first of that year's victims. It was just turning autumn, the air still had the feel of summer during the day, although the nights were growing colder. She had gone to Companion's Field afterward and had mounted Rolan without saddling him. They had not ambled along as was their usual habit; it was rather as if something was drawing both of them to a particular corner of the Field.

Companion's Field was not, as the name implied, a simple, flat field. Rather, it was a rolling, partially wooded complex of several acres in size, containing the Stable for foul-weather shelter, the barn and granary holding the Companions' fodder, and the tack shed—in reality a substantial building with fireplaces at either end. The heart of the field was the Grove, the origin-place of the original Companions, and the location of the tower containing the Death Bell. There were several spring-fed creeks and pools and many secluded, shady copses, as well as more open areas.

Talia's "feelings" led her to one of those secluded corners, a tiny pool at the bottom of an equally tiny valley, all overhung with golden-leaved willows. There was a Herald there, his own Companion nuzzling anxiously at his shoulder, staring vacantly into the water of the pool.

Talia dismounted and sat next to him. "Would you like to talk about it?" she asked, after a long silence.

He tossed a scrap of bark into the pool. "I found him—Gerick, I mean."

"Bad?"

"I can't even begin to tell you. Whatever killed him can't have been human, not even close. And the worst of it was—"

"Go on."

"It was *my* circuit he was riding. If I hadn't broken my leg, it would have been me. Maybe."

"You don't think so?"

"There's been some odd things going on out there on the Western Border, especially on my circuit. I tried to warn him, but he just laughed and told me I'd been out there too long. Maybe, if it'd been me out there—I don't know."

Talia remained silent, knowing there was more he hadn't said.

"I can't sleep anymore," the Herald said at last, and indeed he looked haggard. "Every time I close my eyes, I see his face, the way he was when I found him. The blood—the—pain—Dammit to all the Twelve Hells!" He drove his fist into the ground beside him. "Why did it have to be Gerick? *Why?* I've never seen anybody so much in love with life—why did he have to die like *that?*"

"I wish I had an answer for you, but I don't," Talia replied. "I think we'll only know the *why* of things when we meet our own fates. . . ." Her voice trailed off as she searched for words to bring him some kind of comfort. "But surely, if he loved life as much as you say, Gerick must have made the most of every minute he had?"

"You know—you're right. I used to dig at him for it, sometimes he'd just laugh, and tell me that since he didn't know what was around the corner, he planned to make the most of whatever he had at the moment. I swear, it seemed sometimes as if he were trying to live three men's lives, all at once. Why, I remember a time when—"

He continued with a string of reminiscences, at times almost oblivious of Talia's presence except as an ear in which to pour his words. He only stopped when his throat grew dry, and he realized with a start that he'd been talking for at least a couple of hours.

"Lord of the Mountain—what have I been telling you?" he said, seeing for the first time that his companion was only an adolescent girl. "Look I'm sorry. What is your name?"

"Talia," she replied and smiled as his eyes widened a little in recognition. "There's nothing to apologize for, you know. All I've been doing is listening—but now you're remembering your friend as he lived instead of as he died. Isn't that a better memorial?"

"Yes," he said thoughtfully. "Yes." The strain was gone from his face, and she could no longer sense the kind of tearing, destructive unhappiness that had led her here. There was sorrow, yes—but not the kind that would obsess and possess him.

"I've got to go now, and you should get some sleep before you're ill." She swung up on Rolan's back as he raised eyes that mirrored his gratitude to meet hers.

"Thank you, Queen's Own," was all he said—but the tone of his voice said much more.

The second Herald to die that year fell victim to an avalanche, but the lover he'd left behind had to be convinced that he hadn't been taking foolish risks because they'd quarreled previously. That was an all-night session, and Talia appeared at her first class looking so dragged out that the now-Herald Nerissa, who was teaching it, ordered her back to bed and canceled all her morning work.

The third meant another soul-searching session with Selenay, guilt-wracked over having sent, this time, a young and inexperienced Herald into something she would never have been able to cope with—an explosive feud between two families of the lesser nobility of the East. It had devolved into open warfare between them, and while trying to reconcile the two parties, the Herald had gotten in the way of a stray arrow. Had she had more experience, she would not have so exposed herself.

Of course, Selenay had had no way of knowing that the feud had gotten that heated at the time she sent Beryl—but with the clear vision imparted by hindsight, she felt that she should have guessed.

But for the fourth, just after Midwinter holiday, it was Talia herself that was in dire need of comfort—for the Herald who died was Jadus.

She'd awakened one morning before dawn knowing immediately that something was wrong—that it involved Jadus, and had only taken enough time to pull her cloak on over her bedgown before running to his room. She all but ran into a Healer leaving it, and his eyes told her the truth.

Jadus' passing had been quite peaceful, he told her; Jadus had had no inkling of it, simply hadn't awakened. His Companion was also gone—probably simultaneously.

None of this was any comfort at all.

She retreated to her room and sat on the edge of her bed, staring at the chair he'd spent so many nights occupying, guarding her in her illness. She thought of all the things that she wished now she'd told him—how much he had meant to her, how much she'd learned from him. It was too late for any of that now—and too late to thank him.

"Lovey—I heard—" Keren stood beside her; Talia hadn't even noticed the door opening. As they stared at one another, the Bell began to toll.

As if the bell-tone had released something, Talia began to cry soundlessly. Keren held her on the edge of the bed, and they wept together for their old friend and for all that he'd meant to both of them.

Keren was not the only one to think of Talia when the news spread, for when they looked up at a small sound, Dean Elcarth had taken the chair across from Talia's bed.

"I have to tell you two things, my dear," he said with a little difficulty. "Jadus was a long-time friend of mine; he was my counselor on my internship in fact. He left all of his affairs in my hands. He knew he hadn't much longer to live, and he told me when—he wanted you to have—" Mutely he held out the harp case that held My Lady.

Talia took it in trembling hands and stared at it, unable to speak around the lump of tears in her throat.

"The other thing is this; he was happier these past two years than at any time since he lost his leg. When it came to strict academic subjects, he wasn't a very good teacher; his heart just wasn't in it. The classes we had him teach were just to keep him busy, and he knew it. Until you came, he'd been retreating more and more into the past, living in a time when he'd been useful. You made him feel useful again. And when you were sick—I don't think you realize how much your needing him, both to guard your safety and to chase the nightmares away with his music, made him *alive* again. And being able to counsel and guide you—it meant the world to him."

"He—knew? He knew how much I needed him?"

"Of course he knew; he had the thought-sensing Gift. No matter how well you think you shield, youngling, when you care for someone the way you two cared for each other, things are bound to get through—will you, nill you. And when you started coming to him for advice or for help, and when *he* was the one you came to over the Hulda affair—I don't think he was ever prouder of anything he'd done. He often told me he no longer missed not having a family because now he had a family in you and in the friends you'd brought to him. He was a very lonely man until you came to his door, little one. He died a happy and contented man."

Elcarth dropped his head and rubbed briefly at his eyes, unable to say more.

"I have to go," he said finally, and stood up. Talia caught his hand.

"Thank you—" she whispered.

He squeezed her hand in acknowledgment and left.

It was several months before she could bring herself to touch My Lady—but once she had (though she missed Jadus dreadfully every time she played), she never once neglected to practice.

And when she did, she tried to remember him as he'd been that night, alert and alive, in the chair next to her bed with his harp on his lap, and a loaded crossbow hidden on the floor beside him, with his old cane exchanged for one that held concealed the blade of a sword.

And the incredulous smile of joy that had appeared when she had begged him to play for her.

Or the way he'd looked when he told her and Skif that they could leave the problem of Hulda in his hands—strong again; confident again—*needed*.

And the laughter and joy they'd shared that Midwinter day when Keren had taught her to skate.

Sometimes, it even helped a little. But only sometimes.

CHAPTER 11

“TRIPE! I’M LATE!” Talia swore to herself, finally noticing the time by the sundial in the garden beneath her window. She gathered up the scattered notes around her desk, coerced them into a more-or-less neat pile, and flew out the door of her room.

She’d managed to learn a few shortcuts in the three years she’d been at the Collegium; that and longer legs managed to get her to her classroom scant seconds ahead of Herald Ylsa and the Dean. She ran her fingers through her unruly curls, hoping to smooth them down enough that her race through the halls wouldn’t be blazoned in her appearance.

Three years had made quite a difference in the way she looked. The awkward adolescent whose arms and legs had always seemed a bit too long for her body was gone. Though she’d never be tall, growth and Alberich’s training had honed her into a slender, supple, and athletic young woman. The face she showed to the world was self-confident, but that outward appearance covered a certain shyness and uncertainty that still remained. The muddy color of her hair had finally turned to a rich red-brown. She wore it just touching her shoulders; much to her dismay, since she secretly yearned for straight, midnight-black hair like Sherrill’s, it had remained stubbornly curly. Her eyes now matched her hair, and while she would never be called beautiful, she charmed everyone when she smiled—which she did now more often than not. There was no one in the Collegium or among the full Heralds of the Circle who were acquainted with her who did not care deeply for her.

The older trainees had taken it upon themselves to make it pointedly clear to the Blues that anyone harassing her would find life very uncomfortable indeed. Her teachers tried to keep her challenged, but at the same time went out of their way to coordinate their efforts so as to make it possible for her to keep up with all her commitments. The younger students—for she always had a moment to spare to soothe an anger, encourage the discouraged, or lend an ear to the homesick— frankly adored her. Her own contemporaries had formed a kind of honor guard for her headed by Griffon, always at hand to take over a chore or duty when the inevitable conflicts arose.

She returned all these attentions with an artless gratitude and affection that made it seem a privilege to have helped her.

And yet she still felt a kind of isolation from everyone but her few close friends—Skif, Keren, Sherri, and Jeri. It was almost as if she was *of* the Collegium and Circle, yet not truly at one with them.

A great part of that feeling had to do with the fact that it seemed to her as if she were continually receiving the affection and attention she so ardently craved, and yet was doing little or nothing to earn it. Exposing Hulda had been mostly Skif's work; civilizing Elspeth had been largely a matter of forcing her to take the consequences of her actions and returning her to her previous behavior patterns. It hardly seemed to her that being Selenay's sounding board required much effort on *her* part. She felt—when she had time to think about it—as if she would never truly belong until she earned her place, entirely by her own efforts, and by doing something for the benefit of the Circle that no one else could do.

She little realized that by helping to ease the emotional turmoils of others she was already accomplishing just that. As far as she was concerned, that was the kind of thing anyone would and could do under the same circumstances. Only Elcarth, Herald Kyril (who made a study of Heraldic Gifts), and Ylsa realized how rare her abilities and her Gift were—and how badly they would miss her, were she not there.

But since she still kept most of her inmost doubts to herself, none of them realized she felt this way. They saw only the cheerful exterior that she presented to the world at large.

Only Keren and Rolan ever witnessed the bouts of self-doubt and temper; the fits of self-pity and depression. And neither of those two (like Jadus before them) was likely to betray her trust, since it was given so rarely. For if she had a fault, it was this; even after three years, it was still hard for her to truly trust in others.

Today marked a new phase of her studies, and a strange and somewhat frightening one. Now she was to learn the full use of that ability to sense the distresses of others that had appeared so abruptly under stress. Today was the beginning of her lessons in "Herald's magic."

There were three others in the class besides herself; the twins Drake and Edric from her own year-group (Talia was still unable to tell them apart), and a silent, flame-haired lad from the year-group following Talia's. Neave's abilities had caused mild havoc among the trainees for a brief period until he had been identified as the source of disturbance. He was a "projector"—and he'd inadvertently projected his own nightmares into the dreams of those around him that were at all receptive and unshielded. Since his life up until he'd been Chosen had been rough enough to make even the ex-street-urchin Skif blanch, his nightmares had been grown in fertile ground and given his fellow students several sleepless and terror-filled nights.

As the Dean and Herald entered the room, Talia found she had tensed up all over. These were new and strange waters she was about to dive into; she'd more or less come to terms with the simpler manifestations of her Gift, but there remained her old Hold training to deal with. To Holderfolk, such abilities were "unnatural" at best, and demon-born at worst.

Talia was just grateful that the class was being taught by two so familiar to her. If it had been a stranger facing her, she would have been ready to have a litter of kittens with nerves! She tried to relax—this was nothing to fear; *every* Herald had to learn the working of his or her Gift—and Elcarth caught her eye, and gave her a brief, encouraging smile.

Dean Elcarth surveyed the four of them, noting their understandable nervousness. Only Drake and Edric appeared to be more excited than ill-at-ease—but then, *their* Gift had been a part of them since birth. He smiled reassuringly at Neave and Talia, lifted an eyebrow at the twins, and began his usual speech.

"We put the four of you in a class together because you all demonstrate Gifts in the same 'family' of talents," the Dean began, as his bright, round eyes met each of theirs in turn. "Your Gifts of what we call 'magic' are all in the areas of communication. I want you all to know that although we refer to these things in the world outside these walls as 'magic,' there is nothing *whatsoever* unnatural about them. You have Talents, even as a Bard, an artist, or an artisan. You should never be afraid of what you have been gifted with—rather you should learn how to use these gifts to the benefit of yourselves and others.

"Talia and Neave already know Herald Ylsa; she was instrumental in discovering that both of you had prematurely awakened Gifts, since she is one of the best at the using and detecting 'communications' type abilities that we have among the Circle. For this reason, she will be in charge of this class, and I am merely here to assist her. Don't be afraid to ask her questions; despite her formidable reputation, she doesn't bite—"

"Not hard, anyway," Ylsa interrupted with a smile.

"—and if she doesn't know the answers to your questions, she certainly knows exactly where to look and who to ask! I'll be helping her, since next to Herald Kyril, I'm probably the second choice for an expert at the Collegium. Ylsa, the floor is yours."

"Well," she said, folding her arms and leaning back against the edge of the desk. "Where shall I start? Have any of you questions about all this?"

"Herald," Neave's expression was troubled. "All this—magic—it isn't evil, is it?"

"Is a crossbow evil?" she countered.

"Depends on who's holding it, Herald," one of the twins grinned and answered, "and who it's pointed at."

"Exactly. Your Gifts can be used for evil purposes. They're just like any weapon—and make no mistake about it, they can be weapons if you're so minded. But you wouldn't be sitting here now if you were inclined toward evil. Trust the judgment of your Companion in that, Neave, if you don't trust your own. They don't Choose where evil is—and on the very rare occasion where someone has been corrupted past redemption—and the last was two hundred years ago—they will repudiate their Chosen. So since you and Kyldathar still seem on very good terms, I think you can set your mind at rest about being evil."

"Herald, the Companions seem to be able to make our Gift stronger, somehow," said the other twin. "Edric and I could 'talk' a little to each other before, but since we were Chosen it's been *much* clearer and easier."

"Good!" Ylsa nodded. "I wondered if any of you had made that connection. Yes, the Companions seem to strengthen our Gifts and develop the ones that are latent. You'll probably find that your Gift gains enormously in power when you're in physical contact with your Companion and when you're under the influence of very strong emotions. No one is sure whether there's a connection there, between our bonds with our Companions and very strong emotions. Our Gifts are unfortunately not the kinds of things that yield easily to measurement."

"Herald Ylsa, we've all seen or heard about the 'Truth Spell'—are we going to learn *spells*?" Talia asked. "My folk say all spells are demon-work."

"Yes, you will be learning spells of a sort, though probably not what the Holderfolk had in mind. What *we* call a spell for the most part is an exercise that forces you to concentrate. When you concentrate, you boost your capability; it's as simple as that. The word 'spell' is just a handy term; in point of fact, most of them are rather like meditation chants or prayers of a sort."

"Then, does everybody have this kind of—uh—gift?" Neave asked.

"Again, yes. The catch is that most people don't have enough of the ability for it to be really useful to them. It's just like Talia sings very well but will never be a Bard, and I throw a decent pot but could never be a really *good* potter. As far as that goes, there are some of us whose Gifts are hardly stronger than those of nonHeralds—and even among Heralds a *really* powerful Gift is rare, though we all have enough to enable us to bond with our Companions and use the Truth Spell. From what we can tell, it seems to be that the very strongest gifts tend to be associated with those who become Healers rather than Heralds, al-though the Gifts of communication are very similar to the Healing Gifts. That is why in an emergency you may be called on to assist Healers. Sometimes the very strongest of our variety of Gifts hide themselves; I've known a case or two when persistent *inability* has actu-ally hidden very strong *ability*. Mostly though, it seems that contact with your Companion triggers your Gift and continued development of the bond also develops the Gift to the point where you have direct conscious control of it. Once you can control it, you can be trained in the use of it, and you can learn its limits. Oh, I think I should mention something about the Truth Spell; *that* really is a spell, in the sense of the Bardic tales. It requires a Gift to use, apparently the one that makes the Companion-Herald bond possible. If you have a strong Gift, you'll be able to use it to actually force someone to speak only the truth; if your Gift is weak, you'll only be able to detect whether or not a person is lying. The Truth Spell will be the last thing we'll teach you. Now, if you're all ready, I think we're about at the point where we should stop talking and start doing."

For once, learning did not come easily to Talia. To her extreme frus-tration, mastering the use of her Gift proved to be far more elusive than she had dreamed. The others quickly outstripped her in progress as she strove to get some kind of control on her abilities. Directing her Gift seemed to be a greatly different thing than simply blocking it or letting it direct her actions passively, as she had been doing. It seemed to require a kind of combination of relaxation and concentration that she despaired of ever mastering. Several weeks passed without her attaining much more control than she had had before the class started.

"You know," Ylsa said one day, with a look as if she were slowly realizing something that should have been obvious, "I think we're going after the wrong Gift. I'm not at all sure now that your prime Gift is thought-sensing."

"Well, what could it be?" Talia cried in frustration.

"Everything you've told me and what I've seen for myself points not to the mind, but the heart. Look, your own mind-call to Rolan was fear; the times with Selenay and other Heralds—sorrow, pain, loss. Even what you picked up from me was an emotion—love. Or maybe lust," she winked at Talia, who coughed politely and blushed, "since I'm not sure exactly what you were getting from me that time, and it had been a *long* trip. Seriously, though—you *can* hear thoughts if you're properly prepared or you're in deep trance, but what you receive first and strongest is *emotion*. When there's no emotion involved, and there hasn't been in these training sessions, it's that much harder for you to receive meaning. I didn't think about that because the Gift for emotion-sensing—we call it 'empathy'—is almost *never* seen alone, or in a Chosen. The only times I can ever remember seeing it is in company with the Gift of true Healing, and the Companions never Choose someone with the Healing Gifts, probably because they're needed too much as Healers. What have I been telling you to do all this time?"

"Relax and clear my mind of everything," Talia said, beginning to grasp what Ylsa was saying, "and especially to clear my mind of emotions, *even the ones coming in from outside*."

"So naturally you fail. Our Gifts are tricky things, you know; they depend very strongly on how much we believe in our own abilities. When you failed, you disbelieved a little and made it that much harder the next time. It's time we abandoned this tack and tried something different."

"Like what?"

"You'll see—just keep your shields down. If all this isn't moonshine, I don't want you expecting anything in particular, and maybe having your imagination supply it for you." Ylsa turned to Neave and whispered in his ear. He nodded and left the room, while Talia waited with half-perplexed anticipation for something to happen.

Suddenly she was inundated by terror, and hard upon the terror came a picture—and then it was something more than a picture. It was a vision of a filthy, smoke-filled taproom—a vision that she was a part of, for the room around her and her fellows had vanished. All around her loomed the slack bodies of drunken, half-crazed people; mostly men, but with a few slatternly women sprawled among them. They were very much bigger than she; she seemed to have shrunk down to the size of a ten-year-old. She was trying to slip through them with as little stir as possible, serving their cheap wine, when one of them woke from his daze and seized her arm in a grip that hurt. "Come here, little boy, pretty boy," he crooned, ignoring her struggles to free herself. "I only want to give you something. . . ."

She wanted to scream, knowing very well what it was he wanted, but found her throat so choked with fear that she could barely squeak. It was like a nightmare from which there could be no awakening. She began losing herself completely in panic when something broke the spell she was in.

"Talia!" Ylsa was shaking her, slapping her face lightly. "Talia, block it out!"

"Goddess. . . ." Talia slumped in her seat and held her head in both hands. "What happened?"

"I told Neave to project the most emotional image he could think of at you," Ylsa said, a bit grimly. "We succeeded better than I had guessed we would. You not only received it, you were trapped by it. Well, that answers *that* question—your Gift is empathy, beyond all doubt. And now that we know for certain what your Gift is, we can do more about training you properly."

"Lady of Light," Talia said, burying her face in her hands. "Poor, poor Neave! If you'd seen what I saw . . . how can such filth be allowed to exist?"

"It's not—not here," Neave himself came through the door, looking quite ordinary; far calmer, far more natural than Talia would have believed possible for someone whose mind held such memories. "I'm from outKingdom, remember? Where I come from, an orphaned child of the poor is fair game for whatever anyone wants to do with him. So long as the priests and the Peacekeepers aren't *officially* aware of what's going on, and there's no one to speak for the child, just about anything is tolerated. Are you all right? I could tell something was wrong, but not what. I stopped sending, but you'd already broken off contact. Talia, you had an awfully strong hold on me; I found myself reliving that whole filthy episode—"

"Neave—I'm so sorry—" She strove to express her horror at what he'd gone through, and failed utterly.

He touched her arm hesitantly, his eyes understanding. "Talia, it was long ago and far away. Thanks to people like Ylsa and the Dean, it doesn't even hurt that much anymore. I know now it wasn't anything *I* did that caused it." He licked his lips, his calm shell cracking just a little. "Time does heal things, you know, time and love and help. I just wish that I could somehow make sure that nothing like that ever happens to another child."

"Someday, we hope, that's exactly what the Heralds will accomplish," the Dean said gravely. "Someday—when there isn't a Kingdom on this world that doesn't welcome us. But for now—well, Neave, we save the ones we can, and try not to think too hard about the others, the ones we couldn't save. We can't be everywhere. . . ."

But Elcarth's eyes told them how little it helped, at times, to know that, and how hard it was to forget the ones still trapped in their little hells.

Eventually, Ylsa declared the class to be officially over, saying that there was nothing else she could actually teach them. Now their proficiency depended on their own limits and how well they honed their Gifts with practice.

The end of the class meant that it was time to learn the only "real" magic that they were ever likely to see. It was time to learn the Truth Spell.

"Legend says this was discovered by a contemporary of Herald Vanyel, just before the incursions of the Dark Servants," she told them. "Since Vanyel himself was the last of what were called the 'Heraldic Mages,' this is the last real bit of magic ever created in Valdemar and is about all the 'real magic' we have left except for a few things the priests and Healers use. Most of the rest was lost to the Dark Servants, abandoned because of negative associations, or just plain forgotten. In some ways, it's too bad—it would be nice to still be able to build a fortress like the Palace-Collegium complex and to pave roads the way the old ones did. At any rate, this spell starts with a cantrip; a little rhyme, just like some of the others you've learned—"

With the rhyme came an image they were to hold in their minds, one that made very little sense to Talia, the image of a wisp of fog with blue eyes. While holding this image, they were to recite the rhyme mentally nine times; no more, no less. On the ninth repetition they were to imagine the fog enveloping the person they were casting the spell on.

Ylsa demonstrated on Dean Elcarth; closing her own eyes briefly then staring fixedly at him for a few moments. Within a few heartbeats, Elcarth was surrounded by a faint but readily visible glowing blue nimbus of light.

"I've just put the first stage on him," Ylsa told them. "I'm not forcing the truth out of him, but just registering whether or not he's telling it. Lie for me, Elcarth."

"I'm passionately in love with you, Ylsa."

The glow vanished, while Ylsa and her students laughed.

"Now tell me the truth."

"I consider you to be one of the most valuable assets of the Circle, but I'm rather glad you're not *my* lifemate. You're altogether too difficult a woman and you have a nasty temper."

The glow reappeared, and Ylsa sighed dramatically. "Ah, Elcarth, and here all this time I'd been hoping you secretly cared."

"Elcarth, sir, can *you* see what we're seeing?" Neave asked curiously.

"Not so much as a glimmer," he replied. "But anyone except the person bespelled sees the glow, whether or not they've got a Gift. Why don't you invoke the second stage, Ylsa?"

"If you're ready for it." Again she stared at him; Talia could see no perceptible change in the glow surrounding him.

"How old are you, Elcarth? Try to tell me 'twenty.'"

His face twisted with strain and beads of sweat appeared on his forehead. "T-t-t," he stuttered. "T-fifty-seven." He sighed heavily. "I'd forgotten what it felt like to try and fight Truth Spell, Ylsa. Take it off, would you, before I get tricked into revealing something I shouldn't?"

"Now why would I do something like that to you?" she teased, then closed her eyes briefly again, and the glow was gone. "You banish the spell easily enough—just picture the cloud lifting away from the person, close its eyes, and dissipate."

"You all have Gifts strong enough to bring both stages of the spell to bear," she said a moment later, "so why don't you start practicing? Neave and Talia, with me—the twins with Elcarth."

The feeling of having the second stage of the Truth Spell cast on her was decidedly eerie, Talia found. No matter what she had *intended* to say, she found her tongue would not obey her; only the exact truth came out. In cases where she didn't know the answer to a question, she was even forced to say so rather than temporize.

At last Ylsa declared them all proficient enough to close the class out.

"You know the 'spells'—though if we find out you've been using the Truth Spell as a prank, you'll find yourself in *very* hot water, so don't even consider it! Practice it if you wish, but do so only under the supervision of a full Herald. You know where your strengths and weaknesses lie," she continued. "Just like sparring practice will make you a better fighter, practicing with your Gifts will develop them to their full extent. If you run into any problems that are related to your Gifts, there are three of us who are probably the experts; you can come to any of us, day or night if it's an emergency. Myself, when I'm at the Collegium, the Dean, or Herald Kyril, the Seneschal's Herald. There are books in the Library as well that may help; I recommend you go up there and follow your instincts. Certainly you'll learn more about the abstract theory of our Gifts from them than you will from me, if that's what you want. I never was one for theory. I leave that up to Kyril! *He* enjoys trying to ferret out the 'whys' and 'hows' of our Gifts. I'm content with just knowing the usages, and never mind how it works."

Theirs was the first of the three groups being taught to finish formal training. The other two were much smaller, the 'communication' Gifts being by far and away the most common, and contained, respectively, Griffon and a younger girl, Christa; and Davan with one of Christa's year-mates, a boy called Wulf. Talia was extremely curious about these other Gifts and asked Ylsa about them as the last class broke up.

"The other two general groups have to do with moving things with thought alone, and seeing at a distance," Ylsa said. "We tend to lump them under the names of 'Fetching' and 'Sight.' Oddly enough, the two Heralds best at both those skills happen to work together as a team; Dirk and Kris. Well, maybe it's not so odd. Gifts that are needed tend to appear just before they're needed."

The second name woke a vague feeling of recollection; after a moment of thought, Talia remembered that she'd met Kris before, her first night at the Collegium. "Kris is the one that's too good-looking to be true, isn't he?" she asked Ylsa with a half-smile.

"That's the one. The fact that Dirk and Kris are partners is one reason why we hold these classes—particularly the latter two—all at the same time and for more than one year-group; it makes more sense to wait for a time of several weeks when Dirk and Kris don't have to be out somewhere," Ylsa replied. "Why are you asking?"

"Insatiable curiosity," Talia confessed. "I—kind of wonder how their Gifts are related to my own."

"Seeing's probably the closest; emotions are powerful attractants for the mind's eye. In fact, you have more than a touch of that particular Gift yourself, as you've noticed. I've told you that no one ever has *just* one Gift with no hint of the others, haven't I? You've got enough thought-sensing and Sight to possibly be useful in an emergency—

maybe just a hint of Healing as well. Anyway, the difference between their Gifts and yours is that you will generally have to See things through the eyes of someone present unless there's a *lot* of emotional residuum to hold you, and then it will be very vague. They can See things as if they were observing them directly, even if there's nobody there. There isn't much to watch in that class, though; just the three of them sitting around in trance-states. Quite boring if you're not linked in with them. Dirk's class is something else altogether—*that's* something to see! I know he won't mind; want to peek in on them?"

"Could I?" Talia didn't even try to conceal her eagerness.

"I don't see any reason why not. Queen's Own should probably see some of the other Gifts in action—especially since it seems your year-mate Griffon has one of the rarer and potentially more dangerous of the 'Fetching' family."

"He does? What does he do?" Talia found it difficult to envision the good-natured Griffon as dangerous.

"He's a Firestarter."

Because of Griffon's Gift, Dirk was holding his classes outside, away from any building, and near the well—just in case. Talia could see he had a bucket of water on the cobblestones beside him. He and his two pupils were sitting cross-legged on the bare paving, all three seeming to be too engrossed in what they were doing to notice any discomfort from the stone. He nodded agreeably to Ylsa and Talia as they approached, indicating with an eyebrow a safe place to stand and watch, and then turned his attention immediately back to his two pupils.

Talia discovered to her surprise that she recognized Herald Dirk as the young Herald she'd encountered just outside the capital. She had been far too overcome with bashfulness and the fear that she'd been wrong-doing to take more than a cursory look at him then; she took the opportunity afforded by his deep involvement with his pupils to do so now.

Her initial impression of homeliness was totally confirmed. His face looked like a clay model that had been constructed by someone with little or no talent at all. His nose was much too long for his face; his ears looked as if they'd just been stuck on by guess and then left there. His jaw was square and didn't match his rather high cheekbones; his teeth looked like they'd be more at home in his Companion's mouth than in his. His forehead didn't match any of the rest of his face; it was much too broad, and his overly generous mouth was lop-sided. His straw-colored hair looked more like the thatched roof of a cottage—

provided that the thatcher hadn't had the least notion of what he'd been about. The only thing that redeemed him from being repulsive was the good-natured smile that always hovered around the corners of his mouth, a smile that demanded that the onlooker smile in response.

That, and his eyes—he had the most beautiful eyes Talia had ever seen; brimming with kindness and compassion. The only eyes she could compare them to were Rolan's—and they were the same living sapphire blue as a Companion's.

If she hadn't been so fascinated by what was transpiring, she might have paused to wonder at the strength of response she felt to the implied kindness of those eyes.

As it was, though, Griffon was in the process of demonstrating his gift, and that drove any other thought from her head.

He seemed to be working his way up through progressively less combustible materials; it was evident from some of the residue of this exercise that he'd already attained the control required to ignite normally volatile substances at will. In front of him were the remains of burned paper, shredded cloth, the tarry end of a bit of rope, and a charred piece of kindling-wood. Now Dirk placed in front of him an odd black rock.

"This stuff *will* burn if you get it hot enough, I promise you," he was saying to Griffon. "Smiths use it sometimes to get a really hot fire; they prefer it over charcoal. Give it a try."

Griffon stared at the bit of black stone, his face intent. After a tense moment, he sighed explosively.

"It's no use—" he began.

"You're trying too hard again," Dirk admonished. "Relax. It's no different than what you did with the wood; the stuff's just a bit more stubborn. Give it longer."

Once again Griffon stared at the lump. Then something extraordinary happened. His eyes suddenly unfocused, and Talia's stomach flipped over; she became disoriented for a moment—the experience was something rather as if she'd been part of the mating of two dissimilar objects into a new whole.

The black lump ignited with a preternatural and explosive fury.

"*Whoa!*" Dirk shouted, dousing the fire with the handy bucket of water. It had burned with such heat that the stone beneath it sizzled and actually cracked when the water hit it. There was a smell of scorched rock and steam rising in a cloud from the place it had been.

Griffon's eyes refocused, and he stared at the blackened area, dumbfounded. "Did *I* do that?"

"You certainly did. Congratulations," Dirk said cheerfully. "Now you see why we have this class outside. More importantly, can you do it again, and with a little more control this time?"

"I—think so—" Griffon's eyes once again took on the abstracted appearance they'd had before—and the soaked remains of the black rock sizzled, then began merrily burning away, in sublime indifference to the puddle around them.

"Now damp it," Dirk commanded.

The flames died completely. In seconds the rock was cool enough for Dirk to pick up.

"Well done, youngling!" Dirk applauded. "You've got the trick of it now! With practice you'll be able to call fire right out of the air if you want—but don't try yet. That's enough for today. Any more, and you'll have a headache."

The headaches were something Ylsa had warned Talia's class about, the direct result of overextending a Gift. Sometimes this was unavoidable, but for the most part it was better not to court them. Drake had gotten one one day, showing off; his example had reinforced that prohibition. Ylsa had given them each a packet of herbs to make into a tea that deadened the worst of the pain should they miscalculate and develop one anyway, and had told them that Mero kept a further supply on hand in the kitchen when they ran out.

"Now, Christa—your turn." Dirk moved his attention to the lanky, coltish girl to his left. "There's a message tube, the mate to this one—" he laid a Herald's message container of the kind that Special Messengers usually carried on their belts in front of her, "—on the top of the first bookcase in the Library. It's lying along the top of *Spun of Shadow*. I know this is bigger than anything you've tried before, but the distance is a bit less than you've reached in the past. Think you can visualize it and bring it here?"

She nodded without speaking, and took the message tube in her hands. There was a growing feeling of tension once again; it was plainly perceptible to Talia. She felt as if she were in the middle of two people pulling on her mind—then came a kind of popping noise; now not one, but two message tubes lay in Christa's hands.

Dirk took the new one from her and opened it. He displayed the contents to her with a grin—a small slip of parchment with the words "Exercise one, and well begun" on it. Christa's grin of accomplishment echoed Dirk's.

"Not good poetry, but the sentiment's right. Well, you managed that one. Now let's see if you can get a little farther. . . ."

Ylsa nudged Talia, who nodded reluctantly, and both moved quietly away.

"Gifts like Griffon's have been known to wreak absolute havoc if the owner fails to learn how to control them," Ylsa said gravely once they were out of earshot. "There have been instances in the past when the trainee's teacher, unprepared perhaps for the kind of explosion we saw today, reacted with fear—fear that the pupil in turn reacted to. Sometimes that causes the pupil to block his Gift entirely, making it impossible for him to learn full control; and then, at some later date, during a moment of stress or crisis, it flares up again with a fury that has to be seen to be believed. We've been very fortunate in that this fury has always been turned against the enemies of the Kingdom in the past."

"Lavan Firestorm—" Talia said in comprehension. "I remember now; he almost single-handedly drove back the Dark Servants at the Battle of White Foal Pass. But at Burning Pines his Companion was killed, and the last Firestorm he called up consumed him as well as the enemy."

"There's nothing but bare rock at Burning Pines to this day. Those who were there were just lucky he retained enough hold on his sanity to warn them before he called down the Fires. And there's no guarantee that the Firestorm *couldn't* be turned against friends as well as enemies—rage can often be blind. That's why Dirk makes such a good teacher; he never shows the slightest sign of fear to his pupils. We're lucky to have him in the Circle," Ylsa replied. "At any rate, you've got weapons drill to go to, and I have to report that I'm free for reassignment. I'll see you at dinner, kitten."

Talia continued to practice every night, choosing times when the sometimes volatile emotions of the students of the Collegium were damped by the weariness of day's end. For several weeks she simply observed what she was drawn to—though a time or two she quickly chose some *other* subject to observe after her initial contact proved highly intimate and rather embarrassing. When she became more sure of herself, though, she was tempted by encountering the fear of one of the youngest student's nightmares to try intervening.

To her great delight, she was successful in turning the fear away. Without that stimulus, the dream quickly changed to something more innocuous.

Her success prompted her to try intervention in the emotions of others several times more—though always choosing only to try to redirect the more negative emotions of anger, fear—or once, in the case of a quarrel and a gross misunderstanding on the part of two of the court servants, hatred. Her successes, though not always complete, were enough to encourage her in the belief that such interventions were "right."

There was a side effect to the complete awakening and training of her Gift, and it had to do with Rolan. He was, after all, a stallion—and *the* premier stallion of the Companion herd. And Companions, like their human partners, were always "in season." Rolan's company was much sought after of a night.

And now that Talia's Gift was at full strength, it was impossible to shield him out of her mind.

The enforced sharing of Rolan's amorous encounters vastly increased her education in certain areas—even if it wasn't something she'd have chosen of her own accord.

It was both curiosity and her growing sensitivity that led her to the House of Healing and the Healer's Collegium. Most of the patients there were Heralds, badly injured in the field. Once their conditions had been stabilized they were always sent here, where the combined efforts and knowledge of the Kingdom's best in the Healer's craft could be brought to their aid. There was not the crying need for her in the House of Healing that there had been at other times and places—but the distress was there all the same, and it drew her as a moth is drawn to flame. She was at a loss as to how to gain entrance there until impulse caused her to seek out the one teacher she knew among the Healers— the one who had treated her in her illness; Devan.

Her choice couldn't have been better. Devan had been briefed by Ylsa on the nature of Talia's Gift, and as an empath himself, he thoroughly understood the irresistible drawing power that the place had for her. He welcomed her presence on his rounds of his patients, guessing that she might well be able to accomplish something to aid in their recoveries.

It wasn't easy, but as she had told Selenay, when something needed to be done, she made the time for it. She began getting up an hour or so earlier, breakfasting in the kitchen, and making Devan's early-morning rounds with him, then returning during the time in the afternoon that Elspeth spent riding with her mother.

Talia learned a great deal, and not just about the Healing Gifts. With so many Healers and Healers-in-training available, it was not necessary for her to participate in Devan's treatments, but her observations gave her a profound respect for his abilities. His specialty—all Healers had one form of Healing that they studied more intensively than the others—was the kind of hurts caused by wounding, and what he referred to as "trauma"; injuries acquired suddenly and violently, and often accompanied by shock.

Talia had never quite realized down deep until she began visiting the House of Healing just how hazardous the life of a Herald could be. Until now, she'd only been aware of the deaths; accompanying Devan she saw what *usually* happened to Heralds who ran afoul of ill luck on duty.

"It's the Border sectors that are usually the worst, you know," Devan told her when she remarked that no less than three of his patients seemed to be from Sectors in and around her old home. "Take your home Sector for instance; the normal tour of duty for a Herald is a year and a half. Guess how long it is for the ones that ride the Holderkin Sector?"

"A year?" Talia hazarded.

"Nine or ten months. They're fine until the winter raids coming over from Karse. Sooner or later they catch more than an arrow or an axe, and then it's back here to recover. That's one of the worst, though some of the Sectors up on the North Border are just as bad, what with the barbarians coming down every time the food supply runs short. That's why we have Alberich teaching you combat and strategy, youngling. Get assigned to a Sector like the Holderkin one, and you're often as much soldier as Herald. The Herald in charge may well be the only trained fighter around until an Army detachment arrives."

Later, she asked him why it was that there wasn't anyone from the Lake Evendim area, when she knew from what Keren and Sherrill had told her that they, too, had their share of freebooters.

"Along Lake Evendim it isn't raiders and barbarians. It's pirates and bands of outlaws because it's easy to hide in the shore-caves. Not too many injured end up here because that type of opponent isn't really out to fight, just to thieve and run. Your compatriots usually wind up getting patched up at one of the Healing Temples, and then they're on their way again. We don't have anyone here from Southern Sectors, either."

"Why?"

"Southern's abutted by Menmelith, and they're friendly—but the weather's strange and unpredictable, especially in the summer. Lots of broken bones from accidents—but there, again, they're usually cared for locally unless it's something really bad, like a broken neck or back."

"But there's two from the Northwest corner—and one of them is poor Vostel—" Talia shuddered a little. Vostel was burned over most of his body, and in constant agony when not sustained by drugs. Talia had taken to spending a lot of time with him because the constant pain was a drain on his emotions. He felt free to let down his frail bulwark of courage with her; to weep from the hurt, to curse the gods, to confess his fear that he would never be well again. She did her best to comfort, reassure, and give back some of the emotional energy that his injuries drained from him.

"Northwest is uncanny," Devan replied. "And I say it, who comes from there and should be used to it. Very odd things come out of that wilderness, and don't think I'm exaggerating because I've seen some of them. Just as an example, ninety-nine people out of a hundred will tell you that griffins don't exist outside of a Bard's fevered imagination—the hundredth has been up there and seen them in the sky, and knows them for the deadly reality that they are. I've seen them—I've hunted them, once; they're hard to kill and impossible to catch, and dangerous, just like every weird thing that lives in that wilderness. They say there were wars once somewhere out there fought with magic—magic like in the Bardic tales, not our Gifts—and the things living out there are what's left of the weapons and armies that fought them."

"What do you think?" Talia asked.

"It's as good a way to explain it as any, I suppose," Devan shrugged. "All *I* know is that most people don't believe the half of my tales. Except the Heralds of course; they know better, especially after a griffin's taken a mouthful out of some of them, or a firebird's scorched them for coming too close to her nest—like Vostel. That's probably why I stay here; it's the only place I'll be believed!"

Talia shook her head at him. "You stay because you have to. You're needed too badly here—you couldn't do anything else, and you know it."

"Too wise, youngling," he replied, "You're too wise by half. Maybe I should be glad; you're certainly making it easier to get my patients on their feet again. If I haven't said so before, I appreciate your efforts. We don't have enough mind-Healers to care for the minor traumas; the two we've got have to be saved for the dangerously unbalanced. Now don't look innocent, I know *exactly* what you've been doing! As far as I'm concerned, you can go right on doing it."

For here among the injured she found yet another, and more subtle application of her own Gift. There wasn't the kind of self-destructive sorrow to deal with that came upon those left behind with a Herald's death, but there were other, more insidiously negative emotions to be transmuted.

Self-doubt, so familiar to her, was one of those emotions. There wasn't a Herald in the wards that wasn't prey to it. Often they blamed themselves for their own injuries or the deaths or injuries of those they had been trying to help. And when they were alone so much of the time, with only pain and memory as companions, that self-doubt tended to grow.

It was hardly surprising that some of them developed phobias either, especially not if they'd been trapped or lying alone for long periods before rescue.

And there was a complex muddle of guilt and hatred to be sorted out and worked through for most of them. They hated those who had caused their hurts, either directly or indirectly, and they felt terrible guilt because a Herald was simply not *supposed* to hate anyone. A Herald was supposed to understand. A Herald was supposed to be the kind of person who cured hatreds, not the kind who was prey to them himself. That a Herald was also not supposed to be some kind of superhuman demigod didn't occur to them. That a little honest hatred might be healthy didn't occur to them either.

But the most insidious emotion, and the hardest to do anything about was despair; and despair was more than understandable when a body was plainly too badly hurt to be fully Healed again. It sometimes happened that an injury had been left too long untended to be truly Healed, especially if it had become infected. That was why Jadus had lost his leg in the wars with Karse fought by the Tedrel mercenaries. Healers could realign even the tiniest fragments of bone to allow a crushed limb to be restored—but only if that bone had not yet begun to set. And nerve-damage left too long could never be restored. How did you ease the pain of one who could look at his maimed and broken flesh and know he would never be the same again?

And there was the steady toll on heart and courage inflicted by what seemed to be endless pain—pain such as the burned Vostel was enduring.

All these things called to her with a voice too strong to be denied, begging her to set them aright. So, as she became more deft in the usage of her Gift, she began administering to these injured as well as the bereft, and doing it so subtly that few realized that she'd helped them until after she'd gone. It was hard: hard to find the time, hard to witness the kinds of mental torment that could not be set aright with one simple touch or an out-pouring of grief—but once she began, it was impossible to stop; the needs in the House of Healing drew her as implacably as the anguish left in the wake of death did. She didn't realize—though by now Kyril and one or two others did—that she was only following in the footsteps of many another Monarch's Own. Like

Talia, those who had possessed the strongest Gifts in that capacity wound up ministering not only to the Monarch, but the entire Circle as well. The mounting evidence for these few was that when Talia earned her Whites, she was likely to prove to be one of the Heralds tales are written about. Unfortunately for their peace of mind, the Heralds tales are written about seldom had long or peaceful lives.

CHAPTER 12

"MAKE SURE YOU get the blindfold good and tight," Elspeth told Skif. "Otherwise the test isn't any good."

Skif forbore to comment that he already knew that, and simply asked, "Is Keren done yet?"

"I'll go see." Elspeth ran off.

"Positive you can't see anything? Too tight? Too loose?" he asked Talia, making a few final adjustments to her blindfold.

"Black as a mousehole at midnight," she assured him. "And it's fine—it isn't going to slip any, I don't think, and it isn't uncomfortable."

"Keren says she's ready when you are," Elspeth called from beyond the screen of trees in Companion's Field where Keren stood.

"You ready?"

"Any time."

Skif led Talia carefully around the trees to where Keren stood, hands on her hips and a half-smile curving her lips.

"I took you at your word, little centaur; it's good and complicated," she said as they approached her. "Nobody's ever tried this sort of thing before to my knowledge; it should be interesting."

"Nobody seems to have this kind of Companion-bond either except me," Talia replied. "And I want to see how much of it is really there and how much is imagination."

"Well, this should do the trick. If you're really seeing through Rolan's eyes, you won't take a single misstep. If you're only imagining it, there's no way you'll be able to negotiate *this* maze."

The red and gold leaves had been carefully cleaned from the ground for at least a hundred feet in all directions in front of where Keren was standing, and laid out on the grass was a carefully plotted maze, the boundaries of its corridors marked by a line of paint on the grass. The corridors were only about two feet wide at the most, and it would take careful watching to avoid stepping on the paint. The maze itself was, as Keren had indicated, very complicated, and since the corridors were not demarcated by anything but the paint on the grass, there would be no way the blindfolded Talia would be able to tell where they were by feel.

Rolan stood beside Keren, on a little rise of ground that gave him a good view of the entire maze. According to Talia's plan, *he* would be her eyes for this task. If the bond between them was as deep and strong as she thought, she would be able to traverse the maze with relative ease.

While Keren, Skif, and Elspeth watched in fascination, she set out to make the attempt.

Halfway through, she hesitated for a long moment.

"She's going to end up in a dead end," Skif whispered to Keren.

"No, she's not—wait and see. There's more than one way you can get through this, and I think she just chose the shorter route."

Finally Talia stopped and turned blindly back to her audience.

"Well?" she asked.

"Take the blindfold off and see for yourself."

She had threaded the maze so successfully that there wasn't even a smear of paint on her boots. "It worked—" she said, a little awed. "It really worked!"

"I must admit that this is one of the most amazing things I've ever seen," Keren said, picking her way across the grass followed by Rolan and the other two. "I thought Dantris and I were tight-bonded, but I don't think we could have managed this. Why did you stop halfway through?"

"Rolan was arguing with me—I wanted to go the way I finally did, and he wanted me to take the 'T' path."

"Either would have gotten you out; the one you wanted was the shorter, though. Ready for the second test?"

"I think so. Rolan seems to be."

"All right then—off with you, despoiler of gardens!" Keren slapped Rolan lightly on the rump; he snorted at her, and trotted off. Skif followed beside him.

Keren had a single die, which she threw for a set of twenty passes, as Talia carefully noted down the number of pips. Skif, with Rolan, had a set of six cards, one for each face of the die. Rolan was to indicate which face was up for each pass Keren made—for this time, *he* would be using Talia's eyes. This didn't take long; both of them were soon back, and Skif's and Talia's lists compared.

"Incredible—not even *one* wrong! We're going to have to tell Kyril about this; I don't doubt he'll want to give you even more tests together," Keren said with amazement.

"He's welcome if he wants to," Talia replied. "I just wanted to be sure that I was right about the bond. Now that we're done, I'll tell you what else I was testing. I was shielded the entire time for both tests."

"You're joking, surely!" Skif's mouth fell open.

"I was never more serious. You realize what this means, don't you? Not only is our bond one of the strongest I know of, but if *I* can't shield him out, nobody can block him away from me, either."

"That could be mighty useful, someday," Keren put in. "It means that even if you were unconscious, you could be reached through Rolan. We'll definitely have to tell Kyril about this now."

"Go right ahead. It's hardly something that needs to be kept secret."

"Talia, do you think I'll have a friend like Rolan someday?" Elspeth asked wistfully.

Talia gathered the child to her and hugged her shoulders. "Catling," she whispered. "Never doubt it for a minute. In fact, your Companion-friend may very well be even *better* than Rolan, and that's a promise."

Rolan did not respond to this with his usual snort of human-like derision. Instead, he nuzzled the child gently, almost as if to confirm Talia's promise.

A few evenings later Talia decided to determine exactly what the physical limit of the range of her Gift was.

She did not bother to light a candle in her room, but simply relaxed on her bed in the growing dusk, isolating and calming any disturbing influences in herself until she was no longer aware of her body except as a kind of anchor from which to move outward. She extended her sense of empathy slowly, reaching first beyond her room, then beyond the Collegium, then beyond the Palace and grounds. There were vague pockets in the Palace of ambition and unease, but nothing and no one strong enough to hold her there.

She brushed lightly past them, venturing beyond, out into the city itself. Emotions appeared as vivid colors to her; they were like mists to move through for the most part, with none of the negative sort being strong enough to stay her passage. Once or twice she stopped long enough to intervene; in a tavern brawl, and in the nightmares of a young soldier. Then she passed on.

She ranged out farther now, following the Northern road, moving from contact to contact with those dwelling or camped beside it as if she were following beacons along the wayside. They were like little lanterns along the darkened road, providing mostly guidepoints for her—or perhaps like stepping-stones across a brook since she needed them to move onward. The contacts here were fewer than in any other direction as the Northern road led through some of the most sparsely populated districts in the Kingdom. As Talia's consciousness flowed along this route, she remembered that this was the route Ylsa had been sent out on earlier in the week.

Suddenly, as if merely being reminded of Ylsa's existence were impetus enough, she found herself being pulled Northward, caught by a force too strong and too urgent to resist.

There was growing unease and apprehension as she was pulled along—and growing fear as well. She found herself unable to break the contact or to slow herself and became even more alarmed because of this. She was in a near panic when she was suddenly pulled into what had drawn her.

She found herself *there*. Looking out of another's eyes. Ylsa's eyes.

Ambushed!

Too many—there were too many of them to fight off. Felara lashed out with wicked hooves and laid about her with her teeth, trying to make a path for escape, but their attackers were canny and managed to keep them surrounded. She clamped her legs tightly around Felara's chest to stay with her, knowing she was as good as dead if she was thrown.

She drew her longsword and cut at them, but for every one she laid low, two sprang up to replace him. The sword was not really meant for fighting a-horseback, and before she'd managed to strike more than half-a-dozen blows, it was carried out of her hands by a falling foe, and she was forced to draw her dagger instead. Then, in a well-coordinated move, they all drew back as a horn sounded.

Terrible pain lanced through her shoulder and momentarily filmed her eyes. She looked down stupidly to see a feathered shaft sprouting from her upper chest.

Felara screamed in agony as a second shaft pierced the Companion's flank. Damn the moon! They were illuminated clearly by it—clearly enough to make good targets for the archers that *must* be hidden underneath the trees. Their attackers fell back a little more—and more shafts hummed out of the darkness—

Felara cried once again, and collapsed, trapping her beneath her Companion's bulk. And she couldn't think or move, for the loss and the agony of Felara's death were all too much a part of her.

The archers' work done, the swordsmen closed anew. She saw the blade catch the moonlight, and arc down, and knew it for the one that would kill her—

:Kyril! Tell the Queen—in the shaft!:

Dozens of images flashed and vanished. One stayed. Arrows—ringed with black. Five of them. Hollow black-ringed arrows—

Then unbearable pain, followed by a terrifying silence and darkness, more terrible than the pain—she was trapped in the darkness, unable to escape. There was nothing to hold to, nothing to anchor to—then abruptly, there *was* something in the darkness with her.

It was Rolan—

And she took hold of him in panic fear and *pulled*—

Talia shrieked with a mortal pain not her own—and found herself sitting bolt upright in her bed. For one moment she sat, blinking and confused, and not at all sure that it all hadn't been a far too realistic nightmare.

Then the Death Bell tolled.

"No—oh no, no, no—" She began to sob brokenly in reaction—when a thought stilled her own tears as surely as if they'd been shut off.

Keren.

Keren, who was bound to Ylsa as strongly as to her Companion or her brother—who depended on those bonds. Who, Talia knew, made a habit of communicating with her lover every night she was gone if Ylsa was within range. Who *must* have felt Ylsa's death—if she hadn't been mentally searching for her at the time of the ambush, she would know it by the Herald's bond. And who, prostrated by grief and the shock of Ylsa's death, which she had experienced no less than Talia, might very well lose her hold on responsibility and duty long enough to succeed in death-willing herself.

Talia was still dressed except for boots. She ran for the Herald's quarters without stopping to put them on. She'd never been in Keren's rooms before, but there was no mistaking the fiery beacon of pain and loss that led her onward. She followed it unerringly.

The door was already open when she arrived; Keren's twin slumped next to her, his eyes dazed, his expression vacant. Keren was sitting frozen in her chair; she'd evidently been trying to reach Ylsa when Ylsa was struck down. She was totally locked away within herself. Her face was an expressionless mask, and only the wild eyes showed that she was alive. The look in those eyes was that of a creature wounded and near death, and not very human anymore.

Talia touched Keren's hand hesitantly; there was no response. With a tiny cry of dismay, she took both Keren's cold hands in her own, and strove to reach her with her mind.

She was dragged into a whirling maelstrom of pain. There was nothing to hold on to. There was only unbearable loneliness and loss. Caught within that whirlpool was Keren's twin—and now, Talia as well.

Again she reached blindly in panic for a mental anchor—and again, there was Rolan, a steady pillar to hold to. She reached for him; was caught and held firm. Now, no longer frightened, no longer at the mercy of the pain-storm, she could think of the others.

Keren could not be reached, but perhaps her brother could be freed. She reached for the "Teren-spark," caught it, and held it long enough to try to pull both of them out.

With a convulsive lurch, Talia broke contact.

She found herself on the other side of the room, half-supported by Teren, half-supporting him herself.

"What happened?" she gasped.

"She cried out—I heard her, and found her like *that*. When I tried to get her to wake, when I touched her, she pulled me in with her—" Teren shook his head, trying to clear it. "Talia, I can't reach her at all. We've got to do something! You can reach her, can't you?"

"I tried; I can't come near. It's—too strong, too closed in. I can't catch hold of her, and she's destroying herself with her own grief. Somehow—" Talia tried to shake off the effects of her contact with that mindless chaos and loss. "Somehow I've got to find something to make her turn it outward instead of in—"

Talia's chaotic thoughts steadied, found a focus, and held. With one of the intuitive leaps perhaps only she was capable of, she thought of Sherrill—

Sherrill, daring to follow Keren into the river. Follow *Keren,* that was the key; and now Talia could remember how Sherrill had always seemed to hover at the edge of wherever it was that Keren or Ylsa or both were. And how there had always been a kind of smothered longing in her eyes. Remembered how Sherrill had always kept from intruding *too* closely on them, perhaps fearing that her own presence might spoil something—

Sherrill, who came from the same people as Keren and Teren; from among folk who did not hold that love between those of the same sex was anathema as was so often the case elsewhere.

Sherrill, who had as many lovers as she wished, yet stayed with none.

"Teren, think hard—is Sherrill back from her internship yet?" Talia asked him urgently.

"I don't—I think so—" He was still a little dazed.

"Get her, then. Now! She'll know who the Bell is for—tell her Keren needs her!"

He did not pause to question her, impelled by the urgency in her voice. He scrambled to his feet and sprinted out the door; Talia returned to Keren's side and strove to touch her without being pulled in a second time.

Finally the sound she'd been hoping for reached her ears; the sound of two pairs of feet running up the corridor.

Sherrill led Teren by a good margin, and she plainly had only one goal in her mind—Keren.

Talia relinquished her place as Sherrill seized Keren's hands in her own and knelt by her side; sobbing heartbrokenly, calling Keren's name.

The sound of her weeping penetrated Keren's blankness as nothing Talia had tried had done. Her voice, or perhaps the unconcealed love in that voice, and the pain that equaled Keren's own, broke the hold Keren's grief had held over her.

Keren's face stirred, came to life again—her eyes went to the woman kneeling beside her.

"Sherrill—?" Keren whispered hoarsely.

Something else came forward from the back of her mind, and Talia remembered one thing more—Ylsa, saying "sometimes persistent inability can mask ability"—and Sherrill's own disclaimer of any but the most rudimentary abilities at thought-reading.

Before the wave of their combined grief, and her need to find and give comfort, Sherrill's mental walls collapsed.

Teren and Talia removed themselves and shut the door, giving them privacy to vent their sorrows. But not alone anymore, and not facing their grief unsupported.

Talia leaned up against the corridor walls, wanting to dissolve helplessly into tears herself.

"Talia?" Teren touched her elbow lightly.

"Goddess—oh, Teren, I saw her die! I saw Ylsa die! It was horrible—" Tears were coursing down her face, and yet this wasn't the kind of weeping that brought any relief. Other Heralds were beginning to gather around her; she hadn't had any time to reshield and their raw emotions melded painfully with her own. It felt as if she were being smothered or torn into dozens of little pieces and scattered on the wind.

Herald Kyril, a tall man considerably older than Teren, and accompanied by the Queen, pushed his way to Talia's side and caught hold of one of her hands. With that contact, he managed to shield her mind from the others. It gave her some respite, though the relief was only partial. He could not shield her from her own memories.

"Majesty!" he exclaimed. "*This* is the other presence I sensed!"

Selenay exercised her royal prerogatives and ordered the corridor cleared.

"Kyril—" she said when only Talia remained. "It is possible that she may have the answer—her Gift is empathy, to be as one with the person she touches."

Talia nodded to confirm what Selenay said, her face wet, her throat too choked to speak.

"My lady"—the iron-haired Herald had something about him that commanded her instant attention—"you may be the key to a terrible dilemma. I hear the thoughts of others, it is true, but *only* as words. Ylsa cast a message to me with her last breath, but it means *nothing* to me, *nothing*! But if you can recall her thoughts, you who shared her mind—you alone know the meaning behind those words on the wind. Can you tell us what she meant?"

Those final images sprang all too readily to mind, invoking the rest of the experience. "The arrows—" She gasped, feeling Ylsa's death-throes in every cell of her own body. "—the black-ringed arrows she carried are metal; hollow. What you want is inside them."

"'In the shaft'—of course!" Selenay breathed. "She meant the arrow-shaft!"

Talia closed her hands over her aching temples; she wished passionately that she could somehow hide in the darkness behind her eyes.

"Kyril, are Kris and Dirk in residence?" Selenay demanded.

"Yes, Majesty."

"Then we have a chance to snatch what Ylsa won for us before anyone has an opportunity to find it. Talia, I must ask still more of you. Come with me—Kyril, find Kris and Dirk and bring them with you."

Selenay half-ran down the hall; Talia was forced to ignore her pounding head and urge her trembling legs into a sprint to keep up with her. They left the Collegium area entirely, and entered the portion of the Palace reserved for the Royal Family—a portion of the area dating right back to Valdemar and the Founding.

The Queen opened the door on a room scarcely larger than a closet; round, and with a round table in the center. It was lit by one lantern, heavily shaded, suspended from the ceiling above the exact center of the table. Beneath it, resting on a padded base, was a sphere of crystal. The table itself was surrounded by padded benches with backs to them. As the door closed behind them, the "dead" feeling to the room showed that it was so well-insulated against outside noise that a small riot could take place outside the door without the occupants of the room being aware of it. It was no longer possible to hear even the grim tolling of the Death Bell.

Talia sank onto one of the benches, holding her furiously aching temples and closing her eyes against the light. Her respite was short-lived. The door opened again; Talia raised aching lids to see that Kyril had brought two more Heralds with him, both dressed in clothing that showed every evidence of being thrown on with extreme haste.

With a pang, Talia recognized Dirk and had no difficulty in identifying the angelically beautiful Kris. They took the bench to her left, Kris sitting closest to her. Kyril sat to her immediate right, and Selenay next to him.

"Talia," Kyril said, "I want you to retrace where you sent your mind tonight. I think perhaps there will be enough emotional residue for you to find it again. This is not going to be easy for you; it will require every last bit of your strength, and I think I can predict that what you will find there may be even more distressing than what you already know. I'll try and cushion the effects for you, but since your Gift is tied up with emotions and feelings, it's bound to be painful. Kris will be following you with his sight. Put your hand in his, and don't let go until we tell you to. Dirk will be linked with him, and the Queen will be shielding all four of us from the outside world and the thoughts of others and keeping distractions from us." As he spoke, Kyril took Talia's unresisting right hand into his own.

She had no energy to spare to reply; she simply leaned back into the padded support of the bench back and put herself back into the interrupted trance. The pain of her head interfered with that. There was a whisper, and a hand rested for a brief moment on the one resting in Kris'—"Selenay" her mind recognized absently—and the pain receded. She retraced her movements now with a kind of double inner vision, seeing the swirls of emotion she had followed, and Seeing the actual landmarks with Kris' Gift as well. Darkness did not hamper his sight in the least, for everything seemed to be illuminated from within, living things the most.

Time lost meaning. Then as she began to recognize things she had passed, she began to dread what she would find at the end of the journey.

Finding the site of the ambush again was probably the worst experience she had ever had in her life.

Ylsa's body had been searched—with complete and callous thoroughness. She was only grateful that it was not Keren who was linked in with her, to see the bestial things they'd done to her lifemate. She wanted to retch; started to feel her grasp on the place slip, then felt someone else's strength supporting her. She held to her task until she began to lose herself as her strength faded. She couldn't feel her own body anymore, even remotely. A luminous mist began to obscure her inner vision. She knew she should have been frightened, for she had gone beyond the limits of her own abilities and energies and was in grave danger of being lost, but she could not even summon up enough force to be afraid.

Then, for the third time, she felt Rolan with her, adding his energy to her own, and she held on for far longer than she would have thought anyone would have been able to bear. Then she heard Kris' voice say, "Got it," and felt him loose her hand.

"Your part's over, Talia," Kyril murmured.

She fled back to herself in a rush, and with a tiny sob of release she buried her head in her arms on the table and let the true tears of mourning flow at last. She wept in silence, only the shaking of her shoulders betraying her. The attention of the others was directed elsewhere now, and she felt free to let her grief loose.

Something clattered down onto the table with a faint metallic clash. The sound was repeated four more times.

Dirk's voice, harsh with fatigue, said, "That's the lot."

There was a stirring to her right, a sound of metal grating on metal, and the whisper of paper.

There was utter silence; then the Queen sighed. Her bench grated a little on the floor as she stood. "This is the proof I needed," she said grimly. "I must summon the Council. There will be necks in the noose after this night's work; high-born necks."

There was a whisper of cooler air from the door, and she was gone.

Talia felt Kyril rise beside her. "My place is at the Council board to represent the Circle," he said, then hesitated.

"Go, Kyril," Kris replied in answer to his hesitation. "We'll see to her."

He sighed with relief, obviously having been torn between his responsibilities to Talia and to the Circle. "Bless you, brothers. Talia—" his hand rested briefly on her head. "You are more than worthy to be Queen's Own. This would not have been remotely possible without your help. Oh, damn, words mean less than nothing now! You'll learn soon enough what this night's agony has won for all of us in the way of long-overdue justice. I think—Ylsa would be proud of you."

The door sighed; he was gone.

"Talia?" Someone had taken Kyril's place on her right; the voice was Dirk's. She stemmed the flood of tears with an effort, and regained at least a fragile semblance of control over herself. Surreptitiously drying her eyes on her sleeve, she raised her aching head.

The weariness on both their faces matched her own, and there were tears in Kris' eyes and the marks of weeping on Dirk's cheeks as well. Both of them tried to reach out of their own grief to comfort her, but were not really sure what to say.

"I—think I'd like—to go back to my room," she said carefully, between surges of pain. Her head throbbed in time with her pulse, and her vision faded every time the pain worsened. She tried to stand, but as she did so, the chamber spun around her like a top, the lamplight dimmed, and there was a roaring in her ears. Kris shoved the table out of the way so that she wouldn't crack her skull open on it while Dirk knocked over the bench in his haste to reach her before she fell; then everything seemed to fade, even her own body, and her thoughts vanished in the wave of anguish that followed.

It was Ylsa—and Felara with her. At least, Talia thought it was Felara; the Companion didn't look the same from moment to moment, a fascinating and luminous, eternally shifting form. And *where* they were— it was sort of a ghost of her own room, all gray and shadowy; insubstantial. You could see the Moon and the stars through the walls.

"Ylsa?" she said, doubtfully—for the Herald looked scarcely older than herself.

"Kitten," Ylsa replied, her tone a benediction. "Oh, kitten! You won't remember this clearly—but you *will* remember it. Tell Keren not to grieve too long; tell her I said so! And if she doesn't behave herself and take what Sherri's offering, I'll come haunt her! The darkness isn't the end to everything, kitten, the Havens are beyond it, and I'm overdue. But before I go—I have a few things to tell you, and to give you—"

*   *   *

She woke the next morning with burning eyes and a still-pounding skull, yet with an oddly comforted soul. There had been a dream—or was it a dream? Ylsa, no longer the mutilated, ravaged thing Talia had seen, but miraculously restored and somehow younger-looking, had spoken to her. She'd seemed awfully substantial for a ghost, if indeed that was what she was.

She'd spoken with Talia for a long, long time; some things she'd said were so clear that Talia could almost hear them now—what to tell Keren, for instance, when Keren's grief had ebbed somewhat; to make it clear to Sherri that she was not to consider herself an interloper. Then she'd taken Talia's hand in her own, and done—what?

She couldn't remember exactly, but somehow the anguish of last night had been replaced by a gentle sorrow that was much easier to bear. The memories, too—those that were her own were still crystal clear, but those which had been Ylsa's were blurred, set at one remove, and no longer so agonizingly a part of her. She couldn't remember now what it had felt like to die.

Someone had removed her outer tunic, tucking her into bed wearing her loose shirt and breeches. As she sat up, nausea joined the ache in her skull and her temples throbbed. The symptoms were very easy to recognize; after all, she'd badly overtaxed herself. Now she was paying the price. Ylsa had said something about that, too, in the dream—

She dragged herself out of bed and went to the desk, only to discover that someone had anticipated her need, readying a mug of Ylsa's herbal remedy and putting a kettle of water over the tiny fire on her pocket-sized hearth. She needed only to pour the hot water over the crushed botanicals and wait for them to steep. She counted to one hundred, slowly, then drank the brew off without bothering to sweeten or strain it.

When the pounding in her head had subsided a bit, and her stomach had settled, she sought the bathing room. A long, hot bath was also part of the prescription, and she soaked for at least an hour. By then, her headache had receded to manageable proportions, and she dressed in clean clothing and descended to the kitchen.

Mero was working like a fiend possessed; his round face displaying a grief as deep as any Herald's. He greeted her appearance with an exclamation of surprise; she soon found herself tucked into a corner of the kitchen with another mug of the herb tea in one hand and a slice of honeycake to kill the taste in another.

"Has anything happened since last night?" she asked, knowing that Mero heard everything as soon as it transpired.

"Not a great deal," he replied. "But—they brought her home in the dawn—"

His face crumpled for a moment, and Talia remembered belatedly that Mero and Ylsa had been longtime friends, that he had "adopted" her much as he had taken Elspeth as a special pet, in Ylsa's long-ago student days.

"And Keren?" she asked, hesitating to intrude on his grief.

"She—is coping. Is better than I would have expected. That was a wise thing—a kind thing, that you did; to bring to her side one who could most truly feel and share in her loss and sorrow," he replied, giving her a look of sad approval. "The Book of One says 'That love is most true that thinks first of the pain of others before its own.' She—the lady—she must be proud of you, I think—" he stumbled to a halt, not knowing what else to say.

"I hope she is, Mero," Talia replied with sincerity. "What of the Queen and the Council—and Teren?"

"Teren helps Sherrill to tend his sister; he seems well enough. I think it is enough for him to know that she is safe again. Oh, and Sherrill has been ordered to bide at the Collegium until this newly-woken Gift of hers be properly trained. Kyril himself is to tend to that. As for the rest—the Council are still closeted together. There was some coming and going of the palace Guard in the hour before dawn, however. Rumor says that there are some highborn ones missing from their beds. But—you do not eat—" He frowned at her, and she hastily began to nibble at the cake. "*She* told me, long ago, that those who spend much of themselves in magic must soon replace what they spent or suffer as a consequence." He stood over her until she'd finished, then pressed another slice into her hand.

"It's so quiet," she said, suddenly missing the sound of feet and voices that usually filled the Collegium. "Where is everybody?"

"In the Great Hall, waiting on the word from the Council. Perhaps you should be there as well."

"No—I don't think I need to be," she replied, closing weary eyes. "Now that my head is working again, I know what the decisions will be."

Whether she'd sorted out the confused memories alone, or with the aid of someone—or something—else, she knew now what it was that Ylsa had died to obtain. It was nothing less than the proofs, written in their own hands, of treason against Selenay and murder of many of the Heralds by five of the Court's highly placed nobles. These were the incontrovertible proofs that the Queen had long desired to obtain—and two of the nobles named in those letters were previously unsuspected, and both were Council members. There would be no denying their own letters; before nightfall the heart and soul of the conspiracy begun by the Queen's husband would be destroyed, root and branch. These documents, hidden in the hollow arrows and transported to the dim chamber of the Palace by Dirk and Kris, would be the instruments of vengeance for Ylsa herself, and Talamir, and many another Herald whose names Talia didn't even know. How Ylsa had obtained these things, Talia had no idea—nor, with the effect of the drug she'd been drinking finally taking hold, did she much care.

She began to doze a little, her head nodding, when the Death Bell suddenly ceased its tolling. She woke at the sudden silence; then other bells began ringing—the bells that only rang to announce vital decisions made by the Council. They were tolling a death-knell.

Mero nodded, as if to himself. "The Council has decided, the Queen has confirmed it. They have chosen the death-sentence," he said. "They will probably grant the condemned ones the right to die by their own hands, but if they have not the courage, the executioner will have them in the morning. I wish—" His face registered both grief and fury. "It is not the way of the One, may He forgive me—but I could wish they had a dozen lives each, that they might truly pay for what they did! And I wish that it could be I who metes out that vengeance to them—"

Talia briefly closed her eyes on his raw grief, then took up the task of easing it.

The petals falling from the apple trees were a match for Rolan's coat—and the pristine state of Skif's traveling leathers.

"Do I look that different?" he asked Talia anxiously. "I mean, I don't *feel* any different."

"I'm afraid you do look different," she told him with a perfectly straight face. "Like someone else altogether."

"How?"

"Well, to tell you the absolute truth," she muted her voice as if she were giving him the worst of bad news, "you look—"

"What? What?"

"Responsible. Serious. *Adult*."

"Talia!"

"No, really, you don't look any different." She giggled. "All it looks like is that you fell into a vat of bleach and your Grays got accidentally upgraded."

"Oh, Talia." He joined her laughter for a while, then grew serious. "I'll miss you."

"I'll miss you, too."

They walked together in silence through the falling blossoms. It was Skif who finally broke the silence between them.

"At least I won't be as worried about you now—not like I'd have been if I'd gone last fall."

"Worried? About me? Why? What is there to be worried about *here*?"

"For one thing, you're safer now; there isn't anybody left to be out after your blood. For another, well, I don't know why, but before, you never seemed to belong here. Now you do."

"Now I feel like I've earned my place here, that's all."

"You never needed to earn it."

"I thought I did." They drew within sight of the tack shed, where Skif's Companion Cymry waited, and with her, his internship instructor, Dirk. "Promise me something?"

"What?"

"You won't forget how to laugh."

He grinned. "If you'll promise me that you'll learn."

"Clown."

"Pedant."

"Scoundrel."

"Shrew." Then, unexpectedly, "You're the best friend I'll ever have."

Her throat suddenly closed with tears. Unable to speak, she buried her face in his shoulder, holding him as tightly as she could. A few moments later, she noticed he was doing the same.

"Just look at us," she managed to get out. "A pair of great blubbering babies!"

"All in a good cause." He wiped his eyes on his sleeve. "Talia, I really do have something I'd like to ask you before I leave. Something I'd like you to do."

"Anything." She managed to grin. "So long as it's not going to get me in too much trouble!"

"Well—I never had any family—at least not that I know of. Would—you be my family? My sister? Since it doesn't seem like we were meant to be anything else?"

"Oh, Skif! I—" She swallowed. "Nothing would make me happier, not even getting my Whites. I don't have any family anymore either, but you're worth twelve Holds all by yourself."

"Then, just like we used to on the street—" He solemnly nicked his wrist and handed her his knife; she followed suit, and they held their wrists together . . .

"Blood to blood, till death binding," he whispered.

"And after," she replied.

"And after."

He tore his handkerchief in half, and bound up both their wrists. "It's time, I guess. If I dally around much more, Dirk's going to be annoyed. Well—take care."

"Be very careful out there, promise? If you manage to get yourself hurt—I'll—I'll turn Alberich loose on you!"

"Lord of Lights, you *are* vicious, aren't you!" He turned toward her, and caught her in a fierce hug that nearly squeezed all the breath from her lungs, then planted a hard, quick kiss on her lips, and ran off toward his waiting mentor. As he ran, he looked back over this shoulder, waving farewell.

She waved after him until he was completely out of sight.

She was unaware that she was being watched.

"And off goes her last friend." Selenay sighed, guilt in her eyes.

"I think not," Kyril replied from just behind her.

They had just turned their own Companions loose and had been walking together slowly back to the Palace; the gentle warmth and the perfumed rain of blossoms had made both of them reluctant to return to duty. Kyril had spotted Talia first; they'd turned aside into a copse to avoid disturbing what was obviously meant to be a private farewell.

"Why?" Selenay asked. "Lady knows she's little enough time for making friends."

"She doesn't have to *make* them; they make themselves her friends. As little as I see the trainees, I've noticed *that*. And it isn't just the younglings—there's Keren, Sherrill—even Alberich."

"Enough to hold her here without regret? We've stolen her childhood, Kyril—we've made her a woman in a child's body, and forced responsibilities on her an adult would blanch at."

"We steal *all* their childhoods, Lady; it comes with being Chosen," he sighed. "There isn't a one of us who's had the opportunity to truly be a child. Responsibility comes on us all early. As to Talia—she never really had a childhood to steal; her own people saw to that."

"It isn't fair—"

"Life isn't fair. Even so, given the chance to choose, she'd take being Chosen over any other fate. I know I would. Don't you think she's happier with us than she would be anywhere else?"

"If I could only be sure of that."

"Then watch her—you'll see."

Talia stared as long as anything of Skif and his mentor could be seen, then turned back toward the Collegium. As she turned, Selenay could clearly see her face; with no one watching her, she had erected no barriers. As she turned away, her pensive expression lightened until, as she faced the Collegium most of the sorrow of parting had left her eyes. And Selenay's heart lifted again, as she read all Kyril had promised she would find in those eyes.

Talia sighed, turning back toward the Collegium. As she did so, she felt Rolan reaching tentatively for her. For one long moment after Skif had vanished off on his own, she had felt bereft and terribly lonely. But now—

How could she *ever* be lonely when there was Rolan?

And Skif wasn't the only friend she had; Jeri was off somewhere, but Sherrill was still here—and Keren, Devan, little Elspeth, Selenay—even dear, overly-gallant Griffon.

They were all of them, more than friends; they were kin—the important kind, soul-kindred. Her family. Her *real* family. *This* was where she'd belonged all along; as she'd told Skif, it had just taken her this long to see it.

And with a lighter heart, she turned back down the path that led to the Collegium.

The Collegium—and home.

ARROW'S
FLIGHT

For Carolyn,
who knows why

PROLOGUE

LONG AGO—SO LONG ago that the details of the conflict are lost and only the merest legends remain—the world of Velgarth was wracked by sorcerous wars. The population was decimated. The land quickly turned to wilderness and was given over to the forest and the magically-engendered creatures that had been used to fight those wars, while the people who remained fled to the eastern coastline, there to resume their shattered lives. Humans are resilient creatures, however, and it was not overlong before the population once again was on the increase, and folk began to move westward again, building new kingdoms out of the wilderness.

One such kingdom was Valdemar. Founded by the once-Baron Valdemar and those of his people who had chosen exile with him rather than facing the wrath of a selfish and cruel monarch, it lay on the very western-and-northernmost edge of the civilized world. In part due to the nature of its founders, the monarchs of Valdemar welcomed fugitives and fellow exiles, and the customs and habits of its people had over the years become a polyglot patchwork. In point of fact, the one rule by which the monarchs of Valdemar governed their people was "There *is* no 'one, true way.'"

Governing such an ill-assorted lot of subjects might have been impossible—had it not been for the Heralds of Valdemar.

The Heralds served many functions; they were administrative overseers, dispensers of justice, information gatherers, even temporary military advisors, answerable only to the Monarch and their own circle of peers. Such a system might have seemed ripe for abuse—it would have been, but for the Companions.

To the unknowing eye, a Companion would seem little more than an extraordinarily graceful white horse. They were far more than that. Sent by some unknown power or powers at the pleading of King Valdemar himself, it was the Companions who chose new Heralds, forging between themselves and their Chosen a mind-to-mind bond that only death could sever. While no one knew precisely *how* intelligent they were, it was generally agreed that their capabilities were at least as high as those of their human partners. Companions could (and did) Choose irrespective of age and sex, although they tended to Choose youngsters just entering adolescence, and more boys were Chosen than girls. The one commonality among the Chosen (other than a specific personality type: patient, unselfish, responsible, and capable of heroic devotion to duty) was at least a trace of psychic ability. Contact with a Companion and continued development of the bond enhanced whatever latent paranormal capabilities lay within the Chosen. With time, as these Gifts became better understood, ways were developed to train and use them to the fullest extent to which the individual was capable. Gradually the Gifts displaced in importance whatever knowledge of "true magic" was left in Valdemar, until there was no record of how such magic had ever been learned or used.

So the governing of Valdemar evolved; the Monarch, advised by his Council, made the laws; the Heralds dispensed the laws and saw that they were observed. The Heralds themselves were nearly incapable of becoming corrupted or potential abusers of their temporal power; the Chosen were by nature remarkably self-sacrificing—their training only reinforced this. They had to be—there was a better than even chance that a Herald would die in the line of duty. But they were human for all of that; mostly young, mostly living on the edge of danger—so, it was inevitable that outside of their duty they tended to be a bit hedonistic and anything but chaste. And only seldom did a Herald form a tie beyond that of brotherhood and the pleasures of the moment—perhaps because the bond of brotherhood was so *very* strong, and because the Herald-Companion bond left little room for any other permanent ties. For the most part, few of the common or noble folk held this against them—knowing that, no matter how wanton a Herald might be on leave, the moment he donned his snowy uniform he was another creature altogether, for a Herald in Whites was a Herald on duty, and a Herald on duty had no time for anything outside of that duty, least of all the frivolity of his own pleasures. Still, there *were* those who held other opinions . . . some of them in high places.

Laws laid down by the first King decreed that the Monarch himself must also be a Herald. Thus it was ensured that the ruler of Valdemar could never be the kind of tyrant who had caused the founders to flee their own homes.

Second in importance to the Monarch was the Herald known as the "King's (or Queen's) Own." Chosen by a special Companion—one that never seemed to age (though it was possible to kill him) and was always a stallion—the Queen's Own held the special position of confidant and most trusted friend and advisor to the ruler. Thus the Monarchs of Valdemar were assured that they would always have at least one person about them who could be trusted and counted on at all times. This tended to make for stable and confident rulers—and thus, a stable and dependable government.

For generations it seemed that King Valdemar had planned his government perfectly. But the best-laid plans are still capable of being circumvented by accident or chance.

In the reign of King Sendar, the kingdom of Karse (that bordered Valdemar to the south-east) hired a nomadic nation of mercenaries to attack Valdemar. In the ensuing war, Sendar was killed, and his daughter, Selenay, assumed the throne, herself having only recently completed her Herald's training. The Queen's Own, an aged Herald called Talamir, was frequently confused and embarrassed at having to advise a young, headstrong, and attractive female. As a result, Selenay made an ill-advised marriage, one that nearly cost her both her throne and her life.

The issue of that marriage, the Heir-presumptive, was a female child whom Selenay called Elspeth. Elspeth came under the influence of the nurse Selenay's husband had brought from his own land, and became an intractable, spoiled brat. It became obvious that if things went on as they were tending, the girl would never be Chosen, and thus could never inherit. This would leave Selenay with two choices; marry again (with the attendant risks) and attempt to produce another, more suitable Heir, or declare someone already Chosen and with the proper bloodline to be Heir. Or, somehow, salvage the Heir-presumptive. Talamir had a plan—one that it seemed had a good chance of success—which involved sending the child into fosterage in a remote province, away from the influence of the nurse and Court, with those who could be counted upon to take no nonsense from her.

Then Talamir was murdered, throwing the situation into confusion again. His Companion, Rolan, Chose a new Queen's Own—but instead of picking an adult or someone already a full Herald, Chose an adolescent girl named Talia.

Talia was of Holderkin—a puritanical Border group which did its best to discourage knowledge of outsiders. Talia had no idea what it meant to have a Herald's Companion accost her, and then (apparently) carry her off. Among her people, females held very subordinate positions, and nonconformity was punished immediately and harshly. And since Talia herself was ill-suited to a subordinate role, she was constantly being told that everything she said or did was wrong at best, and evil at worst. She was ill-prepared for the new world of the Heralds and their Collegium. The one thing she *did* have experience in was the handling and schooling of children, for she had been the teacher to her Holding's younger members from the time she was nine.

But she managed—to find a true home among the Heralds, *and* to civilize the Brat. Now the year-and-a-half of Field duty awaited her—and a trial she never dreamed of having to pass.

CHAPTER 1

*T*HWACK!

The flat of Alberich's practice-blade cracked against Talia's ill-guarded side. She hadn't seen the blow coming, she truly hadn't. That had *hurt*, and she would lay money on having a bruise despite the padded jerkin that had absorbed most of the blow. The practice blades may have only been wood, but Alberich tended to wield them all the harder for that.

"Faugh!" he spat in disgust, and came at her again before she had recovered from the last blow. This time he connected with her knife-arm, right at the elbow. She yelped, the arm went numb, and she lost her blade entirely.

The hawklike eyes glared at her with no trace of pity, and the scar-seamed face was a demonic mask as he passed judgment on her performance.

He was at least in his mid-forties, if not older, but he hadn't lost a fraction of his edge or agility in the five years Talia had known him. She was panting with exertion—he might as well have been taking a leisurely stroll. His well-worn, dark leathers (he was the only working Herald in Talia's experience who never wore Whites) showed not so much as a tiny sweat stain. The afternoon sun pouring down on all of them had made him look as thin and insubstantial as a shadow. And he had been just as hard to catch.

"A pity it is that Skif is not here to see you. Die of laughter he surely would!" he growled. "Eighteen you are—one would think you eight. Slow, clumsy, and stupid! Paugh! Had I been a real assassin—"

"I would have died of fright before you touched me."

"Now it is jokes! This is a battle-practice—not a comedy. If I wish amusement, I shall find a jester. Once again—and correctly, this time."

Once she was ready to drop with exhaustion, he turned his attention to Elspeth. Now that both of them deserved special tutelage he had changed the hour of their lessons to one shared by no one else, so that he could give his full devotion to the Queen's Own and Heir-presumptive. Rather than being held on the training grounds outside, the two had their drills in the salle. This was a barn-like building with a sanded wooden floor, lined with mirrors, with high clerestory windows to admit the maximum amount of light. Lessons were always held here during inclement weather, but it was too small for mass practices and classes for the combined Heraldic-Bardic-Healer's Collegium students. Only those "privileged" to receive private lessons with Alberich took those lessons habitually in the salle.

Now that his attention was off her, Talia found her thoughts drifting back to her surprise of this afternoon.

Talia tugged and wriggled impatiently until she had succeeded in getting the supple, soft, white leather tunic over her head. Pulling it into place over the white raime shirt and leather breeches, she finally turned to admire the effect in the polished metal mirror in front of her.

"Havens!" She laughed, not a little surprised, "Why don't the Grays ever look like this?"

"Because," a harsh voice drawled from the next room, "you youngsters would have your minds on anything but your studies if they did!"

Talia laughed, turned back to the mirror, and preened. Today was the anniversary of her first class at Herald's Collegium—a fact that she'd forgotten until Keren and Sherrill (senior Heralds both, and instructors at the Collegium as well as Talia's longtime friends) arrived at her room with their arms full of white uniforms and wearing broad grins.

For the Heraldic Circle had considered—for less than five minutes, all told—had voted—and had passed Talia into full Herald status with the rest of her year-mates—no surprise to anyone in the Collegium, though by tradition the trainees were not to know when they were to be evaluated until the evaluation had already been made *and* they had passed.

Keren and Sherrill had claimed the right to give her the good news.

They didn't even give her a chance to think, either—just appeared at her door, swept her up one on either side, and herded her down the long, dark wood-paneled hall of the Collegium dormitory, down the stairs to the first floor, and out the double doors at the end.

From there they had taken her off to the Seneschal's office to claim her new quarters. Now she stood in the bedroom of the suite she'd chosen, marveling at her reflection.

"I look like a real grownup for a change!"

"That *is* the general idea." Sherrill laughed richly.

She cocked her head to one side, regarding the tiny, slender figure in the mirror. Her unruly red-brown curls were as tousled as ever, but somehow gave an impression now of being tumbled the way they were on purpose. The huge, deep-brown eyes that had been utterly guileless seemed somehow wiser; the heart-shaped face no longer so childlike. And all that change wrought by the magic of a new uniform!

"Talia, your head is going to swell like a spongetoad in rainy season if you're not careful." Keren interrupted her train of thought a second time. By craning her neck to peer around the doorframe Talia could see the riding instructor grinning sardonically from where she was sprawled on the wooden-backed, red-cushioned couch in the other room.

"Don't you know what the Book of the One says?" Sherrill added piously over her mate's shoulder. " 'Great pride shall earn equal humiliation.' "

Talia left her bedroom to join them. They were lounging comfortably in her sparsely-furnished outer room, sharing the lone couch.

"I suppose you're both going to claim that you never spent so much as a minute in front of the mirror when you first got *your* Whites," Talia taunted, strolling toward them with her hands clasped behind her back.

"Who? Me?" Sherrill replied in artificial innocence, lifting an airy hand and batting thick black lashes over wide hazel eyes. "And feed my vanity? W-e-l-l, maybe a *little*."

"I happen to know for a fact that you spent half the day there. I'm told you were trying every hairstyle you could twist that black mane of yours into, seeing which one went best with the new outfits," Keren countered dryly, running her fingers through her own close-cropped, graying brown hair.

Sherrill just grinned and crossed her legs elegantly, leaning back into the cushions. "Since I can't claim equal knowledge of what you did on that august occasion, that's hardly a fair blow."

"Oh, I did my share of mirror-gazing," Keren admitted with mock reluctance. "When you're as scrawny as a sapling and flat as a boy, it's rather astonishing to see yourself in something that actually flatters you. I swear I don't know how they do it—it's the same pattern for everybody, and not that dissimilar from the Student Grays—"

"But Lord, the difference!" Sherri concluded for her. "I don't know *anybody* who doesn't look fantastic in their Whites. Even Dirk manages to look presentable. Rumpled, but presentable."

"Well, what do you think of me?" Talia asked, turning on her toes in front of them, and grinning impishly into Keren's eyes.

"What do I think? That you look fabulous, you young demon. Keep fishing for compliments, though, and I'll likely dump you in the horse trough. Have they told you anything about your internship?"

Talia shook her head, and clasped her hands behind her again. "No. All they said was that the Herald they want to pair me with is in the field, and they won't tell me who it is."

"That's pretty much to be expected. They don't want you to have time to think of things to impress him with," Sherrill replied. Suddenly her eyes sparkled with mischief. "Oh, but I can think of *one* prospect that would give Nerissa a litter of kittens!"

"Who?" Talia asked, head to one side.

"Kris and Dirk are due back in the next few weeks, and Dirk got the last greenie—as you should know, since it was Skif—so it's Kris' turn next! Nessa would *die!*"

"Sherri, it's *only* my internship assignment."

"A year and a half Sector-riding, most of it spent alone together, and you say it's *only* an assignment? Talia, you must have ice water for blood! Do you have any notion of the number of hours Nessa—and half the females of the Circle, for that matter—spend on their knees praying for an assignment like that? Are you sure you don't have leanings our way?"

Talia chuckled, and wrinkled her nose at them. "Quite sure, darlings. Just what is Kris' attraction for Nessa, anyway? She's got most of the males of the Circle panting at her heels as it is."

"The lure of the unattainable, or so I would surmise," Keren supplied, lids half-closed lazily with only a glint of brown iris showing. "He hasn't taken a vow of chastity, but he's so circumspect about his dalliances you'd never know it. It drives Nessa wild, and the harder she chases, the faster he runs. She's as caught up now by the chase as by the face."

"Well, she can chase him all she wants. *I* am not at all impressed by Kris' handsome face," Talia replied firmly.

"Or the gorgeous body—?" interjected Sherrill.

"*Or* the gorgeous body. Nessa can have all the gorgeous bodies in the Circle, for all I care. Holderkin men are handsome specimens, and I can do without them—my father could have given Kris stiff competition in his younger days, and I've told you what kind of a petty tyrant he was. And my late-but-not-lamented brother Justus was actually handsomer, if you favor blonds, and he was the foulest person I've ever known. I'd rather have a good heart and plain packaging."

"Yes, but Kris is a Herald—" Sherrill pointed out, tapping one long finger on her knee for emphasis. "That guarantees the good heart without having to settle for a homely exterior. No handsome, smiling bastards in *our* ranks—"

"Sherri, this is all sheer speculation. Until I find out who I'm interning with, I refuse to worry about the subject," Talia replied firmly.

"You are no fun at all."

"I never said I was."

"Hmm. Dirk's interning that scalawag Skif—" Keren said thoughtfully. "You and Skif were very thick there for a while. In fact, as I recall, you and *he* had a rumor or two floating about your heads. Is that why you aren't interested in Dirk's partner?"

"Maybe," Talia smiled enigmatically. The fact that their "romance" had been entirely without any result was Skif's secret—and hers. The streak of ill-luck and accident that had plagued their meetings had not had any effect on their friendship: except that they had never managed to be more than just that—friends. Oddly enough, though, except for a brief period of anxiety when word had come that Skif had been hurt during his first three months in the field, Talia had thought less of Skif, and more of his counselor. To her own amazement—and for no reason, logical or fanciful, that she could think of—when her thoughts strayed in the direction of the former thief and his internship assignment, it was in Dirk's direction that they tended to wander. This was annoying; she'd met the man all of three times in her life, and had never been in his company for more than an hour or two at most. Yet, that homely face and those wonderful blue eyes kept lingering stubbornly in her thoughts. It did *not* make sense.

She shook her head to free it of those fanciful images. She had little enough time, and had none to spare in daydreams.

"Well, this little wardrobe change of yours ought to surprise little Elspeth," Sherrill said, changing the subject.

"Oh, Lady Bright—" Talia sat down with a thump on one of her cushions, joy extinguished. It almost seemed to her at that moment that the bright sun-rays pouring through her windows had dimmed. "Poor Elspeth—"

"Something up?" Keren asked, one eyebrow rising.

"Just the usual."

"What's usual? You know I don't get around the Court."

"Intrigue rising beyond gossip. She's almost fourteen and still not Chosen; there's muttering in the Court that she's still the Brat under the skin and she'll *never* be Chosen. In Council meetings one or more of the Councilors is usually trying to pressure Selenay into naming an Heir—'pro tem,' as they put it—"

"Who?" Sherrill asked in alarm, sitting straight up. "Who's stirring up the water?"

"You know I can't tell you that! Anyway it isn't just *those* particular Councilors; it's more than half of the Court. Elspeth doesn't say much, but it's got her very depressed, poor baby. Their timing couldn't be worse. She's already moody enough with the normal adolescent woes, and this has got her in near-tears on a regular basis. When I'm not getting my shoulder soggy, I keep finding her at Companion's Field whenever she's free, sort of lurking—"

"Hoping any minute to be Chosen. Gods, no wonder she's wearing a long face whenever I see her. What's Rolan got to say about this?"

"Be damned if I know!" Talia gifted Keren with a look of exasperation. "*You* know he doesn't Mindspeak me in words."

"Sorry." Keren winced. "I keep forgetting."

"He's worried, but it could be as much over the machinations and power-maneuverings at Court as anything else. The current candidates are Jeri, Kemoc, and your oh-so-lovely Kris."

"Wonderful people in and of themselves," Keren observed, "but with some not-so-wonderful relatives lurking in the family trees. One would think Kris' uncle Lord Orthallen would have his hands full enough as chief Councilor without wanting to be the Heir's uncle—"

"*That* man will *never* have enough power to satisfy him," Talia snapped bitterly.

Keren raised an eyebrow at the outburst, and continued. "Kemoc's horde of lazy cousins would swarm the Court, looking for sinecures—and Kemoc's such a soft touch he'd try to manage it. And Jeri—Lady Bright! Her *mother!*"

"We'd have a battle royal every day between Jeri and Lady Indra over how Jeri's Council votes should go. I wish her husband would lock her away. Or buy a gag for her."

"Amen. Pity none of them come without baggage. *Not* my idea of a fun situation. And poor catling caught in the middle."

Talia sighed in agreement. "Speaking of no fun, I'd better scramble. Alberich informed me in no uncertain terms that my new status does not exempt me from his special lessons. I have the sinking feeling that he intends to slap my inflated pride down to pre-student levels, and probably with the flat of his blade."

"Can I watch?" Keren asked wickedly.

"Why not? Elspeth's always there, and there's nothing like being worse at something than a thirteen-year-old girl to really deflate your opinions of yourself. Well, that ought to reinflate *her* self-esteem a bit. Ah, me, it's a pity to have to get these lovely new clothes all over dirt and sweat—"

As they descended the cool darkness of the spiraling staircase, Keren and Sherrill in the lead with their arms casually linked, Talia reflected that bringing them together was probably the best thing she'd ever done. The bond between them was easily as strong as the one Keren had shared with Ylsa—and had Ylsa lived, they might very well have formed one of the relatively rare, permanent threesomes. There was no doubt that they were very good for each other. Poor Ylsa . . .

Talia's chosen living quarters were at the very top of her tower at the end of the Herald's wing. The suites in the four towers were seldom used—probably because they were more than a bit inconvenient. The walk up and down the darkened stone staircase was a long one, but she felt that the view (and the privacy) were worth it.

But the trudge was likely to bring complaints from Talia's friends—and Keren voiced the first of many.

"I'll tell you one thing, my fine young Herald," Keren grumbled a little when they finally reached the ground floor. "Visiting with you on a regular basis is going to keep your friends in shape. Why you chose to roost with the birds is beyond me."

"Do you truly want to know why I chose that particular suite?" Talia asked with a grin.

"Say on."

"Pray remember, if you will, what my Gift is—I'm an empath, not a mindspeaker. Either of you remember who my neighbor was?"

"Mm. Destria, wasn't it?" Sherrill replied after thought. "Turned out to be a good Field Herald, despite her—ah—"

"Randiness," Keren supplied with a hint of grin. "That girl! Anything in Grays *or* Whites, so long as it was male! Havens, when did she ever have time to study?"

"Then you both know about her habit of 'entertaining' with great frequency and—um—enthusiasm. What I couldn't shield I could most certainly hear! Between her nocturnal activities and Rolan's, I got a quite thorough education, let me assure you! That's when I swore my privacy was worth any inconvenience. I don't want to eavesdrop on anyone else's fun ever again, and I certainly don't want anyone eavesdropping on mine!"

"Talia, I don't believe a word of it," Sherrill giggled. "What could you possibly have to fear from eavesdroppers? You're practically a temple virgin compared with the rest of us!"

"You ought to believe it, since it's all true. Well, here's where we part company. Wish me luck—I'm going to need it!"

Pity that they hadn't wished her luck—she might have gotten a few less bruises. Talia fanned herself with a towel while she paced back and forth to keep from stiffening up, and watched Elspeth with unforced enjoyment. The girl was a pleasure to observe, moving through the sparring bout with the grace and agility of a dancer, and making it all seem effortless and easy. She was much better even than Jeri had been at her age, but then she had had the benefits of four years of Alberich's remorseless training; Jeri had only had the finest arms-tutors money could obtain. No amount of money could buy Alberich's expertise.

She ran through the assigned exercises with careless grace. Then, at the end of a bout, she unexpectedly executed one of the spin-and-tumbling-rolls that Alberich had been trying to train into Talia—a move that was *not* one Alberich had been teaching *her*. And she scored a kill on him.

He stared at her in startled amazement for a long moment, as both Talia and Elspeth waited breathlessly for the roar of disapproval they were certain would come.

"Good!" he said at last, as Elspeth's jaw dropped in surprise. "Very good!" Then, lest she dare to grow careless because of the compliment, "But next time must be better."

Despite this unexpected kudos, Talia found when she brought Elspeth a damp towel at the conclusion of the lesson that the girl was subdued and depressed.

"What's wrong, catling?" she asked, seeing how like her mother Elspeth was, despite the brown hair and eyes rather than Selenay's blond and blue. At this moment the shadow on her face matched the one the Queen wore when troubled. She *knew* the answer already, but it would do the girl good to talk it out one more time.

"I can't do anything right," Elspeth replied unhappily. "I'll never be as good as you, no matter how hard I try."

"You can't be serious—"

"No, really, look at you! You spent half your life on a backwoods dirt-farm; now you can't be told from Heralds that were highborn. You got good marks in your classes; I'm abysmal in all of mine. And I can't even manage to be Chosen. . . ."

"I suspect it's the last that's eating at you the most."

Elspeth nodded, the corners of her mouth drooping.

"Catling, we're two different people with wildly different abilities and interests. In the five years I've been here I've never once managed to earn a 'good' from Alberich, much less a 'very good'! I'm still so stiff when I dance that they say it's like dancing with a broom."

"Oh, huzzah, I'm a marvel of coordination. I can kill anything on two legs. That's a *terrific* qualification for being Heir."

"Catling, you've *got* the qualifications. Look, if I live to be two hundred, I will *never* understand politics. Think back a minute. At the last Council meeting, I could sense that Lord Cariodoc was irritated, but *you* were the one who not only knew why and by whom, but managed to placate the old buzzard before he could start an incident. And your teachers assure me that though you may not be the best in your classes, you aren't the worst by any stretch of the imagination. As for being Chosen, catling, thirteen is only the *average* age for that. Think of Jadus—he was sixteen and had been at Bardic for three years! Or Teren, for Lady's sake—a man grown and with two children! Look, it's probably only that *your* Companion just hasn't been old enough, and you know very well they don't Choose until they're ten or better."

Elspeth's mood seemed to be lightening a bit.

"Come on, love, cheer up, and we'll go see Rolan. If riding him will bring some sun to your day, I'm sure he'll let you."

Elspeth's long face brightened considerably. She loved riding as much as dancing and swordwork. It wasn't often that a Companion would consent to bear anyone but his Chosen; Rolan had done so for Elspeth in the past, and she obviously counted those moments among the finest in her life. It wasn't the same as having her own Companion, but it was at least a little like it. Together they left the training salle, and headed for the wooded enclosure that was home to the Companions at the Collegium (partnered, unpartnered, and foals) and that also held the Grove, that place where the Companions had first appeared hundreds of years ago.

And although she took pains not to show it, Talia was profoundly worried. This situation with Elspeth's status hanging fire could not be maintained for much longer. The strain was telling on the Queen, the girl, and the Heraldic Circle.

But Talia had no more notion of how to solve the problem than anyone else.

Talia woke with a start, momentarily confused by the strange feel and sounds of the room in which she found herself. She couldn't see a blessed thing, and over her head was a rattling—

Then she remembered where she was, and that the rattling was the shutter of the window just over the head of her bed. She'd latched it open, and it was rattling in the high wind that must have begun some time during the night.

She turned over and levered herself into a kneeling position on her pillow, peering out into the darkness. She still couldn't see much; dark humps of foliage against barely-lighter grass. The moon was less than half full, all the buildings were dark, and clouds racing along in the wind obscured the stars and the moonlight. The wind smelled of dawn though, and sunrise couldn't be far off.

Talia shivered in the chill, as wind whipped at her; she was about to crawl back under her warm blankets when she saw something below her.

A person—a small person—hardly more than a dim figure moving beyond the fence of Companion's Field, visible only because it was wearing something light-colored.

And she knew with sudden surety that the one below was Elspeth.

She slid out of bed, wincing at the cold wood under her feet, and grabbed clothing by feel, not waiting to stop to light a candle. Confused thoughts tumbled, one over the other. Was the girl sleepwalking? Was she ill? But when she reached unthinkingly and tentatively with her Gift, she encountered neither the feel of a sleeping mind, nor a disturbed one; only a deep and urgent sense of *purpose*.

She should, she realized in some dim, far-off corner of her mind, be alarmed. But as soon as she had touched Elspeth with her Empathic Gift, that sense of calm purpose had infected her as well, and she could no more have disobeyed its promptings than have launched into flight from her tower window.

In a dreamlike state she half-stumbled out into the middle room, fumbled her way to the door, and cautiously felt her way down the spiraling staircase with one hand on the cold smoothness of the metal railing and the other on the rough stone of the wall beside her. She was shivering so hard her teeth rattled, and the thick darkness in the stair-well was slightly unnerving.

There was light at the foot of it, though, from a lamp set up on the wall. The dim yellow light filled the entranceway. And the wood-paneled corridor beyond was lighted well enough by farther wall-hung lamps that Talia felt safe in running down the stone-floored passage-ways to the first door to the outside she could find.

The wind hit her with a shock; it was a physical blow so hard that she gasped. It nearly wrenched the door out of her hands and she had to struggle for a moment she had not wanted to spare to get it closed behind her. She realized that she had gotten only a hint of its force from her window; her room was sheltered from the worst of it by the bulk of the Palace itself.

She found herself at the exterior bend of the L-shaped Herald's wing; just beyond her bulked the Companion's stables. Elspeth was nowhere in sight.

More certain of her ground now than she had been in the unfamil-iar wing of the Palace, Talia would have run if she could, but the wind made that impossible. It plastered her clothing to her body, and drove unidentifiable debris at her with the velocity of crossbow bolts. She couldn't hear anything now with it howling in her ears; she *knew* no one would hear her calling. Now she became vaguely alarmed; with the wind this strong and in the dark, it would be so easy for Elspeth to misstep and find herself in the river—

She mindcalled Rolan for help—and could not reach him—

Or rather, she could reach him, but he was paying no attention to her whatsoever; his whole being was focused on—what it was, she could not say, but it demanded all his concentration; for he was ab-sorbed in it with such intensity that he was shutting everything and everyone else out.

It was up to her, then. She fought her way around the stables toward the bridge that led across the river to the main portion of Companion's Field. It was with incredible relief that she spotted the vague blur of Elspeth ahead of her, already across the river, and headed with utter single-minded concentration in the direction of—

There was only one place she *could* be heading for—the Grove.

Talia forced her pace to the fastest she could manage, leaning at an acute angle into the wind, but the girl had a considerable head start on her, and had already entered the Grove by the time she had crossed the bridge.

The pale blob was lost to sight as the foliage closed around it, and

Talia stumbled over the uneven ground, falling more than once and bruising hands and knees on the stones hidden in the grass. The long grass itself whipped at her booted legs, tangling her feet with each step. She was halfway to the Grove when she looked up from yet another fall to see that it was—gods!—*glowing* faintly from within.

She shook her head, blinking, certain that her eyes were playing tricks on her. The glow remained, scarcely brighter than foxfire, but unmistakably *there*.

She started to rise, when the entire world seemed to give a gut-wrenching lurch, disorienting her completely. She clutched at the grass beneath her hands, as the only reality in a suddenly unreal world, the pain of her bruised palms hardly registering. Everything seemed to be spinning, the way it had the one time she'd fainted, and she was lost in the darkness with the wind wailing in a whirlwind around her and the Grove. There was a sickening moment—or eternity—when *nothing* was real.

Then the world settled, and normality returned with an almost audible *snap*; the wind died away to nothing, sound returned, the disorientation vanished, all in the space of a single heartbeat.

Talia opened her eyes, unaware until that moment that she'd been clenching both eyes and jaw so tightly her face ached. Less than five feet away stood Elspeth, between the supporting shoulders of two Companions. The one on her left was Rolan, and he was back in Talia's awareness again—tired, though; very tired, but strangely contented.

Talia staggered to her feet; the gray light of the setting moon was lightening the sky, and by it, she could make out the girl's features. Elspeth seemed dazed, and if the contrast between the dark mass of her hair and the paleness of her skin meant anything, she was drained as white as paper.

Talia stumbled the few steps between them, grabbed her shoulders and shook her; until that moment the girl didn't seem to realize she was there.

"Elspeth—" was all she managed to choke out around her own nerveless shivering.

"Talia?" The girl blinked once, then dumbfounded her mentor by seeming to snap into total wakefulness, smiling and throwing her arms around Talia's shoulders. "Talia—I—" She laughed, almost hysterical with joy, and for one brief moment Talia feared she'd lost her mind.

Then she let go of the Herald and threw both of her arms around the neck of the Companion to her right. "Talia, Talia, it happened!

Gwena Chose me! She called me when I was asleep, and I came, and she Chose me!"

Gwena?

Talia knew every Companion in residence, having spent nearly as much time with them as Keren, and having helped to midwife many of the foals. *That* name didn't belong to any of them.

And that could only mean one thing; Gwena, like Rolan—and unlike any other Companion currently alive—was Grove-born. But why? For centuries only Monarch's Own Companions had appeared in the Grove like Companions of old.

Talia started to say something—and abruptly felt Rolan's presence overwhelming her mind, tinged with a feeling of gentle regret.

Talia shook her head, bewildered by the sensation that she'd forgotten something, then dismissed the feeling. Elspeth had been Chosen; *that* was what mattered. She remembered the mare vaguely now. Gwena had always been one of the shyer Companions, staying well away from visitors. All her shyness seemed gone, as she nuzzled Elspeth's hair with possessive pride. Rolan, who had been supporting Elspeth on the left, now paced forward in time to give Talia a shoulder to lean on, for her own knees were going weak with reaction, and she felt as drained as if she'd had a three-candlemark workout with Alberich. Birds were breaking into morning-song all around them, and the first light of true dawn streaked the sky to the east with festive ribbons of brightness among the clouds.

"Oh, *catling!*" Talia released her hold on Rolan's mane and flung both her arms around Elspeth, nearly in tears with joy.

It did not occur to either of them to wonder why no one else had been mustered out of bed by that imperative calling both of *them* had answered—and why no one else had noticed anything at all out of the ordinary even yet.

Talia managed to convince Elspeth—not to go back to her bed, because that was an impossibility—but to settle with Gwena in a sheltered little hollow, with a blanket purloined from the stable around her shoulders. Talia hoped that when her excitement faded the child would doze off again; the gods knew she'd be safe enough in the Field with her own Companion standing protective guard over her. She wished devoutly that she could have done the same, but there were far too many things she had to attend to.

The first—and most important—was to inform the Queen. Even at this early hour Selenay would be awake and working, and likely with one or more Councilors. That meant a formal announcement, and not what Talia *really* wanted to do, which was to burst into Selenay's chamber caroling for joy.

However pleased Selenay would be, *that* sort of action would only give the Councilors a very poor impression of the Queen's Own's maturity.

So Talia stumbled back to her room again, through the sweet breeze of a perfect dawn, through bird choruses that were only a faint, far echo of the joy in her heart, to get redressed. And this time, as neatly and precisely as she could manage, cringing inwardly at the grass stains left on the knees of the pair of breeches she'd just peeled off. *Then* she walked—*walked*—decorously and soberly down through the silence of the Herald's wing to the "New Palace" wing that held the suites of Queen and Court.

As usual, there were two blue-clad Guardsmen stationed outside the doors to the Royal chambers. She nodded to them, dark Jon to the right, wizened Fess to the left; she knew both of them well, and longed to be able to whisper her news, but that wouldn't do. It wouldn't be dignified, and it would absolutely shatter protocol. As Queen's Own, she had the right of entry to the Queen's chambers at any time of night or day, and was quickly admitted beyond those heavy goldenoak doors.

As she had expected, Selenay was already hard at work in her dark-paneled outer chamber; dressed for the day in formal Whites, massive desk covered with papers, and both Lord Orthallen and the Seneschal at her shoulders. She looked up at Talia's entrance, startled, blue eyes seeming weary even this early in the day. Whatever brought those two Councilors to her side, it did not look to be pleasant. . . .

Perhaps Talia's news would change all that.

She clued Selenay to the gravity of her news by making the formal half-bow before entering, and that it was good news by a cheerful wink so timed that only Selenay noted it. Protocol demanded exactly five steps across that dark-blue carpet, which took her to exactly within comfortable conversational distance of the desk. Then she went to one knee, trying not to flinch as her bruises encountered the floor. Selenay, tucking a strand of gold hair behind one ear and straightening in expectation, nodded to indicate she could speak.

"Majesty—I have come to petition the right of a trainee to enter the Collegium," Talia said gravely, with both hands clasped upon the upright knee, while her eyes danced at the nonsense of all this formality.

That got the attention not only of Selenay, but of both Councilors.

Only highborn trainees needed to have petitions laid before the Crown, for becoming a Herald often meant renouncing titles and lands, either actual or presumptive.

Talia could see the puzzlement in the Councilors' eyes—and the rising hope in Selenay's.

"What Companion has Chosen—and what is the candidate's name and rank?" Selenay replied just as formally, one hand clutching the goblet before her so tightly her knuckles went white.

"The Companion Gwena has Chosen," Talia barely managed to keep from singing the words, "And her Choice is the Heir-presumptive, now Heir-In-Right, the Lady Elspeth. May I have the Queen's leave to enter the trainee in the Collegium rolls?"

Within the hour Court and Collegium were buzzing, and Talia was up to her eyebrows in all the tasks needed to transfer Elspeth from her mother's custody to that of the Collegium. Elspeth spent the day in blissful ignorance of all the fuss—which was only fair. The first few hours were critical in the formation of the Herald-Companion bond, and should be spent in as undisturbed a manner as possible. So it was Talia's task to see to it that when Elspeth finally drifted dreamily back through the gates of Companion's Field, everything, from room assignment to having her belongings transferred, had been taken care of for her.

And toward day's end it occurred to Talia that it behooved her to take dinner with the Court rather than the Collegium. The Queen might make dinner the occasion for the formal announcement of choice of Heir.

She finished setting up Elspeth's class schedule with Dean Elcarth, and sprinted to her quarters and up the stairs as fast as her sore knees would permit. After a quick wash, she rummaged in the wooden wardrobe, cursing as she bumped her head against one of the doors. After making what she hoped was an appropriate selection, she dressed hastily in one of the velvet outfits. With one hand brushing her hair, half-skipping as she wedged her feet into the soft slippers that went with it, she used the other hand to snatch the appropriate book of protocol from among the others on her still-dusty desk. While wriggling to settle the clothing properly and using both hands to smooth her hair, she reviewed the brief ceremony attendant on the coronation of the Heir. She shot a quick look at herself in the mirror, then took herself off to the Great Hall.

She slipped into her seldom-used seat between Elspeth and the Queen and whispered, "Well?"

"She's going to do it as soon as everyone arrives," Elspeth breathed back. "I think I'm going to die. . . ."

"No you won't," Talia answered in a conspiratorial manner. "You've been doing things like this for ages. Now *I* may die!" Elspeth was relaxing visibly now that Talia was there to share her ordeal.

Talia had only taken meals with the Court a handful of times since she'd arrived at the Collegium, and the Great Hall never ceased to impress her. It was the largest single room in the Palace, its high, vaulted ceiling supported by slender-seeming pillars of ironoak that gleamed golden in the light from the windows and the lamp- and candle-light. There were battle-banners and heraldic pennons that went clear back to the Founding hanging from the rafters. Talia's seat was at the table placed on the dais, which stood at a right angle to the rest of the tables in the Hall. Late sunlight streamed in through the tall, narrow windows that filled the west wall, but the windows to the east were already beginning to darken with the onset of nightfall. The courtiers seated along the tables below her were as colorful as a bed of wildflowers, and formed a pleasing grouping against the panels and tables of golden ironoak.

When the Great Hall was filled, the Queen arose as the stewards called for silence. It would have been possible to hear a feather fall as she began. Every eye in the Hall was riveted on her proud, White-clad figure, with the thin circlet of Royal red gold (it was all she would wear as token of her rank) encircling her raival-leaf golden hair.

"Since the death of my father, we have been without an Heir. I can understand and sympathize with those of you who found this a disquieting and frightening situation. You may rejoice, for all uncertainty is at an end. This day was my daughter Elspeth Chosen by the Companion Gwena, making her a fully eligible candidate for the position of Heir. Rise, daughter."

Elspeth and Talia both rose, Elspeth to stand before her mother, Talia to take the silver coronet of the Heir from the steward holding it. She presented it to the Queen, then retired to her proper position as Queen's Own, behind and slightly to Selenay's right. She was pleased to note that although Elspeth's hands trembled, her voice, as she repeated her vows, was strong and clear. Elspeth caught her eyes and held to Talia's gaze as if to a lifeline.

Elspeth was frightened half to death, despite her lifelong preparation for this moment. She could clearly see Talia's encouraging expression, and the presence of the Queen's Own gave her comfort and courage.

For one panicked moment halfway through her vows, she forgot what her mother had said just the instant before. She felt a flood of gratitude when she noticed Talia's lips moving, and realized that she was mouthing the words Elspeth had just forgotten.

There was more to it than just having a friend at hand, too—with her mental senses sharpened and enhanced by having been Chosen, Elspeth could dimly feel Talia as a solid, comforting presence, like a deeply-rooted tree in a wild windstorm. There would always be shelter for her beneath those branches, and as she repeated the last words of her Oath, she suddenly realized how vital that shelter would be to one who, as ruler, must inevitably face the gales, and more often than not alone. There was also, distinctly, though distantly, the sense that Talia loved her for herself, and as a true friend. And that in itself was a comfort. As she finished the last words and her mother placed the silver circlet on her head, she tried to put all her gratitude to her friend in the smile she gave her.

As the Queen placed the coronet on her daughter's hair, a spontaneous cheer rose that gladdened Talia's heart. Perhaps now the Brat could be forgotten.

But as they resumed their seats and the serving began, the unaccustomed dainties of the Queen's table suddenly lost their appeal as Talia realized that there was yet another ceremony to be endured, one about which she knew nothing. As soon as the powers of the Kingdom could be gathered there must be a great ceremony of fealty in which the Queen's Own would play a significant role. Talia reached blindly for her goblet to moisten a mouth gone dry with panic.

Then she took herself firmly in hand; Kyril and Elcarth, as Seneschal's Herald and Dean of the Collegium, would surely know everything about this occasion—and just as surely would be aware that Talia *didn't*. There was no need to panic. Not yet, anyway.

The meal seemed to be progressing with ponderous slowness. This was Talia's first High Feast—and it seemed incredibly dull. She sighed, and the Queen caught the sound.

"Bored?" she whispered out of the corner of her mouth.

"Oh, no!" Talia replied with a forced smile.

"Liar," the Queen replied with a twinkle. "No one but a moron could avoid being bored by all this. You sit and sit, and smile and smile, till your face and backside are both stiff. Then you sit and smile some more."

"How do you manage this day after day?" Talia asked, trying not to laugh.

"Father taught me a game; Elspeth and I play it now. What are we doing this time, catling?"

"We're back to animals," Elspeth replied, as her mother nodded to an elderly duke in response to some comment he'd mumbled. "You try and decide what animal the courtiers most remind you of. We change each time. Sometimes it's flowers, trees, rocks, landmarks—even weather. This time it's animals, and *he's* a badger."

"Well, if he's a badger, his lady's a watchdog. Look how she raises her hackles whenever he smiles at that pretty serving girl," Talia said.

"Oh, I'd never have thought of *that* one!" Elspeth exclaimed. "You're going to be good at this game!"

They managed to keep straight faces, but it wasn't easy.

Talia sought out Kyril the next day before the thrice-weekly Council meeting to learn that she had three weeks in which to prepare for Elspeth's formal investiture. He and Elcarth pledged to drill her in all she needed to know, from protocol to politics, every day.

The Council meeting in itself was something of an ordeal. She and Elspeth had seats on the far end of the horseshoe-shaped Council table, almost opposite Selenay and the empty place beside her. That empty chair was the seat of the Queen's Own, but Talia could not, under law, assume that place until she had passed her own internship. She and Elspeth had voice on the Council, but no vote. Elspeth's own voting rights were in abeyance until *she* passed internship. The Councilors tended to ignore them because of that lack of voting rights—but not today.

No, today they interrogated both Talia and Elspeth with an ill-concealed eagerness that bordered on greed. How soon did Talia think she'd be out in the field—could the internship be cut back to a year? Or given the importance of her position, and her lack of experience, should it be extended past the normal year-and-a-half? Could Elspeth's education be rushed? What should she be tutored in besides the normal curriculum of the Herald's Collegium? Did *she* feel ready for her new position as Heir? And on and on . . .

From most of the Councilors Talia only received a well-intentioned (if irritating) eagerness to help "the children" (and she cursed—not for the first time—her slight stature that made her seem barely an adolescent). But from others—

Lord Orthallen, one of Selenay's closest advisors (as he had been to her father) regarded both of them with a cool, almost cold, gaze. And Talia felt very like a prime specimen of some unusual beetle on the dissecting table. She got no emotional impressions from him at all; she never had. That was profoundly disturbing for one whose Gift was Empathy—and even more disturbing was the vague feeling that he was not pleased that Elspeth had at last been Chosen.

From Bard Hyron, speaker for the Bardic Circle, she got a distinct feeling that all this was happening far too quickly. And that not enough caution was being exercised. And that *he* didn't quite trust *her.*

Lord Gartheser's feelings were of general displeasure over the whole affair, but she couldn't pinpoint why. There was also a faint overtone of disappointment; he *was* related to Kemoc, one of the three other contenders for the position. Could that be all, though? Or was there something deeper in his motivation?

Lady Wyrist was downright annoyed, but why, Talia couldn't fathom. It might have been simply that she was afraid that Talia would favor her own relations, the Holderkin, who lived in the area Wyrist spoke for. She could hardly know that there was small chance of *that!*

Orthallen was the one who bothered her most, but as the meeting broke up, she knew she would mention this to no one. She had nothing of fact to report; and she and Orthallen had bad blood between them over his treatment (and near-expulsion) of her friend Skif from the Collegium. She knew better than to give Orthallen so powerful a weapon if he *was* an enemy as to seem to be holding a grudge. Instead she smiled sweetly and thanked him for his good wishes. Let him think her an innocent idiot. Meanwhile she would make sure to have one eye on him.

But soon, very soon now, *she* would be gone, on her year-and-a-half internship, and that would take her entirely out of the current intrigues at Court. It would also make it impossible for her to deal with any of it. If Gartheser, Orthallen, or any of the others had deeper schemes, there would be no one near Elspeth who could detect the shadow of the scheming.

She would be gone—and who would watch them then?

CHAPTER 2

T HREE WEEKS TO the investiture. Only three weeks, but they
seemed like three years, at least to Talia.

There was an elaborate ceremony of oaths and bindings to memorize, but that wasn't the worst of it. Talia's main function at this particular rite would be *apparently* to perform the original duties of Heralds,
the duties they had held in the days before Valdemar founded his kingdom, to announce each dignitary by name and all ranks and titles before escorting him or her to the foot of the Throne.

This was, of course, the lesser of her twin functions. In reality the
more important would be using her empathic Gift to assess—and, one
hoped, neutralize—any danger to the Queen and Heir from those
about to come within striking distance of them. The full High Court
ceremonial costumes included a wide variety of instruments of potential mayhem and assassination.

There was one small problem with this; Talia was farmbred, not
highborn. The elaborate tabards of state that a highborn child could
read as easily as a book were little more than bewildering patterns of
gold and embroidery to *her* eyes. And she would be dealing with nobles
who were very touchy over their titles, and apt to take affront if even
the least and littlest were eliminated.

That meant hours closeted in Herald Kyril's office, sitting until her
behind went numb on one of the hard wooden chairs he favored,
memorizing plate after plate from the state book of devices until her

eyes were watering. She fell asleep at night with the wildly colored and imaginative beasts, birds, and plants spinning in mad dances behind her eyes. She woke in the morning with Kyril's voice echoing out of her dreams, inescapably drilling her.

She spent at least another hour of every day in the stuffy Council chamber, with the Councilors engaged in pointless debate about this or that item of protocol for the coming ceremony until she wanted to scream with frustration.

Elspeth, at least, was spared this nonsense; *she* had quite enough on her plate with her new round of Collegium classes and duties. For the next five years or so, once the ceremony was complete, she would be neither more nor less important nor cosseted than any other trainee—within certain limitations. She would still be attending Council sessions once she'd settled in, and certain High Court functions. But these were far more in the nature of duties rather than treats—and were, in fact, things Talia reckoned that Elspeth would really rather have foregone if she'd had any choice in the matter.

When Talia had taken the opportunity to check on her, the girl seemed well-content. She was surely enjoying the new-found bond with her Companion Gwena. Keren had told Talia that every free moment saw the two of them out in the Field together, which was exactly as it should be.

But there was one unsettling oddity about the Council sessions that kept them from sending Talia to sleep—an oddity that, in fact, was contributing to an uneasiness ill-suited to the general festive atmosphere that hovered over Court and Collegium.

Talia was catching Councilors and courtiers alike giving her bewildered, almost fearful glances when they thought she wasn't watching. If it had not happened so frequently, she might have thought she was imagining it, but scarcely a day passed without someone watching her with the same attention they might have given to some outre creature that *might* prove to be dangerous. It troubled her—and she wished more than once for Skif and his talents at spying and subterfuge. But Skif was furlongs away at very best, so she knew she'd have to muddle along beneath the suspicious glances, and hope that whatever rumors were being passed about her (and she had no doubt that they *were* about her) would either be put to rest or come to light where she could confront them.

Another goodly portion of each day she spent helping to train a young Healer, Rynee, who was to substitute for her while she was gone on her internship circuit. Rynee, like Talia, was a mind Healer;

she could never replace Talia, not without being a Herald herself, but she could (and would) try to keep her senses alert for Heralds in stress and distress, and get them somewhat sorted out.

And last, but by no means least, there were exhausting bouts with Alberich, all with the express purpose of getting both Talia and Elspeth prepared for any kind of assassination attempts that might occur.

"I really don't understand why you're doing this," Elspeth said one day, about a week from the date of the ceremony. "After all, I'm the one who's the better fighter." She had been watching from a vantage point well out of the way, sitting cross-legged on one of the benches in the salle, against the wall. Talia was absolutely sodden with sweat, and bruised in more places than she cared to think about—and for a wonder, Alberich wasn't in any better condition than she.

Alberich motioned to Talia that she could rest, and she sagged to the floor where she stood. "Appearances," he said, "partially. I do not wish that any save the Heralds should know how skilled you truly are. That could be the saving of your life, one day. Also it is tradition that crowned heads do not defend themselves; that is the duty of others."

"Unless there's no other choice?"

Alberich nodded.

Elspeth sighed. "I'm beginning to wish I wasn't Heir, now. It doesn't look like I'm going to be allowed to have *any* fun!"

"Catling," Talia panted, "if this is your idea of *fun*—you're welcome to it!"

Elspeth and Alberich exchanged rueful glances that said as plainly as words, *she'll never understand*, and made shrugs so nearly identical that Talia was hard put to keep from laughing.

Finally the day arrived for the long awaited—and dreaded—rite of Elspeth's formal investiture as Heir. The fealty ceremony was scheduled for the evening with a revel to follow. Talia, as usual, was running late.

She dashed from her last drilling session with Kyril to the bathing-room, then up to her tower suite, taking the steps two at a time. She thanked the gods when she got there that one of the servants had had the foresight to lay out her gown and all its accoutrements, else she'd have been later still.

She donned the magnificent silk and velvet creation with trepidation. She'd never worn High Court ceremonials in her life, though she'd helped Elspeth into her own often enough.

She faced the mirror, balancing on one foot while she tied the ribbons to the matching slippers around the ankle of the other.

"Oh, bloody hell," she sighed. She knew what a courtier ought to look like—and she didn't. "Well, it's going to have to do. I just wish . . ."

"You wish what?"

Jeri and Keren rapped on the side of the tower door and poked their heads around the edge of it. Talia groaned; Jeri looked the way she *wished* she looked, gowned and coiffed exquisitely, every chestnut hair neatly twisted into a High Court confection and precisely in place.

"I wish I could look like you—stunning, instead of stunned."

Jeri laughed; to look at her, no one would ever guess this lady was nearly the equal of Alberich in neatly dissecting an opponent with any weapon at hand. "It's all practice, love. Want some help?" Her green eyes sparkled. "I've been doing this sort of nonsense since I was old enough to walk, and mama usually commandeered all the servants in the house to attend *her* preparations, so I had to learn how to do it myself."

"If you can make me look less like a plowboy, I will love you forever!"

"I think," Jeri replied merrily, "that we can manage at least that much."

For the next half hour Talia sat on her bed in nervous anticipation as arcane things happened to her hair and face while Jeri and Keren exchanged mysterious comments. Finally Jeri handed her a mirror.

"Is that *me*?" Talia asked in amazement, staring at the worldly sophisticate in the mirror frame. She could scarcely find a trace of Jeri's handiwork, yet somehow she had added experience and a certain dignity without adding years or subtracting freshness. Replacing her usual disordered tumble of curls was a fashionable creation threaded through with a silver ribbon.

"Do I dare move? Is it all going to come apart?"

"Havens, no!" Jeri laughed. "That's what the ribbon's for, love. It isn't likely to happen this time, praise the Lord, but you know very well what your duty is in an emergency. The Queen's Own is supposed to be able to defend her monarch at swordpoint, then calmly clean her blade on the loser's tunic and go right back to whatever ceremony was taking place. That's why your dress is ankle-length instead of floor-length, has no train, and the sleeves detach with one pull—yes, they do, trust me! I ought to know; I supervised the making of it. It's been a long time since we've had a female Monarch's Own, and nobody knew exactly how to modify High Court gear to suit. At any rate, you could work out now with Alberich without one lock coming loose or losing any part of the costume you didn't want to lose. But don't rub your eyes, or you'll look like you've been beaten." She gathered her things. "We'd better be moving if we don't want to get caught in the mob."

"And you'd better take care of the important part of your costume, childing," Keren warned as they started down the stairs.

Talia had not needed the reminder. The rest of her accessories were already laid out and waiting. A long dagger in a sheath strapped around her waist and along her right thigh that she could reach—as she carefully determined—through a slit in her dress was the first weapon she donned. Then came paired throwing knives in quick-release sheaths for both arms—gifts from Skif, which he had shown her how to use long ago. Even Alberich admitted that Skif had no peer when it came to his chosen weapons. Lastly, were two delicate stilettos furnished with winking, jeweled ornaments that she inserted carefully into Jeri's handiwork.

No Herald was ever without a weapon, especially not the Queen's Own, as Keren had reminded her. The life of more than one Monarch had been saved by just such precautions.

Just as Talia was about to depart, there was a knock at her door. She opened it to find Dean Elcarth standing on her threshold. Towering over him, fair and raven heads side by side, lit by the lantern that cast its light beside her door and looking like living representatives of Day and Night, were Dirk and Kris. Talia had not heard that either of them had returned from the field, and surprise stilled her voice as she stared at the unexpected visitors.

"Neither of these gallants seems to have a lady," the Dean said with mischief in his eyes. "And since you have no escort, I thought of you immediately."

"How thoughtful," Talia said dryly, finally regaining the use of her wits, and knowing there was more to it than that. "I don't suppose you had any other motives, did you?"

"Well, since you *are* interning under Kris, I thought you might like to get acquainted under calmer circumstances than the last time you met."

So Kris *was* to be her counselor. Sherri had been right.

"Calmer?" Talia squeaked. "You call *this* calmer?"

"Relatively speaking."

"Elcarth!" Dirk exclaimed impatiently. "Herald Talia, he's teasing you. He asked us to help you because we know most of the people here on sight, so we can prompt you if you get lost."

"We also know who the possible troublemakers are—not that we expect any problems," Kris continued, a smile warming his sky-blue eyes. "But there's less likely to be any trouble with two great hulking brutes like us standing behind the Queen."

"Oh, bless you!" Talia exclaimed with relief. "I've been worried half to death that I'll say something wrong or announce the wrong person and mortally offend someone." She carefully avoided mentioning assassination attempts, though she knew all four of them were thinking about how useful the pair would be in *that* event.

Kris smiled broadly, and Dirk executed a courtly bow that was saved from absurdity by the twinkle in his eyes as he glanced up at her.

"We are your servants, O fairest of Heralds," he intoned, sounding a great deal like an over-acting player in some truly awful romantic drama.

"Oh, don't be ridiculous." Talia flushed, feeling oddly flattered and yet uncomfortable. "You know very well that Nessa and Sherri make me look like a squirrel, and the last time you saw me, I was passing out at your feet like a silly child and probably looked like leftover porridge. Among friends my name is Talia. *Just* Talia."

The Dean pivoted and trotted down the staircase, seemingly very pleased with himself. Kris chuckled and Dirk grinned; both of them offered her their arms. She accepted both, feeling dwarfed between the two of them. There was barely enough room for all three of them on the stairs.

"Well, you devil, you've done it again," Dirk said to his partner over her head, blinking as they emerged from the half-dark of the staircase into the light of the hall. "I get a scrawny ex-thief with an appetite like a horse for my internee, and look what you get! It's just not fair." He looked down at her from his lofty six-and-a-half feet, and said mournfully to her, "I suppose now that you've gotten a good look at my partner's justifiably famous face, the rest of us don't stand a chance with you."

"I wouldn't go making any bets if I were you," she replied with a hint of an edge to her voice. "I *have* seen him before, you know, and you don't see me falling at his feet worshiping now, do you? My father and brothers were just as handsome. No insult meant to you, Kris, but I've had ample cause to mistrust handsome men. I'd rather you were cross-eyed, or had warts, or something. I'd feel a great deal more comfortable around you if you were a little less than perfect."

Dirk howled with laughter at the nonplussed expression on his friend's face. "That's a new one for you, my old and rare! Rejected by a woman! How's it feel to be in *my* shoes?"

"Odd," Kris replied with good humor. "Distinctly odd. I must say though, I'm rather relieved. I was afraid Elcarth's mind was going, assigning me a female internee. I've only seen you once or twice, remember, and we weren't exchanging much personal information at the time! I thought you might be like Nessa. Around her I start to feel like a hunted stag!" He suddenly looked sheepish. "I have the feeling I may have put my foot in it; I hope you don't mind my being frank."

"Not at all. It's my besetting sin, too."

"Well, you seem unexpectedly sensible. I think we'll do all right together."

"Provided that *I* haven't taken a dislike to *you*." Talia was just a little nettled at his easy assumption that she would fall swift prey to his admittedly charming manner. "Haven't you ever been told not to count your eggs till the hens lay them?"

From the look on Kris' face, that possibility hadn't occurred to him, and he was rather at a loss to deal with it. Dirk didn't help matters by becoming hysterical.

"She's got you there, old boy!" he choked. "Stars be praised, I've lived to see the day when it's *you* that gets put in his place, and not me!"

"Oh, Bright Havens, don't worry about it," Talia said, taking pity on him. "We're both *Heralds*, for pity's sake! We'll manage to get along. It's just for a year and a half. After all, it's not as if somebody were forcing me to *marry* you!"

Kris' expression was indescribable when Talia spoke of being "forced" to marry him as if it were something distasteful.

"I'm fairly sure you didn't insult me, but that certainly didn't sound like a compliment!" he complained forlornly. "I'm beginning to think I prefer Nessa's attitude after all!"

By now they'd had to stop in the middle of the hall, as Dirk was doubled over and tears were streaming down his face. Both of them had to pound on his back in order to help him catch his breath again.

"Holy—Astera—" he gasped. "This is something I never expected to see. Or hear! Whew!" He somehow managed to look both contrite and satisfied at the same time. "Forgive me, partner. It's just that seeing *you* as the rejected one for a change—you should have seen your own face!—you looked like you'd swallowed a live toad!"

"Which means that nothing worse can happen to him for the rest of the week. Now look, none of this is getting us to the ceremony," Talia pointed out, "and we're already running late."

"She's right again," Dirk said, taking her arm.

"What do you mean, 'again'?" Kris asked suspiciously, as they hurried to the Great Hall.

Fortunately, their arrival at the door of the Great Hall prevented his having to answer that question.

Dirk had been having a little trouble sorting out some very odd feelings from the moment that Talia had answered her door. The last time he'd seen the Queen's Own, she'd fainted from total exhaustion practically at his feet, after having undergone a considerable mental and emotional ordeal. He had learned afterward that she had experienced at firsthand the murder of the Herald-Courier Ylsa, and saved Ylsa's lifemate Keren from death-willing herself in shock. Then, without a pause for rest, she had mentally guided him and his partner to the spot where Ylsa had been slain. This slight, fragile-seeming woman-child had aroused all of his protective instincts as well as his admiration for her raw courage. He'd carried her up to her room himself, and made certain she was safely tucked into her bed; then left medicinal tea ready for her to brew to counteract the inevitable reaction-headache she'd have when she woke. He'd known at the time she'd exhausted all her resources—when he heard the whole story later in the day he'd been flabbergasted at her courage and endurance.

And she was so very frail-looking; it was easy to feel protective about her, even though her actions gave the lie to that frail appearance. At least, he'd thought at the time that it was only his protective instincts that she aroused. But the sight of her this time had seemed to stir something a bit more complicated than that—something he wasn't entirely sure he wanted to acknowledge. So he defused the situation as best he could, by clowning with Kris. But even while he was bent double with laughter, there was a vague disquiet in the back of his mind, as though his subconscious was trying to warn him that he wasn't going to be able to delay acknowledgment for long.

Talia was refusing to allow her nerves to show, but they were certainly affecting her despite her best efforts. She was rather guiltily hoping Kris had realized that she had been taking some of that nervousness out on him.

The Great Hall, tables cleared away, and benches placed along the walls, with every candle and lantern lit, gleamed like a box made of gold. The courtiers and notables were dressed in their finest array, jewels and silver and gold ornaments catching the light and throwing it back so that the assemblage sparkled like the contents of a highborn dame's jewelbox. Prominent among the gilded nobles were the bright scarlet of Bards, the emerald green of Healers, the bright blue of the uniforms of high-ranking officers of the Guard and Army, and the brilliant white of Heralds. Each of those to be presented wore over his or her finery the stiff tabard, heavy with embroidery, that marked a family or Guild association. The men and women of the Guards standing duty in their sober midnight-blue and silver ringed the walls, a dark frame for the rest.

The Queen's Own and her escorts assumed their places behind the thrones, Talia in her place behind and to Selenay's right, Kris and Dirk behind and to either side of her. Talia had a feeling that the three of them made a very impressive and reassuring sight to those who had come here fearing to see weakness.

But there was uneasiness, too—the uneasiness she had been sensing for the past three weeks, magnified. And she could not, for the life of her, fathom the reason.

The ceremony began; Talia determined to ignore what she could not change, and did her best to appear somehow both harmless and competent. She wasn't sure just how successful she was, but some of the background of general nervousness *did* seem to decrease after a while.

She tried to will some confidence into the young Heir, who was beginning to wilt under the strain. She tried to catch her eyes and give her a reassuring smile, but Elspeth's expression was tight and nervous, and her eyes were beginning to glaze.

For Elspeth was not faring as well as Talia. The ceremony demanded that she respond to each of her new liegemen with some sort of personalized speech, and about halfway through she began running out of things to say.

Kris was the first, with his musician's ear for cadence, to notice her stumbling and hesitating over her speeches. As the next worthy was being brought before her, he whispered, "His son's just presented him with his first grandchild."

Elspeth cast him a look of undying gratitude as she moved to receive this oath. As the gouty lord rose with difficulty from his knees, she congratulated him on the blessed event. The gentleman's expression as he was escorted away was compounded of equal parts of startlement and pleasure, for he'd no notion that anyone knew other than the immediate members of his family.

Elspeth decided at that moment that Kris was fully qualified for elevation to sainthood, and beamed quickly at both of the Heralds before the next notable arrived.

Dirk caught on immediately and supplied the information for the next. Kris countered with intelligence for the following two. Elspeth began to sparkle under the gratified looks of the courtiers, reviving as quickly as she'd wilted, and Kris and Dirk began to keep score in the impromptu contest. The Queen seemed to find it all she could do to keep a straight face.

Finally, the last dignitary made his oath, and all three Heralds took their places with the Circle to swear their oaths en masse. The Healer's and Bardic Circles followed them, then the various clerics and priests made vows on behalf of their orders and devotees.

And the long ceremony was at last complete—without a mishap.

The Queen's party retired from the dais, leaving it to instrumentalists of the Bardic Circle, who immediately struck up a dance melody.

Talia joined Elspeth in the window-alcove furnished with velvet-padded benches that was reserved for the Queen's entourage. "What were you three up to?" she asked curiously. "I was too far away to hear any of it, but you certainly seemed to be having a good time!"

"These two Heralds that came as your escort—they were wonderful!" Elspeth bubbled. "I ran out of things to say, and they told me exactly what I needed to know. Not big things, but what was most important to them right now—the lords and so forth, I mean. Then they started making a contest out of it, and that was what was so funny, them arguing back and forth about how much something was 'worth' in points. Mother could hardly keep from laughing."

"I can imagine." Talia grinned. "Who won?"

"I did," Kris said from behind her.

"You wouldn't have if I'd thought of the sheep first," Dirk retorted.

"Sheep?" Talia said inquisitively. "Sheep? Do I want to know about this?"

Dirk snickered, and Kris glared at him.

"It's perfectly harmless," Kris answered, with just a hint of irritation. "When Lady Fiona's husband died, she and Guildmistress Arawell started a joint project to boost the fortunes of her family and Arawell's branch of the Weaver's Guild. They imported some sheep with an especially soft and fine fleece much like lambswool from outKingdom—

quite far south. They've finally succeeded in adapting them to our harsher winters; the spring lambing more than doubled their flock, and it seems that everyone is going to want stock or fabric of the wool."

"That's not what we came here for," Dirk said firmly. "Sheep and discussions of animal husbandry—keep your filthy thoughts to yourself, partner!—"

"*My* filthy thoughts? Who was the one doing all the chortling a few minutes ago?"

"—do not belong at a revel. I claim the first dance with you, Talia, by virtue of the fact that my partner is going to have you all to himself for a year and more."

"And since that leaves me partnerless," Kris added, "I would very much like to claim our newest Chosen for the same purpose."

"Mother?" Elspeth looked pleadingly at the Queen. Kris' stunning good looks had made more than a slight impression on her, and that he should want to dance with her was a distinct thrill.

"My dear, this is *your* celebration. If you want to ride your Companion around the Great Hall, you could even do that—provided you're willing to face the Seneschal's wrath when he sees the hoofmarks on his precious wood floor."

Without waiting for further permission, Kris swept the girl into the dance.

Dirk lifted an inquisitive eyebrow at Talia.

"Oh, no," Talia laughed. "You don't know what you're asking. I dance like a plowboy, I have no sense of rhythm, and I ruin my partner's feet."

"Nonsense," Dirk replied, shaking unruly blond hair out of his eyes. "You just never had the right partner."

"Which is you? And I thought Kris was vain!"

"My dear Talia," he countered, swinging her onto the floor, "truth can hardly be considered in the same light as vanity. I have it on the best authority that my dancing more than compensates for my looks."

Shortly, Talia was forced to admit that he was absolutely correct. For the first time in her experience, she began to enjoy a dance—it was almost magical, the way they seemed to move together. Dirk didn't seem displeased by her performance either, as he yielded her to other partners with extreme reluctance.

Kris, on the other hand, despite yearning glances from nearly every young woman present, danced only with women far older than himself, or with Elspeth or Talia.

"I hope you don't mind being used like this," he said contritely, after the sixth or seventh dance.

"Used?" she replied, puzzled.

"As a shield. I'm dancing with you to keep from being devoured by *them*." He nodded toward a group of Court beauties languishing in his direction. "I can't dance just with beldames, Elspeth has to take other partners, and the only Heralds I can trust not to try to carry me off are Keren, Sheri, and you. And those other two don't dance."

"It's nice to know I'm wanted," she laughed up at him.

"Did I just put my foot in it again?"

"No, not really. And I don't mind being 'used.' After all, by now they all know we're assigned together, so they'll assume we're getting acquainted. You can avoid people without anyone's feelings being hurt."

"You *do* understand," he said, relieved. "I hate to hurt anyone's feelings, but they all seem to think if they just throw themselves at me hard enough, I'll *have* to take one of them—short-term, long-term, it doesn't seem to matter. Nobody ever seems to wonder what *I* want."

"Well, what *do* you want?" Talia asked.

"The Collegium," he replied to Talia's amazement. "That's where most of my time and energy go—and where I want them to go. I do a lot of studying on my own: history, administration, law. I'd like to be Elcarth's replacement as Dean and Historian when he retires, and that takes a lot of preparation. I don't have much free time—certainly none to spend on games of courtly love. Or shepherd-in-the-hay."

Talia looked at him with new respect. "That's marvelous; Elcarth's job is the hardest and most thankless I can think of. In some ways, it's even worse than mine. You might just be the one to handle it. I don't think you can serve the Collegium and still give another person a—a—"

"The amount of attention a decent pairing needs," he finished for her. "Thank you—do you know, you're the first person besides Dirk who didn't think I was out of my mind?"

"But what would you do if you *did* find someone you wanted?"

"I don't know—except that it isn't likely to happen. Face it, Talia, Heralds seldom form permanent attachments to anyone or anything. We're friends, always, and sometimes things get more intense than that, but it doesn't last for long. Maybe it's because our hearts are given first to our Companions, then to our duty—and I guess there aren't too many of us with hearts big enough for a third love. Non-Heralds don't seem to be able to grasp that. Not too many Heralds do, for that matter. But look around you—Sherrill and Keren are the *only* life-bonded couple I can think of, and I wouldn't be willing to settle for less than what they've got. Which is why I'm hiding behind you."

"You can't hide forever."

"I don't have to," he replied whimsically. "Just till the end of the revel. After that, I'll be safely in the field, accompanied solely by the only person I've met who thinks I'd be better off cross-eyed and covered with warts!"

Dirk reclaimed her after that; it was during that dance that she noticed that the number of white-clad bodies was rapidly diminishing. "Where's everyone gone?" she asked him, puzzled.

"It's not often that we get this many of us together at one time," he replied, "so as people get tired of dancing, we slip off to our own private party. Want to go?"

"Bright Havens, yes!" she replied with enthusiasm.

"Let me catch Kris' eye." He moved them closer to where Kris was dancing with a spritely grandmother, and tilted an eyebrow toward the door. When Kris nodded, Dirk arranged for them to end the dance next to the exit as the musicians played the final phrase.

Kris joined them after escorting his partner to her seat. "I like that one; she kept threatening to take me home, feed me 'proper'—and then 'train me right,' and I know she wasn't talking about dancing or manners!" He laughed quietly. "I take it Talia's ready to go? I am."

"Good, then we're all agreed," Dirk replied. "Talia, go get changed into something comfortable, find something to sit on, and an old cloak in case we end up outside. If you play any instruments, bring them, too—then meet us in the Library."

"This is like the littles' game of 'Spy'!" she giggled.

"You're not far wrong," Kris answered. "We go to great lengths to keep these parties private. Now hurry, or we'll leave without you!"

She gathered her skirts in both hands and ran lightly down the halls of the Palace. When she reached her tower, she again took the steps two at a time. She paused only long enough in her room to light a lamp before unlacing her dress and sliding out of it. Even though she was in a hurry she hung it up with care—there was no use in ruining it with creases. She changed into the first things that came to hand. She freed her hair from the ribbon, letting it tumble around her face while she carefully stored My Lady in her case, and stuck her shepherd's pipe in her belt. She slung the carrying strap of the harpcase over her shoulder, an old, worn wool cloak from her trainee days over all, picked up one of her cushions, and was ready to go.

Well, almost. Remembering what Jeri had said about the cosmetics, she stopped at the bathing room at the base of the tower for a quick wash, then ran for the Library.

When she swung open the door to the Library, she discovered that the other two had beaten her there—but then, they probably didn't have several flights of stairs to climb.

Kris was all in black, and looking too poetic for words. Dirk was in mismatched bluish grays that looked rather as if he'd just left them in a heap when he'd picked up his clean laundry (which in fact, was probably the case). Both of them looked up at the sound of the door opening.

"Talia! God—you don't dawdle like my sisters do," Dirk greeted her. "Come over here, and we'll let you in on the secret."

Talia crossed the room to where they were standing, the first study cubicle.

"The first to leave always meet here to decide where we're going to convene," Dirk explained, "and they leave something telling the rest of us where that is. In this case—it's this."

He showed her a book left on the table—on harness-making.

"Let me guess," Talia said. "The stable?"

"Close. The tackshed in Companion's Field; see, it's open at the chapter on the special bridles we use," Kris explained. "Last time they had to leave a rock on top of a copy of a religious text; we used the half-finished temple down near the river because we'd met too often around here. A bit cold for my liking, though I'm told those currently keeping company enjoyed keeping each other warm."

Talia smothered giggles as they slipped outside.

The windows of the tackshed had been tightly shuttered so that no light leaked out to betray the revelry within. Both fireplaces had been lighted against the slight chill in the air and as the main source of illumination. The three of them slipped in as quietly as possible to avoid disturbing the entertainment in progress—a tale being told with some skill by a middle-aged Herald whose twin streaks of gray, one at each temple, stood out startlingly in the firelight.

"It'll be quiet tonight," Kris whispered in Talia's ear. "Probably because the Palace revel turned into such a romp. Our revels tend to be the opposite of the official ones."

Heralds were sprawled over the floor of the tackshed in various comfortable poses, all giving rapt attention to the storyteller. There seemed to be close to seventy of them; the most Talia had ever seen together at one time. Apparently every Herald within riding distance

had arranged to be here for the fealty ceremony. The storyteller concluded his tale to the sighs of satisfaction of those around him. Then,
with the spell of the story gone, many of them leaped up to greet the
newcomers, hugging the two men or grasping their hands with warm
and heart-felt affection. Since they were uniformly strangers to Talia,
she shrank back shyly into the shadows by the door.

"Whoa, there—slow down, friends!" Dirk chuckled, extricating
himself from the press of greeters. "We've brought someone to meet all
of you."

He searched the shadows, found Talia, and reaching out a long arm,
pulled her fully into the light. "You all know we've finally got a true
Queen's Own again—and here she is!"

Before anyone could move to greet her, there was a whoop of joy
from the far side of the room, and a hurtling body bounced across it,
vaulting over several Heralds who laughed, ducked, and protected their
heads with their arms. The leaper reached Talia and picked her up
bodily, lifting her high into the air, and setting her down with an enthusiastic kiss.

"Skif?" she gasped.

"Every inch of me!" Skif crowed.

"B-but—you're so *tall*!" When he'd gotten his Whites, Skif hadn't
topped her by more than an inch or two. Now he could easily challenge Dirk's height.

"I guess something in the air of the south makes things grow, 'cause
I sure did last year," Skif chuckled. "Ask Dirk—he was my counselor."

"Grow? Bright Stars, *grow* is too tame a word!" Dirk groaned. "We
spent half our time keeping him fed; he ate more than our mules!"

"You've done pretty well yourself, I'd say," Skif went on, pointedly
ignoring Dirk. "You looked fine up there. Made us all damn proud."

Talia blushed, glad it wouldn't show in the dim light. "I've had a lot
of help," she said, almost apologetically.

"It takes more than a lot of help, and we both know it," he retorted.
"Well, hellfire, this isn't the time or place for talk about work. You
two—you know the rules. Entrance fee!"

Dirk and Kris were laughingly pushed to the center of the room, as
the story teller vacated his place for them. "Anybody bring a harp?"
Kris called. "Mine's still packed; I just got in today."

"I did," Talia volunteered, and eager hands reached out to convey
the harp, still in the case, to Kris.

"Is this—this can't be My Lady, can it?" Kris asked as the firelight
gleamed on the golden wood and the clean, delicate lines. "I wondered

who Jadus had left her to." He ran his fingers reverently across the strings, and they sighed sweetly. "She's in perfect tune, Talia. You've been caring for her as she deserves."

Without waiting for an answer, he began playing an old lullaby. Jadus had been a better player, but Kris was surprisingly good for an amateur, and much better than Talia. He made an incredibly beautiful picture, with the golden wood gleaming against his black tunic, and his raven head bent in concentration over the strings. He was almost as much a pleasure to watch as to listen to.

"Any requests?" he asked when he'd finished.

"'Sun and Shadow,'" several people called out at once.

"All right," Dirk replied, "but I want a volunteer to sing Shadow-dancer. The last time I did it, I was hoarse for a month."

"I could," Talia heard herself saying, to her surprise.

"You?" Dirk seemed both pleased and equally surprised. "You're full of amazing things, aren't you?" He made room beside himself, and Talia picked her way across the crowded floor, to sit shyly in the shadow he cast in the firelight.

"Sun and Shadow" told of the meeting of two of the earliest Heralds, Rothas Sunsinger and Lythe Shadowdancer; long before they were ever Chosen and while their lives still remained tangled by strange curses. It was a duet for male and female voice, though Dirk had often sung it all himself. It was one of those odd songs that either made you hold your breath or bored you to tears, depending on how it was sung. Dirk wondered which it would be tonight.

As Talia began her verse in answer to his, Dirk stopped wondering. There was no doubt who'd trained her—the deft phrasing that made the most of her delicate, slightly breathy voice showed Jadus' touch as clearly as the harp he'd left her. But she sang with something more than just her mind and voice, something the finest training couldn't impart. This was going to be one of the magic times.

Dirk surrendered himself to the song, little guessing that he was surpassing his own best this night as well. Kris knew, as he accompanied them—and he wished there was a way to capture the moment for all time.

The spontaneous applause that shook the rafters startled both Dirk and Talia out of the spell the music had wrapped them in. Dirk smiled with more than usual warmth at the tiny female half-hiding in his shadow, and felt his smile returned.

"Well, we've paid *our* forfeit," Kris said, cutting short the demands for more. "It's somebody else's turn now."

"That's not fair," a voice from the back complained. "How could any of us possibly follow *that?*"

Someone did, of course, by changing the mood rather than ruining it by trying to sustain it. A tall, bony fellow borrowed Talia's pipe to play a lively jig, while two men and a woman bounded into the center to dance to it. That seemed to decide everyone on a dancing-set; Talia reclaimed her pipe to join Kris, someone with a gittern, and Jeri on tambour in a series of very lively round dances of the village festival variety. As these were both strenuous and of an accelerated tempo, those who had felt lively enough to dance were soon exhausted and ready to become an audience again.

Those who didn't feel up to entertaining paid their "entrance fee" in food and drink; Talia saw a good many small casks of wine, cider, and ale ranged along the walls, and with them, baskets of fruit, sausages, or bread and cheese. Stray mugs and odd cups were always accumulating in the tackshed, especially during the hot summer months when Heralds and students were likely to need a draught of cool water from the well that supplied the Companions' needs at this end of the Field. These handy receptacles were filled and refilled and passed from hand to hand with a gay disregard for the possibility of colds or fever being passed with the drink. Like Talia, most of the Heralds had brought cushions from their quarters; these and their saddles and packs were piled into comfortable lounges that might be shared or not. A few murmurs from some of the darker corners made Talia hastily avert her eyes and close her ears, and she recalled Dirk's earlier comments about Heralds "keeping each other warm." From time to time some of these rose from the dark, and either left for more private surroundings or rejoined those by the two fires. And over all was an atmosphere of—belonging. There was no one here that was not cared for and welcomed by all the rest. It was Talia's first exposure to a gathering of her fellows under pleasant circumstances, and she gradually realized that the feeling of oneness extended outside the walls as well—to the Companions in the Field, and beyond that, to those who could not be present this night. Small wonder, with such a warmth of brotherhood to bask in, that the Heralds had deserted the main revelry for this more intimate celebration of their joy at the Choosing of the Heir. It was enough to make her forget the strange uneasiness that had been shadowing her the past three weeks.

As soon as she could manage it, Talia retrieved Skif from a knot of year-mates who seemed bent on emptying a particular cask by themselves.

"Let's go up to the loft," she said, after scanning that perch and ascertaining that none of the amorous had chosen it themselves. "I don't want to disturb anybody, but I don't want to leave, either."

The "loft" was little more than a narrow balcony that ran the length of one side and gave access to storage places in the rafters. Talia noticed immediately that Skif—*very* uncharacteristically—kept to the wall on the stairs, and put his back against it when they reached the loft itself.

"Lord and Lady, it's good to see you!" he exclaimed softly, giving her a repeat of his earlier hug. "We weren't sure we'd make it back in time. In fact, we left all the baggage and the mules back at a Resupply Station; took only what Cymry and Ahrodie could carry besides ourselves. I've missed you, little sister. The letters helped, but I'd rather have been able to talk with you, especially—"

Talia could sense him fighting a surge of what could only be fear.

"Especially?"

"—after—the accident."

She moved closer to him, resting both her hands on his. She didn't have to see him to know he was pale and white-knuckled. "Tell me."

"I—can't."

She lowered her shields; he was spiky inside with phobic fears: of storms, of entrapment, and most of all, of falling. In the state he was in now, she doubted he'd be able to look out a second-story window without exerting iron control—and this from the young man who'd led her on a scramble across the face of the second story of the Palace itself, one dark night!

"Remember me? What I am? Just start at the beginning; take it slowly. I'll help you face it down."

He swallowed. "It—it started with a storm; we were caught out on the trail in the hills. Hills, ha! More like mountains! Gods, it was dark; rain was pouring down so hard I couldn't even see Cymry's ears. Dirk had point, the mules were next, I was tail—it was supposed to be the safest place. We were more or less feeling our way along; sheer rock on one side of us, ravine on the other."

Talia had herself in half-trance, carefully extending herself into his mind. He was fighting down his fear as he spoke and beginning to lose to it.

"The trail just—crumbled, right under Cymry's hooves. We fell; there wasn't even time to yell for help."

Gently, Talia touched the fear, took it into herself, and began working away at it. It was like knife-edged flint, all points and slicing surfaces. As softly as flowing water, and as inexorably, she began wearing away at it, dulling it, muting it.

"We ended up wedged halfway down. Cymry was stunned; I'd broken my arm and most of my ribs, I think; I don't remember much. It hurt too much to think, and where I was stuck, there was a flood of water pouring down the wall like a young waterfall. You know I don't Mindspeak too well, and Dirk's Gift isn't Mindspeech anyway; I couldn't get hold of myself enough to call for help that way, and it was impossible to be heard over the storm."

He was shaking like a reed in a windstorm; she put her arm around his shoulders; supplying a physical comfort as well as the mental. "But Dirk found you," she pointed out.

"The Gods alone know how; he had no reason to think we were still alive." The tension was rapidly draining out of him as Talia shielded him from the phobic memories; not enough to make him forget, but enough to make them less real, less obsessive. "He got ropes around both of us and anchored us where we were; used something to divert the water away from me, and stayed with us, hanging on with his teeth and toenails, until the storm was over. Then he got blankets over us and sent Ahrodie off for help while he got me back up to the trail. I don't remember that part at all; I must have blacked out from the pain." His voice sounded less strained.

The fear was nearly conquered now; time to diffuse the rest of it. "You must have looked like a drowned rat," she replied with a hint of chuckle. "I know you have a fetish for cleanliness, but don't you think that was overdoing it a bit?"

He stared at her in surprise, then began to laugh, shakily. The laughter was half tears as the last of the tension was released. Hysterics—yes, but long needed.

She held him quietly until the worst passed, and he could see past the tears to her face, childlike in the half-dark.

The paralysis of fear that Skif had lived with on a daily basis for the past several months had all but choked the voice out of him as he tried to tell Talia what had happened that awful night. He'd suffered nightmare replays of the incident at least one night a week ever since. It had taken all of his control to repeat it to her—at least at first. But then, gradually, the words had begun to flow more freely; the fear had slowly loosed its grip on him. As he neared the end of his narrative, he began to realize what Talia had done.

It was gratitude as much as release that shook the tears from him then.

"You—you did it to me, didn't you—fixed me like you did with Vostel and the rest of them—?"

"Mm-hm." She nodded, touching his hair in the dark. "I didn't think you'd mind."

"No more nightmares?"

"No more nightmares, big brother. You won't find yourself wanting to hide in a closet during storms anymore, and you'll be able to look down over cliffs again. In fact, you'll even be able to tell the story in a week or two without shaking like a day-old chick, and it should make a good tale to earn the sympathy of a pretty lady with!"

"You—you're unbelievable," he said at last, holding her tightly.

"So are you, to have been coping with all that fear all this time, and not letting it get the best of you."

They sat that way for some time, before the murmur of voices below them recalled them to their surroundings.

"Hellfire! This is supposed to be a party, and you're supposed to be enjoying it," Skif said.

"I am, now that you're all right." She rose to her feet, and gave him a hand up. "Well, I'm going back to the singing, and it seems to me that your year-mate Mavry is looking a bit lonely."

"Hm. So she is," he replied, peering down into the lighted area. "Think I'll go keep her company. And—heart-sister—"

"No thanks needed, love."

He kissed her forehead by way of reply, then skipped lightly down the stairs of the loft and took himself off to the other side of the room, where Mavry willingly made a space for him beside her.

Talia rejoined the musicians just in time for Dirk to claim her for another duet. She had to plead a dry throat before they'd let someone else take the floor.

She didn't notice the passing of time until she caught herself yawning hard enough to split her head in half. When she tried to reckon up how much time had passed, she was shocked.

Thinking she surely *must* be mistaken, she slipped over to the door to look out to the east. Sure enough, there on the horizon was the first hint of false dawn. True dawn was less than an hour away.

She collected her things, feeling suddenly ready to collapse. Dirk, half-propped on a backrest of saddle and several old saddleblankets, seemed to be asleep as she slipped past him, but he cracked an eyelid open as she tried to ease herself out.

"Giving up?" he asked softly.

She nodded, stifling another yawn with the back of her hand.

"Enjoy yourself?" At her enthusiastic nod, he smiled, another of those wonderful warm smiles that seemed to embrace her and close everything and everyone else outside of it. "I'll be heading back to my own bed before long. About this time things start to break up on their own. And don't worry about being expected on duty today. No one will be up to notice before noon at the earliest—look over there." He cocked an eyebrow to his left. Talia was astonished to see the Queen, dressed in old, worn leathers, sharing a cloak and resting her head in easy intimacy on the shoulder of the middle-aged storyteller. And not far from her sat Alberich, finishing the last of a wineskin with Keren, Sherrill, and Jeri.

"How did Selenay and Alberich get in without my noticing?" Talia asked him.

"Easy. You were singing at the time. See, though? You won't be missed. Have a good long sleep—and pleasant dreams, Talia."

"And to you, Dirk," she said.

"They will be." He chuckled, and closed his eyes again. "They most assuredly will be."

CHAPTER 3

TALIA DIDN'T USUALLY sleep long or heavily. Perhaps the cause was that she'd drunk more wine than usual, or perhaps it was just the incredibly late hour at which she'd sought her bed. At any rate, it took having the sun shine directly into her eyes to wake her the next morning.

Since the window of her bedroom faced the east, she'd positioned her bed with the headboard right under the windowsill. That way she always had the fresh air, and her face should remain out of the sunlight until well after the time she normally rose. No matter how cold the winter, she'd never been able to bear the slight claustrophobia that closed shutters induced in her, so the glazed windows themselves and the thin fabric curtaining them were all that stood between her eyes and the sun's rays, and the windows themselves were open, with the curtains moving slightly in the breeze.

As she squinted groggily through the glare, she realized that it must be nearly noon, and as if to confirm this, the noon warning bell at the Collegium sounded clearly through her open window.

Well, the wine she'd indulged in last night had given her a slight headache. She muttered something to herself about fools and lack of judgment and pulled her pillow over her head, tempted to go right back to sleep again. But a nagging sense of duty, (and, more urgently, a need to use the privy) denied her further sloth.

She'd been so tired last night—this morning?—that all she'd been able to do was peel off her clothing, leave it in a heap on the floor, and fall into bed. Now that she felt a little more awake, her skin crawled with the need for a bath. Her hair itched. Her mouth didn't bear thinking about. She groaned. It was definitely time to get up.

She sighed, levered herself out of bed, and set about getting herself back into working condition.

Sitting on the edge of the bed, she rubbed her eyes until they cooperated by focusing properly, then reached for the robe hanging on one of the posts at the foot of her bed. She wrapped it about herself, then collected the clothing on the floor. The soiled clothing went into a hamper; the servant who tended to the Heralds in this section of the wing collected it and sent it to the laundry as part of her duties—and *that* was a luxury that was going to take some getting used to! She'd been lowborn and at the bottom of her Holderkin family's pecking order as a child, and once at the Collegium had fallen naturally in with the tradition that trainees tended to their own needs and shared the common chores. She had become habituated to doing the serving, and not to being waited on herself!

The warmth of the smooth wood beneath her feet was very comforting, and she decided then that she would *not* have any floor coverings in her new quarters. She liked the way the sunwarmed boards felt to bare feet, and she liked the way the wood glowed when the sun touched it.

She rummaged in her wardrobe, and draped a new, clean uniform over one arm, then bundled her bathing things into the other arm and headed for the door.

The bathing-room shared by the other tower occupants was on the bottom floor; that was another disadvantage of having selected a tower room. It was a long walk, and seemed longer for the thinking about it. Talia was the only current occupant though. The other rooms were either unclaimed or their owners were out on circuit. So at least there wasn't going to be any competition for the facilities.

Talia saw a note waiting for her on her door as soon as she opened it. Rubbing her temple in response to the ache behind her eyes, she wondered who could be the early riser after the revelry of the previous night. She took it down and began to skim through it as she headed down the stairs. What she read caused her to stop dead and reread it thoroughly.

It was from Kyril.

I realize this is notice so short as to be nonexistent, he wrote, *but we've had an emergency since last night. The Herald currently riding one of the Northern Border Sectors has had an accident, and we have no one free who knows anything about the area to cover it. Dirk can't—he's already assigned to another Border Sector that needs a Borderbred Herald too badly to reassign him elsewhere. The closest we can come is this—since Dirk is a native of that area, Kris has visited up there fairly often; and you're of Borderer upbringing. Since you haven't been assigned a circuit yet, it seemed to me that assigning it to you as your internship with Kris would solve our problems very neatly. However, this means that you two will have to start as soon as we can get you on the road north; tomorrow, I hope. Please report to me right after the noon meal—or as soon as you read this note!—for a briefing and some final information.*

Her first thought was an irreverent and irrelevant one. She *knew* Kyril hadn't left the revel before her—how *could* he have been awake and ready to handle crises so blasted early in the morning after? Her next was more to the point. Tomorrow! She hadn't expected assignment with so little warning. There wasn't any time to waste; she ran downstairs to the bathing-room. The last thing she wanted to do was give Kyril an impression of carelessness or incompetence.

A good hot bath did a great deal to revitalize her; a dose of willowbark tea took care of the ache in her head. She couldn't do much for the half-cloudy feeling of her mind, but she hoped that being aware that she wasn't quite at her best would compensate for that. Rather than take the time for a full meal she begged cheese, bread, and fruit from Mero. She was far too keyed up to eat much, anyway. This would be the first time that she would meet with Kyril as an equal; up until now, even though she had her Whites, it had still been very much a teacher-student relationship.

She took a few moments of precious time to consult with Rolan before seeking Kyril. It was frustrating not to be able to speak with him in words—but simply Mindtouching with him gave her an added measure of calmness. He reassured her that Kyril would never have expected her to report any earlier than this, and prevented her from changing at the last minute into one of her formal uniforms. And beneath it all was the solidity of knowing that he stood ready to help her if she truly found herself out of her depth on this assignment. Feeling a good bit more confident, she skipped down the tower steps and entered the Palace proper.

A few moments later she had made her way to the administrative area. She paused outside the door of the Records Room—which served as Kyril's office—for a moment to order her mind and calm herself. She pulled the doeskin tunic straight, smoothed her hair; took a deep breath, knocked once and entered.

The Records Room was as neat as Dean Elcarth's office was cluttered. Sun streamed in through the two windows that looked out into the gardens on the west side of the building. Both of them were wide open, and flower-scent wafted in through them. The room was crammed as full of bookshelves as it was possible to be. Kyril's desk stood just under one of the two windows, to take full advantage of the light. Kyril himself was leaning in the window frame, absently watching courtiers stroll in the gardens, and obviously waiting for her. She noticed something anomalous on his desk as he turned from the window to greet her; a quiverful of white arrows.

"Sir?" she said softly; and he turned to smile greeting at her.

Kyril was pleased to see that Talia was looking alert and ready for practically anything. In the past few weeks of working with her, he had come to truly believe all that her Collegium teachers had claimed for her. The Queen's Own was always an outstanding person among Heralds, but Talia bid fair to be outstanding among the ranks of her own kind. He could not for a moment fathom why her reputation, even among her fellow Heralds, was one of being a sweet, but somewhat simple creature. He wasn't altogether certain that *he* would have been able to manage the feat of memorizing all the Kingdom's familial devices and titles in the three weeks she'd taken. Perhaps it was because she was so shy, even yet, and seldom spoke without first being spoken to. Perhaps it was because of her ability with children in general, and the Heir in particular—a strong maternal instinct was not necessarily coupled in anyone's mind with a high intellectual level.

Then again, there weren't too many even among the Heralds who had been her teachers who had seen the *real* Talia. She had not allowed very many of them to come within arm's length, as it were. Kyril was just sorry he had had so little time for her; and he sometimes worried a little about that strange Gift of hers. Empathy that strong—and having seen her exert herself, he *knew* it was very strong—was far more the Gift of Healers. He had been relieved when she'd begun spending so much time with the Healers; *they* would know how to train her properly, if anybody would. If he had only had the time—if Ylsa hadn't been killed—

But Talia seemed to have everything perfectly under control, and if even her own peers tended to underestimate her, that surely wasn't going to harm her any.

Perhaps, though, that tendency to dismiss her lightly was not altogether a bad thing. Kyril had been dealing with Court and Council on a daily basis for something like twenty years, and being underestimated could be a potent and very useful weapon. People might not see past the guileless eyes, and tend to let their tongues run on longer leads in her presence. No, that reputation of hers might well be a very *good* thing for all of them. Certainly the disturbing rumors he'd heard lately about her would not survive much longer if people began comparing the tales of machinations with her reputation as a sweet and uncomplicated innocent.

"Sit, sit." He waved at a chair, taking one himself. "You look none the worse for your late night. I remember *my* first Herald's revel; I thought my hangover was going to last for the next week! I trust you enjoyed yourself." He smiled again as she nodded shyly. "It's the first chance I had to hear you sing. Jadus used to make us all curious, boasting about your abilities. He was certainly right about you! Last night—to tell the truth, I've heard Bards that didn't give performances that moving. You're as good as Jadus claimed, maybe better." She blushed, and he chuckled. "Well, that's neither here nor there. I am very sorry about all the hurry, but we don't like to leave Border Sectors without a Herald for very long; in this case, it's not that there's potential for trouble, but that the people of the Sector feel isolated enough as it is, particularly in winter. They need to know that they're as important to the life of this Kingdom as the capital Sector itself." He regarded her steadily; her answer to his speech would tell him a great deal.

The eyes that met his squarely held faint surprise.

"I—I thought there was always potential for trouble in a Border Sector, sir," Talia ventured. "There're raiders, bandits—lots of problems even if the people themselves never cause them."

"In the general run of things that's true, but the Border in this Sector runs through the Forest of Sorrows, and that's no small protection."

"Then the tale of Vanyel's Curse is true?" Talia was amazed. "Sorrows *does* protect the Kingdom? But . . . how?"

"I wish I knew," Kyril replied, musing half to himself. "They knew things, those old ones, that we've forgotten or lost. They had magic then—real magic, and not our mind-magic; the Truth Spell is just about all we have left of that. Vanyel's Curse is as strong in Sorrows as the day he cast it with his dying breath. Nothing that intends ill to this Kingdom or the people in it lives more than five minutes there; I've seen some of the results with my own eyes. I used to ride Northern myself, back in the days when I was still riding circuits, and not Seneschal's Herald. I've seen bandits impaled on branches as if on thrown spears. I've seen outlaws who starved to death, buried to their waist in rock-hard earth, as if it opened beneath their feet, then closed on them like a trap. What's more—and *this* is what was more frightening than the other things—I've seen barbarian raiders dead without a mark on them, but their faces twisted into an expression of complete and utter terror. I don't know what it was that happened to them, but my guess is that they were truly frightened to death."

Talia shook her head wonderingly. "It's hard to believe. How can a curse know someone's intent?"

"I can't explain it, and neither can any of the old chronicles. It's true nevertheless. You, or I, or any of the people of the Sector can walk that forest totally without fear. A baby could walk through there totally unharmed, because even the forest predators leave humans alone in Sorrows—well, that's the only anomalous thing about the area. The religion is fairly ordinary, the people follow the Lady as Astera of the Stars, and the God as Kernos of the Northern Lights; there's no anti-woman prejudice. In fact, because of Sorrows, we often have females riding circuit there alone. The Herald you're replacing is a woman, in point of fact. You may know her, she was two year-groups ahead of you—Destria."

"Destria? Havens—she isn't badly hurt, is she? What happened?"

"The injury is fairly serious, but not life-threatening. She was trying to rescue half a dozen children during a flood—it's a hard land, Talia, that's the main problem with it—and broke both legs."

"Thank the Goddess for Companions."

"Amen to that; without hers she'd have lain in sleet-born water for hours, probably died of exposure. No, Destria's Sofi managed to get not only her Herald but all the children to safety. All's well there except for the injury. So, that's the gist of the situation, and as I said, I apologize for the short notice. I hope you don't mind too much."

"Not at all, sir," Talia replied. "After all, I had even less notice when I was Chosen, didn't I?"

"Good for you!" Kyril chuckled. "Well, now we come to the reason why I asked you to come here, instead of meeting you for lunch or asking you to meet with both Kris and myself to be told about this. I'm sure you realized a long time ago that there were things we wouldn't teach you until you got your Whites. What I'm about to show you is the best-kept secret of the Heraldic Circle. Haven't you ever wondered why all Heralds are required to become archers?"

"I never thought about it," she confessed, looking puzzled. "It does seem a little odd, now that you mention it. We don't fight with the royal Archers in battle; when we do fight, it's mostly sword or hand-to-hand. We usually don't have to hunt to feed ourselves riding circuit; we carry supplies or depend on the shelters. So why do we have to learn bow?"

"So that you have an excuse to carry arrows wherever you go," Kyril replied. "Not everyone has the kind of mind-reach I have; Lady knows things would be much simpler if they did, because there are plenty of times when the ordinary means of passing information wouldn't do at all. We have to have a foolproof, unambiguous method of passing simple messages, but it has to be impervious to tampering. That's why the Arrow-Code was developed, and thus far no one has broken it. And it all starts with this—"

With skillful and practiced fingers, he carefully broke barbs from the fletchings of a plain white arrow he pulled from the quiver. Talia could see that he was being very precise about which barbs he broke from which fletchings, yet when he was through, it looked as if the arrow had simply been handled too roughly.

"So *that's* why all our arrows are fletched with mud-gannet feathers!" Talia said, enlightened.

"Right. They're nowhere near as suitable as goose, but the barbs are so thick, heavy, and regular it's possible to have the fletching on every arrow we carry absolutely identical—*and* it's possible to literally count barbs for the code. Now this is my pattern. It's registered here, among the secret Records, and even there it's in an encrypted form for added security. Outside of those Records, only four people know it—the Queen, the Seneschal, Elcarth, and Teren, who used to be my partner. Only the Queen, the Seneschal, and Elcarth know how to translate the ciphers we've written the patterns in besides myself. When your internship is over, you'll be given the encryption key as part of what you need to know as Queen's Own. Only two people know every pattern by heart; myself and Elcarth. Now you know why one of the primary prerequisites of both our jobs is a perfect memory!"

Talia smiled, and bit her lip to keep from chuckling.

"This pattern identifies the message carried by the color of the banding on the arrow as coming from me and no one else. Now—" He took a second arrow from the quiver, and broke the barbs in a second pattern. "—this is *your* pattern. When I'm satisfied that you can reproduce it in the dark and behind your back, I'll give you a general idea of the rest of the code."

*   *   *

She was slightly nonplussed to discover that Kyril meant that literally. It took several hours before she could perform that simple task without seeing the arrow she was working on, and without truly thinking about it, with a speed and accuracy that contented him. Meanwhile, the sun crept across Kyril's desk, and her stomach began reminding her that it had been a long time since her last real meal.

Finally Kyril pronounced her competent, and allowed her to give her tired fingers a rest while he explained the remainder of the code to her.

"The rest of it," he told her, "is a bit more complicated, although we've done our best to make the colors mnemonic to the message. Kris will drill you on the full code on your way to your sector, but in general, this is what the simple banding of one color means. White means there's nothing wrong—'all is well, come ahead.' It's usually used just to identify that there's another Herald about, and who it is. Green calls for a Healer to be sent, purple for a priest, gray for another Herald. Brown tells the receiver to watch for a message; there's trouble, not serious, but something that requires elaboration, and something that may delay the Herald sending it in keeping his schedule. Blue means 'treachery.' Yellow calls for military aid, the number of yellow bands on the arrows tells how many units—if you send every yellow-ringed arrow you've got, and we know exactly how many you have, we know to send the entire Army! Red means 'great danger—come with all speed.' Then there's black."

He paused, his eyes holding Talia's. "I pray to Heaven that you never have to send a black arrow, Talia. Sending any black-ringed arrow means there's been or will be death or catastrophe. And there's a variant on the code for black you should also know now rather than later. The black arrow intact except for the fletching pattern means 'total disaster, help or rescue needed.' Break the arrow, send the pieces, and it reads 'disaster, all hope gone. *Do not attempt rescue.*' Remove the head, and it means that the one whose pattern is in the fletching is dead. The broken arrow, the headless arrow—those can actually be of any color so long as the fletching pattern's there. Those are the two we'll always understand—and the ones we never want to see."

Talia felt a peculiar chill thread her backbone, and suddenly the hot, sunny day seemed unaccountably gray and chill. She shook off the feeling, and repeated Kyril's words back to him, verbatim.

"That's all there is," he said, satisfied. "You're as well prepared as any of us is for his first assignment—and you're one of the best Heralds the Collegium has ever turned out. You ought to do just fine, even though this is going to be a tough assignment. Good luck to you, Talia; I look forward to seeing you in another year and a half."

She took her leave of him and despite her hunger, decided it would be a good idea to hunt up Kris. The first place she looked for him, given the situation, was the tackshed. After all, he was only just in from fieldwork; his first move should be to see that needed repairs had already been made to his Companion's gear. That was exactly where he was, in company with Dirk, checking over his harness and tack.

As alert as a wild thing to any hint of movement, Dirk was the first to notice her. "It's our songbird!" he said genially, favoring her with one of those smiles that was almost an embrace. "I expect you have the word? And Kyril's given you the code?"

She nodded, feeling oddly shy, then searched for Rolan's never-used traveling equipment. It was similar to the tack he'd worn when he'd found her, except that the bridle bells were removable, and the saddle was a bit more complicated. Besides the usual girth, it had breast and rump bands like those on warriors' saddles, a far larger number of the snaffles by which objects could be fastened to the skirting, and an arrangement of rings and straps that made it possible for a rider—ill, injured, or unconscious, perhaps—to be belted securely into his seat.

Talia rarely ever bothered with saddle or bridle around the Collegium, but she knew from experience, both her own and Rolan's, that it would mean a great deal in the way of comfort on a ride of more than an hour (for both of them) for her to use the saddle. And as her near-fatal escapade in the river had shown, the otherwise useless reins on the bridle had other functions than guiding her Companion. Had Rolan been wearing his bridle, she could have twined her arms in the reins and let him tow her to shore, for instance.

"Everything in good order?" Kris asked. She nodded an affirmative, feeling awkward and tongue-tied now that she was less than twenty-four hours away from a long journey spent mostly in his company.

"Kris and I haven't taken care of requisitioning your supplies yet," Dirk said, giving her an encouraging, lopsided grin, as if he sensed how she was feeling. "We were waiting for you to catch up with us."

"*We?*" Kris lifted an eyebrow at his partner. "What's this 'we' all about? She happens to be *my* trainee, you know."

"And who's the one who can't ever remember how many furlongs it is to his Sector, and whether or not you need high-energy rations, or even *where* he's going, half the time?"

"Your guess is as good as mine—I don't know of anybody answering that description." Kris grinned.

Dirk heaved a heavy sigh. "No gratitude, that's what it is. All right, sieve-head, let's you and *your* trainee get over to the Quartermaster and show her how it's done."

They arranged themselves with Talia walking between them, and strolled out of the Collegium area of the Palace to the area reserved for the Guard. That is, *they* strolled—Talia had to stretch her legs no small amount to keep up with them. All the time she was constantly aware of the little, warm, sidelong glances Dirk kept throwing at her when he thought she wasn't watching. She wasn't used to being under such intense scrutiny, and it made her a little—not uneasy, precisely—*unsettled* was perhaps the better word.

Like the Heralds, the Guard had their own area of the Palace, although they had nothing that was quite like the Collegium. They did have a training center, and a communal barracks, as well as officer's quarters, and they maintained a number of small rooms as offices. Since the needs of the Heralds and the Guard were quite similar in some areas of supply, the Quartermaster of the Guard also dispensed initial supplies to outbound Heralds. Any other supplies were taken care of at special Resupply Stations in the field.

The Offices of the Guard were entered by a door directly under the shadow of the wall that encircled the entire Palace/Collegium complex. There were a dozen or more officers seated at desks literally crammed together in the relatively small room, all busy with piles of paperwork, but Kris and Dirk seemed to know exactly where they were going. Talia followed as they threaded their way through the maze, while the officers whose work they inadvertently disturbed gave them either glares or friendly winks. Their goal was a desk at the very rear, whose occupant, a grizzled old veteran, looked rather out of place among the younger, obviously townbred officers. He seemed to be hard at his paperwork, but looked up and grinned broadly at the sight of them.

"Wot, ye tired of our faces alriddy?" he jeered. "Or is't ye've got somebody's daddy 'twould like t' see if Heralds bleed red?"

"Neither, you old pirate," Kris replied. "We've got a gap to fill up North, and Kyril, in his infinite wisdom, has decreed that we're best suited to fill it."

The man's face grew serious. "Ah didna hear the Bell—"

"Relax, Levris, it wasn't fatal," Dirk assured him. "A pair of broken legs, or so I'm told. Talia, this is Levris, he's the Quartermaster of the Guard, and as such, those of us on circuit see a lot of him."

The wizened man stood, took her hand like a courtier, and bowed gracefully over it. "'Tis a pleasure," he said gravely, while Talia blushed. "An' a privilege. Ye be Queen's Own, I'm thinkin'—"

"Absolutely right," Kris said, corners of his mouth twitching. "She's my internee."

"Oh, so?" Levris let go of Talia's hand, rested both hands on his hips, and gave him a stern look. "Ye'll not be tryin' any of yer seducin' tricks on her, m'lad, or if Ah come t' hear of it . . ."

Now it was Kris' turn to blush, and Dirk's to hide a grin.

Talia decided to come to his rescue. "Herald Kyril surely wouldn't have assigned us together if he thought there was any harm in the pairing," she pointed out. "And this is *duty*, not a pleasure-jaunt."

"Well, an' that's true," he admitted reluctantly, seating himself again. "So—what Sector?"

"North Border, Sorrows Two," Kris told him. "And since we won't be meeting the outgoing Herald, we'll need the whole kit."

"By t'morrow, Ah s'ppose? And ye'll be wantin' the special rations. Ye might give a man some warnin', next time!" he grumbled, but there was a twinkle in his eye.

"Sure, Levris. We'll make certain to schedule our broken legs from now on—*and* make certain it's convenient for you."

"See that ye do, then." He chuckled, then pulled out a half-dozen forms, and had Kris and Talia sign them all. That done, he shooed them out the way they had come.

"That's all there is to it," Kris said as they returned to the Collegium side. "He'll have everything we'll need ready for us in the morning."

"Provided Herald Sluggard can be persuaded to rise that early," Dirk grinned.

"Now that you've checked over your harness, all you need to do is pack your personal things," Kris continued, ignoring him. "Keep in mind that where we're going it gets cold sooner than here, stays that way for longer, and the cold is more intense. The leaves are already falling up there, though they've just started to turn here. We'll plan on staying mostly in Waystations near the villages; we won't want to get too far from other people if we can help it."

"Nevertheless," Dirk warned both of them, "You'd better also plan on having to spend several nights alone in the wilderness. I lived in that area; you didn't. The villages are far apart, and winter storms can spring up out of nowhere. You may get caught without a Waystation near, so pack the emergency supplies; if you don't use them, there's no harm done, but if you need them, you'll be glad you have them. Plan for the worst possible snow you've ever seen—then overplan."

"Yes, O graybeard." Kris made a face at him. "Holy Stars, Dirk, I visited with your family up there often enough! The way you're fussing, you'd think both of us were green as grass and totally untrained! Talia's no highborn fragile flower, she's a Borderer, too, even if she's from farther south than you."

"Well, better I should remind you needlessly . . ."

"Stow it and rope it down, granther! We'll be *fine*! Anyone would think you were my keeper, not my partner." Now Kris cast a sly, side-long glance at Talia, who was feeling distinctly uncomfortable. "Or is it someone else you're worrying about?"

From the surprise on Kris' face, even he hadn't expected the blush that reddened Dirk's ears.

"Look," Dirk said hastily, "I just don't want you two to get into any trouble. You owe me for too many lost bets, and I'd rather not have to try to collect from your lord father! Is there anything else you'd like advice for, Talia?"

"N-no," she stammered. "I don't think so, anyway. I thank you both. I'd better get back to my quarters and pack."

"Don't forget—take nothing but Whites!" Dirk called after her. "You're on duty every minute in the field. And nothing fancy! It'll only get ruined."

He needn't have said that, about "nothing fancy," she thought a little resentfully. *After all, I'm not some silly townbred chit.* And then she wondered for a fleeting instant why his good opinion of her should seem so important.

Dismissing the thought from her mind, she ran back up the tower stairs and ransacked her wardrobe, laying everything white she could find on the bed. That way she wouldn't overlook a tunic or other article that she might find herself in need of out in the field.

She packed nothing but the doeskin, with the summer and winter changes both—but she packed every stitch of those she had.

Though from the way Dirk talks, she thought wryly, *you'd think it never got warm up there.*

She added a repair kit for leather and one for harness, and then for good measure added a sealed pot of glue, just in case. There'd been times enough back on the Holding when she was on sheep-watch that she'd needed a pot of glue, and not had one to hand. She packed her sewing kit, and a brick of hard, concentrated soap—the special kind that you needed for use on Whites to keep them pristine—just in case it ever became necessary to do her own repairs and cleaning of her clothing. Certainly the village laundrypeople normally tended those jobs, but you never knew. She added a small metal traveling lamp, and extra wicks, because she'd never seen a lamp in the Waystations, and if they stayed more than one night, lamplight was easier on the eyes than firelight. Then her personal gear, her weapons, a precious book or two, some writing supplies. Her bedroll was next, and all the extra blankets she could find; with them, two extra towels besides the others she carried, and a pair of thick sheepskin slippers. Rolan's gear was all with his tack, but just the same she packed a vial of ferris-oil. He liked it; it was good for his hooves and coat and kept the insects away.

Even when she'd packed everything as compactly as she could, it still bulked distressingly large. She stared at the clumsy packs in near-despair, trying to think of something she dared leave behind. Kris would surely think she was an idiot for wanting to bring all this stuff!

"Good packing job," Keren said from the open door behind her. "I intended to come up here and help you cut down on the flotsam, but it looks like I'm not needed."

"Is that meant ironically or seriously?" Talia asked, turning to greet the more experienced Herald with relief.

"Oh, seriously. My counselor made me repack three times for my interning trip, and I never did get my packs down that small—I kept thinking of things I was sure I'd miss. Know what? I ended up sending most of them back here."

"But how is Rolan ever going to carry all this, the supply pack and me, too?"

"Easy, he won't have to. You'll each have a packbeast, probably a mule. Well, maybe not; you're going north, they may give you chirras. Didn't anybody tell you that? You're riding circuit, not carrying messages, so you don't need speed. You can easily hold your speed down to match your packbeasts' without sacrificing anything."

Talia heaved a sigh of relief. "Nobody told me. Kris either assumed that I knew, or left it out deliberately to keep me from overpacking."

"Well, don't go crazy now that you know," Keren warned.

"I won't. In fact, other than begging a couple more blankets and a pillow from Supply, packing all three pairs of my boots, and adding a bit more in the way of towels and soap and the like, there's only one thing more I want to add." Talia tucked her third pair of boots into a pack, tied it shut, and turned to the hearthcorner. There, where she'd left her last night still in her carrying case, was My Lady. She opened the case, detuned the strings for safety in traveling, and added her to the pile.

"Good notion," Keren said. "You may be snowbound at any time, and that'll keep you from tearing out each other's throats from boredom. Not only that, folks up there seldom see a Bard except in summer. You'll be like gifts from the Gods."

"Keren—I'll—" Talia suddenly had a lump in her throat. Now it came home to her; she was leaving, leaving the only place that had ever felt like home, and the only friends she'd ever had. "—I'll miss you."

Keren reached out and hugged her shoulders. "Don't you worry. You'll be fine, I know you will. Kris is a good lad, if a bit too conscious of his own good looks. Little centaur—I'll miss you, too. But don't you dare cry—" she warned, caught between a chuckle and a tear, "—or *I'll* start! Come on, we've just enough time to catch the end of supper, and you must be ready to chew harness."

Supper was rather subdued; nearly everyone had long since eaten and gone, and of those that were left Talia really knew only Keren well. Talia kept glancing around her, realizing how much she was going to miss this place, that had been her first *real* home.

She had expected that Keren would leave her afterward, but to her surprise, the older woman insisted that she come with her to Keren's rooms. She was even more surprised when Keren insisted Talia precede her through the door.

Then she saw who was waiting for them there; almost more people than would fit into the room: Elcarth, Sherri, Jeri, Skif, Teren—even Alberich. Devan made a brilliant patch of green among the Whites in his Healer's robes; the students were well represented by Elspeth. Keren pushed her into the room from behind as she hesitated on the threshold.

"You really didn't think we'd let you go without a proper good-bye, did you?" Skif teased as Talia stared in dumb amazement. "Besides, I know you—you were all set to mope away your last night here alone. Goose! Well, we're not having any of *that*!"

Since that was exactly what she'd expected to be doing, Talia blushed rose-pink, then stuck her tongue out at him.

Skif, knowing very well how prone Talia was to isolating herself just when she needed others the most, had accosted Keren as soon as the news of Talia's assignment had gotten to him. The two of them had put their heads together and quickly put together this little "fare-thee-well" party, designed to keep her from falling into a last-minute melancholy. When Skif saw the expression on Talia's face as she'd realized what they'd done, he felt more than repaid for his effort.

He did his level best the whole evening to project how much his "little sister" meant to him, knowing she'd pick it up. The warmth in her eyes made him feel that he'd at least begun to give her an honest return for the help she'd given him last night. In some ways he was just as glad now that they'd never become lovers, for there was nothing that could have been more satisfying, in the long run, than the open, loving relationship they had instead. He had more than a suspicion that she felt the same.

"So, songbird, how about a tune or three?"

While it wasn't precisely as festive as the celebration the night before had been, everything had been geared to setting her mind at rest and making her feel confident about the morrow. Each of them, with the exception of Devan and Elspeth, had faced the same moment—and each knew some way to make the prospect a positive one. There was a great deal of laughter, plenty of absurd stories, and a palpable aura of caring. They sent her off to bed in good time to get a full night's sleep, and she left with a smile on her face.

Kris answered the tap on his door late that evening, expecting to see Dirk; in fact, he'd already gotten out a bottle of wine and two glasses, figuring that his partner wouldn't let the evening pass without coming by for a farewell drink and chat. He got a fair shock to find his uncle, the Councilor Lord Orthallen, standing in the dim hallway instead.

He managed to stammer out a surprised greeting, which Orthallen took as an invitation to enter. The silver-haired, velvet-robed noble wore a grave expression on his still-handsome, square-jawed face, so Kris had more than a faint suspicion that his visit was *not* just to bid farewell to his nephew.

He directed his uncle to the most comfortable chair in the room and supplied him with the glass of wine intended for Dirk before taking the chair opposite him.

"Well, uncle?" he said, deciding he was too tired to dance diplomatically around the subject. "What brings you here? I know it wasn't just to bid me a fond farewell."

Orthallen raised one eyebrow at his bluntness. "I understand you have the new Queen's Own as your internee."

Kris shrugged. "It's no secret."

"How well do you know her?"

"Not at all," he admitted. "I've seen her twice, worked with her once. She seems nice enough—quite well balanced, all told. Her Gift is an odd one, but—"

"*That* is exactly what is worrying me." Orthallen all but pounced on the opening. "Her Gift. From all anyone has been able to tell me, it *is* a very unusual one for a Herald, much less the Queen's Own. It seems to be one that the Heralds themselves know very little about, and I'm not entirely happy that an inexperienced child should be in her position with a power so . . . out-of-the-ordinary."

"Rolan Chose her," Kris replied warily. "That should be proof enough that she's capable of handling it."

"Yes, but—*emotions*—it's such a volatile area. No black-and-white there, only gray. There are rumors in the Court . . ."

"Such as?"

"That she has fostered an unnatural dependence in the Heir. After all, the child *is* vulnerable to that sort of thing. It was her unnatural dependence on that foreign nurse, Hulda, that led to her nearly being disallowed in the first place. And there are other rumors."

Kris bit back an angry retort; best hear his uncle out. "Go on."

"That Talia has used her power to influence the Council; you can imagine for yourself how easy that would be. If a Councilor were wavering . . . it would be very easy to nudge his emotions, make him feel happier about one side or the other. Or not even that . . . simply *sense* that he is wavering, and *use* that knowledge to persuade him in a more ordinary fashion. By knowing how Councilors stood, it would make it quite simple for her to manipulate them just by tone of voice. . . ."

"That's absurd! *No* Herald would ever use her Gift in any such fashion!"

"So *I* have maintained," Orthallen replied smoothly, "but—the only others Gifted with Empathy are the Healers; Healers put it to very specific and humanitarian use. There is no corresponding protocol of use among Heralds. And, nephew—what if she truly were not aware she was using her abilities? These powers are not material properties one can weigh or measure or hold in one's hand. What if she were doing this sort of thing without even realizing it?"

Kris felt as if he had been hit with a pail of cold water. "I—I suppose it's just barely possible. I don't think it's at all likely, but I can't dismiss the notion out of hand."

Orthallen rose, a satisfied smile creasing his lips. "That is what I hoped you would tell me. I'm counting on you, nephew, to lay these phantoms of doubt to rest. You'll be with her night and day for the next eighteen months, and I'm sure you will be able to tell me on your return that all these rumors are no more than smoke."

"I'm sure I will, uncle," Kris replied, letting him out—but not at all sure in his own mind.

It was just false dawn when Talia woke, and she dressed as quickly as she could, discovering that someone had left a breakfast tray for her outside her door. She had only just finished it when a Guardsman tapped discreetly on the doorframe, explaining that he was there to help her carry her packs down. With his aid she managed to get everything down to the tackshed in one trip.

Bright light from oil lamps along the wall dazzled her eyes as she entered. Waiting in the very center was Rolan; his harness was piled beside him. Next to him was a second Companion stallion, and Talia could see Kris' legs behind him as she and the Guard approached. Tethered beside the strange Companion were two most unusual pack animals.

Talia had never seen chirras before except in pictures, for their heavy coats made summer at the Collegium far too uncomfortable for them. Rather than keep them there, the Circle had a northern farm where they were bred and stabled, and only brought them down on rare occasions like this. Had this been within the normal order of things they would have taken mules from the Collegium stables for the first part of the journey. Then they would have met the Herald they were replacing at the edge of her Sector and exchanged their mules for her chirras.

Talia discovered that pictures and descriptions were inadequate to convey the charm of the northern beasts. The chirras were as tall at the shoulder as a horse, but a much longer neck put their heads on a level with the head of a human on horseback. Instead of hooves they had doglike, clawed feet, except that the feet were almost round and far bigger than Talia would have expected from the overall size of the animal. Both chirras were creamy white with black markings; one had a little cap-like spot on the top of its head, and a matching saddle-marking on its back, the other had a collar of black fur that ran around its throat and down its chest. Their ears were large, resembling rabbit ears, but rounder, with tips that flopped over. Their ears were set on the tops of their skulls and faced forward. Their faces were vaguely rabbit-like. Their brown eyes were very large, gentle, and intelligent. When Talia approached them with her hand held out to them, they scrutinized her closely, then politely took turns whuffling her palm.

Kris was already halfway through his inspection of the beasts and their gear.

"Kind of cute, aren't they? Anybody ever tell you how they manage to live through those blizzards? They've got three layers of fur," he said, bent over and adjusting the girth of the pack-harness, half-hidden by the chirra's bulk. "The outermost is long and coarse, and pretty much waterproof—even frost won't form on it. The middle layer is shorter, and not quite so coarse. The inner layer is what they shed every year; it's dense, very soft and fine, and is what does most of the work of keeping them warm. We'll have to groom them very carefully every night to keep all that fur from getting matted, or they'll lose the warming and waterproofing effect."

"Why are their feet so big?"

"To hold them up on the snow; they'll be able to walk on snow crusts that the Companions will break right through." He moved to the front of his and picked up its forefoot while it whiffled his hair. "Look here—see all the hair between the toes? If you think their feet look big now, wait till they spread them out on snow. You'd think that hair wouldn't make any difference, but it does, like the webbing on snow-shoes. I much prefer chirras over mules in any kind of climate that they can tolerate. They've got sweet tempers, and they're really quite intelligent. If a mule balks, you can't tell half the time if he's being stubborn, or if there's really something wrong. A chirra never balks *unless* there's something wrong."

The chirra next to Talia stretched out his neck and nudged her hand, obviously wanting to be petted. "How much can they carry?" she asked, complying by scratching behind the chirra's ears. It sighed happily and closed its eyes in content.

"Almost half their own weight—as good or better than a mule. Well, look at the packs they're bringing now, and you can see."

Talia was astonished at the size of the pack the stablehands were loading on the chirra she was scratching. It didn't seem the least bit uncomfortable.

Kris looked it over, then eyed the packs Talia had brought down from her room. "They've left enough leeway for you to load those on him as well, Talia. Don't worry, he's smart. If it's going to be more than he can carry, he'll just lie down until we lighten the load."

To her relief, the chirra showed no sign of wanting to lie down after her packs had been strapped on top of the supplies. Kris saw to the distribution of the rest of the supplies and his own belongings, while Talia made sure the chirra's harness was firm, but comfortable, with nothing twisted or binding.

She harnessed Rolan herself, then double-checked her work, and asked him in an undertone, "You don't mind traveling with these beasties, do you?"

He seemed pleased that she had asked the question but conveyed the impression that he was quite pleased with the packbeasts. Without words, Talia got the distinct impression that the chirras, sporting those thick, warm coats, would be more than welcome company on cold winter nights.

She fastened the lead rope of the chirra to the back of Rolan's saddle, and mounted. Kris mounted a fraction of a second later. "Ready?" he asked.

"As ready as any internee, I guess."

"Then let's go."

CHAPTER 4

K RIS TOOK THE lead; they had to go single file in the city. Talia and Rolan followed his chirra out of the gates of the courtyard, past the Collegium and Palace buildings, gray and silent in the early morning light, then down the cobblestoned road to the iron gates leading to city streets themselves, the road she'd ridden up five and a half years previously. She looked back over her shoulder for a last glimpse of the dear, familiar stone buildings, and wondered what she'd be like when she saw them again.

The guard at the gate let them out; it was scarcely an hour until dawn and the streets were not yet crowded. They followed the long spiral outward, passing first through the residential areas that were nearest the Palace—huge buildings belonging to the highest ranked of the nobly-born, some nearly rivaling the size of Bardic or Healer's Collegium, though not that of the Palace itself. Then, crowded far more closely together, the homes of the rich—merchants and craftsmen and Guild officials. Unlike the Palace and the edifices of the nobles, which were the same gray granite as the city walls, these buildings were wooden. Since land within the walls was at a premium, they crowded so closely the eaves touched—and when there was a need to expand, the only direction to take was *up*, which sometimes produced some very strange results. Most of these houses had been constructed of ironoak, a wood nearly as tough and indestructible as steel, but that was where any similarity among them ended. They had been built to some highly individual styles, and often had been added to in years and styles varying wildly from the original. Had the spiraling main street not been wide enough for three carriages, it would never have gotten any sun; as it was, riding through this district so early in the morning was rather like riding down a canyon with sides carved in the most fantastic of shapes. Talia had to fight to keep from giggling as she passed some of these houses, for Skif—to "keep his hand in," or so he claimed—had often paid uninvited visits to the upper stories of some of these places. He'd usually left unsigned notes to be found later, chiding the owners for their lack of security. That was *one* prank the Provost-Marshal would *never* have forgiven him if it had been discovered.

After the street took a sharp right-angle turn, the purely residential district came to an end. Now the lower stories of the buildings were devoted to shops and the work-places of fine craftsmen, or offices, with an occasional expensive hostelry. The upper floors were comprised of apartments or lodgings. At this point they began encountering what little traffic there was this early in the morning. Nearly the only people about were the farmers who had brought their produce in to market, for the only cityfolk moving were those who were buying fresh supplies for their inns. Talia and Kris were able to move at a brisk pace, not having to stop for traffic more than once or twice. The streets were so quiet at this hour that *they* were the chief sources of sound; the ringing of the Companions' hooves, the chime of their bridle-bells, and the click of the chirras' claws on the cobblestones.

It took them nearly an hour to reach the Northern gate; the farther from the center of the city they went, the less wealth was displayed. There were no slums within the Old City; those were outside the city gates, huddling against the walls as if in hopes that those sturdy stone structures might shelter them from the elements. It was in one such district that Skif had grown up, the rather odd section along Exile's Road that led into the West. Talia had never been there; she had seldom been out of the Old City, much less into the New. The one time she'd asked to be taken there, Skif had turned white, and refused. She'd never asked again.

Nor would she go anywhere near that section this time, for Kris' chosen route led past the warehouses and the shipwrights, after crossing over the River just inside the Old City walls and exiting through the North Point Gate. Here there was no activity at all; workers had not yet arrived, and deliveries to the warehouses had yet to be made. So once again, they rode in silence after a sleepy Guardswoman waved them on their way.

Beyond the gate the road widened and changed from stone to that odd substance that wasn't stone and wasn't clay. Talia hadn't thought about it in years, but it occurred to her now to wonder just what it was that paved some of the roadways of this Kingdom.

"Kris?" she called, and he motioned to her to ride up alongside him, now that they were out of the city.

"What *is* this stuff?" she asked, pointing to the surface of the road.

He shrugged. "Another lost secret. Some of the roads leading to the capital are paved with it, a few all the way to the Border; but any roads made later than Elspeth the Peacemaker's time are just packed gravel at best." He saw she was looking about her with unconcealed curiosity. "Haven't you ever been out of the city before?"

"Not very often since I was Chosen," she replied, "and never in this direction."

"Didn't you even go back home for holidays?" he asked, astonished.

"My parents weren't exactly pleased with me, even—or perhaps especially—when they learned I was Chosen," she replied dryly. "Not to put too fine a point upon it, they disowned me. In Hold terms, that means they denied the very fact of my existence. I spent all my holidays here, with Jadus while he was still alive, then with Keren and Ylsa, or with Gaytha Housekeeper and Mero the Collegium cook."

"You've been rather sheltered, then."

"At the Collegium, yes, except for the first year. Not at the Hold, though. Know anything about Holderkin?"

"Not much," Kris admitted. "They seemed so dull, I'm afraid I've forgotten most of what I learned about them as a student."

"Whether or not it's dull depends on whether you were born male or female. Holderkin are originally from outKingdom—Karse, if you're curious. They fled from religious persecution; their religion is based on a dominating, ruling God and a passive, submissive Goddess, and the Karsites are monotheistic. That was . . . oh, two generations ago. They are very secretive, and very intent on maintaining their ways intact. Men have some choice in their lives; women are given exactly two choices—serve the Goddess as a cloistered, isolated votary under a vow of silence, or marry. You make that choice at the mature age of thirteen, or thereabouts."

"Thirteen!" Kris looked aghast.

"Hellfire, Kris, life is hard on the Border! *You* ought to know that, with your partner being a Borderer. There were raiders every winter I can remember. The land is stony and hard to farm. Holderkin don't believe in going to Healers, so a lot of simple injuries and illnesses end in death. If you're not wedded by fifteen, you may not leave any off-spring—and they need every working hand they can get."

"You sound like you *enjoyed* that kind of life—like you approve of it!" Kris was plainly astonished by her attitude.

"I hated it," she said flatly. "I hated every minute that I didn't spend reading or daydreaming. Rolan's Choosing me was the only thing that saved me from a forced marriage with some stranger picked out by my father. I think that the way they confine themselves, their children, and most especially their minds is something approaching a crime. But *most* of the Holderfolk I knew seemed content, even happy, and I have no right to judge for them."

"Fine; you don't judge for them, but what about others who are unhappy as you were, with no Rolan to rescue them?"

"A good point—and fortunately for those would-be rebels, one Elcarth and Selenay thought of after hearing my story. The Holderfolk got their landgrants on condition that they obey the Queen and the laws of this Kingdom. Shortly after I arrived at the Collegium, Selenay had a law passed through the Council that Heralds must be allowed free access to children at all times, in order that they can be certain that the children of this Kingdom are properly educated in our laws, history, and traditions. Heralds whose Gift is Thought-sensing go right into the Holdings now. Anyone willing to sacrifice family ties and standing as I did is free to leave with them, and they make sure the unhappy ones know this. The amazing thing to me is that there was very little objection to the practice after the initial outrage died down. I suppose the Hold Elders are only too pleased that their potential troublemakers are leaving on their own."

Kris seemed a bit bemused. "I can't imagine why anyone would *not* want to leave conditions like that."

Talia shook her head sadly, remembering. It wasn't quite true that she hadn't gone back to the Hold—she had, once, last year. She'd gone back in the hopes of rescuing her sister Vrisa—to discover Vris had changed, changed past all recognition. Vris was a Firstwife now, with status, and three Underwives to rule. She'd regarded Talia as if she were a demon—when she thought Talia wasn't looking, she'd made holy signs against her. In point of fact, she looked and acted enough like Keldar, the Firstwife who'd done her best to break Talia's rebellious spirit, to have been Keldar's younger self. She not only didn't want rescue, she'd been horrified by the idea.

"Kris, it's not my choice to make," she answered wearily. "It's theirs.

All that I care about is that the ones like me now have the option I didn't have before I was Chosen—to escape."

Kris looked at her with curiosity. "Just when I think I have you neatly categorized, you say or do something that turns it all upside down again. I'd have bet that you'd have been willing to lead an army into the Holds to free the women, given the chance."

"Maybe when I didn't know as much about people as I do now," she sighed.

They rode on in silence. The sun rose on their right, turning the sky pink, rose and blue, casting long shadows across their path from the buildings. Before long they had passed beyond the edge of the New City, and there was nothing before them but the occasional farmhouse. Cows were gathering outside barns, lowing to be milked. Now they saw people working, and a light breeze carried to them the smell of cut grain and drying hay, and the sounds of birds and farmbeasts.

"Tell me about yourself," Kris said, finally. "When you're tired of talking, I'll tell you about me. Start with what it was like on the Hold, before you were Chosen."

"It's boring," she cautioned him.

"Maybe—but it's part of you. As your counselor, I need to know about you."

He did his best to keep his opinions to himself while she talked, but he frequently looked surprised by some of what she told him, and actually horrified once or twice. He had, she thought, a hard time conceiving of a culture so alien to his own, so confining and repressive. Talia herself spoke in a kind of detached tone. She felt very distant from the Holderkin and all they meant now. She could think of them without much animosity; as something foreign.

It was noon when she finally grew tired of explaining Hold customs to Kris. She paused for a long drink from her waterskin, suddenly aware that her mouth was very dry, and said firmly, "I think I've talked enough."

"More than that; it's time to break for lunch," he replied. "While we keep to this pace the chirras can go on indefinitely, so whether or not we break depends on whether or not we want to take a rest from riding. How are you feeling?"

"Like I'd like to get off for a while," she admitted. "It's been a long, long time since I spent this many hours riding."

"I'm glad you said that." His answering smile was completely ingenuous and quite charming. "I'm not all that fond of eating in the saddle unless there's no choice. As soon as I spot a place where we can water the chirras and our Companions, we'll take a rest."

They found a Waystation within the half-hour. This one was watered by a well rather than a stream; they took turns hauling up enough water to satisfy the four-footed members of the party, then tethered the chirras so that both Companions and chirras could graze for a bit while they ate their own lunch.

They ate in silence, and Kris seemed to be in no great hurry to move on afterward. He lay back in the soft grass instead, thoughts evidently elsewhere, though he glanced over at Talia once or twice.

Kris was worried, though he was taking pains not to show it. His uncle's words kept coming back to him, and he could not, in all conscience, dismiss them. He'd made a number of assumptions about his trainee, most of them based on her apparent youth and inexperience—and now what she'd told him seemed to indicate that she was anything but inexperienced, and certainly was *not* the simple creature he'd pictured to himself. This child—no, *woman*; he began to wonder now if she'd ever had anything like a "childhood" as he knew the meaning of the term—had been functionally the Queen's Own long before she ever attained her Whites. But she was so tiny, and so guileless, and so very innocent-seeming, that you forgot all about that, and tended to think of her as much younger than she really was.

He didn't think any of that surface was a deliberate act—but he also couldn't tell what lay below the surface, either.

Was she capable of the kind of deliberate misuse of her Gift that Orthallen had described?

"I've got to ask you a question," he said at last. "And please, I don't mean this as any kind of insult. There are some rather unpleasant rumors circulating the Court, and I'd like to know the truth. Have—have you ever used your Gift to influence Elspeth?"

Her reaction was far more violent than he would have expected. *"No!"* she shouted, sitting bolt upright, and actually startling Companions and chirras into shying. "How can you even *think* such a thing?"

Her eyes were hot with anger; her face as white as her uniform.

He met that angry gaze as best he could, acutely aware of how still it was, of the grass under his hands, of the sun on his head. "It's a rumor, I told you; I have to know."

"I have never—I *would* never—do anything like that to anyone. It's—the whole idea is perverted," she choked. "Dammit, I *knew* there had to be some odd things being said about me. I mean, I could tell, people were acting very strangely when they thought I wasn't looking. But this! It's—it's disgusting. Does Elspeth know about this?"

"Not so far as I know—" He broke off at the sudden, pained look she gave him.

She rose to her feet, abruptly. "I've—I've got to go back; I can't leave her to face that alone."

"That's just what you can't do," he said, jumping up and catching hold of both her arms. "Don't you see? If you did that, you'd just be *confirming* the idea in people's heads. Besides, you've been given an assignment, and a set of orders. It's not up to you to decide whether or not you're going to obey them."

She buried her face in her hands for a moment; when she took her hands away he could see her fighting to exert control over herself. "All right," she said, sinking back to the ground. "You're right. You said that there were other rumors. What are they?"

"That you've been using your Gift to influence other people— specifically Councilors on crucial votes. The kindest version of that rumor says that you're not doing it consciously, that you don't realize you're doing it."

"Good God. How am I supposed to answer *that* one?"

Kris didn't have an adequate reply, so he continued. "Another rumor is that you're using your Gift just to *read* people, then using the knowledge of their emotional state to manipulate them into doing what you want."

"Goddess. That's almost close to the truth . . ."

"Again, the kindest version is that you don't realize that you're doing it. People are frightened; your Gift isn't one they've seen outside of a Healer; Mindspeakers have an ethical code they understand, but *this*?"

"So far as I know, there *is* no ethical code," she said, and looked up at him. Her eyes were full of a pain he didn't understand, and a confusion he wished he could resolve. "Is that all?"

"Isn't it enough? They say you're young, you're inexperienced— some say *too* young to be in the position of power that you are, and to be wielding such a strange mind Gift."

"As if," she replied bitterly, "I have any choice in the matter."

And she did not speak to him again until long after they had mounted up and gotten back on the North Road.

Kris bore with her lack of communication up to a point, but finally decided to try and break the deadlock himself. He Mindtouched Tantris, asking him to move in closer to Rolan, until he and Talia were almost knee to knee.

"Just exactly how *does* your Gift work?" he asked, unwilling to bear the tense silence.

"I feel emotions the way Farspeakers hear words," she replied, after turning in her saddle to give him a sober look, one that seemed to be weighing him for some quality. "If the emotions are connected with something strongly enough, I See that. If they're twisted or wrong, or very negative, sometimes I can fix them, like a Healer with a wound. Ylsa said it's a pretty rare Gift to see crop up alone, that it's usually tied up with the Healing Gifts. As you know."

"Interesting," he replied as casually as he could. "So *that's* how you were able to lead me to where Ylsa died. Most Heralds are Mindspeakers, you know, and most of the rest are Farseers, like me. Only a few of us have odd Gifts like yours and Dirk's. And Griffon's—brrr!—that's one I wouldn't want." The sun lost some of its warmth for him as he thought of the demonstration Griffon and Dirk had given him. "Firestarting is a terrible burden, and it's so easy for the power to get out of control . . . and when it does, well, you end up with barrens like at Burning Pines. And it isn't really useful at all except as a weapon. I hope his being born with it now doesn't mean something; Heralds with the really odd Gifts tend to appear when there's going to be a need for them. The last Firestarter was Lavan Firestorm, and you know what *his* era was like—" He flushed, beginning to realize that he was pontificating—but, damn—he wanted to get her mind off the rumors so she'd act normally again. "Sorry. I tend to get carried away when I start discussing Gifts. It's a hobby of mine, one I share with Kyril. It's fascinating to see what kinds of Gifts we have, and to try and see if there are patterns."

"Really?" She perked up a little, a bit more color coming into her cheeks. "Has anybody else ever had my kind of Gift before?"

"Not that I'm aware of among the Heralds, but I must admit that I've only looked into the Gifts of living Heralds, or the really spectacular ones of the past. I can't say that I've ever heard of that ability to Heal the mind, except in a true Healer, but it wouldn't surprise me much to discover that this one's the Gift that distinguishes the Queen's Own from the rest of us. And you seem to have it mostly by itself, and maybe much stronger even than in Healers. Probably the others *have* had it, but not so strongly that anyone noticed it. Nobody seems to have made a study of the Monarch's Own—not like they have with the more ordinary Gifts. And now that I think about it, your primary job is to ensure the mental stability of the Monarch—an ability like the one you have could come in very useful if something *really* went wrong." He was doing his best to imply that he believed her—that he was certain the rumors weren't true. He only wished that he really *could* be that certain.

"I can see that." She was silent, and seemed to be thinking hard. Late afternoon sun was gilding everything, and the early breeze had died. The chirras' eyes were half-closed in the drowsy warmth, and the few sounds to either side of them were those of farmworkers cutting hay and grain, and insects droning in the grass. "So you See, and Dirk Fetches?"

"Right. That's why we work together, and generally don't ride Sectors except when we're shorthanded, the way we have been lately. To put it bluntly, we're Selenay's thieves." He laughed a little. "If I know what I'm looking for, I can generally find where it is from several miles away—more, if I get a 'ride,' like I got from you. Once I know exactly where it is and can fix the location in my mind, Dirk can read the location to Fetch whatever it is to where *we* happen to be. That's how he retrieved Ylsa's arrows."

"That seems to be a lot harder than it sounds . . . rather wearing, too, from the little I've seen."

"Gods, that's an understatement. In a lot of ways, it would be less tiring to run on foot to where it is, get it, and run back. And the heavier the object, the more difficult it is to Fetch. We haven't tried anything much larger than a building brick—and that gave him a reaction-headache that lasted for a week. I was pretty surprised when he had enough energy left to carry you to your room after retrieving those arrows."

"Aha!" She seemed pleased that it had been Dirk who had cared for her. "A mystery solved! I've wondered about that for the last two years. So *he* was the one!"

"He was like a hen with one chick—wouldn't let me do more than trail along, and I was in better shape than he. Said that with all those girls in his family, he knew better than I did what to do with a sick one."

"Can he work with anyone but you?"

"We don't know; he's never tried, since he gets such a good 'fix' from me. Probably, though. One Farseer's a lot like another."

"How long have you two been working together?" she asked curiously.

"Since we both got our Whites. That was another year they were shorthanded, and sent us both out to intern with the same counselor—

Gerick. Well, you know Gerick, he's absentminded; he left a small, but valuable ring at one of the Waystations—it was the Queen's gift to one of the Guildmasters. Rather than spend two hours going back for it, Dirk offered to try Fetching it. I Looked for it, found it had rolled under the bed while we were packing, and gave Dirk the location. That was when we discovered that I gave him the clearest 'fix' he'd ever had to work from. He Fetched the ring, no problem; we started working as a team, and we've been doing things that way ever since."

"It's just that you seem so unlike each other, I find it hard to imagine you two staying together."

Kris laughed, pleased to have gotten onto a safe subject. "You might be surprised. Underneath that jester mask he wears, Dirk's a very serious gentleman. And we have pretty much the same taste in music, reading, even food. . . ."

"In women?" she teased.

"Well . . . that, too," he admitted with a reluctant smile. "And it's really pretty unfair. Poor Dirk—it doesn't matter if he finds the lady first. Once she's seen me she usually goes all 'sisterly' on him. He's mostly pretty good-natured about it, but if I were in his shoes, I'd be damned annoyed!"

"Well, he knows you can't help it. You were born looking like an angel, and he . . . well, he wasn't, and that's all there is to say."

"It's still not fair. You'd think that at least *one* woman would figure out that Dirk the man is worth ten faces like mine."

"I expect someday someone will," Talia replied noncommittally, avoiding his eyes. "Where is he from?"

Her reply was just a bit too casual; her attempt at nonchalance immediately set off mental alerts in Kris' mind, especially following all those questions about his partner. Part of him followed up on the puzzle while he answered her question. He had a very faint suspicion, too tenuous to be even a guess. It was rather like trying to remember a name he'd forgotten. It would probably take a while before he had enough information to make a surmise . . . but now he'd be subconsciously watching for clues.

"The Sector right next to ours, Sorrows One. He's got a huge family up there. He used to haul me home with him for holidays—still does when we're free. Three of his married sisters and their families live with their parents and help run the farm. It's like a madhouse; people everywhere, babies and cats constantly underfoot. It's marvelous madness though. They're wonderful people, and there's never a lonely or dull moment."

He smiled half to himself as he recalled some of those visits, his earlier thoughts gone on the breeze. Dirk's family—they should have been gypsies! All of them crazy, and all of them delightful. He'd been looking forward to another Midwinter Festival with them, but it obviously wasn't going to be *this* year. Well, there was always another time.

Talia's next question broke the strange, apprehensive chill he felt at that thought.

"What about you?"

"Well, let me think. My father is Lord Peregrine; I'm the second son, but my brother is ten years older than I am, and I have nephews and nieces that aren't much younger than you. My parents are both very wrapped up in matters of state, so I was left pretty much in the hands of my tutors, back on the family estate."

"I think I know your father; he's one of the Seneschal's chief assistants. And your mother?"

"She organizes the resupply of the Waystations. I think she would have liked to have been a Herald, but since she wasn't Chosen, this is the closest she can get."

"Weren't there any children your own age on the estate?"

"Not many; their parents seemed to think mine would be angry if their offspring were allowed to 'contaminate' me. I spent a great deal of my time reading."

"Like me—only you didn't have to hide to do it!" she laughed.

"You're wrong there! My tutors seemed to think that my every waking moment should be spent learning something serious, dull, and practical. I had a hiding place up in the oldest tree in the garden. I fixed it up until it was quite impossible to see me from the ground. I smuggled my tales and poetry up there, and escaped at every opportunity." A breeze that stirred the leaves of the trees lining the road to either side of them seemed to chuckle at Kris' childish escapes. "Then, when I was twelve, my parents took me to Court. I don't think it ever entered their heads that the Collegium stood on the same grounds." He smiled. "Even if they'd forgotten, though, I hadn't. I hoped—but when no Companion met me at the Palace gate, I gave the dream up. I was supposed to be presented at Vernal Equinox Festival, and I can remember everything, right down to the fact that one of my bootlacings didn't quite match the other. I was standing next to my father, outside, in the gardens, you know—when there was an unexpected visitor to the Festivities."

Tantris shook his head, making the bells on his bridle sing. Kris chuckled, and reached forward to scratch behind his ears. "I knew what the appearance of a Companion meant, and I kept looking around to see who he had come to Choose. I nearly went out of my mind with happiness, when I finally stopped craning my head around and found he was standing right in front of *me*! Then, when I looked into his eyes. . . ." His voice trailed off.

"It's not like anything else, is it?" Talia prompted softly. "And it isn't something you ever lose the wonder of."

"That it's not," he agreed, speaking half to himself, "and I knew then that I'd never be lonely again. . . ." He shook off the spell, and became matter-of-fact. "Well, my parents were both very proud. They had me installed at the Collegium before I had a chance to turn around. Oddly enough, it's easier to deal with them now that I'm an adult. My father can relate to me as an equal, and I think that my mother forgets half the time that I'm one of her offspring. I really don't think they ever knew what to do with a child."

"They probably didn't, especially with so much time between you and your brother."

"Dirk has no notion how much I envy him his family," he sighed.

"You think not?" Talia smiled. "Then why does he keep bringing you home with him?"

"I never thought about that."

They rode silently for a mile or so.

"Talia, do you ever miss your family?"

"Not after I found other people who really cared about me. I was the scarlet jay among the crows with them; I was more of an outsider among my own family than I ever was at the Collegium. One of those pretty brothers of mine used to steal my books, and call me 'Herald Talia' to make me cry. I'd like to have seen his face when I was Chosen."

"Do you ever think about going back?"

"You know, that used to be a daydream of mine, that I'd somehow magically become a Herald—remember, I didn't know about being Chosen—and I'd come back dressed in my Whites and covered in glory. Then they'd all be envious, and sorry that they were mean to me."

"And now?"

"Well, I went back long enough to try and 'rescue' the sister I'd been closest to only to find she had turned into a stranger. I didn't go any farther into the Holdings, just turned around and came back home. I didn't want to see any of them again. Why bother? My parents pretended I was an outsider, my sibs were either afraid or contemptuous; Heralds are very immoral, you know. What is it Mero's Book says? About how the people you grow up with react to your fame?"

"'No one honors a saint on his hearthstone.'"

"It's true, too. I'm resigned to letting things rest as they are, knowing that my example shows misfits that there *is* an escape."

He didn't seem inclined to further conversation, so she turned her attention back to those unsettling rumors.

Poisonous, that's what they were. Ugly, and poisonous.

And true? said a niggling little doubt.

She wanted to deny any truth to it at all—vehemently. But could she? In all conscience, could she?

The business about Elspeth—no, she could not believe she'd been fostering dependence in the child, not even unconsciously. Once Elspeth had begun acting like a human being again, she'd been pushing her toward *independence*, driving her to make her own decisions and take responsibility for the results.

But the rest—oh, insidious. For a Mindspeaker, it was obvious when he was projecting; it sounded to the recipient a great deal like the Mindspeaker's normal voice, but as if the words were coming from deep inside his own ear. But when *she* projected—would anyone be able to tell she was doing so?

She could tell; sending emotion cost her effort and energy.

But if she were excited or agitated—would she notice the energy expense?

Did she even need to be doing it while she was awake? What about when she was *asleep*? How could she possibly be sure what her irrational sleeping mind was doing?

And what about simply reading people's emotional states? Was she transgressing by doing so, and acting on the knowledge?

How could she *avoid* doing it? It was like seeing color; it was just *there* unless someone was deliberately shielding.

Doubt followed doubt in an insidious circle, each feeding on the one preceding it, until Kris broke the silence.

"This is our first stop—this close to the capital they won't be hungry for news, and it's very unlikely they'd need us to work in any official capacity. Still, it's only good manners to repay them in some way for their hospitality. Small villages don't see trained Bards oftener than once a month, so they're very receptive to even amateur music. Would you be willing to sing if I played?"

"Of course," she replied, grateful for the interruption. "It's only fair that I share the work. Did you notice that I brought My Lady?"

"No!" he exclaimed with delight. "You'll let me play her? I have a smaller traveling harp with me, but it hasn't half the range or the tone of My Lady."

"I let you have her the other night, didn't I? You'll have to retune her. I detuned the strings so they wouldn't snap if the weather changed suddenly." She smiled shyly. "I have good instrument etiquette. Jadus taught me quite well, I assure you."

"He couldn't do otherwise when it came to music. He's the one who taught me in the first place."

"Really? I wonder why he didn't leave her to you?"

"That's easy enough to answer. I didn't take the time to keep him company the way you did," Kris replied with a slightly shamed expression. "He may have given me a little of his skill, but he gave his harp where he'd given his heart—to a lonely little girl, because she'd given him her own."

The village came into view before a surprised Talia had time to form a reply. Children swarmed upon them, chattering and calling questions that both Heralds fielded with chuckles and smiles. Older children ran ahead to alert their elders that there were two Heralds taking the road north, who were clearly planning on spending the night.

Long before they reached the inn at the center of the village square, a crowd had gathered to meet them. The village itself was a large one, with cobblestoned streets and white-plastered buildings of two and even three stories high. Rather than thatched, the roofs were tiled—something Talia had read was more common the farther north one went. With all the shutters thrown open, soft yellow light gleamed through the windows of the houses, as the sun set and candles and lamps were lit.

As Kris had indicated, this village was close enough to the capital that Heralds stopped with fair regularity. Heralds traveling to their Sectors were housed in inns rather than the Waystations, unless they were caught without other shelter, and inns got back a percentage of their taxes for every Herald they entertained. It was possible for an inn on a busy road to be rebated all of its tax if enough Heralds stayed there—and that made Heralds welcomed and sought-after guests.

Under all those strange eyes, Talia regained an outward control, at least; putting on her "public" face and pushing her self-doubts to the back of her mind. It would not do for these people to see her disturbed.

The Innmaster himself welcomed them at his front step and escorted them to the stables. Stablehands tended to the chirras, but the Heralds themselves cared for their Companions. Kris chuckled once or twice— apparently at something that Tantris "said" to him—and Talia felt a tiny twinge of jealousy at their ability to Mindspeak one another.

Once back inside, the Innmaster escorted them personally to their quarters, and gave Talia and Kris small rooms on the second floor— rooms scrupulously, almost painfully clean. Their rooms adjoined one another and each boasted a window, a small table, and a narrow bed that looked surprisingly comfortable.

They were courteously given the use of the bathhouse without any- one pestering them. But once they joined the rest of the guests in the common room for supper, the questions began. The dark-paneled common room overflowed to near-bursting with villagers; tallow-dips in sconces on the walls cast a dim but clear light, so it was easy to see and be seen. The air was seasoned with a pleasant aroma of bread and roasting meat and wood smoke. Though the furnishings were only rough wooden tables and benches, they, and the floor, were sanded smooth and scrubbed clean. The Heralds took their places at a table near the fire, and the rest of the guests gathered around them.

Kris took it upon himself to try and answer them, but when it seemed as if he'd never get more than a mouthful of dinner before it got cold, Talia took her own turn. As Kris had told her, the common people were very well informed this close to the capital: what they wanted most was detail. Much of what they wanted to know centered on the new Heir, a subject Talia knew very well indeed. She satisfied them enough that eventually she and Kris were able to finish their din- ners in peace.

Talia had brought My Lady down with her; while Kris tuned her, she took the time to answer questions from a different source—the children. They seemed to sense that this Herald would not brush them off, ignore them, or give them light answers. They had a thousand questions concerning Heralds and what it took to be one.

Some of the questions gave her pause for thought.

"Why don't Heralds ever stay in one place?" one young boy asked. "We always have the same priest—why don't we keep the same Her- ald?"

"For one thing, there just aren't enough of us to send one to each village, or even one to each group of villages," Talia told him. "For another—tell me, what will happen when your priest grows old and retires, or perhaps dies?"

"They'll send us a new one, of course."

"And he'll be a stranger to all of you. Do you think he'll fit in and be accepted right away?"

"No." The lad grinned impudently. "A lot of the grannies won't really trust him until he's been here for years—if then."

"But a Herald has to have your trust right away, don't you see? If you come to trust the person more than the office, the way you do with your priest, there would be trouble for every new Herald in a Sector."

The boy looked thoughtful at this. "So you move all the time, to make sure it's the job that stays important, not the person doing it. I bet if you stayed in one place too long, you'd get too bound up with the people to judge right, too."

A little startled by this observation, so very accurate, she sent a fleeting thought toward the stable.

Since she wasn't in trance, Rolan couldn't give her more than a vague feeling—but the impression was that he had already noted this boy, and it was very probable that the child was going to receive a hooved visitor in the next year or two.

Armed with this knowledge, she answered the rest of this boy's questions with special care and watched him afterward. She noted that he seemed to be the mentor and protector of some of the little children, urging them forward to talk to her when he knew that they were too shy to go alone. He wasn't above his share of pranking about, she noticed with relief, but his tricks were never those that could *hurt* anyone.

Kris soon had the harp in tune; Talia let him take center stage alone for a while, knowing how much the approving attention would please him. The guests and villagers were loud in their appreciation, and only when Kris was glowing from their applause did Talia add her voice to the harpsong.

The host of the inn eventually decreed they'd tired the Heralds out long enough, and mock-ordered both of them to their beds. Talia was just as pleased; she was feeling the effects of a long day in the saddle, and she thought of her pillow and warm bed with longing.

When they mounted the next morning, just as the sun arose, Talia winced a little as she climbed into her saddle.

"Sore?" Kris asked with a slight smile.

She groaned faintly. "Before this trip is over I'll probably be in agony. I didn't realize I was this badly out of riding trim. I may never be able to get my legs closed again."

"That would make some people happy," he teased, and ducked as she threw an apple core left from her breakfast at him.

"Just for that, maybe I won't give you this." He held up a pouch that jingled faintly.

"Why? What is it?" she asked, curiosity aroused.

"When I picked up our expense money, I *thought* perhaps you might have forgotten your stipend," he replied, tossing the pouch over to her. "You had, so I drew it for you. You're a full Herald now, remember? You earn a stipend."

"Bright Havens!" Her hand flew to her head in embarrassment. "I *did* forget."

"Don't feel badly. After five years of no pocket money, most of us forget. I did. But it comes in very handy, especially when you happen to be at a fair, and see something you just *know* So-and-so would love. Or, for that matter, that *you* can't live without."

"It's a good thing I've got you for a counselor," she replied ruefully. "I'd probably have left my own head back at the Collegium."

Kris just chuckled as he led the way out the gates of the inn onto the road.

As they traveled northward, the road changed from the strange, gray material to packed gravel, to clay, to finally a simple raised and cleared strip between the trees, all the grass worn down by travelers and their mounts and carts.

As the roadway changed, so did the landscape to either side. Farms covered more area—and there were greater stretches of uncultivated land between them, from wide meadows to nearly virgin forest.

The weather changed, growing slowly, but steadily, worse. It rained almost every day, in a steady, penetrating shower. And soon the rains lasted all day, never becoming less than a drippy drizzle, so that the chill water soaked through even their oiled-wool cloaks. The chirras whined in protest at being made to travel at all, and they rode enveloped in miasmas of soggy leaves and wet wool. By the time they reached their chosen resting place each night, they were aching with cold, sodden clear through, and longing for hot wine, hot food, and hotter baths.

Talia's mood was at one with the weather. Her mind kept running in circles on the same subject. *Was* she misusing her Gift? How could she tell? What were the ethics of Empathic sensing, anyway?

From time to time, long skeins of waterbirds called from overhead, flying south, high and fast, their cries coming down on the wind like the calls of lonely spirits. The lost calls echoed in Talia's mind long after they'd passed; sad callings for the answers to questions that could not *be* answered.

And when, at dismal day's end, they saw the lights of the next village and heard the cheerful noise of the inn, those were welcome sights and sounds indeed.

And yet for Talia, the sight of the inn became a prospect she almost dreaded. She found herself scanning the faces of those around her, seeking almost obsessively for some sign that *she* was influencing their moods.

The only interruption to her rounds of intense self-scrutiny came when Kris drilled her in the intricacies of the Arrow Code, or coaxed her into some kind of conversation while they rode.

The farther north they went, the farther apart the villages were. Finally there was little choice as to which village they would rest in overnight; often there would be only one within striking distance. The cultivated areas began to be fewer, the woods and forests thicker and showing less evidence of the hand of man. At long last the weather cleared a bit; the rain stopped, although most days were overcast. At the beginning of the trip, the workers they saw in the fields had hailed them cheerfully, then gotten on with what they were doing. Now almost invariably the farmfolk called them to the roadside and offered them a drink of sweet cider or cold spring water in exchange for a bit of news. This evidence alone made it plain that they were on the very edge of the Kingdom, for at this time of year, there wasn't much time left to get the last of the crops in; and it took a great deal to pull a farmer's attention away from that goal, even for the little time it took to drink a glass and pass a trifle of information.

Talia was just as glad that they met with so few people. Her circling self-doubts were beginning to have an effect on her; her shields were wearing thin and she could feel the press of Kris' emotional state just beyond them—though *he* was trained to mind-block without thinking about it. With ordinary folk it was far worse.

It didn't help her doubts at all that to sense that *he* was still uneasy about *her.*

Kris had done his best to shove his uncle's words into the back of his mind, but he wasn't overly successful. He wanted to bring up the subject with Talia again, but hadn't dared. She seemed edgy and preoccupied in general—and nervous whenever they were around large groups of people, although he doubted that anyone but another Herald would have noticed the nerves behind her "public" face. So he tried to keep the conversation going on other topics.

But behind it all were the unanswered questions. *Was* she misusing her Gift? Was she doing so without realizing it?

And—much more sobering—was she using it to manipulate him?

It was distressing, because he was coming to like her—like her a great deal, more so even than the usual hail-fellow good comradeship that was the norm among Heralds. They were very much alike in many ways. It was horrible to have to suspect a friend of something so insidious.

Because she was becoming that—a friend of the same order as Dirk.

"You know . . ." he said one day, out of the blue, "you're like the sister I never had."

"You're like the brother I wish I had . . ." she replied without seeming to think about it. "That I might have had if Andrean hadn't died in that raid. He was the only one of my sibs who was kind to me, excepting Vrisa. If I'd had you instead of Justus and Keltev, things might have been easier."

"They also might have turned out a lot differently. Would you have been willing to run away if life had been more pleasant?"

"A good point," she conceded. "Probably not. And then where would I be?"

He grinned, while Tantris shook his head mirthfully and made his bridle bells ring. "If what you've told me is true, six years married, and the mother of as many children."

She grimaced, and shifted in the saddle with a creak of leather. "Thank you, no. Hectic as it is, I like the life I'm leading now. Speaking of which, don't we cross into our new Sector today?"

He pulled the map they'd been given out of a pocket on the front of his saddle, consulted it, and peered around under the lowering sky, looking for landmarks. Finally he spotted one, a cluster of three flat-topped hills off to the west of the road. "We'll cross the border before nightfall, and we'll be staying tonight at our first Waystation."

"Because—" She put on a somber mien. " 'Heralds do not stay at inns in the Sector they serve, unless weather prevents them from reaching a Station; this insures that they keep a proper distance and maintain impartiality with the people of their Sector.' I remember."

"You certainly do!" He laughed, cheered by her apparent return to good humor. "That's old Werda to the life!"

"And that's also the reason we either buy the supplies we run out of outright, or wait until we reach a Resupply Station; assuming they're not in the Waystation. Right?"

"High marks; completely correct." He looked about him at the falling leaves, at trees whose branches were almost bare. "I'm sorry that this isn't going to be an easy beginning for you. This is a bad time of year to start riding this Sector. There's going to be snow in the next couple of weeks. Trainees usually aren't faced with conditions this hard at the beginning of their internships."

"I'm Borderbred, remember? *This* is a lot more like the kind of life I was bred to than my life at the Collegium. I'll manage."

"You know," he said soberly, "I know you'll do your best. I know you'll try your hardest. That's all anyone can ask. I trust you, Talia."

At least, he thought to himself, *I think I do.*

CHAPTER 5

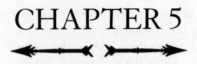

THE BOUGHS OF the nearly leafless trees arched above them, skeletal hands reaching for the gray sky. The road continued before them, a leaf-carpeted tunnel through the bleak, gray-brown forest. The sodden leaves had been flattened by so many rains that the Companions didn't even kick them up; the dense mat only served to muffle the sounds of their hooves. There were no birds, only the occasional sound of a branch cracking somewhere off in the shadows of the underbrush.

Talia and Kris rode well past sunset and on into the dark to reach the Waystation Kris intended to use as their first stop in their new Sector. With the last rays of the sun went the last hint of warmth; as the last dim, red light filtered through the branches, a cold wind began to sigh among them. Kris took the lead, but it was Tantris, with the superior night-sight of Companions, who was really picking out their way, through cold and dark that was enough to drive just about any other consideration from human minds. Talia was strongly considering unpacking her heavy cloak and was definitely glad that all Waystations, however small or primitive, had fireplaces. The wind had a sharp bite to it, and carried a hint of snow along with the cold.

This Station, as it loomed up out of the shadows in front of them, did not appear to be all that small. Hopefully, it was not primitive either.

* * *

One thing was always the first order of business, no matter how late the hour, nor how foul the weather, when Heralds opened a Waystation. Talia dismounted, felt along Rolan's saddle, and took out her firestarter and tinderbox. After no little fumbling and cursing, she managed to get a tiny flame going in the tinder. Protecting it carefully from the wind, she removed a small, fibrous bundle from one of the packs; it had a waxed wick sticking out of it, which she lit at the tiny flame. While Kris pulled off the packs and saddlebags, she tossed it inside and shut the door. He left the packs at her feet, and took Companions and chirras around to the side of the building. While she waited, she shivered in the cold wind, and started a little when an owl cried in the distance. The little, homely sounds Kris was making in the lean-to stable were very welcome against all that dark, with the wind sighing in the boughs of the trees.

She nursed the tiny fire she had going; if it went out, the whole rigmarole was to do over again. When she had counted to one hundred, slowly, she opened the door again. The Station was full of a pungent, oily smoke that was now being swiftly drawn up the chimney with the help of the draft from the open door. And any vermin that had been within the Station were either dead or fled.

Talia hauled the packs and bedrolls inside, then began to get them set up while Kris ducked inside long enough to get grain for the Companions and the chirras who were now in the stabling at the side of the building. She took a rushlight from her saddlebag by feel, and lit it from her bit of tinder. To her immense relief, the place seemed to be quite sturdy, and well maintained and supplied. She threw the bedrolls into the twin bedboxes, then proceeded (wistfully wishing for just a touch of Griffon's Gift) to get a fire going. It took several false starts, but eventually she managed to get a respectable blaze on the cold hearth. Once the flames were high enough to provide illumination as well as warmth, she extinguished the light she'd lit; no sense in wasting what wasn't really necessary, and the rushlights took up so much space in the packs that they didn't carry many of them. She unpacked some of their food supplies and unsealed the vermin-proof cendal-wood bins the Station staples were kept in to put together a reasonable meal, then took two of the larger pots outside to the well to get water for washing and cooking.

Kris seemed to be taking overly long with bedding down the chirras and Companions; she'd managed to heat enough water for both of them to wash, had fixed a meal, and had cleaned herself up and changed into a worn shift and old breeches she kept for sleeping in before he finally appeared. She was about to chide him for being so slow, when she realized that he'd dawdled on purpose.

"Kris, you don't have to be so thrice-blessed chivalrous, you know," she said instead, feeling his reticence sharply, and being irrationally irritated by it. "All the children on the Holdings sleep in the same room until they're thirteen, and you know very well I've shared Waystations and tents with my whole year-group while we were in training. I can't possibly have something you've never seen before—and the same goes for you."

"I'm . . . just not used to having a woman as a partner," he said.

"Then stop thinking of me as a woman." She yawned, bundling herself into her bedroll and blinking at him sleepily through the firelight. Her irritation was gone as quickly as it had come, once she'd reinforced her shielding—although the fact that she'd had to do the latter bothered her; she shouldn't have *needed* to.

"That's easy for *you* to say!" he retorted.

"Then pretend I'm Keren, with no interest in men whatsoever. Because if you don't, one of these evenings I'm going to find an ice statue waiting outside the door—and it'll be you!"

He chuckled, and admitted that she just might be right.

Her heart pounded a little the next day as they approached their first village of their Sector. There was no telling what reception awaited them—or what requests. This far from the capital, a village often didn't even boast its own priest, but shared one with several other villages; and the only representatives of Kingdom law were the Heralds.

Her shields were so very thin; she'd discovered that last night. She couldn't fathom why; shielding had always been second-nature, nearly instinctive—and now they seemed to be eroding, slowly, inexorably. She was frightened by the loss of control and was afraid to tell Kris, afraid her confession would simply reinforce his own doubts about her, and create more stress than she already had.

As they rode in, it appeared as though the entire population of the area had assembled to meet them. Talia thought they must have had lookouts posted, perhaps for the last week or so, waiting for the Heralds they knew were replacing the injured one. The emotional atmosphere— which she felt in spite of her best efforts to shield—was tense, with no hint of why. The village was a small one, single-storied houses of gray wood and darker gray stone, topped with tile roofs, all clustered about a central square. There were no bright-painted shutters here; the wind-driven ice of winter storms would have etched the paint off in a single season. The inn was so small it obviously had no guest-rooms; those overnighting would have to sleep in the common room on the benches when the inn closed for the night. There was no sign of damage to any of the buildings, no hint of disorder; whatever had these folk anxious had nothing to do with their material life. The village folk, though—*they* were dressed in gaudy colors, as if for a festival. So why the feeling of apprehension so thick she could almost smell it?

"Thanks be to the Lady, you've finally come!"

A plump woman who reminded Talia for all the world of a hen bustled forward, pushing before her a young couple of about sixteen or so until they stood less than a foot from Kris' stirrup. Both were dressed in heavily embroidered finery, and the girl was roundly pregnant. They clutched each other's hands as if they were afraid, and neither of them would look at the Heralds. Talia was puzzled beyond her own worries. What was it that could be wrong—that she hadn't sensed?

"The priest took sick and hasn't been able to make his rounds since eight weeks ago," continued the plump woman, tucking a stray strand of hair behind the girl's ear, "and in any case, he hasn't been here since before Midsummer. There hasn't been anyone to marry these two in all that time!"

"Were they properly year-and-day handfasted?" Talia asked, knowing the Border custom, meant to ensure fertility before a permanent bond was made.

"Bright Stars, yes—the priest did it himself last Midwinter!" the woman exclaimed impatiently, while the other villagers nodded in agreement.

Enlightenment dawned on Talia, though Kris was obviously still perplexed about the reason for their obvious apprehension.

"You're both still willing?" he asked. Both gave a very shy assent, but one obviously unforced.

"They're just victims of very bad timing," Talia whispered to him. "And they're afraid we'll disapprove—maybe even refuse to wed them—because they left the formal ceremony so long. They should have wedded as soon as they knew she was with child, but I'll bet a pretty they were so busy with planting that they put it off until after Midsummer, assuming the priest would get here in plenty of time—except that they hadn't counted on him falling ill. Poor babies! They're terribly in awe of us, and they're afraid we'll make difficulties for them because they didn't take care of it right away. We'd be within our right to do so . . . by the letter of the law."

"But not by the spirit," Kris whispered back, relieved that it was so simple. "Well, since everyone's agreed," he said loudly enough for everyone to hear, smiling broadly, "what's holding up the celebration?"

There was a general sigh of tension vanishing, and trestle tables and food began appearing as if conjured by a spell. Before very long the square had been transformed and a proper wedding celebration was in full swing. To save them any further embarrassment, Kris took the young couple off to one side and witnessed their vows, signing their wedding contract as officiating Herald in lieu of a priest.

The young couple returned to enjoy their feast, their shyness nearly gone. They were obviously comforted on two counts: that the Heralds had made no difficulty over the lateness of their vows, and that now their firstborn would have no taint of illegitimacy about it.

The remainder of that day they spent in relative idleness, since there was no use whatsoever in trying to get any official business conducted. The press of people was putting a considerable strain on Talia, but she thought she was succeeding in keeping the strain from showing, even to Kris. She sat mostly on the edge of things, speaking pleasantly when spoken to, but letting Kris take the lion's share of the attention.

And she was even more worried than when they'd first entered this village; her shields hadn't been this fragile since before she'd learned the full use of her Gift. Virtually *anything* would bring them down, and she had to expend ridiculous amounts of energy to put them back up again.

If only she'd never heard those filthy rumors. . . .

The thought of the rumors brought her back full circle to her self-doubt and fear, and the press of emotions became almost painful, until she finally resorted to an old expedient; drinking enough wine to blur the edges of her sensing, and make it all bearable. It was rather too bad that it left her sober enough to negotiate the dark path back to the Waystation with no trouble at all—for that meant she was still sober enough to think.

They returned the next day, ready for business. The people of the village had no grievances that needed settling, but they were eager to hear the news from the capital and the other towns of the Sector. The common room of the inn, dark and smokey as it was, was the only "public" room in the whole village, so that was where they conducted their business. The village storyteller—who doubled as the clerk—sat drinking in every word they spoke, and making copious notes, for it would be his duty to repeat all that the Heralds related for those who were absent from the village, or for those small holders who seldom came to town.

They gave the morning to the decisions of the Queen and Council, how and why those decisions had been reached, and what, if any, laws had been passed to uphold and enforce those decisions; and the afternoon they spent relating the news of the Court and events of major importance to the entire Kingdom—all of which took them until darkness fell, and they returned to the Station again.

This day had lain easier on Talia's wire-taut nerves, for there was nothing to excite anyone's emotions in the dry news they recited, and even if there had been, the storyteller/clerk was too intent on memorizing every word to allow his feelings to intrude. When the two of them returned to the Waystation, Talia made herself a cup of double-strength shamile tea, a strong soporific. She was determined to get to sleep, and to sleep deeply, thinking perhaps weariness was part of the cause of her troubles.

But her dreams were uneasy, and she woke feeling more drained than she had been when she'd gone to sleep.

They spent the third day on the reports of the headman and clerk, and taking the verbal news of the village to be passed on up the line. Kris would carry the headman's written reports until they came to a center of population large enough to boast a messenger, or until they arrived at a Resupply Station, at which point he could send what he had collected south to the capital, together with his own observations on the probable truth or falsehood of the information contained in them.

That was Kris' job. Talia remained in the background the entire time, hoping to be noticed as little as possible, for it seemed that the strain was worst when she was interacting with someone.

But that evening at the Waystation, Kris insisted on hearing Talia's opinion on the reports they'd been given, and the reliability of the headman and clerk who had given them.

"They seemed honest to me," she told him, hoping he had no notion of how much she *had* sensed, against her will. "I didn't have any feeling they were trying to mislead us, hide anything, or hold anything back. As far as I can judge, the only mistakes in their records are honest errors. They were quick enough to correct them, in any event, when you pointed them out."

"Good," Kris said with satisfaction. "That tallies with what I saw. I'm just as glad; I hate calling people out—even when it's blatantly obvious that they're lying to me." He noted both their observations on the cover page of the reports, and sealed them in a waterproof wrapper.

To Talia's relief, he had not seemed to note how much strain she was under.

"I didn't realize we took tax records, too," she said, attempting to distract herself—and him—with questions about routine.

"Always, in Border Sectors; almost never in the interior. We take a duplicate of what they're supposed to give the taxmen when they come next spring. This way, if some disaster should destroy their records, they have at least a partial reckoning on file. It's to their advantage, since if there's a disaster of that magnitude, the village may have lost quite a bit more than the records, and the Queen will be able to judge what aid to give them based on what would have been taxed."

She did not make the same mistake with the tea this night, but instead lay in the darkness of the Station, staring up at the blackness above her head, listening to Kris' quiet breathing and going back to her earliest lessons in shield-discipline. She thought, when she finally was weary enough to sleep, that she might have reinforced her shields enough to carry her through the final day.

The fourth day they went over the clerk-storyteller's accounts of what they'd told him, making corrections or elaborations as required. When the fifth day dawned (much to Talia's relief), they were back on the road again; headed through the village on their way out, but not to do more than pick up their laundry and visit the village bathhouse.

By the time they were well past the village and out into the wilds, it was growing noticeably colder, and both of them were wearing their heavier winter cloaks. The trees were now totally barren of leaves, and the warm, friendly scents of autumn were gone from the wind. Although it seldom rained anymore, the skies continued to be overcast—a featureless slate-gray. They crunched their way through a carpet of dead, brown leaves that had collected on the roadway. Most of the birds and beasts were gone, hibernating, or in hiding now; the loss of foliage and cover made them cautious and quiet, those that were left. The Heralds seldom saw more than the occasional rabbit or squirrel, and never heard much besides the wind in the naked boughs of the trees and the scream of a crow or two. The Companions' bridle bells made a lonely chime against the silence of the sleeping forest.

So far as Talia was concerned, that was all to the good; at least she wasn't having to be continually on guard against her shields failing. But her nerves continued to fray; and as they traveled onward through the bleak woods, she wasn't sure which was worse, being alone in this gloom-ridden wilderness, where the gray and empty forest only fed her depression, or being surrounded by people, with shields slowly going to pieces.

Kris wasn't much happier; he kept wondering if—and how much—of his general feelings of approval toward Talia were manufactured. Was she consciously or unconsciously augmenting them? He was beginning to examine every nuance of feeling, trying to detect if *she* had had a hand in it.

He liked her—Bright Havens, he *wanted* to like her, she was so much like him in so many ways. She was a good partner, taking on tasks without complaining, without needing to be prompted, striving to be a full equal and pull her own weight . . . and yet, and yet . . .

Yet there were those rumors, and his own feelings that he could well have been tampered with without his ever noticing it. "No smoke without fire?" Perhaps. It was so damned hard to tell . . . and the way she was withdrawing wasn't helping.

The next stop was two days distant, which meant an overnight stay in a Waystation midway between the two villages. Kris was no longer even thinking of his partner in terms of being female; *now* the strain on his nerves was because of his suspicions. They repeated their routine of the first night; Talia readying the shelter while Kris took care of the four-footed members of the party. His night-vision was much better than hers; it only seemed logical. And it gave him a chance to consult with Tantris without her around.

Tantris was puzzled, and worried. :*I haven't felt anything, little brother, but . . .*:

"But?" Kris asked aloud.

:*I am not certain that I would. Rolan is disturbed, and refuses to discuss it.*:

"Great."

:*He is senior to me, as you are senior to Talia. If he does not wish to discuss the private affairs of his Chosen, that is his business, and his right.*:

"I know, I know. Look, at least tell me if you pick up anything, all right?"

:*You have my word.*: his Companion replied, :*but I think perhaps . . .*:

"Perhaps what?"

:*You need more expert aid,*: came the reluctant reply.

"Tell me from where, and I'll get it! There isn't anybody in the Circle with a Gift like hers—and I rather doubt that Healer's Empathy is identical."

:True,: came the sigh in his mind, and after that, he could coax nothing more out of Tantris on the subject.

It troubled him deeply. If a *Companion* didn't feel up to the problem . . .

And they did not even have time to reach the gate of the next village before they were met on the road by two different parties demanding justice.

They saw it coming easily enough. "Steady," Kris said as they rode into a press of farmers in heavy brown homespun, who crowded up against the sides of the Companions with their petitions. Talia went pale and strained, and sat Rolan's back absolutely motionless and with lips tightly compressed. Kris did his best to sort out the arguments, then finally lost patience and sharply ordered them all to hold their tongues.

When the clamor died down, he finally managed to ascertain that there were two aggrieved parties, both as alike to his eyes as a pair of crows—brown hair, thick brown beards, nearly identical clothing of brown homespun. After listening to both sides, and putting up with each one interrupting the other until he was ready to take a stick to both of them, he decreed that the argument was moot until third parties could be questioned.

The dispute was a trivial one by *his* lights, over a cow and her calf. The facts were that a bull had somehow made its way into a field containing a cow in season; not surprisingly, the calf resulted. The calf was quite plainly the offspring of the bull in question, nor did the cow's owner deny this. What *was* under dispute was how the bull had gotten at the cow in the first place.

The cow's owner claimed angrily that the owner of the bull had allowed it to stray, and that it had found its own way there, and thus he had incurred no stud fee. He pointed to the damage done to his hedges, and inquired with self-righteous wrath if anyone thought he'd ruin his own enclosure to save himself the fee.

The bull's owner claimed just as vociferously that the owner of the cow had enticed the bull into the pasture with the express purpose of saving himself the stud fee.

Kris felt absolutely helpless; this was *not* an area in which he had any expertise at all. He glanced entreatingly at his internee, who was farm-bred, after all, and should have *some* notion of how to sort it out. Talia was looking a bit white around the lips and eyes, but otherwise seemed in control. He nudged Tantris up beside her, and whispered, "All right, trainee—you know more about this sort of thing than I do. Got any ideas?"

She started just a little; possibly only someone watching for reactions would have noticed it. "I . . . I think so," she said, slowly. "It's like a dispute we had once back at Sensholding."

"Then take over. *I'm* out of my depth."

She asked a few questions of the disputants, then went among the rest of the villagers, making inquiries into the habits of each of the parties in question. It was generally agreed that, while the owner of the cow was parsimonious, he was far too stingy to have ruined his own fences just to save a stud fee. And the bull's owner had a habit of allowing it to stray, being too lazy to fix breaks in his own enclosures until after the beast had escaped yet another time.

But then she surprised Kris by asking a source he never would have considered—some of the children gathered at the edge of the crowd. After sidelong glances to be certain that no one was likely to tell them to hold their tongues, they told Talia that this particular cow was *never* kept in the field where the bull had supposedly found her. She was quite valuable, and her owner always kept her where he could keep an eye on her.

Talia returned to the disputants.

"This is my first judgment," she said, slowly, and with an oddly ex-pressionless tone. "There is no doubt that your bull *did* stray, and since it is quite probable that it did the damage claimed to the fences, you owe this man for the repairs he had to make."

The owner of the bull looked extremely disgruntled; the cow's owner gloated. Talia did not allow him to gloat for long.

"You, on the other hand," she told him—not quite looking at him, "have never kept your cow in that particular field. You must have seen that the bull had broken in, and decided that since the damage was al-ready done, you might as well save yourself the stud fee. So you moved your cow to the field where the bull was. Because of this, my second judgment is that you owe him half the stud fee he would normally have charged you."

Now both of them looked chagrined.

"All things considered, I should think that you are probably even."

They grudgingly agreed that this was the case.

"Don't you leave yet!" she said, turning to the owner of the bull, and showing a little more animation. "You have been letting a potentially dangerous animal roam loose. My third judgment is that anyone who finds your bull roaming and confines it in a safe place for you to take home is entitled to have his cows serviced for nothing to pay him for his trouble. *That* should induce you to take better care of your stock in the future."

The grins creasing the faces of the rest of the villagers made it clear that they considered Talia's rulings to have been equitable and appropriate—and they were certainly popular. Kris smiled and gave her a little nod of approval; she smiled back, tentatively, some of the strain gone from around her eyes.

With children ranging along before and behind them, they continued down to the village itself, which was a slightly larger version of the first village they had served, and actually boasted a "town hall" of sorts. It was there that they set up shop in the single large room that served as a meeting hall, behind an ancient and battered marble-topped table that might well be the oldest object in the village. It was an improvement on the common room of the inn in that it wasn't as smoky or cramped; but the fireplace did little to heat it, and Kris found himself hoping that they would be able to deal with their business and be on their way before he got frostbitten feet and fingers.

But another dispute for arbitration landed on them almost immediately; a problem of the location of the boundary between two neighboring farms. The farmers themselves were not overly concerned about the matter, as they were old friends and had settled the problem over the years by sharing equally both the work and the fruits of the fields in question. They confided to Kris, however, that they feared this could not continue for very much longer; both had more than one son to be provided for, and they feared that tempers were already growing heated on the subject among their offspring. Kris, after a glance at Talia showed him she had no opinion in this matter, agreed that the matter should be settled now, before it developed into a full-blown feud. He promised that they would attend to it as soon as they had discharged their other duties.

The disputants were obliged to be content with that. Kris called for the village records, and while each of them took a turn at relaying the news and the laws, the other searched the records provided by the village clerk for clues to the ownership of the properties in question.

Regrettably, the clues were few, and contradictory. It seemed that both claims were equally valid.

Talia was increasingly reluctant to take any part in the affairs at hand. Her shielding was disintegrating, slowly, but steadily; she was positive of that now. What was worse, she was no longer certain that she was able to keep her own feelings from intruding and influencing those around her, for her instinct-level control over projection was going, too. Kris was trying to put her at ease, but she could sense his own doubts as clearly as if he were shouting them aloud.

And when, the night before they were due to leave, they discussed the problem of the disputed fields at length in the privacy of the Way-station, she was keeping herself under such tight control that she knew she was going to have a reaction-headache from the strain.

"The problem is that the stream they used as the original dividing line has changed its bed so many times that I can't see any way of reconstructing what it was originally," Kris sighed. "And you can't cast a Truth Spell on a stream!"

She hesitated a long moment, drawing invisible patterns on the hearthstone of the Station with a twig. "Do you suppose they'd settle for dividing it equally? You've talked with them more than I have."

"Not a chance," Kris replied flatly, firelight casting ever-changing shadows across his face. "I've talked with the eldest sons, and they're just about ready to come to blows over it. The fathers would be perfectly willing, but the children would never stand for it, and it's the children who will make trouble if they're not satisfied."

"I can't see making this an all-or-nothing proposition," she sighed, after a long pause.

"Neither can I." Kris stared into the flames, thinking. "Among the highborn the way to settle this would be to marry two of the younger children, then deed the land in question to them."

"There's not enough land there to support even one person, much less a family," Talia felt impelled to point out, "even if we could find two of the children willing to marry."

Kris played absently with one of the arrows from his quiver—then looked down at it suddenly, and smiled in inspiration. "What about the hand of Fate?"

"What do you mean by that?"

"Suppose we each took a stand on the opposite sides of the area and shot arrows straight up—then drew a line between where they landed for the new border. If there's no wind tomorrow, where they fall is going to be pretty much at the whim of the Lady. Do you think that would satisfy everyone?"

"That . . . that's no bad notion," she said, thinking hard. "Especially if we have the priest bless the arrows, pray over the fields, that sort of thing. It wouldn't be a human decision anymore; it would be in the hands of the gods—and who's going to dispute the will of the gods? I think both families will be willing to abide by it. Kris, that's a wonderful idea!" She sighed, rather sadly. "I wouldn't have thought of that."

"You did *fine* yourself, earlier," he said, more forcefully than he had intended. "I was totally out of my depth."

"Well, I don't like the idea of anyone allowing livestock to roam at will. Out here on the Border if cattle or hogs get into the forested areas, they're likely to go feral, and then you've got a real problem on your hands."

"Hmn. I knew dogs gone wild could be a problem, but I never knew livestock could." Kris filed that piece of information away for future reference.

"It's a fairly serious problem," she replied absently. "When domestic animals go feral, they have no fear of man the way wild animals do, and what's more, they're familiar with how people act. There was more than one person among Holderkin killed or maimed by feral stock."

"Well, I repeat, you did fine. You shouldn't be afraid to put your say in. That's what this internship is all about."

"I—" she started, then shrank back into herself.

"What?"

"Nothing," she replied, moving back into the shadows where he couldn't read her expression. "I'm just tired, that's all. We should get some rest."

That withdrawal troubled him badly . . . but there didn't seem to be anything he could do about it.

On their way out of town the next day, they stopped to acquire the clerk and the priest; when they presented their solution to the two families in question, both sides were heartily in favor of it. The farmers themselves were willing to agree to any solution to the problem that would defuse the potentially explosive situation between their children. The children of both families were equally certain that the gods would be with them when the arrows flew.

For something that had been under dispute for so long, the end came almost as an anticlimax. The priest blessed arrows, bows, Heralds, fields, families—anything that could possibly pertain to or be interested in the problem. ("If it moves, I'm blessing it," he told the Heralds with a twinkle in his eyes. "And if it doesn't move, I'm praying over it!") Talia and Kris each took a stand on the exact midpoint of the northern and southern boundaries of the disputed plot and launched their arrows; the priest marked the landing point of one, the clerk of the other. The landing places were permanently designated with stone cairns and newly planted trees, the new border was made and drawn on the maps and deeds. Both sides professed themselves satisfied. The Heralds went on their way.

But by now Talia was so withdrawn that Kris could not read her at all; she might as well have been a statue of a Herald. She seemed to have wrapped herself in a cocoon of self-imposed isolation, and nothing he could do or say seemed to be able to break her out of it.

And as for himself, he found himself wondering if both those disputes hadn't been solved a little *too* easily. It would have been child's play for her to have nudged the disputants ever so slightly into a more friendly—or at least less antagonistic—attitude toward one another. And once she was gone, if that was indeed what she had done, the quarrels would break out all over again.

Had he been overly impressed with the way she had handled the first case? Had she been adjusting *his* attitude?

There was simply no way of being sure . . . no way at all.

Talia was coming to realize that all her control had been on a purely instinctive level; that she really didn't *understand* how her own Gift worked. The training Ylsa had given her was the sort given to Mind-speakers, and in the face of this disintegration of control, very little of Ylsa's teaching seemed directly applicable to her current problem. The Healers she'd worked with had never said anything to her . . . perhaps because they'd seen the control and assumed it was conscious rather than instinctive.

For that matter, her Gift might not be much like theirs except in effect. They certainly didn't use *their* Empathy as primary Gift; it was used mostly as an adjunct to Healing.

They certainly weren't confronted with the ethical considerations she found herself facing. When they weren't Healing, they simply shielded. And they didn't work with law and politics.

She longed to tell Kris—and feared to. It would only make things worse, and what could he do, after all? His Gift wasn't even of the same type as hers, and what training he had been given could hardly apply to her.

So she said nothing, endured in miserable self-doubt, and did her best to reverse a situation that was moving increasingly out of control.

CHAPTER 6

T HERE WAS LITTLE of note in any of the towns and villages they passed through on their meandering way to the Border. The worst that they encountered were three cases where the village headmen were obviously trying to cover something up; twice they were lining their own pockets with tax money, once the headman was deliberately omitting his farms and those of his kin from the survey and tax rolls. In all three cases they actually *did* nothing when the cheats were uncovered; that was not their job. Instead, they noted these facts on their reports. When the taxmen arrived in the spring, they would come armed with the truth, and the guilty parties would find themselves paying a stiff penalty. This kept the onus of tax enforcement off the Heralds.

One thing was notable; the farther north they went, the greater the distance grew between communities, and the smaller the communities were. Now it was taking nearly a week's ride to pass from village to village.

Talia remained withdrawn and silent, responding only when spoken to, and never volunteering any opinion. She seemed to warm up a little when they were between villages. She'd talk to Kris then, on her own; she even could be persuaded to sing a little. But as soon as they came within a day's ride of a populated area, the shutters came down, and she locked everything and everyone outside. When she spoke, she had an odd, flat, indifferent quality to her tone. She reminded Kris of himself the first time he'd walked the two-rope bridge on the obstacle course; there was that kind of tautness underneath the mask, as if she expected to fall at any moment. Tantris could tell him nothing, but even Rolan seemed unusually on edge.

There was one other thing to observe about the countryside; these northernmost communities were not only smaller, but they kept themselves behind palisades of strong logs, with gates that were barred at night. There were wolves and other wild beasts prowling the winter nights—and some of those beasts were on two legs. The Forest of Sorrows didn't keep everything out of this Sector, and couldn't prevent outlaws from coming in from the three directions other than the forest Border. Talia and Kris rode with all senses alert and their weapons loose and to hand now, and they bolted the Waystation doors at night.

All of which *might* have accounted for Talia's nerves; except that she supposedly came from Border country herself, and should be used to keeping watch for raiders. Still, Kris reasoned, it *had* been a long time, and she had never been part of the defenders—she had been part of what was being protected.

But that wouldn't account for Rolan's nerves. The Companions were both combat-trained *and* combat-experienced; they were more than guard enough for themselves, their Chosen, and the chirras. Kris watched Talia—unobtrusively, he hoped—and worried, and wondered.

They progressed through several towns and villages; Talia was beginning to feel as if she were falling to pieces, bit by bit. Her shields were eroding to the point where she had very little control over them, and nearly everything was getting through; she *knew* she was not only reading, she was inadvertently projecting, because *Rolan* was becoming as nervous as she was. Her only defense was to withdraw into herself as much as possible, and Kris seemed bound and determined to prevent *that*. She felt lost, and frightened, and utterly alone. There was no one she could turn to for help; Kris himself had said that he thought her Gift was unique. She was certain now that *he* couldn't give her any advice on how to handle it; his own Gift *was* very nearly the kind that could be weighed and measured. Hers wasn't even necessarily detectable. And now it was becoming utterly unpredictable. Her feeling of panic and entrapment grew.

Finally they reached the town of Hevenbeck, very nearly on the Border itself. Talia's unhappiness was a hard knot within her now; the petty problems of the townfolk seemed trivial at this point.

In the previous village they'd had some of their messages catch up with them; one of them had been a brief note to Talia from Elspeth. She'd said only that she was doing well, hoped Talia was the same, and that Talia wasn't to worry about her. And that added to Talia's troubles. She had no notion of what prompted the note, or what could be happening back at the capital at this moment. Elspeth was in her first year as a trainee; like Talia she was the only girl in her year-group. She was probably confused—most certainly overwhelmed—and just entering adolescence to top it all off. *And* she would be having to cope with all the rumors Talia already knew, and whatever had sprung up in her absence. It was quite likely she needed Talia more now than she ever had since she'd been the Brat.

Not to mention the effect of the rumors on the rest of the Heralds.

Would they, like Kris, be tempted to believe them? Or would they dismiss them out of hand and ignore the matter—leaving Elspeth to face them alone?

How was Selenay getting along without her? What if the Queen was turning to Orthallen for advice—Orthallen, whom Talia somehow *could not* bring herself to trust?

She was so engrossed in trying to hold control and deal with these other worries that had begun occurring to her that she was paying scant attention to the petitioners before her—a grim and straitlaced couple who reminded Talia unpleasantly of her own Holderkin relatives.

They were dressed in clothing of faded black and dusty brown; carefully mended and patched as if they were two of the town's poorest inhabitants, although Talia and Kris had been informed by the headman that they were actually one of the wealthiest couples Hevenbeck boasted. Their mouths were set in identical disapproving grimaces as they harked over their grievances in thin, whining voices.

Those voices irritated her no end; their petty spitefulness rasped at her through what was left of her shields, like having sandpaper rubbing over a sunburn. She was grateful when Kris interrupted them.

"You're quite certain this girl is responsible for the missing poultry? There's no chance it could be foxes or other vermin?"

"Our coops are as tight as our house, Herald," the man whined. "More so! She's done it; done it in spite of the good wages we've paid her and the comfortable job she's had with us. I don't doubt she's been selling them—"

"But to whom? You said yourself no one in town will admit to buying fowl from her."

"Then she's been eating them!" the woman retorted. "Greedy she is, that I know for certain—"

Talia forced herself to turn her attention to the serving maid; her garb was even more threadbare than her employers, she was thin and pale, and looked ill-used. She certainly didn't look to Talia as if she'd been feasting on stolen chickens and geese!

The girl briefly raised her eyes—and a disquieting chill threaded Talia's backbone at the strange blank, gray gaze. Then she dropped her regard again, and Talia dismissed her misgiving as another manifestation of her lack of control over her Gift. She wanted away from them all; they made her skin crawl, and all she wanted was to have this nonsense over with so that she could retreat back into the relatively safe haven of the Station.

She spoke without thinking about anything except getting rid of them.

"I can't see where you have any proof of what you're claiming," she interrupted sharply, "and I can't see why you're bringing it before Heralds—"

"Talia, you haven't been listening," Kris said in a low, warning voice. "It isn't just the missing birds—though that's all they seem to be worrying about. There's other things—the runes on their doorstep in blood—the—"

"Kris, this is *ridiculous*!" she exploded. "All they want is an excuse to dismiss that poor child without her wages! Havens, Keldar used to pull that filthy trick once every year—hire some pathetic wench and dismiss her on some trumped-up excuse before her year's wage came due!"

"Talia," Kris said after a pause, his voice full of reluctance, "I hate to have to pull rank on you, but I'm going to have to insist—because you can work Second-stage Truth Spell and I can't. I want you to cast it on all three of them in turn."

"I can't believe you're wasting Truth Spell on something this petty!"

"That's an order, Herald."

She bit her lip at the cold tone of his voice, and obeyed without another word. The First-stage Truth Spell only revealed whether or not the speaker was telling the truth. Second-stage *forced* him to tell it. Much to her surprise, when Kris questioned the couple at some length while she held the spell on them, their story was the same.

Then she transferred the spell to the timid-seeming servant-girl—and mouse became a rabid weasel.

The girl underwent a complete personality change when Talia's spell touched her mind. She stared at her employers, eyes bright and feral, a fierce snarl twisting her lips. "Oh, yes," she hissed softly. "*Oh* yes, I've been taking their birds. It's little enough for all they've done to me—"

"What have they done to you?" Kris prompted.

"Beatings for the least little clumsiness—bread and barley-broth and moldy cheese, meal after meal. They own the biggest flock of hens in the town, and I haven't tasted an egg or a bit of chicken in half a year! My pledged clothing is *her* castoffs, and worn to nothing by the time I get them. When I'm not bruised, I'm hungry, when I'm not hungry, I'm cold! But I'll have my revenge—"

The look of mad hatred she turned on the two made them shrink back away from her, frightened at the transformation in her. And Talia clenched her hands until her nails bit into her palms, endeavoring to hold control in the storm of the rage and hatred she was experiencing.

"—oh, *yes*, I'll have my revenge! That's what the birds were for, you know. I've not been eating them. I've been sacrificing them—giving them to the wolves. They come to me every night now. Soon now, soon they'll teach me how to change my skin for one of theirs, and when I learn—when I learn—"

The mad light in her eyes told clearly what she expected to do to her employers when she'd learned to shift her shape. Talia went cold all over, shaking from head to foot. The beat of the girl's emotions against her crumbling barriers was almost enough to send her fleeing in panic. Her breath froze in her throat, and she could feel herself coming perilously close to insanity herself.

"—and after them, the rest. And my gray brothers and sisters will help, oh, yes—" The maid began to raise her voice, and her words disintegrated into babbling; raving fragments of hatred and imagination.

It was too much for Talia to bear. The girl was shattering her barriers, and about to draw *her* down into madness. She reached out blindly, without thinking, using her Gift in instinctive self-defense, and touched the girl, putting her into a sudden sleep.

The plaintiff couple was speechless; for a long moment, so was Kris.

"I think," Kris said carefully, at last, "that we had better take her and put her into the care of a Healer. I don't know how much of what she said about the way you treated her was the truth, and how much she imagined, but I think perhaps you'd better agree to pay all the Healer's expenses. And if you take another servant—you'd best be careful about her working conditions."

Kris was ominously silent as they rode back to the Station in the gathering dusk. The disposition of the mad girl had occupied all the rest of the afternoon. It had taken the Healer nearly a candlemark to wake her from the deep sleep Talia had thrown over her. And Talia was profoundly shamed, as much for her panicked, unthinking reaction as for the self-centered, willful irresponsibility that had led her to neglect her duty.

"Kris . . . I'm sorry," she said in a subdued, unhappy voice as soon as they were past the city gates. "I didn't mean—I—"

Kris said nothing, and Talia shrank back into herself, the last of her carefully-built self-confidence shattered.

He guesses—surely he guesses. I'm a failure; I can't even control myself enough to complete half a circuit. I can't do anything right.

But he made no reply, not even to condemn; she could only sense that he was thinking, but not what he was thinking about. She rode silently at his side, waiting for the axe to fall, all the way back to the Station. And the fact that it did *not* fall only made things worse.

Kris rode in silence, only now beginning to realize that by not giving her a little comfort and encouragement that he had made a nearly fatal mistake. Her self-esteem was far more fragile than he had guessed. And her nerves were plainly gone. Now he thought he knew why she would venture no judgments at all, and gave him her opinions hesitantly, and only when directly asked for them. When he asked her, back at the Station, she avoided answering all questions about how she was feeling, answering only that she was "all right." He began to wonder if she'd ever recover from the incident . . . and he began to fear that he'd ruined her.

And then, deep in the darkness of the night, the disturbing thought occurred to him that she was slowly going mad, and perhaps taking him with her.

There was snow on the ground as they rode toward the tiny hamlet that bore the dubious distinction of being the settlement that was farthest north and nearest the Border, right up against the Forest of Sorrows itself. Talia, more used to having to exert herself to bolster what was left of her shields than to stretch out to sense the population centers, began wondering if her powers had finally failed her altogether. But, no—there was Kris, so clear to her raw mind that his proximity was almost painful. So it had to be something else.

She finally got up her courage and confided what she had not sensed to Kris. "There's just too much . . . well, 'silence' is the only way I can put it. I can hardly feel anything, and the little I can pick up is as if everyone were sleeping, or unconscious."

"You're certain that the cold's not affecting you?" he asked.

I only wish it would, she thought wistfully, then answered him. "No . . . I don't think so. It was no colder back at Greenhaven, and I could feel the people from a day away."

He considered. "All right then, we'd better pick up our pace to the fastest the chirras can maintain. If there's something wrong, the sooner we get there, the better."

The snow creaked underfoot, and the bridle-bells rang madly as they picked up the pace to a trot. The air was utterly still; the sky cloudless and an intense blue that almost hurt the eyes. Sun filtered through the bare branches of the trees, leaving shadows like blue lace on the snowbanks. It was a beautiful day, and the strange uneasiness Talia was feeling was entirely out of place in it.

The village itself was very quiet as they came within sight of it—too quiet by far. Sheltered between two hills, the cleared area in which it stood showed no tracks on the snow whatsoever, neither coming nor going. The gates stood open, and unattended. Kris' face showed his alarm so clearly that Talia knew without having his emotions battering her that he was as fearful as she. He ordered Talia to remain where she was, and descended the hill they were on to the village gates, taking his chirra inside with him.

He hadn't been inside long when she saw the gates slam shut, and heard the bar slide into its slots. Immediately following this, she saw an arrow arc over the palisade to land in the snow on her side of the wall.

She ran to where it had landed. It bore four rings; three were green, one was red. She checked the fletching pattern; it was Kris' without a doubt. It might have seemed silly for him to have patterned the arrow when she'd watched him enter the village with her own eyes, but this was truly the only way for her to be certain that when the gate slammed shut it had been because *he* had shut it, and not outlaws lairing within.

This could only mean one thing. The entire village had fallen victim to some kind of plague.

Lord and Lady—what do I do—she thought frantically, then staggered as Rolan pushed her impatiently with his nose. She felt his annoyance as plainly as if he'd spoken it. He'd had more than enough of her self-indulgent nerves; this required action, simple action. She knew very well what she had to do, and she'd damn well better get about doing it!

It was as if something within her that had been broken was being splinted together. She forced herself to regain calm, to plan. She wrote a note, telling Kris that she was leaving her chirra tethered to the gate, and that he should take it inside when he saw that she'd left. She took a plain white arrow of her own, tied the note to it, and sent it back across the wall. She went through her packs, removing a map, a skin of water, and a bag of meal for herself and Rolan to share.

Consulting the map, she saw that the nearest Healing Temple lay five days by horse to the east. That meant that she and Rolan could make it in two.

She tethered the chirra, swung herself onto Rolan's back, and they were off.

This was where the ground-devouring pace of the Herald's Companion was worth more than gold or gems. A Companion could travel at the equivalent of an ordinary horse's gallop for hours without tiring. If need be, he could subsist for several days at this punishing pace with little more than water and a handful or two of meal. He would need several days of heavy feeding and rest when the ordeal was over, but a Companion never faltered, and seldom even strained muscles or tendons under the conditions that would kill a horse. Any place a hooved animal could go, a Companion could go, including scrambling over icy, hazardous rock-falls only goats would dare. The only thing his Herald need worry about was whether he was capable of staying on his back!

Talia and Rolan pushed their pace far into the night; she ate and drank in the saddle, even dozed a bit. Their road was clear, and relatively dry; the footing was good, so Rolan exerted himself to the utmost. There was even a full moon, so they could see their way quite clearly. The noise of their passing disturbed whatever wildlife there was, so they rode in a silence broken only by the sound of Rolan's hooves pounding on the frozen ground. It was an eerie journey, like something out of a dream, a wild ride that never seemed to get anywhere. Rolan was relatively fresh, so they continued on until even after the moon had set. Finally, however, even he had to take a brief rest. Not long before dawn, they broke their journey in a tiny clearing alongside the road, beside a stream crowned with an ice-covered waterfall.

Rolan halted right next to the pool below the waterfall, his flanks heaving, his sides steaming in the cold, his breath puffing out and frosting around his nostrils. Talia broke the ice for him, but the water was too cold for him to drink safely. She gave him water from her own waterskin instead, filling it when it was empty, warming it against her body, and letting him drink until he'd had enough. She filled the skin one last time, and had a long drink herself after giving him about a third of the meal she was carrying. Just as the sun rose, striking fire from the bejeweled waterfall, they were ready to resume the grueling run.

They stopped again near noon, for both of them had needs of nature to attend to. That did not take them long at all, and Talia took advantage of the daylight and relatively warm sun to strip his tack off him long enough for it to dry, rubbing him down with the towel she always kept in his saddlebag.

She leaned her head against his flank, knees feeling weak, and not just from the long ride.

Lady help me—Healers have my Gift—how am I ever going to face them? How can I face anyone, falling apart like this? Oh, gods—I can't bear it—

Rolan nudged her shoulder gently; she could almost hear him in words, so clearly did his message come to her. *I'll help you,* the feeling said.

"Oh, Gods—can you?"

The reply was an unqualified affirmative. She sighed, and relaxed, and reached out to him—

And felt her shields coming up, held up by a force from outside herself; felt a calm come over her, and a kind of numbness that was so much better than the pain and stress she'd been living with that she nearly cried.

"How long—?"

His regret seemed to say that he couldn't hold things for very long at all.

"Just make it long enough for us to get there and back. I'll work so hard I'll wear myself out, and *that* will keep things under control. I can't project if I don't have the strength to spare. I'll figure out what's gone wrong, I know I will—if I can just stay away from people for a while—"

Then let's go, his impatient headshake said.

The tack, including the saddle blanket, was dry to the touch, so she lost no time in getting him saddled again and getting on their way, with anxiety riding pillion behind her.

They galloped into the courtyard of the Healing Temple shortly after dusk. Her Whites and her Companion gave her instant attention; Rolan had not even halted when a green-clad novice Healer was at her stirrup to receive her orders. Immediately behind him came two more, one with hot wine with herbs in it for Talia, the other with fresh, warm gruel for Rolan. Both of them consumed their portions with gratitude, while a messenger went to arouse the two Heralds posted to this Temple. Meanwhile another novice lit torches all around the courtyard, and before Talia had finished her wine, a fragile, slender woman whose close-cropped hair flamed red even in the uncertain torchlight came at a dead run across the cobbled court. She had a heavy satchel slung over one shoulder, her green robes were flying, and she was tying a cloak on as she ran.

"I'm Kerithwyn," she said as she reached Talia. "I'm the most experienced Healer here in plague diseases. The other two you asked for will follow as soon as our Heralds are ready, but I'm ready to leave now."

"All right, then; the sooner we get back to Kris the happier I'll be. You're used to riding pillion with a Herald?" Talia held out her hand to aid the Healer astride Rolan.

"You could say that," the woman replied, taking Talia's outstretched hand. She gave Talia an odd look when their hands touched, hesitated a moment, then set her foot on top of the Herald's, and lifted herself onto the pillion pad behind Talia with practiced ease.

"Rolan is a good bit faster than most Companions—so be prepared."

Despite the advance warning, Talia heard the woman gasp a little in surprise as Rolan launched himself back the way they had come.

It was obvious, however, that the woman was no stranger to this kind of transportation. She held her seat without losing her grip on her medicinals or on Talia's belt, but also without any panic-stricken clutching. She kept her cloak tucked in all around her, and kept her head down, taking advantage of the small shelter behind Talia from the wind of their passing. Talia was relieved to learn that she was prepared to eat and doze a-horse, and if anything, was even less willing than Rolan to stop for rest.

They reached the village shortly after midday of the second day of their return. It was still utterly lifeless, and Talia's unpredictable shields had shut down on her, so that she couldn't even sense Kris within.

She had the Healer dismount, then backed Rolan up to the gate to beat a tattoo on it with one of his hind hooves. No matter where Kris was, waking or sleeping, so long as he hadn't fallen ill himself, he'd hear *that*.

She fretted, hands clenching on the reins, when he didn't appear immediately after the pounding. He could so easily have caught the plague himself; they were anything but immune. Kerithwyn stirred uneasily by her stirrup, the same thoughts obviously occurring to her, by the worried look on her face.

But then she heard the bar slide back and the gate cracked open just enough to admit them. She rode straight in without stopping to dismount, the Healer following, and only slid off when they were inside the gates.

"The other two are less than a day behind us, but I was ready immediately, so I came on ahead," Kerithwyn told Kris briskly. "What is the situation?"

Kris was sliding the bar back into place, and when he turned to face them, Talia wanted to weep with pity for him. She could hardly believe how worn-looking he was; he must have been on his feet since she'd left.

"It's bad," Kris said wearily. "It looks like the entire population was hit within a day or two. There were five dead when I got here, and I've lost three more since."

"Symptoms?"

"High fever, delirium, a red rash, and swelling under the jaw and the arms."

Kerithwyn nodded. "Snow fever—that's what we call it anyway. It generally shows up right after the first few snowfalls; after Midwinter it seems to vanish and it never appears in warm weather. How have you been treating them?"

"Trying to get liquids down them, especially willowbark tea, although when the fever seemed to be getting too high, especially in the children, I packed them in snow for a bit to bring it down."

"Excellent job! I couldn't have done better myself," she applauded. "I've got some specific remedy with me, but it will take a little time to do any good, so we'll be doing more of the same with the ones not in immediate danger. I'll start with Healing the worst victims now. Have either of you ever assisted a Healer before?"

"I can't," Kris replied shaking his head, so that his lank hair fell onto his forehead. "The last Healer I spoke to said my Gifts were all wrong. I'm afraid I'll be of more use as a simple pair of hands."

Kerithwyn turned to look at Talia, her look oddly measuring.

She swallowed hard, but answered. "I've never tried, but my Gifts are Empathy and Mindhealing. My instructor said they were Healing types." *If I'm going to be assisting, I can't have shields up anyway, and this is going to take so much energy I won't be projecting either.*

"Empathy in a Herald?" Kerithwyn raised one eyebrow. "Well, you ought to be a great deal of help, then. We'll try it, anyway; the worst that can happen is nothing. Herald, have you isolated the worst cases?"

"They're all in here," Kris pointed to a small house immediately next to the gate. "When it didn't seem to harm them to move them, I put all of the worst of them together."

"Excellent." Kerithwyn gave him about a pound of an herbal mixture, instructing him to make a cauldron of tea with it. He was to give every victim at least a cupful, and drink some himself. As Kris left to follow her instructions and care for Rolan, Kerithwyn entered the house with Talia.

The house was cramped and dark, with the windows kept shuttered against the cold air. Kris had moved as many beds and pallets into the three rooms of the house as he could fit. He had done his best to keep his patients clean and had herbal incense burning on the hearth against the miasma of sickness, but there was still a faint but noticeable odor of illness. So many people crowded together made Talia feel claustrophobic, and the smell made her faintly nauseous. She was only grateful that these people were apparently so deeply unconscious that there was nothing for her to have to try to shield against. Kerithwyn appeared not to notice any of this.

The worst of the sick ones was a frail old woman whose bloated jaws looked grotesque on her thin face.

"Take a chair and sit next to me, Herald," the Healer instructed. "Make yourself comfortable, take my free hand, and drop your shielding"—again that measuring look—"and do whatever it is that you do when you prepare to Mindspeak. I'll take care of the rest."

Talia closed her eyes and forcibly ignored her surroundings and put her anxieties into abeyance by concentrating on an old breathing exercise.

It took her a long, considering moment to determine that she was still capable of going into deep-trance. With everything *else* going merrily to hell, she wasn't entirely certain she'd be able to perform even such a rudimentary exercise as deep-trancing.

Tentative trial proved that fear, at least, was groundless.

Once she achieved the appropriate level of trance-state, the Healer appeared to her inner eyes as a nearly solid core of calming green-and-gold energy.

Gods be thanked, she thought with detached gratitude, *Kerithwyn must be even more of an expert than she claimed.*

It wasn't just that the Healer possessed a controlled power the equal of any of the teaching Healers Talia had dealt with—it was also that Talia herself had nothing to fear from the Healer's presence. Kerithwyn was allowing *no* negative emotions to ruffle the surface of *her* mind!

The patient seemed to be roiling with something dark, muddy-red. Talia observed with detached fascination as the Healer sent lances of light into these sullen eddies, cleaning and dispersing them, and feeding the tiny, flickering sparks she uncovered beneath them until they burned strongly again. As Kerithwyn worked, Talia could both see and feel energy draining from herself to the Healer, replacing what Kerithwyn spent.

Now that she understood what the Healer required, she opened the channel between them to its fullest possible extent and reached for Rolan's support. Energy flowed to the Healer in a steady, powerful stream from the two of them, and the work picked up in pace and sureness. It was all finished in a moment, and Talia felt the contact between them break. She sped up her own breathing, turned her concentration outward, and opened her eyes.

The Healer's gray eyes were filled with approval. "*Very* good, Herald; you grasped the concept quite quickly. Can you continue as well as you have begun?"

"I'll give you all I have."

"In that case, I think that the plague will claim no more victims. As you can see, we have done quite well with this one."

The old woman bore little resemblance to the sick creature she had been when they started. The swelling in her jaws was already more than half gone, and it was clear that her fever was nearly broken. Talia was immensely cheered by the sight. This was the first time in so long that she'd done something right. . . .

They treated every person in the house before the Healer insisted that Talia rest. Talia sought out their packs, remembering that she had seen them when she had entered. Kris had left them all in a heap by the fire. She dug out some dried meat and fruit, but found she had so little appetite that she couldn't even raise enough interest to bite into the rations. Instead of eating, she sagged cross-legged on the hearthstone with her back to the fire, soaking up the heat with her eyes closed, too exhausted to sense anything, and so grateful for the respite that all she wanted to do was enjoy the stillness in her mind.

"Foolish girl! Didn't you learn anything about Gifts at that Collegium of yours?"

Talia opened her eyes in surprise; Kerithwyn was standing over her with a steaming mug in one hand and a bar of something in the other.

"You should know perfectly well that if you don't replenish your energy reserves, you'll be of no use to anyone!" She thrust both articles into Talia's hands. "I know you aren't hungry—eat anyway! Finish these, then go find your partner and make him eat and sleep. He doesn't look like he's done either for a week. Don't worry, when I want you, I'll find you. And make sure your Companions are all right as well."

The block proved to be dried fruit and nuts pressed together with honey. Under other conditions Talia would probably have found it to be revoltingly sweet, but once she'd forced down the first bite, it seemed to gain enormously in appeal, and the rest followed rather quickly. She recognized the liquid for the tea Kris had been feeding the plague victims, and saved one bite of the bar to take the nasty taste out of her mouth.

She looked first for Rolan; Kris had removed his tack, thrown several blankets over him, and led him to the stabling area of the inn. Kris had left food and water within reach, but that was all he'd had time to do.

She groomed and cleaned him, grateful that Companions were intelligent creatures that could be trusted to walk themselves cool. He was obviously tired for the first time in her experience, and equally obviously hungry, but otherwise none the worse for the run. She blanketed him warmly against chill and hunted until she found the grain storage area. She added dried fruit to the sweet-feed and put plenty within easy reach, then made a pot of hot gruel, which Rolan slurped up greedily as soon as it had cooled enough to eat.

It occurred to her, tired as she was, that she ought to check on Tantris. Kris' Companion whickered a welcome and rattled his grain bucket entreatingly. She laughed—how long it had been since the last time she'd laughed!—he had hay, he wasn't about to starve, but he obviously wanted some of the same treatment Rolan was getting. She obliged him as he nuzzled her in thanks. The chirras, loose in a large enclosure that gave them access to the outside and which contained enough fodder for them for a week, were in fine fettle. She changed their water, and went to look for Kris.

It didn't take much persuasion on her part to get him into the bedroll she had laid out on the hearth. He actually fell asleep before he'd finished the rations she'd given him; she gently removed the half-finished meal from his hands and placed it where he would see it when he woke, then took up the task she'd pulled him away from.

All three of them worked like slaves far into the night, snatching food and sleep in stolen moments when no one seemed to need aid too urgently. Oddly enough, the frail-seeming Kerithwyn exhibited the least amount of wear. She showed incredible stamina and tirelessness; she frequently scolded them into taking a rest when she herself had taken fewer breaks than either of them.

All three of them were worn and wan when the longed-for sound of hooves pounding on the gate signaled the arrival of the other two Healers and their Herald-escorts.

The two new Healers—a great, hairy bear of a man, and a round-faced girl who seemed scarcely old enough to have attained full Greens—quickly assumed control from Kerithwyn, who found a flat space, a few blankets, and promptly went to sleep. Both Heralds were experienced in assisting Healers, and sent Talia and Kris to their bed-rolls for their first steady night of sleep since they'd arrived here.

All of them were on their feet the next day, and back to the job at hand. They took it in turn to eat and sleep, and by the end of the week several of their former patients were in good enough shape to begin helping them care for their fellow victims. At that point Kerithwyn told Kris gently but firmly to be on their way.

"We don't need you anymore—no, not even for the usual," she insisted. "Our own Heralds can take care of any disputes; we get the laws and news at least once every month, and we're perfectly capable of re-laying reports. I want you two *out* of here before you catch this plague yourselves."

"But—" Kris protested.

"*Out!*" she replied. "I've had this sort of thing happen to me six times already; this is the seventh. You are *not* shirking your duty. Loris and Herald Pelsin are going to be *staying* here until Midwinter; these people are *not* going to need you! Now go!"

Kris gathered his belongings, acquired some fresh food to supplement the dried—it would stay perfectly sound in the cold—left their reports with the Heralds who had brought the Healers, as well as giving them the written reports on the villages they had already visited to be sent back to the capital.

But Talia did not escape so easily. While Kris was conferring with the other two Heralds, Kerithwyn took her aside just before she was ready to mount Rolan. "Child," she said bluntly, "your shields are as full of holes as last week's target, and if you weren't exhausted, you'd be projecting everything under the sun! You're in such a state that if I had any time, I wouldn't let you leave this place. But I *don't* have either the time or the energy to spare. I don't know what you've been doing, or what you *think* you're doing, but whatever it is, it's dead wrong. You'd better get yourself in hand, girl, and quickly, or you'll be affecting even the unGifted. Now go—and start working on that control."

With those blunt words she turned on her heel and left; leaving Talia torn between running after her and begging her help, and slitting her wrists on the spot.

In the end, though, she gathered the ragged bits of her courage around her, and headed out the gate after Kris.

Kris consulted the map; Kerithwyn had ordered him to find a layover point where the two of them could take a long rest. He told Talia that he thought he'd found a particularly good Waystation for them to use as their resting-place. Talia nodded, sunk in her own misery; Kris was preoccupied with making certain of their current location, and hadn't noticed anything—or at least, he hadn't said anything to her about it. But after what Kerithwyn said . . .

Well, she was going to have to be twice as careful as before, that was all.

They were a full half-day from the village now, and well into the Forest of Sorrows itself. Kris had called a halt around midday, so that they could all get a bite to eat while he checked his bearings. There were several narrow roads through Sorrows, and if they had missed theirs, or mistaken the road for a herd-track, they could get into trouble before nightfall.

But they *were* on the right road, and the Waystation was within easy striking distance.

It was fortunate that it was not too far distant, for just after they had dismounted and taken rations from their packs, the chirras began whuffing, and dancing uneasily.

"Talia, chirras don't misbehave unless there's a good reason," Kris said with a frown of worry, as his jerked the lead rope from his hands for the third time. "Can you tell what's wrong?"

"I don't know . . ." she said doubtfully, still shaking from her confrontation with the Healer, and never having done a great deal of work with animals. "I'll give it a try, though."

She braced herself, and sent herself into the deep-trance in which she had been able to touch animals' minds before. The image of what was causing their unhappiness was clear and sharp—and enough to send her flying back to consciousness with speed. "Snow," she said succinctly, for the image had been crystal clear and highly sharpened by fear. "Lots of it—a big blizzard coming down out of the north. It'll hit us before dusk."

Kris swore. "Then we haven't much time. Let's get moving."

CHAPTER 7

THE CHIRRAS RESUMED their good behavior, as if they understood that Talia had learned what was troubling them. They all pushed on as quickly as they could, but the icy road made it hard for both chirras and Companions to keep their footing, and the clouds piling up from the north were making it as dark as if it were already dusk. Then a bitter wind began, cutting through the trees with an eerie moan. The road they were following had taken a turn to the north about a furlong back, which put the wind right in their faces. Kris and Talia dismounted and fought against it alongside the Companions and chirras. When the first fat flakes began falling, they were already in difficulty.

Within moments it was no longer possible for either Herald to see more than a few feet ahead, and the wind was strong enough to whip the edges of their cloaks out of their benumbed hands. It howled among the tree branches, and ravened on the ground, shrieking like the damned. The trees groaned and creaked in protest, the thinner branches whipping wildly above their heads. It was so hard to be heard above the storm that neither of them bothered to speak, using only hand signals when there was something that *had* to be communicated. This was like no storm Talia had seen before, and she hoped (when she had any thoughts at all through the numbing cold) that it wasn't typical for this Sector.

The snow piled up with frightening speed; ankle-deep, then knee-deep. They completely lost track of distance and time in the simple struggle to place one foot in front of the other. Kris and Tantris found the lane that led to the Waystation more by accident than anything else, literally stumbling into it as they probed the bushes at the side of the road.

The lane soon plunged down between two shallow ridges where they were sheltered from the worst of the wind. They let go of the girths they'd clung to and stumbled along in their Companions' wake, trusting to their mounts' better senses to guide them all to the Station. By the time they achieved it, they could hardly see the path ahead of them. The bulk of the Station loomed up before them out of the gray-white wall of snow only when they were practically on top of it.

The Station probably hadn't been visited since the resupply team had last inspected and stocked it during the summer. A quick survey of the woodpile told them that there wasn't enough stockpiled there to last for as long as they were likely to be snowed in. In frantic haste, they left the chirras tied to the building, removed everything from the packs on their Companions, fastened lead ropes from their own belts to the snaffles on the saddles and went out with axes to look for deadfall.

It was grueling work, especially coming on top of the previous crisis. Talia's arms and shoulders ached with the unaccustomed work; what didn't ache was nearly numb with cold. Her cloak was caked with snow to the point where it creaked and bits of snow fell off when she moved. Her world narrowed to the pain, the axe in her hands, and the deadfall in front of her. More than anything else, she longed to be able to lie down in the soft snow and rest, but she knew that this was the very last thing she should do. Instead, she continued to struggle against pain and the driving snow, using the numbing cold and the ache of overtaxed muscles as a bulwark against despair—the despair that Healer Kerithwyn had evoked with her brusque warning. She drove herself in the gathering gloom until she became aware that she could barely see where her axe was falling. It was nearly night now—true night.

It was time to give up. As Talia and Rolan hauled in the last load while full darkness fell, it was all she could do to cling to his girth as he dragged her and the wood back toward the station. The wind had picked up—something she wouldn't have believed possible—and it was all but tearing her cloak from her body. Her breath was sobbing in her lungs, sending needles of ice and pain through her throat and chest.

She opened the door of the Station, only to blink in surprise—for there was nothing before her but a gloom-shrouded little room with a door on the opposite wall. After a moment, her fatigue-fogged mind managed to grasp the fact that this Station, unlike any other she had seen previously, had an entranceway to buffer the effect of the outside chill.

She fumbled the second door open, Rolan crowding into the entrance after her. Kris had beaten her to the Station with his final load shortly before, and had fumigated it and started a fire in the fireplace. He unfastened her from Rolan; she stumbled thankfully toward the yellow beacon of the fire with half-frozen limbs. He led Rolan into the shelter of the Station itself, and as she collapsed next to the warmth of the flames she saw that he had brought in Tantris and the chirras as well. It made things a bit crowded until he got them all settled, but Talia knew that there was no way anything could live long in the howling winds outside.

She peeled off her snow-caked garments and hung them beside Kris' on pegs above the fireplace. Kris was already taking care of meal preparations, so after she slipped into her woolen shift and old breeches (feeling far too exhausted for a complete change of clothing) she made a nest of the dun-colored blankets from both their bedrolls on top of dry straw in front of the fire. This way they could warm their aching, shivering bodies in comfort while waiting for whatever it was to cook.

She blinked stupidly at the fire, mind and body alike still numb and cold. She held to that numbness, stubbornly, not wanting to face the alternative to numbness. She succeeded; she remained sunk in exhausted apathy long after she normally would have begun to show some signs of life. Kris was standing over her for several minutes before she realized he was there.

"Talia . . ." he began awkwardly, "I know this isn't the time or the place, but there isn't likely to be a better one. I have to talk to you."

Without really realizing it, she rose slowly to her still-benumbed feet, feeling a cold that had nothing to do with the blizzard outside. "Ab-b-b-out what?" she stuttered, fearing the worst.

"Kerithwyn had some words with me before we left," he said, as the despair she'd been holding off with the last of her strength came down on her with the same overwhelming power as storm—and with it, oddly enough, a hopeless kind of rage. "Hell, Talia—she told me you've been holding back on me; that your Gift is totally out of control!"

Something within her shattered, letting loose the storm she'd held pent up for so long.

*   *   *

Kris was expecting anger, denial—*but not this!* He was battered by alternating waves of suicidal despair, and killing rage; the shock of it literally sent him to his knees. His eyes filmed with a red mist. There was a roaring in his ears, behind which he could dimly hear the squeal of an angry horse and the clatter of hooves on stone.

That was what brought him out, before he grabbed a weapon and killed himself, her, or both of them. He built up the strongest shield he could, fought his way to his feet, and rushed her, literally slamming her into the wall behind her with enough force to make his own teeth rattle.

"Stop it!" he shouted at the wild, inhuman thing struggling beneath his hands. "Damn you, *stop* it! Look what you're doing to us!" He wrenched her around violently, so that she could see for herself the unbelievable sight of Rolan backing Tantris into a corner, teeth bared and eyes wild and red-rimmed. *"Look what you're doing to them!"*

She stared—and collapsed so suddenly he didn't even have time to catch her, for she fell right through his hands. She fell and curled into a limp ball on the cold stone floor of the Station, sobbing as if she had lost everything she ever held dear.

And the storm within the Station walls faded away to nothing.

He went to his knees beside her, and gathered her against his shoulder. She didn't resist—didn't even seem to know he was there. He held her while she cried, horrible, tearing sobs that seemed to be ripping her apart inside, while the fire he'd started burned lower and lower, and the storm outside echoed her heartbroken weeping.

Finally, when it seemed possible that the fire might die altogether, he picked her up and put her in the nest of blankets and hay. She curled up, facing away from him and still crying, while he built up the fire, finished the tasks he'd left undone, and returned to her.

He got in beside her, chilled to the bone, and took her equally cold body into his arms again. The violence of her grief seemed to have worn itself out; he shook her a little. "Come on—" he said, feeling more than awkward. "Talk to me, lady—"

"I–I—" she sobbed. "I want to die!"

"Why? Because your Gift got out of control? What kind of attitude is that for a Herald?"

"I'm *no* kind of Herald."

"Like bloody hell!" he interrupted. "Who says?"

"Everyone—you told me—"

"Oh, hell. . . ." *Now* he realized what it was that triggered this whole mess in the first place—himself, telling her the rumors about her. Gods—he *knew* she hadn't a high level of self-esteem—what he'd said back at the start of this trip must have hit her like a punch in the kidneys. He must have started her on a round of self-examination and self-doubt that turned into a downturning spiral she hadn't the power to stop. Her Gift was the sort of thing that would feed on doubt and make it reality—which in turn would feed her doubts, reinforcing them as her loss of control turned rumor into truth.

And *this* was the result. A fully developed Gift without any controls on it whatsoever, and a young woman ready to kill herself the minute he turned his back.

"Listen to me—*dammit* Talia, *listen!*" He shook her again. "If things were that bad, Rolan would have left you. He'd have repudiated *anybody* not worthy of her Whites. Has he made any move like that at all?"

"N-n-n-no . . ."

"Has he even *warned* you?"

The sobs were fading. "N-n-no."

"He's *helped* you, hasn't he? He's kept your damned secret. *He* thinks you're still a Herald. So *act* like one, dammit! Stop emoting and start *thinking.* You're in a mess; now how can we get you out of it?"

She looked up at him for the first time, eyes swollen and red. "We?"

"We," he repeated. "I'm as much to blame for this as you are. I should never have told you those damned stories—should have believed you when you told me they weren't true. I'd be willing to bet it was *my* doubt that made all this worse. Hmm?"

She shook her head, then hid her face against his chest. He pulled her closer, and began stroking her hair and rocking her a little. "Poor baby," he murmured. "Poor scared, lonely baby—here—try this." He reached out and seized a small leather bottle from the top of his pile of belongings beside them, and passed it to her. "One of the standard cures for sensitivity is wine. This ought to blunt your edges good!"

Talia accepted the bottle, took a gulp and almost choked. The stuff was like drinking sweet, liquid fire!

"What—*is*—that?" she asked when she'd stopped gasping for breath.

"Something the Healers make—spirits of wine, they call it. They make it by freezing the wine they make from honey, and throwing away the ice; that's what's left. The one that looks like a bear gave it to me before we left."

Talia took another drink, just a sip this time, and with more caution. It didn't burn the way the first mouthful had, and left behind a very pleasant sensation in her mouth and stomach. And it certainly *did* blunt the edges of both her sensitivity and her raw nerves. *That* was the best thing that had happened to her all day, so she took a third swallow.

"Easy there, little one." Kris laughed, sounding relieved. "That stuff's potent!"

"I can tell," she said, feeling a bit giddy. "But I feel a lot better. Not so raw."

"That was what I hoped," he replied, appropriating the bottle and drinking from it himself. "I suppose we shouldn't be drinking it on an empty stomach, but I figure you need it. Hell, after what I've been through, so do I!"

She had drunk enough that she was just aware of Kris' mental presence; his proximity was no longer painful. "Thanks."

"Don't mention it."

She lay quietly in the circle of his arms, feeling utterly drained, as they continued to share sips of the bottle. The fire popped and crackled, with little bits of blue and green flame among the red and orange. She was finally beginning to feel warm all the way through—something she hadn't thought likely out there in the snow—and relaxed—something she hadn't thought likely ever again. The fire smelled of evergreens, like forest-green incense. The chirras and Companions shifted a little from time to time, rustling the straw Kris had laid down for them. Gods—what she'd almost done to them! She touched with Rolan just long enough to assure herself that he was all right. . . .

His forgiveness and love was so total that tears came to her eyes again.

"Hey," Kris said gently. "I thought we'd agreed there'd be no more of that."

When she didn't reply, he put one hand under her chin, tilted it up, and kissed her.

It was *intended* to be a brotherly kiss.

It didn't stay brotherly for more than an instant.

"Bright Havens!" he breathed in surprise when they finally moved apart.

Talia leaned back into his shoulder; her desire had surprised her as much as it had him, although she knew that was a common enough reaction after great stress. She wasn't aware of him as her counselor or even as a Herald at this moment—only as a friend and an emotional shelter—and knew with certainty that he was as aware of her need as she was of his own. This time she reached for him.

As their mouths met and opened, he gently slipped the shift down past her waist. She shivered in delight as his mouth brushed the back of her neck, the line of her shoulders, as he kissed away her tears; he sighed as she nibbled his earlobe timidly. With her shields gone, they seemed to be feeling every tiny nuance of each other's reactions. As she traced the line of his spine with a feather-like touch, she felt it as much as he—when she tensed and gasped as he found an unexpectedly responsive spot, he tensed in sympathy as well.

Finally their mutual desires grew too impatient to be put off any longer; he slowly let her down on the blankets beside him, sank into her embrace, and entered her.

He was totally unprepared for the stab of pain that was shared as the pleasure had been. He would have withdrawn from her at once, but she clung to him with fierceness and would not let him go.

She'd expected pain, and endured it. What she had not expected was that he would curb his own desire, to bring her past the pain, and finally to patiently wait on her pleasure before taking his own.

She shifted over as he collapsed, then nestled into the curve of his arm again. They curled together in their warm nest, spent and replete, and feeling no urgent need to do anything other than savor the experience they'd shared. For long moments there was no sound at all but the sounds of the fire, and the tiny stirrings of the four at the other end of the station.

He turned his head to look into her dark eyes, wide and drowsy with content. "Why didn't you tell me you were a virgin?" he asked softly.

"You didn't ask," she said sleepily. "Why? Is it that important?"

"I don't think I'd have loved you if I'd known."

"All the more reason not to tell you," she pointed out logically. She nestled closer to him, her head on his chest, pulling blankets over both of them. "But I'm glad it was you."

"Why?"

"Among other things, my gossiping Heraldic sisters were right. It was . . . a lot nicer than I'd been led to believe first times usually are."

"A compliment?" he asked, amused.

"A compliment."

A thought occurred to him. "Wait a minute. I thought you and Skif . . ."

She smiled, the first real smile he'd gotten out of her in weeks. "That's what you were supposed to think. It was awful—we both had horrid schedules, and we were so exhausted that we kept falling asleep before we could get anywhere."

She told him the comic-frustrating tale of their abortive romance, and how it had finally culminated in their swearing blood-brotherhood, rather than bed.

"Poor Skif! And poor Talia," he chuckled. "You knew he'd be teased half to death if that tale got out, didn't you? So you let everyone think otherwise."

"Mm-hmm. Poor Skif . . ." She yawned. "Victim of unrequited lust." She was falling asleep in his arms, and as much as he hated to disturb her, he knew that he'd better.

"Wake up, sleepy. If you don't want to greet the dawn with a head-ache, you'd better have some food in you, and something to drink be-sides that devil's brew. The last thing you need is a hangover in the morning, and as potent as that stuff is, you're likely to wish you had died if you let it give you one. And we may be warm *now*, but we're going to wake up cold and stiff in the middle of the night if we don't make up a better bed. After all we've weathered, I'd hate to see you cramped in knots for want of a little sense."

She yawned hugely but didn't protest. They both rummaged out clean bedclothes and pulled them on. While he ladled stew out of the pot over the fire, she remade their "nest" with everything she could find to use as a blanket. He made hot tea, and they drank it with their meal.

They bedded down in each other's arms after he'd banked the fire, seeing no reason now to return to their practice of separate beds.

"I'm awfully glad this happened now," she said before he drifted off to sleep.

"Why's that, little bird?"

"Two sleep warmer together than two alone . . . and it's getting a lot colder."

Kris was pleased to discover that (unlike some lovers he'd had) Talia was a quiet sleeper; not at all restless, and not inclined to steal the blan-kets (which was, in his opinion, the quickest way to ruin an otherwise satisfactory relationship). He found her presence oddly comforting, and an especially good antidote to the howl of the wind outside.

He woke once when Tantris tickled his mind into wakefulness; he and Rolan wanted out. He was very grateful for the tiny entranceway this Station possessed; it wasn't part of the usual design, but with crowding he could fit one Companion and one chirra inside and still close the door to the interior before opening the outer door. If the ex-terior door had opened directly into the station as was usually the case, every time he had to let them out he'd be letting most of the heat they'd built up out with them.

The wind hadn't slackened in the least, and the snow was still coming down as thickly as before. It was definitely daylight, but he couldn't even tell where the sun was, much less see how high it was. It took all his strength to keep the door from being blown out of his hands; he realized then that this was why they'd awakened him and not Talia. He'd left halters and lead-reins on the chirras, which the Companions used to lead them outside.

One more advantage of chirras, he reflected wryly. *You can't housebreak mules.*

The scrape of a hoof on the door signaled their return. He managed to hold to the door and slammed it behind them, but in spite of the buffering of the entranceway, their exit and re-entrance had stolen a noticeable amount of the heat from the room. He built the fire back up after filling the biggest pot they had with clean snow, then carefully groomed all four of ice and snow. He made sure they were comfortable, and noticed with a smile that all four of them lay in a close-packed group, with chirras on the outside and Companions in the middle.

"You're too clever by half," he told Tantris, and smiled at the Companion's amusement-laden reply.

:Given the choice, would you take the outside? They've got the coats for this, brother-in-soul—we haven't!:

He was grateful for Tantris' nonchalance; both the Companions seemed to be taking the events of the previous night as simply one more obstacle to be met and dealt with, rather than an insurmountable disaster. That heartened him, for he expected to need their help.

He hung the pot full of half-melted snow over the fire, then banked it again before returning to the bed that was looking better by the moment.

When he slipped in beside Talia he got another delightful surprise. Instead of pulling away, Talia actually hugged his chilled body to her warm one until he was no longer shivering, despite being three-quarters asleep herself. *There never*, he reflected as he drifted back to dreams, *was a truer test of friendship!*

When he finally woke of his own accord, he judged that several hours had passed; it was probably late morning or early afternoon. There didn't seem to be any real reason to get up; the winds still howled with the same ferocity outside.

"I wish these Stations had a window," he said drowsily. "It's impossible to tell if it's still snowing or not."

"No, it isn't," Talia murmured sleepily in his ear.

He hadn't realized she was awake. "No, it isn't, what?"

"It's not impossible to tell if snow's still coming down. Listen, and you can hear it on the roof and windward walls. It has a different sound than wind alone. It kind of hisses."

Kris listened; she was right. There was a hissing undertone to the storm outside. "How did you know about that?" he asked, more than a little surprised.

"Comes of sleeping in the attic. There're no windows in the attic of a Hold house, and that's where all the littles sleep. If you wanted to know what kind of weather to dress for, you learned to recognize all the sounds that weather makes. Where are you going?"

"Now that we're awake, I'm going to get the fire built back up."

He got an armload of wood from the stack he'd brought inside earlier, exposed the banked coals, and soon had it blazing again. In spite of the heat given off by the banked coals, the room was icy; the chimney was cleverly baffled, but the wind was still succeeding in stealing some of their heat. He was quite chilled by the time he was satisfied with the state of the fire. When he slid back in beside her, Talia again snuggled up to warm him.

"That's definitely above and beyond the call of duty," he said, when he'd stopped shivering. "Thanks."

"You're welcome. Consider it payback for last night."

He deliberately misunderstood. "Bright Havens, little bird, you keep surprising me! I hadn't the least notion there was such a sensualist under that serene exterior."

She played along. "Why shouldn't there have been?"

"You surely didn't show any sign of it. And you certainly haven't been . . . practicing, shall we say?"

"I hadn't found anyone I was enough at ease with before this except Skif, and that liaison seemed to have a curse on it!" There was rueful laughter in her voice. "But it wasn't that I lacked interest; I never told you about Rolan."

"What's *Rolan* got to do with this?"

"Remember I told you that he's always in the back of my mind? That I always know what he's doing, and I can't shield him out at all?" Her expression was a little shadowed as she realized she couldn't shield anyone out at the moment.

"So?" he prompted. "Why would you want to?"

"Nighttime in Companion's Field gets very interesting . . . and Companion mares share another characteristic with humans besides the gestation period." When he looked blank, she sighed. "They're always 'in season,' oh, wise counselor."

"Good Lord. And if you can't shield him out . . ."

"That means exactly what your filthy mind is thinking."

"Secondhand experience?"

"Something like it."

He pulled her head to rest comfortably on his shoulder. "Talia, I'm sorry I didn't see the state you were in, and I'm sorrier I didn't do anything about it."

"Oh—I—" She sobered immediately when he mentioned her emotion-storm. "Gods, Kris, what am I going to do?"

"We."

"What?"

"We. You, me, Tantris, and Rolan. This is not the total disaster you seem to think it is. Let's take the easy things. First of all, you've learned something you won't forget. Now let me tell you a little something, Queen's Own. The reason you're out here is that you'll see every kind of problem you're likely to run up against at Court—only out here it will be much more clear-cut, much simpler. You learn how to handle it where it's easy to deal with, instead of plunging right in and drowning. Take somebody who's held a grudge for so long it's an obsession. You've seen it once now, would you recognize it again?"

Talia thought about how she'd felt when the girl looked into her eyes; the odd chill she'd sensed. "Yes," she said at last.

"And do you think you could handle it?"

"Maybe . . . I think I'd have to get an assist though."

"Good for you. Before this you'd have said 'yes.' Now you realize you might need help. You're learning, greenie. Now the hard part. Your Gift has gone out of control; we have to get it back under control again. I'll be willing to bet part of the reason for it going was that nobody recognized you need special training—training to keep your own emotional state from feeding back on your Gift. I'm not even certain there *is* such a thing."

"Why do you say that?"

"Because I can't think of another Queen's Own in living memory that has had as powerful a Gift as yours. I've never heard of empathy strong enough to be used as a weapon. Talamir certainly didn't have it—nor Keighvin before him. I don't even know that there's a Healer around with empathy that strong. *Maybe* a Healer could train you, but I wouldn't care to bet money on the idea."

"Then what . . ."

"We'll bloody well *invent* the training. All four of us. First off, your shields are gone. That's likely to be the hardest for you to get back, but I think *maybe* we can deal with it in a different way for now. Hey, Fairyfoot—"

Tantris looked up and snorted. *:Yes, master of the world?:*

"Go ahead, *be* sarcastic."

:You started it.:

"This is serious, Hayburner. Can you impose shields on her from outside?"

Tantris looked at both of them thoughtfully. *:Yes,:* he said after a long pause, *:but not for very long.:*

"If you can, then Rolan can—"

:Has.:

Kris raised one eyebrow. "Huh. I should have anticipated that. All right, I know *I* can; I've reinforced shielding on the kids I was teaching. So if we take it turn and turn about, can we keep her buffered so long as it's just the three of us she's dealing with?"

:I would think so.: Tantris looked at the other Companion measuringly. *:Rolan says to tell you we can probably even handle small gatherings of people.:*

"Better than I'd hoped. Fine. I'll take first watch. When I flag . . ."

:I'll catch,: came the confident answer. *:My pleasure, brother-in-soul.:*

"Did you get the drift of that?" He turned to Talia, setting up shielding around her as he spoke.

"You're—oh, *Gods!*" The relief on her face was a revelation; until that moment he had not realized *how* much strain she was under.

"Right. Now . . . having gotten that taken care of temporarily, we'll deal with the half of the problem that's dangerous to others."

"The projecting—"

"But not now. You're too tired to project past the end of your nose unless I make the mistake of frightening you half to death again, so that can wait. I'm hungry, and I want a bath."

Although they had used the Waymeet village bathhouse frequently, choosing a scrub by way of restorative over the sleep they had had little time for, it had been well over a day since the last time they'd gotten clean. Since both of them had fastidious natures, they were feeling it.

"You go first, then. I want to groom the four-feets, and I'll wash afterward. I can start to smell them now, and if I don't get them pretty well clean, things could get whiffy in here. Since I'm doing Rolan, I might as well do all four of them. There's no need in both of us getting filthy."

Kris sniffed; the air was faintly perfumed with an odor of wet wool and horse-sweat. "You don't have to do all four, but if you insist, I'll let you. You're ruining my lovely self-indulgence, though. If you're going to go all virtuous on me and work, I'll have to find something to do as well." He sighed heavily, and made sad eyes at her.

She made a face at him, feeling like her old self for the first time in weeks. She got dressed, threw her cloak on, then took the first chirra's lead-rein.

Chores kept them occupied for the rest of the day, housekeeping and tending to mending that had been left neglected while they ministered to the plague victims. Talia was just as happy; she was reluctant to face her problems just now when she was so emotionally raw. After a quiet bit of lunch, Kris went to take inventory of their supplies.

There was a half-height door opposite the entrance to the station; it led to a storage shed. Kris found far more supplies there than he had dared to hope—and found some unfamiliar jars and barrels as well. He brought some of those into the Station.

The jars held honey and oil. "Someone near here must have left these after winter set in," Kris said in surprise. "It wouldn't be safe or wise to leave them here in warm weather; they'd go bad or attract animals. That's why they're not standard stock. What's in the barrel?"

"The oil can be used in the lamp, too." Talia opened her barrel. It held what seemed to be dried beans. Kris was perplexed.

"Now why . . ." he began, when Talia remembered something Sherrill had told her.

"Sprouts!" she exclaimed. "To keep us from the winter sickness, if we get stuck here longer than the fruit lasts. We're supposed to soak those in water until they sprout, then eat the sprouts. They do that where Sherrill and Keren come from."

Kris looked sober. "We may need them, too. Even if the fruit holds out, it's dried; not as good for holding off winter-sickness as fresh." He made a mental tally of all their supplies. "I think we can hold out for a month or so," he decided, from experience with being snowed in before. "And from the looks of this storm, that's exactly what may happen. It's still going strong, and by the way the sky looked today, I don't think it's going to be slackening soon."

"Do we have enough fodder, though? Tantris and Rolan are big eaters, and we can't feed them on bark and twigs the way we can with the chirras if supplies run low."

"There's fodder and straw baled and stacked on the other side of the shed where you can't see it, besides on the near side," Kris reassured her. "It almost looks as though whoever was stocking this Station was expecting a storm this bad. It seems odd, but I don't know enough about this area to tell you whether or not this type of weather is typical for this time of year. Dirk would know that better than I."

"Whatever the reason for the abundance of supplies, it's a good thing for us that they're there."

They did something about supper, and Kris retuned the harp. With an inquiring glance in her direction, he began with a song that she'd sung at the Herald's revel. Taking the glance as an invitation, she stretched herself next to him and began to sing quietly. He hummed the low harmonic under his breath; his voice, though no match for Dirk's, was reasonably melodic. Behind them the Companions and chirras pricked their ears up to listen with every evidence of interest.

Suddenly two new voices joined in, wordlessly crooning an eerie descant. Talia and Kris jumped, startled, and stopped—the new voices stopped with the music.

Puzzled, they began again, this time peering into the darkened side of the Station. After a moment, the descant resumed.

"Well, that's what I get for making fun of Dirk's and Harthen's tales!" Kris said in surprise. "Chirras *do* sing!"

Rolan and Tantris were staring at their stable-mates with a kind of ironic astonishment. Evidently *they* hadn't expected the singing either. The chirras, oblivious to everything but the music around them, were reclining with their eyes closed and their heads and necks stretched upward as far as they could reach. Their throats were pulsing, and the humming was, without a doubt, coming from them.

"Don't feel badly. I wouldn't have believed it either," Talia replied. "I mean, they look like sheep, sort of, and sheep don't sing. Probably there aren't too many people playing or singing around them, which would be why more folks haven't heard them. *We* never did; they were always outside in the lean-to."

The chirras joined in happily on almost everything they played, but they particularly seemed to enjoy the livelier tunes. What was utterly amazing—apart from the simple fact that they sang at all—was *what* they sang. They crooned harmonics to the melody rather than following the melody itself, and usually chose the upper range in a descant. They would listen for a verse or two before joining in, but though very simple, their harmonizing always fit. Talia knew a great many human singers who couldn't boast that ability.

They continued on for some time, so fascinated by this inhuman

choir that they forgot any worries they had. They continued until Kris'
fingers were much too tired to play any more. Although he dearly
wanted to go on, after a few fumblings, which caused the chirras to
flatten their ears and stare like a pair of offended old women, he was
forced to admit it was time to give his hands a rest.

"In that case . . ."

"What have I decided? This is going to be rather hard on you, little
bird—"

"And the past few weeks haven't?" she replied bitterly.

"Not like this; it's going to be pretty cruel. The way I figure it, the
two of us *not* shielding, and especially Rolan, are going to be watching
you like cats at a mousehole. The least little indication of projection,
and we're going to jump all over you. After a few days of that, I am
willing to bet that you will by damn not be doing any projecting without knowing that you're doing it!"

"It doesn't sound pleasant," she said slowly, "but it does sound like it
may work."

"Then once we've got you knowing when you're projecting, we'll
move to handling the projection consciously. Then we'll work on you
controlling the level of it. Finally we'll work on getting your shields
back up."

"If you think I can. . . ."

"I bloody damn *know* you can!" he said. "But we are not going to be
doing anything tonight. If you're as worn out as I am—and if you're
not *more* worn out, you're a better man than I, after all you've been
through—you won't be able to do anything, much less work something as delicate as a rogue Gift."

As he spoke, he became acutely aware of his own mental fatigue,
and the strain of holding shields on her. Just as he felt his own control
waver, he felt Tantris slip into his place.

:*My turn, brother,*: the mental voice said firmly. He sighed and sent a
wordless thought of thanks.

Talia readied things for the morning, while he cared for their Companions. She had shed her clothing and was lazily reaching for the
woolen shift she was using as a bedgown, when she found her wrist
caught by Kris' hand.

He had come upon her quietly from behind, and now captured her
other wrist, holding her with her back pressed into his chest. "Surely
you're not sleepy already?" he breathed into her ear, sending delightful
shivers up her back.

"No," she replied, leaning her head back as his lips touched the back of her neck and moved around to the hollow below her ear.

"Good," he drew her down beside him, on top of the blankets he'd spread on the hearthstone, right next to the fire. He stretched himself beside her so that she was between him and the fireplace, feeling truly relaxed for the first time since Elspeth was Chosen.

He cradled her shoulders while his free hand traced invisible patterns on her skin that seemed to tingle—she moved her own hands in half-instinctual response to what she felt from him; at first hesitantly, then with growing surety. Every inch of skin seemed to be doubly sensitive, and she murmured in surprise and delight as his hands did new and entrancing things. Just when she thought for certain that he'd roused her to the uttermost, he moved his seeking mouth elsewhere, and she learned how it was to be fully awakened to desire.

Learning from him, she followed his lead, as he roused her to fever pitch, let her cool a little, then aroused her senses again. Finally, when she was certain neither of them could bear any more, he sought her mouth again and joined with her.

The pain was less than nothing compared to what they shared.

When at last Kris disengaged himself from her, they lay twined together for a long, euphoric moment, still deeply in rapport. He half-rose and handed her the nearly-forgotten shift with one hand while pulling on his own robe. She slipped it on, lazily gathered up the blankets, and remade their bed. She curled up in it with utter contentment as he banked the fire against the night.

"That Gift of yours is not always a bad thing," he said, finally. "Should you ever choose a life-partner, I think I would envy him, little friend. Now I see what they mean about wedding or bedding Healers—especially if all of them have the same kind of Empathy that you do."

"Oh?" Her ears all but perked up with interest. "And what do they say?"

"That you may not get much time with them because they're always likely to be called away—but what time you do get makes up for their frequent absences."

She reached up to pull the blankets more securely about the two of them, and something odd about her hand caught his attention. He captured her wrist again, and held it so that the palm would catch the last of the firelight, frowning a little as he did so.

Her palm was disfigured by a deep, roughly circular scar.

"That," she said quietly, answering the question he did not speak, "is the reason why I was afraid of men for so long—and why I don't trust handsome ones. My brother Justus, with the innocent face of a golden-haired angel and the heart of a demon, did that to me when I was nine years old."

"Why?" The word held a world of shock and dismay.

"He wanted . . . I don't know what he wanted; maybe just to see me hurting. He hated anything he couldn't control. He used to inflict as much pain as he could on the farm animals whenever something had to be done with them. He'd half-drown the sheep, dipping them for insects; he'd cut them terribly, shearing them. Horses he broke *were* broken; there was no spirit in them when he was done. I think it galled him that I could have an escape from the boredom of Hold life that he couldn't ruin—he couldn't stop my reading or dreaming. He ordered me one day to drown a sack of kittens; I tore the sack open instead so that they all escaped. I'm sure he knew that that was exactly what I would do. He backhanded me, knocked me down flat, stepped on my wrist, and used a red-hot poker on my hand. I think that one time he overstepped what he'd intended; I don't think he meant to burn me as badly as he did, at least not after he saw what he'd done. Gods, I'll never, ever forget his face while he was burning me, though." She shuddered, and he held her a little closer. "That— obscene *joy*—I still had nightmares about it right up through my second year at the Collegium. I know they heard me screaming, but no one came very fast because they knew he was setting a task for me and figured I was being punished for slacking. When I didn't stop after a couple minutes, though, one of the Underwives came to check. *After* all the damage was done. When she saw me, he'd already thrown the poker down. He told Keldar Firstwife that he'd hit me for disobedience and I'd grabbed the poker to hit him back, but it had been in the fire too long. He didn't even have to explain why it was that my palm was burned and not my fingers. They believed him, of course, and not me."

"Gods!" He was sickened—and a little more understanding of why she hadn't confided in him.

"It was . . . a long time ago. I'm almost over what it did to me. I think if he were still alive, and subjecting a wife or children to his sadism . . . well, he's not. He managed to get himself killed a year or two after I was Chosen. There was a raid, and he had to prove just how much braver he was than anyone else. And Keltev, who was bidding fair to grow up like him, seems to have learned better, so . . ." She shrugged.

"That's the one who used to tease you about wanting to be a Herald—Keltev? Now I know why you put up with the Blues for so long. You had practice; after Justus they must . . ."

"As far as physical tormenting, they were amateurs. Mental, though . . . they were quite . . . adept. But I'd learned from my sibs that if you give them the satisfaction of knowing they've hit home by acting as if they'd hurt you in any way, they only get worse. And how was I to know I'd be believed?"

"Oh, Talia—" he held her closely against his chest. "Poor little bird!"

"It wasn't so bad as all that," she said softly into his shoulder. "Besides, I've learned better now. I've got people I can love, friends I can trust—my year-mates, my teachers—and now"—she looked up at him a little shyly—"you and Dirk."

"And everyone else in the Circle, little bird," he replied, kissing her softly on the forehead, "I'm just sorry I didn't trust *you*. But we'll fix it. We'll fix it."

She simply sighed assent.

The fire was now little more than glowing coals, and Kris stared at them while he let his mind drift, not yet ready to sleep.

"You know, you and Dirk will get along beautifully," he mused. "Your minds work almost the same way."

"Why do you say that?"

"You wouldn't do anything to save yourself pain, but you dared your brother's anger to save the kittens. That's so much like Dirk it isn't funny. Hurt him . . . he'll just go and hide in himself; but hurt a friend, or something helpless—Gods! He'll sacrifice himself to save it, or he'll rip your heart out because he couldn't. You're two of a kind; I really think you're going to be more than casual friends."

"Do you really think so?" she said, a little too eagerly.

All the pieces fell together, and the suspicion he'd had earlier became a certainty. "Why, Talia," he chuckled, "I do believe you're a bit smitten with my partner!"

He felt the cheek resting on his shoulder grow warm. "A little," she admitted, knowing that it would be useless to deny it.

"Only a little?"

"More than a little," she replied almost inaudibly.

"Serious?"

"I . . . don't know. It depends on him, mostly." She was blushing furiously now. "I'm afraid it could get that way very fast under the right conditions."

"But now?"

She sighed. "Kris, I don't know, I just don't know. And why am I bothering to get my hopes up? I don't know how he feels . . . whether or not he's likely to be the least bit interested in me. . . ."

"*You* may not. I think maybe I do. If I'm reading him right, he's already interested." Kris thought back on the way Dirk had acted right before he and Talia had left. He couldn't stop talking about how envious he was that Kris had gotten her as an intern, and he kept on at great length about her wonderful voice. Normally, since that bitch at the Court had hurt him, he'd paid very little attention to women, except for the occasional ribald remark.

Then he'd hinted that it would be a good notion if they'd all practice together so they could do more as a trio. Holy Stars, he'd never once suggested that they practice together with *anyone* before, not even Jadus.

"For one thing," Kris said slowly, "he wants us to play together on a regular basis. I mean, he wants *us* to play, and *you* to sing."

"He does?" she said in bemusement. "He plays?"

"As well as I do, or better. Since my voice isn't very good, though, and his is, he's kind enough to let me have the playing to myself. Out on the road we play together quite often, but outside of myself hardly anyone in the Circle knows he can."

"And he said I was full of surprises!"

"Oh, you are." He caressed her hair absently. Lord of Lights, they were so well suited to each other. There was a great deal more to both of them than would ever show on the surface. There were depths to both of them that *he* knew he'd never see.

He chuckled a little.

"What's so funny?"

"Bright Havens, I hardly dare think what you might be like in the arms of someone you truly loved! He'd better have a strong heart, or he might not survive the experience!"

"Kris!" she exclaimed indignantly. "You make me sound like the widowing-spider that eats her mate!"

He ruffled her hair. "Maybe I'd better make certain that you and Dirk make a pair of it. He's the strongest man I know."

"Keep this up much longer," she said warningly, "and I'll put snow down your back after you fall asleep."

"Cruel, too. On second thought, maybe I'd better warn him off."

"Do that, and I'll go directly to Nessa when we get back, tell her that you confided your everlasting passion for her to me, but that you're too shy to tell her yourself."

"Not just cruel—vicious!"

"Self-defense," she countered.

"Monster of iniquity," he replied, tugging at her hair until it fell into her eyes. "You know, of all the people I can think of, I can't imagine being able to stand being snowed in with any of them except you and Dirk—especially for as long as *we're* likely to be stuck here."

She grew serious. "Is it really likely to be that long?"

"If it doesn't stop snowing soon, it could easily be a month. This Station is down in a valley and protected by trees. We're not getting the worst of it. I tried to get past the trees earlier, and you can't. The snow has drifted as high as a chirra in some places. Even after the snow stops, we'll have to wait for the Guard to clear the road, because until they do we won't be going anywhere."

"How will anyone know where we are?"

"I told that Healer—the bearish one, I think his name is Loris— where I intended us to hole up. Besides, little bird, this may be all to the good. We may well need all that time to get your Gift back under control again."

"That . . . that's true," she said soberly. "Oh, Kris—do you really think we can?"

He noted with a bit of pleasure, the "we," for it meant she was no longer thinking in terms of dealing with the problem on her own. "Not only do *I* think so, but Tantris and Rolan do. You're not going to argue with them, are you?"

"I . . . I guess not."

"I hear a doubt. No doubts—that's what got you into this mess in the first place. We *will* get you back in control. I may not be a Kyril or an Ylsa, but I *am* a Gift-teacher. I know what I'm doing."

"But—"

"I told you, but me no 'buts'! *Believe*, Talia. In yourself as much as in me. That's the weakest leg your Gift has to stand on right now."

She didn't reply to that; just stared thoughtfully at the fire until her eyes drooped and finally closed, and her slow, steady breathing told him she'd fallen asleep.

He remained awake for much longer, engaged in a struggle with himself he *had* to win, a struggle to set aside a Herald's impartiality and wholeheartedly believe in *her*.

For if he could not—she was certainly doomed, and quite probably so was he. The moment she sensed doubt in him, despair and betrayal would turn her wild Gift against both of them. And he had *no* doubt of how *that* would end.

CHAPTER 8

KRIS PURSUED AN icy apparition through the storm-torn forest, a creature that was now wolf, now wind, now an unholy amalgam of both. It glared back over its shoulder at him through snow-swirls that half obscured it, baring icicle fangs and radiating cold and evil. He shivered, unable to control the trembling of his hands, though he clenched them on his weapons to still their shaking . . .

His weapons—he looked down, surprised to see that his bow was in his hands, an arrow nocked and ready. The beast ahead of him snarled, dissolved into a spin of air and sleet with hell-dark eyes, then transformed back into a leaping vulpine snow-drift. He sighted on it, and more than once, but the thing never gave him a clear target.

Talia was somewhere ahead of him, he could hear her weeping brokenly above the wailing of the wind and the howling of the wind-wolf, and when he looked down he could see her tracks—but he could not seem to spot her through the curtains of snow that swirled around him. He realized then that the wind-wolf was stalking *her*—

He quickened his pace, but the wind fought against him, throwing daggers of ice and blinding snow-swarms into his eyes. The thing ahead of him howled, a long note of triumph and insatiable hunger. It was outdistancing and outmaneuvering him—and it would have Talia before he could reach her. He tried to shout a warning—

And woke with a start. Outside the wind howled like a demented monster. Talia touched his shoulder, and he jumped involuntarily.

"Sorry," she said. "You—you were dreaming, I think."

He shook his head to clear it of the last shreds of nightmare. "Lord! I guess I was. Did I wake you?"

"Not really. I wasn't sleeping very well."

He tried to settle himself, and found that he couldn't. A vague sense of apprehension had him in its grip, and would not loose its hold on him. It had nothing to do with Talia's problems; a quick exchange of thought with Tantris confirmed that she was not at fault.

"Kris, do you think maybe we should move the supplies?" Talia said in a voice soft and full of hesitation.

"That doesn't sound like a bad idea," he replied, feeling at once that somehow his uneasiness was connected with just that. "Why? What made you think of that?"

"I kept dreaming about it, except I couldn't shift anything. It was all too heavy for me, and you wouldn't help. You just stood there staring at me."

"Well, I won't just stand and stare at you now." He began unwinding himself from the blankets. "I don't know why, but I think we'd better follow up on your dream."

They moved everything from behind the Station to either side of the door on the front. Rather than diminishing, the sense of urgency kept growing as they worked, as if they had very little time. It was hard, chilling, bitter work, to manhandle the clumsy bundles of hay and straw through the snow, but neither of them made any move to give up until the last stick and bale was in place.

While there was still light left to see by, they took turns clearing the valley of deadfall. They finally had enough to satisfy Kris when they'd found the last scrap of wood that hadn't vanished into snow too deep to be searched. It would not outlast being snowed in, but there was more than enough to outlast the storm. If, when the storm died, they couldn't reach any more deadfall, they could cut one of the trees surrounding the station, evergreens with a resinous sap that would allow them to burn, even though green.

But when they returned to their shelter, their work wasn't complete. For though there seemed little rational reason to do so, they continued to follow their vague premonitions and moved all the supplies from the storage shed into the Waystation. It made things very crowded, but if they didn't plan on moving around much, it would do.

By the time they finished, they were as chilled and weary as they had been the first night. They huddled over the fire with their bowls of stew, too exhausted even for conversation. The wind howling beyond the door seemed to have settled into their minds, numbing and empty-ing them, chilling them to the marrow. They huddled in their bed in a kind of stupor until sleep took them.

The wind suddenly strengthened early the next morning, causing even the sturdy stone walls to vibrate. They woke simultaneously and cowered together, feeling very small and very vulnerable as they lis-tened with awe and fear to the fury outside. Kris was very glad now that they'd trusted their instincts and moved everything to the leeward side of the Station and within easy reach.

"It's a good thing this isn't a thatched roof like the last Station we were in," Talia whispered to him, shivering against him, and plainly much subdued by the scream of the wind outside. "Thatch would have been shredded and blown away by now."

Kris nodded absently, listening mainly to the sound of the storm tearing at their walls like a beast wanting to dig them out of their shel-ter. He was half-frightened, half-fascinated; this was obviously a storm of legendary proportions and nothing he'd ever seen or read could have prepared him for its power. The Station was growing cold again, heat escaping with the wind.

"I'd better build up the fire now, and one of us should stay awake to watch it. Talia, make a three-sided enclosure out of some of our sup-plies or the fodder, and pile lots of straw in it. We need more between us and the cold stone floor than we've been sleeping on. Leave room for the four-feets; if it gets too cold they'll have to fit themselves in nearer the fire, somehow."

Talia followed his orders, building them a real nest; she also layered another two bedgowns on over the woolen shift. Kris uncovered the coals and built the fire back up—and when he saw the skin of ice forming on their water-kettles, he was glad he had done so.

They crept back into their remade bed and held each other for extra warmth, staring into the fire, mesmerized by the flames and the wail of the wind around the walls. There didn't seem to be any room for human thought; it was all swept away by that icy wind.

Their trance was broken by a hideous crashing sound. It sounded as though a giant out of legend was approaching the Station, knocking down trees as he came. The noise held them paralyzed, like rabbits frightened into immobility. There wasn't anywhere to run *to* in any event. If something brought the Station down, they'd freeze to death in hours without shelter. Neither of them could imagine what the cause could be. It seemed to take several minutes, approaching the Sta-tion inexorably from the rear, finally ending with a roar that shook the back wall and a splintering sound that came unmistakably from beyond the half-door.

They sat shocked into complete immobility, hearts in their throats, for a very long time.

Finally—"Bright Goddess! Was that where I thought it was?" Kris gulped and tried to unclench his hands.

"B–b–behind the Station," Talia stuttered nervously, pupils dilated with true fear. "Where the storage shed is."

Kris rose and tried the door. It wouldn't budge. "Was," he said, and crawled back in beside her.

She didn't venture to contradict him.

Twice more they heard trees crashing to the ground, but never again so close. And as if that show of force had finally worn it out, the wind began to slacken and die. By noon or thereabouts, it had gone completely, and all that remained were the faint ticking sounds of the falling snow. Without the wind to keep it off the roof, it soon built up to a point where even that could no longer be heard.

The Station stopped losing heat. The temperature within rose until it was comfortable again, and the rising warmth lulled them back into their interrupted sleep before they realized it.

The Companions prodded them awake. How long they'd been asleep they had no idea; the fire was dying, but by no means dead, and the silence gave no clue.

Rolan impressed Talia with his need to go out. Immediately. Talia could tell by Kris' face that Tantris was doing likewise.

He looked at her and shrugged. "Might as well find out now as later. We're still here, and under shelter at least," he said, and pulled on fresh clothing while she did the same.

It was not long till dark. The stacked fodder had kept the door clear of snow or they'd never have gotten it open. Beyond the shelter of the bales was a drift that reached higher than Kris' head.

The chirras were not at all perturbed by the sight; they plowed right into it, forcing their way almost as if they were swimming, their long necks keeping their heads free of the snow. The Companions followed and the two Heralds followed them. After making their way through drifts that rose from between the level of Talia's waist to the height of the first one, they suddenly broke into an area that had been scoured down to the grass by the wind.

The forest around them had a quality of age, of power held in check, that was raising the hair on the back of Talia's neck. There was *some-thing* here ... not quite alive, but not dead either. Something ... waiting. Watching. Weighing them. Whatever it was, it brooded over them for several long moments. Talia found herself searching the shadows under the trees until her eyes ached, looking for some sign, and found nothing. But *something* was out there. Something inhuman, almost elemental, and—and at one, in some strange way she couldn't define and could only feel, with the forest itself. As if the *forest* were providing it with a thousand eyes, a thousand ears. . . .

"Where's the road?" Talia asked in a small, frightened squeak.

Kris started at the sound of her voice, looked around, then turned slowly, evidently getting his bearings. The Station from here seemed to be only one taller drift among many. There were new gaps in the circle of trees that surrounded it. "That way—" He pointed finally. "There *was* a tree just beside the pathway in—"

"Which is now across the pathway in."

"Once we get to it, we can have the chirras and Companions haul it clear . . . I hope."

"What about the back of the Station?" She was not certain that she wanted to find out.

"Let's see if we can get back there."

Working their way among the drifts in the deepening gloom, they managed to get to a point where they could see what had happened behind the Station, even though they couldn't get to it yet. Kris whistled.

Not one, but nearly a dozen trees had gone over, each sent crashing by the one behind it, the last landing hard against the side of the Station. The storage shed was gone; splintered.

"At least we'll have plenty of firewood," Talia said with a strained laugh.

"Talia—" There was awe in Kris's voice. "I never believed those stories about Sorrows and Vanyel's Curse before—but *look at the way the trees fell!*"

Talia subdued her near-hysterical fear and really took a good look. Sure enough, the trees had fallen in a straight line, all in the direction of the force of the wind—except the last. There was no reason why it should have deviated that she could see, and had it fallen as its fellows it would have pulverized the Station—and them. But it had not; it had fallen at an acute angle, missing the Station entirely and destroying only the empty shed. It had almost fallen *against* the wind.

"Gods," Kris said. "I—I never would have believed this. I never believed in miracles before." He looked around again. "I . . . this sounds stupid but, whatever you are . . . thanks."

The steady feeling of being watched vanished as he said it. Talia found she could breathe easily again.

"Look, we'd better get back inside. It's nearly dark." Kris gazed up at the sky, and the snow that still fell from it with no sign of slackening.

Subdued by their situation and the destruction outside, they made their meal, ate, and cleaned up in silence. Finally Talia broached the subject that was troubling them both.

"*Can* we get out of here?"

"I'd like to be reassuring and optimistic, and say yes—but truthfully I don't know," Kris replied, resting his chin on his knees and staring into the fire. "It's a long way to the road, and as I've told you, it will be worse beyond the trees. It's going to take us a long time to cut a path there, with no certainty that the Guard will have gotten that far when we do make it."

"Should we try to force our way without cutting a path?"

He shook his head. "The chirras could do it, unburdened, but not Tantris and Rolan. Even if they could, we'd need the supplies. I just don't know."

"Maybe we'd better just concentrate on digging our way out."

"But how can we dig ourselves out with no tools?"

"There's the tree blocking the way, too."

Kris stared at the fire without speaking for a long time. "Talia," he said finally, "Holderfolk never buy anything if they can help it—their miserliness is legendary. What do you know about making shovels?"

"Not much," she replied ruefully, "but I'll try."

"Let's take an inventory of our materials."

They had plenty of rawhide for lashings, lots of straight, heavy tree limbs for handles and bracings, but nothing to use for blades. The un-used bedboxes were so stoutly built that it would be next to impossible to pull the bottoms out, and the shelves were made of board too thick to be useful. There *had* been thinner wood used in the shelves of the shed—but they were fragmented now. Finally Talia sighed sadly and said with reluctance, "The only thing we have to use is the harp case."

"No!" Kris protested.

"There's nothing else. When we leave here we can detune My Lady and wrap her in blankets and cloaks and she should be all right without the case. The wood is light and strong, and it's been waterproofed. It's nearly even the right size and shape. We haven't got a choice, Kris. Jadus wouldn't thank us for being sentimental fools."

"Damn!" He was silent for a moment. "You're right. We haven't any choice."

He got the case from the corner on top of Talia's packs where he'd left it. Wincing a little, he took his handaxe and carefully pried the front and back out of the frame, and handed them to Talia.

She fished a bit of charcoal out of the fireplace and drew something like the blade of a snow-shovel on each piece. She handed him one while she took up the other.

"Try and whittle it to that shape while I do the same."

She shaved delicately at the edges of the wood with the blade of her own axe, with shavings falling in curls next to her. Kris watched her with care until he felt he knew exactly what she was doing, then began on his own piece. There was one blessing; the grain was fine enough that with sharp axes it was relatively easy to shape. When both their pieces approximated the look of a shovel blade, Talia marked holes in the boards for them to drill out with their knives. By the time they'd finished, their wrists and hands were tired and sore.

Talia flexed her hands trying to get some feeling and movement back into them. "Now I need two pieces about so wide," she said, gesturing with her hands about two fingers' width apart, "and as long as the backs of the blades. I expect you'll have to cut them out of the frame."

While Kris further demolished the harpcase, she rummaged in her packs for her pot of glue. When she found it, she placed it in a pot half-filled with water, and put that container over the fire so the glue would melt. Meanwhile she went through the dozen or so branches that looked to be good handle material and picked out the two best.

Once the glue was ready, she showed Kris where to drill holes in the branches, and how to taper the end that was going to be fastened to the blade. Her wrists just weren't strong enough for the job. When he finished the first one, she lashed it to the blade with wet rawhide, stretching the thong as tightly as she could so that it would shrink and bind the shovel to blade as firmly as possible when it dried. Then she cross-braced the back of the blade with a smaller branch cut to fit, lashing it the same way to the handle. Lastly she glued the piece of frame to the back of the shovel blade to act as a stop to keep the snow from sliding off. She lashed another piece of branch to the handle behind the stop to act as a brace, then she glued every join on the whole makeshift shovel, saturating even the rawhide with glue. That finished all she knew how to do; she set the whole thing aside to cure overnight, and started in on the second.

"They're not going to hold up under much rough handling," she sighed wearily when she'd finished. "We're going to have to treat them with a great deal of care."

"It's better than trying to do it with bare hands," Kris replied, taking her hands in his own and massaging them.

"I guess so." She tried to force herself to relax. "Kris, just how does the Guard clear the roads off?"

"They recruit villagers. Then it's teams with shovels; they dig out the worst places, and pack down the rest."

"I don't imagine that it's a very fast process."

"No."

The single word hung in the air between him. Talia was afraid, but didn't want to put more of a burden on Kris than he already had by giving way to her fears.

The silence between them grew.

"I hate to say this," he broke it reluctantly, "but you're projecting. I can feel it, and I know it isn't me, and Tantris just backed me up."

Anger flared a little, followed by despair—

"Dammit Talia, *lock it down*! You're not helping either of us!"

She gulped back a sob; bit her lip hard enough to draw blood, then steadied herself by beginning a breathing exercise; it calmed her, calmed her enough that she actually found the leakage, and blocked it. Kris heaved a sigh of relief, and smiled at her, and she felt a tiny stirring of hope and accomplishment.

Finally he let her hands go and went after the harp; she wasn't in a mood to sing by any means, but he chose nothing that she knew. He seemed more to be drifting from melody to melody, perhaps finding his own release from distress in the music he searched. She listened only; the chirras seemed to have caught the somber mood and did not sing either. She used the harpsong to reinforce her own ritual of calming and did not open her eyes until it stopped.

Kris had risen and was replacing the harp in its corner of the hearth. He returned to her side and stretched himself next to her without speaking.

She was the one who broke the silence.

"Kris, I'm scared. *Really* afraid. Not just because of what's happening to me, but because of all that"—she waved her hand—"out there."

"I know." A pause. "I'm scared, too. We . . . haven't got a good situation here. You—you could have killed us both the other night. You still could. And out there . . . I've never felt so helpless in my life. Between the two, I just wanted to give up. I just wanted to curl up in a ball and hope it all went away."

It cost him to admit that, Talia knew. "I wish I wasn't so messed up; I wish I was bigger and stronger. Or a Farspeaker like Kyril," she replied in a very small voice.

"You can't help what happened. As for being a Farspeaker, I don't think both of us together could reach someone with the Gift to hear us, and if we could, I don't know that it would do any good," he sighed. "We just have to keep on as we have been, and hope we get out of here before the supplies run out. That's the real problem, when it comes down to it—the supplies. Otherwise I wouldn't worry. We've got about enough for a month, but not much more than that. If we run out . . ."

"Kris—you know, we *are* in Sorrows—remember the tree? Maybe— maybe we'll be sent game."

"You could be right," he mused, beginning to brighten. "It would take less magic to send a few rabbits within reach of our bows than it did to divert that tree."

"And maybe we'll get out before we have to worry about it. And you don't have to worry about me, you know. I'm Borderbred. I can do with a lot less than I've been used to eating."

"Let's not cut rations down unless we have to. We'll be using a lot of energy keeping warm."

Gloom settled back over them. Talia decided that it was her turn to dispel it.

"I wonder what things are like back at Court right now. It's almost Midwinter."

"Pandemonium; it's never less. Uncle hates Midwinter; there're so many people coming in for the celebrations who 'just incidentally' have petitions that there are Council meetings nearly every day."

She looked at him unhappily. "I don't get along with your uncle very well. No, that's a lie. I don't get along with him at all. I *know* he doesn't like me, but there's more to it than that. I keep having the feeling that he's looking for a way to get rid of me."

Kris looked flatly astonished. "Whoa—wait just a minute here— you'd better start at the very beginning. I can hardly believe my ears—"

"All right," she replied hesitantly, "but only if you promise to hear me out completely."

"That's only fair, I guess."

"All right; when I first got to the Collegium I had a pretty miserable

time of it as you know. Dirty tricks, nasty anonymous notes, am-
bushes—it was the unaffiliated students, the Blues, but they made it
seem as if it was other trainees that might be responsible so I wouldn't
look inside the Collegium for help. It all came to a head—"

"When they dumped you in the river just after Midwinter—"

"And they meant to kill me."

"What?" he exclaimed.

"It isn't common knowledge. Elcarth and Kyril know; and Sherrill,
Keren, Skif, Teren, and Jeri. Ylsa knew, so did Jadus; I think Alberich
knows. Mero guessed. I'm pretty sure one or more of the others told
Selenay some time later. One of the Blues told me to 'give their greetings to Talamir' just after they threw me in—I think the meaning
there is pretty clear. They expected me to drown, and if it hadn't been
that my bond with Rolan was strong enough for him to know what
had happened—well. But I was delirious with fever when they were
caught and I couldn't tell anyone. They claimed it was all just a joke,
that they hadn't thought I'd get worse than a ducking. Your uncle
backed them up before the Council. So instead of being charged with
trying to kill me, they got their wrists slapped and were sent home to
the familial bosoms."

"That's hardly an indication that—"

"You promised not to interrupt me."

"Sorry."

"The next time we got into it was over Skif. It was right when Skif
was helping me unmask Elspeth's nurse Hulda. I needed to find out
who had sponsored her into Valdemar besides Selenay and Elspeth's
father. Skif went to the Provost-Marshal's office to find the immigration records, and Orthallen caught him there. He dragged him up in
front of Selenay, accusing him of trying to alter the Misdemeanor
Book. And he demanded that Skif be given the maximum punishment
for it—stable duty with the Guard for the next two years on the Border. You know what *that* could have meant. At worst, he could have
been killed; at best, he'd be two years behind the rest of us, and I'd
have been without one of my two best friends all that time—as well as
being without the only person in the Collegium who could possibly
have helped me expose Hulda. I got Skif off, but I had to lie to do it;
and I can tell you that Orthallen was *not* pleased."

Kris looked as if he wanted to interject something, but held his
peace.

"Lastly there's the matter of my internship. Orthallen 'in view of my
youth and inexperience' was trying to pressure the Council into ruling

I should stay out in the field for three years—double the normal time. Fortunately, neither Selenay, nor Elcarth, nor Kyril were having any of that—and pointed out that internships are subject only to the will of the Circle, not the Council."

"Is that all?"

"Isn't it enough?"

"Talia, this all has very logical explanations if you know my uncle. Firstly he couldn't possibly have known about the students' malice— I'm certain of it. He's known most of them since they were in swaddling clothes; he even refers to people grown and with babes of their own as 'the youngsters.' And he probably felt obligated to act as their spokesperson. After all, you had *two* people to speak for you on the Council, Elcarth and Kyril."

"I suppose that's logical," Talia said reluctantly. "But Skif—"

"Oh, Skif—my uncle is a prude and a stickler for convention, I know that for a fact. Skif has been a thorn in his side ever since he was Chosen. Before Skif came, there was never any problem with Heraldic students getting involved in trouble down in town—the unaffiliates and the Bardics, and once in a great while the Healers, but never the Grays."

"Never?" Talia's right eyebrow rose markedly. "I find that rather hard to believe."

"Well, almost never. But after Skif started *his* little escapades—Lord and Lady, the Grays are as bad as the Bardics! It's like the younger ones feel they have to top him. Well, Uncle is not amused, not at all. He's a great believer in military discipline as a cure for high spirits, and I'm certain he never meant anything worse for Skif than that."

"What about me? Why does he keep trying to get between me and Selenay?"

"He's not. You *are* young; his idea of Queen's Own is someone like Talamir. I have no doubt he truly felt a long internship was appropriate in your case."

"I wish I could believe you."

"Holding a grudge is rather childish—and unlike you—"

"I am *not* holding a grudge!"

"Then why are you even refusing to consider what I've told you?"

Talia drew a deep breath and forced herself to calm down. "There is a third explanation for what he's been doing. It could be that he thinks of me as a threat to his influence with Selenay. And I might point out one other thing to you—and that is I am willing to bet the person who told you all about those 'rumors' is your uncle. *And* I'd be willing to bet he asked you to investigate them. *He* knows what my Gift is. He could well know what the effect of hearing that poison would be on me."

Instead of refuting her immediately, Kris looked thoughtful. "That is a possibility; at least over the internship thing. He's very fond of power, my uncle; he's been Selenay's chief advisor for a long time, and was her father's before that. And there isn't a great deal you can do to change the fact that Queen's Own is always going to have more influence than chief advisor. And I hate to admit it," he finished reluctantly, "but you're right about my source of information on the rumors."

Talia figured that now that she'd got him thinking instead of just reacting, it was time to change the subject. She would dearly have loved to have suggested that Orthallen might well have *originated* the rumors, but Kris would never have stood still for the implication that his uncle's conduct was less than honorable.

"Kris—let's try and forget about it, for a few hours, anyway. We've got other things to worry about."

He regarded her soberly. "Like the fact that you had enough energy to project; like the fact that you could do it again."

"Yes." She drew a deep breath. "I could even break down again; I was right on the verge of it this afternoon. If we hadn't had something to *do*, I might have. And I was—maybe hallucinating out there."

"Hell."

"I'll—try. But I thought you'd better be warned."

"Featherfoot?" He looked long at Tantris, then nodded in satisfaction. "He says he thinks he and Rolan can handle you, if it gets bad again. He says it was mostly that Rolan was caught off-guard that things got out of hand the first time."

She felt a heavy burden fall from her heart. "Good. And—thanks."

He gave her a wink. "I'll get it out of you."

She made a face at him, and curled up in the blankets to sleep with a much lighter heart.

They woke at very close to their normal time; there would be no dallying today, nor for many days to come, not if they wanted to reach the road before their supplies ran out. They suited up in their warmest clothes, took the shovels, and began the long task of cutting a path to freedom.

The snow was wet and heavy—an advantage, since it stayed on their shovels better. But the very weight of it made shoveling exhausting work. They took a break at noon for a hot meal and a change of clothing, as what they'd put on this morning was now quite soaked through. They shoveled until it was almost too dark to see.

"We've got to get to that tree and get it moved out of the way while the snow's still like it is now," Kris said over supper. "If it should turn colder and freeze, we'll never be able to get that thing moved. It would be stuck in ice like a cork in a bottle."

"We'll be all right as long as the snow keeps falling a little," Talia replied, thinking back to her days watching the Hold flocks at lambing time. "We'll only have to worry about the temperature falling if the weather changes."

They turned in early, hoping to get to the tree before the end of the next day.

By late afternoon they had reached it, and decided, after looking the massive trunk over, that it would be best if they hacked it in half with their handaxes and hitched the chirras and Companions to the lighter half. When darkness fell, they were slightly more than halfway through the trunk.

Again they rose with the sun and returned to the tree. They managed to cut through it by noon, and after lunch made their attempt to move it.

They had decided the previous night to leave nothing to chance and had made a set of harnesses for themselves from spare rope. They hitched their own bodies right in beside the chirras and Rolan and Tantris.

It turned out that it was just as well that they had decided to do so. Only when all six of them dug in and strained with all their strength did it move at all. All of them gasped and panted with the effort, and over-burdened muscles screamed out in protest, while the tree shifted fraction by minute fraction. It took until dark to haul it clear of their escape route.

As darkness fell, they dragged themselves back into the Station, nearly weeping with aches and exhaustion. Nevertheless, they rubbed the chirras dry and groomed their Companions, fed and watered and blanketed them. Only then did they strip off their own sodden garments and collapse on their bed. They were too bone-weary to think of anything but lying down—and their aching bodies.

Finally, "Do you really *want* supper?" Kris asked her dully; it was his turn to make it.

The very idea of food was nauseating. "No," she replied in a voice fogged with exhaustion.

"Oh, good," he said with relief. "Neither do I."

"I can't seem—to get warm." It took an effort to get the words out.

"Me either." Kris sat up with a low moan. "If you'll get the tea, I'll dig out the honey."

"It's a bargain."

They'd left hot water for tea on the hearth, knowing they'd want it. Neither of them rose any farther than their knees as they dragged themselves to their goals. Talia poured water onto the herbal mixture, spilling half of it as her hands shook with weariness. Kris returned with the jar of honey in one hand, and something else in the other.

He put the jar down with exaggerated care, and Talia spooned three generous dollops into each mug. Fortunately, it was too thick to spill as the water had. She pushed one mug toward Kris, who handed her something in exchange for it.

It was one of the fruit and nut bars Kerithwyn had forced into them back at Waymeet. Talia felt sick at the sight of it.

"I know," Kris said apologetically. "I feel the same way. But if we don't eat something, we'll pay for it tomorrow."

She stirred the honey into her tea and drank it even though it was still so hot it almost scorched her tongue. As heat spread through her, the food began to seem a bit more appealing. As she finished the second mug of tea, she was actually feeling hungry.

Chewing the tough, sticky thing took the last of her energy, though. From the look of things, Kris was feeling the same way. The third cup of tea settled the question entirely. She just barely managed to get underneath the blankets before she was asleep.

She woke with every muscle screaming an angry protest. She shifted position a little, and a groan escaped.

"I wish I was dead—I wouldn't hurt so much," Kris moaned forlornly in her ear.

"Me, too. But I keep thinking of what Alberich always told us."

"Must you remind me? 'The cure that is best for the sore body is more of what made it sore.' Oh, how I wish he was wrong!"

"At least we have to go out long enough to see what we have to deal with beyond the tree."

"You're right." Kris uncoiled himself slowly and painfully. "And we have to wrestle more wood inside."

"And more hay."

"And more hay, right. There's this much, little bird. If you feel like I feel, you couldn't project past your own nose right now!"

They helped each other wash and dress; there were too many places they couldn't reach for themselves without their stiff muscles screaming at them. Talia managed to concoct porridge with fruit in it, making enough to feed them twice more, and tea as well. They would probably be so tired they wouldn't taste either, but it would be solid and warm, and hopefully they wouldn't be so tired tonight that the very thought of food was revolting.

When they opened the door, the glare of the sunlight on all that snow drove them back—for the weather had changed overnight, and the sky was cloudless. Without some kind of protection for their eyes they'd be snowblind in moments.

"Now what?" Talia asked, never having had to deal with this kind of situation before.

Kris thought hard. "Keep your eyes shadowed from above by your cloak hood, and I'll see if I can rig something for the snowglare."

He rummaged through his pack, emerging with a roll of the thin gauze they used for bandages. "Wrap that around your head about twice. It should be thin enough to see through."

It wasn't easy to see through, but it was better than glaring light that brought tears to the eyes.

The tree lay where they had left it, and beyond it was the pathway out. Somewhere.

It was possible to see where it went by the lane between the trees and the absence of underbrush. The problem was that it lay beneath drifts that from where they were standing never seemed to be less than four feet deep.

"Well, at least there're no more downed trees," Talia said, trying to be cheerful.

Kris just sighed. "Let's get the shovels."

The drifts were deep, but at least they were not as wide as the ones in their valley had been. Though the snow was seldom less than two feet deep, it also was rarely more than six. They shoveled and trampled until dusk, then brought in more wood and fodder, ate, and fell into bed.

Talia woke in the middle of the night feeling very cold. Puzzled, she huddled closer to Kris, who murmured sleepily, but didn't wake. Despite this, she kept feeling colder. Eventually she moved warily out of bed; as soon as she did so, the chill of the air struck her like a hammer blow. She slipped her feet into her sheepskin slippers, wrapped her cloak around herself, and quickly moved to pile wood on the fire. When the flames rose, she could see the eyes of the chirras and Companions blinking at her—they had moved out of their corner and nearer to the heat.

"'Smatter?" Kris asked sleepily. "Why's it so cold?"

"The weather changed again. The temperature's dropping," Talia said, thinking about how the wet snow outside must be freezing into drifts like out-croppings of white granite. "I think the luck-goddess just left us."

CHAPTER 9

WHEN AT LAST they slept again, it was restlessly; they woke early, and with a premonition of the worst. The icy chill of the Station did not encourage dawdling; they dressed quickly and went out to discover just how bad the situation truly was.

It wasn't good, by any stretch of the imagination. The snow had frozen, thickly crusted on top, granular and hard underneath. The crust was capable of supporting their weight, and even the weight of the chirras unladen (providing that they held their pace to a snail's crawl), but it would never hold the chirras with even a small pack, or the Companions. And as if that weren't bad enough, it was obvious that their shovels were not sturdy enough to deal with snow this obdurate.

Both Heralds stared hopelessly at the rock-hard place where they'd left off digging the night before and at the now-useless shovels. Finally Talia swore passionately, kicked at a lump of snow, and bit her lip to hold back tears of frustration, and reminded herself *not* to let anything leak.

"Look, Talia, we're not getting anywhere like this," Kris said after a long moment of silence. "You're tired; so am I. One day isn't going to make any difference to us one way or the other—for that matter, neither will two or three. I'm your counselor; well, I counsel that we take a rest, and let our bodies recover, until we can think of a plan that has some chance of getting us out of here."

Talia agreed wearily.

Once back inside, she lit the little oil lamp and surveyed the shambles they'd made of the interior of the Station. "We're obviously going to be here a while, so it's time we stopped living in a goat pen. Look at this! We hardly have room to move."

Kris looked around, and ruefully agreed.

They began cleaning and rearranging with a vengeance. Working in the comparatively warm Station was by far and away easier than shoveling snow had been. Before noon, the Station was cleaned and swept and all was in good order.

"Had any ideas?" Kris ventured over lunch.

"Nothing that pertains to the problem. I did think of something that needs doing, though. Since we're stuck until we can think of a way to handle that snow, we ought to do something about washing our clothing. The only warm things that I have left to wear are what I've got on."

"There's saddle-soap in the Station supplies to clean the leathers," he said, thinking out loud, "and we could empty two of the barrels to wash in."

"I brought more than enough soap for all the rest," she told him, "and the Lord knows we don't have to scrimp on water!"

"All right then, we'll do it! I'm in no better shape than you—and I *hate* wearing filthy clothes."

Under the primitive conditions of the Station, cleaning white clothing was not an easy chore. Again, however, it was easier than the digging and hauling they'd been doing, and a great deal warmer as well. Eventually every clean surface sported a drying garment.

"I never thought I'd want to see another set of student Grays again," Talia said, sitting back on her heels and surveying her handiwork.

"I know what you mean," Kris grinned, looking up from his last pair of boots. "At least the damn things didn't show dirt quite so badly. How are you doing?"

"I'm done, since I did my leathers while you were washing."

"This finishes it for me."

"Well, I still have hot water left—enough for two really good baths. It's too bad we can't fit ourselves into the barrels and soak, but at least we can get really clean."

"Good thinking, little bird. Although after all the soap and water I've been immersed in today, there isn't much that needs to soak!"

Things began to take on a more cheerful appearance once they were clean, especially since they weren't aching from the punishing cold and muscle strain of the past few days.

Talia combed her wet hair out in front of the fire, more than half mesmerized by the flickering flames and the movement of the comb through her hair. The Station had lost the slightly stale odor it had acquired during the blizzard, and now smelled of soap and leather—very pleasant. Bits of old tales began to flicker through her mind— unconnected images dealing with tales of battle, of all things. Battles, and how the Companions themselves used to fight alongside their Heralds. Or were those images unconnected?

"Kris," she said slowly, an idea beginning to form, "the main problem is the hard snow and the ice crust. Our shovels aren't strong enough to break it into pieces. But if we wrapped their legs to keep them from being cut, Rolan and Tantris could—like they were fighting."

"By the Stars of the Lady, you're right!" he exclaimed with excitement. "Not only that, remember how you wondered what good those huge claws did the chirras? They dig themselves hollows to lie in, in dirt *or* in snow. If we could make them understand what we wanted, we could have them dig out chunks of a size we could manage!"

"Havens, Rolan and Tantris can do that!"

Tantris snorted, and Rolan sent Talia a little mental caress.

Kris laughed. "All right, granther—" he said to his Companion, looking happier than he had all day. He turned back to Talia. "The Source of all Wisdom over there seems to think we'll be able to work faster than we did before. He wanted to know why we hadn't thought of this until now."

"Well, *you* two wouldn't have done us much good with the wet snow, now, would you?" Talia asked the two sets of backward-pointing ears. Rolan tossed his head.

"And the chirras would have made more of a mess than they'd have cleared. The snowdrifts weren't stable enough until they froze," Kris added, a little smugly. "So there."

"Did he say anything else?" Talia asked, a little envious of Kris' ability to Mindspeak with his Companion.

"He just told me he's been worried about how hard we've been working—but then he actually *ordered* me to rest tomorrow. You'd think we were trainees."

Talia shook her head ruefully, for there was no doubt that Rolan considered this to be an excellent idea. There was a distinct undertone to *his* mental sending of worry that both of them had been overworking.

"Rolan says the same. I don't think I want to argue. Oh, Bright Havens, I hurt!" Talia stretched aching arms and shoulders. "This has hardly been the rest stop we were ordered to take."

Kris groaned good-naturedly, stretching his own weary muscles. "If anything, I'm more exhausted than I was when we stopped, if that's possible. I'm certainly a lot sorer."

"Then I'll make you an offer; want a backrub?"

"Do you?"

"Oh, Lord, yes," she sighed.

"I'll work on you, then you work on me. Strip, wench—I can't work through four shirts and a tunic!"

"It's only two," she protested with a laugh, "and they're summer-weight at that. While I was cleaning, I wanted to clean everything!" Nevertheless, she complied, stretching out on a pallet of blankets on the hearth. Kris seemed to find every last ache, and drove each one out with deft fingers. Soothed by the gentle hands, she drifted into a half-sleep.

He woke her by tickling the back of her neck. "My turn," he said, as she lazily turned her head.

She sighed with content and rose to her knees, and slipped on a shift (blessedly clean, and warm from the fire) while he took her place on the hearth. She tried to copy what he'd done to her, and hunted for the muscles that were the most tense, and so hurt the most. Before very long she had him as soothed and relaxed as she was, and they basked in the heat of the fire like a couple of contented cats.

"I'll do anything you ask," he murmured happily. "Anything, so long as you don't ask me to move. And as long as you don't stop."

She giggled at the tone of his voice as she gently rubbed his shoulders. "All right, then—tell me about Dirk?"

"Promise not to stop what you're doing?"

"Surely."

"Good," he said with satisfaction. "Because it's a very long story. For one thing, I have to start with his grandfather."

"Oh, come now—" she said, raising an eyebrow. "Is this really necessary, or are you just trying to prolong the backrub?"

"I promise you, it's absolutely necessary. Now, 'once upon a time' when Dirk's grandfather settled his Steading, he lived on the very Border itself. He was quite ambitious, so he added a little more to his lands every year, and only stopped when he had as much as one man could reasonably expect to keep under cultivation with the aid of a moderate number of hands. By then the Border had been pushed back by him and others like him. So now that it was a safer place to live, he married."

"Logical, seeing as he had to have produced at least one offspring to be Dirk's father."

"Quiet, wench. As it happened, their only child was female, but it didn't perturb him that he would be leaving the Steading to her; he fully expected that she would marry in due course, and the place would still be in the bloodline. However, the gods had other ideas in mind."

"Don't they always?"

"First of all, it turned out that his daughter had a really powerful Gift of Healing. Now this was as welcome as it was unexpected, since it's hard to get Healers to station themselves near the Border. There's always more work there than they can handle successfully unless they're stationed with a Temple, and you know how Healers are—they'd rather die than leave something half-done. At any rate, Borderbred Healers always seem to feel they have a duty to serve where they were born, so there was little chance she'd end up anywhere else. Her proud and happy father sent her off to Healer's Collegium, and in due course she returned in her Greens. So far everything had gone according to expectation. However, being the Healer put a crimp in her father's original plans for her. It seemed that the young men of the area were somewhat reluctant to court a person whose attentions could, because of her Gift, never be entirely devoted to anyone person. And this despite the tale I told you about them. Healers are, after all, Healers first and anything else second."

"Like Heralds, or priests. Look at us."

"Point taken. At any rate, not even the rather substantial inducement of her inheritance could lure any of the neighboring farmers or their sons to the nuptial table. The old man began to despair of having his hard-won acreage remain in the family. Then there came the second twist to the plot. Late one autumn night there was a terrible storm."

"I've had my fill of storms."

"Hush, this is a required storm. In fact, it was the worst autumnal storm that part of the Kingdom had ever seen. It began after sunset and lightning downed so many trees that it was completely unnecessary to cut any for firewood that fall. Freezing rain fell from the heavens in sheets rather than drops. There was so much thunder that it was impossible to hold a conversation and impossible to sleep. And in the midst of all this chaos and confusion, there came a knocking on the farmstead door." Kris was very obviously enjoying himself to the hilt.

"A tall, dark, mysterious stranger, no doubt."

"Who's telling this story, you or me? As a matter of actual fact, it *was* a stranger; half-drowned, half-frozen, half-dead and very much bedraggled, but blond, and hardly mysterious. It was a young Bard, only recently graduated from *his* Collegium and starting his journeyman period. He'd lost his way in the storm, fallen into a river, and had all manner of uncomfortable things happen to him. When he pounded on their door, he was already fevered, delirious, and well on his way to a full-blown case of pneumonia."

"I smell a romance."

"You have an accurate nose. Naturally, the young Healer took him in and nursed him back to health. Just as naturally, they fell head over heels in love. Being a man of honor, as well as having his head stuffed full of all those romantic ballads, the Bard begged the old man's permission to wed his daughter in true heroic style. He needn't have worried, because by now the old fellow was beginning to think that *any* son-in-law was better than none. However, he made it a condition of his agreement that they remain on the Steading.

"It rather surprised the old farmer when the—he thought—feckless, footloose Bard agreed with all his heart—subject to the agreement of his Circle of course. How could the old man have known that our Bard was born a farmer, and that entwined with his love of music and his love of the daughter was his love and deep understanding of the land? Well, the Circle agreed—provided he compose a Master's ballad about the storm, courtship, and all; and he settled down happily with all three of his loves—land, lady, and music. Then before the year was out, he had a fourth."

"Dirk. So that's where he got that wonderful voice!"

"And where he learned to play so well. Actually, though, you're a bit ahead of the tale. The first child wasn't Dirk. He has three older sisters, two younger, and a baby brother. When they can be sorted into some semblance of order and organization, they have family concerts. You should hear them all singing together, it's wonderful; I swear even the babies cry in the right keys! Well, grandfather passed to his reward content in the knowledge that the land would remain in the bloodline, since by the time he departed, two of the girls had begun enthusiastically producing enormous broods of their own."

"I was asking about Dirk."

"Talia, my little bird, you can't separate Dirk from his family. They're all alike; see one, you know what the rest are like. How things ever get done in that household I have no idea, since it seems to be formed entirely of chaotic elements."

"Just like a Bard."

"Actually, he's the most organized of the lot. If it weren't for him and the husbands of the sisters, they'd spend all their time flying in circles. There's an incredible amount of love there, though; and it overflows generously on anyone who happens to find himself dragged unwittingly into their midst."

"Like you."

"Like me. Dirk insisted on hauling me home with him the first holiday after we'd met when he found out there wasn't going to be anyone home with me but the servitors. They treated me *exactly* like one of the family, from bathing babies to teary farewell kisses. I was rather overwhelmed. I certainly hadn't expected anything like them!"

Talia chuckled, picturing to herself the reserved, slightly shy young boy that Kris must have been, finding himself in the hands of what must have seemed like a family of madmen.

"Once I got used to them, I had a lot of fun. That's why, every chance I've had, I've gone home with Dirk when he went. Right now four of his sisters are married. Three of them live in extensions to the original house and their husbands share the work on the Steading, because Dirk's father has developed bad knees. The last has his own land to look after, but they're still on hand for every holiday in the calendar. It's a good thing they all get along so well."

"We were talking about Dirk."

"Right." Kris' eyes gleamed with mischief at the impatience in her voice. "He was Chosen even younger than I—only eleven; probably because at eleven he was more mature in a lot of ways than I was at thirteen. We were Chosen the same year, and almost the same month. He told me that Ahrodie Chose him in the middle of the marketplace on Fair Day, and he kept trying to direct her attention to his sister because he thought he was too ugly to be a Herald!"

"Poor child."

"So we went through the Collegium as year-mates. He saw how lonely I was there, and how unused to dealing with other children, and decided that I needed a friend. And since I couldn't seem to make one by myself, he was going to do it for me! In classes, though, I had to help him along, and he was never better than average. It was pretty well accepted by all of us that after our internships he was going to work Border Sectors and I was going to teach. Then we found out how our Gifts dovetailed, and how incredibly well we work together, and everyone's plans were rather abruptly changed."

"And you began working as a team."

"Oh, yes. *And* we discovered that we have a kind of Gift for intrigue as well. The number of situations we've gotten ourselves into would astound you, yet we always seem to extricate ourselves and come home covered in glory."

"Kris, what's he really like?"

"Behind the jester-mask? Very sensitive—that's his heritage coming out. Endlessly kind to the helpless; you should see him some time with a lap full of kittens or babies. Don't think he's soft and sentimental, though. I've seen him slit people's throats in cold blood when they deserved it, and do it from behind in the dark without a pretext of fair play. He says that if they're intending to do the same to him, it doesn't make sense to give them warning. He can be totally ruthless in the cause of Queen, Kingdom, and Circle. Let's see, what else is there? You've danced with him, so you know that his bumbling farmer look is totally deceiving. He's one of the few people that Alberich will accept to act as a substitute with his advanced pupils when Alberich is sick. And for all that, he's terribly vulnerable in certain areas. I helped him get over his broken heart, and I promise you, Talia, that I will personally break the neck of anyone who hurts him like that again."

He was lying with his head turned to one side and pillowed on his arms; Talia could not help but see the fierce, cold hatred in his expression at that moment.

Kris's fierce tone as he spoke the last few words was completely unfeigned. He remembered only too well what Dirk had been like then—broken, defeated—it had been horrible to compare what that bitch had made him into with what he had been before she'd worked her wiles on him. Dirk seldom shed a tear—but he had wept helplessly on Kris' shoulder when she'd ruined his life and his hopes for him. It was a thing he never wanted to witness again. And if he had any say about it, he never would.

Then a painful thought occurred to him. He *knew* Dirk was more than interested in Talia . . . and she *had* been showing evidence of the same sort of feeling. But he and Talia had most of a year to go on her internship, and now that they were intimate, it was damned unlikely they'd go back to their earlier relationship. What the *hell* was he going to do if she started getting infatuated with *him*?

It was more than a possibility; after all, nearly every other female he'd spent any time with had ended up in the same state.

He didn't want to think about it. . . .

"I think it's time to do something about your problem," he said, thinking that trouble might be less likely if he reasserted his position as a figure of authority.

"Like what?" She sat up slowly, and shook her hair out of her eyes, her expression in the flickering firelight a sober one.

"I'm going to take you absolutely back to basics. Back to the very first thing they taught me."

"Shielding?"

"Hell, no, girl," he replied, astounded. "More basic than that—and if shielding was what they taught you first, maybe that's one reason why you're having this problem. I'm taking you right back to the first steps. Ground and center."

She looked puzzled, and shifted a little, curling her legs under her. "Ground and *what*?"

"Oh, Gods," he groaned. "How the hell did you get away with—of course. Ylsa must have thought you knew the basics. Maybe you did . . . instinctively." He bit his lip, thinking hard, staring off into the space beyond his internee. Talia just sat quietly, peering anxiously at him through the half-dark of the Station. "Trouble is, as *my* teacher used to say, instinct is *no* substitute for conscious control."

"I—I guess I've rather well proved that, haven't I?" she replied bitterly.

"Well, once instinct goes, there's no basis for reorganizing yourself." He took a deep breath, acutely aware of the faint smell of soap, straw, and animal that pervaded the Station.

"Gods." She sighed, and rubbed her temple with one hand. "All right—do your worst."

"Don't laugh," he replied grimly. "Before I'm through it may well seem like just that. All right, are you comfortable? Absolutely comfortable?"

She frowned, shifted a little, then nodded.

He settled himself, folding his own legs under him, shifting until the straw under his blanket moved to a more comfortable place. "Close your eyes. You can't sort out what's coming in at you unless you can recognize what's *you* and what *isn't*. That's what my teacher used to call 'the shape inside your skin.' Find the place inside you that feels the most stable, and work out from there. Feel *everything*—then put what you've felt away, because you can recognize it as you."

He was using what he called "teaching voice" with her, a kind of soothing monotone. She'd gone quite naturally into a half-trance, fairly well relaxed. By unfocusing his eyes and depending on Sight rather than vision, he could See every move she made by the shifting energy patterns within her. Sight was a good Gift to have for this situation, maybe better than her own would have been. By looking/not-looking in a peculiar sort of way that made his eyes feel strained, he could see energy fields and fluxes. What he Saw was difficult to describe; it was something like seeing multiple images or "ghosts" of Talia, each one haloed in a different "color." When he Looked at the unGifted or Gifted but untrained, the images didn't quite mesh and the edges were fuzzy and indistinct. In Talia's case the edges were almost painfully sharp and the images were given to flaring at unpredictable intervals—and they were so unconnected they almost seemed to belong to more than one person. If she could find her center, they would fuse into one; if she could ground, the flaring would stop.

"All right, once you've found that stable place, there's a similar place outside of you—in the earth itself. When you feel that, connect yourself to it. Finding the stable place is called 'centering,' connecting yourself to the earth is called 'grounding.'"

He could tell, although his own Gift wasn't anything like hers, that she had *almost* managed both actions. Almost—but not quite. The images were overlapping, but not fusing; and they dimmed and brightened and dimmed again. And he could see that she was off-balance and not-connected, although to *her* it probably seemed as if she'd done exactly as he asked. Poor lady—he was about to do a very cruel thing to her.

He sighed, and signaled Tantris—who gave her a rude mental shove.

A shove that translated into a very physical toppling over.

"Not good enough," he said coldly, as she stared up at him from where she was sprawled with a dazed expression on her face. "If you'd done the thing properly, he wouldn't have been able to budge you. Again. Ground and center."

She tried—much shaken, this time. If anything, she was worse off than before. Tantris hardly flicked her, and she lost internal balance. This time she did not lose physical control, although it was a near thing. She visibly swayed as if beneath a blow.

"Ground and center, girl. This is a baby-lesson, it ought to be reflex. *Reflex*, not instinct. Do it again."

She was exhausted, sweat-drenched, knotted up all over, and shaking with the effort of holding back tears before he let up on her. There *had* been progress, though, and he told her so.

"You're not there yet," he said. "But you're closer. You got a little closer to your true center each time you tried for it—except for the last time; you missed it altogether. That's why we're quitting for a little."

She buried her face in her hands, trembling all over. "I think," she said after a moment, her voice muffled, "that I could come to hate you with very little effort."

"So why don't you?" he asked, masking his apprehension and the cold chill he felt at her words.

She looked up at him, and lowered her hands away from her face, slowly. "Because you're trying to help me, and this is the only way you know how."

He let out the breath he'd been holding in a long sigh of relief. "Lord of Lights," he said thankfully, "you would not believe how glad I am to hear you say that."

"Because if I did hate you, I could quite easily kill you."

"Exactly so. And all the easier while I was working with you—because I have to be completely unshielded to See what you're doing."

She shuddered, and he moved forward to put his arms around her. She tensed for a moment, then relaxed onto his shoulder. "How much more of this . . . ?"

"Until you get it right."

"Gods. And this is only the very beginning?"

"Just the first steps."

She bit back a sob of frustration; he felt it, more than heard it, and ached for her.

And said the cruelest thing yet. "All right, you've had your wallow in self-pity. Now let's get back to work."

And when she stared at him in disbelief, he snapped an order at her like any drill-instructor. "Ground and center, girl, *ground and center.*"

When he finally let up on her, it was so late that he'd had to mend the fire twice; she was physically as well as emotionally drained. She crawled into bed and huddled among the blankets, too spent even to cry.

He was almost as exhausted as she.

He staggered over to the fire and banked it with painful precision, controlling the shaking of his hands with effort. "You almost had it," he said, finally. "You came so close. I think you might have had it, if you'd just had the energy to get there."

She lost the bleak emptiness that had been in her eyes. "I—I thought maybe—"

"Tomorrow we'll try something different; we'll try it in link. Once you *find* your center, you won't lose it again. Gods, it is so frustrating watching you . . . I can *See* you coming close and missing, and I want to scream."

"Well, it's no Festival from inside either," she retorted, then managed a wan smile. "The least you can do, after torturing me all night, is to get in with me and keep me warm."

"Oh, I think I could manage something more personal than that," he replied, dredging up a smile of his own.

Talia fell asleep almost immediately, every last bit of energy exhausted by the efforts of the day. Kris remained awake a bit longer, trying to figure how he was going to fit in the training with the all-too-necessary effort of digging out. Just before he finally slept, Tantris had the last word.

:*Not one day,*: Tantris ordered. :*You're more tired than you thought. You rest tomorrow, too.*:

"I'm fine," Kris objected in a whisper.

:*Hah! You only* think *you are. Wait until tomorrow. Besides, if you can get her centered, you'll be on the way to solving* that *problem. That takes precedence, I think.*:

"I hate to admit it," Kris yawned, "but you're right, Featherfoot."

Kris had not realized how truly bone-weary they were until he woke first the next day to discover that it was well past noon. He woke Talia, and they finished mending all the now-dry garments, putting off the inevitable "lesson" as long as possible by mutual unspoken accord.

Finally it was she who said, reluctantly, "I suppose we'd better . . ."

"Unfortunate, but true. Here—" He sat on the blankets of their "bed," and patted a place in front of him. "I told you I was going to try a different tactic. You've linked in with me before, so you know what it's like."

She seated herself cross-legged, their knees touching, and looked at him warily. "I think I remember. Why?"

"I'm going to try and show you your center. Now, just relax, and let me do the work this time." He waited until she had achieved that half-trance, closed his own eyes long enough to trance down himself, then rested his hands lightly on her wrists. It was little more than a moment's work to bring her into rapport; *that* part of her Gift was still working, almost *too* well. He opened his eyes slowly, and Looked, knowing she could see what he Saw.

She looked, gasped, and grabbed—throwing both of them out of trance and out of rapport.

He had been expecting something of the sort and had been prepared for a "fall." She had *not* been, and sat shaking her head to clear it afterward.

"That was a damnfool move," she said, when at last she could speak.

"I won't argue with that statement," he replied evenly. "Ready to try again?"

She sighed, nodded, and settled herself once more. This time she did not grab; she hardly moved at all.

Finally she broke the trance herself, unable to take the strain. "It's like trying to draw by watching a mirror," she said through clenched teeth.

"So?" he replied, giving her no encouragement to pity herself.

"So I try again."

It was hours later when she met with victory; as Kris had suspected, when she centered properly, it was with a nearly audible *snap*, a great deal like having a dislocated joint pop back into place. There was a flare of energy—and a flash of something almost like pain—followed by a flood of relief. Kris had Tantris nudge her—then shove her, with no effect.

"Ground!" he ordered; she fumbled her way into a clumsy grounding with such an utter lack of finesse that his other suspicion—that she'd never done grounding and centering properly before—was pretty much confirmed. It was then that he realized that her shields hadn't just gone erratic, they'd collapsed; and the reason they'd collapsed was that they'd never been properly based in the first place.

"All right," he said quietly. "Now you're properly set up. Can you see now why it's important?"

"Because," she answered slowly, "you have to have something to use as a base to build on?"

"Right," he agreed. "Now come out of there."

"But—"

"You're going to find it yourself, this time. *Without* my help. Ground and center, greenie."

"Ground and center. Dammit, that's *not* right." "Do it again. Ground and center." "Again, and faster." "Dammit, it should be *reflex* by now! Again."

Talia held to her temper by the most tenuous of holds. If it hadn't been for the concern he was feeling, so overwhelming that she could sense it with no effort at all, she'd have lost her temper hours ago. Ground and center, over and over, faster and faster—with Tantris and Rolan shoving at her when she least expected it.

The first time they'd pushed her before she was properly settled, she'd literally been knocked out for a moment; she came to with Kris propping her up, expression impassive.

"Tantris *hit* me," she said indignantly.

"He was supposed to," Kris replied, letting her go.

"But I wasn't ready! It wasn't *fair!*" She stared at him, losing the tenuous hold she'd had on her emotions. It felt like betrayal; it felt horribly like betrayal—

"Damn right, it wasn't fair." He answered the anger and hurt in her voice with cool contempt. "Life isn't fair. You learned that a long time ago." He felt the anger then—hers; it couldn't be coming from anywhere else, since beneath his veneer of contempt, he was worried and no little frightened. He was taking his life in his hands by provoking her, and was all too conscious of the fact. "Dammit, you're leaking again. *Lock it down!*" The anger died; she flushed with shame. He didn't give her a chance to get back into the cycle of doubt and self-pity. "Now; ground and center—and get centered *before* they can knock you over."

He didn't even let her stop when they ate; snapping at her to center at unexpected moments, letting Tantris or Rolan judge when she was most off-guard and choosing then to push at her. It wasn't until *he* was exhausted, so exhausted he couldn't properly See anymore, that he called it quits for the night.

She undressed for bed in total silence; so barricaded that there was nothing to read in her face or eyes. He waited for her to say something; waited in vain.

"I'm not sorry," he said finally. "I know it's not your fault you got out of Grays half-trained, but I'm not sorry I'm doing this to you. If you don't learn this the hard way, you won't learn it right."

"I know that," she replied, looking up at him sharply. "And I'm *not* angry at you—not now, anyway. I'm mostly tired, and Gods, my head hurts so I can hardly think."

He relaxed, and reached for the container of willowbark on the mantelpiece, handing it to her with a rueful smile. "In that case, I can assume it's safe to come to bed?"

"I wouldn't murder you there, anyway," she replied with a hint of her old sense of humor. "It would get the blankets all sticky."

He laughed, and settled himself, watching her make herself a cup of herbal tea for her headache. Before today he hadn't been sure—but now he dared to believe she *would* tame that wild Gift of hers. It wouldn't be too much longer before centering *would* be reflex. Then it was only a matter of time, to build back what she'd lost.

"Kris? Are you still awake?"

"Sort of," he answered drowsily, lulled by the warmth and his own weariness.

"I just want to say that I appreciate this. At least, I do when you're not pounding on me."

He chuckled, but made no other reply.

"I need you, Kris," she finished softly. "That's something I don't forget even when I'm angriest. I really need you."

It took a while for the sense of that to penetrate—and when it did, it almost shocked him awake again. If he hadn't been so tired—

As it was, guilt followed him down into sleep. She needed him. Good Gods; what if it was something more than need?

Talia waited until Kris' deep and even breathing told her he really had fallen asleep, and carefully extricated herself from the bed without waking him. She always thought better with some task in her hands, a holdover from her childhood, so she took her cup of willowbark tea and set about polishing some of the bright bits of metalwork on Rolan's tack. The cloak she'd wrapped around herself kept the chill off her back, and the fire in front of her gave off just enough heat to be pleasant. Thusly settled in, she put her mind to the myriad problems at hand.

The fire crackled cheerfully; she wished *she* could feel cheerful. Lord and Lady, what an unholy mess she'd gotten into! The storm alone would have been bad enough; *any* of the problems would have been bad enough. To have to deal with all of them together . . .

At least she'd made a start, some kind of start, on getting herself re-trained. Kris seemed happier, after this afternoon's work. He had been right about one thing; now that she knew what "being centered" felt like, she'd never lose the ability to find that firm base again. She'd wanted to kill him this afternoon, and more than once—but she was learning in a way that would make her stronger, and now that she was calmer, she could appreciate that.

She needed him, more than she'd ever needed anyone else.

But—Lord and Lady—what if it was something more complicated than need, or even need and the kind of feeling she had for Skif?

He *was* handsome; handsome as an angel. And despite a certain smug vanity, a man she'd be more than proud to have as a friend. Look at the way he was taking his life in his hands—literally—for the sake of getting her back in control of herself and her Gift. He was kind, he was gentle, he was considerate, and with the way her mind had been playing tricks on her lately, it was more than a possibility that she'd unconsciously used her Gift to influence the way he thought about her. Even to the point of getting him into bed with her—

Lady knew *she* was no beauty. And if she had influenced him in that, she could have caused an even deeper attraction.

She clenched her hands on her mug so hard they ached. That was one thing she had *not* wanted. At least not originally. But now?

She liked Kris well enough. Well enough—but not *that* well.

She *was* attracted to Dirk, there was no question about that. And strongly; more strongly than she'd ever felt about anyone.

It was almost, she decided a bit reluctantly, as if Dirk was some hitherto-unrecognized, hitherto-unmissed, other half of herself, and that she'd never again feel whole after having met him unless—

Unless what?

Heralds seldom made any kind of long-term commitment; contenting themselves with the close friendship of the Circle, casual, strictly physical liaisons, and the bonds of their Companions. And truly, few Heralds she knew were at all dissatisfied with that kind of life. Realistically speaking, the job was far too dangerous to make a lifebond possible or desirable. Look what had happened to Keren when Ylsa died; if Sherrill hadn't had exactly what she needed *and* been right on the spot, she might very well have death-willed herself in bereavement.

And she'd only seen Dirk a handful of times.

But for Heralds, sometimes only once was enough.

Her mind drifted back years.

It was late one night that they'd all been gathered in Keren's room over hot mulled wine and sometimes ribald conversation. Somehow the subject turned from bawdy jokes to the truth behind some of the legends and tales told by outsiders about Heralds: they were laughing at some of the more absurd exaggerations.

"Take that love-at-one-glance nonsense," Talia had giggled. "Someone ought to really take the Bards to task over that one. How could anyone know from the first meeting that someone they've just met will be a lifepartner?"

"Oddly enough, that's not an exaggeration," Sherrill had replied soberly. "When it happens with Heralds, that's generally exactly the way it happens. It's almost as if there were something, something even deeper than instinct, that recognizes the other soul." She'd shrugged. "Metaphysical, sentimental, but still true."

"Do you mean to tell me that both of you had that happen?" Talia had been incredulous.

"As a matter of fact, the very first time I set eyes on Keren," Sherrill replied. "Notwithstanding the fact that I was just under fourteen at the time."

Keren nodded. "Ylsa and I knew when we met midway through our third year—until then we'd never done more than wave at each other across the room since we had had very different schedules. We did wait, though, until we were both sure that it was something solid and not ephemeral, and until we'd completed our internships, before committing to each other."

"And I didn't want to intrude on what was obviously a lifebond."

"You would have been welcome. To tell you the truth, we'd wondered a little—"

"But I didn't know that at the time, did I?" Sherrill had laughed. "Truly, though, Talia, anyone I've ever talked to that has seen a lifebond has said the same thing; that was the way it was for Selenay's parents, for instance. It either happens the first time you meet, or never."

"And if it's not a lifebond, there's nothing you can do to make it one—to make it more than a temporary relationship, no matter how much you want it to be something more," Keren had continued. "My twin found that out."

Talia must have looked intensely curious, although she hadn't actually asked anything, because Keren continued after a moment.

"Remember I've told you once or twice that I've got a niece and nephew almost your age? Well, they're Teren's. Not only were we not Chosen at the same time, but it took seven years for his Companion to come for him. By then I was a field Herald—and he was married and working the sponge-boat. Then it happened. He was Chosen. And the wife he had thought he was contented with turned out to mean less to him than he'd ever dreamed. He *wanted* to love her, he really did. He tried to make himself love her—it didn't work. He went through an incredible amount of soul-searching and guilt before concluding that the emotion wasn't there and wasn't going to be, and that his real life was with the Circle and his Companion. And to tell the truth, his wife—now ex-wife—didn't really seem to care. His children were adopted into our family and she turned around and married into another with no sign of regret that *I* could see. So you see," she had concluded, "if you're a Herald, you either have a lifebond and recognize it at once, or you live your life without one."

Talia sighed.

If she were going to be honest with herself, she had to admit that this seemed to be exactly what had happened to her with regard to Dirk. *Seemed* to be—that was the key. How did she know that this wasn't some fantasy she was building in her own mind?

It didn't feel much like a fantasy, though. It was more like a toothache; or perhaps the way Jadus had felt about his missing leg. He'd said it had often seemed as if it were still there, and aching.

Well, there was something in Talia that ached, too.

Fine. What about Kris?

What she felt for Kris . . . just wasn't that deep. Yes, she needed him—his support, his expertise, his encouragement. But "need" was just not the same as "love." Or rather, the emotion she felt for him was a different kind of love; a comradeship—actually closer to what she felt for Rolan or Skif or even Keren than anything else.

But if *Kris* had become infatuated with *her*—Gods, it almost didn't bear thinking about.

Granted, he certainly wasn't acting very lover-like. And earlier—he almost seemed to be throwing Dirk at her. Outside of bed he was treating her more like Alberich treated a trainee who had gotten some bad early lessoning and needed to have it beaten out of him. Except in the digging out, when he treated her as an absolute equal; neither cosseting her nor allowing her to take more than her share of the work.

Provided her mind hadn't been tricking both of them—which was a very real possibility.

"Oh, hellfire," she sighed.

At least she'd managed to clarify *some* of her feelings. And there wasn't anything she could do about it anyway—not until she had her Gift under full control, and could sort out what was "real" and what wasn't. She drank the last of the stone-cold tea, and put up the harness, then slipped back into bed. Right now the only thing to do was to enforce the sleep she knew she needed badly. It was best to just try and take things a day at a time.

Because at this point, she had more pressing problems to deal with.

If she couldn't get her Gift back under control, this would all be very moot. . . .

For she was quite well aware of how close she'd come to driving both Kris and herself over the edge. It could happen again, especially if he did something to badly frighten her—and if it did—

If it did, it could end, only too easily, in his death, hers, or both.

CHAPTER 10

WELL, THERE WAS one way, Talia knew, to keep herself under control—and that was to work herself into a state of total exhaustion. So in the morning she rose early, almost before the sun, and she began pressing herself to her limits—making each day blur into the next in a haze of fatigue. It became impossible to tell what day it was, or even how long they'd been there.

Talia usually woke first, at dawn, and would prod Kris into wakefulness. One or the other of them would prepare not only breakfast, but unleavened cakes with some form of soup or stew: something that could remain untended most of the day without scorching, simply because they both knew that by the time they came in, they would have barely enough energy to eat and perform a sketchy sort of wash before collapsing into bed.

After a hearty breakfast of fruit and porridge, she would wrap the Companions' legs against the sharp edges of the ice-crust while Kris haltered the chirras, and all six occupants of the Station would troop out into the cold to begin the day's work.

Rolan and Tantris would move up first, and break the crust of ice and the hard snow beneath by rearing to their full heights and crashing down on it with their forelegs, or backing up to it and kicking as hard as they could. They would move back, and Talia and Kris would then take their places; picking up the chunks that had broken off and heaving them to either side of the trail they were cutting. The chirras would use their powerful foreclaws on what remained until they were halted by snow too packed for them to dig or crust too slippery to get a grip on. Then the Heralds would move the chunks they'd dislodged, scoop up the loose snow, and let the Companions take over again.

They would work without a break until the sun reached its zenith, then take begrudged time for a hasty lunch. On their return, they would work until darkness. Each day the trips to and from the Station got longer; sometimes it was only that which kept Talia working. There were times, too many times, when their progress was limited to a few feet for a whole day of back-breaking labor; and she knew the Station itself was furlongs from the road. It was when their measured progress amounted to little more than a dozen paces that the temptation to give up was the strongest.

When darkness fell, Kris would tend the Companions while Talia groomed the chirras, checking them thoroughly for any sign of injury or muscle strain during the process of grooming them. Rolan and Tantris, of course, could be relied upon to tell their Chosen if *they'd* been hurt, but the chirras were another story. And if one of the chirras had to drop out of the work, their progress would be halved.

Finally Kris or Talia—usually Talia—would ensure that everyone was well supplied with food and water and blanketed against the night chill before they wolfed down their own dinners and sought their bed.

It was the hardest physical labor either of them had ever performed. The constant cold seeped into their very bones, and their muscles never stopped aching. It wore them down, a little more each day. They had strictly rationed their own supplies, and the food they were taking in was not equaling the energy they were expending. They were getting thinner, both of them, and tougher, physically. It was a change Talia hardly noticed, because it was so gradual, but once in a while she would think vaguely that her friends would have been surprised to the point of shock by the way she looked.

Kris continued to hammer at her through the first week of digging out, until centering and grounding *had* become reflexive. After that, he left her in peace, only offering an occasional bit of weary advice. Talia's control over Empathic projection came and went, at unpredictable intervals, although Kris evidently never noticed her projecting involuntarily. If he had, he would have pounced on her; of that she was certain. Her shielding *was* returning now that she had something to form a firm base for it, but it was the thinnest of veils, hardly even enough to know that it was there. She worked at control with nearly the same single-minded obsession she was giving the physical labor of digging out.

The only pauses in their routine were the two occasions when they again ran out of clean clothing. Those two days were given over to a repeat of their washday, and to brave attempts to revive one another's faltering spirits. As tired as Talia was, it was easy to become depressed. Kris wasn't quite so much the pawn of his emotions, but there were times Talia found herself having to pull him out of despair. The endless cold did not help matters any, nor did the fact that they had, indeed, needed to cut green wood to use in their fire. The green wood, even when mixed with seasoned, gave off much less heat. Talia felt as if she'd never be warm again.

But one afternoon, nearly a month from the time they'd first reached the Station, she looked up from their task in sudden bewilderment to realize that they'd finally reached the road.

And the road was as drift-covered as the path out had been.

"Now what?" Talia asked dully.

"Oh, Gods." Kris sat down on a chunk of snow with none of his usual grace. This was a scenario he'd never contemplated; he'd always assumed that once they broke out, the main road would be cleared as well. He stared at the icy wilderness in front of them and tried to think.

"The storm—it must have spread farther than I thought," he said at last. "The road crews should have been within sensing distance by now, otherwise."

He felt utterly bewildered and profoundly shaken—for once at a total loss for a course of action. He just gazed numbly at the unbroken expanse of snow covering the road, unable to even think clearly.

Talia tried to clear her mind—to stay calm—but the uncanny silence echoed in her ears. And that feeling of someone watching was back.

She glanced apprehensively at Kris, wondering if *he* was sensing the same thing she was—and in the next breath, certain it was all originating in *her* mind.

The feeling of being watched was, if anything, more intense than it had been before. And ever-so-slightly ominous. It was very much akin to the uneasy queasiness she used to have whenever Keldar would stand over her at some chore, waiting and watching for her to make the tiniest mistake. Something out there was unsure of her—mistrusted her—and was waiting for her to slip, somehow. And when she did—Panic rose in her, and choked off the words she had intended.

*　　*　　*

Kris stared at the unbroken ice crust as if entranced, unable to muster enough energy to say anything more. Gradually, though, he became aware of a feeling of uneasiness—exactly as if someone were watching him from under cover of the brush beneath the snow-laden trees. He tried to dismiss the feeling, but it continued to grow, until it was only by sheer force of will that he was able to keep from whipping around to *see* who was staring at the back of his neck—

It wasn't entirely an unfriendly regard . . . but it was a wary one. As if whatever it was that was watching him wasn't quite sure of him.

He tried to shield, to clear his mind of the strange sensations, only to have them intensify when he invoked shielding.

And now he was seeing and hearing things as well—slight forms that could only be caught out of the corner of his eye, and slipped into invisibility when he tried to look at them directly. And there seemed to be sibilant whisperings just on the edges of his hearing—

All of which could well be from a single source. Talia had told him once already that she thought she was hallucinating; she could well be drawing him into an irrational little nightmare-world of her making.

"Talia!" he snapped angrily, more than a little frightened. *"Lock it down!"*

And he whipped around to glare at her, enraged, and just about ready to strike out at her for her lack of control.

Talia forgot the strange watcher; forgot everything except Kris' angry—and untrue—accusation. She flushed, then paled—then reacted.

"It's *not* me!" she snapped. Then, when he continued to stare at her with utter disbelief, she lost the control she had been holding to with her psychic teeth and toenails.

This time, at least, the Companions were prepared, and shielded themselves quickly. Kris, however, got the full brunt of her fear of the situation and her anger at him. He rose involuntarily to his feet and staggered back five or six paces, to trip and fall backward into the hard snow, his face as white as hers, and unable to do more than raise his arms in front of his face in a futile gesture of warding.

And the watcher stirred—

Talia froze; the feeling that some power was uncoiling and contemplating striking her down was so powerful that she was unable even to breathe. Somehow she cut off the emotion-storm—and simultaneous with her resumption of control, Rolan paced forward slowly, to stand beside her. He faced, not her, but the watching forest, his whole posture a silent challenge.

There was a feeling of vague surprise—and the sensation of being watched vanished.

Talia felt released from her paralysis and wanted to die of shame for what she'd nearly done to Kris. As he blinked in surprise, she turned blindly away from him, leaned against a tree-trunk and wept, her face buried in her arms.

Kris stumbled to his feet, and put both arms around her. "Talia, little bird, please don't—" he begged. "I'm sorry; I didn't mean—I lost my temper. It'll be all right. It's got to be all right—I'm sorry. I'm sorry—"

But dreary days of grinding labor and nights of too little rest had taken their toll of his spirit as well. It was only when the tears started to freeze on both their faces that they were able to stop sobbing in dejection and despair.

"It—that thing watching—"

She shook with more than cold. "I—don't want to talk about it," she said, looking uneasily over her shoulder. "Not here—not now."

"It wasn't you—"

"No. I swear on my life."

He believed her. "All right, let's handle what we've got; the storm was worse than we thought," he said, getting control of himself again. "This is the very northernmost end of the road. They can't be more than a few days away, and we aren't running short of food yet. We'll be all right—especially if we start rationing ourselves."

"We won't need as much food if we rest," Talia said, drying her eyes on the gauze she'd used to protect them from sunglare.

"And we can plant a signal so that they know we're here. I can get the crust to hold me a good distance, and you're lighter than I am; about an hour's scramble will do. Wait here."

He mounted Tantris and the two of them headed back to the Station, vanishing from sight down the narrow little valley they'd cut. Talia waited for their return, occasionally looking warily over her shoulder. Whatever had been watching her had been within a hair of striking her; why she was certain of this, she had no idea, but she could not rid herself of the thought. She had no idea what had deterred it, but she did not want it to catch her unaware. She clung to Rolan's neck, and waited, exerting every bit of control she had. For it seemed to her that the watcher had only acted when it appeared that she was attacking Kris. If that *was* the case, she had no intention of inadvertently invoking it again.

It was at least a candlemark—and far too long for her peace of mind—before she saw Kris and Tantris trotting back. He carried four white arrows, two long branches, and some bright blue rags.

"These will show up at a distance. Here, pattern these, will you?" He dismounted and handed her two of the arrows, and began working on his two. "We tie the arrows to the stick, and plant the stick out in the middle of where the road is. When the crews find them, they'll know we're here, and still alive. They'll even know for certain it's us if they happen to have a Herald with them—surely anyone with them will have been given our patterns."

"Why are we doing this?"

"If we don't, they might not clear the road this far. This is just the northernmost loop; it isn't strictly needed to get between Waymeet and Berrybay. It takes longer to go around than to cut through Sorrows, but nobody travels much in the winter except Heralds. And nobody knows *where* we've been 'lost.'"

He handed her one of his arrows in exchange for hers. Both of them tied the arrows to one of the branches, and made them as conspicuous as possible with fluttering rags.

"You go toward Waymeet, I'll go toward Berrybay," he said, preparing to climb up on the snow crust. "Plant yours at the first crossroads you come to. I'll do the same. Hopefully the road crews will find *one* of them before they give up."

"Kris—what if it snows again?"

"Talia, for the love of the Goddess, don't even *think* that. Walk as far as you can, but be back here by dusk."

Talia had never felt so lonely. There was scarcely a sound from the white woods on either side. She could hear the creaking sounds of Kris carefully making his way across the snow crust behind her, sliding his feet so as not to break it. Even so, she heard the crunch that meant he'd fallen through at least once before he got too far away for the sounds to carry to her. It was a measure of his own dejection that he didn't even have the spirit to swear.

She set out herself, often having to detour around high drifts that she didn't dare try and climb. Her eyes ached from tears and snowglare, and she was as tired as she'd ever been in her life. She was grateful that she was lighter than Kris; the snow crust was holding beneath her without any such mishaps as he had had.

The silence was eerie—frightening. As frightening in its way as the howl of the storm had been. Talia was shivering long before she reached her turnaround point, and not just from cold. There were no sounds of birds or animals, no indication that anything else lived and moved here besides herself. That horrible feeling of something watching might be gone, but there was still something uncanny about the Forest of Sorrows, something touched with the chill of death and the ice of despair. Whatever power held sway here, it was unsleeping and brooding; she *knew* it beyond doubt, and somehow knew she was feeling only the barest touch of its power—and she didn't really want to trust to the supposed protection of her Whites by venturing too far alone. She was more than relieved to find a half-buried crossroads sign; that meant she could plant her gaudy staff in the snowcrust at the peak of a drift and retrace her steps.

She was never so glad to see another human being as she was to see Kris, picking his way across the snow, coming toward her.

Back in the Station, Talia surveyed what was left of their supplies. "They'd better come soon," she said, trying to keep doubt out of her voice. "Even if we're careful, we don't have much. It'll probably last for a week, but not much more."

"If they're as worried as I think—as I hope—they'll be working around the clock, even by torchlight," Kris said, sheer exhaustion making his voice toneless. "It just can't be too much longer."

"They may not recognize us as Heralds at all," she replied, trying to joke a little. "I doubt they've ever seen Heralds looking so shabby. I've had to practically rub holes in my things to get them white again. Our appearance is hardly going to enhance the Heraldic image."

She screwed her face up in imitation of an old man's grimace, and croaked, "Heralds? Yer be not Heralds! Yer be imposters, for certain sure! Gypsies! Scalawags! And where got ye them whitewashed nags, eh? Eh?"

Kris just stared at her for a long moment, then suddenly began to laugh as helplessly as he'd wept earlier. Perhaps it was their weariness that made them as prone to near-hysterical hilarity as to tears. Talia began to giggle herself, then crow with laughter. They collapsed into their bed-nest together, legs too weak to stand up, and for a long time could hardly stop laughing long enough to breathe. No sooner would one of them get himself under control, and the other start to follow suit, when one look would set them both off again.

"Enough—please—" Kris gasped at last.

"Then don't keep looking at me," Talia replied, resolutely staring at a stain on her boots until she got her breath back.

"Berrybay has a Resupply Station," Kris said, doing his best to maintain a serious subject. "We *can* get new uniforms there, and we can get our leathers bleached and re-treated. I'll warn you, though, the sizes will only be approximate."

"Just so that the Whites *are* white and not gray, or full of holes."

"I don't suppose you know enough sewing to alter what we get?" Kris asked wistfully. She could tell by his expression that his fastidious nature was mildly disturbed by the notion that he would be looking considerably less than immaculate in outsize uniforms.

Talia raised an eyebrow in his direction. "My dear Herald, I'll have you know that by my third year at the Collegium I was *making* Whites. I may very well have made some of *your* wardrobe."

"Strange thought." He pulled off his boots, slowly. "It—it *wasn't* you playing tricks on my mind?"

"No," she replied. "Not until you shouted at me."

"Gods—I think I must be going mad."

She was rubbing her white, cold feet, trying to restore circulation. "Don't—please—it's the isolation, the worry," she responded, with a clutching of fear in her chest. "Not enough rest, not enough food—"

"Are making me see things? Are *you* seeing things?"

"No," she admitted, "but—it seems like the forest is—watching. Almost all the time."

Kris started. Talia saw him jump, and bit her lip.

"It's nothing," he said. "Just—Tantris says you're right. He says the forest *is* watching us. Dammit—I thought it was you, doing things to me. Sorry."

"Kris—I lost it again—" Tears stung her eyes.

"Hey, not as bad as last time—and you got control back by yourself. Right?"

"Sort of. Whatever it was—when I turned on you, it suddenly felt like it was going to do something to *me* if I touched you. That was when I got scared back into sense."

"And you got control back. However it happened, *you* got control back. Don't give up on me, little bird. And don't give up on yourself, either."

"I'll try," she said, a faint tremor in her voice. "I'll try."

Leaden silence hung between them, until he took it upon himself to break it. "Jadus left you his harp, so I assume that you know how to play it, but I've never once heard you do so. Would you?"

"I'm nowhere near as good as you are," she protested.

"Humor me," he insisted.

"All right, but you may be sorry." She curled into the blankets to try and keep a little warmth in her legs and back and took the harp from him when he brought it from its corner.

This was the first time she'd played in front of anyone but Jadus. The way the firelight caught the golden grain of the wood brought back those days with a poignant sadness. She rested her hands on the strings for a moment, then began playing the first thing that came to memory.

The song was "Sun and Shadow," and Kris was very much aware from the first few notes that she performed it quite differently than he did. Where he and Dirk emphasized the optimistic foreshadowing of the ultimate solution to the lovers' trials, and made the piece almost hopeful in spite of its somber quality, she wandered the lonely paths of the song's "present," where their respective curses seemed to be dooming the pair to live forever just out of one another's reach. She was correct in insisting that she wasn't as technically adept a player as Kris, but she played as she sang—with feeling, feeling that she made you hear. In her hands "Sun and Shadow" could tear your heart.

The last notes hung in the air between them for long moments before he could clear his throat enough to say something.

"I keep telling you," he managed at last, "that you underestimate yourself."

"You're a remarkably uncritical audience," she replied. "Would you like her back, or shall I murder something else?"

"I'd like you to play more, if you would."

She shrugged, but secretly was rather pleased that he hadn't reclaimed My Lady. Her mood was melancholy, and it was possible to find solitude by losing herself in the music—solitude that it wasn't possible to create when he was playing or she was singing. She continued, closing her eyes and letting her hands wander through whatever came to mind, sometimes singing, sometimes not. Kris listened quietly, without comment. The few times she looked up, his face was so shadowed that she couldn't read his expression. Eventually she ran out of music fitting her mood, and her hands fell from the harpstrings.

"That's all I know," she said into the silence that followed.

"Then that," he replied, taking the harp from her, "is enough for one night. I think it is more than time enough for bed."

She had doubted she'd be able to sleep, but the moment she relaxed, she was lost to slumber.

*   *   *

Three days later the Station seemed to have shrunk around them and felt very confining, especially to Talia, who had always had a touch of claustrophobia. Her temper was shortened to near nonexistence . . . and she feared losing it. Greatly feared it.

"Kris—" she said, when his pacing became too much for her to bear. "Will you go out? Will you *please* go somewhere?"

He stopped in midstep, and turned to eye her with speculation. "Am I driving you out of patience?"

"It's more than that. It's—"

"That feeling of being watched. Is it back?"

She sagged with relief. "You feel it, too?"

"Not now. I did a little while back."

"Am—I sending both of us mad?" She clenched her hands so hard that her nails left marks in her palms.

He sat on the floor at her feet, took her hands in his, and made her relax them. "I don't think so. If you'll remember, *Tantris* told me that the forest was watching us."

"What *is* it?"

"I only have a guess; it's Vanyel's Curse. It's made the whole forest aware somehow."

"I don't think it likes me," she said, biting her lip.

Kris had the "listening" look he wore when Tantris Mindspoke him. "Tantris says that *he* thinks it's disturbed by you; you're a Herald, but you're a danger to me, another Herald. It isn't sure what to do with you."

"So as long as I stay in control, it will leave me alone . . ."

"I would surmise." He rose to his feet. "And to keep you from losing control, *I* am going out."

Kris had decided to flounder his way down the road toward Waymeet, in hopes of meeting with a road crew. He entered the Station to have an entirely unexpected and mouthwatering aroma hit him full in the face.

"I'm hallucinating," he said, half-afraid that once again he really *was*. "I'm smelling fresh meat cooking."

"Pretty substantial hallucinations, then, since you're going to have them for supper," Talia replied, with a sober face. Then, unable to restrain herself, she jumped up from the hearth to throw her arms around him in a joyful hug. "Two squirrels and a rabbit, Kris! I got them *all*! And there'll be more—the fodder is attracting them! I didn't even lose or break any arrows!"

"Bright Havens—" he said, sitting down with a thump, hardly daring to believe it.

There was no denying the stewed meat and broth Talia ladled out to him, however. They ate every scrap, the first fresh food they'd had in weeks, sucking the tiny bones dry, then celebrated with exuberant loving. They fell asleep with untroubled hearts for the first time in many days.

They were awakened the next morning very early; the chirras were stirring restlessly, and both Companions seemed to be listening to something.

Rolan was overwhelmingly relieved and joyful, and Talia went deeper to find out why.

"Tantris says—" Kris began.

"There're people coming!" Talia finished excitedly. "Kris, it's the road crew!"

"There's a Herald with them, too. Tantris thinks they'll reach us sometime after noon."

"Have they reached our marker yet?"

"Yes. The Herald had his Companion broadcast a Mindcall to ours when he found it. I might even have met them yesterday, if I hadn't gone in the wrong direction—idiot that I am!"

"How were you to know? How many are there?"

"Ten, not counting the Herald."

"Should we go out and try to dig the path out farther to meet them?"

"No," Kris said firmly. "The little we can do won't make much difference, and I'm still tired. We'll pack up, straighten things up here, and meet them where the path meets the road."

It seemed strange to see the Station barren of their belongings, with only the empty containers that the supplies had been stored in to tell of their presence there this past month. It took longer than Talia had thought it would to repack everything; they did not leave the Station until almost noon.

When they reached the road, they could see the newcomers in the far distance. They waved and shouted, and could tell by the agitated movements of the other figures that they'd been spotted. The work crew redoubled their efforts, and before too long—though not soon enough for Talia and Kris—the paths met.

"Heralds Talia and Kris?" The white-clad figure that was first through the gap was unfamiliar to both of them, though his immaculate uniform made them uncomfortably conscious of the pitiful condition of their own.

"Yes, Herald," Kris answered for both of them.

"Praise the Lady! When the Guard learned that you hadn't stayed at Waymeet and hadn't arrived at Berrybay, and that you'd left on the very eve of the storm, we all feared the worst. Had you been caught in it, I doubt you would have survived even one night. This was the worst blizzard in these parts in recorded history. Oh, I'm Tedric. How on earth did you manage?"

"We were warned by our chirras in time to make the Waystation, but I doubt that we'd be in any shape to greet you now if it hadn't been stocked by someone other than the regular Resupply crew," Kris replied. "Whoever it was, he seems to have had an uncannily accurate idea of how much provender we'd need, and what kinds."

"That's the Weatherwitch's doing," said one of the work crew, a stolid-looking farmer. "Kept at us this fall till we got it stocked to her liking. Even made us go back after first snow with some odd bits—honey 'n oil, salted meat 'n fish. We had it to spare, praise Kernos, and she's never yet been wrong when she gets one o' these notions, so we went along with it. Happen it was a good thing."

"Praise Kernos, in very deed! I see you've got your gear. Come along with me and I'll have you warm and dry and fed before nightfall. I'm with the Resupply Station outside of Berrybay. I've got plenty of room for both of you, if you don't mind sharing a bed."

"Not at all," Kris replied gravely, sensing Talia struggling with the effort of maintaining what little shielding she had against the pressure of fifteen minds. "We've been sleeping on straw next to the hearth for warmth. Right now a camp cot would sound like heaven, even if I had to share it with Tantris!"

"Good. Excellent!" Herald Tedric replied. "I'll guide you both back; these good people know what they're doing, and they certainly don't need me in the way now that we've found you."

The members of the work crew made polite noises, but they obviously agreed with him.

"Fact is, Herald," the red-faced farmer whispered to Kris, "Old Tedric's a good enough sort, but he don't belong out here. He's too old, and his heart's more'n a mite touchy. Waystation Supply post was supposed to be a pensioning-out position, if you catch my meaning. He ain't the kind to sit idle, even though he hasn't the health to ride circuit no more. We're supposed to be keepin' an eye on him, make sure he don't overdo—job's set up so's he could feel useful, but wouldn't have to do anything straining. Guard's supposed to do all his fetching and carrying for him. But what with this storm and all, Guard's busy clearing the roads, seein' to the emergencies—when he found out you two was missin', nothing would do but that he go out with us. Gave us a real fright a time or two, gettin' short of breath and blue-like when we thought we might've found bodies. Good thing you turned up all right, or I reckon we'd have had a third body on our hands."

This put things in an altogether different light. Kris felt a sudden increase in respect for the talkative and seemingly feckless Herald. On closer examination he saw that Tedric was a great deal older than he had first appeared, partially because he was bald as an egg, and partially because he had the kind of baby-soft face that tends not to wrinkle with age. His Companion cosseted him tenderly, flatly refusing to race headlong down the road so that he could prepare the Station for his guests.

Talia and Kris took turns telling him what had transpired from the time they discovered the plague in Waymeet.

"So you're the Queen's Own, the one with the Gift for emotions and mind Healing?" he asked Talia, peering at her short-sightedly. She could sense his faint unease around her, even through the shields Rolan was holding, and mentally shrank into herself. "I wonder if you could do something for the Weatherwitch?"

"Considering that we obviously owe her our lives, I'll certainly be glad to try," Talia replied, trying not to show her own unease and her real dismay at being asked to *use* her wayward Gift. "Just who is she, and why do you call her the Weatherwitch?"

"Ah, it's a sad story, that," he sighed. "A few years ago, it would be, when I'd only just been assigned this post, there was a young woman named Maeven in Berrybay who'd gone and had herself a Festival child—that's a babe that no one will claim, and whose mother hasn't the faintest notion who the father might be. People being what they are, there was a certain amount of tsk-ing, and finger-pointing, until the poor girl heartily wished the babe had never been conceived, much less born. That's what made what happened to her all the worse, you see. You know, 'be careful what you ask for, you might get it'? I'm sure she often wished the child gone, and when the accident happened, she blamed herself. She was taking her turn working at the mill, and she left the little one alone for longer than she should have. Poor mite was just beginning to crawl about, and it managed to wriggle free of the basket she'd left it in. It crawled straight to the millrace, fell in, and drowned. She was the one to find the body, and she went quite mad."

"But why 'Weatherwitch'?" Kris asked.

"She must have had a Gift, and her going off her head freed it altogether, because she started being able to predict the weather. She'd be acting just as usual, dandling that rag-doll she got in place of her babe—then out of nowhere she'd look straight *through* you, and tell you that you'd better see that the beans got taken in because it was going to hail that night. Then, sure enough, it would. People in Berrybay and for a bit around took to coming to her any time the weather looked uncertain. She began to be able to See the weather that was coming days, then weeks, then months in advance. That's why the villagers heeded her when she told them to stock the Station. I wish they'd told me, I'd have laid in a good deal more on my own."

"You stocked it very well, and we've nothing to find fault with," Kris replied reassuringly. "I'm afraid, though, that you'll find we've used up just about everything that was there."

"That will be no problem," Tedric said cheerfully. "I'll be glad to have a little task to turn my hand to. Most of my work's done in the summer, and winter's a bit of a slow time for me. But it looks to me as if you could use a full resupply yourselves."

"I'm afraid so," Talia said as Tedric shook his head over the state of their uniforms. "I don't think the fabric is going to be good for much except rags."

"I've got plenty of stock back at the Station, and I'm no bad hand with a needle," Tedric replied. "I think I can refit you well enough so that you won't be looking like crow-scares. I've got all the necessaries for bleaching and refinishing your leathers, so we won't have to replace those, and your cloaks still look in fairly good shape, or will be after we clean them. If you don't mind staying a bit, I can turn you out looking almost like the day you left to take this sector."

"That sounds fantastic!" Kris said with obvious thankfulness.

"I can help with the altering, sir," Talia added.

The old Herald twinkled at her. "But who tailors the tailor, then? And surely you wouldn't deny an old man the pleasure of helping fit a pretty young lady, would you?"

Talia blushed, and to cover it, settled My Lady wrapped in her blankets in a new position on her lap. Without the harpcase to protect her, Talia elected to carry her personally.

"What's this?" Tedric asked and brightened to learn it was a harp.

"Which of you is the musician?" he asked eagerly.

"We both are, sir," Kris replied.

"But he really plays a great deal better than I do," Talia added. "And Herald Tedric, we'd truly appreciate it if you could find someone to make a new traveling case for her while we're here. We had to destroy the old one to make snow shovels."

"The cabinetmaker would be proud to oblige you," Tedric said with certainty. "In fact, he may even have something already made that will fit. Midwinter Fair is at the Sector capital in a few weeks, and he's been readying a few instrument cases to take there, as well as his little carved boxes and similar trumperies. He's known for his work on small pieces as well as furniture, you see. I'll make a note to start stocking shovels in our Stations from now on. Not every Herald has harpcases to sacrifice."

They passed the village of Berrybay just before sunset, Talia finding herself grateful for the shielding Rolan was supplying her, and reached the Resupply Station with the coming of the dark. The place was much larger than Talia had expected.

"Bright Havens!" she exclaimed. "You could house half the Collegium here!"

"Oh, most of it isn't living quarters—it's mostly haybarn, warehouse, and granary. I do have three extra rooms in case some need should bring a number of Heralds this far north, but only one of those rooms has a bed; any more than two would have to make up beds on the floor. But let's take first things first. I expect you'd both appreciate a hot bath. It will pleasure both of you to know I have a real bathing-room, just like the ones at the Palace and Collegium. While you're getting washed, I'll find some clean clothing for you to wear until we get your new outfits altered and your leathers cleaned. As soon as you're feeling ready, there'll be supper. How does that strike you?"

"It sounds wonderful—especially the part about the hot bath!" Talia replied fervently, as they dismounted in the station's stable.

"Then take yourselves right in that door over there—I'll tend to your beasts and friends. Go up the staircase, then take a sharp right. The copper's all fired up. I've been doing it every day on the chance that we'd find you. The room you'll be using is sharp left."

They each took a small pack and Talia took her harp, and entered the door he'd indicated. Tedric hadn't exaggerated, though it only held a single bed the bathing-room was identical in every other way to the ones at the Palace.

"Which of us goes first?" Talia asked, thinking longingly of clean hair and a good long soak.

"You. You look ready to die," Kris replied.

"I'm feeling the strain a bit," she admitted.

"Then get your bath. I can wait."

When tight muscles were finally relaxed, and the grime that had accumulated despite her best efforts ruthlessly scrubbed away, she wrapped herself with towels and sought their room. She found that Tedric had preceded them there; on the bed were laid out fabric breeches and shirts of something approximating their sizes.

The approximation was far from exact. It was obvious that if these articles were representative of the kinds of clothing held in storage, there was a great deal of work that was going to have to be done.

She stretched out on the bed for just a moment . . . only to fall completely asleep.

Kris had taken himself downstairs again to talk in private with Tedric. He hadn't missed the older man's initial unease around Talia—nor the fact that he had already known that Talia was Queen's Own and what her Gift was. The identity of an internee was not supposed to be generally known, and the Gift of the Queen's Own wasn't generally even a matter of public knowledge among the Heralds themselves.

He decided that he was a bit too tired for diplomacy, and bluntly asked the older man where he'd gotten his information about Talia.

"Why . . . rumors, mostly," Tedric supplied in astonishment. "Although I didn't credit the half of them. I can't imagine a *Herald* misusing a Gift, and I can't believe the Collegium would allow anyone out who was poorly trained. And I've said so. But I must tell you, there are a lot of eyes and thoughts up here—and, I regret to say, some of them hoping to catch a Herald in failure."

After a covering exchange of pleasantries, Kris climbed the stairs with a worried soul. He found Talia asleep on the bed, and took his towels without waking her.

He lay back in his hot bath to soak, his mind anything but relaxed. If anyone discovered the state Talia was in, not only would her reputation be finished, but the reputation of Heralds as a whole and that of the Collegium would be badly damaged. The faith Heralds themselves had in the Collegium would be shaken if they knew how poorly counseled she'd been.

For that reason, they *dared* not abort the circuit and head back; that would be the signal of failure certain critics of the system had been waiting for. Nor could Kris himself let any senior Herald know the true state of things and how poorly controlled Talia was—for that would lead to a profound disturbance in the ranks of the Heralds them-selves, a disturbance that could only roll all the way back to Selenay and Elspeth, with all the attendant problems it would cause them.

It would be up to Kris, and to Talia herself, to get her back to the functional level she had before this whole mess blew up in their faces.

It was with that sobering reflection he finished his bath, and went to get dressed and wake her.

She woke from her nap in a fairly good mood, giggling a little at the way she looked in the outsized garments Tedric had supplied.

"It's because two-thirds of the Heralds are men, little bird," Kris re-plied. "And all the Resupply Stations get the same goods. So most of the clothing stored here will be made to fit men. I expect when he gets a chance to look, he'll find some things close to your size. If you think you look silly, look at me."

The waist of his breeches was a closer fit than hers, but the legs were huge and baggy and much too long, and the sleeves of his shirt fell down past his fingertips.

"I expect most of what he has is in two categories, large, and 'tent.' At any rate, it's better to have to cut down than try to piece on more fabric."

They descended the staircase to join their host, Kris barefoot and Talia in her sheepskin slippers since their boots were so stiff from re-peated soaking and drying that it was too much of an effort to try to pull them on. In any case, the dwelling was very well heated, and Kris' bare feet caused him no discomfort.

They found the old Herald puttering about in his room that seemed to combine the functions of kitchen and common room. He chuckled to see them, looking like two children clothed in their parents' cast-offs.

"I just took what was nearest to hand," he said apologetically. "I hope you don't mind."

"They're clean, and dry, and warm." Kris smiled. "And right now, that's all we care about. I must say that what I smell would have me pleased to come to table in a grain sack, if that's all there was to wear."

Tedric looked very flattered, and seemed to have no recollection of Kris's earlier interrogation. "When one lives alone, one acquires hob-bies. Mine is cooking. I hope you don't find it inferior to what you're used to."

Talia laughed. "Sir, what we're 'used to' has been porridge, stew made with dried meat and old roots, half-burned bannocks, and more porridge. I have no doubt after the past month that your meal will taste as wonderful as your bathtub felt!"

Venison with herbs and mushrooms was a definite improvement over the meals they'd been making. A mental check assured them that Tedric had seen to Rolan, Tantris, and the chirras in the same generous fashion. Both the Companions were half-asleep, with filled bellies, drowsing in heated stalls.

When their own hunger was truly satisfied, Kris helped Tedric clear away the remains of the meal while Talia ran back upstairs for My Lady.

"You seemed so interested in which of us was the musician that I thought we'd repay you for your hospitality," Kris said, taking the harp and beginning to tune her.

"One doesn't hear a great deal of music out here," Tedric replied, not troubling to keep the eagerness from his eyes. "I think it's the one thing that I really miss by being stationed here. When I rode circuit I was always running into Bards."

The old Herald listened with a face full of quiet happiness as they played and sang. It was quite plain that he had missed the company of other Heralds, and equally evident that he had told the simple truth about missing music out here on the Border. Of course, it was very possible that the traveling Bards had simply not noticed this Station, half-hidden off the road and placed at a bit of a distance from Berrybay. It was just as possible that Tedric's work kept him so busy during the summer (the only time journeyman Bards were likely to come this way) that he could not spare the time to seek the village when Bards came through. Kris made a mental note to send a few words to that effect when they sent their next reports. Old Tedric should not have to do without song again if he could help it.

When they finally confessed themselves played out, Tedric instantly rose and insisted that they seek their bed.

"I don't know what possessed me, keeping you up like this," he said. "After all, I'll have you here for as long as it takes to outfit you. Perhaps I'll hide all the needles for a week or two!"

When they rose the next morning—somewhat reluctantly, as the featherbed they'd shared had been warm and soft and hard to leave— they discovered that he had already put their leathers and boots to soak in his vats of bleaching and softening solution. Talia helped him take some of their ruined garments apart to use as patterns, and they began altering the standard stock. Tedric was every bit as good with a needle as he'd claimed. By day's end they were well on the way to having their wardrobes replenished, and it was not possible to tell that the garments had not been made at the Collegium; by week's end they were totally re-outfitted.

Once their outfitting was complete, they set about discharging their duties to the populace of Berrybay.

The rest and the tranquillity had been profoundly helpful in enabling Talia to firm up what control she had gotten back over her Gift. She had enough shielding now to hold against the worst of outside pressure on her own; that wasn't much, but it was better than nothing. And she felt her control over her projective ability would hold good unless she were frightened or startled—or attacked. If any of those three eventualities took place, she wasn't entirely certain *what* she'd do. But worrying about it wouldn't accomplish anything.

She almost lost her frail bulwarks when they entered the village. Kris had warned her that the rumors had reached this far north, but the knowledge had not prepared her.

When they set up in the village hall, she caught no few of the inhabitants giving her sidelong, cautious glances. But what was worse, was that the very first petitioners wore charms against dark magic into her presence.

She tried to keep up a pleasant, calm front, but the villagers' suspicion and even fear battered at her thin shields and made her want to weep with vexation.

Finally it became too much to stand. "Kris—I've got to take a walk," she whispered. He took one look at the lines of pain around her eyes, and nodded. He might not be an Empath, but it didn't take *that* Gift to read what the people were thinking when they wore evil-eye talismans around one particular Herald.

"Go—come back when you're ready, and not until."

She and Rolan went out past the outskirts of the village. Once away from people, she swore and wept and kicked snow-hummocks until her feet were bruised and her mind exhausted.

Then she returned, and took up the thread of her duties.

By the second day the unease was less. By the third, the evil-eye talismans were gone.

But she wondered what the reaction of the villagers was going to be when they sought out the Weatherwitch on the morning of the fourth.

*   *   *

The depression surrounding the Weatherwitch's unkempt little cottage was so heavy as to be nearly palpable to Talia, and to move through it was like groping through a dark cloud. The Weatherwitch sat in one cob-webbed, dark, cold corner, crooning to herself and rocking a bedraggled rag doll. She paid no heed at all to the three who stood before her. Tedric whispered that the villagers brought her food and cared for her cottage—that she was scarcely enough aware of her surroundings to know when a meal was placed before her. Kris shook his head in pity, feeling certain that there was little, if anything, that Talia could do for her.

Talia was half-attracted, half-repelled by that shadowed mind. If this encounter had taken place a year ago, she would have had no doubt but that she could have accomplished something, but now?

But having come, and having sensed this for herself, she could *not* turn away.

She half knelt, and half crouched, just within touching distance, on the dirty wooden floor beside the woman. She let go of her frail barriers with a physical shudder of apprehension, and let herself be drawn in.

Kris was more than a little afraid for her—knowing nothing, really, of how her Gift worked, he feared it would be only too easy for her to be trapped by the madwoman's mind—and *then* what would he do? Talia remained in that half-kneeling stance for so long that Kris' own knees began to ache in sympathy. At length, her breathing began to resume a more normal pace and her eyes slowly opened. When she raised her head, Kris extended his hand to her and helped her to her feet again.

"Well?" Tedric asked, not very hopefully.

"The gypsy family who died of snow-sickness two months ago—the ones in the Domesday Book report; wasn't there a child left living?" she asked, her eyes still a little glazed.

"A little boy, yes," Kris answered, as Tedric nodded.

"Who has him?"

"Ifor Smithwright; he wasn't particularly pleased, but *somebody* had to take the mite in," Tedric said.

"Can you bring him here? Would this Smithwright have any objection if you found another home for the child?"

"*He* wouldn't object—but *here*? Forgive me, but that sounds a bit mad."

"It *is* a bit mad," Talia said, slumping with weariness so that Kris couldn't make out her expression in the shadows, "but it may take madness to cure the mad. Just . . . bring him here, would you? We'll see if my notion works."

Tedric looked rather doubtful, but rode off and returned less than an hour later with a warmly-wrapped toddler. The child was colicky and crying to himself.

"Now get her out of the house; I don't care how," she told Tedric wearily, taking the baby from him and soothing it into quiet. "But make sure that she leaves that doll behind."

Tedric coaxed the Weatherwitch to follow him out with a bit of sweet, after persuading her to leave her "infant" behind in the cradle by the smokey fire. Talia slipped in when her back was turned. Seconds after that, a baby's wail penetrated the walls of the cottage, and the madwoman started as if she'd been struck.

It was the most incredible transformation Kris had ever seen. The half-crazed, wild animal look left her eyes, and sense and intelligence flooded back in. In a few seconds, she made the transition from "thing" to human.

"J-Jethry?" she faltered.

The baby cried again, louder this time.

"Jethry!" she cried in answer, and ran through the door.

In the cradle was the child Tedric had brought, perhaps something under a year old, crying lustily. She scooped the child up and held it to her breast, holding it as if it were her own soul given back to her, laughing and weeping at the same time.

No sooner did her hands touch the child, when the last, and perhaps strangest thing of all, happened. It stopped crying immediately, and began cooing back at the woman.

Talia was not even watching; just sagging against the lintel, rubbing her temples. The other two could only watch the transformation in bemusement.

At last the woman took her attention from the baby she held and focused on Talia. She moved toward her hesitantly, and halted when she was a few steps away.

"Herald," she said with absolute certainty, "*you* did this—you brought me my baby back. He was dead, but you found him again for me!"

Talia looked up at that, eyes like darker shadows on her face, and shook her head in denial. "Not I, my lady. If anyone brought him back, it was you. And it was you who showed me where to find him."

The woman reached out to touch Talia's cheek. Kris made as if to interfere, but Talia motioned him away, signaling him that she was in no danger.

"You *will* reclaim what was yours," the Weatherwitch said tonelessly, her eyes focused on something none of them could see, "and no one will ever shake it from you again. You will find your heart's desire, but not until you have seen the Havens. The Havens will call you, but duty and love will bar you from them. Love will challenge death to reclaim you. Your greatest joy will be preceded by your greatest sorrow, and your fulfillment will not be unshadowed by grief."

"'There is no joy that has not tasted first of grief,'" Talia quoted softly, as if to herself, so softly that Kris could barely hear the words. The woman's eyes refocused.

"Did I say something? Did I see something?" she asked, confusion evident in her eyes. "Was it the answer you were looking for?"

"It was answer enough," Talia replied with a smile. "But haven't you more important things to think of?"

"My Jethry, my little love!" she exclaimed, holding the child closely, her eyes bright with tears. "There's so much I have to do—to make it up to you. Oh, Herald, how can I ever thank you enough?"

"By loving and caring for Jethry as much as you do now; and not worrying what others may say about it," Talia told her, motioning to the other two to leave, and following them quickly.

"Bright Havens!" Tedric exclaimed, a little uneasily, when they were out of earshot of the cottage. "That was like old tales of witchcraft and curse-lifting! What kind of strange magic did you work back there?"

"To tell you the truth, I'm not very sure myself," Talia said, rubbing tired eyes with the back of her hand. "When I touched her this morning, I seemed to see a kind of—cord? tie?—something like that, anyway. It was binding her to something, and I seemed to see that page in the report about the gypsies. I know outlanders aren't terribly welcome here, so I took a chance that the survivor wouldn't find a new home very easily. You confirmed what I guessed, Tedric. And it just seemed to me that what she needed was a second chance to make everything right. Am I making sense?"

"More sense than I hoped for. It's hardly possible that he could be— hers? Is it?" Kris said hesitantly.

"Kris, I'm no priest! How on earth can I answer that? All I can tell you is what I saw and felt. The little one is about the same age as hers would have been and they certainly seem to recognize each other, if only as two lost ones needing love. I won't hazard a guess after that."

"This is a terribly callous thing to ask, I know," Tedric said, looking a good bit less anxious now that the "magic" was explained away as rational common sense. "But—she won't lose her powers now that her mind is back, will she?"

"Set your fears at rest; I think you and the people of Berrybay can count on their Weatherwitch yet," Talia replied. "Speaking from personal experience, I can tell you that such Gifts rarely lie back down to rest once you've roused them. Look at what she said to me!"

"'Love will challenge death to reclaim you,'" Kris quoted. "Strange—and rather ambiguous, it seems to me."

"Prophecy has a habit of being ambiguous," Tedric said wryly. "It's fortunate that she's able to be more exact when it comes to giving us weather-warnings. Come now; you and Rolan are tired and hungry, Talia, both of you. You deserve a good meal, and a good night's rest before you take the road again."

"And prophecy to the contrary, my heart's desire at the moment is one of your venison pies followed by a convivial quiet evening and a good sleep in your featherbed, and I hardly think I need to seek out the Havens to find *that*!" Talia laughed tiredly, linking arms with Tedric and Kris, while Rolan followed behind.

Well, she had weathered *this* one. Now all she had to do was continue to survive.

CHAPTER 11

"WELL, LITTLE BIRD," Kris said lazily. "It's almost Midsummer. You're halfway done. Evaluation, please."

Talia picked idly at the grass beside her. "Is this serious, or facetious?"

"Quite serious."

The sun approached zenith, and a warm spot created when the white-gold rays found a gap in the leaves of the tree overhead was planted just on Talia's right shoulder blade. Insects droned in the long grass; occasionally a bird called, sleepily. They were at the Station at the bottom of their Sector where they had first entered, back last autumn. Today or the next day a courier-Herald would make a rendezvous with them, bringing them the latest laws and news; until then, their time was their own. They had been spending it in unaccustomed leisure.

She thought, long and hard, while Kris chewed on a grass stem, lying on his back in the shade, eyes narrowed to slits.

"It's been horrid," she said finally, lying back and pillowing her head on her arm. "I wish these past nine months had never happened. It's been awful, especially when we first get into a town, and they've heard about me, but . . ."

"Hmm?" he prompted when the silence had gone on too long.

"But . . . what if this . . . my Gift going rogue . . . had happened at Court? It would have been worse."

"You would have been able to get help there," he pointed out, "better than you've gotten from me."

"Only after I'd wrecked something. Gods, I hate to think—letting loose that storm in a packed Court . . ." she shuddered. "At least I've got projection under control *consciously* now, rather than instinctively. Even if my shields aren't completely back."

"Still having shield problems?"

"You know so, you've seen me in crowds. There are times when I hate you for keeping me out here, but then I realize that I *can't* go back until I have my shields back. And we can't let anyone know about this mess until it's fixed; not even Heralds."

"So you figured that out for yourself."

"It didn't take much; if people knew that the rumors were at least partially true, they'd believe the rest of it. I've watched you playing protector for me every time we meet another Herald. And there's something else. I can't go back until I figure something out."

"What?"

"Not just the 'how' of my Gift, but the 'why' and the 'when.' It's obsessing me, because those rumors about manipulation come so close to the truth. I *have* used my Gift to evaluate Councilors, and I *have* acted on that information. When does it start becoming manipulation?"

"I don't know . . ."

"Now I'm more than half afraid to use the Gift."

"Oh, hell!" He flopped over onto his side, hair blowing into his eyes. "Now *that* bothers me. Hellfire, none of this would have happened to you if I'd just kept my mouth shut."

"And it might well have happened at a worse time—"

"And might *not* have." Those blue eyes bored into hers. "What's gone wrong is as much my fault as yours."

She had no answer for him.

"Well, the situation went wrong, but I *think* we're turning it around," he said at last.

"I hope so. I think so."

"Well, you're handling everything else fine."

There was an uneasiness under his words; she was sensitive enough now to tell that it had something to do with her, personally, not her as a Herald.

Oh, Gods. She did her best to hide her dismay. She had done her level best to keep their relationship on a friend/lover basis, and *not* let her Gift manipulate him into infatuation, or worse. Most of the time she thought she'd succeeded—but then came the times like these, the times when he looked at her with a shadowed expression. She knew, now, that she didn't want anything more from him, for as her need of him grew less, her feelings had mellowed into something very like what she shared with Skif.

But what of him?

"I wonder what Dirk's up to," he said, out of the blue. "He's Sector-riding this term, too."

"If he has any sense, being glad he's not having to eat your cooking." She threw a handful of grass at him; he grinned back. "Tell me something, why do you keep calling me 'little bird'?"

"Good question; it's Dirk's name for you. You remind him of a woodlark."

"What's a woodlark?" she asked curiously. "I've never seen one."

"You normally don't see them; you only hear them. Woodlarks are very shy, and you have to know exactly what you're looking for when you're trying to spot one. They're very small, brown, and blend almost perfectly with the bushes. For all that they're not very striking, they're remarkably pretty in their own quiet way. But he wasn't thinking about that when he named you; woodlarks have the most beautiful voices in the forest."

"Oh," she said, surprised by the compliment, and not knowing quite how to respond.

"I can even tell you when he started using it. It was just after you'd fainted, and he'd picked you up to carry you to your room. 'Bright Havens,' said he, 'she weighs no more than a little bird.' Then the night of the celebration, when we all sang together, I caught him staring at you when you were watching the dancers, and muttering under his breath—'A woodlark. She's a shy little woodlark!' Then he saw me watching him, and glared for a minute, and said, 'Well, she is!' Not wanting to get my eyes blackened, I agreed. I would have agreed anyway; I always do when he's right."

"You two," she said, "are crazy."

"No milady, we're Heralds. It's close, but not quite to the point of actual craziness."

"That makes me crazy, too."

"You said it," he pointed out. "I didn't."

Before she could think of a suitable reply, they heard a hail from the path that led to their Station and scrambled to their feet. It was their courier—and their courier was Skif.

"Welladay!" he said, dismounting as they approached him. "You two certainly look hale and healthy! Very much so, for a pair who were supposed to have come near perishing in that Midwinter blizzard. Dirk was damned worried when I talked to him."

"If you're going to be seeing him sometime soon, or can find a Bard to pass the message, you can tell him that we're both fine, and the worst we suffered was the loss of Talia's harpcase," Kris said with a laugh.

"If? Bright Havens, I haven't got any *choice*! I've been flat ordered to find him when I'm done with briefing you, on pain of unspecified torture. You'd have thought from the way he was acting that neither of you had the mother-wit to save yourselves from a wetting, much less a blizzard."

Kris gave Talia another odd, sidelong glance.

"You'd best bring your Companion and whatever you've brought for us on up to the Waystation," she said. "It's going to take you a while to pass everything to us, and to make sure we've got it right."

"A while, O modest Talia? With you, I've got no fear that it'll take long." Skif grinned. "I know quite well that you can memorize faster than I can, and Kris was my Farseeing teacher, so I know he's just as quick. I'll turn Cymry loose and let her kick her heels up a little; I can lead the pack mule afoot."

"We'll take her tack for you," Kris offered. "No use in you carrying it when we're unburdened."

Skif accepted the offer gladly, and they strolled up the path toward the Station together; Kris with the saddle and blanket balanced over one shoulder, Talia with the rest of the tack, Skif with the saddlebags.

"I've brought you two quite a load," he told them as they approached the station, "Both material and news. Hope you're ready."

"More than ready," Talia told him. "I'm getting pretty tired of telling the same old tales."

"Don't I just know! Well, I've got plenty of news, personal and public, and more than you may guess. Do you want your news first, or your packs?"

"Both," Kris said with the charming smile of a child. "You can tell us the personal news while we gloat over our goodies."

"Why not?" Skif chuckled. "I'll start with the Collegium and work my way outward."

The first bit of news was that Gaytha and Mero had surprised nearly everyone by suddenly deciding to wed. They had had themselves handfasted just before Skif had left, and were to be wedded in the fall. Kris' jaw sagged over that piece of news, but Talia, recalling things she'd seen over holidays while still a student, nodded without much surprise.

Keren had broken her hip during the past winter. She'd slipped and taken a bad fall trying to rescue a Companion foal from beneath a downed tree (the foal was frightened silly, but otherwise emerged from the ordeal unscathed. The same—obviously—could not be said for poor Keren). Sherrill had taken on Keren's duties as riding instructor as well as her own scheduled classes. When Keren's bones were healed, she decided that it was getting to be time to think about training a successor anyway, so they were currently sharing the classes.

Alberich had at last retired from teaching all but the most advanced students; to no one's surprise, he had appointed Jeri to take his place.

Companions had Chosen twenty youngsters this spring, the largest number yet. For the first time in years the Collegium was completely full. No one knew whether there should be rejoicing or apprehension over this sudden influx of Chosen; the last time that the Collegium had been full had been in Selenay's father's time; there had been the Tedrel Wars with Karse on the Eastern Border shortly thereafter and every one of the students had been needed to replace those Heralds that had sought the Havens when it was over.

Elspeth was doing unexpectedly well, and Talia rejoiced to hear it. Elcarth had taken her heavy schedule and lightened it by a considerable amount, and she had responded by working like a fiend incarnate on those classes that were left. She seemed determined to prove that she was not ungrateful for the respite, and that she did not intend to shirk her remaining responsibilities.

There was little news of the Court, but none of that was good. The rumor-mills had been churning away; mostly working on the grist of Elspeth and the absent Talia. About half of it was elaboration on the rumors they already knew, the rest concerned Elspeth's supposed unfitness for the Crown—that she was too pliant, too much of a hoyden, not bright enough—and too dependent on the Heralds in general and Talia in particular to make all her decisions for her.

Kris noted without comment the brief shadow of pain that veiled her face.

"But I've told anybody who's bothered to bring up the subject that whoever started these tales had holes in his skull. Elspeth's nothing but a normal tomboy—like Jeri, and they were perfectly willing to consider Jer as Heir! And I told 'em nobody who knows you would even consider the idea that you might be misusing your Gift! So that's that.

All right, it's your turn," Skif ordered. "You two have to tell me the whole tale of your blizzard. I've been strictly charged by half the Circle to bring back every detail. If you leave one thing out, I'm not entirely certain of my safety when I get back!"

Kris told most of it, from the plague at Waymeet to the arrival of Tedric—leaving out the disintegration of Talia's control.

"Sounds grim," Skif said when they'd finished. "I'm surprised you didn't tear each other's throats out—from boredom if nothing else. Of course, you were too busy digging out to have time to be bored."

Kris inhaled his wine, and nearly choked to death trying to keep from laughing.

Talia covered her blushes by pounding his back—then took over the conversation with a stern glance in his direction that almost sent him into another fit.

"It was a good thing we had the harp with us," she said, firmly restraining the urge to set both her hands around his throat and strangle him. "Music did a lot to keep us going. And we discovered something really strange, Skif. Did you know that those stories the Northerners kept telling us about how chirras sing are true?"

"You've been on circuit too long," he replied with a disbelieving grin.

"She's telling the truth, Skif," Kris asserted. "Chirras do sing—well, hum is more like it. They do it intentionally, though, and I've heard worse harmonics coming from human throats."

"Can you prove this? Otherwise I'm going to have a hard time convincing anyone else, much less myself."

"Are you planning on spending the night with us?"

"So long as I'm not in the way."

"You can stay if you clean up dinner," Talia teased. "We'll cook for you, but you'd better do your share of the work."

"Anything is better than having to eat my own cooking!" Skif replied with a hearty sigh. "When I was interning, Dirk absolutely refused to let me cook anything after the first two meals I ruined. I don't blame him. I'm the only person I know that can boil an egg for an hour, and have it turn out half scorched and half raw."

"Then you'll get your demonstration after dinner."

When they had finished their evening meal, Talia called the chirras up from the lake to the Waystation and gave the demonstration Skif had demanded. As the first notes rose from the packbeasts' long throats, Skif's eyes widened in disbelief. A quick look around, however, soon proved to him that there was no trickery involved. After the first two songs he relaxed and admitted that he found the weird harmonics quite pleasant, if at first startling.

When they tired of singing, they began trading road-tales. Skif had by far the largest stock of funny stories, since his assignment as courier put him in contact with a wide variety of situations (in one case, he'd had to rescue his contactee at the meeting point from an amorous and overly enthusiastic cow). But in the midst of what Skif had thought was one of his more amusing anecdotes, Talia suddenly excused herself and walked out into the night with some haste.

"Did I say something wrong?" Skif said, bewildered, since she had been giving every evidence of enjoying the story until then. "What's the matter with her?"

"I have no more idea than you—" Kris started to say. Then he thought of something.

"Just wait a moment." He closed his eyes and Mindcalled to Tantris. The answer he got made him half-smile, although he spared a flash of pity for Talia.

"She'll be back in a little while," he told the puzzled Skif. "When she's less—shall we say—uncomfortable."

Skif was annoyed. "Just what is that supposed to mean?"

"Skif, your Cymry's a mare."

"That was fairly obvious."

"Rolan's a stallion, a stallion that hasn't been near a Companion mare for several months. Talia's Gift, in case you've forgotten, is Empathy; and unlike most of us, she tells me that Rolan is *always* with her— 'in the back of her head,' she calls it."

"What?" Skif was bewildered; then realization dawned. "Oh-ho. I forgot a little experiment we did. You can't shield out your Companion with a bond that tight, can you?"

"That's it—not on that level, you can't. And with her Gift thrown in, it's even more . . . overpowering. As I recall, you can barely Mindspeak, right? So you're protected from Cymry's sporting. Needless to say, the same is not true for Talia."

Skif's chuckle was just a touch heartless. "Too bad your Tantris isn't a mare."

"I've had that thought a time or two myself," Kris admitted, joining the chuckle.

Skif sobered abruptly. "Look—Kris, I know it's none of my business, but are you and Talia—you know—?"

"Damned right it's none of your business," Kris said calmly. He'd been expecting the question, assuming that Skif was only waiting to get him alone. "So why are you asking?"

"Kris, it's part of my job to notice things. And I've noticed that while you aren't cuddled up like courting doves, you're both a lot easier with each other than I've ever seen either of you around anyone else." Skif paused, then remained silent.

"You were obviously planning on saying more; go on."

"I owe Dirk. I owe him my life; by all rights he should have left us when Cymry and I fell into that ravine while I was interning. He had no way of knowing we were still alive, and the trail was washing out under him with every second he stayed. But he didn't leave; he searched all through that downpour until he found us, and if he hadn't, we wouldn't be here now. He's been acting damned peculiar whenever anybody mentions Talia. He was starting to act that way when you two left, and it's gotten worse since then. Dear old 'I'm-indifferent-to-women' Dirk came close to tearing my heart out and feeding it to me when I couldn't give him any more information about you two than rumor—and I would bet my hope of the Havens that it wasn't over *your* welfare. So if you two are more than friends, I want to know. Maybe I can break it to him gently."

"Oh, Gods," Kris said weakly. "Oh *Gods*. I don't know, Skif—I mean, I know how I feel, which is that I'm quite fond of her, and that's all; but I don't know how she feels. I'm afraid to find out."

"I have the suspicion that there's a lot more going on here than you've told me," Skif replied. "You want to make a full confession?"

"Gods—I'd better go back a few years—look, the reason Dirk pretends to be indifferent to women is because he was so badly hurt by one that he came within a hair of killing himself. It was that bitch, Lady Naril; it was when we were first assigned to Court. She wanted me, I wasn't having any. So she used Dirk to get at me."

"Don't tell me—she played the sweet innocent on him. She tried working that one on me, but I'd had warning."

"I wish Dirk had. By the time I knew what was happening, it was too late. He was flopping like a stranded fish. She used him to set up a meeting between us; and at that point she handed me an ultimatum; either I became her lap-dog, or she would make Dirk's life hell for him. Unfortunately she hadn't counted on the fact that Dirk was jealous as well as devoted. He'd stayed within earshot, and he heard the whole thing."

"Good Gods!" Skif couldn't manage more than that.

"Verily." Kris closed his eyes, trying to shut out the memory of how

Dirk had looked when he confronted them. It had been ghastly. Even his eyes had been dead. But what had followed had been worse. Kris had made a hasty exit, and when he'd gone, Naril had taken Dirk to pieces. If only he'd known, he'd *never* have left them alone—

"But—"

"He was shattered; absolutely shattered. I think it was only Ahrodie that kept him from throwing himself in the river that night. Now you tell me he's acting like—"

"Like a man with a lifebond, if you want to know the truth. He's close to being obsessed."

"Talia *was* showing signs of the same thing, but now—I just don't *know*, Skif. We—started sleeping together during that blizzard. There were a lot of other complications that I can't go into, and now I don't know *how* she feels. But I'm mortally afraid she's gotten fixated on me."

And he was Dirk's best friend. Gods, Gods, it was happening all over again—

"Well, what are you going to do about it?" Skif asked.

"I'm going to break it off, that's what, before it gets too serious to be broken off. If it *is* a lifebond, once the infatuation is nipped in the bud, she'll swing back to Dirk like a compass needle. But for Lord's sake, don't let Dirk know about any of this." Kris rubbed his forehead, feeling almost sick with remorse.

"No fear of that—" Skif broke off what he was saying to nod significantly in the direction of the door behind Kris.

Talia entered and resumed her abandoned seat, looking much cooler and more composed.

"Better?" Kris asked in a sympathetic undertone.

"Much," she sighed, then faced Skif. "As for you, you troublemaker, I hope you're prepared to cosset a pregnant Companion in another couple of months!"

"Now Talia," he chortled heartlessly, "Cymry's been at her games with every stallion I've rendezvoused with, and nothing like that has happened yet."

"Every other stallion wasn't Rolan," she said with a wry twist to her lips. "Serves you right, too, for not warning me, you smug sadist. Or don't you remember your history, and the extraordinary fertility of Grove stallions—*particularly* the Companion of the Queen's Own?"

"Kernos' Spear! I never once thought of that!"

Both Kris and Talia laughed at the expression on Skif's face.

"I'd be willing to bet a full wineskin that Cymry didn't think of that either," Kris added.

"You just won," Skif said, reaching behind him into his pile of belongings, and throwing a leather bottle at the other Herald. "Oh, well—no harm without a trace of good. This will keep me off the road, but it will also keep me from having to do my own cooking. I'd better start thinking of ways to make myself useful around the Court and Collegium. Hope Teren likes being courier—he's the only one free at the moment, now that the new babies are done with Orientation."

He settled into his bedroll with a much bemused expression.

The next day was involved in memorizing all Skif had to impart to them. When both of them were letter-perfect, in the early afternoon, Skif packed up the few bits he had of his own personal gear and supplies, and headed back the way he'd come.

"How much did you tell him?" Talia asked, watching him depart.

"Only that we've had some complications I can't go into; I had to tell him, he noticed you weren't looking too well. That's all." He gave her yet another of those odd, sidelong glances.

"Lord—poor Elspeth, facing those damned rumor-mongers all by herself! Gods—I *need* to be there—and I *can't* be there—"

"That's right. You can't. Going back now won't do you any good, and might do her harm."

"I know, but it doesn't stop me from wanting to—"

"Look at it this way—with all the rumors that are bound to start about *me* and you, maybe they'll forget about the others."

"Oh, Gods"—she blushed—"have I *no* privacy?"

"Not as a Herald, you don't."

They walked back to the Station; Kris was brooding about something, Talia could see it in the closed expression he wore, and sense it in the unhappy unease that lurked below the surface of his thoughts.

It was an unease she shared. She couldn't tell exactly what was bothering him—except that it had to do with her *and* with Dirk. She wondered if this was a sign that her worst fear was true, that he *had* become far more involved with her than he'd intended.

She didn't want to hurt his feelings—but damn it all, it wasn't *him* she wanted! If only he'd *talk* to her. . . .

They read their letter-packets in silence; Talia's was mostly brief notes, and not very many of them. But the last letter had Talia very puzzled; it was enormous, from the thickness of the packet, and yet she couldn't recognize the handwriting on the outside. She frowned at it, recalling for a moment the evil days when virulent and anonymous letters were a daily occurrence. Then she steeled herself and broke open the seal, telling herself that there was no reason why she shouldn't pitch it into the fire if it turned out to be of that ilk.

To her shock and delight, it was from Dirk.

The actual letter was not very long, and the phrasing was stilted and formal, yet just to know that he'd written it gave her a delightfully shivery feeling. The content was simple enough; he hoped that her close association with his partner would lead to a closer friendship among the three of them, since they all shared the common interest of music. It was in light of this common interest that he had (he said) made bold to write her. He had been assigned to the Sector that contained most of the Kingdom's papermills and printing houses and was the headquarters of the Printer's and Engraver's Guild. This meant that music and books that were difficult to obtain elsewhere were relatively common there. He had bought himself a great deal of new music, and had thought that Talia and Kris should have copies also.

It was what he hadn't said that both excited and worried Talia. The letter was so bland that it could have reflected either polite indifference to her, or been an attempt to conceal the same sort of obsession that she was feeling.

Still, it was definitely odd for him to have sent the music manuscripts to Talia instead of to Kris.

Kris coughed uneasily, and she looked up to meet his eyes.

"What's the matter?" she asked.

"Dirk's letter," he replied. "I'm usually lucky to get a page, maybe two—but this approaches perilously the size of an epic!"

"That's odd."

"That's an understatement. He rattles on about nothing like a granny-gossip at a Fair, and it's what he *doesn't* write about that's the most interesting. He dances verbally about doing his very best to avoid the subject of my internee. That's not easy to do in a letter this size! He doesn't mention you until the very end, and then only to say that he's sent you some music that we all might like to try together some time. It's as if he's afraid to write your name for fear he'll give something away."

Talia swallowed a lump that had suddenly appeared in her throat.

"Here's the music he sent," she replied, handing him the packet.

"Bright Havens, this must have cost him a fortune!" Kris began sorting it into two piles, one for each of them—when something slipped out from amid the music manuscripts.

"Hm? What's this?" He picked it up; it seemed to be a slim book bound in brown leather. He leafed through it.

"This—without any doubt—is intended for you," he said soberly, handing it to her.

It was a book of ballads, among them, the long version of "Sun and Shadow."

"How do you know he didn't buy it for himself?" she asked doubt-fully. "Or you?"

"Because I happen to know he has two copies of that same book, both bound in blue, which happens to be *his* favorite color. One he keeps at his room, the other travels with him. And he knows I have the book, I'm the one that showed it to him. No, it's no accident that this was among the manuscripts—and it's undoubtedly the reason why he sent them to you instead of me."

"But—"

"Talia, I have to talk to you. Seriously."

Gods—here it came.

"I—" he began, looking almost tortured. "Look, I like you a lot. I think you're one of the sweetest ladies to wear Whites. And I probably should never have let you get involved with me."

"What?" she said, unable for a moment to comprehend what he was trying to say.

"Dirk is worth twenty of me," he continued doggedly, "and if you stop to think about it, you'll realize I'm right about that. You're seeing more in our relationship than exists—than *can* exist. I just can't give you anything more than friendship, Talia. And I can't let you ruin your life and Dirk's by letting you go on thinking—"

"Wait just a damned minute here," she interrupted him. "You think that *I'm* infatuated with *you*?"

He looked surprised by her reaction. "Of course," he replied—in an insultingly matter-of-fact tone.

All the tension that had been building up inside her came to a head. She'd been putting up with his occasional air of superiority, the slight condescension he used whenever later evidence proved that some deci-sion of his that she'd opposed turned out to be right. And there was an underlying resentment on her part at his unvoiced attitude that getting her Gift under control was now largely a matter of "will" and not the slow rebuilding of something that had been shattered past recognition.

It was that "of course" that had been the spark to set the pyre alight. She turned on him angrily, fists clenching unconsciously. "Of course?

Just because every other female falls languishing at your feet? You think I've no mind of my own?"

"Well," he replied, taken aback, and obviously intending to try to say something to placate her.

"You—you—" she was at a total loss for words. All this time, she'd been wasting, worrying about *him*, about hurting *his* feelings. And he had been blithely assuming that just because she'd been sleeping with him, she was *obviously* going to be fixated on him. Even now, he was still bewildered, perfect features blank with perfect astonishment.

She pulled back her right arm, and landed a perfect punch right on the end of that perfect chin.

Kris found himself staring up at her from the ground in front of the Station door, with a jaw that felt dislocated.

"You conceited *peacock*! *Humor* me, will you? At least—" she snarled "—you can't accuse me of misusing my Gift *this* time!"

He lifted one hand and felt along his jawline, a little dazed. "No. That was a physical attack, all right . . ."

But by the time he answered, she had turned on her heel and stalked off toward the tiny lake, into the darkness. By the time he gathered his wits and came after her, there was no sign of her beyond a little pile of clothing next to the blankets they'd spread there earlier in the day.

Now he was beginning to become angry—after all, he hadn't meant to insult her!—and a little worried, as well. He began stripping off his own clothing to go in after her. As he waded in through the shallows, he saw something moving across the lake, coming toward him. Before he had any idea of what she intended, she pulled both his legs out from beneath him and yanked him under the water. Coughing and spluttering, he broke the surface again to see her bobbing just out of reach.

She was laughing at him.

"Bitch!" he yelled, and dove furiously after her. But when he reached the place where she had been, she was gone, and the surface of the pond was undisturbed. He peered around in the dim light, trying to locate her, when hands grasping his ankles gave him just enough warning to hold his breath this time. Once again he was pulled under, and once again she escaped without his laying a finger on her.

This time when he surfaced and gasped for air, he did not immediately set out after her. When he didn't move, she called mockingly, "That's not going to save you, you know," and dove under, vanishing.

He waited for her to surface, ready to catch her before she'd fully located him. When she didn't, he waited for currents that would tell him she was somewhere nearby, beneath the water.

Nothing happened, and he began to be a little concerned. She'd been under an awfully long time. He struck out for the spot where he'd last seen her.

He had no sooner begun to move when she erupted from the water immediately behind him. Hands on his shoulders drove him under. He kicked free and came thrashing back up, to find her a bare fingerlength out of reach.

"Infatuated fool, am I? *Stupid*, am I? Then why can't you catch me?"

He kicked off after her, windmilling the surface energetically. She didn't seem to be expending half the effort he was, yet she sped through the water with ease, remaining out of reach with a laziness that galled. From time to time she'd vanish altogether, and this was the signal that he'd better hold his breath, because shortly after her disappearance he would find himself pushed or pulled under the surface again.

And no matter how hard he tried, he couldn't catch her even then.

Finally he took refuge in the shallows, and waited for her to follow. Now *he* was angry; humiliated, and angry, and ready to take her apart.

She rose, dripping, out of the water just out of reach. He glared at her—

And suddenly realized he'd put himself in a worse position than before. He was stark naked—he could probably pound her into the ground like a tent peg if he could get his hands on her—but if she could get even the tiniest amount of leverage to get a knee in—

Oh, she could *hurt* him.

Anger, frustration, and acute embarrassment chased each other around inside of him until he was nearly vibrating with conflicting impulses—while she glared back, just as angry as he was. Until something of his inner confusion communicated itself to her—and she collapsed to her knees, laughing helplessly.

His anger ran away like water.

He was completely exhausted; when anger stopped giving him an energy boost, he felt it. He turned his back on her, climbed out of the water, and dragged himself onto the waiting blanket without bothering to reach for a towel or his clothing.

As he lay face down, panting, he heard footsteps behind him.

"No more—please!" he groaned. "You've won; I've lost. I'm an idiot. And a boor. Truce!"

"You give up too easily." Talia laughed deep in her throat, like a cat purring. "And you deserved what you got. Keren's right; every so often you start to think you can have everything your own way, and you ought to have a lesson."

She sat down beside him, and he moved his head enough to see that she'd donned her short undershift and was toweling her hair vigorously.

"Where did you ever learn to swim like that?"

"Sherrill," she replied. "Oh, I've been able to swim since I was very little, but my efforts were a lot like yours; loads of thrashing to little purpose. After the time I was dumped in the river, Alberich detailed Sherrill to teach me the efficient way to swim, and how to keep from drowning under most conditions. Next winter she gave me a 'final exam' by pushing me off the bridge fully clothed. Obviously, I passed— though a pair of my boots is still probably residing at the bottom of the river. Good thing I'd almost outgrown them."

"Remind me never to anger either of you while swimming."

"Count Keren in on that, too. She's just as good. Poor, abused Kris." He could almost see her eyes sparkling with mischief. "Are you half-drowned?"

"Three-quarters. And completely worn out."

"Forgive me, but I doubt that." She ran a delicate finger along his spine.

He gritted his teeth and remained unmoving, trying his best to ignore the shivery-pleasant sensations she was causing. When he didn't respond, except for goose bumps, she simply laughed again, and began stroking him delicately from neck to knees.

He was determined not to yield, and held himself as quiet as possible.

"Stubborn, hmm?" she chuckled.

Before he had any notion of what she intended, she began fondling him in such a way that his original intentions went flying off in every direction.

"Witch!" he said fiercely, and flipped over so quickly that he managed to get her pinned beneath him.

"I thought you were supposed to be worn out."

"I'll show you how worn out I am," he muttered, and began tormenting her in return, playing teasingly with every part of her that he could reach. She simply chuckled throatily and returned kind for kind. He held out as long as he physically could—but the conclusion was foregone. It left them both dripping with sweat, and drained as well as sated.

"Lord of Lights," he said when he was able to speak. "If that's an example of what Rolan does to you, I'm glad Tantris isn't a mare! By the time we finished this circuit, I'd be worn to a shadow."

Instead of replying, she sighed, rose, and took the few steps to the water's edge, plunging gracefully back into the pond.

When she returned, clean and dripping, she seemed to have regained a more tranquil mood. Kris took a brief dip himself, and by the time he got back she was dry again, wearing her sleeveless tunic against the cooling breeze. He dried himself off and handed her the bottle Skif had left with them. She took a long pull at it and gave it back.

"So it's Midsummer's Eve, hmm? We never celebrated Midsummer on the Holdings," she said. "And I was always at the Collegium during holidays after I was Chosen."

"Not celebrate Midsummer? Why not?" he asked in surprise.

"Because, according to the Elders, it has no religious significance and is only a frivolous and lewd excuse for licentiousness. That's a quote, by the way. What do people usually do, Midsummer's Eve?"

"Your Elders have a little right on their side." He couldn't help smiling. "On Midsummer's Eve at sunset, there are picnics in the woods. People always *begin* in large groups, but by this time of night they've usually paired off. The excuse to sleep out tonight is that you need to sleep in the forest in order to find the freshest flowers in the morning. Believe it or not, when morning arrives, people *do* manage to pick flowers."

She took a long pull on the bottle. "For their lady-loves?" She probably hadn't meant it to sound cynical, but it did.

Kris was too tired to take offense. "No, for every female, no matter who. There's no female of any age that lacks a garland or bouquet; those that have no relatives get them from anyone that can claim the remotest acquaintance with them. No one is left out, old or young. Women who have been or are about to be mothers get baskets of fruit as well. That day there are more picnics in the woods—family picnics, this time, with a bit more decorum—and music and tales in the evening. Bards love it; they're sure to leave with their pockets full of coin, their hair full of flowers, and a young lady or gentleman on each arm. It's rather like a Birthing-Day celebration, but on a bigger scale."

"Holderfolk don't celebrate Birthing-Days either—except to deliver a lecture on responsibility," she said tonelessly.

"When *is* your Birthing-Day?" he asked curiously.

"Midsummer's Eve. Tonight. Which is no doubt why I'm such a demon-child, having had the bad taste to be born on such a licentious night."

"So *that's* why you've been so off-color!" Kris snatched at the excuse to turn her mood around. "You should have told me!"

"I'm being more than a bit of a bitch, aren't I? I'm sorry. First I get mad and knock you down, then I make a fool out of you, knowing damn well that I could probably swim rings around you, then I half-drown you, and I conclude by doing my best to ruin the rest of the evening by being sour. I'm being rotten, and I apologize."

"You've put up with my moods often enough. You're entitled to have off times yourself."

"Well, I think I've caught up for the next hundred years or so."

"I'm sorry I didn't talk to you about—you and me—before," he said, as the bottle came and went.

"I wish you had. You've been leaving me in knots because *I* was afraid I'd manipulated you into being fixated on *me*. I couldn't imagine why you'd be making love to me unless it was because my Gift had warped you. I'm not exactly the gods' gift to men. And I've been mostly a problem to you on this trip."

"Oh, Gods—" He was at a complete loss for words for a long time. Finally he handed her the bottle, and caught her hand when she moved to take it. "Talia, you are a completely lovable and lovely person; I care for you because you deserve it, not because your Gift manipulated me. Dirk may well be lifebonded to you—and if that's true, I couldn't be happier. It would satisfy one of *my* dearest wishes, that both of you should find partners who deserve you. And if those partners should be each other—that would make me one of the happiest people in this Kingdom."

"I—" she said hesitantly, "I don't know quite what to say."

"Just don't hit me again. That's one response to being at a loss for words I'd rather you didn't repeat. Now, what else is bothering you?"

"I'm tired. I'm tired of having to struggle for what seems to come easily to everyone else. I'm tired of having responsibility for the whole damned Kingdom on my back. I'm tired of being alone, and fighting my battles alone."

"Well—"

"Look, I know it has to be this way, but I don't have to smile and pretend I *like* it! And last of all, I'm feeling rotten because nobody has ever given me a Midsummer garland or a Birthing-Day present."

"Makes sense."

The bottle was more than half empty; they'd shared it equally, and Kris was beginning to see things through a very delightful haze.

"How does it make sense?" she demanded irritably.

"Because if you could have what you wanted, you wouldn't be upset, but you can't so you are." It seemed like a brilliant deduction to Kris, and he examined the statement with delight.

Talia shook her head as she tried to reason it out. "That just doesn't come out right, somehow," she complained.

"It will after another drink." He passed her the bottle.

When the last drop of liquor was gone, so was her ill temper.

"I—am fairy—very—glad that we've got something to shleep—sleep on right here," Kris said carefully. "Ish—it's much nicer, you can see the stars, and I can't walk anymore anyway."

"Stars are nice," she agreed. "Not moving's nicer."

"See the Wain?"

"Who?"

"The Wain—those stars jusht over the big pine there. Five for the bed 'n the axle, two for th' wheels, three for th' tongue."

"Wait a minute." She peered at the stars, trying to get them to form up properly, and was delighted when she finally did. "What's the rest of 'em?"

"Right next t' the Wain's the Hunter. There's the two little stars for his belt, two more for's shoulders, four for's legs—" He realized by her steady breathing that she had fallen asleep.

He reached over for the second blanket and covered them both with it, without disturbing his floating head much. He lay back, intending to think a little—but a little thinking was all he managed, since he, too, was soon drowsing.

The next morning he woke before she did, and remembered the conversation of the night before. He moved very carefully, hoping that he wouldn't wake her, and on being successful moved off into the woods on a private search.

Talia woke to an incredibly subtle perfume wreathing around her. She opened sleep-blurred eyes to see where it was coming from, to discover that someone had placed a bouquet by her head.

"What?" she said sleepily, trying to think why there should be flowers beside her. "Who?"

"A joyous Midsummer to you, Herald Talia, and a wonderful Birthing-Day as well," Kris said cheerfully from a point behind her. "It's a pity that more of your friends couldn't deliver trifles, but you'll have to admit that we *are* a bit far from most of them. I trust you'll accept this one as a token of my profound apology for insulting you last night. I didn't intend to."

"Kris!" she exclaimed, as she sat up and took up the flowers, breathing the exquisite fragrance with hedonistic delight. "You didn't need to do this—"

"Ah, but I did. It wouldn't be Midsummer unless I gathered at least one bouquet. Besides, that scent you're enjoying is supposed to be a sovereign remedy for hangover."

"Is it?" she laughed.

"I have no idea," he admitted. "Part of my hangover always includes a stopped-up nose. Look at the stems, why don't you?"

Holding the bouquet together was a silver ring, of a design of two hands clasped together. It was the token a Herald only gave to the friends he loved best.

"Kris—I don't know what to say—"

"Then say 'Thank you, Kris, and I accept your apology.'"

"Thank you, love, and I *do* accept your apology—if you'll accept mine."

"I would be only too pleased to," he said, giving her a cheerful grin. "Dear heart, I'd intended to give you that at Midwinter, but since you said you'd never had a Birthing-Day gift, the opportunity was too good to pass by. And it had damn well better fit—you wouldn't believe how hard it is to get someone's ring size without them knowing! It goes on the right hand, little bird; the left is reserved for another purpose."

Talia slipped it on, vowing to discover when Kris' Birthing-Day was so as to return the gesture with interest. "It's perfect," she said as he sat down next to her with a very pleased expression.

She threw her arms around him, completely happy for the first time in months, and opened a tiny channel of rapport deliberately so that he could know what she couldn't say in words.

"Hoo—that's as intoxicating as what we were drinking last night, little bird!"

She took the hint and closed the channel down again, but she could tell that he had enjoyed the brief thrill.

"What are these flowers? I've never smelled anything so wonderful in my life! I think I could live on the scent alone."

"A little deep-woods northern flower that only blooms at this time of year. It's called 'Maiden's Hope.' I thought you might like it."

"I love it." She continued to breathe in the scent of the flowers with her eyes half-shut. Kris thought with amusement that she looked rather like a young cat in her first encounter with catmint, and told her so.

"I can't explain it—it smells like sunrise, like a perfect spring day, like the heart's desire—"

"How about like breakfast?" he replied comically.

"*Breakfast?* Oh well, if that's your heart's desire—" She laughed at him and rose smoothly to her feet. "It is my turn, so I guess I'd better reward you for being so outrageously nice to me after I tried to murder you last night."

"And since you seem so enamored of those flowers, I'll see that you have some in your wedding garland if I have to nurture them in a hot-house myself."

"I thought you had a black thumb." She removed one of the creamy white blossoms and tucked it behind one ear.

"For you, little bird, my thumb will turn green. I never break my promises if I can help it, and this is one I definitely intend to keep."

"Then I'd better keep my promise of breakfast. Where will I get my flowers if I let you wither away of starvation?"

They gathered their scattered belongings and returned arm-in-arm to the Waystation.

CHAPTER 12

GEESE HONKED OVERHEAD, heading south. It had been one of those rare, glorious golden autumn days—far too lovely a day to spend indoors, so Talia and Kris had been hearing petitions stationed behind a wooden trestle table set out in front of the inn door. Their last petitioner had been a small boy leading a very large plowhorse, and he had given them a message.

Talia scanned the letter, and handed it without comment to Kris. He read it in silence, while the scruffy child who had brought it scuffed his feet uneasily through the pile of golden leaves at his feet.

Kris returned the message to her, as she braced her arm on the rough wood of the trestle table and leaned her chin on one hand. "How long ago did all this happen?" she asked the boy.

"'Bout two days," he said, combing dark hair out of his eyes with his fingers. "Feud, though, tha's been on years. Wouldn't be s'bad this time 'cept fer th' poisoned well. Tha's why granther sent me. Reckons in settlin' now, 'fore somebody gets killed."

Talia looked up at the position of the sun, and added figures in her head. "I'm for riding out now," she said, finally. "Advice?"

Kris brushed more leaves off the table, and glanced back over his shoulder at the inn behind them. "We don't have any more petitions to be heard, but riding out to a place that isolated is going to take the rest of the afternoon. We'll have to ride half the night to make up the time, and we won't have the chance to reprovision until we get to Knowles Crossing."

Talia's shields chose that moment to go down; she felt the boy's anxiety with enough force to make her nauseous while she fought them back into place. She couldn't manage more than half strength; could still feel the child fretting after they were up. "I take it that means you think we should reprovision now, and wait until tomorrow morning."

"More or less."

"Well, I don't agree; let's wrap things up here and move out."

She could feel *his* disapproval as they followed behind the child, perched like a toy on the back of an enormous, thick-legged horse that was more used to pulling a plow than being ridden.

"You let the boy manipulate you," he said, finally, as their mounts and chirras kicked up swirls of leaves.

"I didn't. A poisoned well is a serious business out here. It indicates a situation gone out of control. Are you willing to have deaths on your conscience because we dallied a day, buying supplies?" She whispered, but her tone was angry.

He shrugged. "My opinion doesn't matter. *You* are the one giving the orders."

She seethed. They argued frequently these days—now and again it was something a bit more violent than an argument. Kris often seemed to take a stand opposing hers just for sheer obstinacy.

"You bastard," she said as the reason occurred to her. The boy looked back at her, startled. She lowered her voice. "You are just opposing me to see if I *can* be manipulated, aren't you?"

He grinned, ruefully. "Sorry, love. It was part of my orders. Including manufacturing emotions, since you can sense them. Face it, if anybody is going to be able to warp your decisions, it would be your counselor. But now that you know—"

"You can stop giving me headaches," she replied tartly. "Now, let's get down to business."

"You could have used your Gift back there," he said, as they settled at last into their bed. It had taken a long, hard ride through the moonless, frosty night to reach their Station once the feud had been settled. And it had taken a lot of negotiating to *get* it settled.

"I—I still haven't figured out the ethics of it," she answered slowly. "Having it, and having people's emotional states shoved in my face is bad enough. I *still* don't really know when it's right to use it."

"Damn. What if it had been the only way to take care of the problem? Then what would you have done?" Kris was worried about this; he was afraid that if an emergency arose and the only way to deal with it was by exercising that Gift, she might well freeze. And if it came to using it offensively, the likelihood of her freezing was all the greater.

"I don't know." A long pause, as she settled her head on his shoulder. "The only other people I know of with Empathy are Healers—and they are never going to come into contact with the situations *I* have to deal with. *Where* are the boundaries?"

He sighed, and held her, that being the only comfort he could offer her. "I don't know either, little bird. I just don't know."

Kris leaned his aching head against the cold stone mantelpiece of the Station fireplace. This had *not* been a good day. By now the rumors about her had spread everywhere they went. Although this was *not* their first visit to Langenfield, the villagers met Talia with unease and a little fear—and often wearing evil-eye talismans; they were obviously uncomfortable with her judgment and her abilities.

Talia had given no impression of anything but confidence, intelligence, and rock-steady trustworthiness, despite the fact that Kris knew that she had been trembling inside from the moment she passed the village gates.

This situation had been one she'd had to face over and over again, every time they entered a new town.

He felt Talia's hand touch his shoulder. "I'm the one that should have the headache," she said softly, "not you."

"Dammit, I *wish* you'd let me do something about this—"

"What? What can you do? Give them a lecture? I have to *win* their trust, and win it so firmly that all their mistrust starts to look foolish in their *own* eyes."

"I could make it seem like I'm the one taking the lead."

"Oh, that's a *great* idea. Then all they'll do is wonder if I'm manipulating you like a puppet," she retorted bitingly.

"Then I could back you up, dammit!" He met her anger with anger of his own. They glared at each other like a pair of angry cats, until Talia broke the tension by glancing down. Kris followed her glance to see that her hands were clenched into tight fists.

"Damn. I was all set to give you another love-pat, wasn't I?" she asked, chagrined. "This—Gods, between my shields being erratic, and having to face this same situation over and over—I'm like a harpstring tuned too high."

Kris forcibly relaxed his own tight muscles, including *his* fists. "I should know better than to provoke you. Intellectually, I understand. You have to face the battle and win it *on your own*. But emotionally— it's a strain on both of us, and I can't stop wanting to help."

"That's why I love you, peacock," she said, putting both hands around his face and kissing him. "And—Havens! Wait here—it's been such a rotten day, I totally forgot!"

He stared after her in puzzlement, as she dashed out the Station door and returned, brushing snow from her shoulders. "I left this in a pocket on my saddle so I wouldn't forget it—and then I go and forget it!" She pressed a tiny, wrapped parcel in his hand. "Happy Birthing-Day."

"How did you—" He *was* surprised. "I—"

"Unwrap it, silly." She looked inordinately pleased with herself.

It was a ring, identical to the one he'd given her months ago. "I—" He swallowed the lump that had appeared in his throat. "I don't deserve this."

"In a pig's eye! You've earned it a dozen times, and more, even if you *do* tempt me to kill you once a week."

"Only once a week?" He managed a grin to match hers.

"You're improving—or I am. Now I *did* remember to get a nice fresh pair of quail, honeycake, and a very good bottle of wine." She slid her arms around his, stood on tiptoe, and kissed the end of his nose. "Now, shall we make this a proper Birthing-Day celebration, or not?"

Now came the stop she was dreading above all the others; Hevenbeck.

There hadn't been a more pleasant winter afternoon on this entire trip; cold, crystal-clear air, sunlight so pure it seemed white, a cloudless and vibrant blue sky above the leafless, white boughs of the grove of birch they were passing through. Snow on the ground sparkled; the air felt so clean and crisp it was almost like drinking chilled wine. Talia let the cheer of the day and of the others elevate her own spirits; after all, there was no reason to think that the people of Hevenbeck would be any worse than the rest of what she'd dealt with. It was unlikely in the extreme that anyone except the old miser and his wife would remember her or that she'd nearly let her own troubles distract her from what could have become a serious situation!

They were several miles from Hevenbeck, when Talia was suddenly struck by a wall of fear, pain, and rage! She reeled in her saddle, actually graying out as Kris steadied her. She came back to herself feeling as if she'd been hit with a warhammer.

Kris was still holding her, keeping her from falling off of Rolan's back. "Kris—" she gasped, "FarSee to Hevenbeck—"

Then it was her turn to steady him, as he willed himself into deep trance. Her head still rang with the fierce anguish of the emotions she'd encountered; she breathed deeply of the crisp air to try and clear it, and clamped down her shields—and for once, they actually worked, right up to full strength.

It hardly seemed as if he'd dropped into his trance before he was struggling up out of it again, blinking his eyes in confusion.

"Northern raiders—" he said with difficulty, still fogged with trance. "—though how they got past Sorrows—"

"Damn! And no help nearer than two days. How many?"

"Ten, maybe fifteen."

"Not *too* many for us to handle, I don't think—"

"I'd hoped you would ride your internship without seeing any fighting," he said hesitantly.

She jumped down off Rolan and headed for the chirras, her feet crunching in the snow. "Well, we haven't got a choice; trouble's there, we'd better deal with it."

"Talia, I'm just a Herald, but you're the only Queen's Own we've got—"

"I also shoot better than you do," she said crisply, sliding his sword and dagger out of his pack and reaching over the chirra's furry back to hand them to him. "If it'll make you feel any better, I promise not to close in for hand-to-hand unless I have to. But you handed over responsibility, and unless you overrule me, I say I'm going. Ten to fifteen aren't too many for both of us—but they could be for one alone."

"All right." Kris began strapping his weapons on, while Talia led the chirras off the road entirely. With snow creaking beneath her feet, she took them into the heart of a tangled evergreen thicket out of view of the roadway. There she tethered them lightly, the scent of bruised needles sharp in her nostrils, and backed out, breaking the snow-cake to powder and brushing it clear of footprints with a broken branch.

She laid a gloved hand lightly on Rolan's neck, as his breath steamed in the cold air. "Tell them to stay there until dark, loverling," she murmured. "If we're not back by then, they can pull themselves loose and head back to the last village."

Rolan snorted, his breath puffing out to hang in front of his nose, and stared fixedly at the thicket.

"Ready?"

He tossed his head.

"How about you?" She looked to Kris, whose face was pale, and whose mouth was set and grim.

"We'd better hurry. They were about to break down the gate."

She stripped the bridle bells from both sets of harness, and vaulted into the saddle with a creaking of leather. "Let's do it."

They made no effort to come up quietly, just set both Companions to a full gallop and hung on for dear life. White hills and black trees flashed past them; twice the Companions vaulted over fallen tree-trunks that the villagers had not yet cleared away from the roadbed. As they galloped up over the last hill, the sun revealed the plight of the village in merciless detail; black of ash, red of blood, orange of flame, all in high contrast against the trampled snow.

The raiders were just breaking through the palisade gate as they came galloping up. Enormous iron axes swung high, impacting against the tough ironoak of the gate with hollow thuds. The noise the bandits were making covered the approach of the two Heralds entirely, between the sound of the axes against the wood and the war-cries they were shrieking. Three or four of their number lay dead outside the palisade, blood soaking into the snow about them. The gate came down just as the Heralds got into arrow-range—most of the rest surged through the gates and into the village. There were still a handful of reivers outside; to her relief, Talia saw nothing among them but hand-weapons—no bows of any kind.

Rolan skidded to a halt, hooves sending up a shower of snow, as Talia pulled an arrow from the quiver at her saddle-bow without looking, and nocked it. She aimed along the shaft, feeling her own hands strangely calm and steady, and shouted—her high, young voice carrying over the baritone growls of the raiders. They turned; she found her target almost without thinking about it, a flash of pale skin above a shaggy dark fur—and loosed.

One of the raiders took her arrow squarely in the throat; he clutched at it, crimson blood welling round his fingers and spotting the snow at his feet. Then he fell, and she was choosing a second target; there was no time to think, only to let trained reflexes take over.

Talia's next two arrows bounced harmlessly off leather chest-armor and a battered wooden shield; Kris had not stopped when she had, but had sent Tantris hurtling past her, charging headlong into the gap where the gate had been while the reivers were busy protecting themselves from her covering fire. That seemed to decide the ones still left outside; they rushed her.

She got off one more shot, picking off her second man with a hit in his right eye. He went down; then Rolan warned her he was going to move. She clamped her legs tight around his barrel, as he pivoted and scrambled through the churned-up mud and snow along the palisade. When they were still within arrow-range he pivoted again, hindquarters slewing sideways a little, mane whipping her chest. She already had an arrow nocked; she sighted again, and brought down a third with a solid hit in his chest where an armor plate had fallen off and not been replaced.

A puff of breeze blew a cloud of acrid smoke over the palisade; she coughed and her eyes watered as she groped for another arrow. The remaining three men came on, howling, spittle flecking beards and lips, as her fingers found another shaft in the rapidly emptying quiver.

The nearest, bundled in greasy bearskins, stopped and poised to throw his axe. That was long enough for her to sight and loose. Her arrow took him in the throat, and he flung the axe wildly, hitting only the palisade, as he collapsed. Then Rolan charged the two that were left.

Talia clung with aching legs and arrow-hand while he reared to his full height and smashed in the head of the first one in his path. It was a horrible sound, like a melon splitting open; Talia felt the shock as Rolan's hooves connected, heard the surprised little grunt the man made. Blood and fear and stale grease-and-sweat smell stank in their nostrils. The last one was too close for arrow shot. Talia felt at her belt for her throwing dagger, pulled it loose, and cast it at short range. This one had worn no chest-armor at all. He stopped short, his eyes surprised; his sword fell from his hand and his free hand felt at his chest. He looked down stupidly at the dagger protruding from his ribs, then his eyes glazed over, and he fell.

Talia and Rolan raced for the gate; she glanced behind her for possible foes and saw they were leaving red hoofprints behind them.

She was met with a chaos of burning buildings and screaming people; they thundered inside, and skidded to a halt, confused for a moment by the fear and smoke. Talia felt, more than saw, a fear-maddened ox charging down the single street; saw out of the corner of her eye a child running straight into its path. Rolan responded to her unspoken signal; whirled with joint-wrenching suddenness and leapt forward; she leaned out of the saddle, clinging to the saddle-bow, and scooped up the child as Rolan shouldered the oncoming animal aside. Then he leapt again, giving Talia the chance to deposit the baby on a doorstep. Kris was nowhere to be seen—but neither were the raiders.

Talia vaulted off Rolan's back and began grabbing hysterical townspeople; without stopping to think about it she began forcibly calming them with her Gift, and organizing them into a fire brigade. All the while she fought the urge to flee away, to somewhere dark and quiet, and be sick. She kept seeing those surprised eyes—*feeling* the fear and pain just outside of her shields.

But there was no time to think—just to act. And pray that her shields *stayed* up—or she had no idea of what might happen under such a load.

Kris appeared when the fires were almost out; face smudged with smoke, Whites liberally splashed with blood, eyes dull. Tantris stumbled along beside him. Talia left her fire-brigade to deal with what was left, just as cheering villagers appeared in his wake, waving gore-encrusted scythes and mattocks. She limped to his side; only now was she noticing she'd sprained her left ankle, and wrenched her right shoulder when she'd caught up that child. He lifted his eyes to meet hers and she saw reflected in them her own bleak heart-sickness.

She took the bloody sword from his unresisting hand, fought down her own revulsion, and touched his hand; hoping to give him the ease she could not yet feel.

He sighed, and swayed; and leaned against Tantris for support. Tantris was as blood-speckled as Rolan, and had a shallow cut along one shoulder. "They wouldn't surrender, and wouldn't run," he said, voice harsh from the smoke and the shouting. "I don't know why. The Healer's dead; that poor mad girl with him. There's about ten more dead and twice as many wounded. Thank Gods, thank Gods, no children. That couple—burned to death trying to save their damned chickens. Three houses burned out at the other end of the village—" He stared at the townsfolk cheering and laughing and dancing awkwardly in the bloody snow and churned-up mud. "They think the battle's over. Goddess, it's just beginning—the ruined foodstores, the burned out houses, and the worst of winter yet to come—"

"It—it's not like in the ballads, is it?"

"No," he sighed, rubbing his eyes with a filthy hand. "It never is—and we have a job to do."

"Then let's get the chirras back and set about it."

Their second stopover at Waymeet, by contrast, was almost embarrassing, Kris being hailed as the village's hero for having remained behind to tend the ill while Talia went for help. It became necessary to remind the grateful people of the rules that governed a Herald's behavior on circuit, else they would have been feasted at a different house every night, slept in the best beds in the village, and come away with more gifts than the chirras could carry.

That stop went a long way toward raising their spirits. *Both* their spirits—for there were no evil-eye talismans on display in Waymeet, and there were no odd sidelong glances at Talia. And her shields were holding—were still holding—

They stopped with Tedric at Berrybay; he proved to be more than delighted to welcome them, and a two-day rest with him—and a chance to cry out their heart-sickness on the shoulder of someone who would truly understand—completed their cure.

When they were back to making normal conversation Tedric mentioned, with the pleasure of a child in a new toy, that since their visit, the wandering Bards had taken to stopping overnight with him, and that scarcely a month went by now without at least one arriving on his doorstep.

Kris thought of his report, and smiled to himself.

Maeven Weatherwitch and her adopted child were thriving. Her ability to Foresee had actually grown. The grateful people of Berrybay allocated a portion of their harvests to her so that she need not take the chance of losing the Gift to hunger or an accident in the fields. Best of all, the local priestess of Astera was training her to become her own successor.

And Talia's shields continued to hold.

They rode through the early Spring leaves (scarcely more than buds) on their last few stops for this circuit. Come Vernal Equinox, scarcely more than a month away, they would turn their chirras over to the next Herald assigned to this circuit and would be on their way back to the Collegium.

It was over—it was almost over. Talia felt her control was back, and more certain than before. Her shields were back, and stronger. Now if only . . .

If only she could ease the aching doubt in her mind . . . the rights and the wrongs. . . .

The unanswered questions kept her up nights, staring into the darkness long after Kris had fallen asleep at her side. For if she could not find an answer for herself, how could she ever again dare *use* the Gift she'd been born with, except in utterly circumscribed circumstances?

Birds newly-arrived from the south sang in the budding bushes all around them; trees seemed to be covered with a mist of green. Talia was not expecting trouble, so when Kris asked her to deliberately drop her shields and cast her senses ahead to Westmark, what she encountered caught her completely off-guard. The force of emotion she felt sent her slumping forward as if from a blow to the head. Kris urged Tantris in close beside her and steadied her in the saddle as she shook her head to clear it.

"What is it?" he asked anxiously. "It can't be—"

"It's not raiders, but it's bad. There's death, and there's going to be more unless I get there fast," she said. "You bring on the chirras while I go ahead."

She sent Rolan into his fastest gallop, leaving Kris and the pack-beasts far behind. They flashed through beams of sunlight cutting between the trees like spirits of winter come to invade the spring. She narrowed her eyes against the rush of greening wind in her face, and the whipping of Rolan's mane, trying to sort out the images she'd gotten. She had touched the terrible, mindless violence of a mob, and two sources of fear—one, the fear of the hunted; the other, the fear of the hopeless. Underneath it, like a thin stream of something vile, had lurked a source of true and gloating evil.

Even above the pounding of Rolan's hooves, she heard the mob as she neared the outer wall of Westmark, a sturdy and skilled piece of brick-layer's work, dull red behind the pale mist of opening leaves. She heard the hair-raising growl long before she saw the mob itself. She had no need to be in trance to feel the turmoil of emotions, though by the grace of the Lady they hadn't yet found their victim. She could almost taste his fear, but it wasn't the panic of the caught creature yet.

As she came within sight of the mob, a single figure burst from under cover of the town gates and ran for his life straight toward her, his feet kicking up yellow road-dust as he ran toward her. At the sight of him, the people hunting him howled and plunged through the gates after him.

He seemed determined to cast himself under Rolan's hooves if it was necessary to do so in order to reach her. With all the skill burned into both of them by Keren, she and Rolan avoided him and wheeled around in a wrenchingly tight circle, putting Rolan's bulk between the fugitive and his hunters.

The stranger seized the pommel of her saddle in a white-knuckled death-grip and gasped: "Justice—"

She remained in the saddle, certain that if all else failed, she could have him up behind her and be away before any of the mob could react. But at the sight of her Companion and her unmistakable uniform, the crowd slowed, began muttering uncertainly, and finally stopped several feet away.

When she spoke, a silence fell upon them. "Why do you hound this man to his death?" she demanded, pitching her voice to be carrying and trumpet-clear.

The crowd before her, no longer the mindless mob now that their momentum was broken, stirred uneasily. Finally one man stepped forward; by his fine dark umber wool and linen clothing, prosperous, and no farmer.

"That trader's a murderer, Herald," he said. "A foreigner and a murderer. We reckon on giving him his due."

"Nay—" the man at her saddle panted, olive skin gone yellow-pale, large dark eyes wide with fear. "Trader, yes, and foreign. But no murderer. This I swear."

An angry growl arose at his words.

"*Hold!*" she shouted, pitching her voice to command before they could regain their mob unity. "It is no crime to be a foreigner, and the Queen's word grants Herald's justice to anyone within the bounds of this Kingdom who would claim it. This man has claimed justice of me; I *will* give it to him. You who call him a murderer—did any of you see him kill?"

"The body was in his wagon, and still warm!" the spokesman protested, rubbing his mustache uneasily.

"So? And was the wagon then so secured that none could enter it but he? No? Then how can you be certain that the body was not put there to turn suspicion upon this one—already suspect because of being foreign?"

The dismay she felt told her that they had not considered the possibility. These were not evil people—that thread of viciousness she had sensed was not coming from one of *them*—they were only thoughtless, and easily led while in the herd-mentality of the mob. Confronted with someone who made them think, they lost their taste for blood.

"This will be done by the law, or not at all," she said firmly. "Let every man, woman and child not bedridden assemble in the square. At this point there is not one of you above suspicion. Let the body be brought to me there."

The man clinging to her pommel was slowly regaining his courage and his breath. "I have heard of your kind, Lady Herald," he said, obviously nervous, by the sweat only now beginning to bead his generous forehead; but equally obviously willing to trust her. "I swear to you that I did not do this evil deed. You may put me to the ordeal, if you will."

"There will be no 'ordeal,' and nothing to fear if you are truly innocent," Talia told him quietly. "I do not know what you have heard of us, but I pledge you that you shall have exactly what you asked of me—justice."

The trader walked beside her as she rode Rolan into the town gates, past the substantial bulks of the brick houses, and on to the cobblestoned square. Exactly as she had ordered, every ambulatory person in the town that day was assembled there. They had left an empty space for her in the middle, and in this space there lay a long, dark-draped bundle—plainly, the victim.

Talia picked out two dozen robust-looking, mortar-bespeckled citizens, and ascertained by questioning them under her Gift that they could not have had anything whatsoever to do with the crime, as they had all been engaged in moving the town wall outward. She set these men, armed with cudgels, to guarding the exits to the square, since once the killer realized that he or she was about to be uncovered, he might try for an escape and Talia did not intend that he should succeed.

Then she removed the blanket. The young woman—girl, almost—had been beaten severely, and her neck was broken. She had been pretty; her clothing was well-made, not badly worn, but had been ripped in many places. Whoever was guilty of this was brutal and violent, and nothing Talia sensed in the trader corresponded to the kind of mind that could batter a young girl to death. The crime *did* match that thread of evil she'd sensed before she confronted the mob, however.

"Who was this child?" she asked, after giving her own nerves a moment to steady.

"My stepdaughter." A square-jawed, bearded man stepped forward, his face hard, his brown eyes unreadable. Talia noted that he did not address her with the honorific "Herald." This might mean much, or nothing.

"When was she found, and by whom?"

"About an hour ago, Herald," a thin, graying woman in a floury apron spoke up. "My boy found her. I'd sent him to the trader with the money for some things I'd asked him to set aside for me." She pushed forward a lanky blond lad of about fifteen with a sick expression and greenish face.

"Tell me what you found, as exactly as you can remember it," Talia ordered, pity making her move to shield him from view of the body.

"Ma," he gulped, eyes fixed on her face. "Ma, she sent me like she said, with egg money for some fripperies she'd asked the trader to hold for her. When I got to the wagon, the trader weren't there, but he's told us to go in and wait for him times afore when he weren't there, so I did. It were kinda dark inside, and I stumbled over something. I flung the door open to see what I were a-fallin' over. It were Karli—" He swallowed hard, his face growing greener. "I thought maybe she were sick, maybe drunk even, so I shook her. But her head rolled so funny—" He scrubbed his hand against his tunic in an unconscious effort to rid it of the contamination he'd felt from touching a corpse.

"Enough," Talia said gently. The poor child could never have seen violent death before, much less touched it. She remembered how she had felt after the fight at Hevenbeck, and tried to put her sympathy in her eyes. "Have any of you ever seen this girl with the trader before?"

Several people had, volunteering that she'd had huddled, whispered conferences with him, conferences that broke off if any came near. Feet scuffled uneasily on the cobblestones as she continued her interrogations as thoroughly and patiently as she could, and she could hear little whispers at the edge of the crowd. She wished she could hear them clearly, for they might tell her a great deal.

The man who claimed to be the murdered girl's stepfather spat angrily and interrupted. "We're wasting time! Anyone with eyes and ears knows the scum killed her! He wanted her, no doubt, then killed her when she refused him—or if she did not refuse, for fear she'd make him wed her after."

Talia's eyes narrowed. This hardly sounded like a grief-stricken parent.

"*I* am the instrument of the Queen's Justice, and it is I and no one else who will decide when we are wasting time," she said coldly. "Thus far I have seen nothing to implicate this man, beyond him speaking with the girl. I am sure she spoke to many. Did she not speak daily even to you? Does this make you a suspect?"

Was it her imagination, or did he pale a trifle?

"Trader, what say you?"

"May I speak all the truth?" he asked.

Now *that* was an odd way to answer. "Why need you ask?"

"Because I would not malign the dead before her kith and kin, but what I would say may not meet with the approval of those here."

"Wait but a moment, trader," she answered, and closed her eyes. She took a moment to pass deeply into trance and invoke once again the "Truth Spell." There were two stages of this spell. The first stage could be cast by any Herald, even those with only a touch of a Gift. It caused a glow, invisible to the speaker, but quite apparent to anyone else, to form about the speaker's head and shoulders. The second stage, (and one which required not just a Gift, but a powerful "communication" Gift), could, when invoked, force the speaker to tell *only* the truth, regardless of his intentions. Talia's Gift was sufficient to enable her to bring both forms of the Truth Spell into play, and she invoked them now. As the blue glow formed about the trader's head, she could hear a sudden intake of breath, then sighs of relief. These people might never have seen Truth Spell in action in their lives, but they knew what it was, and they trusted in the power of the spell and the honesty of the wielder.

"Tell all the truth freely. You cannot hurt her in the Havens, and it is your own life you are defending."

"She came to me several times, yes," he said. "She wished me to take her with me when I left here."

"Why?" Talia asked.

"Because she wished to escape—what and why she would not say. She said that no one would believe her if she were to say what it was. She first offered me money, but I dared not risk the damage to my trade if these people were made wroth. Still, she persisted. In the end, she agreed that she would 'disappear' a day before I was to leave so that it would seem I had naught to do with it, and as payment she offered herself," he sighed. "It was wrong, surely, but I am only flesh, and she was comely. It did not seem so evil that I should have pleasure of her in return for an escape she desired so badly. I was to have met her on the road outside of town tomorrow night, after dusk. After I spoke to her this morning, I did not see her again alive."

The glow did not falter, nor did Talia feel the drain of energy that would have indicated that the trader was being forced to tell the truth. The crowd, which had been watching the glow intently, sighed again. Now it was obvious to everyone that the trader could not be guilty—but then, who was?

"Lies! All lies!" The stepfather broke free of his neighbors and plunged forward with the apparent intent of strangling the trader with his bare hands. Rolan reared, ears laid back, and snapped at him, keeping him away, as Talia herself drew her dagger with a hiss of metal—and in the rush of his anger and—and yes, *fear*—Talia Saw the scene his emotions carried and knew the truth.

"Hold him!" she ordered, and several strong men rushed him and pinioned his arms against his sides, despite his struggles.

Despite what she knew, she could not accuse him solely on the basis of what she'd Seen. But from the rest of what she'd picked up, she might not need to.

"Karli's sister—where is she?" Talia demanded, and many hands pushed the pale, shrinking girl forward, a girl of about fourteen, with a sweet, timid face and dark eyes and hair.

"I don't want to force you to speak," Talia told her in a soft voice no one else could hear, "but I will if I have to. Will you tell us the truth about this man who calls himself your father, and be free?"

She had cringed when shoved before Talia, but the Herald's kindly voice and the reassurance she was trying to show revived her—and the last words, "be free," seemed to set new courage in her. She stood up straighter, and stared at her stepfather with hate.

"Yes. Yes!" Her voice was shrill with defiance. "I'll tell the truth. It was *him*—our so-kind father—that Karli wanted to escape from! And why? Because he has been making us lie with him every night since mother died!"

The accusing words rang in the sudden silence. The villagers stared at the girl and her stepfather in stunned amazement.

"Lying slut!" the man screamed into the shocked quietude, struggling against the hands that held him.

"I speak nothing but the truth!" she shouted back, her eyes dilated with fear—and something more, something of anger and rage and shame. "When we cried, when we fought, he beat us, then he raped us. Karli swore she'd escape somehow, but he found out, said he'd teach her to mend her ways."

"She lies!"

"Do I? Then hold him for six months and wait," she laughed wildly. "You all know he hasn't let a male older than five near me since last winter. I would have gone with Karli, but how could I earn a copper, bulging with child? *His* child—*his* bastard!" She broke down, sobbing hysterically, and one of the women darted forward without hesitation to throw a shawl around her in a protective maternal gesture, followed by others, who formed a comforting circle around the girl, shielding her from the sight of her ravisher and glaring at him with hate-filled and disgusted eyes.

Talia confronted him, shaking with outrage, but somehow controlling her own revulsion. "You went seeking the child, and found her with the trader. You decided to confront her, teach her a lesson. You became angry when she defied you, thinking herself safe because she was in a public place. You beat her, and killed her, then hid her body in the trader's wagon, knowing he'd be blamed, knowing that if he was killed before I arrived no one would ever look farther for the real murderer."

She was transferring the Truth Spell to him even as she accused him, forcing him to speak his real thoughts when next he opened his mouth.

It worked more thoroughly than she had imagined it would. "Yes— and why not? Do I not feed and clothe them? Am I not their owner? They are mine, like their slut of a mother! She died without giving me my money's worth, and by the Gods, it is their duty to fill her place!"

Talia was nauseated by the mind behind those words. No punishment seemed adequate to her to fit what he had done. An odd, disinterested corner of her weighed all the facts—and coldly made a thought-out, logical decision.

Her revulsion and anger built until she could no longer contain it— and then it found the outlet that matched the decision she'd come to. She *forced* rapport on him—not the gentle sharing she had had with Kris, but a brutal, mental rape such as she had not dreamed she was capable of. Then with a sidewise twist, she pulled the stepdaughter into the union—and forced her memories into his mind, forced him to *be* her through all her pain-filled and horrified experiences.

He gave a single gargling howl, stiffened, then dropped to his knees. His startled captors released him, but he was in no shape to take advantage of the situation. When they pulled him to his feet, his mouth hung slack and drooling, and there was no trace of sanity left in his eyes. Talia had locked him into a never-ending loop, as he re-lived, over and over, every waking moment that his stepdaughter had spent as his victim.

The villagers moved away from her, one involuntary pace.

Now she'd just shown them what she could do.

"Herald?" one of the men said timidly, looking at her with respect tinged with fear. They knew that she had punished him herself even if they had no idea how. "What must we do with him?"

"What you please," she said wearily, "and according to your own customs. Whether he lives or dies, he has been dealt with."

As they took him away, one of the women caught her attention. "Herald, we have heard you have a mind-magic. Is there aught you can do for this girl? And—I am a midwife. Would you take it amiss if she should 'lose' the child? Though I am not Gifted, I learned my craft among Healers. It can be done with no harm to her."

In for a lamb—she thought, and nodded.

The people were dispersing, too shocked and appalled even to whisper among themselves. Talia stumbled wearily to the knot of women, and knelt beside the shivering, sobbing girl. She eased into trance, and probed as Kerithwyn had taught her. She could "read," though she could not act on what she read. It was as she had suspected; the girl was too young, the not-born malformed. She transferred her attention to the girl's mind and began laying the foundation for a healing that time and courage could complete without any further intervention on Talia's part—imprinting as forcefully as she could that none of this had been the girl's own fault. Lastly, she sent the girl into a half-trance which would last for several days, during which the damage done to her body, at least, could be mended.

She stood, bone-weary, and faced the midwife. "What you suggest would happen eventually, and it will be easier on her body if it were to happen now. She hates what she bears as much as she hates the father, and the cleansing of her body may bring some ease to her heart. And—tell her that *she* was never to blame for this. Tell her until she believes it."

The midwife nodded without speaking, and she and the others led the half-aware girl to her house.

Only the trader was left. His eyes brimmed with tears and gratitude; the proximity of his clean, normal mind was infinitely comforting to Talia. After the running sewer of the stepfather he seemed like a clear, sparkling stream.

"Lady Herald"—he faltered at last—"my life is yours."

"Then take it, and do good with it, trader," she replied, burying her face in Rolan's neck, feeling her Companion's gentle touch slowly cleansing her of contamination.

The trader's footsteps receded.

And the sound of three sets of hooves was approaching. They rang with the unmistakable chime of Companion hooves on stone—and were accompanied by the soft sound of gently-moving bridle bells.

Oh, Goddess, help me! she thought. *No more—I can't bear any more.*

But the hooves continued to approach, and then she heard footsteps and felt hands take her shoulders. She looked up. It was Kris.

"I saw the end, and I heard the rest from the midwife," he said quietly. "But—"

"But—you made a judgment *and* a punishment, Herald," said a strange voice, a female voice, age-roughened, but strong. Talia looked beyond Kris to see two unfamiliar faces; a woman about Keren's age, but strongly and squarely-built, and a young man perhaps a year or two older than Kris, with mouse-brown hair. Both wore the arrows of Special Messengers on the sleeves of their Whites.

Special couriers—their Companions must have sensed the trouble, and brought them to help.

And they were senior Heralds. "You *did* use your Gift on that man, did you not?" the young man asked, somberly.

"Yes," she replied, meeting their eyes. "I did. And I would do the same if the circumstances warranted it."

"Do you judge that to be an ethical use of your Gift?"

"Is shooting raiders an ethical use of my hands?" she countered. "It's part of me; it is totally in my control, it does not control me. I made a reasoned and thought-out decision—*if* the man ever accepts his own guilt and the fact that what he did was *wrong*, he'll break free of the compulsion I put on him. Until then he will suffer exactly as he made his victims suffer. That seemed to me to be far more in keeping with his crime than imprisoning or executing him. So I judged, and meted out punishment; I stand by it—and I would do it again."

She regarded them both with a certain defiance, and somewhat to her surprise, they both nodded with a certain amount of satisfaction.

"Then I think that *we* are not needed here after all," said the woman. "Clear roads to you, brother—sister—"

They wheeled their Companions and rode back out the gates without a single backward glance.

That left only Kris.

"You did very well, Herald Talia," he said gently.

She stood wearily in the firm grasp of his hands, with his voice recalling her to duty. She longed beyond telling to lay that duty on him, and she knew that if she asked, he would take it.

But if she laid it on anyone, she would be proving false to her calling. If this were a normal circuit, there would be no Kris to take up the burden of her tasks because she felt too worn, too sickened, too exhausted—and yes, too cowardly, too cowardly to face all those people and prove again to them that their trust was not misplaced, that a Herald could bring healing as well as punishment. And they must be shown yet again that though a Herald had powers the guilty had to fear, the innocent would never feel them. She must face the fear in those faces and turn it back into trust. Kris could not do that for her, and if he were not here, she would not even have the brief luxury of imagining that he could.

She sighed, and hearing the weariness, the pain in that sigh, Kris almost wished that she'd ask for him to take over. His heart ached for her, but this was the trial by fire that every Herald had to face, soon or late, and she most of all. No matter what the personal cost, a Herald's duty must come first. She had proven that her Gift was under her control. She had proven that she was willing to accept the ethical and moral responsibilities that particular Gift laid upon her. Now she must prove she had the emotional and mental strength to carry any job she undertook to its end.

She had no choice, and neither did he. They had accepted this responsibility along with every other aspect of becoming a Herald. But— he hurt for her.

She looked up, and must have seen his thoughts writ plainly in his eyes.

"I'd better locate the Town Council, the Mayor, and the Clerk," she said, pulling herself up straight and schooling her face into calm. "There's work to do."

As Kris watched her walk away, head high, carriage confident, nothing reflecting her inner agony, he felt a glow of pride.

Now she was truly a Herald.

Kris preceded her to the Waystation nearest the town and had all in readiness when she rode up, shoulders slumped in exhaustion. The rules governing both of them allowed him to do that much for her, at least. She sought their bed long before he, and was apparently asleep by the time he joined her, but in the darkness he felt her shaken with silent tears, and gathered her into his arms to weep herself to sleep on his shoulder.

The second day she took reports and news, and began settling grievances. Kris winced to see how warily the townsfolk regarded her, like some creature from legend—powerful, and not necessarily to be trusted. It was well that this was such a large place, for after her performance of the previous day, it might have been difficult to find those willing to have her sit in judgment over them—except that there was no choice in the matter here. Anyone with a grievance to settle before a Herald in a place this size must register that fact in writing; with the witness of their own words, there was not one of them bold enough to deny his original will.

Talia had the right to choose the order of their judgments; normally she did not exercise that right, but she chose otherwise this time. Wisely, she picked those cases to settle that required tact, understanding, and gentleness to come first. Gradually the townsfolk began to relax in her presence, began to lose their fear of her. By the third day, they were laughing at the occasional wry jest she inserted into her comments. By day's end, the fear was forgotten. By the fourth day, when she took her leave of them, she had regained their trust in Heralds, and more. Kris was so proud of her that he fairly shone with it as they rode on to their next stop.

The gods must have agreed with him, for they were kind to Talia in this much, at least. There were no further crises for the rest of the circuit.

"I can't believe it's over."

"You'd better," Kris laughed, "since that's the rendezvous point ahead of us. And unless my eyes are deceiving me—"

"They're not. That's a Companion grazing, and I think I see two mules."

"So tonight is the last we'll spend in a Waystation for a while. Sorry?"

"That I won't be eating your cooking or mine, or sleeping on straw? Be serious!"

Kris chuckled, and squinted against the light of the westering sun. "Hark!" he intoned melodramatically. "Methinks our relief hath heard the silver sound of our Companions' hooves."

"Or the rattling of your few thoughts in your empty head—" Talia kneed Rolan and they galloped into the lead. "It's Griffon!"

Sure enough, it was Talia's year-mate, who had gotten into Whites at the same time, but evidently finished his own internship early. She slid off Rolan's back after both of them had pulled up beside him with a clattering of hooves and jangling of bridle bells, and delivered a hearty kiss and embrace that sent him blushing as red as ever she had. He greeted Kris with such obvious relief that both of them were hard put to keep from chuckling at his bashfulness.

"There's an inn just a half hour down the road from here," he told them, stammering a trifle. "They're expecting you. I thought you'd probably rather sleep soft tonight, so when Farist caught the edges of Rolan's sending, I rode down there and warned them."

"Right, and thanks!" Kris answered for both of them, touched by the unexpected courtesy. "Seems like it's been forever since we had real beds."

"Not true," Talia interrupted him. "We had a real bed just a bit over four months ago, with Tedric."

"So we did, but it still seems like forever. That reminds me though; my first bit of advice to you is to always plan to stop at the northernmost Resupply Station; it's right near Berrybay. Tedric is a good host, loves having company, and his cooking—!" Kris rolled his eyes heavenward in mock ecstasy.

"And *my* first bit of advice is to watch out for the other northern-most surprise—" Briefly Talia outlined the plague's symptoms and described how it had decimated Waymeet.

They took turns detailing some of the hazards and pitfalls of this circuit, then turned their chirras and their remaining supplies over to him. Griffon helped them load their own gear on his mules, and by the time it was dusk, he was well settled into the Station and they were ready to be on their way.

As the lights of the inn shone through the darkness ahead of them, Kris sensed Talia's involuntary shiver.

"I know," he told her softly. "Now it's over—and now is when it *really* starts to get hard. But you're ready. Trust me, little bird, you *are* ready."

"You're sure?" she replied in a small, doubtful voice.

"As sure as I've ever been of anything in my life. You've been ready since Westmark. If you can handle that, you can handle anything; touchy nobles, Heirs with adolescent traumas, heart-wounded Heralds—"

"Mooncalf Heralds with lifebonds?" she asked with a tinge of sarcasm.

"Even that. *Especially* that. You haven't let it get in the way of anything yet, and you won't now. You're ready, dearheart. And if you *dare* make a liar out of me—"

"You'll what?"

"I'll—I'll commission a Bard to write you into something scathing."

"Great Goddess!" She reeled in the saddle, clutching her heart as if stabbed, her high spirits restored. "A death worse than Fate!"

"See that you behave yourself then." He grinned. "Now come on—there's dinner waiting, and soft feather beds; and after that—"

"Yes," she sighed, staring down the road to the south. "Home. At last."

ARROW'S FALL

Dedicated to:
Andre Norton for inspiration;
Teri Lee
for early encouragement;
and
my husband Tony
for being understanding
about my ongoing affair
with a word processor.

PROLOGUE

LONG AGO—SO LONG ago that the details of the conflict are lost and only the merest legends remain—the world of Velgarth was wracked by sorcerous wars. With the population decimated, the land was turned to wasteland and given over to the forest and the magically-engendered creatures those peoples had used to fight those wars, while the people that remained fled to the eastern coastline, for only in those wilderness areas could they hope to resume their shattered lives. In time, it was the eastern edge of the continent that became the site of civilization, and the heartland that in turn became the wilderness.

But humans are resilient creatures, and it was not overlong before the population once again was on the increase, moving westward, building new kingdoms out of the wilds.

One such kingdom was Valdemar. It had been founded by the once-Baron Valdemar and those of his people who had chosen exile with him rather than face the wrath of a selfish and cruel monarch. It lay on the very western-and-northernmost edge of the civilized world, bounded on the north and northwest by wilderness that still contained uncanny creatures, and on the far west by Lake Evendim, an enormous inland sea. Travel beyond Valdemar was perilous and uncertain at the very best of times, and at the worst a traveler could bring weird retribution on innocents when the creatures he encountered back-trailed him to his point of origin.

In part due to the nature of its founders, the monarchs of Valdemar welcomed fugitives and fellow exiles, and the customs and habits of its people had over the years become a polyglot patchwork. In point of fact, the one rule by which the monarchs of Valdemar governed their people was "There is no 'one true way.'"

Governing such an ill-assorted lot of subjects might have been impossible—had it not been for the Heralds of Valdemar.

The Heralds had extraordinary powers, yet never abused those powers; and the reason for their forbearance—in fact for the whole system—was the existence of creatures known as "Companions."

To one who knew no better, a Companion would seem little more than an extraordinarily graceful white horse. They were *far* more than that. The first Companions had been sent by some unknown power or powers at the pleading of King Valdemar himself—three of them, at first, who had made bonds with the King, his Heir, and his most trusted friend, who was the Kingdom Herald. So it came to be that the Heralds took on a new importance in Valdemar, and a new role.

It was the Companions who chose new Heralds, forging between themselves and their Chosen a mind-to-mind bond that only death could sever. While no one knew precisely *how* intelligent they were, it was generally agreed that their capabilities were at least as high as those of their human partners. Companions could (and did) Choose irrespective of age and sex, although they tended to Choose youngsters just entering adolescence, and more boys were Chosen than girls. The one common trait among the Chosen (other than a specific personality type: patient, unselfish, responsible, and capable of heroic devotion to duty) was at least a trace of psychic ability. Contact with a Companion and continued development of the bond enhanced whatever latent paranormal capabilities lay within the Chosen. With time, as these Gifts became better understood, ways were developed to train and use them to the fullest extent of which the individual was capable. Gradually the Gifts displaced in importance whatever knowledge of "true magic" was left in Valdemar, until there was no record of how such magic had ever been learned or used.

Valdemar himself evolved the unique system of government for his land: the Monarch, advised by his Council, made the laws; the Heralds dispensed the laws and saw that they were observed. The Heralds themselves were nearly incapable of becoming corrupted or potential abusers of their temporal power. In all of the history of Valdemar, there was only one Herald who had ever succumbed to that temptation. His motive had been vengeance—he got what he wanted, but his Companion repudiated and abandoned him, and he committed suicide shortly thereafter.

The Chosen were by nature remarkably self-sacrificing—their training only reinforced this. They had to be—there was a better than even chance that a Herald would die in the line of duty. But they were human for all of that; mostly young, mostly living on the edge of danger—so, it was inevitable that outside of their duty they tended to be a bit hedonistic and anything but chaste. They seldom formed any ties beyond that of their brotherhood and the pleasures of the moment—perhaps because the bond of brotherhood was so *very* strong, and because the Herald-Companion bond left little room for any other permanent ties. For the most part, few of the common or noble folk held this against them—knowing that, no matter how wanton a Herald might be on leave, the moment he donned his snowy uniform he was another creature altogether, for a Herald in Whites was a Herald on duty, and a Herald on duty had no time for anything outside of that duty, least of all the frivolity of his own pleasures. Still, there were those who held other opinions. . . .

Laws laid down by the first King decreed that the Monarch himself must also be a Herald. This ensured that the ruler of Valdemar could never be the kind of tyrant who had caused the founders to flee their own homes.

Second in importance to the Monarch was the Herald known as the "King's (or Queen's) Own." Chosen by a special Companion—one that was always a stallion, and never seemed to age (though it was possible to kill him)—the King's Own held the special position of confidant and most trusted friend and advisor to the ruler. This guaranteed that the Monarchs of Valdemar would always have at least one person about them who could be trusted and counted on at all times. This tended to make for stable and confident rulers—and thus, a stable and dependable government.

It seemed for generations that King Valdemar had planned his government perfectly. But the best-laid plans can still be circumvented by accident or chance.

In the reign of King Sendar, the kingdom of Karse (that bordered Valdemar to the south-east) hired a nomadic nation of mercenaries to attack Valdemar. In the ensuing war, Sendar was killed, and his daughter, Selenay, assumed the throne, herself having only recently completed her Herald's training. The Queen's Own, an aged Herald called Talamir, was frequently confused and embarrassed by having to advise a young, headstrong, and attractive female. As a result, Selenay made an ill-advised marriage, one that nearly cost her both her throne and her life.

The issue of that marriage, the Heir-presumptive, was a female child Selenay called Elspeth. Elspeth came under the influence of a foreigner—the nurse Hulda, whom Selenay's husband had arranged before he died to be brought from his own land. As a result of Hulda's manipulations, Elspeth became an intractable, spoiled brat. It became obvious that if things went on as they were tending, the girl would never be Chosen, and thus, could never inherit. This would leave Selenay with three choices; marry again (with the attendant risks) and attempt to produce another, more suitable Heir, or declare someone already Chosen and with the proper bloodline to be Heir. Or, somehow, salvage the Heir-presumptive. Talamir had a plan—one that it seemed had a good chance of success.

At this point Talamir was murdered, throwing the situation into confusion again. His Companion, Rolan, Chose a new Queen's Own—but instead of picking an adult or someone already a full Herald, he Chose an adolescent girl named Talia.

Talia was of Holderkin—a puritanical Border group that did its best to discourage knowledge of outsiders. Talia had no idea what it meant to have a Herald's Companion accost her, and then (apparently) carry her off. Among her people, females held very subordinate positions, and nonconformity was punished immediately and harshly. She was ill-prepared for the new world of the Heralds and their Collegium that she had been thrust into. But the one thing she *did* have experience in was the handling and schooling of children, for she had been the teacher to her Holding's younger members from the time she was nine.

She managed to salvage the Brat—and succeeded well enough that Elspeth was Chosen herself just before Talia was sent out on her internship assignment.

During that assignment she and Kris, the Herald picked to be her mentor, discovered something frightening and potentially fatal—not only to themselves, but to anyone who happened to be around Talia. Due to the chaos just after her initial training in her Gift, she had never *been* properly trained. And her Gift was Empathy—both receptive and projective—strong enough to use as a weapon. It wasn't until it had run completely wild that she and Kris were able to retrain her so that her control became a matter of will instead of instinct.

She still had moments of misgiving about the ethics of her Gift.

She also had moments of misgiving on another subject altogether; another Herald. Dirk was Kris' best friend and partner—and Talia, after being with him only a handful of times, none intimate, was attracted to him to the point of obsession. There *was* a precedent for such preoccupation; very rarely, Heralds formed a bond with one another as deep and enduring as the Herald-Companion bond. Such a tie was referred to as a "lifebond." Kris was certain that this was what Talia was suffering from. Talia wasn't so sure.

This was just one minor complication for an internship that included battle, plague, intrigue, wildly spreading rumors about *her*, and a Gift that was a danger to herself and others.

At last the year-and-a-half was over, and she was on her way home.

Home—to an uncertain relationship, a touchy adolescent Heir, all the intrigues of the Court—and possibly, an enemy; Lord Orthallen, who just happened to be Kris' uncle.

CHAPTER 1

*W*E COULD BE *brother and sister,* Kris thought, glancing over at his fellow Herald. *Maybe twins—*

Talia sat Rolan with careless ease—an ease brought about by the fact that they'd spent most of their waking hours in the saddle during her internship up north. Kris' seat was just as casual, and for the same reason. After all this time they could easily have eaten, slept—yes, and possibly even made love a-saddle! The first two they *had* accomplished, and more than once. The third they'd never tried—but Kris had heard rumors of other Heralds who had. It did *not* sound like something he really was curious enough to attempt.

They figured on making the capital and the Collegium by early evening, so they were both wearing the cleanest and best of their uniforms. Heraldic Whites—those for field duty—were constructed of tough and durable leather, but after eighteen months they only had one set apiece that would pass muster, and they'd been saving them for today.

So we're presentable. Which isn't saying much, Kris mourned to himself, surveying the left knee of his breeches with regret. The surface of the leather was worn enough to be slightly nappy—which meant it was inclined to pick up dirt. And dirt *showed* on Whites—after riding all day they both were slightly gray. Maybe not to the casual eye, but *Kris* noticed.

Tantris curvetted a little, and Kris suddenly realized that he and Talia's Rolan were matching their paces.

:On purpose, two-footed brother,: came Tantris' sending, tinged with a hint of laughter. *:Since you two are so terribly shabby, we thought we'd take attention off you. Nobody's going to notice you when we're showing off.:*

:Thanks—I think.:

:By the way, you couldn't pass for twins; there's too much red in her hair, and she's too little. But sibs, yes. Although where you got those blue eyes—:

:Blue eyes run in my family,: Kris replied with feigned indignation. *:Both father and mother have them.:*

:Then if you were going to be sibs, your mother must have been keeping a Bard in the wardrobe for Talia to have hazel eyes and curly hair.: Tantris pranced and arched his neck, and one of his sapphirine eyes flashed a teasing look up at his Chosen.

Kris stole another glance at his internee, and concluded that Tantris was right. There *was* too much red in her hair, and it was too curly to have come out of the same batch as his own straight, blue-black locks. And she barely came up to his chin. But they both had fine-boned, vaguely heart-shaped faces—and more than that, they both *moved* the same way.

:Alberich's training. And Keren's.:

:Probably.:

:You're prettier than she is, though. The which you know.:

Kris was startled into a laugh, which made Talia glance over at him quizzically.

"Might one ask—?"

"Tantris," he replied, taking a deep breath of the verdant air, and chuckling. "He's twitting me on my vanity."

"I wish," she answered with more than a little wistfulness, "that just once I could Mindspeak Rolan like that."

"You ought to be glad you can't. You're saved a lot of back-talk."

"How far are we from home?"

"A little more than an hour." He took in the greening landscape with every sign of satisfaction, now and again taking deep breaths of the flower-laden air. "A silver for your thoughts."

"So much?" She chuckled, turning in her saddle to face him. "A copper would be more appropriate."

"Let me be the judge of that. After all, *I'm* the one who asked."

"So you did."

They rode in tree-shadowed silence for several leagues; Kris was minded to let her answer in her own time. The soft chime of bridle bells and their Companions' hooves on the hard surface of the Trade Road made a kind of music that was most soothing to listen to.

"Ethics," she said at last.

"Whoof—that's dry thinking!"

"I suppose it is—" She plainly let her thoughts turn inward again; her eyes grew vague, and he coughed to recapture her attention.

"You went elsewhere," he chided gently, when she jumped a little. "Now, you were saying—ethics. Ethics of what?"

"My Gift. Specifically, using it—"

"I thought you'd come to terms with that."

"In a situation of threat, yes. In a situation where there *was* no appropriate and just punishment under normal procedures."

"That—child-raper."

"Exactly." She shivered a little. "I thought I'd *never* feel clean again after touching his mind. But—what could I have done with him? Ordered his execution? That . . . wouldn't be *enough* of a punishment for what he did. Imprison him? Not appropriate at all. And much as I would have liked to pull him to bits slowly, Heralds don't go in for torture."

"What *did* you do to him? In detail, I mean. You didn't want to talk about it before."

"It was a—kind of twist on a mind-Healing technique; it depended on the fact that I'm a projective Empath. I can't remember what Devan called it, but you tie a specific thought to another thought or set of feelings that *you* construct. Then, every time the person thinks that thought, they also get what *you* want them to know. Like with Vostel— every time he would decide that *he* was to blame, he'd get what *I* put in there."

"Which was?"

She grinned. " 'So *next* time I won't be so stupid!' And when he'd be ready to give up from pain, he'd get, 'But it isn't as bad as yesterday, and it'll be better tomorrow.' Not words, actually; it was all feelings."

"Better, in that case, than words would have been," Kris mused, shooing a fly away absently.

"So Devan said. Well, I did something like that with—that *thing*. I took one of the worst sets of his stepdaughter's memories, and tied *that* in to all of his own feelings about women. And I kept point-of-view, so that it would appear to him as if he were the victim. You saw what happened."

Kris shuddered. "He went mad; he just collapsed, foaming at the mouth."

"No, he didn't go mad. He locked *himself* into an endless repetition of what I'd fed him. It's an appropriate punishment; he's getting exactly

what he put his stepdaughters through. It's *just*, at least I think so, because if he ever changes his attitudes he can break free of it. Of course
if he does"—she grimaced—"he *might* find himself dancing on the end
of a rope for the murder of his older stepdaughter. The law prevents the
execution of a madman; it *doesn't* save one who's regained his sanity.
Lastly, what I did should satisfy his stepdaughter, who is, after all, the
one we *really* want to come out of this thing with a whole soul."

"So where's the ethical problem?"

"That was a stress-situation, a threat-situation. But—is it ethical
to—say—read people during Council sessions and act on my information?"

"Uh—" Kris was unable to think of an answer.

"You see?"

"Let's go at it from another angle. You know how to read people's
faces and bodies—we've all been taught that. Would you hesitate to use
that knowledge in Council?"

"Well, no." She rode silently for a few moments. "I guess what
will have to be the deciding factor is not *if* I do it but *how* I use the
information."

"That sounds reasonable to me."

"Maybe too reasonable," she replied doubtfully. "It's awfully easy to
rationalize what I want to do—what I have no choice about in some
cases. It's not like thoughtsensing; I have to actively shield to keep people out. They go around shoving their feelings up my nose on a regular
basis, especially when they're wrought up."

Kris shook his head. "All I can say is, do what seems best at the time.
Really, that's all any of us do."

:Verily, oh Wise One.:

Kris ignored his Companion's taunting comment. He was going to
question her further, but broke off when he caught the sound of a horse
galloping full out, heading up the road toward them, the hoofbeats
having the peculiar ringing of a Companion.

"That—"

"Sounds like a Companion, yes. And in full gallop." He rose in his
stirrups for a better view. "Bright Lady, *now* what?"

Steed and rider came into sight as they topped the hill.

:That's Cymry—: Tantris' ears were pricked forward. *:She's slim. She
must have foaled already.:*

"It's Cymry," Kris reported.

"Which means Skif—and since I'll bet she just foaled, it isn't a
pleasure-ride that takes them out here."

The last time they'd seen the thief-turned-Herald had been a bit over nine months ago, when he'd met with them for their half-term briefing. Cymry had spent the time frolicking with Rolan, and both she and her Chosen had forgotten about the nearly-supernatural fertility of the Grove stallions. The result was foregone—much to Cymry's chagrin as well as Skif's.

Talia knew Skif better than Kris did; they'd been very close as students, close enough that they'd sworn blood-brotherhood. They had been close enough that Talia could read him better at a distance than Kris could.

She shaded her eyes with her hand, then nodded a little. "Well, it isn't a disaster; there's something serious afoot, but it isn't an emergency."

"How can you tell at this distance?"

"Firstly, there's no emotional-surge. Secondly, if it were serious, he'd be absolutely expressionless. He looks a bit worried, but that could be for Cymry."

Skif spotted them and waved wildly, as Cymry slowed her headlong pace. They hastened theirs—to the disgruntlement of the pack-mules.

"Havens! Am I ever glad to see you two!" Skif exclaimed as they came into earshot. "Cymry swore you were close, but I was half-afraid I'd have to ride a couple of hours, and I hate to make her leave the little one for that long."

"You sound like you've been waiting for us—Skif, what's the problem?" Kris asked anxiously. "What are you doing out here?"

"Nothing for you; plenty for her. Mind you, this is strictly under the ivy bush; we don't want people to know you've been warned, Talia. I slipped out on behalf of a lady in distress."

"Who? Elspeth? Selenay? What—"

"Give me a minute, will you? I'm *trying* to tell you. Elspeth asked me to intercept you on your way in. It seems the Council is trying to marry her off, and she's not overly thrilled with the notion. She wants you to know so you'll have time to muster some good arguments for the Council meeting tomorrow."

Skif reined Cymry in beside them, and they picked up the pace. "Alessandar has made a formal offer for her for Ancar. Lots of advantages there. Virtually everybody on the Council is for it except Elcarth and Kyril—and Selenay. They've been arguing it back and forth for two months, but it's been serious for about a week, and it looks as if Selenay is gradually being worn down. That's why Elspeth sent me out to watch for you; I've been slipping out for the past three days, hoping to catch you when you came in and warn you what's up. With you to back her, Selenay's got full veto—either to table the betrothal until Elspeth's finished training, or throw the notion out altogether. Elspeth didn't want any of the more excitable Councilors to know we were warning you, or they might have put more pressure on Selenay to decide before you got here."

Talia sighed. "So nothing's been decided; good. I can deal with it easily enough. Can you get on ahead of us? Let Elspeth and Selenay both know we'll be there by dinner-bell? I can't do anything now, anyway, but tomorrow we can take care of the whole mess at Council session. If Elspeth wants to see me before then—I'm all hers; she'll probably find me in my rooms."

"Your wish is my command," Skif replied. As all three knew, Skif knew more ways than one in and out of the capital and the Palace grounds. He'd make far better time than they could.

They held their pace to that of the mules as Skif sent Cymry off at a diagonal to the road, raising a cloud of dust behind him. They continued on as if they hadn't met him; but Kris traded a look of weary amusement with her. They weren't even officially "home" yet, and already the intrigues had begun.

"Anything else bothering you?"

"To put it bluntly," she said at last, "I'm nervous about coming back home—as nervy as a cat about to kitten."

"Whyfor? And why *now*? The worst is over. You're a full Herald— the last of your training's behind you. What's to be nervous about?"

Talia looked around her; at the fields, the distant hills, at anything but Kris. A warm spring breeze, loaded with flower-scent, teased her hair and blew a lock or two into her eyes so that she looked like a worried foal.

"I'm not sure I ought to discuss it with you," she said reluctantly.

"If not me, then who?"

She looked at him measuringly. "I don't know. . . ."

"No," Kris said, just a little hurt by her reluctance. "You know. You just aren't sure you can trust me. Even after all we've shared together."

She winced. "Disconcertingly accurate. I thought bluntness was *my* besetting sin."

Kris cast his eyes up to the heavens in an exaggerated plea for patience, squinting against the bright sunlight. "I am a Herald. You are a Herald. If there's one thing you should have learned by now, it's that you can *always* trust another Herald."

"Even when my suspicions conflict with ties of blood?"

He gave her another measuring look. "Such as?"

"Your uncle, Lord Orthallen."

He whistled through his teeth, and pursed his lips. "I thought you'd left that a year ago. Just because of that little run-in you had with him over Skif, you see him plotting conspiracy behind every bush! He's been very good to *me*, and to half a dozen others I could name you, and he's been invaluable to Selenay—as he was to her father."

"I have very good reasons to see him behind every bush!" she replied with some heat. "I think trying to get Skif in trouble was part of a long pattern, that it was just an attempt to isolate me—"

"Why? What could he possibly gain?" Kris was fed up and frustrated because this wasn't the first time he'd had to defend his uncle. More than one of his fellow Heralds had argued that Orthallen was far too power-hungry to be entirely trustworthy, and Kris had always felt honor-bound to defend him. He'd thought Talia had dismissed her suspicions as irrational months ago. He was highly annoyed to find that she hadn't.

"I don't know why—" Talia cried in frustration, clenching her fist on her reins. "I only know that I've never trusted him from the moment I first saw him. And now I'll be co-equal in Council with Kyril and Elcarth, with a full voice in decisions. That could put us in more direct conflict than we've ever been before."

Kris took three deep breaths and attempted to remain calm and rational. "Talia, you may not like him, but you've never had any problems in keeping your dislike out of the way of your decision-making that *I've* ever seen—and my uncle is very reasonable. . . ."

"But I can't read the man; I can't fathom his motives, and I can't imagine *why* he should feel antagonism toward me—but I *know* he does."

"I think you're overreacting," Kris replied, still keeping a tight rein on his temper. "I told you once before that it isn't *you* that's offended him—assuming that he really is offended—but because he's probably feeling like a defeated opponent. He expected to take Talamir's place as Selenay's closest advisor when Talamir was murdered."

"And cut out the role of Queen's Own?" Talia shook her head violently. "Havens, Kris; Orthallen is an intelligent man! He can't have imagined that was possible! He hasn't the Gift, for one thing. And I am *not* overreacting to him."

"Now, Talia—"

"Don't patronize me! You're the one who was telling me to trust my instincts, and now you say my instincts can't be trusted, because they're telling me something you don't want to believe?"

"Because it's childish and silly." Kris snorted.

Talia took a deep breath and closed her eyes. "Kris, I don't agree with you, but let's not fight about it."

Kris bit back what he wanted to say. At least she wasn't going to force him to stay on the defensive. "If you want."

"It—it isn't what I want. What I *want* is for you to believe and trust in my judgment. If I can't have that—well, I just don't want to fight about it."

"My uncle," he said carefully, trying to be absolutely fair to both sides, "is very fond of power. He doesn't like giving it up. That in itself is probably the reason he's been displaying antagonism toward Heralds and you in particular. Just be firm and cool and don't give an inch when you know you're in the right. He'll settle down and resign himself; as you said, he's not stupid. He knows better than to fight when he can't win. You'll never be friends, but I doubt that you need to fear him. He may be fond of power, but he has always had the best interests of the Kingdom at the forefront of his concerns."

"I wish I could feel as confident about that as you do." She sighed, then shifted in her saddle, as if trying to ease an uncomfortable position.

Kris began to make a retort, then thought better of it, and grinned. At this point a change of subject was called for. "Why don't you worry about something else—Dirk, for instance?"

"Beast." She smiled when she saw he was laughing at her.

"So I am. I'm sure he'll tell me the same. Oh, well, the best thing you can do for that little trouble is to let affairs take their natural course. Soon or late, he'll come to the point—if I have to push him myself!"

"Callous, too." She pouted mischievously at him.

"Believe it," he replied agreeably. "I'm going to enjoy teasing the life out of both of you."

Talia schooled herself to remain calm. As she had told Skif, there was nothing to be done *right now*. There were other things she wanted to find out before she took that Council seat in the morning, too—like whether the rumors that she had "misused" her Gift to manipulate others were still active. And who was keeping them active, if they were. At this point, it was a bit too late to try and find out who had originated them.

As they approached the outer city and its swirling crowds, she was made aware of just how much more sensitive her Gift of Empathy had become. The pressure of all those emotions ahead of her was so strong she found it hard to believe that Kris could be unaware of it. She wished, not for the first time, that her Gift included Mindspeech; it would have been comforting to consult with Rolan the way Kris could with Tantris. She'd forgotten what living around so many people was like—and having had her Gift go rogue on her had made her more sensitive than she had been before she left. It wasn't going to be easy to stay tightly shielded day and night, but her enhanced perception was going to demand just that. She felt a flicker of reassurance from Rolan, and smiled faintly despite her anxiety.

They made their way down the increasingly crowded road into the outer city, outside the ancient defensive walls, which had sprung up over several generations of peace. The inner city held the shops, the better inns, and the homes of the middle class and nobility. The outer was given over to the workshops, markets, rowdier hostels and taverns, and the homes of the laborers and poor.

The crowds of the outer city were noisy and cheerful. As when she had first ridden into the capital, Talia found herself assaulted on all sides by sight, scent, and sound. The myriad odors of cookshops, inns, and food vendors vied with the less savory smells of beasts and trade.

The pressure of all the varied emotions of the people around her threatened to overwhelm her for one brief moment, until she firmed up her shields. *No*, she thought with resignation, *this* is not *going to be easy.*

The road led through a riot of color and motion, and the noise was cacaphonic, confusion without mirroring some of her own confusion within.

The leather-workers kept to a section here, outside the North Gate, and both Talia and Kris were caught off guard by a puff of acrid, eye-burning fumes that escaped from a vat somewhere nearby.

"Whew!" Kris gasped, laughing at the tears in his eyes and Talia's, "Now I remember why Dirk and I usually backtracked around to the Haymarket Gate! Oh, well, too late now!"

The brief pause they made to clear their vision gave her a chance to finish making her shielding automatic. Back in their Sector—once she'd *gotten* her shields back—she'd tended to leave them down when it was only the two of them together. Shielding expended energy, and at that point she hadn't any to spare. Now she put in place the safeguards that would ensure that her shields stayed up even when she was unconscious—and felt a brief surge of gratitude to Kris for having re-taught her the *right* way to shield.

*   *   *

Kris kept a careful eye on her as they made their way through the crowds. If she were going to break, *now* would be the time, under the pressure of all these emotions.

:I wasn't worried.:

:You weren't, hm? Maybe I should ask her to favor you with one of those emotional backlashes.:

:No, thank you, I had one. Remember? Rolan nearly brained me.: Tantris' sending took on a serious coloration. *:You know, you really shouldn't tease her about Dirk. Lifebonds aren't easy to bear when the pair hasn't acknowledged it.:*

Kris looked at his Companion's back-tilted ears in astonishment. *:You're sure? I mean, she certainly shows every symptom of lifebonding, but—:*

:We're sure.:

:Do you by any chance know when—?: he asked his Companion.

:Dirk was the first Herald she ever saw; Rolan thinks it might have been then.:

:That early? Lord and Lady, that would be one powerful bond. . . .: Kris continued to watch her with a little bemusement as the thought trailed away.

Tradesmen and their patrons screamed cheerfully at one another over the din of vehicles, squalling children, and bawling animals. Yet for all that the populace seemed to ignore the presence of the two Heralds passing through their midst, a path always seemed to clear itself before them, and someone beckoned them on by a smile or a wave of a hat. The Guard at the outer gate saluted them as they passed through; the Guardfolk were no strangers to the comings and goings of Heralds. They rode through the tunnel that passed under the thick, gray-granite walls of the old city, and the din lessened for just a moment. Then they emerged into the narrower ways of the capital itself. It lacked only an hour until the evening meal and the streets were as crowded with people as Kris had ever seen them. It was not quite as noisy here in the old city, but the streets were just as full. After months of small towns and villages, Kris found himself marveling anew at the crush of people, and the closely-built, multi-storied stone houses. For many months, the chime of bells on their Companions' bridles had been the loudest sound they heard; now that sound was completely engulfed in the babble around them.

The streets had been designed in a spiral; no one could move straight to the Palace grounds—as in most older cities that had been built with an eye to defense. Kris led them on a course that wound ever inward. The din died away behind them as they left the streets of shops behind and entered the inner, residential core. The modest houses of the merchant class gradually gave way to the more impressive buildings owned by the wealthy or noble, each set apart from the street by a private wall enclosing the manse and a bit of garden. Eventually they made their way to the inner beige-brick wall surrounding the Palace and the three Collegia—Bardic, Healer's, and Herald's. The silver-and-blue-clad Palace Guard stationed at the gate halted them for a moment, while she checked them off against a list of those expected to be arriving. Careful records were kept on when a Herald should come in from the field—in the case of those arriving from distant Sectors, this calculation was accurate within a stretch of two or three days; in the case of those arriving from nearby Sectors, expected arrival time was accurate to within hours. This list was posted with the Gate Guard—so when a Herald was overdue, *someone* knew it, and something could be done to find out why, quickly.

"Herald Dirk in yet?" Kris asked the swarthy Guardswoman casually when she'd finished.

"Just arrived two days ago, Herald," she replied, consulting the roster. "Guard then notes he asked about you two."

"Thank you, Guard. Pleasant watch to you." Kris grinned, urging Tantris through the gate she held open, with Rolan following closely behind.

Kris continued to watch Talia carefully, feeling a surge of gratified pride as he noted her behavior. The past few months had been living hell for her. Control of her Gift had been based entirely on instinct, rather than on proper training—and no one had ever realized this. The rumors that she had used it to manipulate—worse, that she had done so unconsciously—had pushed her off-balance. His own doubts about the truth of those rumors had been easy for her to pick up. And for someone whose Gift was based on emotions, and who was frequently prey to self-doubt, the effect was bound to be catastrophic.

It was at least that. She'd lost all control over her Gift—which unfortunately remained at full strength. She'd lost the ability to shield, and projected wildly. She'd very nearly killed them both on more than one occasion.

We were just lucky that during the worst of it, we were snowed in at that Waystation. It was just the two of us, and we were isolated long enough for her to get back in charge of herself.

And then she'd met the rumors again—this time circulating among the common folk. More than once they'd regarded her with fear and suspicion, yet she had never faltered in the performance of her duties or given any indication to an outsider that she was anything except calm, thoughtful, and controlled. She'd given a months' long series of performances a trained player couldn't equal.

It was vital that a Herald maintain emotional stability under all circumstances. This was especially true of the Queen's Own, who dealt with volatile nobles and the intrigues of the Court on a daily basis. She'd lost that stability, but after working through her trial had managed to get it back, and more.

He managed to catch her eyes, and gave her an encouraging wink; she dropped her solemn face for a moment to wrinkle her nose at him.

They passed the end of the Guard barracks and neared the black iron fence that separated the "public" grounds of the Palace from the "private" grounds and those of the three Collegia. Another Guard stood at the Gate here, but his position was mainly to intercept the newly-Chosen; he waved them on with a grin. From here the granite core of the Palace with its three great brick wings and the separate buildings of the Healer's and Bardic Collegia was at last clearly visible. Kris sighed happily. No matter where a Herald came from—*this* place, and the people in it, were his real home.

Talia felt a surge of warmth and contentment at the sight of the Collegium and the Palace—a feeling of true homecoming.

Just as they passed this last gate, she heard a joyful shout, and Dirk and Ahrodie pounded up the brick-paved pathway at a gallop to meet them. Dirk's straw-blond hair was flying every which way, like a particularly windblown bird's nest. Kris vaulted off Tantris' back as Dirk hurled himself from Ahrodie's; they met in a back-pounding, laughing, bear hug.

Talia remained in the saddle; at the sight of Dirk her heart had contracted painfully, and now it was pounding so hard she felt that it must be clearly audible. Her anxieties concerning Elspeth and the intrigues of the Court receded into the back of her mind.

She was tightly shielded; afraid to let anything leak through.

Dirk's attention was primarily on her and not on his friend and partner.

Dirk had been watching for them all day—telling himself that it was Kris whose company he had missed. He'd felt like a tight bowstring, without being willing to identify why he'd been so tense. His reaction on finally seeing them had been totally unplanned, giving him release for his pent-up emotion in the exuberant greeting to Kris. Though he seemed to ignore her, he was almost painfully aware of Talia's presence. She sat so quietly on her own Companion that she might have been a statue, yet he practically counted every breath she took.

He knew that he would remember how she looked right now down to the smallest hair. Every nerve seemed to tingle, and he felt almost as if he were wearing his skin inside out.

When Dirk finally let go of his shoulders, Kris said, with a grin that was bordering on malicious, "You haven't welcomed Talia, brother. She's going to think you don't remember her."

"Not remember her? Hardly!" Dirk seemed to be having a little trouble breathing. Kris hid another grin.

Talia and Rolan were less than two paces away, and Dirk freed an arm to take Talia's nearer hand in his own.

Kris thought he'd never seen a human face look so exactly like a stunned ox's.

Talia met the incredible blue of Dirk's eyes with a shock. It felt very much as if she'd been struck by lightning. She came near to trembling when their hands touched, but managed to hold to her self-control by a thin thread and smiled at him with lips that felt oddly stiff.

"Welcome home, Talia." That was all he said—which was just as well. The sound of his voice and the feeling of his eyes on her made her long to fling herself at him. She found herself staring at him, unable to respond.

She looked a great deal different than he remembered; leaner, as if she'd been fine-tempered and fine-honed. She was more controlled—certainly more mature. Was there a sadness about her that hadn't been there before? Was it some pain that had thinned her face?

When he'd taken her hand, it had seemed as if something—he wasn't sure what—had passed between them; but if she'd felt it, too, she gave no sign.

When she'd smiled at him, and her eyes had warmed with that smile, he'd thought his heart was going to stop. The dreams he'd had of her all these months, the obsession—he'd figured they'd pop like soap bubbles when confronted with the reality. He'd been wrong. The reality only strengthened the obsession. He held her hand that trembled very slightly in his own, and longed with all his heart for Kris' silver tongue.

They stood frozen in that position for so long that Kris thought with concealed glee that they were likely to remain there forever unless he broke their concentration.

"Come on, partner." He slapped Dirk's back heartily and remounted Tantris.

Dirk jumped in startlement as if someone had blown a trumpet in his ear, then grinned sheepishly.

"If we don't get moving, we're going to miss supper—and I can't tell you how many times I dreamed of one of Mero's meals on the road!"

"Is that all you missed? Food? I might have known. Poor abused brother, did Talia make you eat your own cooking?"

"Worse," Kris said, grinning at her. "She made me eat *hers!*" He winked at her and punched Dirk's arm lightly.

When Kris broke the trance he was in, Dirk dropped Talia's hand as if it had burned him. When Talia turned a gaze full of gratitude on Kris, presumably for the interruption, Dirk felt a surge of something unpleasantly like jealousy at the thanks in her eyes. When Kris included her in the banter, Dirk wished that it had been *his* idea, not Kris'.

"Beast," she told Kris, making a face at him.

"Hungry beast."

"He's right though, much as I hate to agree with him," she said softly, turning to Dirk, and he suppressed a shiver—her voice had improved and deepened; it played little arpeggios on his backbone. "If we don't hurry, you *will* be too late. It doesn't matter too much to me—I'm used to sneaking bread and cheese from Mero—but it's very unkind to keep *you* standing here. Will you ride up with us?"

He laughed to cover the hesitation in his voice. "You'd have to tie me up to keep me from coming with you."

He and Kris remounted with a creak of leather, and they rode with Talia between them; that gave Dirk all the excuse he needed to rest his eyes on her. She gazed straight ahead or at Rolan's ears except when she was answering one or the other of them. Dirk wasn't sure whether he should be piqued or pleased. She wasn't favoring either of them with a jot more attention than the other, but he began to wish very strongly that she'd look at him a little more frequently than she was.

A dreadful fear was starting to creep into his heart. She had spent the past year and a half largely in Kris' company. What if—

He began scrutinizing Kris' conduct, since Talia's was giving him no clues. It seemed to confirm his fears. Kris was more at ease with Talia than he'd ever been with any other woman; they laughed and traded jokes as if their friendship had grown through years rather than months.

It was worse when they reached the Field and the tackshed, and Kris offered her an assist down with mock gallantry. She accepted the hand with a teasing hauteur, and dismounted with one fluid motion. Had Kris' hand lingered in hers a moment or two longer than had been really necessary? Dirk couldn't be sure. Their behavior wasn't really loverlike, but it was the closest he'd ever seen Kris come to it.

They unsaddled their Companions and stowed the tack safely away in the proper places after a cursory cleaning. Dirk's was pretty much clean; but Talia's and Kris' needed more work than could be taken care of in an hour—after being in the field for so long, it would all have to have an expert's touch. Dirk kept Talia in the corner of his eye while she worked, humming under her breath. Kris kept up his chatter, and Dirk made distracted, monosyllabic replies. He wished he could get her alone for just a few minutes.

He had no further chance for observation. Keren, Sherrill, and Jeri appeared like magicians out of the thinnest air, converged on her, and carried her off to her rooms, baggage and all, leaving him alone with Kris.

"Look, I don't know about you, but I am starved," Kris said, as Dirk stared mournfully after the foursome, Talia carrying her harp "My Lady" and the rest sharing her packs. "Let's get the four-feets turned loose and get that dinner."

"Well?" Keren asked, her rough voice full of arch significance, when the three women had gotten Talia and her belongings safely into the privacy of her room.

"Well, what?" Talia replied, glancing at the graying Riding Instructor from under demure lashes while she unpacked in her bedroom.

"What? *What!* Oh, come *on,* Talia"—Sherrill laughed—"you know exactly what we mean! How did it go? Your letters weren't exactly very long *or* very informative."

Talia suppressed a smile, and turned her innocent gaze on Keren's lifemate. "Personal or professional?"

Jeri fingered the hilt of her belt-knife significantly. "Talia," she warned, "if you don't stop trying our patience, Rolan just *may* have to find a new Queen's Own tonight."

"Oh, well, if you're going to be *that* way about it—" Talia backed away, laughing, as Sherrill, hazel eyes narrowed in mock ferocity, curled her long fingers into claws and lunged at her. She dodged aside at the last moment, and the tall brunette landed on her bed instead. "—all right, I yield, I yield! What do you want to know first?"

Sherrill rolled to her feet, laughing. "What do you think? Skif hinted that you and Kris were getting cozy, but he wouldn't do more than hint."

"Quite cozy, yes, but nothing much more. Yes, we were sharing blankets, and no, there isn't anything more between us than a very comfortable friendship."

"Pity," Jeri replied merrily, throwing herself onto Talia's couch in the outer room, then twining a lock of her chestnut hair around one finger. "We were hoping for a passionate romance."

"Sorry to disappoint you," she replied, not sounding sorry at all. "Though if you're thinking of trying in that direction—"

"Hm?" Jeri did her best not to look *too* eager, but didn't succeed very well.

"Well, once he's managed to shake Nessa loose—"

"Ha!"

"Don't laugh, we think we know a way. Well, once she's no longer hot on the hunt, he's going to be *quite* unpartnered, and he's just as— um—pleasant a companion as Varianis claims. Jeri, don't lick your whiskers so damned obviously, he's not a bowl of cream!"

Jeri looked chagrined and blushed as scarlet as the couch cushions, as Sherrill and Keren chuckled at her discomfiture. "I wasn't that bad, was I?"

"You most certainly were. Keep your predatory thoughts to yourself if you don't want to frighten him off the way Nessa has," Keren admonished with a wry grin. "As for you, little centaur, he seems to have cured your man-shyness rather handily. I guess I owe Kyril and Elcarth an apology. I thought assigning him to you was insanity. Well, now that our prurience has been satisfied, how did the work go?"

"It's a very long story, and before I go into it, have you three eaten?"

Three affirmatives caused her to nod. "Well *I* haven't yet. You have a choice; you can either wait until I'm done with dinner for the rest of the gossip—"

They groaned in mock-anguish.

"Or you can check me in and bring me something from the kitchen. If Selenay or Elspeth need me, they'll send a page for me."

"I'll check her in." Jeri shot out the door and down the spiral staircase.

"I'll go fetch you a young feast. You look like you've lost *pounds*, and when Mero finds out it's for you, he'll probably ransack the entire pantry." Sherrill vanished after Jeri.

Keren stood away from the wall she'd been leaning against. "Give me a proper greeting, you maddening child." She smiled, holding out her arms.

"Oh, Keren—" Talia embraced the woman who had been friend,

surrogate-mother, and sister to her—and more—with heartfelt fervor. "Gods, how I've missed you!"

"And I, you. You've changed, and for the better." Keren held her closely, then put her at arm's length, surveying her with intense scrutiny. "It isn't often I get to see my hopes fulfilled with such exactitude."

"Don't be so silly." Talia blushed. "You're seeing what isn't there."

"Oh, I think not." Keren smiled. "The gods know *you* are the world's worst judge when it comes to evaluating yourself. Dearling, you've become all I hoped you'd be. But—you didn't have the easy time we thought you would, did you?"

"I—no, I didn't." Talia sighed. "I—Keren, my Gift went rogue on me. At full power."

"Great good gods!" She examined Talia even more carefully, gray eyes boring into Talia's. "How the hell did that happen? I thought we'd trained—"

"So did everyone."

"Wait a moment; let me put this together for myself. You finished Ylsa's class; now let me remember . . ." Keren's brow creased in thought. "It *does* seem to me that she mentioned something about wanting to send you to the Healers for some special training, that she didn't feel altogether happy about handling an Empath when her own expertise was Thought-sensing."

Keren turned away from Talia and began pacing, a habit the younger woman was long familiar with, for Keren claimed she couldn't think unless she was moving.

"Now—*I'd* assumed she'd taken care of that because you spent so much time with the Healers. But she hadn't, had she? And then she was murdered—"

"As far as Kris and I could figure, the Heralds assumed that the Healers were giving me Empath training, and the *Healers* assumed the *Heralds* had already done so because I *seemed* to be in full control. But I wasn't; it was all instinct and guess. And when control went—"

"Gods!" Keren stopped pacing and put both of her hands on Talia's shoulders. "Little one, are you *sure* you're all right now?"

Talia remembered only too vividly the hours of practice Kris had put her through; the painful sessions with the two Companions literally attacking her mentally. "I'm sure. Kris is a Gift-teacher, after all. He took me all the way through the basics, and Rolan and Tantris helped."

"Oh, really? Well, well—*that's* an interesting twist!" Keren raised an eloquent eyebrow. "Companions don't intervene that directly as a rule."

"I don't think they saw any other choice. The first month we were all snowed in at that Waystation—then we found out that those damned rumors had made it up to our Sector and we didn't *dare* look for outside help. It would have just confirmed the rumors."

"True—true. If I were on the Circle, I think I would be inclined to keep all this under the ivy bush. Letting the world know that we blundered that badly with you won't do a smidgen of good, and would probably do a *lot* of harm. Selected people, yes; and this should *certainly* go down in the annals so that we don't repeat the mistake with the next Empath—but—no, I don't think this should be generally known."

"That was basically Kris' thinking, and I agree. You're the first person to know besides the two of us. We'll both be telling Kyril and Elcarth, and I think that's all."

"Ye-es," Keren said slowly. "Yes. Let *those* two worry about who else should know. Well, what ends well *is* well, as they say."

"I *am* fine," Talia repeated emphatically. "I have absolute control now, control not even Rolan can shake. In a way, I'm glad it happened; I learned a lot—and it's made me think about things I never did before."

"Right, then. Now, let's take these rags of yours down to the laundry chute—yes, all of them; not even one outfit for tomorrow. After being in the field, they'll all need refurbishing. Here—" She dug into Talia's wooden wardrobe, and emerged with a soft, comfortable lounging robe. "Put that on. You won't be going anywhere tonight, and in the morning Gaytha will have left a pile of new ones at your doorstep—though from the look of you, they'll be a bit loose, since she'll have had them made up from the old measurements. We've all got a lot of news to catch up on. Oh, and I've got a message from Elspeth; 'Thank the Lady, and I'll see you in the morning.'"

"Well, my old and rare, we have got a *lot* of news to catch up on."

Dirk nodded, his mind so fully occupied with things other than his dinner that he never noticed that he was munching his way through a heap of ustil greens, a vegetable he despised with passion.

Kris noticed, and had a difficult time in keeping a straight face. Fortunately the usual chaos of the Collegium common room at dinner gave him plenty of opportunity to look in other directions when the urge to break into a howl of laughter became too great. It was the height of the dinner hour, and every wooden bench was full of students in Grays and instructors in full Heraldic Whites, all shouting amiably at one another over the din.

"So, how did *your* stint go? We greatly appreciated that music, by the way, both of us. We've got a goodly portion of it memorized by now."

"Sh—you did? You do? That's—" Dirk suddenly realized he was beginning to babble, and ended lamely, "—that's very nice. I'm glad you liked it."

"Oh, yes; Talia especially. I think she values your present more than anything anyone else sent her. She certainly has been taking very good care of it—but that's like her. I'm giving her highest marks; she is one *damn* fine Herald."

Now Dirk took advantage of the noise and clatter at the tables all about them to cover his own confusion. "Well," he replied, when he finally managed to clear his head a bit of the daze he seemed to be in, "it sounds like you had a more entertaining trainee than I did. And a more interesting round. Mine was so dull and normal Ahrodie and I sleepwalked through most of it."

"Lord of Lights—I wish I could claim that! Don't forget, 'May your life be interesting' happens to be a very potent curse! Besides, I seem to remember you claiming that young Skif had you worn to a frazzle before the circuit was over."

"I guess I did," Dirk chuckled. "Did you know his Cymry dropped a foal, and he blames it all on you two?"

"No doubt, since neither of them have an ounce of shame to spare between them." Kris ducked as a student burdened with a stack of dirty dishes taller than he was inched past them. "Lord, I hope that youngling's got one of the Fetching Gifts, or he's going to lose that whole stack in a minute—yes, Skif and Cymry deserve what they got. Poor Talia would have been ready to skin both of them given the chance. . . ."

"Oh?"

Kris was more and more pleased by Dirk's reactions. He needed no further urging, and related the tale with relish, stopping short of the fight—which had been *caused*, in an obscure sort of way, by Dirk—and the swimming match that followed. He insisted then that they ought to take themselves out of the way of those students assigned to clearing tables.

"Fine; my room or yours?" Dirk was doing his damnedest to keep his feelings from showing. Unfortunately, Kris knew him too well;

that deadpan dicing face he was putting on only proved he was considerably on edge.

"Good gods, not yours—we'd be lost in there for a week! Mine; and I still have some of that Ehrris-wine, I think. . . ."

The tales continued over the wine and a small fire, both of them lounging at full length in Kris' old, worn green chairs. And every other sentence Kris spoke seemed to have something to do with Talia. Dirk tried his best to seem interested, but not as obsessed as he actually was. Kris let the shadows hide his faint smile, for he wasn't fooled a bit.

But not once did Kris let fall the information Dirk *really* wanted to know—and finally, emboldened by the wine, he came out and asked for it.

"Look, Kris—you're the soul of chivalry, but we're blood-brothers, you can tell me safely! Were you, or weren't you?"

"Were we what?" Kris asked innocently.

"S-sleeping together, you nit!"

"Yes," Kris answered forthrightly. "What did you expect? We're neither one of us made of ice." He figured that it was far better for Dirk to hear the truth—and to hear it in such a way that he took it for the matter-of-fact thing that it was. Talia and Dirk were probably tied neck-and-neck for the position of his "best friend." And that was *all* he and Talia meant to each other. He could no more conceive of being in love with her than with the close friend he now faced. He watched Dirk covertly, weighing his reaction.

"I—I suppose it was sort of inevitable—"

"Inevitable—something more. Frankly, during that first winter it was too blamed *cold* to sleep alone." He launched into the whole tale of their blizzard-ordeal—with editing. He didn't dare reveal how Talia's Gift had gotten out of control. Firstly, it wasn't anything Dirk needed to know about. Secondly, he was fairly certain it was something that should be known by as few as possible. Elcarth and Kyril, certainly—but he was pretty well certain it just wouldn't be ethical to go around telling anyone else without Talia's express permission.

He concluded the tale with a certain puzzlement; Dirk seemed to have suddenly gone dumb, and very soon pled exhaustion and left for his own room.

Oh, Lord. Of all the damned situations to be in—his very best friend in the entire world with his hooks quite firmly in the first woman Dirk had even wanted to *look* at in years.

It wasn't fair. It wasn't any damned fair. No woman in her right mind was even going to want to look at him with Kris around. And Kris—

Kris—was *he* in love with Talia? And if he were . . .

Gods, gods, they certainly belonged together.

No, dammit! Kris could have any female he wanted, Herald or no, without even lifting a finger! By all the gods, Dirk was going to fight him for this one!

Except that he hadn't the faintest idea how to go about fighting for her. And—Kris was like a brother, more than a brother. This wasn't any kind of fair to him—

He lay sleepless for hours that night, staring into the darkness, tossing and turning restlessly, and cursing the nightjar that was apparently singing right outside his window. By dawn he was no closer to sorting out his own feelings than he had been when he threw himself down to rest.

CHAPTER 2

"TALIA!"

Elspeth greeted Talia's appearance at breakfast with a squeal, and a hug that threatened to squeeze the last bit of breath out of her. The last year and a half had added inches to the young Heir's height; she stood a bit taller than Talia now. Time had added a woman's curves to the wraithlike child as well. Talia wondered, now that she'd seen Elspeth, if her mother truly realized how much growing she'd done in the time Talia had been gone.

The wood-paneled common room was full of youngsters in student Grays, as most of the instructors had eaten earlier. The bench-and-table-filled room buzzed with sleepy murmuring, and smelled of bacon and porridge. Except for the fact that she recognized few of the faces, and the fact that the room was completely full, it all looked the same as it had when Talia was a student; she slid into the warm, friendly atmosphere like a blade into a well-oiled sheath, and felt as if she had never left.

"Bright Lady, catling, you're going to break all my ribs!" Talia protested, returning the hug with interest. "I got your message from Keren—I take it Skif *did* tell you I got in last night, didn't he? I rather expected to find you on my doorstep."

"I had foal-watch last night." One of the duties imposed on the students was to camp in Companion's Field around the time of a foaling, each taking the watch in turn. Companions did not foal with the ease of horses, and if there were complications, seconds could be precious in preserving the life or health of mare and foal. "Skif told me you were here, and that he'd given you my screech for help—so I knew I didn't need to worry anymore, and I certainly didn't need to disturb *your* sleep."

"I heard Cymry dropped. Who else?"

"Zaleka." Elspeth grinned at Talia's bewildered look of nonrecognition. "She Chose Arven just after you left. He's twenty if he's a day, and when Jillian was here during break between assignments—well, you know Jillian, she's as bad as Destria. Seems her Companion was like-minded. We haven't half been giving Arven a hard time over it! Zaleka hasn't dropped yet, but she's due any day."

Talia shook her head, and slipped an arm around the Heir's shoulders. "You younglings! I don't know what the world's coming to these days—"

Elspeth gave a very unladylike snort, narrowed her enormous brown eyes, and tossed her dark hair scornfully. "You don't cozen me! I've heard tales about you and *your* year-mates that gave me gray hairs! Climbing in and out of windows at the dead of night with not-so-ex-thieves! Spying on the Royal Nursemaid!"

"Catling—" Talia went cold sober. "Elspeth—I'm sorry about Hulda." She met Elspeth's scrutiny squarely.

Elspeth grimaced bitterly at the name of the nursemaid who had very nearly managed to turn her into a spoiled, unmanageable monster—and came close to eliminating any chance of her being Chosen.

"Why? You caught her red-handed in conspiracy to keep *me* from ever getting to be Heir," she replied with a mixture of amusement and resentment—the amusement at Talia's reaction, the resentment reserved for Hulda. "Sit, sit, sit! I'm hungry, and I refuse to have to crane my neck up to talk to you."

"You—you aren't angry at me?" Talia asked, taking a seat beside Elspeth on the worn wooden bench. "I wanted to tell you I was responsible for her being dismissed, but, frankly, I never had the courage."

Elspeth smiled a little. "You didn't have the courage? Thank the Lady for that! I was afraid you were perfect!"

"Hardly," Talia replied dryly.

"Well, why not tell me your end of it now? I just got it secondhand from Mother and Kyril."

"Oh, Lord—where do I begin?"

"Mm—chronologically, as you found it out." Elspeth seized a mug of fruit juice from a server and plumped it down in front of her seat-mate.

"Right. It really started for me when I tried to get to know you. Hulda kept blocking me."

"How?"

"Carrying you off for lessons, saying you were asleep, or studying, or whatever other excuse she could come up with. Catling, I was only about fourteen, and a fairly unaggressive fourteen at that; *I* wasn't about to challenge her! But it just happened too consistently not to be on purpose. So I enlisted Skif."

Elspeth nodded. "Good choice. If there was anybody likely to find out anything, it would be Skif. I know for a fact he still keeps his hand in—"

"Oh? How?"

Elspeth giggled. "Whenever he's in residence he leaves me sweets hidden in the 'secret' drawer of the desk in my room. With notes."

"Oh, Lord—you haven't told anybody, have you?"

Elspeth was indignant. "And give him away? Not a chance! Oh, I've told Mother in case he ever gets caught—which isn't likely—but I swore her to secrecy first."

Talia sighed in relief. "Thanks be to the Lady. If anybody other than Heralds found out . . ."

Elspeth sobered. "I know. At worst he could be killed before a Guard knew he was a Herald and it was a prank. Believe me, I know. Mother was rather amused—and rather glad, I think. It can't hurt to have somebody with skills like *that* in the Heralds. Anyway, you re-cruited Skif . . ."

"Right; he began sneaking around, and discovered that Hulda, rather than being the subordinate as everyone thought, had taken over control of the nursery and your education. She was drugging old Melidy, who was *supposed* to be your primary nurse. Well, that seemed wrong to me, but it wasn't anything I could prove because Melidy *had* been ill—she'd had a brainstorm. So I had Skif keep watching. That was when he discovered that Hulda was in the pay of someone un-known—paid to ensure that you could never be Chosen, and thus, never become Heir."

"Bitch." Elspeth's eyes were bright with anger. "I take it neither you nor he ever saw who it was?"

Talia shook her head regretfully, and took a sip of fruit juice. "Never.

He was always masked, cloaked, and hooded. We told Jadus, Jadus told the Queen—and Hulda vanished."

"And I only knew that I'd lost the one person at Court I was emotionally dependent on. I'm not surprised you kept quiet." Elspeth passed Talia a clean plate. "Oh, I might have gotten angry if you'd told me two or three years ago, but not now."

There was a great deal of cold, undisguised anger in the Heir's young brown eyes. "I still remember most of that time quite vividly."

Talia lost the last of her apprehension over the indignation in Elspeth's voice.

"There's more to it than just my being resentful, though," Elspeth continued. "Looking back at it, Talia, I think that woman who called herself my 'nurse' would quite cheerfully have strangled me with her own hands if she thought she could have profited and gotten away with it! Yes, and enjoyed every minute of it!"

"Oh, come now—you weren't that much of a little monster!"

"Here, you'd better start eating or Mero'll throw fits at us when we get downstairs to clean; he's fixed all your favorites." Elspeth took some of the platters being passed from hand to hand, and heaped Talia's plate with crisp oatcakes and honey, warm bacon, and stir-fried squash, totally oblivious to the incongruity of the Heir to the Throne serving one who was technically an underling. She had indeed come a long way from the Royal Brat who had been so very touchy about her rank. "Talia, I lived with Hulda most of my waking hours. I *know* for a fact she enjoyed frightening me. The bedtime stories she told me would curl the hair of an adult, and I'd bet my life that she got positive pleasure out of my shivers. And I can't tell you why I feel this way, but I'm certain she was the most coldly self-centered creature I've ever met; that nothing mattered to her except her own well-being. She was very good at covering the fact, but—"

"I don't think I doubt you, catling. One of your Gifts is Mindspeech, after all, and little children sometimes see things we adults miss."

"You *adults*? You weren't all *that* much older than me! You saw a fair amount yourself, and you'd have seen more if you'd been able to spend more time with me. She was turning me into a little copy of herself, when she wasn't trying to scare me. Once she'd cut me off from everyone else so that there was no one to turn to as a friend, she kept schooling me in how I shouldn't trust anyone but her—and how I should fight for every scrap of royal privilege, stopping for no one and nothing on the way. There's more, something that turned up after you left. When they told me the truth, I got very curious."

"Which is why I call you 'catling' "—Talia interrupted with a grin— "since you're fully as curious as any cat."

"Too true. Curiosity sometimes pays, though; I started going through the things she left, and doing a bit of discreet correspondence with my paternal relatives."

"Does your mother know this?" Talia was a bit surprised.

"It's with her blessing. By the way, I get the feeling that Uncle-King Faramentha likes me as much as he disliked my father. We've gotten into quite a cozy little exchange of letters and family anecdotes. I like him, too—and it's rather too bad we're so closely related; he's got a whole tribe of sons, and I think anybody with a sense of humor like his would be rather nice to get to know. . . ." Elspeth's voice trailed off wistfully, then she got back to the subject at hand with a little shake of her head. "Anyway, *now* we're not altogether certain that the Hulda who left Rethwellan is the same Hulda who arrived here."

"What?"

"Oh, it's so much *fun* to shock you. You look like somebody just hit you in the face with a board!"

"Elspeth, I may kill you myself if you don't get to the point!"

"All right, I'll be good! It's rather late in the day to be checking on these things now, but there was a span of about a month after Hulda left the Royal Nursery in Rethwellan to come here where she just seems to have vanished. She wasn't passed across the Border, and no one remembers her in the inns along the way. Then—poof!—she's here, bag and baggage. Father wasn't among the living anymore through his own stupid fault, and she had all the right papers and letters; nobody thought to doubt that she *was* the 'Hulda' he'd sent for. Until now, that is."

"Bright Lady!" Talia grew as cold as her breakfast, thinking about the multitude of possibilities this opened up. Had the unknown "my lord" she and Skif had seen her conspiring with brought her here? They had no way of knowing if that one had been among those traitors uncovered and executed after Ylsa's murder, for neither of them had ever seen his face. They thought he had been, for there were no other stirrings of trouble after that, but he *might* only have gone to ground for an interval. Had even "my lord" guessed that she was not what she seemed? And where had she vanished to after she was unmasked? No one had seen her leave; she had not passed the Border, at least by the roads (and that was an echo of what Elspeth had just detailed), yet she was most assuredly gone before anyone had a chance to detain her.

And who—or what—had given her warning that she had been uncovered? A danger that Talia had long thought safely laid to rest had suddenly resurrected itself, the cockatrice new-hatched from the dunghill.

"Mero is going to have my hide," Elspeth warned, and Talia started guiltily and finished her meal. But she really couldn't have told what she was eating.

"—and that was the last incident," Kris finished. "The last couple of weeks were nothing but routine; we finished up, Griffon relieved us, and we headed home."

He met the measuring gazes of first Elcarth, then Kyril. Both of them were shocked cold sober by his revelation of the way Talia's Gift had gone rogue—and *why*. They had evidently assumed this interview was going to be a mere formality. Kris' tale had come as an unpleasant surprise.

"Why," Kyril asked, after a pause that was much too long for Kris' comfort, "didn't you look for help when this first happened?"

"Largely because by the time I knew something was really wrong, we were snowed into that Waystation, Senior."

"He's got you there, brother." Elcarth favored the silver-haired Seneschal's Herald with a wry smile.

"By the time we got out, she was well on the way to having her problems solved," Kris continued doggedly. "She had the basics, had them down firmly. And once we got in with people again, we found that those rumors had preceded us. At *that* point, I reckoned we'd do irreparable harm by leaving the circuit to look for other help. We'd only have confirmed the rumor that there was something wrong by doing so."

"Hm. A point," Kyril acknowledged.

"And at that point, I wasn't entirely certain that there *was* anyone capable of training her."

"Healers—" Elcarth began.

"Don't have Empathy *alone*, nor do they use it exactly the way she does—the way she *must*. She's actually used it offensively, as I told you. They rarely invoke the use of it outside of Healing sessions; she is going to have to use it so constantly it will be as much a part of her as her eyes and ears. At least," Kris concluded with an embarrassed smile, "that's the way I had it figured."

"I think that in this case you were right, young brother," Kyril replied after long thought, during which time Kris had plenty of leisure to think about all he'd said, and wonder if he'd managed to convince these two, the most senior Heralds in the Circle.

Kris let out a breath he didn't even realize he'd been holding.

"There was this, too," he added. "At that point, letting out word that we, and the Collegium, had failed to properly train the new Queen's Own would have been devastating to *everyone's* morale."

"Bright Goddess—you're right!" Elcarth exclaimed with consternation, his eyebrows rising to meet his gray cap of hair. "For that to become well known would be as damaging to the faith of Heralds as it would to that of nonHeralds. I think, given the circumstances, you *both* deserve high marks. You, for your good sense and discretion, and your internee for meeting and overcoming trials she should never have had to face."

"I agree," Kyril seconded. "Now, if you'll excuse us, Elcarth and I will endeavor to set such safeguards as to ensure this never happens again."

With a polite farewell, Kris thankfully fled their presence.

In the hour after breakfast, Talia covered a great deal of ground. She first left the Herald's Collegium and crossed to the separate building that housed Healer's Collegium and the House of Healing. The sun was up by now, though it hadn't been when she'd gone to breakfast, and from the cloudless blue of the sky it looked as if it was going to be another flawless spring day. Once within the beige brick walls, she sought out Healer Devan, to let him know of her return, and to learn from him if there were any Herald-patients in the House of Healing that needed her own special touch.

She found him in the still-room, carefully mixing some sort of decoction. She entered very quietly, not wanting to break his concentration, but somehow he knew she was there anyway.

"Word spreads quickly; I knew you'd gotten back last night," he said without turning around. "And most welcome you are, too, Talia!"

She chuckled a little. "I should know better than to try and sneak up on someone with the same Gift I have!"

He set his potion down on the table before him, stoppered it with care, and turned to face her. As a smile reached and warmed his hazel eyes, he held out brown-stained hands in greeting.

"Your aura, child, is unmistakable—and right glad I am to feel it again."

She took both his hands in her own, wrinkling her nose a little at the pungent odors of the still-room. "I hope you're glad to see me for my own sake, and not because you need me desperately," she replied.

Much to her relief, he assured her that there were *no* Heralds at all among his patients at the moment.

"Just wait until the Midsummer storms South, or the pirate-raids West, though!" he told her, his dark eyes rueful. "Rynee will have her Greens by winter; she's got every intention of going back South to be stationed near her home. You're back in good time; you'll be the only trained mind-Healer besides Patris here when she leaves, and it's possible we may need you for patients other than Heralds."

Next she returned to the Herald's Wing for an interview she had not been looking forward to.

She knocked hesitantly on the door to Elcarth's office; and found that not only was Elcarth there, but that the Seneschal's Herald was with the Dean.

During the next hour she reported, as dispassionately as she could, all that had happened during her internship. She did not spare herself in the least, admitting fully that she had concealed the fact that she was losing control over her Gift; admitting that she did not confess the fact until forced to by Kris. She told them what Kris had not; that she had nearly killed both of them.

They heard her out in complete silence until she had finished, and sat with her hands clenched in her lap, waiting for their verdict on her.

"What have *you* concluded from all this?" Elcarth asked unexpectedly.

"That—that no one Herald can stand alone, not even the Queen's Own," she replied, after thought. "Perhaps *especially* the Queen's Own. What I do reflects on all Heralds, and more so than any other just because I'm so much in the minds of the people."

"And of the proper usage of your Gift?" Kyril asked.

"I—I don't really know, entirely," she admitted. "There are times when what I need to do is quite clear. But most of the time, it's so—so nebulous. It's going to be pretty much a matter of weighing evils and necessity, I guess."

Elcarth nodded.

"If I have time, I'll ask advice from the Circle before I do anything irrevocable. But most of the time, I'm afraid I won't have that luxury. But if I make a mistake . . . well, I'll accept the consequences, and try and make it right."

"Well, Herald Talia," Elcarth said, black eyes bright with what Talia finally realized was pride, "I think you're ready to get into harness."

"Then—I passed?"

"What did I tell you?" Kyril shook his head at his colleague. "I knew she wouldn't believe it until she heard it from our lips." The iron-haired, granite-faced Herald unbent enough to smile warmly at her. "Yes, Talia, you did very well; we're quite pleased with what you and Kris have told us. You took a desperate situation that was not entirely of your own making, and turned it around, by yourselves."

"*And* we're satisfied with what you told us just now," Elcarth added. "You've managed to strike a decent balance in the ethics of having a Gift like yours, I think. So now that you've had the sweet compliments, are you ready for the bitter? There's a Council meeting shortly."

"Yes, sir," she replied. "I've been . . . warned."

"About more than just the meeting, I'll wager."

"Senior, that would be compromising my sources—"

"Lord and Lady!" Elcarth's sharp features twitched as he controlled his urge to laugh. "She sounds like Talamir already!"

Kyril just shook his head ruefully. "That she does, brother. Well enough, Talia—we'll see you there. You'd best be off; I imagine Selenay is wanting to discuss a few things with you before the Council meeting itself."

Talia knew a dismissal when she heard one, and took her leave of both of them, with a light foot to match her lightened heart.

"Talia—" Selenay forestalled all formality by embracing her Herald warmly. "—Bright Lady, how I have *missed* you! Come in here where we can have a little privacy."

She drew Talia into a granite-walled alcove holding a single polished wooden bench, just off the corridor leading to the Council chamber. As usual, she was dressed as any of her Heralds, with only the thin circlet of royal red-gold that rested on her own golden hair proclaiming her rank.

"Let me get a good look at you. Havens, you look wonderful! But you've gotten so *thin*—"

"Having to eat my own cooking," Talia replied, "that's all. I would have tried to see you last night—"

"You wouldn't have found me," Selenay said, blue eyes dark with affection. "I was closeted with the Lord Marshal, going over troop deployments on the Border. By the time we were finished, I wouldn't have been willing to see my resurrected father, I was that weary. All those damn maps! Besides, the first night back from internship is always spent with your closest friends, it's tradition! How else can you catch up on eighteen months of news?"

"Eighteen months of gossip, you mean." Talia grinned. "I understand Kris and I caused a little ourselves."

"From your offhand manner can I deduce that my thoughts of a deathless romance are in vain?" Her eyes danced with amusement and she pouted in feigned disappointment.

Talia shook her head in mock exasperation. "You, too? Bright Havens, is everyone in the Collegium determined to have us mated, whether we will or no?"

"The sole exceptions are Kyril, Elcarth, Skif, Keren, and—of all people—Alberich. They all swore that if you ever lost your heart, it wouldn't be to Kris' pretty face."

"They . . . could be right."

Selenay noted her Herald's faintly troubled expression, and deemed it prudent to change the subject. "Well, I'm more than happy to have you at my side again, and I could have used you for the past two months."

"Two months? Is it anything to do with what Elspeth sent Skif out to us for?"

"Did she? That minx! Probably—she hasn't been any more pleased over the Council's actions than I have. I've gotten an offer for Elspeth's hand, from a source that is going to be very difficult for me to refuse."

"Say on."

Selenay settled back on the bench, absently caressing the arm of it with one hand. "We received an envoy from King Alessandar two months ago, a formal request that I consider wedding Elspeth to his Ancar. There's a great deal to be said for the match; Ancar is about Kris' age, not too great a discrepancy as royal marriages go; he's said to be quite handsome. This would mean the eventual joining of our Kingdoms, and Alessandar has a strong and well-trained army, much larger than our own. I'd be able to spread the Heralds into his realm, and his army would make Karse think twice about ever invading us again. Three quarters of the Councilors are for it unconditionally, the rest favor the idea, but aren't trying to shove it down my throat like the others are."

"Well," Talia replied slowly, twisting the ring Kris had given her, "you wouldn't be hesitating over it if you didn't feel there was something wrong. What is it?"

"Firstly, unless. I absolutely *have* to, I don't want Elspeth sacrificed in a marriage of state. Frankly, I'd rather see her live unwedded and have the throne go to a collateral line than have her making anything but a match that is *at least* based on mutual respect and liking." Selenay played with a lock of hair, twisting it around one of her long, graceful fingers, thereby betraying her anxiety. "Secondly, she's very young yet; I'm going to insist she finish her training before making a decision. Thirdly, I haven't seen Ancar since he was a babe in arms; I have no idea what kind of a man he's grown into, and I want to know that before I even begin to seriously consider the match. To tell the truth, I'm hoping for her to have a love-match, and that with someone who is at least Chosen if not a Herald. I saw for myself the kind of problems that can come when the Queen's consort is not co-ruler, yet has been trained to the idea of rule. And you know very well that Elspeth's husband will not share the Throne unless he, too, is Chosen."

"Good points, all of them—but you have more than that troubling you." Talia had fallen into reading the Queen's state of mind as easily as if she'd never been away.

"Now I know why I've missed you! You always manage to ask the question that puts everything into perspective!" Selenay smiled again, with delight. "Yes, I do, but it wasn't the kind of thing I wanted to confess to the Council, or even to Kyril, bless his heart. They'd put it down to a silly woman's maunderings and mutter about moon-days. What's bothering me is this: it's too pat, this offer; it's too perfect. Too much like the answer to everyone's prayers. I keep looking for the trap beneath the bait, and wondering why I can't see it. Perhaps I'm so in the habit of suspicion that I can't trust even what I know to be honest."

"No, I don't think that's it." Talia pursed her lips thoughtfully. "There is something out of kilter, or you wouldn't be so uneasy. You've Mindspeech and a touch of Foreseeing, right? I suspect that you're getting foggy Foresight that something isn't quite right about the idea, and your uneasiness is being caused by having to fight the Council with no real reasons to give them."

"Bless you—that's exactly what it must be! I've been feeling for the past two months as if I were trying to bail a leaky boat with my bare hands!"

"So use Elspeth's youth and the fact that she *has* to finish her training as an excuse to stall for a while. I'll back you; when Kyril and Elcarth see that I'm backing you, they'll follow my lead," Talia said with more confidence than she actually felt. "Remember, I have a full vote in the Council now. Between the two of us we have the power to veto even the vote of the full Council. All it takes is the Monarch and

Queen's Own to overturn a Council vote. I'll admit it isn't politic to do so, but I'll do it if I have to."

Selenay sighed with relief. "How have I ever managed all these years without you?"

"Very well, thank you. If I hadn't been here, I expect you'd have managed to stall them somehow—even if you had to resort to Devan physicking Elspeth into a phony fever to gain time! Now, isn't it time to make our entrance?"

"Indeed it is." Selenay smiled, with just a hint of maliciousness. "And this is a moment I have long waited for! There are going to be some cases of chagrin when certain folk realize you are Queen's Own in truth, vote and all, and that the *full* Council will be in session from now on!"

They rose together and entered the huge, brass-mounted double doors of the Council chamber.

The other members of the Council had assembled at the table; they stood as one as the Queen entered the room, with Talia in her proper position as Queen's Own, one step behind her and slightly to her right.

The Council Chamber was not a large room, and had only the horseshoe Council table and the chairs surrounding it as furnishings, all of a dark wood that age and much handling had turned nearly black. Like the rest of the Palace, it was paneled only halfway in wood; the rest of the room, from about chin-height to the ceiling, being the gray stone of the original Palace-keep. A downscaled version of Selenay's throne was placed at the exact center of the Council table, behind it was the fireplace, and over the fireplace, the arms of the Monarch of Valdemar; a winged, white horse with broken chains about its throat. On the wall over the door, the wall that her throne faced, was an enormous map of Valdemar inscribed on heavy linen and kept constantly up-to-date; it was so large that any member of the Council could read the lettering from his or her seat. The work was exquisite, every road and tiny village carefully delineated. The chair to the immediate right of the Queen's was Talia's; to the immediate left was the Seneschal's. To the left of the Seneschal sat Kyril, to Talia's right, the Lord Marshal. The rest of the Councilors took whatever seat they chose, without regard for rank.

Talia had never actually used her seat until this moment; by tradition it had to remain vacant until she completed her training and was a full Herald. She had been seated with the rest of the Councilors and had done nothing except voice an occasional opinion when asked, and give her observations to Selenay when the meetings were over. While her new position brought her considerable power, it also carried considerable responsibility.

The Councilors remained standing, some with visible surprise on their faces; evidently word of her return had not spread as quickly through the Court as it had through the Collegium. Selenay took her place before her chair, as did Talia. The Queen inclined her head slightly to either side, then sat, with Talia sitting a fraction of a second later. The Councilors took their own seats when the Queen and Queen's Own were in their places.

"I should like to open this meeting with a discussion of the marriage envoy from Alessandar," Selenay said quietly, to the open surprise of several of her Councilors. Talia nodded to herself; by taking the initiative, Selenay started the entire proceedings with herself on the high ground.

One by one each of those seated at the table voiced their own opinions; as Selenay had told Talia, they were uniformly in favor of it, most desiring that the match be made immediately.

Talia began taking stock of the Councilors, watching them with an intensity she had never felt before. She wanted to evaluate them *without* using her Gift, only her eyes and ears.

First was Lord Gartheser, who spoke for the North—Orthallen's closest ally, without a doubt. Thin, nervous, and balding, he punctuated his sentences with sharp movements of his hands. Though he never actually looked directly at Orthallen, Talia could tell by the way he oriented himself that his attention was so bound on Orthallen that no one else made any impression on him at all.

"There can be *no* doubt," Gartheser said in a rather thin and reedy voice, "that this betrothal would bring us an alliance so strong that no one would ever dare dream of attacking us again. With Alessandar's army ready to spring to our rescue, not even Karse would care to trifle with us. I venture to predict that even the Border raids would cease, and our Borders would be truly secure for the first time in generations."

Orthallen nodded, so slightly that Talia would not have noticed the motion if she had not been watching him. And she wasn't the only one who caught that faint sign of approval. Gartheser had been watching for it, too. Talia saw him nod and smile slightly in response.

Elcarth and Kyril were next; Elcarth perched on the edge of his chair and looking like nothing so much as a gray snow-wren, and Kyril as nearly motionless as an equally gray granite statue.

"I can see no strong objections," Elcarth said, his head slightly to one side. "But the Heir *must* be allowed to finish her training *and* her internship before any such alliance is consummated."

"And Prince Ancar must be of a suitable temperament," Kyril added smoothly. "This Kingdom—forgive me, Highness—this Kingdom has had the bitter experience of having a consort who was *not* suitable. I, for one, have no wish to live through another such experience."

Lady Wyrist spoke next, who stood for the East; another of Orthallen's supporters. This plump, fair-haired woman had been a great beauty in her time, and still retained charm and magnetism.

"I am totally in favor—and I do *not* think this is the time to dally! Let the betrothal be as soon as possible—the wedding, even! Training can wait until *after* alliances are irrevocable." She glared at Elcarth and Kyril. "It's my Border the Karsites come rampaging over whenever they choose. My people have little enough, and the Karsites regularly reive away what little they have! But it is also my Border that would be open to new trade with our two Kingdoms firmly united, and I can see nothing to find fault with."

White-haired, snowy-bearded Father Aldon, the Lord Patriarch, spoke up wistfully. "As my Lady has said, this alliance promises peace, a peace such as we have not enjoyed for far too long. Karse would be forced to sue for a lasting peace, faced with unity all along two of its borders. Renewing our long friendship with Hardorn can only bring a truer peace than we have ever known. Though the Heir is young, many of our ladies have wedded younger still—"

"Indeed." Bard Hyron, so fair-haired that his flowing locks were nearly white, was speaker for the Bardic Circle. He echoed Father Aldon's sentiments. "It is a small sacrifice for the young woman to make, in the interests of how much we would gain."

Talia noted dubiously that his pale gray eyes practically glowed silver when Orthallen nodded approvingly.

The thin and angular Healer Myrim, spokeswoman for her Circle, was not so enthralled. To Talia's relief she actually seemed mildly annoyed by Hyron's hero worship; and something about Orthallen seemed to be setting her ever so slightly on edge. "You all forget something— though the child *has* been Chosen, she is not yet a Herald, and the law states clearly that the Monarch *must* be a Herald. There has never been a reason strong enough to overturn that law before, and I fail to see the need to set such a dangerous precedent now!"

"Exactly," Kyril murmured.

"The child is just that; a child. Not ready to rule by any stretch of the imagination, with much to learn before she is. Nevertheless, I am—cautiously—in favor of the betrothal. But only if the Heir *remains* at the Collegium until after her full training is complete."

Somewhat to Talia's surprise, Lord Marshal Randon shared Myrim's mild dislike of Orthallen. Talia wondered, as she listened to that scarred and craggy warrior measuring out his words with the care and deliberation of a merchant measuring out grain, what could have happened while she'd been gone to so change him. For when she'd last sat at the Council board, Randon had been one of Orthallen's foremost supporters. Now, however, though he favored the betrothal, he stroked his dark beard with something like concealed annoyance, as if it galled him, having to agree with Orthallen's party.

Horselike Lady Kester, speaker for the West, was short and to the point. "I'm for it," she said, and sat herself down. Plump and soft-spoken Lord Gildas for the South was equally brief.

"I can see nothing to cause any problems," said Lady Cathan of the Guilds quietly. She was a quiet, gray, dovelike woman, of an outer softness that masked a stubborn inner core. "And much that would benefit every member of the Kingdom."

"That, I think, is a good summation," Lord Palinor, the Seneschal, concluded. "You know my feelings on the matter. Majesty?"

The Queen had held her peace, remaining calm and thoughtful, but totally noncommittal, until everyone had spoken except herself and her Herald.

Now she leaned forward slightly, and addressed them, a hint of command tingeing her voice.

"I have heard you all; you each favor the match, and all of your reasons are good ones. You even urge me to agree to the wedding and see it consummated within the next few months. Very well; I can agree with every one of your arguments, and I am more than willing to return Alessandar's envoy with word that we will be considering his offer with all due gravity. But one thing I cannot and *will* not do—I will never agree to anything that will interrupt Elspeth's training. That, above all other considerations, must be continued! Lady forbid it, but should I die, we cannot risk the throne of Valdemar in the keeping of an untrained Monarch! Therefore I will do no more than indicate to Alessandar that his suit is welcome—and inform him in no uncertain terms that serious negotiations cannot begin until the Heir has passed her internship."

"Majesty!" Gartheser jumped to his feet as several more Councilors started speaking at once; one or two growing angry. Talia stood then, and rapped the table, and the babble ceased. The argumentative ones stared at her as though they had forgotten her presence.

"My lords, my ladies—forgive me, but any arguments you may have are moot. My vote goes with the Queen's decision. I have so advised her."

It was fairly evident from their dumbfounded expressions that they had forgotten that Talia now carried voting rights. If the situation had not been so serious, Talia would have derived a great deal of amusement from some of the dumbfounded expressions—Orthallen's in particular.

"If that is the advice of the Queen's Own, then my vote must follow," Kyril said quickly, although Talia could almost hear him wondering if she really knew what she was doing.

"And mine," Elcarth seconded, looking and sounding much more confident of Talia's judgment than Kyril.

There was silence then, a silence so deep one could almost hear the dust motes that danced in the light from the clerestory windows falling to the floor.

"It seems," said Lord Gartheser, the apparent leader of those dissenting, "that we are outvoted."

Faint grumbling followed his words.

At the farthest end of the table, a white-haired lord rose; the faint grumbling ceased. This gentleman was the one Talia had been watching so closely, and the only one who had not spoken. Orthallen; Lord of Wyvern's Reach, and Kris' uncle. He was the most senior Councilor, for he had served Selenay's father. He had served Selenay as well, throughout her entire reign. Selenay often called him "Lord Uncle," and he had been something of a father-figure to Elspeth. He was highly regarded and respected.

But Talia had never been able to warm to him. Part of the reason was because of what he had attempted to do to Skif. While he did not have the authority to remove any Chosen from the Collegium, he had tried to have the boy sent away for two years' punishment duty with the Army. His ostensible reason was the number of infractions of the Collegium rules Skif had managed to acquire, culminating with catching him red-handed in the office of the Provost-Marshal late one night. Orthallen had claimed Skif was there to alter the Misdemeanor Book. Talia, who had asked him to go there, was the only one who knew he had broken into the office to investigate Hulda's records. He was going to try to see who, exactly, had sponsored her into the Kingdom, in an attempt to ferret out the identity of her co-conspirator.

Talia had saved her friend at the cost of a lie, saying that she had asked him to find out whether her Holderkin relatives were claiming the Privilege Tax allowed those who had produced a child Chosen.

Since that time she had been subtly, but constantly, at loggerheads with Orthallen; when she first began sitting on the Council it seemed as if he had constantly moved to negate what little authority she had. He had openly belittled so many of her observations (on the grounds of her youth and inexperience) that she had very seldom spoken up when he was present. He always seemed to her to be just a little too careful and controlled. When he smiled, when he frowned, the expression never seemed to go any deeper than the skin.

At first she had chided herself for her negative reaction to him, putting it down to her irrational fear of males; handsome males in particular, for even though past his prime, he was a strikingly handsome man—there was no doubt which side of Kris' family had blessed him with his own angelic face. And there was no sin in being a trifle cold, emotionally speaking, yet for some reason, she was always reminded of the wyvern that formed his crest when she saw him. Like the wyvern, he seemed to her to be thin-blooded, calculating, and quite ruthless— and hiding it all beneath an attractively bejeweled skin.

But there was more to her mistrust of him now—because she had more than one reason to suspect that *he* was the source of those rumors about her misusing her Gift, and she was certain that he had started them because he *knew* how such vile rumors would affect an Empath who was well-known to have a low sense of self-esteem. She was equally certain that he had deliberately planted doubts in Kris' mind— *knowing* that she would feel those doubts and respond.

But this time she had cause to be grateful to him; when Orthallen spoke, the rest of the Councilors paid heed, and he spoke now in favor of the Queen's decision.

"My lords, my ladies—the Queen is entirely correct," he said, surprising Talia somewhat, for he had been one of those most in favor of marrying Elspeth off with no further ado. "We have only one Heir, and no other candidates in the direct line. We should not take such a risk. The Heir must be trained; I see the wisdom of that, now. I withdraw my earlier plea for an immediate betrothal. Alessandar is a wise monarch, and will surely be more than willing to make preliminary agreements on the strength of a betrothal promised for the future. In such ways, we shall have all the benefits of both plans."

Talia was not the only member of the Council surprised by Orthallen's apparent about-face. Hyron stared as if he could not believe what he had heard. The members of his faction and those opposed to him seemed equally taken aback.

The result of this speech was the somewhat reluctant—though unanimous—vote of the Council to deal with the envoy just as Selenay had outlined. The vote was, frankly, little more than a gesture, since together Selenay and Talia could overrule the entire Council. But though the unanimous backing of her stance gave Selenay a position of strong moral advantage, Talia wondered what private conversations would be taking place when the Council session concluded—and who would be involved.

The remaining items on the Council's agenda were routine and mundane; rescinding tax for several villages hard hit by spring floods, the deployment and provisioning of extra troops at Lake Evendim in the hope of making life difficult enough this year that the pirates and raiders would decide to turn to easier prey, the fining of a merchant-clan that had been involved in the slave-trade. The arguments about just how many troops should be moved to Lake Evendim and who would fund the deployment went on for hours. The Lord Marshal and Lady Kester (who ruled the district of the fisherfolk of the lake) were unyielding in their demands for the extra troops; Lord Gildas and Lady Cathan, whose rich grainlands and merchant-guilds would supply the taxes for the primary support of the effort, were frantic in their attempts to cut down the numbers.

Talia's sympathy lay with the fisherfolk, yet she could find it in her heart to feel for those who were being asked to delve into their pockets for the pay and provisioning of extra troops who would mostly remain idle. It seemed that there was no way to compromise, and that the arguments would continue with no conclusion. *That* would be no solution for the fisherfolk, either!

Finally, as the Lord Marshal thundered out figures concerning the numbers needed to keep watch along the winding coastlines, a glimmering of an idea came to her.

"Forgive me," she spoke into one of the sullen silences. "I know little of warfare, but I know something of the fisherfolk. Only the young, healthy, and whole go out on the boats in season; unless my memory is incorrect, the old, the very young, pregnant women, those minding the young children for the rest of the family, and the crippled remain in the temporary work-villages. Am I right?"

"Aye—and that's what makes these people so damned hard to defend!" the Lord Marshal growled. "There isn't a one left behind with the ability to take arms!"

"Well, according to your figures, a good third of your troopers would be spending all their time on coastwatch. Since you're going to have to be feeding that many people anyway, why not provision the dependents instead, and have *them* doing the watching? Once they're freed from having to see to their day-to-day food supplies, they'll have the time for it, and what does a watcher need besides a pair of good eyes and the means to set an alert?"

"You mean use *children* as coastwatchers?" Gartheser exclaimed. "That—that's plainly daft!"

"Just you wait one moment, Gartheser," Myrim interjected. "I fail to see what's daft about it. It seems rare good sense to me."

"But—how are they to defend themselves?"

"Against what? Who's going to see them? They'll be *hidden,* man, in blinds, the way coastwatchers are *always* hidden. And I see the girl's drift. Puttin' them up would let us cut down the deployment by a third, just as Gildas and Cathan want," Lady Kester exclaimed, looking up like an old gray warhorse hearing the bugles. "Ye'd still have to provision the full number, though, ye old tightfists!"

"But they'd not have to pay 'em," one of the others chuckled.

"But—children?" Hyron said doubtfully. "How can we put children in that kind of vital position? What's to keep them from running off to play?"

"Border children are not very childlike," Talia said quietly, looking to Kester, and the Speaker for the West nodded emphatic agreement.

"Silverhair, lad, the only thing keepin' *these* children off the boats is size," Kester snorted, though not unkindly. "They're not your soft highborns; they've been *working* since their hands were big enough to knot a net."

"Aye, I must agree." Lady Wyrist entered this argument for the first time. "I suspect your fisherfolk are not unlike my Holderkin—as Herald Talia can attest, Borderbred children have little time for childish pursuits."

"All the more chance that they'll run off, then," Hyron insisted.

"Not when they've seen whole families burned out by the selfsame pirates they're supposed to be watching for," said Myrim. "I served out there. I'd trust the sense of any of those 'children' before I'd trust the sense of some highborn graybeards I could name."

"Well said, lady!" Kester applauded, and turned sharp eyes on the Lord Marshal. "Tell ye what else, ye old wardog—an ye can persuade these troopers of yours to turn to and lend a hand to a bit of honest work now and again—"

"Such as?" The Lord Marshal almost cracked a smile.

"Taking the landwork; drying the fish and the sponge, mending the nets and lines, packing and crating, readying the longhouses for winter."

"It might be possible; what were you planning to offer?"

"War-pay; with the landwork off my people's hands, and knowing their folk on land are safe, we should be able to cover the extra bonus ourselves, and *still* bring in a proper profit."

"With careful phrasing, I think I could manage it."

"Done, then. How say you, Cathan, Gildas?"

They were only too happy to agree. The Council adjourned on this most positive note. Selenay and Talia stood as one, and preceded the rest out; Kyril a pace behind them.

"You *have* been learning, haven't you?" Kyril said in Talia's ear.

"Me?"

"Yes, you; and don't play the innocent," Elcarth joined his colleague as they stood in a white-clad knot outside the Council Chamber door, waiting for Selenay to finish conferring with the Seneschal on the agenda for the afternoon's audiences. He pushed a lock of gray hair out of his eyes and smiled. "That was cleverly done, getting the Border Lords on your side."

"It was the only way to get a compromise going. Cathan and Gildas would have agreed to anything that saved them money. With the Borderers and those two, we had a majority, and everybody benefited." Talia smiled back. "It was just a matter of invoking Borderer pride, really; we're *proud* of how tough we are, even as littles."

"Lovely. Truly lovely." Selenay joined them. "All those sessions of dealing with hardheaded Borderers in the middle of feuds taught you more than a little! Now tell me this; what would you have done if you *hadn't* absorbed all that fisherfolk lore from Keren, Teren, and Sherrill? Sat dumb?"

"I don't think so, not when it was obvious that there'd never be agreement." Talia thought for a moment. "I think . . . if one of you hadn't done so first . . . I would have suggested an adjournment until we could dig up an expert on the people of the area, preferably a Herald who has done several circuits there."

"Fine—that's what I was about to do when you spoke up; we are beginning to think as a team. Now I have a working lunch with Kyril

and the Seneschal. I don't need you for it, so you can go find something to gulp down at the Collegium. At one I have formal audiences,
and you have to be there. Those will last about three hours; you're free
then until seven and Court dinner. After dinner, unless something
comes up, you're free again."

"But Alberich is expecting you at four"—Elcarth grinned at Talia's
groan—"and Devan at five. Welcome home, Talia!"

"Well," she said with a sigh, "it's better than shoveling snow, I guess!
But I never thought I'd begin missing field work so soon!"

"Missing field work already?"

Talia turned to find Kris standing behind her, an insolent grin on
his face. "I thought you told me you'd never miss field work!"

She grinned back. "I lied."

"No!" He feigned shock. "Well, what of the Council meeting?"

She wanted to tell him everything—then suddenly, remembered
who he was—who his uncle was. Anything she told him would quite
likely get back to Orthallen, and Kris would be telling Orthallen in all
innocence, never dreaming he was handing the man weapons to use
against her by doing so.

"Oh—nothing much," she said reluctantly. "The betrothal's being
held off until Elspeth's finished training. Look, Kris, I'm sorry, but I'm
rather short on time right now. I'll tell you later, all right?"

And she fled before he could ask anything more.

Lunch was a few bites snatched on the run between the Palace and her
room; audiences required a slightly more formal uniform than the one
she'd worn to the Council session. Talia managed to wash, change,
and get back in time to discuss the scheduled audiences with the Seneschal. Talia's role here was as much bodyguard as anything else, although her duties included assessing the emotional state of those
coming before the Queen and giving her any information that seemed
appropriate.

The audience chamber was long and narrow; the same gray granite
and dark wood as the rest of the old Palace. Selenay's throne was on a
raised platform at the far end. Behind the throne the wall had been
carved into the Royal arms; there were no curtains for assassins to hide
behind. The Queen's Own spent the entire time positioned behind the
throne to the Queen's right, from which position the Queen could
hear her least whisper. Petitioners had to travel the length of the chamber, giving Talia ample time to "read" their emotional state if she
thought it necessary to do so.

The audiences were quite unexciting; petitioners ranged from a smallholder seeking permission to establish a Dyer's Guildhouse on his property to two noblemen who had called challenge on each other and were now trying desperately to find a way out of the situation without either of them losing face. Not once did she deem the situation grave enough to warrant "reading" any of them.

When the audience session concluded, Talia sprinted back to her room to change into something old and worn for her weapons drill with Alberich.

Walking into the salle was like walking into the past; nothing had changed, not the worn, backless benches against the wall, not the clutter of equipment and towels on and beneath the benches, not the light coming from the windows. Not even Alberich had changed so much as a hair; he still wore the same old leathers, or clothing like enough to have been the same. His scar-seamed face still looked as incapable of humor as the walls of the Palace; his long black hair held neither more nor less gray than it had the last time Talia had seen him.

Elspeth was already there, going full out against Jeri under Alberich's critical eye. Talia held her breath in surprise; Elspeth was (to her judgment, at least) Jeri's equal. The young weapons instructor was not holding anything back, and more than once only saved herself from a "kill" by frantically wrenching her body out of the way of the wooden blade. Both of them were sodden with sweat when Alberich finally called a halt.

"You do well, children; both of you." Alberich nodded as he spoke. Both Elspeth and Jeri began walking slowly in little circles to keep their muscles from stiffening, while drying their faces with old towels. "Jeri, it is more work you need on your defense; working with the students has made you sloppy. Elspeth, if it was that you were not far busier than any student should be, I would make you Jeri's assistant."

Elspeth raised her head, and Talia could see she was flushed with the praise, her eyes glowing.

"However, you are very far from perfect. Your left side is too weak and you are vulnerable there. From now on you are to work left-handed, using your right only when I tell you, to keep from losing your edge. Enough for today, off to the bath with you—it is like your Companions you smell!"

He turned to Talia, who bit her lip, then said, "I have the feeling I'm in trouble."

"In trouble? It *is* possible—" Alberich scowled; then unexpectedly smiled. "No fear, little Talia; it is that I am well aware how few were the chances for you to keep in practice. Today we will start slowly, and I will determine just how much you have lost. *Tomorrow* you will be in trouble."

Talia was thanking the gods an hour later that Kris had insisted they both keep in fighting trim as much as possible. Alberich was reasonably pleased that she had lost so little edge, and kept his cutting remarks to a minimum. Nor was she the recipient of more than one or two bruising *thwacks* from his practice blade when she'd done something exceptionally stupid. On the whole, she felt as if she'd gotten off very lightly.

Another run, this time to wash and change yet again, and she was back at Healer's Collegium, going over the past eighteen months with Devan and Rynee. Both were blessedly succinct; there had not been any truly major mental traumas for Rynee to deal with among the Heraldic Circle. As a result, Talia was able to flee to Companion's Field just as the warning bell for supper sounded at the Herald's Collegium.

Rolan was waiting at the fence, and she pulled herself onto his back without bothering with going for a saddle.

"I think," she told him, as he walked off into a quiet copse, "that I may die of exhaustion. This is worse than when I was a student."

He lipped her booted foot affectionately; Talia picked up a projection of reassurance and something to do with time.

"You think I'll get used to it in a few days? Lord, I hope so! Still—" She thought hard, trying to remember just what the Queen's schedule was like. "Hm. Council sessions aren't more than three times a week. Audiences, though, they're every day. Alberich will torture me every day, too. But I *could* reschedule, say, Devan before breakfast and just after lunch—save weapons drill for just before dinner, so I'm only changing twice a day. You, my darling, whenever I can squeeze a free moment."

Rolan made a sound very like laughing.

"True, with the tight bond *we* have, I don't have to be with you physically, do I? What did you think of the audiences?"

To Talia's delight, he hung his head and did a credible imitation of a human snore.

"You, too? Lord and Lady, they're as bad as State banquets! Why did I ever think being a Herald would be exciting?"

Rolan snorted, and projected the memory of their flight across country to get help for the plague-stricken village of Waymeet, following that with the fight with the raiders that had attacked and fired Hevenbeck.

"You're right; I think I can live with boredom. What do you think of how Elspeth's coming along?"

To her surprise, Rolan was faintly worried, but could give her no clear idea why he felt that way.

"Is it important enough to trance down to where you can give me a clearer idea?"

He shook his head, mane brushing her face a little.

"Well, in that case, we'll let it go. It's probably just the usual rebelliousness—and I can't say as I blame her. Her schedule is as bad as mine. *I* don't like it, and I can't fault her if she doesn't either."

Talia dismounted beside a tiny, spring-fed pool, and sat in the grass, watching the sun set, and emptying her mind. Rolan stood beside her, both of them content with a quiet moment in which to simply be together.

"Well, I'm into it at last," she said, half to herself. "I thought I'd never make it, sometimes. . . ."

This had been the first day she had truly *been* Queen's Own—with all the duties and all the rights; from the right to overrule the Council to the right to overrule Selenay (though that was one she hadn't exercised, and still wasn't sure she had the nerve for!); from her duty to ease the fears of her fellows in the Circle to the duty to see to the Heir's well-being.

It was a frightening moment in a way, and a sobering one. On reflection, it almost seemed as if the Queen's Own best served the interests of Queen and country by *not* being too forward; by saving her votes for the truly critical issues and keeping her influence mostly to the quiet word in the Queen's ear. That suited Talia; she hadn't much enjoyed having all eyes on her this afternoon—especially not Orthallen's. But Selenay had been more at ease just because Talia was *there*; there had been no mistaking that. In the long run, that was what the job was all about—giving the Monarch one completely honest and completely trustworthy friend. . . .

The dying sun splashed scarlet and gold on the bottoms of the few clouds that hung in the west, while the sky above them deepened from blue to purple, and the Hounds, the two stars that chased the sun, shone in unwinking splendor. The tops of the clouds took on the purple of the sky as the sun dropped below the horizon, and the purple tinge soaked through them like water being taken into a sponge. The light faded, and everything began to lose color, fading into cool blues. Little frogs began to sing in the pool at Talia's feet; night-blooming jacinth flowers opened somewhere near her, and the cooling breeze picked up the perfume and carried it to her.

And just when she was feeling totally disinclined to move, a mosquito bit her.

"Ouch! Damn!" She slapped at the offending insect, then laughed. "The gods remind me of my duty. Back to work for me, love. Enjoy your evening."

CHAPTER 3

A S IF THAT tiny insect bite had been an omen, things began to go
wrong, starting with the weather.

The perfect spring turned sour; it seemed to rain every day without
a letup, and the rain was cold and steadily dismal. The sun, when Talia
actually saw it, gave a chill, washed-out light. Miserable, that was what
it was; miserable and depressing. The few flowers that managed to
bloom seemed dispirited, and hung limply on their stems. The damp
crept into everything, and fires on the hearths all day and all night did
little to drive it out. The whole Kingdom was affected; there were new
tales reaching the Court every day of flooding, sometimes in areas that
hadn't flooded in a hundred years or more.

This was bound to have an effect on the Councilors. They worked
like heroes at all hours to cope with emergencies, but the grim atmosphere made them quarrelsome and inclined to snipe at each other at
the least opportunity. Every Council session meant at least one major
fight and two ruffled tempers to be soothed. The names they called
each other would have been ample cause for dueling anywhere else.

At least they treated Talia with that same lack of respect—she came
in for her share of sniping, and that was a positive sign, that she had
been accepted as one of them, and their equal.

The sniping-among-equals was something she could cope with,
though it was increasingly difficult to keep her temper when everyone
around her was losing theirs. Far harder to deal with in any rational

way were Orthallen's subtle attempts at undercutting her authority. Clever, those attempts were; frighteningly clever. He never said anything that anyone could directly construe as criticism; no, what he did was hint—oh, so politely, and at every possible opportunity—that perhaps she was a bit young and inexperienced for her post. That she might be going overboard because of the tendency of youth to see things always in black and white. That she surely meant well, but . . . and so on. It made Talia want to scream and bite something. There was no way to counteract him except to be even more reasonable and mild-tempered than he. She felt as if she were standing on sand, and he was the flood tide washing it out from under her.

Things were not going all that well between herself and Kris either.

"Goddess, Talia," Kris groaned, slumping back into his chair. "He's *just* doing what he sees as his duty!"

Talia counted to ten, slowly, counted the Library bookshelves, then counted the rings of the knothole in the table in front of her. "He was claiming *I* was overreacting at the same time that Lady Kester was calling Hyron a pompous peabrain at the top of her lungs!"

"Well—"

"Kris, he's said the same damn things every Council session and at least three times *during* each session! Every time it looks as if the other Councilors are beginning to listen to what I'm saying, he trots out the same speech!" She shoved her chair away from the table, and began pacing restlessly, up and down the length of the vacant Library. This had been a particularly bad session, and the muscles of her neck felt as tight as bridge cables.

"I just can't see anything at all sinister in my uncle's behavior—"

"*Dammit, Kris*—"

"Talia he's old, he's set in his ways—you're frighteningly young to him, *and* likely to usurp *his* position! Have some pity on the man, he's *only* human!"

"So what am I?" She struggled not to shout, but the argument was giving her a headache. "I'm supposed to *like* what he's doing?"

"He's not doing anything!" Kris scowled, as if he had a headache, too. "Frankly, I think you're hearing insult and seeing peril that *isn't* there."

Talia turned abruptly, and stared at him, tight-lipped, fists clenched. "In that case," she replied, after a dozen slow, careful breaths of dust-laden air, "maybe I should take my irrational fantasies elsewhere."

"But—"

She turned again and all but ran down the staircase. He called something after her, in a distressed voice. She ignored it, and ran on.

So now they didn't talk about much of anything anymore. And Talia missed that; missed the closeness they used to have, the way they used to be able to confide their deepest secrets to each other. Truth to be told, she missed that more than the physical side of their relationship—though now that she was no longer used to being celibate she missed that, too. . . .

Then there was her relationship—or more accurately, lack of one—with Dirk.

His behavior was baffling in the extreme; one moment he would seem determined to get her alone somewhere, the next, he shied away from even being in the same room. He would be lurking in the background everywhere she went for a day or two, then just as abruptly would vanish, only to reappear in a few days. Half the time he seemed determined to throw Kris at her, the other half, equally determined to block Kris from getting anywhere near her—

Talia saw her elusive quarry leaning on the fence surrounding Companion's Field. He was staring, broodingly, off into the far distance. For a wonder, it wasn't raining, although the sky was a dead, dull gray and threatening to pour any moment.

"Dirk?"

He jumped, whipped about, and stared at her with wide, startled eyes.

"W-what are you doing here?" he asked, somewhat ungraciously, his back pressed hard against the fence as if that barrier was all that was keeping him from running away.

"The same as you, probably," Talia replied, forcing herself *not* to snap at him. "Looking for my Companion, and maybe somebody to ride with."

"In that case, shouldn't you be looking for Kris?" he asked, his expression twisted as if he'd swallowed something very unpleasant.

She couldn't think of a reply, and chose not to answer him. Instead she moved to the fence herself, and stood with one booted foot on the first railing and her arms folded along the top, mimicking the pose he had held when she saw him.

"Talia—" He took one step toward her—she heard his boot squelch in the wet grass—then stopped. "I—Kris is—a very valuable friend. More than friend. I—"

She waited for him to say what was on his mind, hoping that *this* time he'd finish it. Maybe if she didn't look at him, he'd be able to speak his piece.

"Yes?" she prompted when the silence went on so long she'd almost suspected him of sneaking away. She turned to catch his blue, blue eyes staring almost helplessly at her before he hastily averted them.

"I—I've got to go—" he gasped, and fled.

She was ready to scream with frustration. This was the fourth time he'd pulled this little trick, *starting* to say something, then running away. And with things somewhat at odds between herself and Kris, she really didn't feel as if she wanted to ask Kris to help. Besides, she hadn't seen Kris much since their last little set-to.

With an exasperated sigh, she Mindcalled Rolan. They both needed exercise—and he, at least, would be a sympathetic listener.

Kris was avoiding Talia on purpose.

When he'd first returned, his uncle had taken time out to give him familial greetings; that was only to be expected. But Orthallen lately seemed to be going out of his way to speak to his nephew two or three times a week, and the conversation somehow always turned to Talia.

Not by accident, either. Kris was mortally sure of that.

Nor were they pleasant conversations, though they seemed to be on the surface. Kris was beginning to get an impression that Orthallen was *looking* for something—weaknesses in the Queen's Own, perhaps. Certainly, whenever he happened to say something complimentary about Talia, his uncle would always insinuate a "Yes, but surely . . ." in a rather odd and confiding tone.

Like the latest example.

He'd been on his way back from a consultation with Elcarth about some of his latest Farseeing pupils, when Orthallen had just "happened" to intercept him.

"Nephew!" Orthallen had hailed him, "I have word from your brother—"

"Is anything wrong?" Kris had asked anxiously. The family holdings were in the heart of some of the worst flooding in a generation. "Does he need me at home? I'll be free in a few weeks—"

"No, no; things are far from well, but it's not an emergency yet. The smallholders have lost about a tenth of their fields, in total; obviously some are worse off than others. They've lost enough livestock that the spring births are barely going to make up for the losses—oh, and your brother lost one of his Shin'a'in cross-bred stallions."

"Damn—he's not going to find another one of those in a hurry. Are we needing any outside help?"

"Not yet. There's enough grain in storage to make up for the losses. But he wanted you to know exactly how things stood, so that you wouldn't worry."

"Thank you, uncle. I appreciate your taking the time to let me know."

"And is your young protégée settling in, do you think?" he then asked smoothly. "What with all the emergencies that have come up lately, I wonder if she has more than she can cope with, sometimes."

"Havens, Uncle, I'm the *last* one to ask," Kris had said with a little impatience. "I hardly see her anymore. We both have duties, and those duties don't let us cross paths too often."

"Oh? Somehow I had gotten the impression that you Heralds always knew what was happening in each others' lives."

Kris really hadn't been able to think of a response to that; at least not a respectful one.

"I only asked because I thought she looked a bit careworn, and I thought perhaps she might have said something to you," Orthallen continued, his cold eyes boring into Kris'. "She has a heavy burden of responsibility for one so young."

"She's equal to it, Uncle. I've told you that before. Rolan wouldn't have Chosen her otherwise."

"Well, I'm sure you're correct," Orthallen replied, sounding as if he meant the opposite. "Those rumors of her using her Gift to manipulate—"

"Were absolutely unfounded. I told you that. She has been so circumspect in even *reading* others that she practically has to be forced to it—" Kris broke off, wondering if he was saying too much.

"Ah," Orthallen said after a moment. "That is a comfort. The child seems to have a wisdom out of keeping with her years. However, if she should feel she's having problems, I would appreciate it if you'd tell me. After all, as the Queen's eldest Councilor, I should be aware of possible trouble. I'd be only too happy to help her in any way I can, but she still seems to be carrying over that grudge from her student days, and I doubt she'd ever give me the correct time of day, much less confide in me."

Kris had mumbled something noncommittal, and his uncle had gone away outwardly satisfied—but the whole encounter had left a very bad taste in Kris's mouth. He was regretting now the fact that he'd confided to his uncle in one of those early conversations his belief that

Talia and Dirk were lifebonded; the man had seized on the tidbit as avidly as a hawk on a mouse. But at the same time, he didn't want to have to face Talia herself with these suspicions awakened; she'd get it out of him, no doubt of it. And while she wouldn't *say* "I told you so," she had a particular look of lowered eyelids and a quirk at one corner of her mouth that spoke volumes, and he wasn't in the mood to deal with it.

Besides, it was only too possible that she'd infected *him* with her paranoia.

If only he could be sure of that—but he couldn't. So he avoided her.

Dirk straddled an old, worn chair in his room, staring into the darkness beyond the windowpane. It was nearly dusk—and as black as midnight out there. He felt as if he were being torn into little bits.

He couldn't make up his mind *what* he wanted to do; part of him wanted to battle for Talia by all means fair or foul, part of him felt that he should be unselfish and give Kris a clear field with her, part of him was afraid to find out what *she* thought of all this, and a fourth part of him argued that he really didn't want any commitments to females anyway—look what the *last* one had gotten him.

The last one. Lady Naril—oh, gods.

He stared at the sullen flickers of lightning in the heart of the clouds above the trees. It had been so long ago—and not long enough ago.

Gods, I was such a fool.

He and Kris had been posted to the Collegium, teaching their specialties—Fetching and Farsight. It had been *his* first experience of Court and Collegium as a full Herald.

I was a stupid sheep looking for a wolf.

Not that he hadn't had his share of dalliances, even if he'd always had to play second to Kris. He hadn't minded, not really. But he'd been feeling a little lost; Kris had been born to Court circles, and flowed back into them effortlessly. Dirk had been left on the outskirts.

Then Naril had introduced herself to him—

I thought she was so pure, so innocent. She seemed so alone in the great Court, so eager for a friend. And she was so young—so very beautiful.

How could he have known that in her sixteen short years she'd had more men in her thrall than a rosebush had thorns?

And how could he have guessed she intended to use *him* to snare Kris?

Gods, I was half out of my mind with love for her.

He stared at the reflection in the window, broodingly. *I saw only what I wanted to see—that's for certain. Lost most of my few wits.*

But there had been just enough sense left to him that when she'd asked him to arrange a private meeting between herself and his friend, he'd hidden where he could overhear her. The artificial grotto in the garden that she had chosen was secluded—but had ample hiding space in the bushes to either side of the entrance.

Dirk probed at the aching memory as if it were a sore tooth, taking twisted pleasure from the pain. *I could hardly believe my ears when I heard her issuing Kris an ultimatum: come to her bed until she tired of him, or she would make my life a living hell.*

He had burst in on them, demanding to know what she meant, crazy-wild with anger and pain.

Kris had slipped away. And Naril turned to him with utter hatred in her enormous violet eyes. When she'd finished what she had to say to him, he'd wanted to kill himself.

Again he stared at his reflection. *Not everything she said was wrong—* he told himself sadly. *What woman with any sense would want me? Especially with Kris in reach. . . .*

It had been a long time before he'd stopped wanting to die—and a longer time before life became something he enjoyed instead of something he endured.

Now—was it all happening again?

He was doing his level best to come to terms with himself, and being stuck at the Collegium with Talia in sight at least once a day wasn't helping. The whole situation was comical, but somehow when he tried to laugh it off, his "mirth" had a very hollow sound even to his ears. He had thrown himself into his work, only to find that he was watching for her constantly out of the corner of his eye. He couldn't help himself; it was like scratching a rash. He knew he shouldn't, but he did it anyway, and it gave him a perverse sort of satisfaction. And even though it troubled him to watch her, it troubled him more not to.

Gods, gods—what am I going to do?

The reflection gave him no answer.

After three weeks of rain, the weather had cleared for a bit. To Talia's great relief, things were emotionally on a more even keel, at least where the tempers of Court and Collegium were concerned. The evening had been warm enough to leave windows open, and the fresh air had made a gratifying change in the stuffiness of her quarters. Talia was fast asleep when the Death Bell shattered the peace of the night with its brazen tolling.

It woke her from a nightmare of flame, fear, and agony. That nightmare had held her in a grip so tenacious that she expected to open her eyes to find her own room an inferno. She clutched the blankets to her chest, as she slowly became aware that the air she breathed was cool and scented with night mist, not smoke-filled and choking. It took several moments for her to clear her mind of the dream enough to think clearly again, and when at last she did, it was to realize that the dream and the Death Bell's tolling had related causes.

Fire—her nails bit into her palms as she clenched her hands. When fire was involved, the Herald most likely to be involved with it was—Griffon! Dear gods—let it not be Griffon, not her year-mate, not her friend—

But as she stared unseeing into the darkness and forced herself into a calmer frame of mind, she *knew* without doubt that it was not Griffon, after all. The name and the face that hazed into her now-receptive mind were those of a student of the year following hers—Christa, whom she remembered as one of Dirk's pupils in the Gift of Fetching.

And in many ways, this was an even greater tragedy, for Christa had still been on her internship assignment.

When the pieces were all assembled from the various fragments the Heralds at the Collegium had "read" when the Death Bell began ringing, the result was almost as confusing as having no information at all. This much alone they knew; Christa was dead; the Herald assigned as her counselor, the cheerfully lascivious Destria, was badly hurt, and the cause had something to do both with raiders and a great fire.

The information they received from the Heralds stationed with the Healing Temple to which Destria had been carried was nearly as fragmentary. Their Gifts of Mindspeech weren't nearly as strong as Kyril's or Sherrill's. But they made it plain that Destria needed more help than they could provide—and that there was urgent need of a different kind of aid. They were sending Destria back to Healer's Collegium and the Palace, and with her would come clarification.

Within the week they came; one uninjured Herald, Destria (a pitiful thing carried on a litter swung between two Companions, one of them Destria's Sofi), and a battered and bruised farmer whose clothing still bore the smoke stains and ash of a fire. All three of them had to have traveled day and night with scarcely a pause to rest to reach the capital so quickly.

Selenay called the Council into immediate session, and the petitioner came before them. He sagged wearily into the chair they set for him, his eyes sunken deeply into their sockets, his hair so full of ash it was hard to tell what color it was. It was plain he had wasted not even a single hour, but had gotten on with the journey without taking time for his own comfort. And the tale he told, of well-armed, organized raiders, and the near-massacre of everyone in his town, was enough to chill the blood.

They had given him a seat, since he was plainly too weary to stand for very long, and he seemed like an omen of doom, sitting before the Council Table, both hands bandaged to the elbow. The taint of smoke had so permeated his clothing that it was carried even to the Councilors, and the smell of it brought his message home with terrible force.

"It was slaughter, pure and simple," he told the Council in a voice roughened by the smoke. "And we walked into it like silly sheep. Up until this spring we've had so much problem with brigands, little bands of them, pecking away at us, that we'd come to expect them, like spring floods. Then, when they all vanished this winter—gods, you'd think we'd have had the sense to realize something was up. But we didn't; we just thought they'd gone off to richer pickings. Ah, fools, fools and blind!"

He dropped his face into his hands for a moment, and when he lifted it again, there were tears on his cheeks from eyes already red. "They'd gotten together, you see; one of the wolves had finally proved the strongest, and they'd gotten together. We'd prided ourselves on having put the village in an unassailable valley; sheer rock to our back and sides, and only one narrow pass that let into it. We couldn't be starved or forced out from thirst; we had our own wells, and plenty of food stockpiled. Well, they had an answer to that. A handful of them killed the sentries, and poisoned the dogs that patrolled the heights, then rained fire arrows down on the village by night. We build with wood and thatch, mostly; the buildings went up like pitch torches. The rest waited outside the pass, and picked off those of us that got as far as the cleft. Have you ever seen rabbits running before a grass fire? That was us—and they were the hungry wolves waiting for dinner to leap into their jaws. Men I've known all my life I watched getting their legs shot out from underneath them. Children hardly old enough to be wearing knives, too—even graybeards and grannies. Anybody likely to be able to take up a weapon. They shot to cripple, not to kill; dead mouths can't tell where they've hid their little treasures, y'see. A good half of those they shot may never walk right again. A good quarter bled to death where they lay. And a full quarter of the children burned to death in the houses they set fire to."

A muted murmur of horror crept around the table; Lady Kester hid her own face in her hands.

A beam of late afternoon sunlight spotlighted the speaker as it poured in through the high windows. It touched him with a clear gold that made his eyes seem even more like burned-out pits in his face. "Your Heralds were not far; overnighting in a Waystation, I think. How they knew our plight, I'll never know—must've been more of your magic, I guess. They came charging up on the backs of the raiders, two of 'em like a blessed army. Those white horses—the Companions—they *were* damn near an army by themselves. They broke up the ambush at the head of the pass, got them scattered off into the woods for a bit. Then the older one started getting us organized, got us clearing the snipers off the heights; the younger one took off into the burning buildings, hearing cries and looking for somebody to save, I guess. The older one didn't even notice she was gone—until—"

He swallowed hard, and his hands were shaking. "I heard screaming, worse than before; the older Herald, she jerked like she'd been shot. She shouted at us to take the brigands before they got themselves over their fright, then she headed into the fires herself; I followed—my hands were too burned to hold a weapon, but I thought I might be able to help with the fires. The younger one had gotten trapped on the second floor of one of the houses; I was right behind the older one and I could see her against the fire. Calm as you please, she's tossing younglings out to their parents. At least I *think* she was tossing 'em—she'd have a little one in her hands one moment, then the next, his mum or dad would be holding it. The older one ran up, started shouting at her to jump. She just shook her head, and turned back one more time—the floor collapsed then. That damn horse of hers crashed through the wall and went in after her—the other Herald was right on his heels. She'd no sooner cleared the door when the whole roof caved in. We got her out, but the other—"

One of Selenay's pages brought him wine, and he drank it gratefully, his teeth chattering against the rim of the tankard.

"That's what happened. For us, we beat 'em back, but we didn't get more than a handful of them compared to the numbers we know they've got. They're comin' back, we know they are. 'Specially since they must know the Heralds are—gone. We lost half the town—most of the able-bodied. I was about the only one that could make the ride here. We need help, Majesty, m'lords—we need it bad—"

"You'll have that help," Selenay pledged, her eyes hard and black with anger as she stood. "This isn't the first incursion of these bastards we've heard of, but it's by far and away the worst. It's obvious to me that there is no way we can expect you folk to handle brigands as organized as these are. Lord Marshal, and good sir, if you'll come with me we'll mobilize a company of the Guard." She looked inquiringly at the rest of the Council.

Lady Cathan spoke for all of them. "Whatever is needed, Highness. You and the Lord Marshal are the best judge of what that is. We'll stand surety for it."

Talia nodded, with all the other Councilors. What Selenay had told the man was true; for the past few months there had been tales of bandits growing organized in Gyrefalcon's Marches. Sporadic raids had occurred before this—but never had the brigands dared to put an entire town to the sword! It was obviously more than local militia could handle; the entire Council was agreed on that.

Talia slipped away then, knowing with certainty that Selenay did not need her at the moment, and that another most definitely did. The tug at her was unmistakable. She opened the door to the Council chamber just enough to slip through—and once she was out into the cool, dark hallway, broke into a run.

She ran out through the old Palace and passed the double doors of Herald's Collegium—then down the echoing main hall, heading for the side door and for Healer's. She felt the pull of a soul in agony as clearly as if she were being called by voice. She all but collided with Devan, who was on his way to look for her.

"I might have known you'd know," he said gratefully, hitching up his green robes so that he could run with her. "Talia, she's fighting us, and we can't get past her shielding to do even the simplest painblocks. She blames herself for Christa, and all she wants to do now is die. Rynee can't do anything with her."

"That's what I thought; Lord and Lady, the guilt is so thick I can almost *see* it. Well, let's see if I can get through to her."

They had accomplished a certain amount of Healing at the site of the battle, while Destria was still unconscious; enough to enable moving her safely. She still was a most unpretty sight, lying on a special pad in one of the rooms reserved for burn patients. The room itself was bare stone; scrubbed spotless twice a day when unoccupied, and not so much as a speck of dust was ever allowed to settle there. The one window was sealed tight so that nothing could blow in. Everything that was brought in was removed as soon as it was no longer needed, and scalded.

It was a tribute to the onsite Healers that Destria was still among the living. The last person Talia had seen with burns like hers had been Vostel, who had taken the full fury of an angry firebird on his fragile flesh. Where her burns had been relatively light—though the skin was red, puffed, and blistering—she was unbandaged. But her arms and hands were wrapped in special poultices of herbs and the thinnest and most fragile of tanned rabbit and calfskin, and Talia knew that beneath those bandages the skin was gone, and the flesh left raw. They had laid her on a pallet of lambskin, tanned with the wool on; the fibers would cushion her burned skin and prevent too much pressure from being exerted on it. Talia knelt at the head of the pallet and rested both her hands on Destria's forehead. Destria's face and head were the only portions of her that were relatively untouched. As Talia reached into the whirlwind of pain, delirium, and guilt with her Gift, she knew that this was likely to be the hardest such fight she'd ever faced.

Guilt, black and full of despair, surrounded Talia from all directions. Pain, physical and mental, lanced through the guilt like red lightning. Talia knew her first priority was to find out *why* the guilt existed in the first place, and where it was coming from—

That was easy enough; she simply lowered her shielding a fraction more, and let herself be drawn in where the negative emotions were the thickest.

The fading core that was Destria spun an ever-tightening cocoon of bleakness around herself. Talia reached for that cocoon with a softly glowing mental "hand" and withered it until that which was Destria stood cringing before her.

Talia paid no heed to her attempts at escape, but drew her into a rapport in which nothing was hidden; not from her—and not from Destria. And she let Destria read *her* as she strove to begin the Healing of the other Herald's mental hurts.

I failed—that was the most overwhelming. *They counted on me, and I failed.*

But there was something more, something that kept the guilt feeding on itself until Destria loathed her own being. And Talia found it, hiding underneath, festering. *And I failed because I wanted something for me. I failed because I was selfish; I don't deserve my Whites—I deserve to die.*

This was something Talia was only too familiar with; and was something Rynee wouldn't understand. Healers were firm believers in a little honest selfishness; it kept a person sane and healthy. Heralds, though—well, Heralds were supposed to be completely unselfish, totally devoted to duty. That was nonsense, of course; Heralds were only people. But sometimes they started to believe in that nonsense, and when something went wrong, because of their natures, the first people they tended to blame were themselves.

So now Talia had to prove to Destria that there was nothing wrong with being a Herald *and* human. No small task, since Destria's guilt was akin to doubts she shared about herself.

How often had she berated *herself* for wanting a little corner of life to call her own—some time when she didn't *have* to be a Herald—when she had been so tired of having to think first of others before taking the smallest action? How many times had she yearned for a little time to be lazy, a chance for a bit of privacy—and then felt guilty because she had?

And hadn't she had been ready to assume that she *was* guilty of unconsciously using her Empathy to manipulate others?

Hadn't she been angry enough to strangle someone more than once, and then been angry at herself for giving in to the weakness of rage?

Oh, she understood Destria's self-loathing, only too well.

Rynee and the rest of the Healers watched soberly, sensing the battle Talia fought, though (except for the perspiration beading Talia's brow) there were no outward signs of a struggle. They all remained in the same positions they had first taken as the shadows cast through the window lengthened almost imperceptibly and the light slowly faded; and still there was no outward indication of success or failure.

Then, after the first half-hour, Rynee whispered to Devan, "I think she's getting somewhere; Destria threw me out after the first few minutes and wouldn't let me in again."

When a full hour had passed, Talia sighed, then carefully broke her physical contact with the other Herald, and slumped with exhaustion, her hands lying limply on her thighs.

"Go ahead; I've got her convinced for now. She won't fight you at the moment."

As she spoke, the waiting Healers converged on Destria like worker-bees on an injured queen. Rynee, whose Gift of Healing was (like Talia's) for minds rather than bodies, helped Talia to her feet.

"Why couldn't *I* get through to her?" she asked plaintively.

"Simple; I'm a Herald, you're not," Talia said, edging past the Healers and out into the hall. "She reacted to you the way you would react to a nonHealer trying to tell you that a gut-stab was nothing to worry about. Gods, I'm *tired*! And I'll have it all to do again tomorrow, or she'll fight you again. And *then*, when I finally convince her permanently that it wasn't her fault, I'll have to convince her she isn't going to revolt men with—the way she'll look when you're done. And that the scarring isn't some punishment set on her for being a bit randy."

"I was afraid of that." Rynee bit her lip. "And she is going to scar; I can't tell you how badly yet, but there's no getting around it. Her face wasn't touched, but the rest of her—some of it isn't going to be at all pretty. The only burn victim I've ever heard of that was as bad was—"

Despite her weariness, Talia's eyes lighted when she saw an idea begin to form behind Rynee's frown. "Out with it, milady—you've the same Gift as I have, and if you've gotten a notion it's probably going to work." She paused in the hallway and leaned against the wood-paneled wall; Rynee rubbed the bridge of her long nose with her finger.

"Vostel—what does he do now? Could he be recalled here for a while?" she asked finally, hope in her cloud-gray eyes.

"Relay at the Fallflower Healing Temple; and yes, anyone on relay work can be replaced. What are you thinking of?"

"That he'll be the best 'medicine' for her; he went through it all himself. He knows how it hurts, and when it'll stop, and how you have to force yourself to work through the pain if you intend to get the full use of your limbs back. And he's a Herald, so she'll believe what he says. Besides all that, despite the old scars he's still a better-than-passable-looking man. And he *doesn't* believe in the fates dealing out arbitrary punishments for a little healthy hedonism."

Talia chuckled in spite of herself. "Oh, very good! If we have him at her side coaxing and encouraging, he'll do half our work for us! You're right about his beliefs, too. All I had to do was keep reassuring him that the pain *would* end, and that he wasn't being a coward and a whiner for occasionally wanting to give up. I've no doubt they'll find each other quite congenial when Destria's back to something like her old self and her old appetites. I'll see Kyril and get Vostel sent here as soon as he can be replaced; he'll be here by the time she starts to need him."

Talia moved away from the wall and stumbled as her knees wobbled a little. They had only gotten a few feet down the hall, and already her exhaustion was threatening to overwhelm her. Rynee steered her toward a soft and comfortable-looking padded bench, one of many

placed at intervals along the walls, for Healers were apt to catch odd-
ments of rest wherever and whenever they could.

"And you—you get yourself down onto that couch and take a short
nap. I'll wake you, but if you don't take some recovery time you won't
be of any use to any of us. You know the saying—never argue with a
Healer—"

"And I never do!"

"See that you keep it that way."

About a week later Talia was on her way from the Audience Chamber
to her own room to change for arms practice, and her mood was a
somber one. The audiences were no longer dull, and that was unfortunate. More and more often those seeking audience with the Queen
were from Gyrefalcon's Marches reporting the depredations of what
was obviously a small army of bandits. It was the wild and rocky character of the countryside that had let them organize without anyone
realizing it; that same wild countryside enabled them to vanish before
the Guard could pin them down.

Orthallen was using the existence of these bandits as a political
tool—a tactic that disgusted Talia, considering the suffering that they
were causing, not to mention that they were preying on some of the
lands supposedly in his jurisdiction.

She had just endured one such session.

There were six Heralds out there now—along with the Guard company Selenay had sent. The Heralds were organizing the common folk
to their own defense, since the Guard could not be everywhere at once.
One of those Heralds, Herald Patris, sent a messenger that had only
arrived today.

"They seem to know exactly where the Guard is at all times," Patris had written. "They strike, and are away before we can do anything. They know these hills of stone and the caves that honeycomb
them better than we guessed; I suspect them of traveling a great deal
underground, which would certainly answer the question of how they
move about without being spotted. At this point, we are beyond saving the livestock or the harvest; Majesty, I must be frank with you. It
will be all we can do just to save the lives of these people. And I must
tell you worse yet—having stripped them of all possessions, the bastards have taken to carrying off the only thing these folk have left.
Their children."

"Great Goddess!" Lady Wyrist had exclaimed.

"I'm on it, Majesty," Lady Cathan had said grimly at almost the same moment. "They won't get children out past my Guildsmen—not after that slaver scandal—with your permission?"

Selenay had nodded distractedly, and Lady Cathan sprinted from the room in a swirl of colorful brocades.

"Majesty," Orthallen said then, "it is as I have been saying. We need a larger standing army—and we need more autonomy in *local* hands. If I had been given two or three companies of the Guard and the power to order them, this emergency would *never* have become the disaster it is!"

Then the debate had broken out—yet again. The Council had split on this issue of granting power at the local level and increasing the size of the Guard; split about equally. On Orthallen's side were Lord Gartheser, Lady Wyrist, Bard Hyron, Father Aldon, and the Seneschal. Selenay—who did not want the size of the army increased, because to do so would mean drafted levies and possibly impressment—preferred to keep the power where it was, with the Council, and was lobbying for hiring professional mercenaries to augment the existing troops. Backing her were Talia, Kyril, Elcarth, Healer Myrim, and the Lord Marshal. Lady Kester, Lord Gildas, and Lady Cathan remained undecided. They weren't especially pleased with the notion of foreign troops, but they also weren't much in favor of hauling folk away from their lands and trades either.

Talia was pondering the state of things when her sharp ears caught the sound of a muffled sob. Without hesitation she unshielded enough to determine the source, and set out to find out was wrong.

Her sharp ears led her into a seldom-used hallway near the Royal Library, one lined with alcoves which could contain statues or suits of plate-mail or other large works of art, but which were mostly vacant and screened off by velvet curtains. This was a favored place for courting couples during great revels, but the lack of seating tended to confine assignations to those conducted standing.

She had a little problem finding the source of the sob, as it was hiding itself behind the curtains in one of those alcoves along this section of hall. Only a tiny sniffle gave her the clue as to which of three it was.

She drew the heavy velvet curtain aside quietly; curled up on a cushion purloined from a chair in the audience chamber was a child.

He was a little boy of about seven or eight; his eyes were puffy from crying, his face was smeared where he'd scrubbed tears away with dirty fingers, and from the look of him, he hadn't a friend in the world. She thought that he must have been adorable when he wasn't crying, a dark-haired, dark-eyed cherub; the uniform Selenay's pages wore, sky-blue trimmed in dark blue, suited his fair complexion. He looked up when the curtain moved, and his face was full of woe and dismay, his pupils dilated in the half-light of the hall.

"Hello," Talia said, sitting on her heels to bring herself down to his level. "You look like you could use a friend. Homesick?"

A fat tear trickled slowly down one cheek as he nodded. He looked very young to have been made one of Selenay's pages; she wondered if he weren't a fosterling.

"I was, too, when I got here. There weren't any girls my age when I first came, just boys. Where are you from?"

"G-g-gyrefalcon's Marches," he gulped, looking as if her sympathy had made him long for a comfortable shoulder to weep on, but not daring to fling himself on a strange adult.

"Can I share that pillow?" she asked, solving the problem for him. When he moved aside, she settled in with one arm comfortingly around his shoulders, projecting a gentle aura of sympathy. That released his inhibitions, and he sobbed into the velveteen of her jerkin while she soothingly stroked his hair. He didn't need her Gift, really. All he needed was a friend and a chance to cry himself out. While she gentled him, she pummeled her memory for who he could be.

"Are you Robin?" she asked finally, when the tears had slowed a bit. At his shaky affirmative she knew she'd identified him correctly. Robin's parents, who held their land of Lord Orthallen, had prevailed on Orthallen to take their only child to the safest haven they knew— Court. Understandable, even laudable, but poor Robin didn't see their reasoning. He only knew that he was alone for the first time in his young life.

"Haven't you found any friends yet?"

Robin shook his head and clutched her sleeve as he looked up to read her expression. When he saw that she was still sympathetic and encouraging he took heart enough to explain.

"They—they're all bigger an' older. They call me 'tagalong' an' they laugh at me . . . an' I don't like their games anyway. I—I can't run as fast or keep up with 'em."

"Oh?" She narrowed her eyes a little in thought, trying to remember just what it was she'd seen the pages playing at. You took them so for granted, they were almost invisible—then she had it.

"You don't like playing war and castles?" That was understandable enough, when fighting threatened his parents.

The flicker of the oil-lamp opposite their alcove showed her his sad, lost eyes. "I—I don't know how to fight. Da said I wasn't old enough to learn yet. That's *all* they want to do—an' anyway, I'd rather r-r-read—but all my books are still at h-h-home."

And if she knew the Seneschal, he'd strictly forbidden the pages to enter the Palace Library. Not too surprising, seeing as most of them would have played catapults using the furniture, with the books as ammunition. She hugged his slight shoulders, and made a quick decision.

"Would you like to be able to read and take lessons at the Herald's Collegium instead of with the pages?" Selenay had all of her pages schooled, but for most of them it was a plague to be endured or a nuisance to be avoided.

He nodded, his eyes round with surprise.

"Well, my master Alberich is going to have to wait a little; you and I are going to go see Dean Elcarth." She rose and offered her hand; he scrambled to his feet and clutched it.

Fortunately there were plenty of other youngsters being schooled at the Collegia—though few were as young as this one. They were the unaffiliated students—the "Blues"—who belonged to no Collegium, but were attending classes along with the Bardic, Healer, and Heraldic students. They, too, wore uniforms, of a pale blue, and not unlike the page's uniform. A good many of them were well-born brats, but there were others that were well-intentioned—those studying to be builders, architects, or scholars in many disciplines. They'd be well pleased to welcome Robin into their ranks, and they'd probably adopt him as a kind of mascot. Talia knew she'd have no trouble in arranging with Selenay for this little one to spend most of his time at the Collegium when he wasn't standing his duty—and at his age, his "duty" was probably less than an hour or two a day. She was pretty certain she'd be able to convince Elcarth as well.

She was right. When she took the child to Elcarth's cramped office, piled high with books, the Dean seemed to take to Robin immediately; Robin certainly did to him. She left him with Elcarth, the gray-haired Herald explaining some of the classes, Robin snuggled trustingly against his chair, both of them oblivious to the dust and clutter about them. It seemed that she'd unwittingly brought together a pair of kindred spirits.

So it proved; she met Robin from time to time thereafter—once or twice when he'd unthinkingly sought her out as a never-failing wellspring of comfort for homesickness, the rest of the time trudging merrily about the Collegium, his arms loaded with a pile of books almost as tall as he—and more than once, in the Library, with Elcarth. Once she found both of them bent over an ancient tome of history written in an archaic form of the language that little Robin couldn't read himself, but just knew Elcarth could—and said so. He was convinced that Elcarth was the original fount of all knowledge. He was bringing Elcarth all his questions, as naturally as breathing.

Until now Talia frequently found both of them immersed in something so dry that she needed a drink just thinking about it! Kindred souls, indeed.

CHAPTER 4

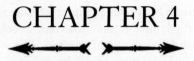

D IRK SPRAWLED IN his favorite chair in his quarters, a battered old piece of furniture long ago faded to indeterminate beige, but one that was as comfortable as an old boot. He wished that he could be as comfortable inside as he was outside.

He stared at the half-empty glass in his hand morosely. He shouldn't be drinking on such a fine night. He was drinking far too much of late, and he knew it.

But what's a man to do when he can't sleep? When all he thinks of is a certain pair of soft brown eyes? When he doesn't know whether to betray his own heart or his best friend?

The only cure for his insomnia was to be found at the bottom of a bottle; so that's where he usually was at day's end.

Of course the cure had its drawbacks; wretched hangovers, increasingly ill temper, and the distinct feeling that avoiding problems was the coward's way out. He longed for a field assignment—oh, gods, to get away from the Collegium and Her! But nothing of the kind was forthcoming—and anyway, they wouldn't assign anything to Kris or him until their current batch of students was fully trained in the use of their Gifts.

Their students—gods, there was another reason to drink.

He finished the glass without even noticing he'd done so, eyes burning with unshed tears.

Poor little Christa. He wondered if anyone else had figured out she had been using her Gift to save the little ones in that fire.

Any time I close my eyes, I can almost see her—

The self-conjured vision was horrific. He could picture her only too easily; surrounded by an inferno, steadfastly *concentrating* with all her soul—because moving anything alive by means of the Fetching Gift was hard; hard and dangerous—while the building went up in flames around her. And it was all his fault that she'd sacrificed herself that way.

He raised his glass to his lips, only to discover that it was empty already.

I'm drinking this bottle too fast—

And the way she'd died—it was all his fault.

Before Christa had finished training with him she'd asked him if it was possible to move *living* things by Fetching. Anyone else he'd have told "no"—but she was so good, and he was so infernally proud of her. So he told her the truth, and what was more, done what he'd never done before and showed her how; how to move live creatures without smothering them, without twisting them up inside. And he'd told her (gods, how well he remembered telling her) that when it had to be done, it was far safer to move a living thing from your hands to where you wanted it to go, than from where it was to your hands.

I am definitely drinking this too fast—the bottle's half empty already.

That was why she'd gone in to send the babies out, not Fetched them out to her. If only he'd known when he'd taught her what he'd discovered since, researching in the Library—that under great stress it was often possible for someone with their Gift to transport *themselves* short distances. He'd *meant* to tell her—but somehow he never found the time.

Now she's dead, horribly, painfully dead, because I "never found the time."

He shook the bottle, surprised to find it empty already.

Oh, well, there's another where that one came from.

He didn't even have to get up; the second bottle was cooling on the windowsill. He reached out an unsteady hand and somehow managed to grab the neck of it. He'd already taken the cork out when he was sober, then stuck it back in loosely. If he hadn't, he'd never have gotten the bottle open.

Gods, I'm disgusting.

He knew this was not the way to be handling the problem; that he should be doing what his heart was telling him to do—find Talia, and let *her* help him work it all out. But he couldn't face her. Not like this.

I can't let her see me like this. I can't. She'll think I'm—I'm worse than what Naril called me.

Besides, if he did go to her, she'd read the rest of what was on his mind, and then what would he do? Gods, what a tangle he'd gotten himself into.

I—I need her, dammit. But—do I need her more than Kris does? I don't know. I just don't know.

He couldn't ask Kris for help, not when Kris was the other half of the problem. And music was no longer a solace, not when every time he played he could hear *her* singing, haunting every line.

Damn the woman! She steals my friend, she steals my music, she steals my peace of mind—

In the next instant he berated himself for even thinking such things. That wasn't fair, it wasn't her fault. She hadn't the least notion of what she'd done to him.

And so far as he'd been able to tell, she really hadn't been spending all that much time with Kris since she'd gotten back. Maybe there *was* hope for him, after all. She and Kris surely weren't behaving like lovers.

But what would he do if they *were* in love?

For that matter, what would he do if they *weren't?*

The level in the bottle continued to go down as he tried—and failed—to cope.

Robin trotted happily down the hall to the Herald's quarters. He adored the Heralds, and was always the first to volunteer when someone had a task that would involve his helping them in any way. In this case it was twice the pleasure, for the Queen's Own, Herald Talia, had come looking for a page to return some manuscripts she'd borrowed from Herald Dirk for copying. Robin loved Herald Talia better than all the others put together—excepting only Elcarth. Heralds were wonderful, and Talia was even more than usually wonderful; she always had time to talk, she never told him he was being a baby (like Lord Orthallen did) when he was homesick. His Mama had told him how important Lord Orthallen was, but so far as Robin was concerned, Talia was worth any twelve Orthallens. He had often wished he could make her smile the way she could cheer him up. She wasn't looking very happy lately and anything he could do to make her brighten a little, he would, and gladly.

There was a swirl of somber robes ahead of him—one of the Great Lords. Maybe even his own Lord. Robin kept his eyes down as he'd always been told to do. It wasn't proper for a little boy to gawk at the Great Lords of State, especially not when that little boy was supposed to be running an errand. If it *was* Orthallen, it was important for him to see that Robin was properly doing his duty.

So it was rather a shock, what with the fact that he was watching where he was going and all, when he tripped and went sprawling face-first, all his scrolls flying about him.

If the one ahead of him had been a fellow page, he would immediately have suspected he'd been tripped a-purpose. But a Great Lord could hardly be suspected of a childish prank like that.

The Great Lord paused just a moment, papers fluttering around his feet, then went on. Robin kept his eyes down, blushing scarlet in humiliation, and began collecting them.

Now that was odd. That was *very* odd. He'd had fourteen scrolls when he'd been sent on this errand. He knew, because he'd counted them in Talia's presence twice. Now he had fifteen. And the fifteenth one was sealed, not just rolled up like the others.

He could have gotten muddled, of course.

But he could almost hear Dean Elcarth's voice in his ear, because he'd asked Elcarth just this very week what he should do if he was asked to do something that didn't seem quite right, or if something happened in the course of his duties that seemed odd. One of the older boys had been sent on a very dubious errand by one of the ladies of the Court, and there'd been trouble afterward. The page involved hadn't had the nerve to tell anyone until it was too late, and by then his memory was all confused. So Robin had asked the wisest person he knew what he should do if he found himself in a similar case.

"Do it, don't disobey—but remember, Robin," Elcarth had told him, "remember *everything;* what happened, who asked you, and when, and why, and who was with them. It may be that what you're being told to do is perfectly legitimate. You could have no way of knowing. But if it isn't, you could be the only person to know the real truth of something. You pages are in a very special position, you know, people look at you, but they really don't see you. So keep that in mind, and if anything ever happens around you that seems odd, remember it; remember the circumstances. You may help someone that way."

"Isn't that being a little like a sneak?" Robin had asked doubtfully.

Elcarth had laughed and ruffled his hair. "If you ask that question, you're in no danger of becoming one, my little owl. Besides, it's excellent training for your memory."

Very well then. Robin would remember this.

There was no answer when Robin tapped at Herald Dirk's half-open door. When he peeked inside, he could see Herald Dirk slumped in a chair at the farther end of the room by his open window. He seemed to be asleep, so Robin slipped inside, quiet as a cat, and left the scrolls on his desk.

Talia didn't need a summons that morning; anyone with the vaguest hint of her Gift of Empathy would have come running to the Queen's side. Emotional turmoil—anger, fear, worry—was so thick in the air Talia *could* taste it, bitter and metallic.

She caught the first notes of it as she was dressing, and ran for the royal chambers as soon as she was decent. The two Guards outside the door looked very uncomfortable, as if they were doing their level best to be deaf to the shouting behind the double doors they guarded. Talia tapped once, and cracked one door open.

Selenay was in her outer chamber, dressed for the day, but without her coronet. She was sitting behind her worktable in her "public" room; there was a sealed scroll on the table before her. With her were Lord Orthallen (looking unbearably smug), a very embarrassed Kris, an equally embarrassed Guardsman, and an extremely angry Dirk.

"I don't give a fat damn how it got there—*I didn't take it!*" Dirk was shouting as Talia glanced at the sentry outside and entered. She shut the door behind her quickly. Whatever was going on here, the fewer people there were who knew about it, the better.

"Then why were you trying to hide it?" Orthallen asked smoothly.

"I wasn't trying to hide it, dammit! I was *looking* for my headache-powders when this idiot barged in without a by-your-leave!" Dirk did look slightly ill; pale, with a pain-crease between his brows, his sapphire-blue eyes thoroughly bloodshot, his straw-blond hair more than usually tangled.

"We have only your word for that."

"Since when," Talia said clearly and coldly, "has a Herald's word been subject to cross-examination? Your pardon, Majesty, but what in the Havens' name is going on here?"

"I discovered this morning, that some rather sensitive documents were missing," Selenay answered, looking outwardly calm, though Talia knew she was anything but untroubled. "Lord Orthallen insti-gated a search, and he found them in Herald Dirk's possession."

"I haven't been anywhere near the Palace wings for the past week! Besides, what use could I possibly make of the damned things?" Dirk's mental anguish was so intense that Talia wanted to weep.

"Look, Uncle, you *know* my quarters are just down the hall from his. I can pledge the fact that he didn't leave them all last night."

"Nephew, I know this man is your friend."

"If I have to be brutally frank, then I will be," Kris said, flushing an angry and embarrassed red. "Dirk couldn't have moved anywhere because he wasn't in any shape to move. He was dead drunk last night, just like he's been *every* night for the past couple of weeks."

Dirk went almost purple, then deathly white.

"So? Since when has inability to move physically hampered anyone with *his* Gift?"

Now it was Kris' turn to pale.

"I haven't heard an answer to a very good question—Orthallen, what on earth would Dirk *want* with those documents?" Talia asked, trying to buy a little time to think.

"They would put someone in this Court in a rather indelicate position," Orthallen replied. "And let us say that the person is entangled with a young lady with whom Herald Dirk was at one time very much involved himself. Their parting was somewhat acrimonious. His motivation could be complex—revenge, perhaps. Blackmail, perhaps. The Queen and I have been attempting to keep this situation from escalating into scandal, but if anyone excepting us saw the contents of these letters, it could throw the entire Court into an uproar."

"I can't believe I'm hearing a Councilor accuse a *Herald* of blackmail!" Talia cried out indignantly.

"You just heard my nephew—his best friend—say he's been drinking himself insensible every night for the past few weeks. Does *that* sound like normal behavior for a Herald?" Orthallen turned to the Queen. "Majesty, I am not saying that this young man would have purloined these documents were he in his proper mind, but I think there is more than enough evidence to indicate that—"

"Orthallen," the queen interrupted him, "I—"

"Wait just a moment—don't anyone say anything." Talia held one hand to her temple, feeling pain stab through her head. The hot press of the emotions of those around her was so intense she was getting a reaction-headache from trying to shield herself. "Let's just assume for one moment that Dirk is telling the absolute truth, shall we?"

"But—"

"No, hear me out. Under that assumption, in what *way—other than someone deliberately going into his room and planting them there*—could those documents have gotten where they were found? Dirk, were they there after dinner?"

"Before I started drinking, you mean?" Dirk replied bitterly. "No. My desk was perfectly clean, for a change. When I woke up this morning, there were about a dozen scrolls there, and this was one of them."

"Fine. I know if someone had gone into your room that normally didn't belong there, you'd have woken up, no matter what. I can tell you that *I* sent Robin to you last night with those poems I borrowed. There were exactly fourteen scrolls, and *that* wasn't one of them. Now unless Lord Orthallen would like to accuse *me* of purloining those documents—"

"I still had them after you left, Talia," the Queen said, a distinct edge to her voice.

"I also know that none of the Heralds would wake up for a page entering their room unless the page deliberately woke them. The little devils are too ubiquitous; practically invisible, and we all *know* they're harmless. So, it is possible that some time between when Robin left me and when he got to your room, Dirk, an extra scroll got added to his pile."

"Guard," Selenay addressed the fourth person in the room, and the Guardsman turned to the Queen with gratitude suffusing his face. "Fetch Robin, please, would you? He'll be having breakfast in the page's room about now. Just ask for him."

The Guard left, plainly happy to be out of the situation.

When he returned with Robin, Talia took the child to one side, away from the others, and closer to the Queen than to Orthallen. She spoke quietly and encouragingly, taking the initiative before Orthallen had a chance to try and bully him.

"Robin, I gave you some papers to take to Herald Dirk last night. How many were there?"

"I—" He looked troubled. "I *thought* there were fourteen, but—"

"But?"

"I fell down, and when I picked them up, there were fifteen. I know, because Dean Elcarth told me to remember things that were funny, and that was funny."

"When did you fall down?"

"Near the staircase, by the lion tapestry."

"Was anyone else nearby? Did you run into anyone?"

"I wasn't running," he said indignantly. "There was a m'lord, but—m'lady, Mama always told me not to stare at m'lords, so—I didn't see who it was."

"Bright Stars!" Orthallen suddenly looked shamefaced—almost horror-stricken—though somehow Talia had the feeling that he was putting on an act. Certainly there was nothing she could sense empathically behind his expression. "That was *me*—and I had the scroll at the time. Stars, I must have dropped it, and the child picked it up!" He turned to Dirk, a faint flush creeping over his face, and spread his hands with an apologetic grimace. "Herald Dirk, my most *profound* apologies. Majesty, I hardly know what to say."

"I think we've all said quite enough for one morning," Selenay replied tiredly. "Dirk, Kris, I am terribly sorry. I hope you'll all put this down to an excess of zeal. Talia—"

Talia just shook her head a little, and said, "We can all talk about it when we've cooled down. Right now is not the time."

Selenay gave her a smile of gratitude as Orthallen used this as a cue to excuse himself.

Talia was not sorry to see him leave.

Selenay detailed the Guard to escort Robin back, and asked Talia, "Have you had anything to eat yet? I thought not. Then go do so, and I'll see you in Council."

The three Heralds left together, the Guardsman right behind them, escorting a mystified Robin back to the page's quarters. Talia could feel Dirk seething, and braced herself for the explosion.

As soon as they were a sufficient distance from the Queen's chambers that they were likely to have no audience, it came.

"Thanks a lot, *friend*!" Dirk all but hissed. "Thanks ever so much, *brother*! How I ever managed without your help, I'll never know!"

"Look, Dirk—I'm sorry—"

"Sorry! Dammit, you didn't even believe me! My best friend, and you didn't believe a single word I said!"

"Dirk!"

"Then telling everyone I'm some kind of drunken fool—"

"I didn't say that!" Kris was beginning to get just as angry as Dirk was.

"You didn't have to! You implied it very nicely! *And* gave your precious uncle more ammunition to use on me!"

"Dirk, Kris has every right to worry about you if you've been acting oddly. And Kris, Dirk's right. Even I could tell you didn't believe him without having to read you." Talia knew she should have kept her mouth shut, but couldn't help herself. "And he's right about Orthallen."

They both turned on her as one, and spoke in nearly the same breath.

"And I don't need any more help from you, 'Queen's Own'—"

"Talia, I'm getting very tired of listening to your childish suspicions about my uncle—"

She went white-lipped with anger and hurt. "*Fine, then*—" she snarled, clenching her fists and telling herself that she *would not* deliver a pair of hearty blows to those stubborn chins. "I wash my hands of both of you! You can *both* go to Hell in a gilded carriage for all of me! With purple cushions!"

Unable to get another coherent word out, she spun on her toe and ran to the closest exit, and didn't stop running until she reached the Field and the sympathetic shoulder of Rolan.

"*Now* look what you've done!" Dirk sneered in triumph.

"What *I've* done?" Kris lost what little remained of his temper and groped visibly for words adequate to express his anger. "Gods, I hope you're satisfied—now that you've managed to get her mad at both of us!"

In point of fact, a nasty little part of him Dirk hadn't dreamed existed *was* pleased, for now, at least, they were on an equally bad footing with Talia. He could hardly admit it, though. "Me? All *I* did was defend myself—"

"I," Kris interrupted angrily, "have had just about enough of this. I'll talk to you about this mess if and when you decide to stop behaving like a damn fool and when you quit drinking yourself into a stupor every night. Until then—"

"This is just a little too public a place for you to start making threats."

Kris bit back the angry words that he knew would put any hope of reconciliation out of reach. "Far too public," he replied stiffly, "and what we have to say to each other is far too private, and can and should wait until then."

Dirk made an ironic little bow. "At your pleasure."

There didn't seem to be any way to respond to that, so Kris just nodded abruptly, and stalked off down the corridor.

Dirk found himself standing alone in the deserted corridor, temples pounding with a hangover, feeling very much abused. He wanted to feel vindicated, and all he really felt like was a fool. And very much alone.

By the time Talia arrived for her weaponry lesson, Alberich had heard the rumors that Kris and Dirk had had a falling-out. He was not too terribly surprised when Talia appeared for her practice session wearing an expression so coldly impassive it might have been a mask. Few even at the Collegium would have guessed how well he could read the Queen's Own, or how well he knew her. She had quite won his heart as a student—so very alone, and so determined to do everything perfectly. She seldom tried to make excuses for herself, and never gave up, not even when she knew she had no chance of success. She had reminded him of times long past, and a young and idealistic student-cadet of Karse—and his sympathy and soul had gone out to her. Not that he would ever have let her know. He never betrayed his feelings to his students while they were still students.

He had a shrewd idea of how matters stood with her in regard to her feelings about Dirk and Kris. So he had a fairly good idea what her reaction to the quarrel might be.

This afternoon the lesson called for Talia to work out alone against the Armsmaster. She did not hold back in the least—began attacking him, in fact, with blind fury as soon as the lesson began. Alberich let her wear herself out for a bit, scar-seamed face impassive, then caught her with a feint not even a beginner would have fallen for and disarmed her.

"Enough—quite enough," he said, as she stood white and drained and panting with exhaustion. "Have I not told you many times, it is with your intellect you fight, not with your anger? Anger you are to leave at the door. It will kill you. Look how you have let it wear you out! Had this been a real fight, your anger would have done half your enemy's work for him."

Talia's shoulders sagged. "Master Alberich—"

"Enough, I have said it," he interrupted, picking up her blade from the floor. He took three soundless steps toward her, and placed one callused hand on her shoulder. "Since the anger cannot be left at the door, you will confide it?"

Talia capitulated, letting him push her gently toward the seats at the edge of the floor. She slumped dispiritedly down onto a bench pushed up against the wall as he seated himself beside her. After a long moment of silence, she gave him a brief outline of the morning's events. She kept her eyes for the most part on a beam of the late afternoon sunlight that fell upon the smooth, sanded, gray-brown wooden floor. No sound penetrated into the salle from the outside, and the ancient building smelled of dust and sweat. Alberich sat beside her, absolutely motionless, hands clasped around the ankle that rested on his right knee. Talia glanced at him from time to time, but his harsh, hawklike face remained unreadable.

Finally when she had finished, he stirred just a little, raising his hand to rub the side of his nose.

"I tell you what I have never admitted," he said after a long pause, tapping his lips with one finger, thoughtfully. "I have never trusted Lord Orthallen. And I have served Valdemar fully as long as he."

Talia was taken aback. "But—"

"Why? Any number of small things. He is too perfect the servant of the State, never does he take for himself any reward. And when a man does not claim a reward visibly, I look for a reward hidden. He does not openly oppose the Heraldic Circle, but when others do, he is always just behind them, pushing, gently pushing. He is everyone's friend—and no one's intimate companion. Also, my Companion does not like him."

"Rolan doesn't either."

"A good measure by which to judge the man, I think. I believe that your suspicions are correct; that he has been striving to undermine your influence with Selenay. I think that since he has failed at that, he turns to eliminating your friends, to weaken your emotional base. I think he well knows how it hurts you to see young Dirk injured."

Talia blushed.

"You are the best judge of the truth of what I say." He shifted on the hard, worn bench and recrossed his legs, ankle over knee. "My guess— he knows Kris is your partisan; he could not get Kris to repudiate you so he decided to set the two great friends at odds with each other in hopes you would be caught in the middle."

"Me? But—"

"If he is of the mind to undermine your authority, this is one way of it," Alberich added quietly, hands clasped thoughtfully over one knee. "To chip away at those supporting you until they are so entangled in their own misfortune that they can spare no time for helping you."

"I see what you're getting at, now. He's removing my support in such a way that *I'm* set off-balance. Then, when I'm in a particularly delicate position, give me a little shove"—Talia flicked out a finger—"and with no one to advise me or give me backing, I vacillate, or start making mistakes. And all the things he's been whispering about my not being quite up to the job look like something more than an old man's mistrust of the young. I thought you didn't deal with Court politics . . ." She smiled wanly at her instructor.

"I said I do not play the game; I never said I did not know how the game was played." His mouth turned up a little at one corner. "Be advised, however, that I have never told anyone of my suspicions because I seemed to be alone in them—and I did not intend to give Lord Orthallen a reason to gaze in my direction. It is difficult enough being from Karse—without earning high-placed enemies."

Talia nodded with sympathy. It had been hard enough on her during *her* first years at the Collegium. She could hardly imagine what it had been like for someone hailing from the land that was Valdemar's traditional enemy.

"Now I do think he has miscalculated, perhaps to his eventual grief. It is that he has badly underestimated the unity of the Circle, I think, or it is that he cannot understand it. Among the courtiers, such a falling out as is between Kris and Dirk would be permanent—and woe betide she caught between them!"

Talia sighed. "I know they'll make up eventually—Lord of Lights, though, I'm not sure I can deal with the emotional lightnings and thunders till they do! Why couldn't Ahrodie and Tantris get their hooves into this and straighten it out?"

"Why do you not?" Alberich retorted. "They are our Companions and friends, *delinda,* not our overseers. They leave our personal lives to ourselves, nor would any of us thank them for interfering. Yes, they will most probably be whispering sensible things into their Chosen's minds, but you know well they will not force either of the two into anything."

She sighed wistfully. "If I were a little less ethical, I'd fix both of them."

"If you were a little less ethical, you would not have been Chosen," Alberich pointed out. "Now, since the anger is gone, shall we return to the exercise of the body in place of the tongue?"

"Do I have a choice?" Talia asked, as she rose from her place on the bench.

"No, *delinda*, you do not—so guard yourself!"

Elspeth had encountered Orthallen during one of her rare moments of leisure; she was dawdling a bit on her way back to her suite in the Palace to dress for dinner with the Court. She took dinner with the Court once a week—"to remind everyone" (in her own wry words) "that they still have an Heir."

She was standing before an open second-story window; some of the gardens were directly below her. She was wearing a rather wistful expression and hadn't realized there was anyone else in the corridor with her until Orthallen touched her elbow.

She jumped and started back (one hand brushing a hidden dagger) when she realized who it was and relaxed.

"Havens, Lord-Un—Lord Orthallen, you startled me out of a year's life!"

"I most sincerely hope not," he replied, "But I do wish you would continue to call me 'Lord-Uncle' as you started to. Surely now that you're nearly through your studies you aren't going to become formal with me!"

"All right, Lord-Uncle, since you ask it. Just remember to defend me for my impudence when Mother takes me to task for it!" Elspeth grinned, and leaned back on the window-frame a little.

"Now what is it that you were watching with such a long face?" he asked lightly, coming close enough to look out of the window himself.

Below the window were some of the Palace gardens; in the gardens a half-dozen couples—children of courtiers or courtiers themselves—ranging from Elspeth's age upward to twenty or so. They were involved in the usual sorts of activities that might be expected from a group of adolescents in a sunny garden in the spring. One couple was engaged in a mock-game of "tag," one girl was embroidering while her gallant read to her, two maids were giggling and gasping at the antics of two lads balancing on the basin of a fountain, one young gentleman was peacefully asleep with his head in the lap of his chosen lady, two couples were simply strolling hand in hand.

Elspeth sighed.

"And why aren't you down there, my lady?" Orthallen asked quietly.

"Havens, Lord-Uncle, where would I get the time?" Elspeth's reply was impatient and a touch self-pitying. "Between my classes and everything else—besides, I don't know any boys, at least not well. Well, there's Skif, but he's busy chasing Nerissa. Besides, he's even older than Talia."

"You don't know any young men—when half the swains of the Court are near dying just to speak to you?" Orthallen's expression of incredulity held as much of bitter as playful mockery, though Elspeth was so used to his manners that she hardly noted it.

"Well, if they're near-dying, nobody told *me* about it, and nobody's bothered to introduce us."

"If that's all that's lacking, I will be happy to make the introductions. Seriously, Elspeth, you are spending far too much of your time among the Heralds and Heraldic Students. Heralds make up only a very small part of Valdemar, my dear. You need to get to know your courtiers better, particularly those of your own age. Who knows? You may one day wish to choose a consort from among them. You can hardly do that if you don't know any of them."

"You have a point, Lord-Uncle," Elspeth mused, taking another wistful glance out the window, "But when am I going to find the time?"

"Surely you have an hour or two in the evenings?"

"Well, yes, usually."

"There's your answer."

Elspeth smiled. "Lord-Uncle, you're almost as good at solving problems as Talia!"

Her face fell a trifle then, and Orthallen's right eyebrow rose as he took note of her expression.

"Is there some problem with Talia?"

"Only—only that there's only one of her. Mother needs her more than I do, I know that—but—I wish I could talk to her the way I used to when she was still a student. She doesn't have the time anymore."

"You could talk to me," Orthallen pointed out. "Besides, Talia's first loyalty is to your mother; she might feel obliged to tell her what you confided in her."

Elspeth did not reply to this, but his words made her very thoughtful.

"At any rate, we were speaking of those young gentlemen who are perishing to make your acquaintance. Would you care to meet some of them tonight, after dinner? In the garden by the fountain, for instance?"

Elspeth blushed and her eyes sparkled. "I'd *love* to!"

"Then," Orthallen made her a sweeping bow, "it shall be as my lady commands."

Elspeth thought a great deal about that conversation as she sat through dinner. On the one hand, she trusted Talia; on the other, if there *were* a conflict of loyalties there was no doubt to whom her first allegiance was due. She hadn't thought about it before—but the idea of her mother knowing *everything* about her wasn't a comfortable one.

Especially since Selenay didn't appear to be taking Elspeth's maturity very seriously.

But Elspeth had gained inches since Talia had gone—and with the inches, a woman's curves. She was taking more care with her appearance; she'd seen the glances given some of her older friends by the young males of the Collegium and recently those glances had seemed very desirable things to collect. She found that lately she was looking to the young men of Collegium and Court with an eye less bemused and more calculating. And to the eyes of a stranger—

She'd looked at herself in her mirror before dinner, trying to appraise what she saw there. Lithe, taller than Talia by half a head, wavy sable hair and velvety brown eyes—the body of a young goddess, if certain people were to be believed, and the look of one more than ready to know more of life—yes. There was no doubt that to a stranger, she looked more than ready to be thinking about wedding or bedding, certainly old enough by the standards of the Court.

Or so Elspeth thought, setting her chin stubbornly. Well, if her mother wouldn't see on her own that Elspeth was quite fully grown now, perhaps there were ways to bring that knowledge home to her.

And, she thought, catching sight of Lord Orthallen among a group of quite fascinating-looking young men, *it just might be rather exciting as well. . . .*

CHAPTER 5

THE WEATHER, WHICH had briefly taken a turn for the better, soured again. Talia's mood was none too sweet either.

The rains returned, and with them, spoiled tempers among the Councilors. Again Talia found herself spending as much time intervening in personal quarrels as helping to make decisions. Orthallen, strangely enough, seemed content now to let her alone. He brooded down at his end of the Council table like some huge white owl, face blank and inscrutable, pondering mysterious thoughts of his own. This alarmed her more than it reassured her. She took to examining every word she intended to say, and weighing it against all the possible ways Orthallen might be able to use what she said against her at some later date.

Dirk split his free time either lurking in her vicinity or hiding out in the wet. The one was as frustrating as the other. Either she didn't see him at all, or she saw him but couldn't get near him. For whenever she tried to approach him, he turned pale, looked around—wearing a frantic expression—for the nearest exit, and escaped with whatever haste was seemly. He seemed to have a sixth sense for when she was trying to catch him; she couldn't even trap him in his rooms. Either that, or he somehow knew when she was at the door, and pretended he wasn't there.

Kris all but hibernated in *his* room. And Talia was determined *not* to see him until he apologized for what he'd said to her. While their quarrel of itself was of no great moment, she was tired to death of having to justify her feelings about his uncle. After her little talk with Alberich, she was certain—with a surety that came all too seldom—that in the case of Orthallen she was entirely in the right, and he was entirely in the wrong. And *this* time she was going to hold out until he acknowledged the fact!

Meanwhile she made up for the absence of both of them by trying to be everywhere at once.

She was shorting herself of sleep to do so, and still felt there was much she wasn't doing. But there was just so much *work;* Selenay had asked her to take on the interviews of petitioners from the flooded areas, Devan needed her with three profoundly depressed patients, and there were all those quarrels among the Councilors.

It was with heartfelt gratitude that she found the sessions with Destria going well; Vostel's arrival put the cap on their success. It was plain to Talia that his reaction to Destria's appearance comforted her immensely. It helped that he regarded her scars as badges of honor and told her so in as many words. And as Rynee had thought, he was of tremendous aid when they began Destria's rehabilitative therapy—for he had gone through all this himself. He coaxed her when she faltered, bolstered her courage when it ran out, goaded her when she turned sulky, and held her when she wept with pain. He was doing so much for her that she needed Talia's Gift less with every day.

Which was just as well, for Selenay needed it the more. As soon as one crisis was solved, another sprang up like a noxious weed, and Selenay's resources were wearing thin. And when some of the choices she made turned out to be the wrong ones—as, soon or late, happened—Talia found herself exercising her good sense and Gift to the utmost.

A drenched and mud-splattered messenger from Herald Patris stood before the Council; when the door-Guard had learned his news, he'd interrupted the session to bring him there himself.

"Majesty," the man said, with a blank expression that Talia found very disconcerting, and which made her very uneasy, "Herald Patris sends this to tell you that the outlaws are no more."

He held out a sealed message pouch as those at the Council board erupted in cheers and congratulations. Only the Queen, Kyril, and Selenay did not join in the rejoicing. There was something about the messenger's expression that told them there was much he had not said.

Selenay opened the message and scanned it, the blood draining from her face as she did so.

"Goddess—" the parchment sheet fell from her nerveless fingers, and Talia caught it. The Queen covered her face with trembling hands, as the tumult around the Council table died into absolute silence.

Her Councilors stared at their monarch, and at an equally pale Queen's Own, as Talia read Patris' grim words in a voice that shook.

"'We ran the brigands to earth, but by the time they were brought to bay, the temper of the Guard was fully aroused. We cornered them at their own camp, a valley overlooked by Darkfell Peak. It was then that they made the mistake of killing the envoy sent to parley. At that point the Guard declared "no quarter." They went mad—that is the only way I can describe it. They were no longer rational men; they were blood-mad berserkers. Perhaps it was being out here too long, chasing phantoms—perhaps the foul weather—I do not know. It was hideous. Nothing I or anyone else could say or do was able to curb them. They fell on the encampment—and the outlaws were slaughtered to the last man.'"

Talia took a deep breath, and continued. "'It was not just the outlaws themselves; the Guard slew every living thing in their bolt-hole, be it man, woman, or beast. But that was not the worst of the horrors, though that was horror enough. Among the dead—'"

Talia's voice failed, then, and Kyril took the message from her, and continued in a hoarse half-whisper.

"'Among the dead were the very children we had hoped to save. All—all of them, dead. Slain by their captors when it became obvious that they would get no mercy from the Guard.'"

The Councilors stared in dumb shock, as Selenay wept without shame.

Selenay blamed herself for not replacing the Guard companies with fresher troops or for not sending someone who could have controlled the weary Guardsmen no matter what strain the troops were under.

Nor was the murder of the children the only tragedy, although it was the greatest. Vital intelligence had been lost in that slaughter— who their leader had been, and whether or not he had been acting under orders from outside the Kingdom.

It took days before Selenay was anything like her normal self.

The one blessing, so far as Talia was concerned, was that Orthallen exercised a little good sense and chose to back down on his militant stance for more local autonomy; just as well, for Lady Kester's people began having the expected troubles with pirates and coastal raiders, and the promised troops had to be shifted to the West. But before they

could reach their deployments, Herald Nathen was seriously hurt leading the fisherfolk in beating off a slaving raid.

And that opened up another wonder-chest of troubles.

Nathen himself came before them, although the Healers protested that
he was not yet well enough to do so. He was a sharp-featured man, not
old, but no longer young; brown-haired, brown-eyed—quite unre-
markable except for the intensity in those eyes, and an anger that kept
him going when nothing else was left to him. He sat, rather than stood,
facing the entire Council. He was heavily bandaged, with his arm
bound against his side, and still physically so weak he could scarcely
speak above a whisper.

"My ladies, my lords—" he coughed, "—I did not dare trust this to
anyone but myself. Messengers can be waylaid, documents purloined—"

"My lord Herald," Gartheser said smoothly, "I think you may be
overreacting. Your injuries . . ."

"Did *not* cause me to hallucinate what I heard," Nathen snapped, his
anger giving him a burst of strength. "We captured a prisoner, Councilors; I interrogated him myself under Truth Spell *before* I was hurt.
The brigands are serving those slavers we thought banished!"

"*What?*" Lady Cathan choked out, as she half-stood, then collapsed
back into her seat.

"There is worse. The slave-traders are not working unaided. I have
it by my prisoner's confession *and* by written proofs that they have been
aided and abetted by Lord Geoffery of Helmscarp, Lord Nestor of La-
verin, Lord Tavis of Brengard, and TradeGuildsmen Osten Deveral,
Jerard Stonesmith, Petar Ringwright, and Igan Horstfel."

He sank back into his own chair, eyes still burning with controlled
rage, as the Council erupted into accusation and counter-accusation.

"How could this have occurred without your knowledge, Cathan?"
Gartheser demanded. "By the gods, I begin to wonder just how assid-
uous you were in rooting out the *last* lot—"

"You were right up there in the front ranks to accuse me the last
time, Gartheser," Cathan sneered, "but I seem to remember you were
also the one who insisted I do all the dirty work. I am only one woman;
I can't be everywhere at once."

"But Cathan, I *cannot* see how this could have escaped your knowledge," Hyron protested. "Those four named are of first-rank."

"And the other three are Kester's liegemen," added Wyrist, suspiciously. "I'd like to know how *they* managed to operate a slaving ring
under Kester's nose."

"And so would I," Lady Kester snapped. "More than you, I reckon."

And so it went, as Selenay mediated the strife among her Councilors. Talia had her hands full seeing that she remained sane during all of it.

All this, of course, meant that she had no time to pay heed to her own problems—most particularly that of the rift between Dirk and Kris, Kris and herself, and Dirk and herself.

It was bad enough that the quarrel existed—but to add yet another pine-bough to the conflagrations, Rolan was causing her considerable discomfort.

He was the premier stallion of the Companion herd and while Talia had been on internship, had only had another stallion—Kris' Tantris—for company. Now he was making up for his enforced celibacy with a vengeance—and the partner he dallied with most often was Dirk's Ahrodie.

And Talia shared it—couldn't block it if she tried. Not that she blamed Rolan; Ahrodie was sweet, attractive, and a most cooperative partner. She ought to know; she was on the empathic receiving end of all of it. But to have this going on, two and three times a week, while she positively ached for Ahrodie's Chosen—well, it was unpleasantly like torture. Rolan evidently had no notion of what he was doing to his Chosen, and Talia refused to spoil his pleasure by letting him know.

So she lost further sleep at night; either in suffering through what Rolan was unknowingly inflicting on her or in dreams in which she worked desperately to knit up some undefined but important object that kept unraveling.

She didn't see Elspeth except at training sessions with Alberich, occasional meals, or now and again with Gwena out in the Field. She seemed a little distracted, and maybe a touch shy, but that was normal for a girl just into puberty, and besides, Talia had her hands full to overflowing. So Talia never once worried about her—until one day she realized with a chill of foreboding that she hadn't seen the girl in several days, not even at arms practice.

Well, that could have been simple circumstance, but it was a situation that needed rectifying. So Talia went looking for her.

She found the Heir in the garden, which was not a place where Elspeth usually spent any time. But she was reading, so she could have decided simply that she needed some fresh air.

"Hello, catling," Talia called cheerfully, seeing Elspeth's head snap up at the sound of her voice. "Are you waiting for someone?"

"No—no, just got tired of the Library—" Had she hesitated a fraction of a second before denying that? "Say, you've been so busy, I'll bet
you haven't heard the latest scrape Tuli's gotten himself into, and I'll *bet*
you could use a good laugh—"

With that, Elspeth kept the conversation on Collegium gossip, and
then pled tasks elsewhere before Talia could gain control of the situation.

The incident left Talia very disconcerted, and when she began seeking the girl out on a regular basis, she only got repetitions of the same.
Then Talia began to take note of the specific changes in the girl's behavior. She was secretive—which was unlike her. There was just the
vaguest hint of guilt in the way she evaded Talia's questions.

Talia took an indirect approach then, and began checking on her
through her year-mates and teachers. What she found made her truly
alarmed.

"Havens," Tuli said, scratching his curly head in puzzlement. "*I* don't
know where she is. She just sort of vanishes about this time of day."

"Uh-huh," Gerond agreed, nodding so hard Talia thought his head
was going to come off. "Just lately. She's swapped me chores a couple
times so she had the hour free—an' she *hates* floorwashing! Somethin'
wrong?"

"No, I've just been having trouble finding her today," Talia replied,
taking care to seem nonchalant.

But she was unnerved. These two were Elspeth's closest friends
among her year-mates, and they only confirmed what Talia had begun
to fear. There were gaps of an hour or so in Elspeth's day during which
she was vanishing, and no one seemed to have any idea of where she was.

It was time she checked her other sources—the Palace servants.

Talia perched herself on a settle, next to the cold fireplace in the Servant's Hall. She had come to her friends—for many of the servants *were*
her friends, and had been since she was a student—rather than raise
anyone's attention by having them come to her. Seated about her were
a half-dozen servitors she had found to be the most observant and most
trustworthy. Two of them, a chambermaid called Elise and a groom
named Ralf, had pinpointed the guilty parties when a group of the
"Blues" (or unaffiliated students) had tried to murder her as a student
by attacking her and throwing her into the ice-covered river. Elise had
seen several of Talia's attackers coming in mucky, and thought it more
than odd; Ralf had spotted the entire group hanging about the stable

earlier. Both had reported their observations to Elcarth when word spread of the attempt on Talia's life.

"All right," Talia began, "I have a problem. Elspeth is going off somewhere about midafternoon every day, and I can't find out where or why. I was hoping one of you would know."

From the looks exchanged within the group, she knew she'd found her answer.

"She's—this goes no farther, young Talia—" This from Jan, one of the oldest there. He was a gardener, and to him, she would *always* be "young" Talia. Talia nodded and he continued. "She's hangin' about with young m'lord Joserlin Corby's crew. Them as is no better'n rowdies."

"Rowdies!" Elise snorted. "If 'tweren't for their highborn da's, they'd been sent home long ago for the way they paw over every girl they can catch unawares." "Girl" here meant "female servant"; if Elise had intended to say that the young men had been mishandling other females, she'd have said "m'ladies." Not that this difference was very comforting; it meant that they were only confining unwanted attentions to the women who dared not protest overmuch.

"It's said," added another chambermaid, "that at home they gets t' more'n pawings."

"Such as?" Talia replied. "You know I won't take it elsewhere."

"Well—mind, m'lady, this is just tales, but it's tales I hear from *their* people—this lot is plain vicious."

Besides forcing their attentions on the servants of their estates, it seemed that "Corby's Crew" was given to so-called pranks that were very unfunny. A cut saddle-girth before a rough hunt was no joking matter, not when it nearly caused a death. And some of these same adolescents were the younger brothers and sisters of those who had tried to murder Talia.

But thus far—that anyone knew—Elspeth had not been a participant in any of their activities. It seemed that at the moment she was simply being paid elaborate court to—something new to her that she evidently found very enjoyable. But it could well be only a matter of time before they lured her into some indiscretion—then used that indiscretion to blackmail her into deeper participation.

Elspeth's good sense had probably protected her so far, but Talia was worried that it might not be enough protection for very much longer.

This required active measures.

She tried to set a watch on the girl, but Elspeth was very clever and kept eluding her. She tried once or twice to read her with a surface probe, but Elspeth's shields were better than Talia's ability to penetrate without forcing her.

Something was going to have to be done, or among the three of them, Elspeth, Dirk, and Kris were going to drive her mad in white linen.

So she decided to try to do something about Dirk first, as being the easiest to get at—and since he wasn't talking to Kris, the way to him was through her blood-brother Skif.

"I'm as baffled as you are, little sister," Skif confessed, running a nervous hand through his dark curls. "I haven't got the vaguest notion why Dirk's making such an ass of himself."

"Lord and Lady," Talia moaned, rubbing her temple and collapsing onto an old chair in Skif's room, "I'd hoped he'd have said *something* to you—you were my last hope! If this doesn't clear up soon, I think I'm going to go rather noisily mad!"

When she had finally given up on trying to manage the problem of Dirk by herself, and had sought out Skif's aid, he'd invited her up to his quarters. He'd been to hers a time or two, but this was the first time she'd seen his. Skif's room was much like Skif himself: neat, decked with odd weapons, and thick with books. Lately Talia hadn't had much time to devote to picking her own rooms up, and she found his quarters a haven from chaos. He had only one window, but it looked out over Companion's Field—always a tranquilizing view.

"First things first—this bond you've got. Kris was right. It's a lifebond—and he's got it, too. I have no doubt whatsoever of that. I can tell by the way he looks at you."

"He looks at me? When? I never *see* him anymore! Since the fight he spends all of his time out in the mud."

"Except at meals—any meal you take at the Collegium—he spends so much time watching you that he hardly eats. And I think he knows your schedule by heart. Any time you might be passing under a window, he's got an excuse to be near that window." Skif paced the length of the room restlessly as he spoke, his arms folded. "He's wearing himself to a thread. That's why I wanted to talk to you alone here."

"I don't know how I'm supposed to be able to help when the man won't let me near him."

"Oh, great!"

"He acts like I was a plague-carrier. I've *tried* to get him alone; he won't let me. And that was before all this mess with the argument with Kris. Now it's twice as bad."

"Havens, what a mess." Skif shook his head ruefully. "He hasn't said anything to me. I can't imagine why he's acting this way. I've had it though, and I know you're at your wits' end. It's about time we brought this out into the sunlight. Since he won't talk to you, I'm going to make damned sure he talks to me. I'm going to have it out with him as soon as I can corner him, and I'll do it if I have to trap him in the bathing-room and steal his clothes! I'm going to get things settled between him and Kris and him and you if I have to tie you all together in a bundle to do it!"

Neither of them had reckoned on the whims of Fate.

Dirk had been fighting what he thought was a slight cold—one of the many varieties that were currently decimating Court and Collegium alike—for about a week. Perversely he refused to care for it; continuing to escape Talia and Kris by retreating into the dismal weather out-of-doors. In a bizarre way, he didn't really *mind* feeling miserable; concentrating on his symptoms kept him from thinking about Her and Him. Physical misery provided a relief from emotional misery.

So he ducked in and out of the cold and rain, day after day, getting soaked to the skin more often than not, but not doing much about it except to change his clothing. Added to that, the emotional strain was taking a greater toll on him than anyone—including himself—realized.

It was midweek, and Talia was taking dinner with the Collegium instead of the Court. She was watching Dirk out of the corner of her eye the entire time, and hoping that Skif was going to be able to fulfill his promise. She was worried—very worried. Dirk was white to the ears; he kept rubbing his head as if it ached. She could see him shiver, although the common-room was warm. He seemed to be unable to keep his mind on what anyone was saying, and he couldn't speak more than two words in a row without going into a fit of coughing.

She could also see that Kris was watching him, and looking just as concerned.

He pushed his food around without eating much. Kris finally seemed to come to some conclusion, visibly steeled himself, and walked over to sit down next to him.

Kris said something to him, which he answered with a shake of his head. Then he stood up—and Kris had to catch him as he started to crumple.

Kris had decided he'd had enough. He couldn't stand watching his dearest friend fret himself to pieces—and he'd come to some unhappy conclusions over the past couple of weeks. He'd gone over to sit next to Dirk before the Herald was aware that he was even in the common room, and spoke his piece before Dirk had a chance to escape.

"I was wrong; I was wrong to put so much trust in my uncle, wrong to have doubted you, and wrong to have said anything about your private life. I apologize. Are you going to forgive me, or will I have to throw myself from the battlements in despair?"

Dirk had started a little when Kris first began speaking in his ear, but hadn't moved away. He'd listened with a mixture of relief and bemusement, then shook his head with a weak smile at Kris' last sally. Then he stood up—

And the room faded from before his eyes, as he felt his legs give under him.

Half a dozen instructors and field Heralds made a rush for him as Kris caught him. They lowered him back down into his seat, as he protested weakly that he was all right.

"I—" He coughed, rackingly. "I just was dizzy a minute—" He bent over in a fit of coughs, unable to continue, hardly able to catch his breath.

"Like Hell!" replied Teren, one hand on his forehead, "You're on fire, man. You're for the Healers, and I don't want to hear any nonsense out of you about it."

Before he could regain enough breath to object, Teren draped one of his arms over his own shoulders, while a very worried Kris did the same on Dirk's other side. The rest surrounded the three of them, allowing no opportunity to escape, and escorted them out the door.

By the time they'd reached their goal, his breath was rattling in his chest and there was little doubt of what ailed him. The Healers isolated him and ran everyone else off, and there was very little that anyone could do about it.

Talia had turned ashen when he'd collapsed, and had left her dinner uneaten, waiting for Kris' return.

Kris finally reappeared, to be engulfed by everyone who'd been present, demanding to know what the Healers had said.

"They tell me he has pneumonia, and it's going to get a lot worse before it gets better," he replied, his voice carrying easily across from the doorway to the bench where Talia sat. "And they won't let anyone see him for at least a day or two."

Talia made a little noise like a strangled sob, stood quickly, and pushed blindly away from the table. The knot of people surrounding Kris had blocked the door nearest her; she stumbled against benches twice as she fled to the door opposite and to her room. She ran all the way down the corridors of the Collegium and through the double doors leading to the Herald's Wing. She hurled herself up the darkened spiral staircase of the tower that held her room, pushed the door open and flung herself down on the couch in the outer room of her suite, sobbing with a lost despair she hadn't felt since that awful moment in the Waystation. . . .

She hadn't closed the door behind her in her flight, and wasn't in much shape to pay attention to sounds around her. She only realized that she was not alone when she heard someone settle beside her, and somehow knew it was Keren and Sherrill.

She tried to get herself back under control, but Keren's first words, spoken in a tone of such deep and unmistakable love that Talia hardly believed her ears, completely undid her.

"Little centaur, dearheart, what cause tha' greeting?"

Keren had slipped into the dialect of her home, something she only did on the rarest of occasions, and then mostly with her twin or her lifemate—moments of profound intimacy.

That broke down the last of her reserve, and she turned with gratitude into Keren's arms and wept bitterly on her ready shoulder.

"Everything's gone wrong!" she sobbed. "Elspeth isn't talking to me anymore, and I *know* there's something going on—something she doesn't want either Selenay or me to know about—but I can't find out *what*! And Dirk—and Kris—we fought, and now they won't talk to me either and—and—now Dirk's sick, and I can't *bear* it! Oh, gods, I'm a total failure!"

Keren, wisely, said nothing, and let the hysterical words and tears wear themselves out. Sherrill meanwhile went quietly about the room, closing the door and lighting candles against the growing darkness. That done, she seated herself at Keren's feet to wait.

"For tha' problem of Elspeth I can think of no solution," Keren said thoughtfully when Talia was in a better state to listen. "But if there was anything truly wrong, her Gwena would surely seek out Rolan—and thee would know."

"I hadn't even thought of that." Talia looked up into Keren's eyes from where she rested on her shoulder, crestfallen at her own stupidity.

"Why should thee? She's never given thee anxiety before." Keren almost smiled.

"I'm not thinking very clearly. No, that's not true. I'm not thinking *at all.* It's wrong of me, but—Keren, I don't know how much longer I can bear this trouble with Dirk without flying to pieces. Keren, I want to be with him so much sometimes I think it would be easier to die!"

Keren sighed. "Lifebond, then, is it? And with Dirk—gods, what a tangle! Well, that explains *his* madness, for certain. Lady only knows what cracked notion the lad has in his head, and 'tis sure the thing's got him all turned round about."

"We know how it can be—an agony." Sherrill rose from her place, sat next to Talia, and slipped her arm around Talia's waist, joining Keren in supporting her. "It's hellish, being pulled inside out by something that can't be denied and won't be turned to anything else. Is anyone trying to help you get this straightened out?"

At Talia's nod, Keren pursed her lips thoughtfully. "I can't think of anything at all to help thee, little centaur. First it's a matter of getting Dirk and Kris speaking, then getting Dirk's mind made up about thee. Hopefully the first is done already. But the second—my best guess is that he's gotten confused somewhere, and has been chasing his own tail. Time, dearling. That's all it will take. Time."

"If I can just hold out a little longer—" Talia relaxed herself with an effort while Keren and Sherrill held her in a circle of love and comfort for long moments.

"You know we understand, dearling," Sherrill said at last for both of them. "Who better? Now, let's change the subject. We're determined to make you smile again."

With that she and Keren took turns telling her the most hilarious stories that they could think of—mostly of some of the goings-on at the Collegium during her absence. No few of them were libelous; all of them were at least undignified. Talia wished profoundly that she had been present to witness the grave and aloof Kyril picking himself out of the fish pond with a strand of waterweed behind his ear. Between the two of them, they soon had her laughing again, and had drained at least some of the tension from her.

Finally, Keren nodded to her lifemate and gave Talia a comforting hug. "I think you're cheered enough to survive the night, dear one," the older woman said. "Yes?"

"I think so," Talia replied.

"Then let tomorrow take care of tomorrow, and have a good long sleep," Keren advised, and she and Sherrill departed as quietly as they had come.

Talia wandered back into her bedroom to shed her uniform. She dressed for bed, then changed her mind and wrapped a robe about herself and settled down on her couch with a book. She must have dozed off without meaning to, because the next thing she knew, Kris was standing beside her and touching her arm lightly to wake her, and the candles were burned down to stubs in their holders.

He was hardly what she expected to see. "Kris!" she exclaimed joyfully, then fear took the place of joy. "Is Dirk—worse?" she asked, feeling the color drain from her face.

"No, little bird, he's no worse. I've just come from there. He's asleep, and the Healers say he'll be all right in a week or two. And we're friends again. I thought you'd want to know—and I wanted to make up with you, too."

"Oh, Kris—I—I've never been so miserable in my life," she confessed. "I was so *angry* with you, that I swore I wasn't going to speak to you until you came to me and apologized, but my pride isn't worth wrecking our friendship over."

His expression softened a little, and she realized he'd been tensed against her answer. "I've never been so miserable either, little bird. And I've never felt like quite so much of an idiot."

"You aren't an idiot. Your uncle is—"

"My uncle is—not what I thought," he interrupted. "I have to apologize to you, like I apologized to Dirk. I was wrong about my uncle. I'm not certain what his problem is, but he is trying to undermine you. And he's trying to wean me away from you. I've extracted information from the unwary often enough that I ought to have recognized it when he was doing it to me—but I didn't until just recently. He became a little too eager, and failed to cover his trail." Kris' expression was troubled. "I *hope* that what he did to Dirk was unintentional, but I'm afraid I can't be certain anymore. I wish I *knew* what his game is. At the moment if I were to hazard a guess, it would be this: he wants the postion he had as Selenay's closest advisor, and he wants me slightly disaffected from the Heralds so that my family loyalty is just a trifle stronger than my loyalty to the Circle. You were right; I was wrong."

"I—I'm almost sorry to hear you say that." A little breeze from the open window behind her made the candles flicker and stirred locks of his hair as she assessed his rueful expression. "What happened to change your mind?"

"Mostly that he tried too hard after the squabble; as I said, he tried to pump me for information about you, and made one too many slighting remarks about Dirk. You were right, that he has a grudge against you, though why, I have no idea. And I think he used that incident with the scrolls as a chance to get at you through Dirk . . . and as a

chance to come between *me* and Dirk. I can only hope he didn't man-
ufacture it, too."

She almost said angrily that the dropped scroll was no accident, that
Orthallen *had* manufactured the incident, but decided to hold her
tongue. He was in a receptive mood, but the quickest way to close his
mind would be to make further accusations. "I have to admit I'm of
two minds about this. I'm glad you're coming around to my way of
thinking, but I'm sorry to have changed your faith in your uncle."

"Don't be, it isn't you that has problems, it's him."

"Well, this is the first time anything has gone right in weeks. Kris,
I'm glad we're friends again."

He dropped easily to the floor beside her couch. "So am I. I've
missed talking to you. But as for things not going right . . . I don't
know about that." He grinned ironically. "That advice you gave me on
how to deal with Nessa certainly worked."

"I meant to ask you about that," she said, grateful for the way they
dropped back into easy conversation, and glad of his company. "I noticed she seems to be pursuing Skif these days."

He sighed, and drooped like a mime displaying dejection. "Once
she had her way with me, she was off to other conquests. Oh, the perfidy of women! When will I ever learn? My heart is forever broken!"

"That's the first time I ever heard that 'forever' equaled the time it
takes to boil an egg," she replied wryly.

"Oh, less, I assure you. I had a chance to drop Skif a word on the
subject of the fair Nessa. Now he happens to be very appreciative of
Nerissa's quite real charms. So now that he knows the means of keeping her attention—which is to play hard-to-get—she may very well
find herself in the position of hunter-turned-hunted."

"Like the old man said about that handfasted couple in Fivetree . . .
do you remember?"

Kris screwed his face up into a fair imitation of the old man's age-
twisted countenance. "Lor' help you, Herald!" he croaked. "Chased
'er? 'Deed he did, in very deed. Chased 'er till *she* caught *him*!"

Talia smiled wistfully. "We had some good times out there, didn't
we?"

"There'll be more. Don't worry, little bird. I'll get this tangle straightened as soon as the Healers will let me near to talk to Dirk. You know,
this illness may be a blessing in disguise; he won't be able to avoid me *or*
find something that urgently needs his attention, and hopefully he'll
believe the things I tell him."

He stood to leave, and Talia gently touched his hand in thanks.

"Take heart, little bird. Things will get better. I can always slip Dirk love-potions with his medicines!" He winked, and ran lightly down the staircase.

She laughed, feeling much eased, and rose; laying her book down on the table beside the couch. She went slowly about the room and extinguished her lights, and then went to bed with a happier heart and mind.

By the next morning Talia felt far more optimistic—and far readier to tackle her problems face on. And since Dirk was out of reach, the logical problem to tackle was Elspeth.

Now she was determined to corner Elspeth and confront her about her behavior. Council and Court kept her occupied most of the day, she missed the girl at arms practice by scant moments. Finally she tried tracking her down after dinner—but Elspeth managed to elude Talia again. She had no doubt this time that it was no accident, but a purposeful avoidance.

Talia was badly worried. All her instincts told her that things were about to come to a head. She opened her shields and was unsuccessfully trying to locate the girl when she felt an urgent and unmistakable summons from Rolan. With a sinking heart she left the Collegium and ran for the Field. When she reached the fence that surrounded it she saw her worst fears realized. Waiting with Rolan was Elspeth's Gwena, both of them like marble statues in the moonlight.

The images she received from both of them—especially Gwena— were blurred and chaotic, though there was no mistaking Gwena's anxiety. Talia touched both their necks and concentrated in an effort to make some sense of the images. Finally she got a series that came clear . . . and Orthallen was at the center of them. Orthallen, and a young courtier who was his creature, one of "Corby's Crew"—and they were planning Elspeth's disgrace!

She threw herself onto Rolan's back without a moment's hesitation. He galloped at full speed to the fence that separated the Field from the barn and stables of the ordinary horses, with Gwena barely keeping up beside him. They vaulted the fence like a pair of great white birds, and headed straight for the haybarn. Talia flung herself off Rolan's back before they had fully stopped.

As she sprinted for the barn, she heard a young male voice murmuring something in the darkness, and she flung open the great door with a strength she never even knew she had.

Moonlight poured in on the pair disclosed, and Talia saw with relief

that matters had not yet had a chance to proceed very far between Elspeth and her would-be lover. *He* was rattled considerably by Talia's
sudden appearance. If Elspeth was, she wasn't showing it.

"What do *you* want?" Elspeth asked flatly, refusing pridefully to
snatch her jerkin closed where it was unlaced.

"To prevent you from making the same mistake your mother did,"
Talia replied just as coldly. "The mistake of thinking that fine words
mean a lofty mind, and a pretty face goes with a noble heart. This
young peacock has little more in *his* mind except to put you in a position where you have no choice but to take him as your consort or disgrace yourself, your mother, and your Kingdom."

"You're wrong!" Elspeth defended him passionately. "He *loves* me!
He told me so!"

"And you believed him, even when your own Companion would
have nothing to do with him?" Talia was white-hot with anger now.
Elspeth was not willing to listen to reason. Very well then, she should
have evidence that she *would* accept—in plenty.

Talia ruthlessly forced rapport on the young courtier. His petty evil
was no match for some of the minds Talia had been forced to touch,
though his slimy slyness made her skin crawl. Before Elspeth had a
chance to shield herself, Talia pulled her in as well—and forced her to
see for herself the true thoughts of one who had *claimed* that he cared
for her.

With a cry of revulsion, Elspeth tore herself away from him and fled
to the opposite side of the barn, while Talia released her mind from the
enforced union. She was less gentle with the young popinjay. She had
him in a crushing mental grip, and fed his fear without compunction as
he gazed at her in dumb terror.

"You will say nothing of this to anyone," she told him, burning
each word into his mind. "Because if you dare, you'll never sleep
again—for every time you shut your misbegotten eyes, *this* is what
you'll see—"

She tore the memory of his worst nightmare out of the bowels of
recollection and flung it in his face, brutally invoking terror and forcing that on him as well. He whimpered and groveled at her feet until
she threw him violently out of rapport.

"Get out of here," she growled. "Get out, go back to your father's
holding, and don't come back."

He fled without a single backward glance.

She turned to face Elspeth, trying to control her anger by slowing
her breathing. "I thought better of you than that," she said, each word

built of ice. "I thought you would have had better taste than to let a creature like that touch you."

Elspeth was crying, but as much out of anger as unhappiness. "Fine words from the Herald Vestal," she spat. "First Skif, then Kris—and now who? Why *shouldn't* I have my lovers as well as you?"

Talia closed her hands into fists so tightly that her nails cut her palms. "I think I hear the Brat speaking," she replied. "The little bitch who wants all the glory of being the Heir, but none of the responsibilities. Oh, Hulda taught you very well, didn't she? Grab and take—snatch all you can, think only of yourself, and never mind what repercussions your actions may have on others. Others don't matter. Oh, no, not now that you're Heir. After all, your word is law, right? Or it should be. And if somebody tries to make you see reason, well, dredge up the worst you can about them and throw it in their faces—then they'll be afraid to try and stop you from doing what you want. Well, that doesn't work with me, young woman. For all the importance it has, I could be sleeping with men, women, or chirras, because *I'm* not the Heir. You seem to have conveniently forgotten that you will sit on the Throne when your mother dies. You may have to make a marriage of state to save us from a powerful enemy. That was what this business with Alessandar and Ancar was all about, or have you forgotten that, too? No one will want you *or* respect you outKingdom after dallying with a petty schemer like *he* is. And I, at least, have never been intimate with anyone that I didn't know, and who wasn't willing to let me inside his thoughts. He wouldn't let you do that, would he? Didn't that make you the least bit suspicious? Lady's Breasts, girl—where was your *mind*? Your own Companion wouldn't have anything to do with him! Didn't that *tell* you anything? If you're so hot to have a man between your legs, why the *hell* didn't you choose a fellow student or someone from the Circle? *They* will at least never betray you and they know when to keep their mouths shut!"

Elspeth burst into frantic tears. "Go away!" she wailed. "Leave me alone! It wasn't like that at all! I thought—I thought—he loved me! I hate you—I never want to see you ever again!"

"That pleases me very well," Talia snapped. "I'm ashamed that I wasted so much of my time trying to help a damned fool."

She stalked out of the barn, vaulted onto Rolan's back, and returned to the Palace without a backward glance.

But before she was halfway there, she was already rueing half of what she had said.

*   *   *

She reported to Selenay in an agony of self-accusation.

The Queen was in her private quarters, which were as spartan as her public rooms were opulent. She had wrapped herself in a robe of old and shabby brown velveteen, nearly the same age and color as the couch she curled up on. Talia stood before her, unable to look her in the eyes, as she related the entire bitter tale.

"Goddess, Selenay, I couldn't have made a bigger mess of the situation if I'd planned it out in advance," she finished, rubbing one temple and very near to weeping with vexation. "I'm as big an idiot as I accused Elspeth of being. I let all my training go flying merrily out the window, let my own problems get the better of me, and completely lost my temper. Maybe you'd better send me back through the Collegium with the babies again."

"Just wait a moment. I'm not sure that your reaction was the wrong one, and I'm not sure that you didn't do the right thing," the Queen replied thoughtfully, candlelight reflecting in her wide eyes. "Sit down, little friend, and hear me out. Firstly, we've been very gentle with Elspeth up until now insofar as exposing her to the kind of emotional blackmail and double-dealing perfidy that we *both* know is fairly commonplace at Court. Well, now she's learned that deceit can arrive packaged very attractively, and that isn't a bad thing. She was hurt and frightened—but that will send the lesson home the more deeply. I believe you were correct in thinking that this experience will prevent her from making the same kind of mistake I made. That's not to say that you didn't overreact and say some things you shouldn't have, but on the whole, I think the good will outweigh the mistakes."

"How can you say that after the way I've alienated her? I'm supposed to be her friend and counselor!"

"And when, in all the time you've known her, have *you* ever lost your temper with her? Not *once*. So she learns something else—that it's possible to go too far with you, and that you're as human and fallible as the rest of us. I doubt she'll ever provoke you that far again."

"There isn't likely to be another chance," Talia said bitterly. "Not the way I've fouled things up."

"I disagree." Selenay shook her head emphatically. "Since you've been gone I've gotten to know my daughter very well. She meant what she said . . . for now. She has a temper, but once it cools she doesn't hold a grudge. And when she realizes that you were right—and acting in her defense—she'll come around. If you were to disappear for a while, I think she'll eventually realize that while you *did* overreact, so did she."

The Queen pondered for a moment. "I think I have the perfect solution. Remember Alessandar's marriage proposal? I intended to make a state visit there in the next few weeks, and I wanted to send an envoy on ahead to look the prince over. As my own personal advisor you would be perfect for that, the more especially as I intend to send Kris as well. I heard about the quarrel between Kris and Dirk, and I had figured on giving *them* a bit of time for things to cool as well. I *was* going to send Dirk and Kyril, until Dirk fell ill last night, so I'll separate the pair by sending Kris off."

"*That's* mended," Talia sighed.

"I still want to send Kris; he has the manner and the blood to be acceptable, and I would as soon keep Kyril here. You and Kris worked outstandingly well as a team, and I trust your judgment completely. I think that rather than canceling the visit, I'll move the date up and send the two of you on ahead to spy things out for me. I'll take Elspeth with me. And I'll have a word with Orthallen about those protégés of his." Selenay's eyes grew cold. "It's about time he stopped being their defender and stopped letting them use his good name to get away with whatever they please."

Talia realized then that she had *not* told Selenay her belief that Orthallen had put the boy up to the attempted seduction. But—what proof did she have? Nothing, except the vague image of Orthallen in the boy's mind—and that could have been because he was hoping to escape punishment by sheltering behind his protector. *Best not to mention it*, she thought wearily. *I'm not up to going through the same arguments I faced with Kris.*

"By the time we all meet again," Selenay was saying, "Elspeth will have had time to think. Do you think you could be ready in the morning? The sooner you drop out of Elspeth's sight, the better."

"I could be ready in an hour," Talia replied. "Although I'm not sure you should be so quick to trust me after tonight."

"Talia, I trust you even more," Selenay replied, as Talia seemed to read understanding in her eyes. "You've come to me hot from the quarrel to claim it was all your fault—how many people, how many Heralds, even, would have done the same? But you haven't told me what has set you so on edge. Is it something to do with Kris? Did you get caught in the middle of his feud with Dirk? If you have problems with Kris, I'll send a different Herald with you."

"Kris?" Talia's honest surprise seemed to relieve the Queen. "No, thank the Lady, we've more than made up our differences, just as he and Dirk made up. Bright Havens, if anything he'll help straighten out this awful tangle! It's nothing that can't be worked out with time, just like this row with Elspeth; it's just that the time it's taking to set everything straight is driving me out of patience and out of temper."

"Good. Then the plan stands. You and Kris will leave in the morning."

"Selenay, if you don't think it's a bad idea . . ." Talia began hesitantly.

"I doubt that it would be. What is it you'd like to do?"

"I'd like to write a note of apology to Elspeth and leave it with you. There's no doubt in my mind that I was partially in the wrong, that I overreacted, and that I said a great many hurtful things because I was unhappy and I wanted to hurt someone else. I certainly was far too hard on her. You can use your own judgment whether or not to give it to her, and when."

"It sounds reasonable to me," Selenay replied, "although a bit unnecessary. We'll be following a week or two behind you, and apologies are always more effective in person."

"That's quite true—but you never know what's likely to happen, and you may want to give it to her before you start off. I don't like the idea of leaving unfinished business behind me, especially something as wretched as this. Who knows? I might never get another chance."

"Bright Havens, dear! I should hire you out as my official doom-sayer!" Selenay laughed, but it was a little uneasy.

Talia shook her head with a vague smile. "Gods, I'm seeing everything miserable just because I'm miserable. I will leave that note with you, but because the catling may well decide to be a human being again once I've left. Now—are they expecting any two Heralds, or Dirk and Kyril? Will there be any problem with me showing up?"

"The underlings are probably just expecting two Heralds," Selenay said. "I hadn't specified. I'll send the appropriate papers with you, of course. The guards on Alessandar's side of the Border will send the specifics on ahead of you. I've heard he has some special way of relaying messages, faster than birds or couriers. I would appreciate it if you could find out more details on that, if it's possible. It might not be. . . ."

"It depends on whether it's supposed to be kept secret from allies or not—or whether it's a secret at all. We'll do our best." Talia managed half a smile. "You know, having the two of us on this assignment will work rather well at ferreting secrets out. Anybody involved with state secrets will be nervous; I can pick that up, and Kris can follow my anchor to Farsee what's going on. My Queen, you are very sly."

"Me?" Selenay contrived to look innocent, then caught her eyes squarely. "Are you *sure* you're ready for this? I won't send you if you don't feel capable of political intrigue and all the rest that this will entail. It is likely to be simple and straightforward, but it *could* involve ferreting out secrets, and at the very least you'll be dealing with the same amount of scheming you have here."

"I'm ready." Talia sighed. "It can't be worse than the mess I've already been dealing with."

CHAPTER 6

"**I** FEEL LIKE I'm running away."

Talia's voice was quiet, but in the hush of pre-dawn Kris had no trouble hearing her.

"Don't," Kris replied, tightening Tantris' girth with a little grunt.

Their Companions stood patiently side by side in the tackshed, as they had so many times during Talia's internship, waiting for their Chosen to finish harnessing them. The rain that had blown up just past midnight had died away to nothing, but the skies were still overcast; both Heralds wore their cloaks against the chill damp. Tantris and Rolan were being decked out in full "formal" array; the silver brightwork gleamed in the light from the lantern just above Tantris' shoulder and the bridle bells tinkled softly as the Companions shifted. The homey scent of leather and hay made Talia's throat ache with tears she refused to shed.

"Look, there isn't anything either of us can do here at the moment, right?" Kris threw his saddlebags over Tantris' hindquarters and fastened them to the saddle's skirting. "Elspeth won't talk to you, and Dirk can't. So you might as well be doing something useful—something different. There won't be anybody who's going to *need* you during the few weeks we'll be gone, will there?"

"No, not really." Talia had been very busy this past evening; her lack of sleep was apparent from the dark circles under her eyes. "Destria is doing fine; anything she needs now Vostel is more than competent to give her. I talked to Alberich; he took me to see Kyril. They promised me that they'd keep an eye on your uncle—I'm sorry, Kris. . . ."

"Don't apologize; I'm just a little surprised you managed to convince Kyril he needed watching. Tantris, *stand*, dammit!"

"I didn't, really, Alberich did."

"Huh. Alberich? Nobody convinces *him* of anything; he must have had reasons of his own to agree with you." He digested this in silence for a moment. Tantris shifted over another step.

"Alberich is going to have a word or two with Elspeth, too," she continued after the silence had become a little uncomfortable. She ran her hands down Rolan's legs to confirm that the bindings on his pasterns and fetlocks were firm. "And Keren promised to beard Dirk in his lair as soon as she can bully her way past the Healers. So did Skif."

"Skif said as much to me. Poor Dirk, I could almost feel sorry for him. He's not likely to get much sympathy from either of those two." Tantris' bridle bells tinkled as he shifted again.

"Sympathy isn't what he needs," she replied a little waspishly, straightening up. "He's been wallowing in self-pity long enough . . ." her voice trailed off, and she concluded shamefacedly: "For that matter, so have I."

"Work is the best cure I know for self-pity, little bird," Kris said, self-consciously. "And—hey!"

With that last step Tantris had managed to shift over far enough that Kris and Talia were trapped between the two Companions, breast-to-breast.

:Kiss and make up, brother-mine. And be nice. She's having a hard time.:

Kris sighed with exasperation, then looking down at Talia's wistful eyes, softened.

"It'll be all right, little bird—and you have every reason to feel sorry for yourself." He kissed her softly on the forehead and the lips.

She relaxed just a little, and leaned her head for a short moment on his shoulder. "I don't know what I've done to deserve a friend like you," she sighed, then took hold of herself. "But we have a long road ahead of us—"

Tantris had moved away so that they were no longer trapped, and Kris could hear him laughing in his mind. "—and we've got a limited time to cover it," Kris finished for her. "And since my Companion has decided to cooperate again, we ought to get moving." He gave Tantris' harness a final tug and swung into the saddle. "Ready to go?"

"As ready as I'll ever be."

They took with them only what Tantris and Rolan could carry. They needed to carry no supplies; they would be housed and fed at inns along the way until they reached the Border, and thereafter would be using the hostels of King Alessandar. They also needed to bring a minimum in the way of personal belongings. The Queen and her entourage would be following at a pace geared to her baggage train, and they would bring whatever might be required for the term of official visits. Selenay and Alessandar were long-time allies; he and her father had been that rarest of things among rulers—personal friends. Although it was a slim chance, the possibility of Elspeth being willing to make a marriage with Alessandar's own heir was not to be dismissed offhand. Alessandar had not been discouraged by Selenay's initial reply to his offer—rather he had urged this visit on her, so that she and Elspeth could see Ancar for themselves. He had argued convincingly that such marriages took years to arrange; even were they to agree now, Elspeth would be past her internship when it became a reality.

Since Selenay had not seen the young man since he was an infant, on the occasion of his naming and her last state visit, she agreed. This would be the ideal time for such a visit. Since the Collegium was about to go into summer recess, she *could* bring Elspeth with her. She was still determined that Elspeth would not be forced into any marriage unless the safety of the entire realm rested on it. She was equally determined that any young man that Elspeth chose, be he royal or common, would at least be of the frame of mind to agree with the principles that governed her Kingdom. If possible, he should be of Heraldic material himself. Ideally, Elspeth's consort would be someone who was either Chosen already or who would be Chosen once he was brought to the attention of the Companions. If this came to pass, it would fulfill Selenay's highest hopes, for the Heir's consort would be co-ruler if also a Herald.

Besides preceding their Monarch and making certain all was in readiness for her, Kris' and Talia's primary duty was to examine the proposed bridegroom—and to determine how his own people felt about him—for themselves; and then give Selenay their opinions of his character. It was no small trust.

This was all in the back of Talia's mind as they rode away in the darkness before dawn. Troubling her thoughts was her feeling that, in spite of the importance of this mission, she was running away from unfinished business by accepting it.

She had labored for hours over the simple note to Elspeth, tearing up dozens of false starts. It still wasn't right; she wished she'd been able to find better words to explain why she had overreacted, and nothing she could say would unspeak some of the hurtful things she'd said. The incident was evidence that she and Elspeth had drawn apart during Talia's interning, and the rift that had come between them needed to be healed, and quickly. She couldn't help but berate herself for not seeing it when she'd first returned.

Then there was Dirk . . .

She couldn't help but think she was being cowardly. Anyone with any courage at all would have remained, despite everything. And yet— what could she truly do back there besides fret? Kris was right; Elspeth would refuse to speak with her, and Dirk was out of bounds in the Healers' hands.

It seemed appropriate that they rode away through darkness, and that the sky was so gloomy and overcast there was no bright dawn at all, merely a gradual lightening of the dark to gray, leaden daylight.

Kris was not very happy with himself at the moment. *:I haven't been doing too well by my friends lately, have I?:* he sent to Tantris' backward-pointing ears.

:No, little brother, you haven't,: his Companion agreed.

He sighed, and settled himself a little more comfortably in the saddle. Now that he looked back on it, there were things he *should* have done. He should have told Dirk right off about the way Talia felt— about Dirk, and about himself. When Dirk started acting oddly, he should have had it out with him. He should never have let things get to the point where Dirk was leaning on the bottle to cope.

Lord and Lady, I'd be willing to bet gold he thinks it's me Talia's in love with. Gods, gods, I've been tearing his heart and soul into ragged bits and I never even noticed. No wonder he picked a fight with me, no wonder he was drinking. Ah, Dirk, my poor brother—I did it to you again. How am I going to make it up to you?

Then there was Talia. He should have believed that Talia wasn't indulging in a grudge. He should have known, what with all the time he'd spent with her, that she wasn't inclined to hold grudges, even though she wasn't inclined to forgive a hurt too easily. He should have believed that her feeling about his uncle was rooted in fact, not dislike. Alberich obviously believed her—and the Armsmaster was hardly noted for making hasty judgments.

:Might-have-beens don't mend the broken pot,: Tantris said in his mind. *:Little brother, why didn't you do these things?:*

Good question. Kris thought about that one while the road passed under Tantris' hooves. There weren't many folk out this early, so they had the road to themselves, and there was nothing to distract him.

One thing at a time. Why hadn't he done anything about Dirk?

He came to the sobering conclusion that he hadn't done anything because he hadn't seen the problem until Dirk was drinking himself to sleep every night. And he hadn't seen it because he was so pleased with himself for the completion of a successful assignment on his own—so wrapped up in a glow of self-congratulation—that he hadn't noticed anything else. He'd been like a child on holiday; selfishly intent only on his own pleasures now that the onerous burden of school was done with for the nonce. Teaching the classes in Farseeing was so very easy for him that it was like having no duty at all, and he'd been spending the rest of his time up to his eyebrows in his own pleasures.

:Very good,: Tantris said dryly. :Now don't go overboard in beating your breast about it. I wasn't too remiss in enjoying myself, either. It had been a long time to be out—and Ahrodie and I missed each other.:

:Hedonist,: Kris sent, a little relieved that his Companion was being so reasonable.

:Not really. We're as close as you and Dirk—in a slightly different fashion. More like you and Talia, really.:

Yes, Talia—it was easy to figure out why he'd been so slow to see her plight. Orthallen was, in all honesty, a politician, a schemer, and power-hungry. Kris had been forced to defend his uncle's actions to other Heralds more than once, although never against an accusation of deliberate and malicious wrongdoing. Kris knew Orthallen never did anything for just one reason; yes, he might well manage to gain a little more power, influence, or put someone in his debt by the things he did, but there was always a profit for the Kingdom as well. Heralds though—the use of authority for personal benefit bothered them, probably because such usage was forbidden them, both by training and by inclination. Most Heralds weren't highborn, and didn't grow up with the intrigue and politics that were a part of the rhythm of Court life. Things Kris accepted matter-of-factly disgusted them. But the fact was that Heralds were very sheltered creatures—except the ones who lived and worked in the Court, or were highborn. Court politics were a reality most Heralds could remain blissfully unaware of, for they dealt only with the highest level of Court life—the Queen, her immediate entourage, and the Seniors—where for all intents and purposes, the politicking didn't exist. It was at Orthallen's level, the mid-to-upper level nobility, that the competition was fiercest. And it was very possible he had seen only the political implications of the ascension of the new Queen's Own. More than possible. Most likely . . .

Which meant he'd seen Talia as a political rival to be trimmed down; seen her *only* as a political rival. Her duties and responsibilities as a *Herald*—Orthallen probably didn't understand them, and certainly discounted them as irrelevant. Old Talamir had been no threat to Orthallen, but this quick, intelligent, *young* woman was.

All of which boiled down to the fact that Talia was likely dead-accurate in reading Orthallen's motives toward her.

Yes, Kris had dealt with fellow Heralds' censure of his uncle before. But Talia's accusations had been different—and he had been as shocked by the idea that a member of his family could be suspected of *real* wrongdoing as Talia had been that a Herald was accused of it. He'd taken it almost as an attack on himself, and had reacted just as unthinkingly.

:I wish you'd spoken your mind to me before this,: Kris told Tantris, just a hint of accusation flavoring the thought.

:It doesn't work that way, little brother,: Tantris replied, *:and you know that perfectly well. We only give advice when we're asked for it. It isn't our job to interfere in your personal lives. How do you think poor Ahrodie was feeling, with her Chosen making a muck of things and not even talking to her, hm? And Rolan can't even properly talk with his Chosen. But now that you are finally asking—:*

:Impart to me your deathless wisdom.:

:Now, now, there's no need to be sarcastic. As it happens, I don't like Orthallen either, but he's never given anyone any real evidence of ill-will before this. All I've ever had to go on were my instincts.:

:Which are far better than any human's,: Kris reminded him.

:Well, don't blame yourself for not seeing anything,: Tantris continued. *:But when someone like Talia insists on a thing, it's probably a good idea to lay aside* your *feelings about it and consider it as dispassionately as possible. Now that she's got that Gift of hers in full control, her instincts in these matters are as good as mine.:*

:Yes, graybeard,: Kris thought, his good humor somewhat restored by the fact that Tantris wasn't trying to make him feel guilty about the mess.

:Graybeard, am I?: Tantris snorted and shook his mane. *:We'll see about that.:* And he performed a little caracole, a half-buck that shook Kris' bones, and a kick or two before settling back down to his original steady pace.

*   *   *

While Rolan could not Mindspeak Talia as Tantris could Kris, he was making his feelings abundantly clear. It was quite plain to Talia that her Companion thought she was indulging in a good deal more self-pity than the occasion warranted. Perversely, his disapproval made her feel all the sorrier for herself.

Eventually he gave up on her, and let her wallow in her misery to her heart's content.

The weather, unseasonable for the edge of summer, was certainly cooperating; it was a perfect day for being depressed. The chill, leaden skies threatened rain, but it never quite made up its mind to fall. The few people they met on the roadway were taciturn and scant in their greetings. The threat of rainfall made folk in the villages they passed inclined to stay indoors.

Because they were traveling light, they would make the best possible time to the Border, even though they would be stopping to rest at night. According to Kyril, it was probable that they would proceed still on their own as far as the capital, since the Companions would be able to make far better time than any steeds the King could send with an escort. Which meant, given the probable speed of Selenay and her entourage, they would have several days at least to assess the prince and the situation before one of them rode back to meet the Queen on the Border.

That likeliest would be Kris; Talia, as Queen's Own, was the better choice for envoy. Although her reason acknowledged the wisdom of this, her emotions rebelled, wanting it to be *her* who made that first contact with Selenay—and with Elspeth—and possibly, with Dirk, if he was well enough by then.

Nothing was going as she would have chosen; and on top of it all, she had been experiencing an odd foreboding about this trip from the moment Selenay mentioned it. There was no reason for it, yet she couldn't shake it. It was as if she were riding from bad into worse, and there was no way to stop what was coming.

Talia remained turned inward, determined to control her own internal turmoil by herself. Weeping on Kris' shoulder would accomplish nothing. Rolan was a solace—but this was a matter of dealing with her own emotions and her own control. A Herald, she told herself for the thousandth time, was supposed to be self-sufficient, able to cope no matter how difficult the situation. She would, by the Havens, control herself—there was no excuse for her own emotional weakness. She had learned to control her Gift—she would learn to school her emotions to the same degree.

The hard pace they were setting left little opportunity for conversation, but Kris was very aware of her unhappiness. Talia had told him in detail about the confrontation with the Heir as they were saddling up. He was sadly aware that there was little he could do to help her; it was extremely frustrating to see her in such emotional pain and be unable to do anything constructive about it. Not long ago, he would have fled the prospect of emotional demands. Now in the light of this morning's introspection his sole regret was that he could not find some way to help.

When she'd lost control over her Gift, there had been something he could do. He was a teacher; he knew the fundamentals of training any Gift, and he had Tantris and Rolan to help him with the specifics of hers. Now . . .

Well, maybe there was one small way in which he could help her. If he talked to his uncle, perhaps he could make him understand that Talia was *not* a political threat. With that pressure off, the problem of dealing with Elspeth and Dirk might assume more manageable proportions.

They stopped for a brief lunch at an inn, but mindful of the time constraints they were under, they ate it standing in the stable-yard.

"How are you doing so far?" he asked around a mouthful of meat pie.

"I'm all right," she replied. She'd already bolted down her portion so fast she couldn't have tasted it. Now she was giving Rolan a brisk rubdown, and was putting far more energy into Rolan's currying than was strictly necessary.

"Well I know you haven't ridden much at forced pace; if you have any problems, let me know."

"I will," was her only reply.

He tried again. "I hope the weather breaks; it's bad for riding, but I would think it's worse for crops."

"Uh-huh."

"We'll have to ride right up until dark to make Trevale, but the inn there should make up for the ride. I've been there before." He waited. No response. "Think you can make it that far?"

"Yes."

"Their wine is good. Their beer is better."

"Oh."

"Their hearthcats have two tails."

"Uh-huh."

He gave up.

They stopped long after dark when Kris was beginning to go numb in his legs, and staggered into an inn neither of them really saw. The innkeeper saw that both of them were exhausted, and wisely kept his other customers away from them, giving them a table right on the hearth and a good dinner.

The inn was a big one, and catered to traders, carters, and other mercantile travel. The common room was nearly full, and noisy enough that Kris did not attempt conversation. Talia was just as glad; she knew she wasn't decent company at the moment, and she rather hoped he'd ignore her until she was. After a meal which she did not even taste and choked down only because she needed to fuel her body, they went straight to their beds. She was able to force herself to sleep, but she could do nothing about her dreams. They were tortured and nightmarish, and not at all restful.

They again left before dawn, rising before any of the other guests of the inn, breaking their fast with hot bread and milk before swinging up into their saddles and resuming the journey.

Talia, having found no answers within, began resolutely turning her attention without. The skies had begun clearing, and by late morning they were able to roll up their cloaks and fasten them behind their saddles. When birds began voicing their songs, her spirits finally began to lighten. By noon she had managed to regain enough of her good humor to speak normally with Kris, and the whole mess she'd left behind her began to assume better proportions. She was still conscious of a faint foreboding, but in the bright sunlight it seemed hardly more than the remnants of her nightmares.

Toward midday Talia suddenly perked up and became more like her old self, for which Kris was very grateful. Riding next to a person who strongly resembled the undead of the tales was not his idea of the way to make a journey.

Diplomatic missions were not entirely new to Kris, though he'd not been senior Herald before. This *was* Talia's first stint as an envoy, and they really needed to talk about it while it was possible to do so unobserved.

Kris was relieved by her apparent return to normal, and ventured a tentative prompting. She responded immediately with a flood of questions, and *that* was more like the Talia he knew, but he could not help but note (with a feeling of profound sympathy) her dark-circled eyes. While he was no Empath, he knew her sleep must have been scant.

By the time they reached the Border itself at the end of a week of hard riding, things were back on their old footing between them. They had discussed every contingency that they could think of between them (ranging from the possibility that Ancar should seem to be perfect in every way, to the possibility that he was a worse marital prospect than Selenay's late consort) and talked over graceful ways to get them all out if the latter should be the case. Kris was fairly sure she was ready to face whatever the fates should throw at her.

As they rounded a curve, late in the afternoon of the fourth day of the journey, Talia got her first sight of the Border. The Border itself, here where two civilized and allied countries touched, was manned by small outposts from each Kingdom.

On the Valdemar side stood a small building, a few feet from the road, and a few feet from the simple bar that marked the Border itself. It served as dwelling and office for the two pairs of Guardsfolk stationed there. The pair on duty were checking the papers of an incoming trader; they looked up at the sound of hoofbeats, and grinned to see the two Heralds. The taller of the two left the trader's wagon and took down the bar for them, waving them through with an elaborate mock bow.

A few lengths farther on was a proper gate, marking Alessandar's side of the Border. It was manned by another pair of guards, this time in the black-and-gold uniforms of Alessandar's army. With them was a young man in a slightly more elaborate uniform; a Captain of Alessandar's army.

The Captain was young, friendly, and quite handsome; he passed them in without more than a cursory glance at their credentials.

"I've been waiting for you," he told them, "but I truly didn't expect you here this soon. You must have made very good time."

"Fairly good," Kris replied, "and we started out a bit sooner than planned. We've been out in the field for the last year or so. Field Heralds are used to being ready to go at a moment's notice."

"As opposed to folks with soft bunks at Court, hm?" The Captain grinned. "Same with us. That lot stationed at Court couldn't have a half-day of maneuvers without a full baggage train and enough supplies to feed a town. Well, I do have some basic orders about what to do with you . . ."

"You do?" Talia said, raising her eyebrows in surprise.

"Oh, it isn't much—just wait until you arrive, then inform the capital."

Talia recalled then what Selenay had said, that Alessandar was rumored to have some new system of passing messages swiftly. She also remembered that Selenay had asked her to find out what she could about it.

Evidently Kris had gotten similar instructions.

"Now *how* are you going to get further instructions about us in any reasonable amount of time?" Kris asked. "I know the nearest authority is several days away on horseback, and you don't have Heralds to carry messages quickly."

The young Captain smiled proudly. "It's no secret," he replied, his brown eyes frank. "In fact, I would be honored to show you, if you aren't too tired."

"Not likely—not when you're offering to show us what sounds like magic!"

The Captain laughed. "From what *I* understand, you're fine ones to talk about wonders and magic! Well, one man's magic is another man's commonplace, so they say. Come along then, and I'll show you."

Out of courtesy to him, since he was afoot, Talia and Kris dismounted and walked with him up the packed-gravel roadway to his outpost; a building much bigger than the one on the Valdemar side, and shaded on three sides by trees.

"Will it interest you to know that I may very well get my orders within a matter of hours, if someone is found of high enough rank to issue them before the sun sets?"

"That's amazing! We can't even do that," Talia replied. "But what does the sun setting have to do with it?"

"You see the tower attached to the outpost?" He shook dark hair out of his eyes as he pointed to a slim, skeletal edifice of gray wood. This tower rose several feet above the treetops, and was anchored on one side to the main barracks of the Border station. It had had both of them puzzled since it seemed to have no real use except perhaps as a lookout point.

"I must admit we were wondering about that," Kris told him. "Are forest fires that much of a danger around here? I wouldn't have thought so, what with all the land under cultivation."

"Oh, it's not a firetower, though that's where the design is from." The young Captain laughed. "Come up to the top with me, and I'll show you something to set you on your ears."

They followed him up the series of ladders that led to the broad platform on the top. Once there, though, Talia didn't see anything out of
the ordinary—just two men in the black uniform tunics of Alessandar's
army, and an enormous concave mirror, as wide as Talia was tall. Although it was not quite perfect, its surface a bit wavering, it was an
impressive piece of workmanship. Talia marveled at the skill that had
gone into first producing and then silvering such an enormous piece of
glass.

The mirror stood on a pivoting pedestal, and as they watched, one
of the two men turned it until it reflected a beam of the westering sunlight at the southwestern corner of the platform. When he'd done that,
the second man picked up a smaller mirror about three handspans
across and took his position in the beam of reflected light.

That was when Talia realized just how they were going to pull off
the trick. It was a very clever variant on the old scheme of signaling
across distance by means of the sun flashing off a reflective object. It
was clever because in this case there was no need to hope that the sun
was in the correct position when you needed to send a message.

The Captain smiled broadly as he saw understanding in their faces.
"It was the idea of some savant in Ancar's entourage. We started building these towers last year at all the outposts; when we realized how
useful they are we sped up the building and put towers up as fast as we
could get the mirrors for them. We have relay towers all across the
Kingdom now," he continued, with cheerful pride. "We can transmit
a message from one end of the Kingdom to the other in a matter of
hours. That's rather better than you Heralds can do, from what I understand."

"That's quite true, but anyone who knows your code has no trouble
in learning the content of any messages you send," Kris pointed out.
"That makes it a bit difficult to keep anything secret, doesn't it?"

The Captain laughed. "In that case, the couriers need never fret that
there will be no job for them, true? Solan," he addressed the man holding the smaller mirror, "tell them down the line that Queen Selenay of
Valdemar's two envoys are here, and waiting for instructions on how to
proceed."

"Sir!" The signalman saluted smartly, and carried out his orders. In
the far distance the Heralds could just barely make out what might be
the top of another tower above the treetops. Shortly after their man
had completed his message, a series of flashes winked back at them
from this point.

"He's repeating our entire message back to us," the Captain explained. "We started this check after a few too many misreadings had caused some serious tangles. Now if he's mistaken any of it, we can correct him before he sends it on."

"Sir. Message correct, sir," the signalman replied.

"Send the confirmation," the Captain ordered, then continued his commentary. "Now the closer you get to any of the major cities, especially the capital, the more men we have on each tower. That makes sure that several incoming messages can be handled at once. If the originator doesn't get confirmation, he assumes that there was a momentary jam-up, and keeps sending until he does."

"It's really brilliant," Talia said, and she and the Captain exchanged a grin at her pun, "but what do you do on cloudy days or at night?"

He laughed. "We go back to the old, reliable courier system in bad weather. We back it up by making our posting stations part of the tower system, so as soon as the clouds break or the sun rises, the message can be relayed. Even when conditions have been at their worst the towers usually still manage to beat the courier. At night, of course, we can signal with lanterns, but that won't be of any help in this case, since no one is going to want to trouble envoys with orders after they've presumably retired. That's assuming anyone highborn enough to issue those orders is willing to take the time to do so after the sun sets!"

They followed him back down the ladders. Once back on the ground, since neither of them showed any signs of fatigue, he gave them a tour of the post that lasted until darkness fell. Talia was intrigued, and not just by the signal towers. This was more than simply a Border-guard station; there was a company of Alessandar's army on permanent duty here. When not patrolling the road for bandits or standing watch on the relay tower, the men (there were no women in Alessandar's army) performed policing functions for local villages.

It was an interesting contrast to the Valdemar system, where Selenay's soldiery was kept in central locations, and shifted about at need. But then, Alessandar had a much larger standing army.

In addition to the army company, there were four Healers—all women—permanently assigned here. There were three buildings, not including the tower; the barracks, the Border station where the Healers lived and where Customs checks were made and taxes collected from those passing across the Border, and a kind of all-purpose building that included the kitchen and storage facilities.

"Well," the Captain said with resignation, when the tour was over and no one had appeared from the tower with a message. "It looks like the folks at the other end couldn't find anyone with enough authority to issue orders about you before it became too late. That means you'll have to spend the night here—unless you'd rather recross the Border?"

"Here will be fine, providing it's no imposition," Kris answered.

The Captain looked doubtfully from Kris to Talia and back again, and coughed politely.

"I haven't got private quarters for you," he said a bit awkwardly. "I could easily find you space in the barracks, of course, and the young lady could take a bed with the Healers, since they're all women. But if you'd rather not be separated . . ."

"Captain, Herald Talia and I are colleagues, nothing more." Kris looked sober enough, but Talia could read his amusement at the Captain's embarrassment.

"Your arrangements are perfectly fine," Talia said smoothly. "We're both used to barracks-style quarters; I promise you that they're quite a luxury compared with some of the Waystations I've spent my nights in."

Talia had been careful to use "I" instead of "we" in speaking of the Waystations. She saw out of the corner of her eye Kris winking at her to congratulate her on her tact.

"If that's the case, I'll escort you to the officer's mess for some dinner," the Captain replied, apparently relieved that they'd made no awkwardness over the situation.

His attitude made Talia wonder if other guests at this outpost had been less than cooperative, or if it was simply that he'd heard some of the more exaggerated tales about Heralds.

While somewhat restrained by the presence of outsiders, the officers were a very congenial lot. They were terribly curious about Heralds, of course, and some of the questions were as naive as any child's. If all of Alessandar's people were as open-handed and content with their lot as these men were, Talia was inclined to think he was every bit as good a ruler as Selenay.

Although Kris got a real bed, Talia had to make do with a cot in the Healer's quarters. She didn't mind in the least. The nightmares that had plagued her nightly all the way here had left her so weary she thought that she could quite probably sleep on a slab of stone.

This night, however, the nightmares seemed to have been partially thwarted. That might have been due to the soothing presence of the Healers bedded all around her. After all, she *was* an Empath; Kris was not. There had been enough bad fortune this spring that it was possible she might well have been picking up the general air of disaster *everyone* was sharing lately. She'd thought she'd made her shields strong enough to block just about anything, but she *had* been stressed, and that put a strain on her shielding.

Or the fact that the nightmares went away might have been just because she had worn herself out past the point of being disturbed by them. For whatever reason, she slept soundly for the first time since leaving, and had only the vaguest memories of disturbing dreams in the morning.

CHAPTER 7

I F KRIS HAD been deaf, he *might* have been able to sleep through the noise of the night guards coming in and the day guards getting up. Since he wasn't, he made a virtue of the inevitable and got up with them. He found Talia, still sleepy-eyed, waiting for him in the mess hall; she'd had the foresight to claim two breakfasts from the cook. Their host put in an appearance just as they were finishing.

"Well, I've got your instructions. I'm to give you maps, and you're not to wait for an escort but to go on to the capital. You're to check in with relay stations at sunset before you stop for the night."

"Sounds simple enough," Kris replied. "I really wanted to get on—not that your hospitality isn't appreciated, but I'd rather not strain your resources. Just as well we're not going to have to wait for an escort."

"I'll admit I was glad to hear I didn't need to supply you with one," their host said frankly. "I'm shorthanded enough, and if half of what I've heard is true, none of our beasts could ever hope to keep pace with yours, anyway."

"It's true enough," Kris replied with pardonable pride. "There isn't a horse born that can match the speed and endurance of a Companion."

"All right, what you'll do is follow the main road to the capital—it's easy enough—and stay overnight at Alessandar's hostels. They'll always be on the main square of town; there'll be a Guardpost nearby, and they'll look like inns. The only difference between a hostel and an

inn is that the sign outside will have a wheat sheaf in a crown. Oh—
you do speak our language, don't you?"

"Perfectly," Kris replied in Hardornen.

"Oh, good—I thought they wouldn't have sent anybody that didn't,
but you never know—and once you get a few miles off the Border nobody speaks Valdemaren."

"I can't say that surprises me too much," Talia put in, in slow, clear
Hardornen. "Once you get a few miles off *our* Border no one except
Heralds speaks *yours!*"

"Right then, you can be on your way as soon as you're ready. Here's
your map," he handed Kris a folded packet, "and best of luck to you."

"Thanks," Kris said, both of them rising and heading for the door.

"And don't forget," he called after them as they headed for the stables, "Check in with the relay towers every night. The capital wants to
be able to keep track of you."

The first day passed without incident. Alessandar's people seemed as
content as Selenay's; they were friendly, and looked quite prosperous,
at least from a distance.

"Isn't there supposed to be a village along here soon?" Talia asked
around noon.

Kris pulled the map they'd been given out of his beltpouch and consulted it. "Assuming I haven't been misreading this—let's see if we can
find a native."

One more turning of the road brought them to a grove of trees in
the road-side corner of a fenced field. Beneath those trees was a group
that could have been exchanged for farmers of Valdemar without anyone noticing the difference. They were stolidly munching their way
through a dinner of thick, coarse bread and cheese, but when one of
them noticed that the two Heralds were approaching them with purpose, he stood, brushed crumbs off his linen smock, and met them
halfway.

"Eh, sir, and can I be of any help to ye?" he asked, as friendly as the
Captain had been.

"I'm not quite used to this map," Kris replied, "and I wonder if you
could tell me how far it is to Southford?"

"That be just a league or so a-down the road; there's that hill yonder
in the way, or ye could see it from here." The man grinned. "A'course,
if the hill bain't there, ye wouldn't have to ask, eh?"

Kris laughed along with him. "That's only true," he said, "and thank
you."

"Nice man," Talia commented when Kris returned to her side. "He could have been one of ours." She squinted across the fields of swiftly-growing green grain, and Kris followed her gaze. "They seem to be thriving, too. So far Alessandar gets high marks from me."

"Ah," Kris replied, "but it isn't Alessandar that's the prospective bridegroom."

"That's true." The face she turned toward him was a sober one. "And I wish I didn't know so many tales of black-sheep sons. . . ."

They were to stay only at the hostels, or so their orders went, so as sunset neared they checked the map for the first town ahead of them likely to have one.

The hostels were an innovation of Alessandar's, and were meant to serve as a courtesy to those moving about his Kingdom on official business. They were rather like well-run inns, save that there was no fee. Court officials, envoys of other Kingdoms, and clergy were permitted unlimited use of these facilities.

They first reported their progress to one of the relay stations in a village along the way, as had been requested. The station was easy enough to find, as it towered over every other structure in the village.

"Will ye be stayin' here, or movin' on past dark?" asked the grizzled veteran who greeted them.

"Moving on," Talia replied, "We plan on making—Keeper's Crossing, was it?" She looked to Kris for confirmation.

He checked the map and nodded.

"That's a ways—but you know best. Guess the tales 'bout them horses o' yours must be true." He looked over Rolan and Tantris with an appraising and approving eye. "Useta be cavalry, meself. Can't say I've ever seen neater beasts. Ye came all the way from the Border since this mornin'?"

Rolan and Tantris preened under his admiring gaze and curvetted a little, showing off. "That we did, sir," Kris answered with a smile.

"Don't look winded—don't even look tired—just exercised a mite. Lord Sun, I'd not have believed it if I hadn't a' seen it. Well, if ye can make that kinda time, ye'll be at the Crossings 'bout a candlemark after sunset. Hostel's in the town square, right-hand side as you come in."

"Many thanks," Talia called as they turned the Companions' heads back to the road.

"Fair wind at yer back!" he called after them, his admiring gaze following them until they were out of sight.

*　　*　　*

The hostel was indeed like an inn, complete with innkeeper. They had been told that the accommodations were as plain as the food, but adequate.

They showed their credentials to the businesslike Hostelmaster when they dismounted at the door. He examined them quite carefully, paying close attention to the seals of Valdemar and Hardorn. When he was satisfied that they were genuine, he summoned a stableboy with a single word. The lad came at a run to take the Companions, and the Hostelmaster waved them inside.

The common room was hot, smoky, and crowded, and it took them a little time to find themselves places at smooth, worn wooden trestle-tables. Finally Talia squeezed in beside a pair of travelers in priestly garb—apparently from the rival sects of Kindas Sun-Kindler and Tembor Earth-Shaker. They were having a spirited discussion of the deficiencies of their various congregations and simply nodded to her as she took her place on the very end of the bench. Kris sat opposite her, with his neighbor a thin, clerkly-looking sort with ink-stained fingers, whose sole interest was the contents of the stoneware platter in front of him.

A harried serving girl placed similar platters before the two Heralds; meat, bread, and stewed vegetables. A boy followed her with a tray of wooden mugs of thin ale, and the keys to their rooms.

They ate quickly; the food wasn't anything to linger over, and Talia's bench, at least, was so crowded she had barely enough room to perch. And there were more people coming in, waiting with expressions of impatience for seats. With their hunger appeased, they took their keys and their mugs to the other side of the lantern-lit room, where there was a fire and a number of benches and settles scattered about.

Talia felt curious eyes on them—not hostile, just curious. She decided that they were the only foreigners among the guests, for she couldn't detect any accents among those speaking. She picked a seat, and took it quickly, feeling very conspicous in her white uniform that stood out so sharply in the otherwise dark room.

"Heralds out of Valdemar, be you?" asked a portly fellow in brown velvet as Kris took a corner of a bench.

"You have us rightly, good sir," Talia answered him.

"Don't see Heralds often." His inquisitive glance left no doubt but that he was curious about what brought them.

"You should be seeing more before summer's over," Talia replied with what she hoped was just enough friendliness. "Queen Selenay will be making a visit to your King. We're here to help get things ready for her."

"Ah?" he replied, his interest piqued. "That so? Well—maybe things be taking a turn for the better, after all."

"Have things been bad lately?" she asked as casually as possible. "Valdemar's had its share of troubles, what with floods and all."

"Oh, aye—floods and all," he replied, a bit too hastily, and turned to the men on the other side of him, joining the conversation in progress.

"'Scuse me, milady, but could you tell me what the grain prices look to be on your side of the Border?" A tall, thin merchant interposed himself between Talia and the man she had first spoken to, and it would have been plain rudeness to ignore him. He kept her engaged with so many questions that she had no chance to ask any of her own. Finally she'd had enough of being monopolized, and signaled Kris that she was ready to leave.

When Kris yawned, pled fatigue, and rose to head for his room and bed, Talia followed. The guest rooms were monklike cells arranged along the walls; they had no fireplaces or windows, but slits in the walls near the ceiling gave adequate ventilation. Kris raised one eyebrow interrogatively at her as he unlocked his door; she gave him the little nod that meant she'd learned something interesting, and the hand motion that meant they'd talk about it later.

Even without a window, Talia knew when it was sunrise. She wasn't much surprised to discover that Kris had beaten her to breakfast by a few minutes. No one else was even stirring. She didn't pay much attention to what she was eating; some kind of grain porridge with nuts and mushrooms, she thought. It was as bland as the dinner had been.

"The boy is harnessing for us," Kris said around a mouthful. "We can be on the road as soon as you're ready."

She washed down the last bite of the gluey stuff with a quick gulp of unsweetened tea. "I'm ready."

"Then let's get going."

They cantered out the village until they reached the outskirts before settling back to a slower pace.

"Well?" Kris asked, when they were well out of earshot of the village.

"There's something not quite right around here," Talia replied, "but I can't put my finger on anything. All I've got is a feeling—and that no

one wants to talk about 'bad times' around here. It may just be an isolated case of discontent—"

She shook her head, suddenly feeling dizzy.

"What's the matter?"

"I don't—know. I feel a little funny all of a sudden."

"You want to stop a minute?" Kris asked, sounding concerned.

She was about to say "no" when another wave of disorientation hit.
"I think I'd better—"

Their Companions moved over to the grassy verge of the road on
their own. Rolan braced all four legs and stood rock-still, while waves
of dizziness washed over her. She didn't dismount—she didn't dare; she
was afraid she wouldn't be able to get back up again. She just clung to
the saddle, and hoped she wouldn't fall off.

"Want to go back?" Kris asked anxiously. "Think you need a
Healer?"

"N-no. I don't think so. I don't know—" The disorientation didn't
seem quite so bad, after a bit. "I think it's going away by itself."

Then, as the dizziness faded, so did the empathic awareness of those
around her; an awareness she always had, no matter how tightly
shielded.

"Goddess!" Her eyes snapped open and she looked frantically around
her, as Kris grabbed her elbow, anxiously. "It's—" She unshielded. It
was the same. She could sense nothing, not even Kris, beside her. "It's
gone! My Gift—"

Then it was back—redoubled. And she, unshielded and wide open,
bent over in physical pain at the mental clamor of what seemed to be
thousands of people. Hastily she shielded back down—

Only to have the clamor vanish again.

She remained bent over, head in hands. "Kris—Kris, what's happening to me? What's wrong?"

He was steadying her as best he could from his saddle. "I don't
know," he said tightly, "I—wait—wasn't there some kind of mushroom in that glop they fed us?"

"I—" she tried to think. "Yes. Maybe."

"Goatsfoot," he said grimly. "It has to be. That's why you're getting
hit and I'm not."

"Goatsfoot? That—" She sat up slowly, blinking tears away. "That's
the stuff that scrambles Gifts, isn't it? I thought it was rare—"

"Only Thoughtsensing and Empathy and yes, it is rare in most
places. It's not *common* around here, but it's not rare either, and it's been
a wet spring, just what goatsfoot likes. The damned fools must have

gotten hold of a lot and just chucked it in the food without checking beyond seeing that it was edible."

She was able to think a little clearer now. "This is going to make anything I read pretty well worthless for the next couple of days, isn't it?"

He grimaced. "Don't even try; it'll make you sick. Those damned fools were just lucky they didn't have a Healer overnighting there! If you can ride, I think we'd better go back—"

"I can ride, if we take it easy. Why?"

He had already turned Tantris' head back the way they had come. "What if they have more of that stuff—and a Healer as a guest tonight?"

"Great good gods!" She let Rolan follow in Kris' wake.

It wasn't more than a league back; they hadn't traveled far before the effect of the fungus hit her. She fought off successive waves of dizziness and disorientation, and was vaguely aware that they'd stopped and Kris was giving someone a sharp-tongued dressing-down. She caught frantic apology; it seemed genuine enough—what her Gift was feeding at her was anything but a reliable gauge. Waves of paralyzing fear, apprehension, guilt—followed immediately by waves of delirious joy, intense sexual arousal, and overwhelming hunger.

Finally, another "blank" moment, and she drew a shuddering breath of relief.

"Little bird?"

She opened her eyes to look down on Kris standing at her right stirrup.

"Do you want to stay here? I can go back to the signal tower and get them to send a message that you've been taken ill—and whose fault it is."

"No—no. I'll be better—better away from people. You can shield; they can't. I won't fall off; Rolan won't let me."

"If that's the way you want it . . ."

"Please—" She closed her eyes. "Let's get out of here—"

She heard him mount; felt Rolan start off after him. She didn't open her eyes; the disorientation didn't seem so bad when she could keep them closed. And she was right; as distance increased between herself and the village, the worst of the effects decreased. She felt a second shield snap up around her—Kris'—then a third—Rolan's—

She opened her eyes cautiously. It was like looking up through water, but bearable. She felt Kris touch her arm, and saw that he was riding beside her.

"This couldn't have been on purpose," she asked, slowly. "Could it?"

He gave the idea serious thought; she could tell by the blank expression on his face. "I don't think so," he said at last. "They couldn't have

known what hostel we'd overnight in, and they couldn't have counted
on goatsfoot being available. They swore they only had that one batch,
that it was in a lot of edible fungus some boy sold them this morning. I
made them dump the rest of the porridge in the pig trough. No, I
think it's just a damned bad accident. Can you go on?"

She closed her eyes, and took a kind of internal tally. "Yes."

"All right, then let's get on with it. I'd like to get you to bed as
early as we can."

But Talia wondered—because with the relay towers, someone *could*
have known what hostel they intended to stay in—and as a former
farmchild, she knew that *some* mushrooms could be preserved indefinitely when dried. . . .

Kris pushed both of them to the limit, hoping to get Talia into the
haven of a bed long before sundown. He managed; better still, that
night they were the only travelers making use of the hostel. The quiet
did her some good; so did the rest. Unfortunately, he knew from old
lessons that there was no remedy for goatsfoot poisoning except time.

The accident was more than annoying; he really needed her abilities
on this trip. Without them, they'd have to go on wit alone.

With a good night's sleep she was back to normal—except that her
Gift was completely unreliable. She was either completely blocked, or
so wide open she couldn't sort out what emotion was coming from
whom.

Neither one of them wanted her to try projecting under *these* conditions. They couldn't predict what would happen and didn't really want
to find out.

So he pushed to make the best time they could to the next hostel—
and hoped they could make training, wit, and skills serve.

When Kris stopped to try to inquire about hostels at noon, people
seemed overly quiet, and not inclined to talk much beyond the simple
courtesy of answering their questions. And the townspeople in the
hamlet they finally reached were the same; hurrying to be about their
business and showing only furtive curiosity about the strangers who
had ridden in.

That night the Guard at the relay station they reported to was cold
and somewhat brusque, and advised them against changing their plans
for stopping at Ilderhaven.

"Them at the capital need to know where ye be; they'll be takin' it
amiss if they can't find ye should they need ye," he said, making it

sound as if "they" would be taking it more than "amiss" if the Heralds changed their stated plans.

Kris exchanged a flickering, sober glance with his partner, but made no retort.

At the hostel, which held a scant handful of travelers, they split up, each taking a likely prospect, and began trying to eke a little more information out of them.

Talia had chosen a shy priestess of one of the Moon-oriented orders, and hoped she could get something useful out of her without her Gift. She began her conversation with ordinary enough exchanges; the difficulties women faced when making long journeys, commiseration over the fact that men in authority seemed to take them lightly—Hostelmasters serving the men in the room first, no matter what the order of their arrival was, and much more in the same vein. Carefully, over the entire evening, she began steering the talk to the topics that seemed to be the most sensitive.

"Your King—I must say, he certainly seems to be a good ruler," Talia said casually, when the topic of Alessandar came up. "From what I can see, everyone seems to be prospering. That ought to be making for good days with your temple."

"Oh, yes . . . Alessandar is a fine ruler to us; things have never been better . . ." The priestess trailed off into hesitant uncertainty.

"And he has a fine, strong son to follow him? Or so I'm told."

"Yes, yes, Ancar is strong enough . . . has there been much flooding in Valdemar? We've never seen the like of it this spring."

Had there been uneasiness when the woman spoke Ancar's name?

"Flooding, for fair. Crops and herds wiped out, rivers changing course even. Young Elspeth has been at the Queen to let her be about the countryside doing what she can—but of course that's out of the question while she's still in schooling. Once she's older though, I've no doubt she'll be the Queen's own right hand. Surely Ancar has been seeing to things for his father?"

"No . . . no, not really. The . . . the factors take care of all that, you know. And . . . we really don't want to be seeing Ancar . . . it isn't fitting for someone in his station to be going among the common folk. He has his own Court—has since he came of age, you know. He has—other interests."

"Ah," Talia replied, and allowed the conversation to turn to another topic.

*   *   *

"Not very conclusive," Kris mused. "But it's looking odd."

Talia nodded; they'd waited again until they were on the road before talking.

"I've gotten a similar sort of impression," he began.

"As if things were reasonably well *now*, but that folk are not entirely sure of what the morrow might bring."

"*Damn* that goatsfoot! If we could just have some idea how deeply this goes—if it's more than just the usual worries about 'better the straw king than the lion king'—*gods*, we need your Gift!"

"It's still not reliable," she told him regretfully.

"Well, we just have to muddle along on our own." He sighed. "This is exactly the kind of reason we've been sent on ahead, and we *have* to have clearer information than we've got. Selenay can't act on anything this vague."

"I know," she said, biting her lip. "I know."

That night Talia tackled an elderly clerk. When she brought up the topic of the King, he was voluble in his praise of Alessandar.

"Look at these hostels—wonderful idea, wonderful! I remember when I was just a lad, my first post as tax-collector—Lord Sun, the inns I had to stay in, verminous, filthy, and costing so high you wondered why they didn't just put a knife to your throat and have done with it! And he's cleaned out most of the brigands and robbers, him and his Army; Karse daren't even think about invading anymore. Oh, aye, he's a great King—but he's old . . . ."

"Surely Ancar—"

"Well, that's as may be. The Prince is a one for protocol and position; he doesn't seem to be as open-handed as his sire. And there's the rumors. . . ."

"Oh?"

"Oh, you know, young m'lady—there's always rumors."

Indeed there were rumors; and now Kris actually suspected listeners, so he signaled Talia to wait to talk until they were on an open stretch of road the next day, with no one else near.

She told him what she'd gotten, and what she'd guessed.

"So Ancar has his own little Court, hm?" Kris mused. "And his own circle of followers and hangers-on. I can't say as I like the sound of that. Even if the Prince is innocent and fair-minded, there's likely to be those that would use him in a situation like that."

"He doesn't sound innocent or fair-minded from the little I've pried out of anyone," Talia replied. "Granted in fairness—he may just be a naturally cold and hard man. Goddess knows he's seen enough warfare at his age to have turned him hard."

"Oh? This is news to me—say on."

"At fourteen he participated in a series of campaigns that wiped out every trace of the Northern barbarians along their North Border. That set of campaigns lasted almost two years. At seventeen he led the Army against the last raid Karse ever dared make on them—and again, the raiders were utterly wiped out. At twenty he personally mounted a campaign against highwaymen, with the result that nearly every tree from here to the capital was bearing gallows' fruit that summer."

"Sounds like he should be regarded as a hero."

"Instead of with fear? It was apparently the *way* he conducted himself that has people afraid. He makes no effort to hide the fact that he enjoys killing—and he's utterly, utterly ruthless. He hanged more than a few of those 'highwaymen' on merest suspicion of wrongdoing, and lingered with a winecup in his hand to watch while they died."

"Lovely lad. Sounds like just the mate for our Elspeth."

"Don't even say that as a joke!" Talia all but hissed. "Or haven't you been granted any of the tales of his conduct with women? *I* was told it isn't a good idea to attract his attention, and to stay out of his sight as much as possible."

"Probably more than you; if you believe what you hear, young Ancar's taste runs to rape, and the younger, the better, so long as they're nubile and attractive. But that's the tale only if you read between the lines. Nobody's told me anything about that straight out."

:They haven't said anything straight out about the wizards he keeps either,: Tantris put in unexpectedly.

"What?" Kris replied in surprise.

:I've been keeping my ears open in the stable. The hostelkeepers have been frightening the stablehands into line with threats about turning them over to Ancar's wizards if they don't move briskly and keep to their work.:

"So? That's an old wives' trick."

:Not when it's being used on "stableboys" old enough to have families of their own. And not when the threat genuinely terrified them.:

"Lord of Light, this is beginning to look grim—" Kris relayed Tantris' words to Talia.

"We've *got* to find someone willing to speak out," she replied. "We daren't turn back with nothing in our hands but rumors. Selenay needs *facts*—and if we turned back now, we might well precipitate a diplomatic incident."

"I agree," Kris replied, even more firmly. "And if we're being watched, well—we just might not reach the Border again."

"You think it's possible? You think he'd dare?"

"I think he would, if what the rumors hint at is true, and enough was at stake. And the only way we're going to get any idea of what Ancar is like and what his plans are, is to get in close to him. And I'm afraid we *need* that information; I'm afraid more than Elspeth's betrothal hinges on us now."

"That," she replied, "is what I feared you'd say."

A day from the capital they finally found someone who would discuss the "rumors." It was pure luck, plainly and simply.

As they rode into town, Talia spotted a trader's caravan that she thought she recognized. Traders' wagons were all built to the same pattern, but their gaudy painting was highly individual. The designs rarely included lettering, since most of a trader's customers were far from literate, but they were meant to be memorable for the selfsame reason. And Talia thought she remembered the design of cheerful blue cats chasing each other around the lower border.

A few moments later, she saw the shaggy black head of the bearded owner, and couldn't believe her good fortune. This trader, one Evan by name, was a man who owed Talia his life. He had been accused of murder; she had defended him from an angry mob and found out the real culprit. Having cast Truth Spell on him and touched his mind, she knew she could trust not only his words, but that he would not betray them to anyone.

His wagon was parked in a row of others, in the stable-yard of the "Crown and Candle," an inn that catered to trade.

When they reached the hostel, and settled down to dinner, Talia tapped Kris' toe with her own. They didn't like to use this method of communicating; it was awkward and very easy to detect unless their feet were hidden. But the hostel was nearly empty, and they'd been given a table to themselves in the back; she reckoned it was safe enough this time.

Follow my lead, she signaled.

He nodded, eyes half closed, as if in response to a thought of his own.

"I saw an old friend today," she said—and tapped *Trader—Truth Spell*—knowing that he would readily remember the only circumstance that combined those two subjects.

"Really? Wonder if we could get him to stand us a drink?"

And—*Information source?*—he tapped back.

"Oh, I think so," she replied cheerfully. Yes.

"Good! I could stand a drop of good wine. This stuff is not my idea of a drink." *Reliable?*

"Then I'll see if we can't talk him into a round or two." *Yes—Debt of honor.*

"Hm." He pushed his stew around with a bit of bread. *Gods—your Gift?*

Back.

Do it.

She summoned one of the little boys that hung around the hostel hoping for just such an opportunity to earn a coin, and sent a carefully worded message to Evan. He replied by the same messenger, asking her to meet him, not at his inn, but at his wagon.

He did not seem surprised to see Kris with her. He opened the back of the wagon and invited both of them inside the tiny living area. The three of them squeezed into seats around a tiny scrap of a table, and Evan poured three cups of wine, then waited expectantly.

Talia let down her shields with caution, and searched about the wagon for any human presence near enough to hear anything. There was nothing, and no one.

"Evan—" she said quietly, then, "traders hear a lot. To come straight to the point, I need to know what *you've* heard about Prince Ancar. You know you can trust me—and I promise we aren't being spied on. I'd know if we were."

Evan hesitated, but only a moment. "I . . . expected something of this sort. If I did not owe you so very much, Lady Herald—but there it is. And you have the right of it, a trader hears much. Aye, there's rumors, black rumors, about young Ancar. Five, six years agone, when he first came of age and warranted his own court, he began collecting some unchancy sorts about him. Scholars, he calls 'em. And, aye, some good has come of it—like the signal towers, some aqueducts and the like. But in the last year his scholars have gotten more of a reputation for wizardry and witchcraft than they have for knowledge."

"Well, now, isn't that what they say of Heralds here, too?" Kris smiled uneasily.

"But I never heard anyone say your witchcraft was anything but of the Light, young man," Evan replied, "and I've never heard anything but darksome tales of late where Ancar's friends are concerned. I've heard tales that they raise power with the spilling of blood—"

"How likely?" Kris asked.

Evan shrugged. "Can't say. To be fair, I've been places where the same is said of the followers of the One, and you of Valdemar know how wrong *that* is. This I *can* tell for true—he has in the past year turned to wenching. Wenching of the nastier sort. He has his way with any poor young maid that catches his eye, highborn or low, and none dare gainsay him—and his tastes run to leaving them with scars. Well, and that isn't all. He has men of his own about the countryside these days—'intelligencers' they call themselves. They claim to be like you twain, being the King's eyes and ears, to see that all's well—but I misdoubt that they're speaking their information in any ears but Ancar's, and I doubt the King knows they exist."

"I don't like that," Talia whispered.

"I don't either. I've been questioned by 'em fair often since I crossed the Border, and I mislike some of the questions they're asking. Who bought like they'd gotten prosperous, who'd told me aught, who bends knee to what god—aye, you can believe old Evan the Shrewd became Evan the Stupid 'round 'em."

His expression changed to one of thick-headed opacity. "Aye, milord, no, milord, talk t' *me* milord?" He wiped the look from his face. "Even let 'em cheat me right royally t' convince 'em. That's not the end of it. I've heard from those I trust that Ancar has raised his own private Army; at least three thousand men, and all of them the scum of the prisons, given their lives on condition they serve him. Well, I'll likely be gone before I find what this was all about, but I pity anybody who's here when Ancar takes the throne. Oh, yes"—he shook his head—"I pity them."

They rode away from their hostel the next morning with grim faces, and paused in a little copse of trees just outside of town, where they could see anyone approaching, but no one could see them.

"I don't like it," Talia said flatly. "My vote is to turn around and head back for the Border—but there's the fact that a move like that could be construed as an insult."

She wanted badly to run; she was more afraid now than she'd ever been except when she'd lost control over her Gift. She was feeling very like she was walking into something she couldn't handle now, too—but this was exactly why Selenay had sent them in the first place—to uncover anything that might threaten Valdemar. And there was just the faintest of premonitions that some of this might lead back to Orthallen.

"All the more reason to stick it out," Kris replied soberly. "We've heard the rumors; we need to learn *exactly* how much danger there is, or we can't properly advise the Queen of the situation. We don't learn the depth of the problem by turning tail and running. And like I said before—if we turn now, they might decide we've learned something, and stop us before we made it back across the Border. If we stick, we should be able to bluff our way out."

"Kris, it's dangerous; we're playing with fire, here."

"I know it's dangerous, but no more dangerous than any number of other missions Dirk and I pulled off. And we have to find what his long-term plans are, if there's any chance at all to do so."

"I know, I know." Talia shivered. "But Kris, I don't like it. I feel like I'm walking into a darkened room, knowing that as soon as I light a candle I'll discover I've walked into a den of serpents and the door's been locked behind me."

"You're the ranking Herald, little bird. Do we go on and find out exactly what the situation is and whether or not there's immediate threat to the Kingdom, or do we head back to Selenay with what we know now—running like our tails are on fire and hope they can't stop us?"

"How could we get back if they come after us?"

Kris sighed. "I wouldn't give very good odds. What we'd have to do is cut across country, avoiding roads—unfamiliar country, I might add, and we'd have to go night and day. *Or* we send Rolan and Tantris back alone, with messages, get rid of our rather conspicuous uniforms, steal disguises, try to get back afoot. With accents that damn us and every 'intelligencer' in the country knowing our exact descriptions. Frankly, the odds are with playing stupid and bluffing our way out."

"Could I pretend to be sick again?"

"Then they'd expect us to go straight to the capital and the King's Healers, not head back to our Border."

Talia shut her eyes and weighed all the possible consequences; then bit her lip, and steeled herself for the decision she knew she had to make.

"We go on," she said, unhappily. "We haven't got a choice."

But when they met their escort just outside the capital at the end of a six-day journey from the Valdemar Border, Talia almost heard the click of the lock behind her.

They announced their arrival at the gates of the city, and were asked, courteously enough, to wait. After about an hour, spent watching the usual sort of foot-and-beast traffic pass in and out of the city, there was a blast of trumpets and the common folk vanished from the vicinity as if whisked away by a spell.

Talia had expected an official escort; she had *not* expected that they would be met by what amounted to a royal procession. For that was exactly what emerged from the city gates.

Prancing out of the gateway came a procession of dozens of brightly-bedecked nobles and their liveried attendants, all mounted on high-bred palfreys.

Prince Ancar and his entourage rode at the head of it. Talia had *definitely* not expected *him*—and from the very brief flash of surprise on his face, neither had Kris.

Ancar rode toward them through a double row formed by his mounted courtiers and his guards; it was all very staged, and meant to impress. It impressed Talia, but hardly in the way she assumed he intended. On seeing him for the first time, Talia felt like a cat that has suddenly been confronted by a viper. She wanted to arch her back, hiss, and strike out at him.

"Greetings, from myself, and my honored Father," he said coolly, bowing slightly but not dismounting. "We have come to escort the envoys of Queen Selenay to the palace."

Talia was mortally certain that the "we" he used was the royal plurality, and noted that his horse was at least two hands higher than either Companion, allowing his head to be that much higher than theirs.

Gods—I don't think he's left anything to chance—

There was no superficial reason for the violent feeling of animosity that struck her; as they exchanged courtesies the Prince seemed perfectly amiable. He was darkly handsome with smooth, even features and a neat black beard and mustache. He spoke to them fairly enough and accorded them every honor. As he rode beside them, back into the city and toward the palace, he discoursed on neutral topics—the harvest to come, the recent spring floods that had occurred in both countries, his wish for continuing good relations between the two Kingdoms. All perfectly natural topics, and all spoken in tones of good-will.

None of this made the slightest bit of difference to Talia. There was something indefinably evil about the man, something cold and calculating, like a snake judging when it would be best to strike.

He was paying very little attention to Talia, who was riding with Kris between them; as if, because of her sex, she was not quite of an exalted enough station for him to bother with. That was all to the good; since he was busy directing his attention to Kris, she decided that this was no time for ethical quibbling; she would try to probe him. This was neither diplomatic nor particularly moral, but she didn't much care. There was something lurking beneath the smooth, careful surface of this cultivated Prince, and she was determined to discover what it was.

She was stopped by a powerful shield—one unlike anything she had ever touched before. There were no cracks in it that she could discover, not by the most careful probing. Startled, she cast a surreptitious glance at Ancar; he continued his conversation without seeming the least disturbed. So *he* was not the one doing the shielding. Who was?

Then her sharp glance was intercepted by a nondescript man in gray riding to the left of the Prince. He looked at her with eyes like dead brown pebbles, then permitted himself a faint smile and a nod. She shivered, and looked hastily away.

They couldn't reach the Palace grounds any too soon for Talia, who only wanted out of the Prince's presence. When they reached the courtyard of the Palace the entire entourage dismounted and dozens of liveried grooms appeared to lead the horses away—and with them, their Companions. Shaken by the encounter with the Prince's mage, Talia scanned the grooms quickly for any evidence of harmful intent.

Thank the gods—

To her relief there was nothing there but admiration for the beautiful creatures and the honest wish to make them comfortable. She tried to link with Rolan, and caught an impression of concern, but in the confusion it was hard to make out what the concern was for.

Kris began to say something—the Prince interrupted him before he'd even gotten a single syllable out.

"The Palace is quite remarkable," said Ancar, a kind of glint in his eye that Talia didn't understand and didn't at all like. "You really *must* see it *all*."

What could they do but consent?

And the Prince seemed determined that they see every inch of his father's Palace, conducting them all over it himself. He kept himself at Kris' side, and one of his ubiquitous toadies at Talia's, effectively separating them. They couldn't even signal to one another—and Talia was nearly stiff with apprehension before the enforced tour was over. Her anxiety, carefully concealed, redoubled every moment they spent in his presence, and she longed for one single moment alone with Kris. It almost seemed as if the Prince were deliberately attempting to prevent any contact between the two Heralds that did not take place under his gaze, for he kept them at his side until it was nearly time for the state banquet that was to welcome them.

*   *   *

At last they were left alone in their sumptuous suite.

Talia scanned about her for listeners, but could detect none. But then—could she if they were shielded?

Make discretion the better part, then.

"Lord of Light," she sighed. "I didn't think I could ever be so tired. . . ."

Hand-sign; *Trap—listeners?* She sat down on a couch, and patted the fabric next to her in invitation.

He took a seat next to her, and her hand. Squeezed. *Gift?*

She squeezed back. *Shields?*

His eyebrows arched in surprise. *How?*

"Did you see that odd little man on the Prince's right?" she asked. *Him.* "I wonder what on earth he could be." *Shielded Ancar. Maybe more.*

"Who knows? Some sort of tutor, maybe." *Trouble.*

"Hm. I could use a little air." *For true.*

They moved to the open window, arms around one another, lover-like.

"Little bird," Kris whispered in her ear, "There's another problem—there aren't enough guards visible here."

Talia giggled and nuzzled his neck. "I'm not sure I understand you," she murmured back.

He laughed, and kissed her with expertly feigned passion. "Look, Selenay is well-loved, so she keeps a minimum of guards about her for safety—but they're still there, still visible. Alessandar is just as highly regarded, so I would expect to see about the same number of guards. I didn't see them. If they're not *in* sight, they must be *out* of sight. Why should he hide his guards? Unless he doesn't know that they're hidden—and if you can hide one, you can hide a dozen just as easily. I don't like it."

"Kris, please—" Talia whispered urgently. "I've changed my mind about staying. I think we should get out of here. Now. Tonight."

"I agree; I think we've walked into a bit more than we can handle by ourselves." He led her back to the couch, where they continued the mock-loveplay. "I've got no doubt now after seeing that magician and watching the way people react to Ancar that every one of the rumors is true. So we'd better leave tonight—but not quite yet. I want to find out what's going on with Alessandar first." He stayed quiet for a moment, deep in thought, hands resting in the small of her back, and face buried in her hair. "I think we should send substitutes into the banquet and do some spying before we leave."

"All right, but I'll do the spying. If I unshield I'll be able to detect people coming long before you would."

"Could you tell if there's a shielded spy watching us by the shield on him?"

"Alone—no."

"I see what you're getting at. Link—"

By linking their two Gifts, her Empathy and his Farsight, they were able to scan their entire vicinity for "null" areas. And discovered, to their mutual chagrin, that there *were* no spies, shielded or otherwise.

"Well—" he pulled away from her, embarrassed. "I certainly feel like a fool."

"Don't." She ran her hands nervously through her hair, and smiled wanly at him. "Better we take the precaution needlessly. If we send in substitutes, won't they be recognized?"

"No one from the Prince's party will be at the banquet, remember? There won't be anyone there who's ever seen us. And if we use a couple of the servants there should be no problems. After all, no one ever looks at servants. The two they assigned to us should do. They're enough like us in size and appearance that our uniforms will fit reasonably well. I'll get their attention, and you deep-trance, and take them over."

Talia shivered. She didn't like doing this, but Kris couldn't. His Gift of Farsight would do him no good in implanting a false personality. It was only by virtue of the fact that her Gift of Empathy was a particularly strong one that Talia could do it at all—this was normally a trick only Mindspeakers could manage.

Kris rang for the two who had been assigned to them. As he had pointed out, they were similar enough in height and build to the two of them that the uniforms should fit well enough to cause no comment.

The servants arrived, and with them, their baggage; Kris instructed them in the unpacking of the formal uniforms. While he engaged their attention, Talia put herself into deep-trance.

Forgive me—she thought, then reached out and touched their minds—lightly—*there*—first the man, then the woman—

Kris caught them as they fell, easing them down onto the bed.

Talia insinuated herself carefully into their minds, sending their real selves into a kind of waking sleep.

Now—for the next part she would need help—

:Rolan?:

In a moment he was with her, still anxious, but in agreement with the plan, or at least as much of it as she was able to show him without being able to Mindspeak him in words instead of images.

Together they emplanted false personalities and memories in their two substitutes; he could do some things she couldn't, she could make them *believe* that they were the foreigners. For the next several hours the servants would be a sketchy sort of Kris and Talia, and remain that way until they returned to these rooms after the banquet. Their behavior would be rather stilted and wooden, but the formal etiquette such occasions demanded would cover most of that.

Talia let Rolan go, and eased herself up out of trance, feeling very stiff, quite exhausted, and just a bit guilty.

"Is it—"

"They're ready," she replied, moving her head around to ease the stiffness in her neck, and getting slowly to her feet. "Let's get some clothes on them."

They clothed the pair in the waiting formal Whites as if they were dealing with two dolls, it being easier to handle them in the entranced state. Talia cut their hair in imitation of Kris' and her own, and applied her skill with makeup to both of them. When she'd done, they bore at least enough of a superficial resemblance to the two of them to get them safely through the doors.

"All right." Kris looked at her as they got the two substitutes on their feet. "I'm for the stables. It's going to take a little time to find the Companions and their tack without being detected. If I can, I'll get everything and get them all saddled up. If you have the chance, you meet me at the stable doors."

"Fine," Talia replied nervously. "I'm going to sneak up to the second floor and the minstrel's gallery. I ought to learn something there; with luck I may be able to pick up something from one of Ancar's toadies, and I'll definitely be able to probe Alessandar and find out if he knows what his son is up to. I won't take long, if I can help it."

"If the worst happens, and you have to run for it, tell Rolan, and I'll pick you up on the run in the courtyard." Kris gave her a tight grin, and she returned it.

Talia took her substitute by the elbow; Kris did the same with his. Together they led them as far as the doors to the suite; then Talia released their minds and gave hers a little push. The young woman blinked once, then her implanted personality took over. She took the young man's arm; he opened the door, and led her toward the banquet hall. Kris and Talia followed behind them long enough to be certain that the ruse would work, then separated.

Thanks to the Prince's enforced tour they were both familiar with the layout of the entire Palace. Kris made for one of the servants' stairs that led to the stables; once she saw him safely on his way, Talia headed for the gallery that overlooked the banquet hall.

She dropped all her shielding and slipped from shadow to shadow along the corridor, taking another of the servants' stairs to the second floor. The activity in the banquet hall aided her; the servants hadn't yet had time to light more than a few of the candles meant to illuminate the maze of corridors. She detected no one as she moved to the wall that backed the gallery.

She sensed the presence of many men as she paused there, hiding herself in the folds of drapery along the wall. This was very wrong. There were to be no minstrels playing in the gallery until much later this evening; at the moment they were playing from behind a screen on the floor of the hall. There should be no one at all in the gallery at this time.

She closed her eyes and carefully extended her other sense past the wall, hoping that one of them might be nervous enough to let her read what he was seeing, carried on the wind of his emotions.

It was easy—too easy. The images came charging into her mind— she knew who and what they were, and what their intent was, and her heart leapt into her throat with terror.

Ranged at about three-foot intervals around the gallery, which ran the entire circumference of the hall, were crossbowmen. Their weapons were loaded and ready, and each had a full quiver of bolts beside him. These were not members of Alessandar's guard, nor soldiers from his army; these were ruthless killers recruited personally by Ancar.

The Prince was impatient, and no longer prepared to wait for his father's natural death to bring him to the seat of power. He was also ambitious, and not content with the prospect of ruling only one kingdom. Here in one room sat his father and everyone who might be opposed to Ancar's rule, as well as the two Heralds who might have warned their Queen of his intent. The opportunity was far too tempting for him to pass by. Once the banquet was well underway, the doors would be locked—and all who might oppose Ancar's desires would die.

With the exception of the Heralds; Ancar's orders concerning *them* were to disable, not kill. And if anything, that frightened Talia even more.

Ancar must have had this whole scheme planned for months, and had only waited for the perfect moment to put it in motion. The six days' warning he'd had when they crossed the Border was sufficient for him to mobilize what was already prepared.

When the slaughter was over he would ride with his own army to the Border, overwhelm the Queen and her escort as soon as they'd crossed it, kill her, seize Elspeth, and present himself as Valdemar's ruler by fait accompli.

Talia longed for Kyril's ability to Farspeak; even at this distance she would have been able to get some kind of warning back to the Heralds near the Border. And she would have been able to Mindcall Kris, and warn him as well. All she could do was to Mindcall to Rolan, carrying her message on a burst of purest fear, and hope he could convey the whole to Kris through Tantris.

She slipped back to the staircase as silently and carefully as she had come, and made her way down to the lower floor.

The hall here was lighted well, and Talia feared to set foot in it; feared it doubly when she sensed the presence of more of Ancar's men standing at intervals along it, presumably to take care of any stragglers. She clung, half paralyzed with terror, to the inside of the door, and tried to think. Was there any other way out?

Then she recalled the smaller rooms of state, meant for receptions and the like, that faced the forecourt on the second floor. Many of them had balconies, and windows or doors that opened out onto the balconies. For the second time she climbed the staircase, heart pounding, her Empathic-sense extended to the utmost.

She moved along the wall, between it and the musty draperies lining it, until she came to the door of one of those rooms. Mercifully it was unoccupied and unlocked; not even a single candle was lit within. She crept out from behind the drape, ignoring the itch of dust in her eyes and nose, and slipped inside.

There was only the gleam of torchlight and moonlight through the windows, but that was enough to show her a room with a polished-wood floor empty of all furniture. She edged around the walls, grudging the time, but not wanting to silhouette herself against those windows for anyone passing by the hall door.

The door to the balcony was locked, but from the inside. Talia realized this after an instant of panic-stricken struggle with it. The catch was stiff, but finally gave. She eased the door open and stepped out onto the balcony, crouched low so as to be below the balustrade. A moment's surveillance of the courtyard showed no eyes to be watching it; she slipped over the balustrade and was about to drop to the court, when the killing began.

With her Empathic senses extended as they were, that nearly killed *her* along with the rest. She felt the deaths of dozens of people in her own flesh; she lost her grip on the railing and dropped to the cobble-stones below. Shock, pain, and fear drove any other thoughts out of her, she could not even move to save herself. She was falling—and couldn't think, couldn't move, couldn't do anything but *react*—react to the agony, the terror—and the anguished guilt of Alessandar's guards seeing him pinned to his throne by dozens of crossbow bolts before they themselves were cut down—

But Alberich had foreseen the day when something like this might happen; he had drilled her until some reactions had become instinctive. Though her mind might be helpless beneath that onslaught, her body wasn't—

She twisted in midair, rolled into a limp ball—hit the pavement feet-first, and turned the impact into a tumble that left her sprawled and bruised, but otherwise unharmed.

Her face twisted with agony as she struggled to her feet and staggered toward the entrance to the stable area, trying to shut her shields down and the pain out. It seemed like an eternity between each stumbling step, yet she had hardly taken half a dozen when she heard the pounding of hooves on stone and saw a white form surging toward her.

It was Rolan—unsaddled. He did not pause as he passed her, knowing that she would not be able to mount unless he came to a dead stop. Hard on his heels came Tantris carrying Kris—who was leaning over as far as he dared, one hand wrapped in Tantris' mane, the other extended toward her, his legs clenched so tightly she could almost feel the muscles ache. As Companion and rider passed her, Talia caught him, hands catching forearms, as she leaped and Kris pulled her up in front of him. Tantris had had to slow a trifle, and Rolan was ahead of him, but they'd not had to stop.

But there was one last obstacle to pass—the narrow passage between the inner and outer walls that led to the portcullis and the outer gate. And Talia had succeeded in shielding herself once again—so they had no warning that the walls were manned.

They galloped straight into a hail of arrows.

It was over in seconds. Fire lanced through Talia's shoulder—just as Tantris screamed in agony, shuddered, and crashed to the ground. She was thrown forward and hit the ground stunned, with the impact breaking off the shaft of the arrow and driving the head deeper. But more agonizing than her own pain was what Kris was enduring.

Rolan paused in his headlong flight—the marksmen had let the unburdened beast go by. There was one thought only in Talia's mind besides the agony of pain—that *one* of them must escape.

"Rolan—*run!*" she screamed with voice, heart, and mind.

He hesitated no longer, but shot through the gate just as the portcullis came crashing down, so close that she felt the sharp pain and his surge of fear as it actually carried away a few hairs from his tail.

Kris lay crumpled beside the motionless body of Tantris, so racked with agony that he could not even cry out. She tried to rise, and half-stumbled, half-dragged herself to his side. She took his pain-tortured body into her arms, desperately trying to think of *anything* that would help him. He was transfixed by arrows so that he looked like a straw target—but a target that bled; it had been his body and Tantris' that had shielded her. Even in the flickering torchlight she could see that his Whites were dyed in creeping scarlet blotches that spread while she held him. She groped mindlessly for the Healing energy Kerithwyn had used; not sure what she could do with it, but driven beyond sanity with the overwhelming need to take the burden of his torment from him. She felt a kind of pressure building within her, as it had in those past times when desperation had driven her to pass the bounds of what she knew. It built past the point where she was conscious of anything outside of herself, conscious even of the agony lancing her own shoulder—

Then it found sudden release.

She opened her eyes to find Kris' own eyes holding hers; free from pain and feverishly clear. Although she could feel his pain still, *he* could not. She had somehow come to stand between it and him.

But he was dying, and they both knew it.

She looked around, expecting to see soldiers surrounding them.

"No."

Kris' hoarse whisper brought her attention back to him. "They—it is a maze. While I live, they will not come."

She understood. His Gift had shown him that there was a maze of stairs and corridors to traverse before the soldiers reached an entrance to this area. But it had also shown him how little time he had left.

"Kris—" She couldn't get anything more past the tears that rose and choked off her words.

"No, little love, little bird. Weep for yourself, not for me."

She nearly fell to pieces with grief at his words.

"I don't fear Death; gladly, willingly would I seek the Havens, if I but knew my Companion waits for me there—but to leave you—how can I leave you with all my burden and yours as well?" He coughed, and blood showed at the corner of his mouth. Somehow he managed to raise one hand to touch her cheek; she seized it with her own and wept into it.

"It isn't fair—to leave you alone—but warn them, heartsister. Somehow warn them. I cannot carry the task to the end, so it ends with you."

She nodded, so choked with tears she could not speak.

"Oh, little bird, I love you—" He seemed to be trying to say more when another spate of coughing shook him. He looked up again, but plainly did not see her; his eyes brightened and gladdened as if he were seeing something wonderful and unexpected. "So—bright! T—"

For one fleeting moment Talia sensed—joy; joy and the touch of awe and a strange glory that was like nothing she'd ever sensed before. Then his body shuddered once in her arms, and the light and life left his eyes. He went limp within her embrace—and then there was nothing but the empty husk she held.

The soldiers came then, tore them apart, and took her away; she was too numb with shock and grief to resist.

CHAPTER 8

HER GUARDS WERE anything but gentle.

They bound her hands behind her and kicked and shoved her down countless rock-faced corridors and a flight of rough stone stairs; when she stumbled they kicked her until she rose, when she faltered they sent her onward with blows. They gave her a final push that sent her sprawling into the center of a bare room. There they put her in the custody of three hulking brutes, creatures who looked more beast than man.

These three stripped her to the skin, indifferent to the agony of her shoulder, and brutally searched her. Then one by one, they raped her with the same brutality and indifference. By that time, she was nearly senseless with shock and pain, and it hardly seemed to matter. It was just one more torture. She couldn't even concentrate enough to use her Gift to defend herself, and when she'd tried feebly to fight back, the one using her had knocked her head against the stone floor so hard she was barely conscious.

When they had finished with her they hauled her to her feet by one arm, and threw her into a dirt-floored, stone-walled cell, then tossed what was left of her bloodstained clothing in behind her. It was the cold that finally roused her, cold that chilled her and made her shake uncontrollably, and awoke her lacerated shoulder to new pain. She roused enough then to crawl to where they'd tossed her things and pull them on over her abused flesh.

Not surprisingly, nothing had been done about the wound in her shoulder, which continued to bleed sluggishly.

I've—got to do something—she thought, through the pain and cold clouding her mind—*got to—get it out.*

She got a firmer grip on reality; thought she remembered that the arrows she'd seen the guards carrying had had leafpoints. *Right*— She steeled herself against the inevitable, got a good grip on what was left of the slippery, blood-soaked shaft, and pulled.

It came free—she passed out briefly as it did. When her vision cleared, she bound the wound with one hand using a scrap from her shredded shirt as a bandage, and hoped that this would at least stem the blood loss.

Selenay. Elspeth. She had to warn the Queen—

That goad was driving her past the point where she should have collapsed, and continued to drive her. She had to warn the others. For that she *must* stay aware—and alive, much as she longed to die. She curled in on herself, forcing herself into trance, driving herself regardless of the pain of her brutalized body. With this much pain behind it, even *she* should be able to reach the Border.

But she met with the same wall that had protected the Prince from her probe. She battered herself against it like a wild bird against the bars of a cage, and with as much effect. There were no cracks, no weak points in it. Try as she might, she could not reach her Mindcall past it. Weeping with bitter pain and tortured frustration, she gave up, and lay in a hopeless huddle on the floor in the darkness.

There was no way of telling how long she lay there before an anomalous sound roused her from a nightmare of shock, pain, and confused grief. She listened again. It was the sound of someone whispering.

"Herald! Lady Herald!" The voice sounded vaguely familiar.

"Herald!" It was coming from a small opening in the ceiling.

She crawled on hands and knees across the dirt floor to lie beneath it, for her legs trembled so much she doubted they'd hold her, and coughed several times before she could speak.

"I'm—here."

"Lady Herald, it's me, Evan—Evan, the trader from Westmark in Valdemar. The one you talked to a day ago."

As she reached out tentatively with her Gift she wondered briefly if this, too, was a trap.

Gods—if it is—but what do I have to lose? Please, Lady—

She nearly fainted with relief when her Gift confirmed that it was the same man.

"Oh, gods—Evan, Evan, Lady bless you—" She gulped and got control over her babbling. "Where are you?"

"Outside the walls in the dry moat. Some of my acquaintances have worked in the Palace and Guard and told me of these ventilation holes. I arrived after you, late this evening—I was drinking with some of the Guard when—there were screams. They told me some of what was happening, and warned me to hold my tongue if I wanted to live. They aren't bad men, but they are afraid, Herald, very much afraid. The Prince is making no secret now that he has evil magicians, and an entire army that answers only to him."

—if only I'd overruled Kris—he'd be alive now—

"Later they told me they'd captured you—I—couldn't leave you without trying to help. I bribed a guard to learn which cell they had taken for you. Lady—" He seemed to be groping for words. "Lady, your friend is dead."

"Yes—I—I know." She bowed her head as the tears fell anew and she did not try to hold them back.

He was silent for a long moment. "Lady, you saved my life; I am still in your life-debt. *Is* there some way I can help you? The Prince means to keep you living; I am told he has plans for you."

Hope rose to faltering life. "Can you help me escape this place?"

And died. "No, Lady," he said sadly. "That would require an army. I would gladly try alone—but it would not serve you. You would still be here, and I would be quite dead."

Half a dozen ideas flitted through her mind; one stayed.

"Are these holes straight? Could you lower something to me, or bring something up?"

"If it were something small, yes, Lady; easily done. My guide told me that they were quite straight, and unobstructed."

"Can you find me two arrows—if you can, see that the barbs of the fletching are heavy—and—" She faltered, and forced herself to continue. "—and at least ten drams of argonel."

"Have they hurt you, Lady? There are safer ways to ease pain than argonel. And Lady, that much—"

"Trader, do not argue. I have my reasons, and argonel it must be. Can you do it?"

"Within the hour, Lady."

There was a thin whisper of sound as he left. She propped herself against the wall and tried to use the pain-deadening tricks she'd been taught to ease her shoulder and her throbbing loins. She would not let herself hope that the trader would keep his promise, but strove to remain passive, unfeeling, in a kind of numbness. It was still dark when she heard a scratch and the trader's voice.

"Lady, I have all you asked for. It's coming now."

She pulled herself up the wall and reached for the bundle that dangled from the ceiling with her good hand, feeling more of the injured shoulder muscles tear as she reached up.

"The bottle holds fourteen drams, and it is full."

"May the Lord of Lights and the Fair Lady shine on you, friend, and all your kin and trade—" she replied fervently, loosening the stopper enough to catch the distinctive sweet-sour odor of argonel. The bottle *was* completely full. "Leave the string. You will be taking something up in a moment and doing me another service—one last office that will free you of life-debt entirely."

"I am yours to command," he replied with simple sincerity.

She snapped the head from the first arrow by holding it under one foot. She let the tears flow freely as she patterned it with Kris' fletching pattern, grateful that she'd been made to learn to do the task in the dark, and finding it hard to continue with the memory fresh of him teaching her his own pattern. The headless arrow—code for a Herald dead. Now for the most important half of the message—code for herself; and code for the mission in such ruins that no attempt at rescue should be made. She broke the second arrow in half and patterned the fletching as her own. She tore the remains of one sleeve from her shirt, secured the arrows into a compact bundle with it, and fastened the whole to the string dangling down from the hole in the ceiling.

"Trader, pull it up."

It gleamed for a moment against the stone, then was gone.

"Now listen carefully. I want you to leave now, before dawn, before the Prince tries to seal the city. You must get outside the city gates."

"There is a guard at the night-gate I know I can bribe."

"Good. Just out of sight of the guardpost on the main highway that runs from the Triumph Gate there is a shrine to the god of wayfarers."

"I know the place."

"My horse will find you there." The one thing that damned magician *couldn't* block was her bond with Rolan! "Tie the bundle around his neck, just as it is, then take whatever plan seems good to you. If I were you, I would make a run for the Border; you'll be safe enough on the Valdemar side. Know that you have all my thanks and all my blessings."

"Lady—a horse?"

She remembered then that he was Hardornen, and couldn't know how unlike horses the Companions were.

"He is more than horse; think of him as a familiar spirit. He will return to my people with my message. Will you do this for me?"

He was close to weeping himself. "Is there nothing more I can do?"

"If you do that, you will have done more than I dared hope. You take with you all my gratitude, and my blessings. Now go, please, and quickly."

He did not speak again, and she heard the scrape that signaled his departure.

She felt for her contact with Rolan. Her bond with him was at too deep a level for the magician even to sense, let alone block. Although alternating waves of pain and faintness threatened to overwhelm her, she managed to remain aware until she knew with total certainty that Rolan had gotten her message-bundle from the trader.

Rolan did not need any instructions to know what to do. Her contact with him weakened and faded as she weakened with effort and blood loss and he headed for the Border at his fastest pace, until it vanished altogether as he reached the edge of her fast-shrinking range. By then it was almost dawn.

Now, there were just two more tasks, and she would be able to give way to her anguish, her hurts, her grief.

First, the bottle. The trader had been right to be nervous about argonel. It was chancy stuff. Sometimes even the normal dose of four drams killed—but the Healers used it now and again to end the suffering of one they could not save. It had the advantage that no matter how great the overdose, there were no painful side effects such as there were with other such drugs—nothing but a peaceful drifting into sleep. If four drams could kill, fourteen should make death very sure.

Using the broken-off arrowhead, she scraped a hole in the floor beneath the pile of molding straw that was supposed to be her bed, a hole just deep enough to bury the bottle. Alessandar had not been the kind of monarch that often used his dungeons; by the grace of the gods the floors were packed earth rather than stone, with a pit dug in one corner for a privy.

She would not use the drug yet—not until she was *certain* that the Queen had received the warning. *Soon, Bright Lady—make it soon—*

Then she scraped a second hole, and a third, and hid the arrowhead from the broken arrow and the one she'd pulled from her own shoulder. If by some mischance they should find the bottle, she could still cut her wrists with one of them.

Her shoulder was aflame with pain and bleeding again, and a little gray light was creeping down the ventilation hole when she'd finished.

She lay on the straw and let herself mourn at last.

Tears of sorrow and of pain were still pouring from her eyes when blood loss and exhaustion finally drove her into unconsciousness.

When she came to herself again, there was a single spot of sunlight on the floor, making the rest of the room seem black by comparison. She blinked in hurt and confusion, as the door clanked once and opened.

She saw one of her jailors strolling toward her, wearing a sadistic grin and unfastening his breeches as he walked. For the space of a second she was ready to cry out and shrink away from him—but then a cold and deadly anger came over her, and abruptly she could bear no more. She took all her agony and Kris' (still rawly part of her), all her loss, all her hatred, and hurled them into his unprotected mind in a blinding instant of forced rapport.

Hatred couldn't sustain her long—she couldn't maintain it for more than a single moment—but that moment was enough.

He screamed soundlessly, and flung himself wildly at the door, nearly knocking himself senseless when he reached it. He slammed it after himself, and threw the bolt home. She could hear him babbling in panic to his comrades on the other side. As she slumped back, she knew that they would not dare to molest her again, not unless the magician was with them. That was very unlikely. *That* one was too busy protecting his Prince and keeping her from Mindspeaking to have time to spare to protect menials so that they might amuse themselves.

They shoved in a pail of water and a plate of some sort of slop later in the day. She ignored the food, but drank the stale, fusty-tasting water avidly. Her terrible thirst woke her to the fact that she was beginning to feel both overheated and chilled.

Gingerly she touched the skin next to the arrow-wound. It was hot and dry to the touch, and badly swollen.

She was taking wound-fever.

While she was still able, she relieved herself down the privy hole in the corner, telling herself that she should be grateful that there was nothing in her stomach and bowels to make a flux of. It was cold comfort, that. She pulled the bucket within reach of the straw and propped herself against the wall in case someone should try to take her un-aware. When the hallucinations and fever-dreams began, she was more or less ready for them.

There was no pattern to the fever. When she was able to think, she would tend to herself as best she could. When the fever took her, she endured.

There were horrible visions of the slaughter in the banquet hall, and the victims paraded their death-wounds before her and mutely asked why she hadn't warned them. In vain she told them that she hadn't known—they pressed in on her, shoving mutilated limbs and dripping wounds in her face, smothering her—

Her bestial guards multiplied into a horde, and used her, and used her, and used her—

Then Kris came.

At first she thought it was going to be another dream like the first, but it wasn't. Instead, he was whole, well; even happy—until he saw her. Then, to her distress, he began weeping—and blamed himself for what had happened to her.

She tried to put on a brave face for him, but when she moved, she hurt so much that her fragile pretense shattered. He shook off his own distress at that, and hurried to kneel at her side.

He somehow drove away some of the pain, spoke words of comfort, bathed her feverish brow with cool water. When she whimpered invol-untarily as movement sent lances of hurt through her shoulder, he wept again with vexation at his own impotence, and berated himself for leaving her alone. When the other, horrible dreams came, he stood them off.

The next time she came to herself, she found that there was a scrap torn from her sleeve near the bucket, still damp. After trying to puzzle it out, she decided that she'd done it herself, and the dream had been a ra-tionalization of it.

As delirium began to take her again, she tried to tell herself that it was unlikely that her hallucinations would include Kris a second time.

But they did, and Kris continued to guard her from the hideous vi-sions, all the while trying to give her courage.

Finally she gave up even trying to pretend to hope, and told Kris about the argonel.

"No, little bird," he said, shaking his head at her. "It isn't your time yet."

"But—"

"Trust me. Trust me, dearheart. Everything is going to come out fine. Just try to hold on—" He faded into the stone, then, as she woke once more.

That puzzled her. Why should a fever-dream of her own making be trying to urge her to live, when she only wanted release?

But for the most part, she simply suffered, and endured the waiting, watching for some sign that her message had safely reached Selenay. The Queen and her entourage should have reached the Border about two days after she and Kris had ridden through the palace gates. They would have been expecting Kris about three or four days after they arrived—a week after she'd been thrown in here. With luck and the Lady with him, Rolan should reach them about that time. She added the days in her head—that meant he would reach the Queen in six to ten days at his hardest gallop—six if he could take the open roads, ten if he had to backtrack and hide.

When Hulda first appeared, at the end of the third day, Talia thought initially that she was another hallucination.

If it hadn't been that Hulda's sharp features and strange gray-violet eyes were unmistakable, Talia wouldn't have recognized her. She was swathed in a voluptuous gown of burgundy-wine velvet, cut low and daringly across the bosom, and there were jewels on her neck and hands and the net that bound her hair. But most amazing of all, she appeared to be hardly older than Talia herself.

She stood peering into the darkness, eyes darting this way and that; a cruel smile touched her lips when she finally spotted Talia huddled against the wall. She moved from the center of the room with an odd, gliding step to stand above Talia, eyes narrowed in pleasure, and nudged her sharply with one dainty shoe.

The pain she caused made Talia gasp and pull in on herself—and her heart leapt into her throat when she realized that the woman was still standing there—real, and no hallucination.

When Talia's eyes widened with shock and recognition, Hulda smiled. "You remember me? How very touching! I had no hope you'd have any recollection of little Elspeth's adored nurse."

She moved a few steps farther away and stood artfully posing in the light that came through the ventilation hole. "And how low the mighty Herald has fallen! You'd have been pleased to see me brought so low, wouldn't you? But I am not caught so easily, little Herald. Not half so easily."

"What—what are you?" The words were forced out almost against Talia's will.

"I? Besides a nurse, you mean?" She laughed. "Well, a magician, I suppose you'd call me. Did you think the Heralds held all the magic there was in the world? Oh, no, little Herald, that is far, far from being the case."

She laughed again, and swept out of the cell, the door clanging shut behind her.

Talia struggled to think; but—Lord and Lady, this meant there was more, much more at stake here than she'd dreamed.

Hulda—so young-looking, and claiming to be a magician. And she hadn't any trace of a Gift, Talia knew *that* for certain. Put that together with the mage who guarded Ancar and kept her from Mindspeaking to other Heralds—gods protect Valdemar! That meant that old magic, *real* magic, and not just Heraldic Mind-magic, was loose in the world again. And in the hands of Valdemar's enemies—

And Hulda had been—*must* have been—playing a deeper game than anyone ever guessed, and for far longer. But to what purpose?

Hulda came again, this time after dark, bringing some kind of witch-light with her. It was an odd, misty ball that gave off a red glare that flickered and pulsated; it floated in behind her and hovered just above her shoulder, bathing the entire cell in an eerie, reddish glow.

This time Talia was more or less ready for her. She was free from delirium for the moment, and feeling light-yet-clear-headed. She had managed to put her own emotions and the helplessness of her position in the back of her mind, hoping for some stroke of luck that might bring her a chance to strike back at her tormentors.

She had figured that Hulda was warded, even as the Prince was; she probed anyway, and discovered her guess was correct. So rather than making any other moves, she simply shifted her weight where she sat so that she might be able to get to her feet at a moment's notice.

Hulda smiled mockingly; Talia glared right back.

"You might rise to greet me," she mocked. "No? Well, I shan't ask it of you. You'll be dancing to my little Prince's tunes soon enough. Or should I say, 'King'? I suppose I should. Aren't you at all curious as to why and how I came here?"

"I have the feeling you'd tell me whether I cared or not," Talia said bitterly.

"Spirited! You're right, I would. Oh, I spent years looking for a child like Ancar—one of high estate, yet one who could readily incline himself to what I would teach him. Then once I found him, I knew within a year that one land would never be enough for him. So once I taught him enough that he could do without me for a time, I turned my attention toward finding him a suitable mate. Dear Elspeth seemed so perfect—" She sighed theatrically.

"Oh?"

"You are so talented, little Herald! What volumes of meaning you convey with a single syllable! Yes, dear Elspeth seemed perfect—coming from a long line of those Gifted magically, *and* with such a father! Plotting against his own wife! Delicious!"

"If you're trying to convince me that treachery is inherited, you're wasting your breath."

She laughed. "Very well then, I'll be brief. I intended Elspeth to be properly trained and eventually consolidate an alliance with Ancar. As you probably guessed, I substituted myself for the original Hulda. Things were progressing quite well—until you intervened."

This time the glance she shot at Talia was venomous. "Fortunately I was forewarned. I returned to my dear Prince, and when he was of an age to begin taking part in the making of plans, we put together a quite tidy plot."

She began pacing the room, restlessly, the folds of her vermillion gown collecting loose dirt from the floor, dirt which she ignored.

"What *is* it," Talia asked the ceiling above her head, "what is it about would-be tyrants that makes them speak and posture like third-rate gleemen in a badly-written play?"

Hulda pivoted sharply about and glared, her hands twitching a little as if she'd like to settle them about Talia's neck. Talia braced herself, hoping she'd try. Granted, she was as weak as water, but there were some tricks Alberich had taught her. . . .

"Haven't you got anything better to do than boast about your petty triumphs to a captive audience?" she taunted.

Hulda's face darkened with anger; then to Talia's disappointment she regained control of herself, and slowly straightened and smoothed the folds of her gown while she calmed her temper.

"You're to be a part of this, you know," she said abruptly. "Ancar wanted both of you alive, but you alone will do. We'll all ride together to the Border and wait for your Queen there. She'll see you with us, and be reassured. Then—"

"You don't seriously think you'll get me to cooperate, do you?"

"You won't have a choice. Just as my Prince's servant can keep you from sending your little messages, so I can take control of your own body from you—particularly since you're in rather poor condition at the moment."

"You can try."

"Oh, no, little Herald. I can bring in more help than you could ever hope to hold against. I will succeed."

She laughed, and swept out the door then, the witchlight following.

As Talia had hoped, on the tenth day of her captivity, the door to her cell opened, and Prince Ancar and his magician stood before her. And with him was Hulda.

She was in another of the periods of clear-headedness between bouts of delirium. She debated facing them standing, but decided that she didn't have the strength. She simply stared at them with undisguised contempt.

"My messengers have sent signals telling me that the Queen of Valdemar has turned back at the Border," Ancar said, gazing at her with basilisk-eyes. "And now they say she gathers an army to her side. Somehow you warned her, Herald. How?"

She returned him stare for stare. "If you two are so all-powerful," she asked contemptuously, "why don't you read my thoughts?"

His face reddened with anger. "*Damn* you Heralds and your barriers—" he spat, before Hulda managed to hush him.

Talia stared at him in astonishment. *Brightest Lady—he can't read me—they can't read me, can't read Heralds—no wonder we almost caught Hulda before—* For one moment, she felt a stirring of excitement, but it faded. The information was priceless—and useless. It only meant they would not be able to pluck truth from her thoughts, and so would never know when and if she lied.

So start now. Tell them a truth they would never believe. According to Elspeth, Hulda had never believed that the Companions were more than very well trained beasts. She had been convinced it was the Heralds who picked the Chosen, not the Companions.

So. "My horse," she said after a long pause. "My horse escaped to warn them."

Ancar smiled, and ice rimed her blood. "An imagination, I trow. You should have been a Bard. This will only delay things, you must realize. I have been working toward my goals for years, and I can easily compass a little more delay." He turned toward Hulda, and brushed his lips along her hair. "Can't I, my dear nurse?"

"Easily, my Prince. You have been a most apt pupil."

"And the pupil has exceeded the teacher, no?"

"In some things, my love. Not in all."

"Perhaps you will be interested to hear that I know of your quarrel with the young Heir, little Herald. It would seem that she is quite crestfallen, and determined to make it up with you, since my informant tells me she is most eager to be meeting with you again. A pity that won't happen. It would have been amusing to watch the meeting—and you under my dear nurse's control."

Talia tried not to show any reaction, but her concentration slipped enough that she bit her lip.

"Do tell her who our informant is, my love," Hulda murmured in Ancar's ear.

"None other than the trusted Lord Orthallen. What, you are not surprised? How vexing. Hulda discovered him, you know—found that he had been working at undermining the Heralds and the Monarchs so long and so cleverly that no one even guessed how often he'd played his cards."

"Some of us guessed."

"Really?" Hulda pouted. "I *am* disappointed. But have you guessed why? Ancar has promised him the throne. Orthallen has wanted that for so very long, you see. He thought he had it when he arranged for an assassin to take Selenay's father in battle. But then there was Selenay—and all those Heralds who persisted in protecting her. He decided to do away with them first—it's a pity how little luck he's had. He has been so surprised at the way you keep eluding his traps. He'll be even more amazed when Ancar gives him the dagger instead of the crown. But I *am* disappointed that you had guessed at his perfidy already."

"My poor dear—two disappointments in one day." Ancar turned his cold gaze back on Talia. "Well, since you have denied me one pleasure, you can hardly blame anyone but yourself when I use you for another, can you? Perhaps it will make up for the entertainments your actions denied my dear nurse."

"Ah, but be wary of this wench, my lord King," Hulda cautioned. "She is not without weapons, even now. Your servant must not let the barrier break for even a moment."

He smiled again. "Small chance of that, my love. He *knows* the penalty should he fail to keep her trapped within her own mind. Should he weaken, my heart—he becomes *yours*."

She trilled with delight as he signaled to the hulking guards that stood behind him.

They seized Talia and dragged her to her feet, pinioning her arms behind her back. Anguish threaded her body as the wound broke open anew, but she bit her lip and suffered silently.

"Stubborn as well! How entertaining you will be, Herald. How very entertaining."

He turned and led the way from the cell with the magician and Hulda in close attendance and the guards following with Talia. There was a long corridor that smelled of mold and damp, and an iron door at the end of it. Beyond it was the smell of fear, and blood.

They shackled her arms to the cold stone above her head, putting an almost intolerable strain on her wounded shoulder.

"I consider myself an artist," Ancar told her. "There is a certain artistry in producing the most pain without inflicting permanent damage, or causing death." He removed a long, slender iron rod from the fire and regarded the white-hot tip thoughtfully. "There are such fascinating things to be done with this, for instance."

As from a century distant she recalled Alberich discussing some of the more unpleasant realities of becoming a Herald with a small knot of final-year students in which she was included.

"The possibility of torture," Alberich had said on that long ago afternoon, "is something we cannot afford to ignore. No matter what it is that the stories say, anyone can be broken by pain. There are mental exercises that will enable one to escape, but they are not proof against the worst that man can devise. All I can advise you if you find yourself in the hopeless situation is that you must lie; lie so often and with such creativity that your captors will not know the truth when they hear it. For the time will come when you will tell them the truth—you will be unable to help yourself. But by then, I hope, you will have muddied the waters past any hope of clarity. . . ."

But Ancar did not want information; he was getting that in plenty from Orthallen. All he wanted was to make her hurt. She was damned if she'd give him satisfaction before she had to.

So the "fascinating things" failed to drive a sound from her, and the Prince was displeased.

He proceeded to more sophisticated tortures, involving complicated apparatus. He handled all of this himself, his long hands caressing the bloodstained straps and cruel metal as he described in loving detail what each was to do to her helpless body.

Talia did her best to keep herself shielded, and to retreat behind those mental barriers to pain and the outside world she had long ago learned to erect, but as he continued his entertainment, her barriers and shielding gradually eroded. She became nauseatingly aware of every emotion he, Hulda, and the nameless magician were experiencing. The intensely sexual pleasure he derived from her pain was worse than rape; and she was in too much agony to block it out. Hulda's pleasure was as perverted, and as hard to bear. In fact, both of them were erotically aroused to a fever-pitch by what they were doing to her, and were a scant step from tearing the clothing from each other's backs and consummating their passion there and then.

Twice she tried to turn her agony back on him, but the magician always shielded him. The magician was deriving nearly as much enjoyment from this as Ancar and his "dear nurse" were, and Talia wished passionately (while she was still thinking coherently enough to wish) to be able to strike out at all of them.

After a time, she was no longer capable of anything but screaming.

When they crushed her feet, she was not even capable of that.

They dragged her back to her cell when her voice was gone, for the Prince did not derive half the pleasure from her torture when she could not respond to his experiments. He stood over her, gloating, as she lay unable to move on the straw where they'd left her.

"So, child, you must rest, and recover, so that we can play my games again," he crooned. "Perhaps I will tire of the game soon; perhaps not. No matter. Think on tomorrow—and think on this. When I tire of you, I shall still find a use for you. First my men will again take their pleasure of you, for they shall not mind that you are no longer as attractive as you once were; some of them would find your appearance as stimulating as *I* do, my dear. Then you shall be *my* messenger. How will your beloved Queen react to receiving her favorite Herald, but a small piece at a time?"

He laughed, and swept out with Hulda at his side, already fondling one of her breasts as the door thudded shut behind him.

It took every last bit of her will, but she remained where she was until it was dark, dark enough that she knew that no one would be able to see what she was doing. She rolled to one side then, pushed aside the straw, and uncovered the place where she'd buried her precious bottle of argonel. It had been the knowledge that she had it that was all that had sustained her this day, and she prayed that they had not searched the cell and found it.

They hadn't.

She kept her mind fastened on each tiny movement, knowing that otherwise she would never be able to continue.

Her fingers were so swollen as to be all but useless, but she had anticipated that. She managed to scrape back the loosely-packed dirt with the sides of her hands, clearing away enough so that she could get her teeth around the neck and pull the bottle out of the hole that way.

The effort nearly caused her to black out and left her gasping and weeping with pain, unable to stir for long moments. When she could move again, she braced the bottle between wrists rubbed raw and pulled the stopper out with her teeth.

She lay for a long, long moment again, while her mind threatened to retreat into blackness. That would only be a temporary escape, and she needed a permanent one.

She spat the stopper out and rolled onto her side while her body howled in anguish, and poured the entire bottle into her mouth. It burned all the way down her raw throat, and burned in her stomach where it lay like molten lead. It felt as if it were eating a hole through to the outside.

She wept with pain, conscious of nothing but pain, for what seemed to be an eternity. But then numbness began to spread from the fire, pushing the pain before it. It spread faster as it moved outward, and soon she could no longer feel anything, anything at all. Her mind seemed to be floating in warm, dark water.

A few thoughts remained with her for a while. Elspeth; she hoped the child really had forgiven her—she hoped the next Queen's Own would love her as much as Talia did. And Dirk. Perhaps it was the best thing that he should *not* know how much she loved him; he would be spared much anguish that way. Wouldn't he? She was glad of one thing; that he and Kris had made up before they'd left. It was going to hurt him badly enough when he learned of Kris' death as it was.

If only she'd been able to tell them—if only she'd known for certain about Orthallen. *He* still was there, the unsuspected enemy, waiting to try yet again. And Ancar—master of magicians and possessed of an army of killers. If only she could tell them somehow. . . .

While she still had the strength and the will, she tried again to Mindcall, but was foiled by the mage-barrier.

Then her will went numb, and all she could do was drift.

It was odd . . . Bards always claimed that all the answers came when one died, but there were no answers for her. Only questions, unanswered questions, and unfinished business. Why were there no answers? One would think that at least one would know *why* one had to die.

Maybe it didn't matter.

Kris had said it was bright. The tales all said the Havens were bright. But it wasn't bright. It was dark—darkness all around, and never a hint of brightness.

And so lonely! She would have welcomed anything, even a fever-dream.

But perhaps that was just as well, too. In the darkness that damned magician couldn't find her to bring her back. If she fled away far enough, he might get lost in trying to find her. It was worth the effort—and the warm, numbing darkness was very soothing, if the loneliness could be ignored.

Perhaps elsewhere, where the mage couldn't follow, she would find the Havens . . . and there would be light.

She let the darkness pull her farther along, closing behind her, and thoughts began to numb and fall away as well.

As she retreated away down into the darkness, her very last thought was to wonder why there still was no light at all, even at the end of it.

CHAPTER 9

WHEN THE QUEEN and her entourage set out at last, Dirk was part of her honorguard despite the vehement protests of Healers and fellow Heralds that he was not well enough for such an expedition.

He had responded that he was needed. This was true; the Collegium had suspended classes and all Heralds normally teaching were serving as bodyguards, with the sole exceptions being those too sick or old to travel. He also argued that he was far healthier than he looked (which was not true), and that he would rest just as well at the easy pace of the baggage train as he would fretting in the infirmary (which was marginally true). The Healers threw up their hands in disgust when Selenay agreed to his presence, and pronounced her to be insane and him to be the worst patient they had ever had since Keren.

He knew very well that Teren and Skif had quietly detailed themselves to keep an eye on him, not trusting his protestations of health in the slightest. He didn't care. *Anything* was worth not being left behind—even being hovered over.

But he was right about the leisurely quality of the journey—this was to be an easy trip; the most exciting thing likely to occur would be when they met Talia or Kris at the Border. The bodyguard of Heralds was more because of tradition than suspected danger. After all, Alessandar was a trusted ally and a firm friend of Valdemar, and it was as likely for harm to come to Selenay and Elspeth in her own capital as it was for them to come to harm in Hardorn. Dirk figured he should be as safe with them as in his own bed.

There were other reasons why Dirk wanted to accompany the others, although none that he was willing to disclose to anyone else. His enforced idleness had given him ample time for thought, and he was beginning to wonder if he hadn't made a bad mistake in his assumptions about the relationship between Talia and Kris. While he hadn't precisely left the field clear, Kris hadn't spent much (if any!) time alone with her since they'd returned. Instead, he'd had a brief fling with Nessa, then returned to his old semi-monastic habits. Nor had Talia sought him out. He knew these things to be facts, since he'd been keeping track of their whereabouts rather obsessively. Now that he thought back on it, Kris' frequent paeans of praise for the Queen's Own seemed less like those of a lover lauding his beloved, and more like a horsetrader trying to convince a reluctant buyer! And the one whose company Talia *had* been seeking was the one person who had been trying to avoid her—himself.

Then there was that odd incident with Keren, right after he'd damn near collapsed. She'd bullied her way past the Healers the morning Kris and Talia had left, while he was still fairly light-headed with fever, and had delivered a vehement lecture to him that he couldn't quite remember. It was maddening, because he had the shrewd notion that it was important, and he couldn't quite bring himself to confront Keren again and ask her what her diatribe had been all about. But if what vague memories he *did* have were not totally misleading—and they very well could be—she'd spoken of lifebonds, and more than once. And she'd gone on at some length about what an idiot he was being, and how miserable he was making Talia feel.

Besides all that, he had had some very frightening dreams that he didn't think could all be laid to the fever, and had been entertaining very uneasy feelings about the whole expedition from the moment he had learned that Talia and Kris were gone. If something were to go wrong, he wanted to know about it firsthand. And he wanted to be in a position where he could do something, not just wonder what was happening; although in the kind of shape he was in, he was not too sanguine that he'd be able to do much.

Technically, he was still an invalid, so he was sent to the rear of the company before the baggage animals, to share Skif's bodyguard duty on Elspeth. Skif's Cymry had foaled in early spring, and the youngster was just barely old enough to make this kind of easy trip.

Elspeth was anxious, and Dirk had a notion that he and Skif were the best possible company for the young Heir; the antics of Cymry's offspring and Skif's easy patter kept her spirits up, and Dirk was more than willing to talk about the one subject that overwhelmed her with guilt and dominated her thoughts—Talia.

Selenay had given Talia's note to Elspeth when the Heir had searched for the Queen's Own without success and had finally demanded to know what her mother had done with her. She had recalled her promise of many years' standing with heartfelt remorse almost as soon as Talia had turned her back on her and ridden away. "I'll never get mad at you," she had pledged. "No matter what you say, unless I go away and think about it, and decide what you told me just wasn't true."

And a great deal of what Talia had said that night, though harsh, *was* true. She hadn't thought past her own pleasure and her own wishes. She hadn't once considered her "affair" in the light of the larger view.

Her would-be lover's betrayal had hurt—but not nearly so much as the thought that she'd driven away a friend who truly loved her with that broken promise. Talia's words had been ugly, but not unearned—and Elspeth had returned her own share of harsh and ugly words.

If truth were to be told, though Elspeth was even more ashamed when she thought about it, the name-calling had begun with her. She wanted desperately, now that she'd read the note, to make her own apologies and explanations, and to regain the closeness they'd had before Talia's stint in the field. Her remorse was very real, and she had the urge to talk about it incessantly.

She found a sympathetic ear in Dirk, who never seemed to find her own repetitive litany boring.

She gradually managed to purge some of her guilt just by pouring her unhappiness into his ears, and slowly it became less obsessive.

But it was still very much with her.

"Daydreaming, young milady?"

The smooth, cultivated voice startled Elspeth out of deep thought.

"Not daydreaming," she corrected Lord Orthallen, just a shade stiffly. "Thinking."

He raised an inquisitive eyebrow, but she wasn't about to enlighten him.

He nudged his chestnut palfrey a little closer; Gwena responded to her unspoken twinge of revulsion and moved away.

"I must admit to being caught up in a great deal of thought, myself," he said, as if unwilling to let her escape from him. "Thought—and worry—"

Damn him! she thought. *He is so smooth—he makes me want to trust him so much! If Alberich hadn't said what he did to me—*

:I'd trust Alberich with my life,: Gwena said unexpectedly in her mind. *:I wouldn't trust that snake with my hoof-parings!:*

:Hush, loveling,: she replied the same way, amusement at her Companion's vehemence restoring her good humor. *:He won't catch me again.:*

"Worry about what, my Lord?" she asked ingenuously.

"My nephew," he replied, surprising the boots off her with his expression and the tinge of *real* concern in his voice. "I wish that Selenay had consulted me before sending him on this mission. He's so young."

"He's quite experienced."

"But not in diplomacy. And not alone."

:Bright Havens, loveling, I could almost believe he really is *anxious!:*

:He is.: Gwena sounded just as surprised. *:And somehow—somehow that frightens me. What does he know that we don't?:*

"It's a simple mission to an ally," she said aloud. "What could possibly go wrong?"

"Nothing, of course. It's just an old man's foolish fancies." He laughed, but it sounded forced. "No, never mind. I actually came back here to see if you were pining over one of those young men you've left back at Court."

"Them?" She produced a trill of very artificial gaiety. "Lady bless, my lord, I can't for the life of me wonder what I ever saw in them. I never met a pack of puppies with emptier heads in my life! I'm afraid they bored me so I was only too pleased to escape them—and I think I'd better head to the rear and take my turn making sure poor Dirk doesn't fall out of his saddle. Farewell, my lord!"

:Oh, that's putting a kink in his tail, little sister!: Gwena applauded as she spun and cantered to the rear. *:Well done indeed!:*

"Dirk?" Elspeth cantered up next to him.

"What imp?" He'd been almost half-asleep; the sun was gentle and warm, Ahrodie's pace was smooth, and the gentle chime of bridle bells and the ringing of hooves on the road had been very soporific.

"Do you think it'll be Talia that meets us on the Border?" Elspeth's tone was wistful, her face full of undisguised hope. Dirk hated to disappoint her, but he didn't have much choice.

He sighed. "Not likely, I'm afraid. Fact is, as Queen's Own she's really your mother's first representative, so chances are she'll still be with Alessandar."

"Oh." She looked rather crestfallen, but apparently was feeling like continuing the conversation. "Are you feeling all right? You've been coughing a lot."

She looked sideways at him with a certain amount of concern in her glance.

"Don't tell me *you're* going to nursemaid me," Dirk replied with some exasperation. "It's bad enough with those two playing mother-hen." He nodded back in the direction where Skif and Teren were riding, just out of earshot.

The bright noontide sun, so welcome after all those weeks of cold rain, made their white uniforms difficult to look at without squinting; Teren positively glistened.

And how in blazes, Dirk found himself wondering, *does he manage to look so immaculate with all the dust we're kicking up?*

Elspeth giggled. "Sorry. It does get to be a bit muchish, doesn't it? Now you know how I feel! It was all right back at the Collegium, but I can't even slip off into the woods to—you know—without two Heralds pounding up to bodyguard me!"

"Don't blame anybody but your mother, imp. You're the only off-spring. She should have whelped a litter, then you wouldn't have these problems."

Elspeth giggled even harder. "I wish some of the courtiers could hear you, talking about her like she was a prize bitch!"

"They'd probably call me out for insulting her. She, on the other hand, might very well agree with me. What are you doing for classes since you're not warming a desk?"

Much to his own surprise, Dirk realized he was interested in hearing Elspeth's answer. Some of the lethargy of his illness was ebbing, replaced by a little of his old energy, and he was beginning to realize that a good deal of his mental distress had vanished as well. Whether this was as a result of mending his quarrel with Kris or something else he had no idea, but it was a welcome change.

"Alberich told Skif to teach me knife-throwing. I'm getting pretty good at it, if I can be forgiven a boast. Watch—"

Her hand flicked out sideways and forward, and a small knife appeared almost magically, quivering in the bole of a tree ahead of them. Dirk hadn't even seen it leave her hand.

"Not bad—not bad at all."

Elspeth cantered up to retrieve it, cleaning the blade of sap on her sleeve, then rejoined Dirk. "He gave me a wrist sheath with a trick release—see?" She pushed up her sleeve to display it proudly. "Just like Talia's."

"So that's where she got them! Figures it'd be him. If there's a way to hide anything, that boy knows it." Dirk grinned, and realized with surprise that it had been a long while since he'd smiled. "Not that I've got any objections, mind you. I'm just as glad you've got a hidden sting, imp."

"Whyfor? Mother wasn't all that happy about my learning 'assassin's tricks,' as she so tactfully put it. It was only my saying that Alberich ordered it that made it right with her."

"Call me a little more pragmatic, but if you know the assassin's tricks, you're one up on the assassin—and there's only one of you, imp. We can't afford to lose you."

"Funny, that's just what Skif said. I guess I'm out of the habit of thinking of myself as important." She grinned, and Dirk thought fleetingly that a charming young woman had been born out of the haughty Brat Talia had taken in charge. No small miracle had been wrought there.

"I hope you're also learning that in a dangerous situation you react with reflexes, not with your head."

She made a face. "Am I not! It hasn't been so long ago that Alberich, Skif, and Jeri were ambushing me every time I wasn't looking, solo or in groups! Anyway, other than that, I'm just supposed to be talking with Heralds. I guess they figure I'll pick things up by contamination, or something."

"That's a fine way to talk about your elders! Although I hate to admit it—but with Skif, 'contamination' is pretty accurate."

"Do I hear my name being taken in vain?"

Skif nudged Cymry up to ride beside them.

"Most assuredly, my fine, feathered felon. I was just warning our innocent young Heir about associating with you."

"Me?" Skif went round-eyed with innocence. "I am as pure—"

"As what they shovel out of the stables."

"Hey, I don't have to sit here and be insulted!"

"That's right." Elspeth giggled. "You could ride off and let us insult you behind your back like we were doing already."

As if to echo her, a bold scarlet jay called down filthy names on him just as he rode beneath it. It hopped along the branch that overhung the road and continued catcalling after he'd passed.

"I do believe I am outnumbered—you're even getting the wildlife on your side! It's time, as Master Alberich would say, for a strategic re-treat."

He reined Cymry in and dropped back to resume his place beside Teren, making a face at Elspeth when he saw she was sticking her tongue out at him. Dirk was hard put to keep a straight face.

But a moment later Elspeth's mood abruptly shifted. "Dirk? Can I ask you something?"

"That's what I'm here for, imp. Part of it, anyway."

"What's evil?"

Dirk nearly lost his teeth. Philosophy was *not* what he was expecting out of Elspeth. "Ouch! Don't believe in asking the easy ones, do you?"

He sat silent for a long moment, aware after a sidelong glance at her that he had won Elspeth's heart forever by taking her question seri-ously. "Have you ever asked Gwena that one?" he said at last. "She's probably a better authority than I am."

"I did—and all she did was look at me like I'd grown horns and say, 'It just *is*!'"

He laughed, for the answer sounded very like the kind of response Ahrodie used to give him. "They do seem to have some peculiar blind spots, don't they? All right, I'll give it a try. This isn't the best answer by a long road, but I think it might be somewhere in the right direc-tion. It seems to me that evil is a kind of ultimate greed, a greed that is so all-encompassing that it can't ever see anything lovely, rare, or pre-cious without wanting to possess it. A greed so total that if it can't possess these things, it will destroy them rather than chance that some-one else might have them. And a greed so intense that even having these things never causes it to lessen one iota—the lovely, the rare, and the precious never affect it except to make it want them."

"So—'good' would be a kind of opposite? Unselfishness?"

He frowned a little, groping for the proper words. "Oh, partially. Evil can't create, it can only copy, mar, or destroy, because it's so taken up with itself. So 'good' would also be a kind of self*less*ness. And you know what a lot of sects preach—that ultimate good—Godhead—can only be reached by totally forgetting the self. What brought this on?"

"When Skif mentioned Master Alberich—he—I—" She hesitated, looking shamefaced, but Dirk did his best to look kind and under-standing, and his expression evidently encouraged her to continue. "You know about what happened—with Talia and me. I was still angry with her the next day, even though I was almost as angry with myself; well, that showed up in practice. Master Alberich made me stop, and took me out to the Field for a walk to cool off. You know, I never thought he was—I don't know, understanding, I guess. Nice. He seems so hard, most of the time."

"Perhaps that's to mask the softness underneath," Dirk replied quietly. He knew Alberich better than almost any other Herald, except for Elcarth and Jeri; and despite all the time he spent in the field, he had come as close as anyone was ever likely to get to the Armsmaster. "Being easy with any of us might be a quick way to get us killed in the field. So he's hard, hopefully harder than anything we'll have to face. That doesn't make him less a human, or less a Herald. Think about it a minute. He's the *one* teacher in the Collegium whose lessoning will make a difference whether we live or die. If he eliminates one little thing—no matter for what reason—it might be the cause of one of his pupils finding an early grave. You can't say that about any other instructor in the Collegium. You might notice the next time the Death Bell rings that you won't see him anywhere around. I don't know where he goes, but I saw him leaving, once. He looked like he was in mortal agony. I think he feels more than most of us would credit him with."

"I guess I know that now. Anyway, he started talking, and you know how it is with him, when he talks, you automatically listen. Somehow I ended up telling him about everything—about how, since Talia seemed so busy, I started talking to Lord-Un—I mean, Lord Orthallen. And how that was why I—started being with—some people. The wild crowd, I guess. That boy. Lord Orthallen introduced us; he told me he thought I ought to be spending more time with the other people of the Court. It all made sense when *he* was saying it, and the boys he introduced me to seemed so . . . attentive. Flattering. I . . . like the attention; I told Alberich that. That's when he said something really odd, Alberich, I mean. He said, 'I tell you this in strictest confidence, Herald to Herald, for I think I would have to guard my back at all times should he come to learn of it. Lord Orthallen is one of the only three truly evil persons I have ever encountered. He does nothing without a purpose, my lady, and you would be wise never to forget this.'"

She glanced at Dirk; he had the feeling she wanted to see the effect of her words.

He made no effort to hide that he was quite sobered by them. The first time she had spoken Lord Orthallen's name, it had felt as if a cloud had passed between himself and the gentle warmth of the sun. And her account of Alberich's words had come as something of a revelation.

"I'm not sure what to say," he replied finally. "Alberich is hardly inclined to make hasty judgments though; I'm sure you realize that. But at the same time, I am hardly one of Orthallen's supporters. I'll just say this; Kris and I quarreled largely because Orthallen insisted he be there when I was accused, and because Orthallen did his best to force him to make a choice between himself and me. I can't think why he would want to do that—except for what I already have said about evil; that it can't see a precious thing without wanting to own or destroy it. And our friendship, Kris' and mine, is one of the most precious things in my life."

Elspeth rode silently by his side for a good many miles after that, her face very quiet and thoughtful.

This was only the first of many such conversations they were to have. They discovered that they were very much alike, sharing a bent toward the mystical that might have surprised those who didn't know them well.

"Well?" Elspeth asked aggressively, "Why *don't* they interfere? If I'm making an ass of myself, why won't Gwena *say* anything?"

Dirk sighed. "Imp, I don't know. Have you ever asked her?"

Elspeth snorted, sounding rather like her own Companion when impatient. "Of course—after I'd made a total fool of myself I asked her right off why she didn't just forbid me to have anything to do with that puppy."

"And what did she tell you?"

"That I knew very well Companions didn't do things that way."

"And they don't . . . until we, their Chosen, come to them." Dirk harbored no small amount of chagrin for not having asked Ahrodie's advice when he'd quarreled with Kris.

"But *why*? It isn't *fair*!" At Elspeth's age, Dirk knew from his *own* experience, "fair" achieved monumental importance.

"Isn't it? Would it be fair to us, in the long run, if they stepped in like nursemaids and prevented us from falling on our noses every time we tried to learn to walk?"

:Good answer, Chosen,: Ahrodie told him, :Even if a bit simplistic.:

:Unless you've got a better one—:

:Oh, no!: she said hastily. :You go right on as you were!:

"You mean, we have to learn from experience by ourselves?" Elspeth asked, as Dirk fought down a grin at Ahrodie's hurried reply.

Elspeth brooded over that while Gwena and Ahrodie amused themselves by matching paces with such absolute precision that they sounded like one Companion rather than two.

"Don't they *ever* interfere?" she asked, finally.

"Not in living memory. In some of the old chronicles, though . . ."

"Well?" she prompted, when his silence had gone on too long.

"*Some* Companions, very rarely, have intervened. But only when the situation was hopeless, and only when there was no other way out of it except by their aid. They were always Grove-born, though, and the only one of those we have now is Rolan. And they have *never* done so except by freely volunteering, which is why Heralds never ask them to."

"Why only then? Why shouldn't we ask?"

"Imp—" He was doing his best to try and express what until now he had only sensed. "What's the one governing law of this Kingdom?"

She looked at him askance. "Are you changing the subject?"

"No. No, I'm not, trust me."

"There *is* no 'one true way.'"

"Take it a step further. Why are the clergy *forbidden* by law to pray for Valdemar's victory in war?"

"I . . . don't know."

"Think about it. Go away, if you like, and come back when you're ready."

She chose not to leave his side, and simply rode next to him with her expression blank and her attention turned so inward that she never noticed Skif coming up from behind them.

Skif pulled up on Dirk's other side, and gave the young Heir a long and curious look.

"Isn't this a bit deep for her?" he asked, finally. "I mean, I've been trying to follow this, and I'm lost."

"I don't think so," Dirk replied slowly. "I really don't. If she weren't ready, she wouldn't be asking."

"Lord and Lady," Skif exclaimed, shaking his head in honest bewilderment, "I give up. You *are* two of a kind."

At length the party reached the Border; Selenay ordered that they make camp there on the Valdemar side since the outpost was far too small to accommodate all of them. The last of the baggage train actually reached it very near dark, and so the Queen was hardly surprised that neither of the two envoys was waiting for them when they arrived. But when the next day passed, she felt a building uneasiness. When two more went by without any sign whatsoever, the uneasiness became alarm.

"Kyril"—Selenay did not remove her gaze from the road as she spoke to the Seneschal's Herald—"I have the feeling something has gone terribly, terribly wrong. Am I being alarmist?"

"No, Majesty." Kyril's usually controlled voice held an unmistakable tremor of strain.

Selenay looked at him sharply. Kyril's brow was lined with worry. "I've tried Farspeech; I can't reach them—and Kris, at least, has enough of that Gift to be able to receive what I send. He's done so in the past. I don't know what's gone awry, but Majesty, I—I am afraid for them."

She did not hesitate. "Order the camp moved back from the Border, and now. There's a good place about half a mile back down the road; it's a flattish hill, barren except for grass. Should there be need, it won't be hard to defend."

Kyril nodded. He did not seem surprised by her paranoia.

"When you've gotten the rest on the move," she continued, "order the local reserves of the Guard to meet us there. I'm going to have the Border Guards stand alert and keep a watch down the Hardorn side of the trade road."

Her Companion, Caryo, came trotting up at her mental summons, and she pulled herself up on the Companion's bare back, without bothering to call for saddle or bridle. As she rode away, Kyril was going in search of the Herald in charge of the camp to begin seeing to the first of her orders.

The new camp was uncomfortable, but as Selenay had planned, was far more easily defensible than the old. When the Guardsmen arrived, Selenay ordered them to bivouac between their camp and the Border. She had sentries posted as well—and ominously, she noticed that the Companions began taking up stations about the perimeter, providing their own kind of sentry-duty.

Elspeth attached herself to Dirk and seldom left his side. Neither of them voiced their fears until late in the fifth day, a day spent in an atmosphere of tension and anxiety.

"Dirk," Elspeth finally said, after Dirk watched her try to read the same page in her book ten times, and apparently never once see a word of it, "do you suppose something's happened to them?"

Dirk hadn't even been making a pretense of doing anything but watching the road. "Something must have," he answered flatly. "If it had been simple delay, they would have gotten word to us. It's not like Kris—"

He broke off at the sight of her frightened eyes.

"Look imp, I'm sure they'll be all right. Kris and I have gotten out of a lot of tight situations before this, and Talia's no faint-hearted Court flower. I'm sure they're making their way back to us right now."

"I hope you're right . . ." Elspeth said faintly, but she didn't sound to Dirk as if she really believed his words.

For that matter, he wasn't sure he believed them either.

The sixth day dawned, with Selenay—in fact, all of them—waiting for the axe to fall.

Late in the afternoon, when one of the lookouts—a Herald with Farsight as well as Mindspeech—reported that a Companion was approaching at speed, the entire encampment was roused within moments, and lined the roadside. Selenay was one of the first; eyes straining to catch the first glimpse.

She, Kyril, and several others of her immediate entourage stood in a tense knot at the edge of the encampment. She noticed vaguely that Dirk, Teren, Skif, Elspeth, and Jeri had formed their own little huddle just within earshot. None of them moved or spoke. The sun beat down on them all without pity, but no one made a move to look for shade.

As Dirk waited with mouth going dry with unspoken fear, a second lookout sprinted up and whispered in the Queen's ear. Selenay grew pale as ice; Elspeth clutched Dirk's arm and the rest stirred uneasily.

Then a dust-cloud and hoofbeats signaled the arrival of the Companion, and hard on the sound itself Rolan pounded into their midst.

Rolan—alone. Without saddle or bridle; gaunt, covered with dust and sweat, and completely exhausted, a state few had ever seen a Companion in before.

He staggered the last few feet up the hill to the Queen, tearing a bundle from his neck with his teeth and dropping it at her feet. Then he sagged with exhaustion, standing motionless except for his heaving flanks and his quivering muscles, head nearly touching the ground, eyes closed, suffering written in every line of him.

Keren was the first to break from her shock. She ran to him, throwing her cloak over him for lack of any other blanket and began to lead him to a place where he could be tended properly, step by trembling step.

Selenay picked up the filthy, stained package with hands that shook so hard she nearly dropped it, and undid the knots holding it together.

Into the grass at her feet fell two arrows; one headless, one broken.

A ripple of shocked dismay passed over the crowd. The Queen felt as frozen as a snow-statue.

As Kyril bent to pick them up, Elspeth whimpered once beside her, and swayed with shock. Jeri caught and supported her just as Dirk's agonized cry of negation broke the silence.

Selenay started, and turned to see Dirk struggling to break away from Skif and Teren.

"Damn you, let me *go!*" he cried in agony, as Skif held him away from Ahrodie. "I've got to go to her—I've got to help her!"

"Dirk, man, you don't even know if"—Teren choked out the words—"if she's still alive."

"She's *got* to be. I'd know if she weren't. She's *got* to be!" He fought them still, as Kyril's low tones carried to where they stood.

"The headless arrow is Herald Kris," he said, his expressionless face belying the anguish in his voice. "The broken is Herald Talia."

"You see? I was right! Let me *go!*"

Skif caught his chin in one hand and forced his head around so that Dirk was forced to look him in the eyes, with a strength that matched Dirk's own, even augmented by the latter's frenzy. There were tears flowing freely down his cheeks as he half sobbed his words. "*Think,* man! That's the broken arrow she sent. She was as good as dead when she sent it, and dammit, she knew it. There's no hope of saving her, but she gave us the warning to save ourselves. Do you want to kill yourself, too, and make us mourn three of you?"

His words penetrated Dirk's madness, and the wild look left his eyes, replaced by anguish and torture.

"Oh, *gods!*" The fight left him, and he sagged to his knees, buried his face in his hands, and began weeping hoarsely.

At this moment Selenay wished with all her aching heart that she could do the same. But this message could have only one meaning; a friend to her and her people had suddenly turned his coat, and her land was in danger. Her Kingdom and the lives of her folk were at stake and she had her duty just as surely as any other Herald. There was no leisure time to spend on personal feelings. Later, when all was safe, she would mourn. Now she *must* act.

She emptied herself of emotion, knowing she'd pay for this self-denial later. There was the Guard to be alerted, the Lord Marshal to be brought; her mind filled with plans, making it easier to ignore (for the moment) the sorrow she longed to give vent to.

She gave orders crisply, sending one Herald after another flying for his Companion, carrying messages to warn, to summon, to prepare. She turned on her heel with Kyril at her side and strode hastily to her tent. Those with experience in armed conflict followed; as did those who might still be needed to bear messages. Those who were not of either group headed for the baggage train to break out the weaponry, or down the hill to organize the tiny force of the Guard to protect the Queen.

Left in their wake were Skif, Teren, and Dirk.

Skif reached out his hand to his friend, then pulled it back. Dirk was curled in on himself, still kneeling in the dust of the road. Only the shaking of his shoulders showed that he still wept.

Skif and Teren stood awkwardly at his side for long moments, both unsure of what, if anything, they could do for him. Finally Teren said in an undertone, "He won't try anything stupid now. Why don't we give him a little privacy? Ahrodie's the only one likely to be able to comfort him at all."

Skif nodded, biting his lip to keep from sobbing himself; and they withdrew after the others, as Ahrodie moved up beside Dirk and stood with her head bowed next to his, almost, but not quite, touching his shoulder.

Lost in his own travail, Dirk heard nothing of another approaching, until a hand lightly touched his shoulder.

He raised his head slowly, peering through blurred, burning eyes, to see that the one touching him was Elspeth. Grief matching his stared out of her eyes, and her features were as tear-streaked as his own. It was growing dark; the last rays of sunset streaked the sky like bloodstains and stars were showing overhead. He realized dimly that he must have been crouching there for hours. And as he stared at her, he began to have the beginnings of an idea.

"Elspeth," he croaked. "Do you know some place no one is likely to be right now? Some place quiet?"

"My tent, and the area around it," she said. He thought he had surprised her out of her own tears by the question. "I'm at the back of the camp, not close to mother's tent. Everybody is with her right now."

"Can I use it?"

"Of course—why? Have you—can you—oh, Dirk, have you thought of something? You have—you have!"

"I think . . . maybe . . . I might be able to 'Fetch' her. But I need a place where my concentration won't be broken."

Elspeth looked hopeful—and dubious. "It's an awfully long way."

"I know. That doesn't matter. It isn't the distance that worries me, it's the weight. I've never Fetched anything that big before; gods, nothing alive even close to that size." His face and heart twisted with pain. "But I've got to try—something, anything!"

"But Kris—" Her voice broke. "Kris isn't here to See for you—no, wait—" she said, kneeling next to him as his hope crumpled. "I can See. I'm not trained, but I've got the Gift. It came on me early—it's been getting a lot stronger since I was Chosen and I know I've got more range than anybody else I've talked to. Will I do?"

"Yes! Oh, gods, yes!" He hugged her shoulders and they rose together and stumbled through the dusk to her tent.

Elspeth slipped inside the tent and tossed two cushions out for them to sit on. Dirk set his hands lightly on her wrists and calmed his own thoughts as best he could. He tried to pretend to himself that this was just another student he was training in her Gift, and began coaxing her into a light trance. The last of the light faded, and the stars grew brighter overhead, while they sat oblivious to their surroundings. She was silent for a very long time, and Dirk began to fear that her untrained Gift would be useless against all that distance, despite the power of the emotions fueling it.

Then, abruptly, Elspeth whimpered in fear and pain and her own hands closed convulsively on his wrists. "I've found her—oh, gods! Dirk, they've done such horrible things to her! I—think I'm going to be sick—"

"Hold on, imp. Don't break on me yet! I need you—*she* needs you!"

Elspeth gulped audibly, and held. He followed her mind to where it had reached, found his target, took hold, and pulled with all his strength.

He could not tell how long he strove against the weight of it—but suddenly pain rose in a wave to engulf him, and he blacked out.

He found himself slumped over, with Elspeth shaking him as hard as she could.

"All of a sudden—you stopped breathing," she said fearfully. "I thought you were dead! Oh, gods, Dirk—it—it's no good, is it?"

He shook his head numbly. "I tried, Goddess save me, I *tried*. I found her all right, but I can't pull her here. I just don't have the strength."

He felt hot tears splash on his hand from Elspeth's eyes, and decided they would make a second attempt. He knew with conviction that he'd rather die in trying to bring Talia back than live with the knowledge that he wasn't brave enough to make the second trial.

But before he could say anything, the matter was taken out of his hands.

:Man,: said a voice in his mind. *:Dirk—Herald.:*

The voice was not Ahrodie's; it was masculine. He looked up to find three Companions standing beside them; Ahrodie, Elspeth's Gwena, and leading them, Rolan. They had moved up on them without so much as a twig stirring. Behind them, at the edge of the enclosure that held Elspeth's tent, were gathered more Companions—every Companion in the encampment, down to Cymry's foal.

Rolan looked ghostlike, gaunt, and seemed to glow, and the back of Dirk's neck prickled at the sight of him. He looked like something out of legend, not a creature of the solid, everyday world.

:You have the Gift and the will to use it. She has the Sight. We have the strength you need.:

"I—but—are you saying—"

:That we may yet save her, if our love and courage are enough. But—be prepared—if we succeed, it will not be without high cost to you. There will be great pain. You may die of it.:

Wordlessly, Dirk looked at Elspeth, and knew by her nod that Rolan had spoken to her as well.

Dirk looked into Rolan's glowing eyes—and they *were* glowing, a sapphirine light brighter than the starshine. "Whatever the cost is, we'll pay it," he said, knowing he spoke for both of them.

They stood up and made room for the three Companions between them. They stood in a circle; Rolan, Elspeth, Gwena, Ahrodie, and Dirk. Elspeth and Dirk clasped hands and rested their arms over the backs of the Companions, obtaining the needed physical contact among the five of them in that way.

It was much easier for Elspeth to find her target the second time.

"I have her," she said softly when she'd touched Talia again, then sobbed. "Dirk—I think she's dying!"

Once more Dirk sent his own mind along the path Elspeth had laid for him, took hold, and pulled.

Then a second strength was added to his, and it built, and grew. Then another joined the second, and another. For one awful, pain-wracked moment—or was it an eternity?—Dirk felt like the object of a tug-of-war game, being pulled apart between two forces far greater than his own. Only his own stubbornness kept him to the task, as he felt his mind being torn in two. He held; then felt himself being stretched thinner and thinner, tighter, and tighter, quivering like a harpstring about to snap. All his strength seemed to flow out of him; he felt consciousness fading again, fought back, and held on with nothing left to him but his own stubborn will. Then, one of the two forces broke—and not theirs. And together they pulled their target toward them, cushioning and protecting it against further damage.

Their combined strength was enough. Barely, but enough.

The conference of war was proceeding in Selenay's tent, with Council members, Officers of the Army and Guard, and Heralds perched wherever there was room. Kyril was pointing out weak spots in their own defenses—places that appeared to be candidates to be attacked—on the map laid over her table. Then a cry of horror from someone standing just outside the tent flap made everyone look up with startlement.

Someone shoved tent flap and those standing inside it abruptly out of the way, and Elspeth stumbled inside, face paper-white and drained, pushing others from her path. Following her was Dirk, who looked even worse. When those inside saw what he bore in his arms, the cry of horror was echoed inside the tent as well—for it was a mangled, bloody wreck of a human body and it had Talia's face.

No one moved—no one but Dirk and the Heir. Elspeth emptied Selenay's bed of the five Heralds perched on the edge of it, pushing them out of the way without a word. Dirk went straight to the bed and set Talia down gently on it. Without even looking around he reached out a blood-smeared hand and seized the most senior Healer present by the arm, pulling her to Talia's side. Then he straightened up with exaggerated care, moved two or three steps out of the way, and passed out, dropping to the ground like a felled tree.

When the furor was over and Selenay had a chance to look around, she discovered that Elspeth had done the same—but less dramatically and more quietly, in the corner.

Elspeth's recovery was rapid—which, as she remarked somewhat astringently, was fortunate for the sanity of those who could not imagine how the impossible rescue had been accomplished.

She was the center of attention for all those who were not involved with the attempt to save Talia. Kyril was her particular demon, insisting on being told every detail so many times she thought she could recite the tale in her sleep, and coming up with countless questions. Eventually Elspeth's patience reached a breaking point, and she told him, in a quiet, but deadly voice, that if he wanted to know any more he should ask his own Companion about it—*she* was going to see what she could do about helping the Healers with Talia and Dirk.

*   *   *

Healer Thesa was worried; Dirk's recovery was not as rapid. He was still unconscious the next day, and it was some time before she and the other Healers diagnosed the problem as a relapse of his pneumonia coupled with incredible psychic strain. She had charge of his case; her old friend Devan had charge of Talia's, though they shared every germ of expertise they had on both cases. Dirk had inadvertently brought the bottle Talia had drunk the argonel out of with her; and the traces of it within the bottle told Devan what it was they had to fight besides her terrible injuries. Within a day or two he and Thesa decided between them that they had done all they possibly could for both of the patients under the primitive conditions of the encampment. They decided that while it was dangerous to move them, it was far more dangerous to leave them there. There might be warfare waged there at any moment, and they both badly needed the expert touch of the teachers at the Healer's Collegium.

Yet there was no time to spare—and assuredly no Heralds to spare—to move them back to the capital. Instead, after a hasty conference, Thesa and her colleague decided to take the patients a few miles up the road, and install them in the stone-walled home of the Lord Holder, who gladly gave up his dwelling to the Queen—and was equally glad to move himself and his family well out of the way of possible combat.

The Queen had called for all the Healers of the Collegium that could be spared. The Lord Holder's residence was more than half fortress; it was readily defensible at need. The Healers were installed there as soon as they arrived with Thesa organizing them as soon as Dirk began showing signs of improvement. Thesa knew with grim certainty that although they had only Talia and Dirk to treat now, if there should be war, they would have other patients, and soon.

Elspeth spent most of her time there; her mother had asked her—*asked* her, and not ordered her, a sign that Selenay trusted her good sense and was tacitly acknowledging that she was becoming adult—to stay with the Healers and some other of the officials of the Court who began arriving as she called them.

"But—" Elspeth began to protest, until the haunted expression in her mother's eyes stopped her. "Never mind. What do you want me to do?"

"I'm giving you powers of regency," Selenay replied. "The rest of the Kingdom isn't going to cease to exist while we wait here. You've sat through enough Council meetings, catling; you have a good idea what to do. You handle the day-to-day needs of the Kingdom unless you *have* to have a decision from me. And one other thing—if the worst happens, you and the Council and whatever Heralds are left escape together into the west and north; Sorrows should hold you safe."

"But what about you?" she asked, around a lump in her throat.

"Elspeth—if it goes that badly—you'll be their new Queen."

That was an eventuality Elspeth preferred not to contemplate. She had enough worries as it was. Talia looked far more dead than alive, and the Healers were obviously baffled and frightened by something about her condition, though they would not reveal to Elspeth what it was.

It was stalemate at the Border, and stalemate in the sickroom, and in neither case could Elspeth do anything about the matter. It was not a position she enjoyed—and she began to realize just how often it was a position the Queen was in. All she could do was pray.

So she did, with a fervor that matched that of her ancestor, King Valdemar—and she hoped that fervor would make her prayers heard.

CHAPTER 10

$\longleftarrow\!\!\!\!\!\longleftarrow\!\!\!\!\!\mbox{---}\!\!\!\!\!\longmapsto\!\!\!\!\!\longrightarrow$

DIRK CAME TO himself shortly after being put in the Healers' hands, but he was confused and disoriented, as well as fevered. And the reaction-backlash he was suffering had him near-blind with a headache no amount of herb tea could remedy. They had to darken his room almost completely until the pain ebbed. In living memory—or so Healer Thesa told him multitudinous times—no Healer had ever seen anyone suffering from a case of backlash as profound as his—not and still be alive to tell about it.

Once again he found himself alone in a small room—but this time it was not in the House of Healing. For several days it was all he could do to feed himself and respond to the orders the Healers gave him. This time he was far too weak to even protest at the regime the Healers directed for him—unlike his previous encounter with them. For a while he remained pliant and well-behaved—but as he recovered, he began to grow suspicious and worried when his questions about Talia remained unanswered or were evaded.

The more they evaded the subject, the more frustrated and angry he became. He even queried Gwena, as soon as his reaction-headache wore off. Gwena couldn't help; she tried to tell him what was wrong with Talia, but her answers were frightening and confusing. She couldn't seem to convey more than that there *was* something seriously ailing the Queen's Own. Finally he decided to take matters into his own hands.

*   *   *

Little Robin had been brought by Lord Orthallen—although he had
the feeling that his lord did not realize it. The boy was a part of his
household, though Orthallen seemed to have long since forgotten the
fact; and when the order came to pack up the household and move to
the Border, Robin found himself in the tail of the baggage train, with
no small bewilderment. He'd been at a loss in the encampment, wandering about until someone had seen him and realized that a small
child had no place in a camp preparing for warfare. So he was sent
packing; first off with Elspeth, then pressed into service by the Healers.
They'd set him to fetching and carrying for Dirk, thinking that the
child was far too young to be able to pick anything up from the casual
talk around him, and that Dirk wouldn't think to interrogate a child as
young as he.

They were wrong on both counts.

Robin was very much aware of what was going on—not surprising,
since it concerned his adored Talia. He was worried sick, and longing
for an adult to talk to. And Dirk was kind and gentle with him—and
had he but known it, desperate enough for news to have questioned the
rats in the walls if he thought it would get him anywhere.

Dirk knew all about Robin and his adoration of Talia. If anyone knew
where she was being kept and what her condition was, that boy would.

Dirk bided his time. Eventually the Healers stopped overseeing his
every waking moment. Finally there came a point when they began
leaving him alone for hours at a time. He waited then, until Robin was
sent in alone with his lunch—alone, unsupervised, and more than
willing to talk—and put the question to him.

"Robin," Dirk had no intention of frightening the boy, and his tone
was gentle, "I need your help. The Healers won't answer my questions,
and I need to know about Talia."

Robin had turned back with his hand still on the doorknob; at the
mention of Talia's name, his expression was one of distress.

"I'll tell you what I know, sir," he replied, his voice quavering a little. "But she's hurt real bad and they won't let anybody but Healers see
her."

"Where is she? Do you have any idea who's taking care of her?"

The boy not only knew *where* she was, but the names and seniority
of every Healer caring for her—and the list nearly froze Dirk's heart.
They'd even pulled old Farnherdt out of retirement—and he'd sworn
that no case would ever be desperate enough for them to call on him.

"Robin, I've got to get out of here—and I need you to help me, all right?" he said urgently.

Robin nodded, his eyes widening.

"Check the hall for me—see if there's anybody out there."

Robin opened the door and stuck his head out. "Nobody," he reported.

"Good. I'm going to get dressed and sneak out. You stand just outside, and if anybody comes this way, knock on the door."

Robin slipped out to play guard, while Dirk pulled on his clothing. He waited just a few moments more, then left his room, giving Robin a conspiratorial wink on the way out, determined to discover the truth.

The Healer in charge was Devan. Though not the most senior, he was the one with the most expertise and the strongest Gift for dealing with wounds and trauma. He was also one of Talia's first and best friends among the Healers, and had worked with her on many other cases where Heralds were involved. There were times when loving care was more important than seniority—and Devan would have been one of Dirk's first choices to care for her, had he been consulted.

Dirk had a fairly good idea of where to find him at this hour—and most castle-keeps were of the same design; Devan would be in the still-room, just off the herb garden near the kitchen—snatching lunch with one hand while he worked with the other. Dirk used all his expertise at shadow-stalking to avoid being caught while making his way to the little first-floor workroom, redolent with the odors—pleasant, and not so pleasant—of countless medicines.

He heard someone moving about behind the closed door, and slipped inside quickly and quietly, shutting it behind him and putting his back up against it. Devan, his back to the door, didn't seem to notice his presence.

"Devan, I want some answers."

"I've been expecting you," the Healer said calmly, without taking his attention from the task in front of him. "I thought you might not be satisfied with what you were being told about Talia. I said so, but I wasn't in charge of your case, and Thesa felt you shouldn't be worried."

"Then—how is she?" Dirk demanded and at the sight of the Healer's gloomy face, asked fearfully, "Is she—?"

"No, Herald," Devan replied with a sigh, stoppering the bottle he'd been decanting liquid into and turning to face him. "She's not dying; not yet, anyway. But she isn't alive, either."

"What's that supposed to mean?" Dirk asked, becoming angry. "What do you mean, 'she's not alive'?"

"Come with me, and you'll see for yourself."

The Healer led the way to a small room in the infirmary, one of several that were interconnected, such as were used for patients that needed to be isolated. There was little there besides a bedside table with a candle and the bed in which Talia lay without moving.

Dirk felt his throat constrict; she looked as if she'd been laid out for a funeral.

Her face was pale and waxen. By watching very closely, Dirk could see that she was breathing—but just barely.

"What's wrong with her?" His voice cracked with strain.

Devan shrugged helplessly—feeling a lot less helpless than he looked, now that Dirk had finally approached him. "I wish we knew. We think we counteracted the argonel in time—well, the pain she was in neutralized a great deal of it, and if we hadn't taken care of the rest she *would* be dead; argonel doesn't allow for mistakes. We've restored some of the blood loss, we're doing painblockages on most of the major injuries—we've done everything we can to restore her, but she simply doesn't wake. No, it's more than that—it's as if 'she' wasn't there anymore, as if we were dealing with an unensouled body. The body works, the reflexes are all there, it breathes, the heart beats—but there's no one 'home.' And we don't have the slightest notion why. One of the older Healers speculates that her soul has 'gone somewhere,' perhaps trying to escape some kind of mental coercion. I suppose that's possible; tradition claims many mages have had Gifts like ours, and used them for evil purposes. It may be she encountered one of them, along with her other trials. It's possible that now she fears returning to herself, not knowing she is in the hands of friends again. We were willing to try almost anything—"

"So?"

"So we asked Herald Kyril to help. He was here for a solid day, holding her hand and Mindcalling her. He pushed himself to his limits, pushed himself until he had a reaction that sent him into a state of collapse. It did no good at all. Frankly, I don't know what else we could try—" he glanced sideways at Dirk. Devan had something in mind, but from what he understood about this young man, Dirk would have to be lured into it very carefully. "—unless—"

"Unless what?" Dirk snatched at the offered scrap.

"As you know, her Gift was Empathic. She did not Mindhear or Mindcall very well. It may be that Kyril simply wasn't able to reach her. I suppose if someone who had a strong emotional bond with her were to try calling her, using that bond, she might hear. We tried communicating with her Companion, but he apparently had no better luck than Kyril, and possibly for the same reasons. Herald Kris had a strong emotional tie with her, but . . ."

"Yes."

"And no one can think of anyone else."

Dirk gulped and closed his eyes, then whispered, "Could . . . I try?"

Devan almost smiled despite the grimness of the situation. *Come on, little fishy,* he thought, trying to imbue his will with all the coercive force of a Farspeaking Herald. *Take the nice bait. I know all about your lifebond. Keren told me about the night you fell ill—and about your performance over the death arrows and how you rescued her. But if you don't admit that lifebond exists you might as well be calling into the hurricane for all she'll hear you.*

He pretended to be dubious. "I just don't know, Herald. It would have to be a very strong emotional bond."

The answer he was praying for came as a nearly inaudible whisper. "I love her. Is that enough?"

Devan almost cheered. Now that Dirk had admitted the existence of the lifebond, the idea stood a chance of working. "Then by all means, do your best. I'll be just outside if you need me."

Dirk sat heavily in the chair next to the bed, and took one bandaged, unresisting, flaccid hand in his own. He felt so helpless, so alone . . . how in the names of all the gods could you call through emotions? And . . . it would mean letting down barriers to his heart he'd erected years ago and meant to be permanent.

But they couldn't have been permanent, not if she'd already made him admit that he loved her. It was too late now for anything but complete commitment—and besides, he'd been willing to die to save her, hadn't he? Was the lowering of those barriers any greater a sacrifice? Was life really worth anything if she wasn't sharing it?

But—where was he going to find her?

Suddenly he sat ramrod straight; he had no way of knowing how or where to call her from, but Rolan must!

He blanked his mind, and reached for Ahrodie.

She settled gently into his thoughts almost as soon as he called her.
:Chosen?:

:I need your help—and Rolan's,: he told her.

:Then you've seen—you know? You think we can help to call Her back?

Rolan has been trying, but cannot reach Her, not alone. Chosen, my brother, I had been hoping you would understand and try!:

Then the other came into his mind. *:Dirk-Herald—she has gone Elsewhere. Can you See?:*

And amazingly, as Rolan projected strongly into his mind, he could See—a kind of darkness, with something that flickered feebly at the end of it.

:Do you call her. We shall give you strength and an anchoring. You can go where we cannot.:

He took a deep breath, closed his eyes, and sent himself into the deepest trance he'd ever managed, trying to send out his love, calling with his heart, trying to use his need of her as a shining beacon to draw her back through the darkness. And somewhere "behind" him Rolan and Ahrodie remained, a double anchor to the real world.

How long he called, he had no way of knowing; there was no time in the currents through which he dove. Certainly the candle on the table had burned down considerably when the faint movement of the hand he held broke his trance and caused his eyes to fly open in startlement.

He could *see* color coming back into her face. She moved a little, winced, and moaned softly in protest. Her free hand reached for her temple; her eyes opened, focused, and saw him.

"You . . . called me."

It was the faintest of whispers.

He nodded, unable to speak through a throat choked with conflicting joy and doubt.

"Where—I'm home? But how—" Then intelligence and urgency flooded into her eyes. And fear; terrible fear. "Orthallen—oh, my God—Orthallen!"

She began struggling to rise, whimpering involuntarily in pain, but driven beyond caring for herself by some knowledge only she possessed.

"Devan!" Dirk could see she had something obsessively important to impart. He knew better than to try and thwart her if the need was *that* urgent—and her evident fear coupled with *that* name could mean worse trouble than anyone but she knew. So instead of trying to prevent her, he gave her the support of his arms, and called for help. *"Devan!"*

Devan nearly broke in the door in his haste to respond to Dirk's call. As he stared at Talia, dumbfounded, she demanded to know who was in authority. Devan saw she would heed nothing he told her until he gave her what she wanted, and recited the all-too-brief list.

"I want—Elspeth," she said breathlessly, "and Kyril—the Seneschal—and Alberich. Now, Devan." And would not be gainsaid.

When Devan sent messengers for the four she had demanded, she finally gave in to his insistent urgings to lie quietly.

Dirk remained in the room, wishing passionately that he could take some of the burden of pain from her, for her face was lined and white with it.

The four she had sent for arrived at a run, and within a few moments of one another. From the despair on their faces, it was evident they had expected to find Talia at least at Death's door, if not already gone. But their joy at seeing her once again awake and aware was quickly turned to shock and dismay by what she had to tell them.

"So from the very beginning it has been Orthallen?" Alberich's question appeared to be mostly rhetorical. He didn't look terribly surprised. "I would give much to know how he has managed to mindblock himself for so long, but that can wait for a later day."

Both Kyril and the Seneschal, however, were staggered by the revelation.

"Lord *Orthallen?*" the Seneschal kept muttering. "Anyone else, perhaps; treason is always a possibility with any highborn—but not Orthallen! Why, he predates me in the Council! Elspeth, can you believe this?"

"I . . . I'm not sure," Elspeth murmured, looking at Alberich, and then at Dirk.

"There . . . is a very simple way . . . to prove my words." Talia was lying quite still to harbor her strength; her eyes were closed and her voice labored, but there was no doubt that she was very much alive to everything about her. "Orthallen . . . surely knows . . . where I was. Call him here . . . but do not let him know . . . that I have . . . recovered enough to speak. Devan . . . you will painblock . . . everything. Then . . . get me propped up . . . somehow. I . . . must seem to be . . . completely well. His reaction . . . when he sees me with Elspeth . . . should tell us . . . all we need to know."

"There is no way I will countenance anything of the sort!" Devan said angrily. "You are in no shape to move a single inch, much less—"

"You will. You must," Talia's voice was flat, implacable, with no tinge of anger, only of command. But Devan folded before it, and the look in the eyes she opened to meet his.

"Old friend, it *must* be," she added softly. "More than my well-being is at stake."

"This could kill you, you know," he said with obvious bitterness, beginning to touch her forehead so that he could establish the pain-blocks she demanded. "You're forcing me to violate every Healing Oath I ever swore."

"No—" Dirk couldn't quite fathom the sad, tender little smile she wore. "I have it . . . on excellent authority . . . that it isn't my time."

She got other protests from the rest when she decreed that only she and Elspeth should receive Orthallen.

With total painblocks established she was able to speak normally, if weakly. "It has to be this way," she insisted. "If he sees you, I think he might be able to mask his reaction. At the least he'll be warned by your presence. With us alone, I think it will be genuine; I don't think he'll bother trying to hide it initially from two he doesn't consider to be physically or mentally threatening."

She relented enough to allow them to conceal themselves in the room next door, watching all that went on through the door that linked the two, provided they keep that door open only a bare crack. Once everyone was in place, they sent for Orthallen.

It seemed an age before they heard his slow, deliberate footsteps following the pattering ones of the page.

The door opened; Orthallen stepped inside, his head turned back over his shoulder, dismissing the page before he closed the door behind himself. Only then did he turn to face the two that awaited him.

Talia had set her stage most carefully. She was propped up like an oversized doll, but to all appearances was sitting up in bed normally. She was a deathly white, but the relatively dim light of their single candle concealed that. Elspeth stood at her right hand. The room was entirely dark except for the candle that illuminated both their faces— concealing the fact that the door behind the two of them was propped open a tiny amount.

"Elspeth," Orthallen began as he turned, "this is an odd place for a meet—"

Then he truly saw who was in the room besides the Heir.

The blood drained swiftly from his face, and the condescending smile he had worn faded.

As he noted their expressions, he grew even more agitated. His hands began trembling, and his complexion took on a grayish tinge. His eyes scanned the room, looking for anyone else who might be standing in the shadows behind them.

"I have met Ancar, my lord, and seen Hulda—" Talia began.

Then the staid, poised Lord Orthallen, who always preferred words over any other weapon, did the one thing none of them would ever have expected him to do.

He went berserk.

He snatched his ornamental dagger from its sheath at his side, and sprang for them, madness in his eyes, his mouth twisted into a wild rictus of fear.

For the men hidden behind the door, time suddenly slowed to an agonizing crawl. They burst through it, knowing as they did so that by the time they reached the two women, anything they did would be far too late to save them.

But before anyone else even had time to react, before Orthallen had even moved more than a single step, Elspeth's right hand flickered out sideways, then snapped forward.

Halfway to them, Orthallen suddenly collapsed over Talia's bed with an odd gurgle, then slid to the floor.

Time resumed its normal pace.

Elspeth, white-faced and shaking, reached out and rolled him over with her foot as the four men reached her side. There was a little throwing dagger winking in the candlelight that fell on Orthallen's chest. Blood from the wound it had made stained his blue velvet robe black. It was, Dirk noted with an odd, detached corner of his mind, perfectly placed for a heart-shot.

"By my authority as Heir," Elspeth said in a voice that quavered on the edge of hysterics, "I have judged this man guilty of high treason, and carried out his sentence with my own hand."

She held to the edge of the bed to keep her shaking legs from collapsing under her, as Talia touched her arm with one bandaged hand—in an attempt, perhaps, to comfort and support her. Her eyes looked like they were going to pop out of her head, and dilated with shock. When Devan threw open the door to the hall, she looked at him pleadingly.

"And now," she said in a strained voice, "I think I'd like to be sick. Please?"

Devan had the presence of mind to get her a basin before she lost the contents of her stomach; she retched until she was totally empty, then burst into hysterical tears. Devan took charge of her quickly, leading her off to clean herself up and find a quiet place where she could vent her feelings in peace.

Kyril and Alberich removed the body, quickly and efficiently. The Seneschal wandered after them, dazed and shaken. That left Dirk alone with Talia.

Devan reappeared for a moment before he could say or do anything. The Healer removed the cushions that had been propping her up, and got her lying down again to his own satisfaction. He pressed his hand briefly to her forehead, then turned to Dirk.

"Stay with her, would you? I took some of the painblocks off before they do her an injury, but all this would have been a heavy strain if she had been healthy. In the shape she's in—I can't predict the effect. She may very well be perfectly all right; she seems in no worse state than she was before. If she starts to go into shock, or looks like she's relapsing—or really, if you think *anything* is going wrong, call me. I'll be within hearing distance, getting Elspeth calmed."

What else could he do, except nod?

When Devan left, he turned hungry eyes back toward Talia. There was so much he wanted to say—and had no idea of how to say it.

Now that the impetus of the emergency was gone, she seemed confused, disoriented, dazed with pain. He could see her groping after coherent thought.

Finally she seemed to see him. "Oh, gods, Dirk—Kris is *dead*. They murdered him—he didn't have a chance. I couldn't help him, I couldn't save him. And it's all my fault that it happened—if I'd told him we had to turn back when we first knew something was wrong, he'd still be alive."

She began to weep, soundlessly, tears trickling slowly down her cheeks; she was plainly too exhausted even to sob.

Then it hit him—

"Goddess—" he said. "Kris—oh, *Kris*—"

He knelt beside her, not touching her, while his shoulders shook with the sobs she was too weary to share—and they mourned together.

He had no idea how long they wept together; long enough for his eyes and throat to go raw. But flesh has its limits; finally he got himself back under control, carefully wiped her tears away for her, and took a seat beside her.

"I knew what happened to him," he said at last. "Rolan made it through with your message."

"How did—how did I get here?"

"I Fetched you—" he groped for the right words. "I mean, I had to, I couldn't leave you there! I didn't know if it would work but I had to try! Elspeth, the Companions, we all Fetched you together."

"You did that? It—I've never heard of anything like that. It's like— like some tale. But I was lost in the dark." She seemed almost in a state of shock now, or a half-trance. "I could see the Havens, you know, I could see them. But they wouldn't let me go to them—they held me back."

"Who? Who held you back?"

"Love and duty—" she whispered as if to herself.

"What?" She wasn't making any sense.

"But Kris said—" Her voice was almost inaudible.

He had feared before. Now he was certain. It *had* been Kris whom she loved—and he'd prevented her from reaching him. He hung his head, not wanting her to see the despair on his face.

"Dirk—" Her voice was stronger, not quite so confused. "It was *you* who called me. You saved me from Ancar, then brought me out of the dark. Why?"

She'd hate him for it, but she deserved the truth. Maybe one day she'd forgive him.

"I had to. I love you," he said helplessly, hopelessly. He stood up to leave, his eyes burning with more tears—tears he dared not shed—and cast one longing glance back at her.

Talia heard the words she'd been past hoping for—then saw her hope getting ready to walk out the door. Suddenly everything fell into place. Dirk had thought that Kris was the one she'd been in love with!

That was why he'd been acting so crazy—wanting her himself, yet fearing to try to compete with Kris. Havens, half the time he must have loathed himself for a very natural anger at his best friend who had turned rival. No *wonder* he'd been in such a state!

And now Kris was gone, and he thought that she'd want no part of him, the constant reminder, the second-best.

Damn the man! Stubborn as he was, there would be no reasoning with him. He would never believe anything she told him; it could take months, years to straighten it all out.

Her mind felt preternaturally clear, and she sought frantically for a way out of her predicament—and found one in memory.

"*. . . just like with a Farspeaker.*" Ylsa's words were clear in her memory. "*They almost always begin by hearing first, not speaking. You're feeling* *right now—but I suspect that one day you'll learn how to project your own feelings in such a way that others can read them, can share them. That could be a very useful trick—especially if you ever need to convince someone of your sincerity!"*

Yes, she'd done that without really thinking about it already. There was the forced rapport, and the kind of rapport she'd shared with Kris and Rolan. And the simpler tasks of projecting confidence, reassurance—this was just one step farther along—

She reached for the strength and the will to *show* him, only to discover that she was too drained, too exhausted. There was nothing left.

She nearly sobbed with vexation. Then Rolan made his presence felt, filling her with his love—and more—

Rolan—*his* strength was there, as always, and offered to her with open-hearted generosity.

And she had the knowledge of what to do and how to do it.

"Wait!" she coughed, and as Dirk half-turned, she projected everything she felt into his open mind and heart. All her love, her need for him—forcing him to see the truth that words alone would never make him believe.

Devan heard a strange, strangled cry that sounded as if it were something torn from a masculine throat. He whirled and started for Talia's room, fearing the worst.

He paused for a moment at the door, steeled himself against what he was likely to see, and opened it slowly, words of comfort on his tongue.

To his total amazement, not only was Talia still living—but she was actually clear-eyed and smiling, and trembling on the knife-edge between laughter and tears. And Dirk was sitting on the side of her bed, trying his best to find some way of holding her without hurting her, covering every uninjured inch of her that he could reach with kisses and tears.

Half stunned, Devan slipped out before either of them noticed him, and signaled a page passing in the hall. He absently noted that it was one whose face he had seen often in this corridor, though he couldn't imagine why the child should have spent so much time here. When the boy saw who it was that had summoned him and what door he had come out of, he paled.

Incredible, Devan thought wryly. *Is there anyone who isn't worried to death about her?*

"I need a messenger sent to the Queen, preferably a Herald-courier, since a Herald is the only one likely to be able to find her without looking for hours, and this is fairly urgent," he said.

The page's mouth trembled. "The Lady-Herald, sir," he said in an unsteady treble. "Is she—dead?"

"Lord of Lights, no!" Devan suddenly realized that he felt like laughing for the first time in days, and shocked the child with an enormous grin. "In fact, while you're getting me that messenger, spread the news! She's very much with us—and she's going to be very, very well indeed!"

CHAPTER 11

DIRK'S PURE JOY could not last for long; all too soon he recalled that there were far more important issues at stake than just his happiness. Talia alone knew what had transpired in Ancar's capital; might know what they could expect. Surely, surely there was danger to Valdemar, and only she might be able to guess how much.

He sobered; she caught his mood immediately. "Orthallen isn't the only enemy," he said slowly.

She couldn't have gotten any paler, but her eyes widened and pupils dilated. "No—how long—was I—"

"Since we Fetched you? Let me think—" he reckoned it up. He'd been unconscious for two days; then spent six more recovering from backlash. "Just about eight days." He guessed at what she'd ask next. "We're in Lord Falthern's keep, right on the edge of the Border."

"Selenay?"

"Devan's sent for her. You're in pain—"

"No choice, you know that." She managed a wan smile. "I—"

She forgot what she was about to say completely as Selenay fairly flew in the open door, face alight with a fierce joy.

"You see, Majesty." Alberich was close on her heels. "It is only the truth I told you." Dirk was astonished to see that the Armsmaster's face wore a nearly identical expression.

"Talia, Talia—" Selenay could manage no more before she was overcome with tears of happiness. She took the hand that Dirk had not claimed gently in her own, holding it with every care, lest she cause more pain. Alberich stood beside her, beaming as if it had all been his doing. Never in his entire life had Dirk seen the Armsmaster smile so broadly.

"Selenay—?"

The anxiety in Talia's voice penetrated even their joy, and brought them abruptly back to earth.

"There's still danger?"

Talia nodded wearily. Dirk arranged the bedding so that she was spared as much pain as he could manage, and she cast him a look that made him flush with pleasure. "Ancar—has his own army."

"And he may attack with it?"

"*Will* attack. Has to, now. He meant to kill you. Then take Elspeth."

"God of Light—"

"Last I knew—planned to take Border. He—has to have—missed me. Can't guess his reaction—but he has to assume—I lived long enough to talk."

"So we're in as much danger as before, maybe more." Selenay stood, jaw clenched in anger. "He'll have a fight on his hands!"

"Magicians. He has magicians. *Old* magic. Kept me from Mindcalling—kept Heralds from knowing Kris was dead; don't know what else they can do. Just know they can block us. And Orthallen— kept him well informed."

"Orthallen?" Selenay lost some of her anger; now she looked bewildered. "Orthallen—Lady help me, I still can't believe it of him— Goddess—he was Kris' *uncle!*"

"He was unpleased that you had sent the lad, Selenay," Alberich reminded her. "I think that we know the reason, now. And his grief at hearing—that was unfeigned."

"But over—perhaps a bit too soon," the Queen replied, biting her lip. "Though he had never been one for making much of a show of feelings."

"He killed your father," Talia whispered, her eyes closed again, exhausted with the effort of speaking for so long. "During the battle— sent an assassin in the confusion."

"He—" Selenay went white. "I never guessed—I *trusted* him!"

Silence then; the silence before the tempest.

"Dirk?" Talia opened her eyes very briefly, only to close them quickly, as if she found her vision wavering when she did so.

He needed no other clue than the dazed way she looked at him; he touched her cheek gently and went looking for Devan himself.

When he came back, he brought with him not only Devan but three other Healers as well. By then the little room was rather crowded; Kyril was back, and Elspeth with him. The Seneschal had returned and had brought the Lord Marshal. Candles had been brought, lighted and stuck on every available surface; the room was bright and a little warm and stuffy.

"I hate to ask this of you and of her, Devan," Selenay said, looking guilty, "but we haven't got the choice. Can you Healers hold her together long enough for her to tell us what we need to know?"

Dirk wanted to protest—then his rebellion subsided. He knew what he'd be doing in Talia's place; using his last breath to gasp out every bit of information he could. Why should she be any different?

"Majesty," Devan bowed his head in resignation. "I will say that I do not approve, and we will not let her kill herself with exhaustion."

"But you'll do it?"

"Like Talia, we have no choice." The Healers surrounded her, touched her lightly, and went into their Healing trances. She sighed; her pain-twisted expression eased and she opened her eyes, which were alert and clear again.

"Ask—quickly."

"Ancar—what can we expect from him?" the Lord Marshal spoke first. "How large is this private army? What kind of men does he have in it?"

"Prison scum; about three thousand. No mercenaries I heard of. But they're trained, well trained."

"What about the standing army? Will he use them?"

"I don't think yet. He murdered Alessandar; don't think he controls officers in the regular army yet. Have to put down rebels in the corps before he can use them. Needs to replace all officers with his own puppets."

"Do you think—can we expect defections?"

"I think so. Whole Border Guard may come over when they learn what happened. Welcome them, but Truth Spell them."

"Where was his own army last?"

"Just outside the capital."

"Does he know you know about his three thousand?"

"No." Her eyes were almost unnaturally bright. "He didn't ask any questions of me, ever."

"The more fool, he. A bit overconfident, wouldn't you say, Alberich? So," the Lord Marshal mused, stroking his beard, his black brows knitted in thought. "Twelve to fourteen days of forced marching would get them here. Much cavalry?"

"I don't think so; these were prison scum before he recruited them. But they're trained to work together, been training for at least three years. He also has magicians. Old magic, real magic, like in tales. If he thinks he'll come up against Heralds, he'll use them."

"How good are they?" asked Kyril.

"Don't know. One of them kept me from Mindspeaking, from probing Ancar, from defending myself, and kept Kris' passing from reaching you here—but he couldn't block empathic link with Rolan. Gods—this is important—they can *block* us, but they *can't read* us. Ancar let that slip—said something about 'damn Heralds and your barriers.'"

"Which means they can't possibly use their magic to learn our plans, especially not if *we* keep shields up?" Kyril asked, with hope in his eyes.

"Think so. Didn't even bother to try to read me, and Hulda is a mage, too—taught Ancar; I don't know how good they are. This isn't mind-magic; can't guess how it works."

"Orthallen," said the Seneschal. "How long has he been working against the Queen?"

"Decades; he had an assassin take the King during battle."

"Who was he working with?"

"Nobody then. Wanted the Throne for himself; just took advantage of Tedrel Wars."

"When did he change?"

"When Hulda contacted him. He thought he was using her."

"That was years ago—!"

"Right. She came to groom Elspeth as Ancar's consort. She found Orthallen, worked with him. He warned her in time to escape. Later Ancar offered him the Throne in exchange for information and internal help."

"The magicians—?" said Kyril, anxiously.

"Not much I can tell. Told you about the mindblock. Same mage kept Ancar shielded. Hulda shielded herself, I think. She looked physically about twenty-five years old. Could have been illusion, but don't think so. She's old enough to have been actually Ancar's nurse—makes her at least forty. Saw her make a witchlight—" Talia pulled her bandaged hand away from Dirk's for a moment, and pulled her loose gown away from her shoulder. Selenay and Elspeth gasped, and the Seneschal bit back an exclamation at what was revealed there—a handprint, burned into the flesh of her chest as if with a branding iron. "She did that, while they were—playing with me. Just laid her hand there, casually. Like it was easy as breathing. Rumors were they can do worse; lots worse."

The four Healers were beginning to look drawn; even with their aid, Talia was visibly fading.

"Tired—" she said, begging with her eyes for a rest.

"We've got enough to go on for now," Selenay looked to each of the others and they nodded in confirmation. "We can get our defenses organized, at least. Rest, my brave one."

She led the others out; one by one the Healers disengaged themselves. As they did, Talia seemed to wilt, and more than a little. Devan caught Dirk's shoulder before he had a chance to panic.

"She'll live; she just needs rest and a chance to heal," he said wearily. "And she's going to get at least some of both right now—if I have to post guards to keep people out!"

Dirk nodded, and returned to her side. She opened her eyes with an effort.

"Love—you—" she whispered.

"My own—" His throat closed for a moment, and he fought down a renewal of tears. "I'm going to leave you for a while; Devan says you need rest. But I'll be back as soon as he lets me!"

"Make it—soon—"

He left, walking backward; she keeping her eyes on him until the door closed.

As Alberich had suspected would be the case, when dawn came, the bivouac on the Border as well as the smaller collection of Councilors and officials at the Keep were in an uproar. Units of the Guard—heartbreakingly small—arrived every hour. Tales, more or less garbled, of what had occurred the previous night were spreading like oil from a shattered urn, and were just as potentially flammable. Talia slept in an induced Healing-trance, blissfully unaware of the confusion.

The Guard was easiest to deal with; the Lord Marshal simply called all the officers together, and with Alberich present to verify exactly what had been said and done, related to them the entire true story. The officers of the Guard, for the most part, had never associated closely with Orthallen; thus, while they were shocked by his betrayal, they took the tale at its face value. They were far more worried about the army Ancar would bring against them, for they numbered something around a thousand to Ancar's three thousand. The magicians they dismissed out of hand.

"My lord," one veteran officer said, his face as scar-seamed as Alberich's. "Begging your pardon, but there's nothing we can *do* about mages. We'll leave that in the hands of those that deal with magic—"

His gaze flickered to Alberich; the Armsmaster gave him a barely perceptible nod.

"—we've more than enough on our plate with what's coming at us."

And Ancar's army *was* on its way; Alberich and the Lord Marshal knew that for a fact. There were two Heralds in Selenay's entourage gifted with Farsight who had also been in Hardorn on more than one mission. They had bent their talents beyond the Border during the night, at Alberich's urging. They had seen Ancar's army, plainly camped for a few hours' rest. More disturbingly, they had "looked" again for that army with the coming of dawn—and found nothing, nothing but empty countryside.

"So there's at least one mage with them," Kyril deduced, as the war-leaders conferred over breakfast. "And he's concealing their movements from our Farsight somehow." Knowing what they now knew about mages being in Ancar's entourage—however little that was—Kyril and Alberich had been made co-equal with the Lord Marshal. Their task was to lead the assembled Heralds in combat—either by steel or by Gift. One of the Heralds' most important tasks was communications; each officer would have a Mindspeaking Herald with him at all times, and Kyril would be with Selenay to coordinate all of them. That was the trick that had won the Tedrel Wars for them, the one thing no other army could match.

"Doesn't matter," the Lord Marshal replied, "at least not at the moment. We know where they *were*; we know by that how fast they've come, and how soon they're likely to get here. We also know those mages haven't been moving 'em somehow—else they wouldn't have needed all the horses your Heralds 'saw.'"

"My lord?" One of his officers had appeared beyond the open tent flap, saluting smartly. He was scarcely old enough to have grown a beard; morning sun gilded his fair hair, and he was having a difficult time repressing a grin. "We're getting the recruits you warned us of."

"Recruits?" Kyril said, puzzled, as Alberich nodded.

The Lord Marshal gave a brief snort that might have been a laugh. "You'll see, Herald. Bring them on up here, lad; we've got two here that can test them."

"All of them, sir?"

"How many are there?" The Lord Marshal was surprised now.

"Over a hundred, sir."

"Lady Bright—aye, bring them all up. We'll get them sorted out, somehow."

As the three Warleaders left the tent to stand in the brilliant sunlight, there was a small dust-cloud in the vicinity of the trade road. As those who made the cloud neared, Kyril and Alberich saw that those at the front of the crowd that approached afoot were wearing the black-and-gold uniforms of Alessandar's regular army.

It appeared that the entire force guarding the Border, from officers to Healers and all their dependents, had defected when they had learned of Alessandar's murder.

Elspeth had the joyous task of breaking the news to the rest of the Council. There was no such accord among the political leaders of Valdemar as there was among her military leaders.

Lord Gartheser was speechless with outrage and shock; Bard Hyron was dazed. Lady Kester and Lady Cathan, still seething over Orthallen's accusations of complicity with the slavers, were surprised, but not altogether unhappy. Father Aldon had closeted himself in the tiny chapel of the Keep; Lord Gildas was with him. Healer Myrim made no attempt to conceal the fact that Orthallen's treachery had not surprised her. Nor did she conceal that his demise gave her a certain grim satisfaction. But then, she might well be forgiven such uncharitable thoughts; she was one of the four Healers who were tending Talia's wounds.

Once the bare bones had been told to the Councilors as a group, Elspeth went to each of these Councilors in turn, privately. She gave a simple explanation of what had occurred, but would answer no questions. Questions, she told them, must wait until Talia had recovered enough to tell them all more.

Long before then, Ancar's army arrived.

Alberich was beginning to feel hopeful. The ranks of Valdemar's forces had been swelled to nearly double the original size by deserters—partisans of Alessandar—from across the Border. The Lord Marshal was fairly dancing with glee; with the exception of the dependents, every one of the men and women who sought sanctuary with them was a well-trained fighter or Healer—and every one burned with hatred and anger for the murder of their beloved King.

For the true tale had been spread to the countryside, from the capital westward, by a most unexpected source—the members of Trader Evan's clan.

Evan, it seemed, had taken to heart Talia's warning to flee—and done more than that. He had spread the word among the traders of his own clan as he fled; they in turn had carried the tale farther. Close to the capital, the people were cowed and afraid, too frightened to dare even escape; but close to the Border where Ancar's hand had not yet fallen so heavily, and where Alessandar had been served out of love, feelings ran high. High enough, that when two or three Border officers decided to defect to Valdemar's side of the Border, nearly the entire contingent of the regular army stationed in the area chose to come with them.

Ancar surely had not anticipated this, nor would Ancar have any way of knowing they had gone. A small group of volunteers had remained behind at the signal towers and continued to send messages and information—all of it false.

"They'll fade into the villages when Ancar has gone by," the Captain who had hosted Kris and Talia told Alberich. "They've got civilian clothing at hand now. If they can, they'll come across to us, but all the men who volunteered have families, and they won't leave 'em."

"Understandable," Alberich replied. "If it is that we win this battle, we shall post watchers to guide them here at every likely crossing. If not . . ."

"Then it won't matter a damn, because Ancar will have us all," the Captain answered grimly.

The Lord Marshal, with his forces doubled, was in no doubt as to the outcome.

"Randon," Selenay said anxiously, as they waited for some sign that Ancar was within striking distance, "I know it's your job to be confident, but he still has us outnumbered three to two—"

They were standing, as they had every day since the Border had been alerted, at the top of the highest hill in the vicinity. Ancar's mages probably could mask the movements of his troops from Farsight, but they'd be hard put to eliminate the dust-cloud of their passing, or the disturbance of birds, or any one of a number of other signs of the movement of many men. From this hill there was a clear line-of-sight for miles into Hardorn. Trained watchers were posted here, but Selenay and the Lord Marshal also spent most of their time not otherwise occupied squinting into the bright sunshine alongside them.

"My lady, we have more on our side than he can guess at. We have a thousand trained fighters besides our own that he knows *nothing* about. We have the choice of battleground. And we have the Heralds to ensure that there are *no* botched orders or misheard messages, or commands that come too late to be effective. The only thing I fear are his mages." Now doubt did shadow the Lord Marshal's eyes, and creep into his voice. "We have no way of knowing what they can do, how many he has, or if we can counteract them. And *they* may turn the day for him."

"And Heraldic Gifts for the most part are not much use offensively," Selenay added, sobered by the thought of the mages. "If only we had one of the Herald-mages alive today."

"Lady-Queen, will I do?"

Selenay whirled, startled. As she and Randon had been absorbed in watching the Border and in their conversation, two Heralds had climbed the hill behind them. One was Dirk, pale, but looking better than he had in days.

The other, so begrimed with dust that his Whites were gray, his face lined with exhaustion, but sporting a self-conscious grin despite his weariness, was Griffon.

"I brought him right here as soon as we'd pried him off his saddle, Majesty," Dirk said. "This lout just may be our answer to the mages— remember his Gift? He's a *Firestarter*, Majesty."

"Just point out what you want to go up in flames—or who," Griffon added. "I guarantee it'll go. Kyril hasn't found anything that'll block me yet."

"That's no boast, Majesty; I trained him, I know what he can do. He's limited to line-of-sight, but that should be good enough."

"But—you were riding circuit up North," Selenay said, dazed with the sudden turn in their fortunes that brought Griffon there when he was most needed. "How did you even find out we were under threat, much less get here in time?"

"Pure, dumb, Herald's luck," Griffon replied. "I ran into a Herald Courier whose Gift just *happens* to be Foresight; her message was delivered and we were—ah—passing an evening together. That night she got a really strong vision; all but dragged me out of bed and threw me into the saddle stark naked. She took over my circuit, I rode for the Border as fast as Harevis could carry me. And here I am. I just hope I can do you some good."

The setting sun was turning the clouds bloody when one of the lookouts reported the first long-awaited sign of Ancar's army. Selenay prayed that the blood-red of the sunset was not an ill omen for her forces, even while she and the Lord Marshal issued the first of the orders for the battle to come.

The Lord Marshal had chosen as the battlefield a low, bare hill just on the Valdemar side of the Border. It had woods to the rear and the left of it, and open fields to the right. What Ancar couldn't know—and what even now the scouts and skirmishers heading into the woods intended to keep him from learning—was that the woods to the rear of the hill had flooded with the bursting of an earthen dam earlier this spring. Water lay two and three feet deep all through them, and the hitherto-spongy ground was a morass of mud.

Others besides those skirmishers were moving into the woods to the left of the chosen field—the thousand or so fighters who had defected to Valdemar. In groups of a hundred or thereabouts, each with a mind-speaking Herald, they were taking positions to lie in wait past any point where Ancar's scouts would be allowed to penetrate.

Teren slapped at another mosquito, and curbed his irritation. The ground was high enough here that they weren't up to their rears in mud, but the stinging insects were having a rare old party—not only acres of newmade marsh to lay eggs in, but this unexpected bonus of humans as refreshments! It was dark, the air was damp, and it was chilly. Wythra didn't like it any better than he did; he could hear his Companion blowing impatiently in the darkness to his right.

:Twin?: he mind-sent. *:We're in position, how about you?:*

:The same,: was Keren's reply, with an overtone of exasperation, *:and up to our armpits in goddamn midges!:*

:Mosquitos here.:

:Count your blessings,: came her retort. *:The midges are crawling into people's armor and you beat yourself black and blue trying to get them.:*

:They're everywhere—: That had the unmistakable overtones of Keren's stallion Dantris, and he was irritated. Unlike most other Heralds, the twins could Mindspeak as well with each other's Companions as with their own. *:Even fellis-oil isn't helping,:* Dantris concluded in annoyance.

:Sounds like you may have more casualties from the wildlife than in battle.: Teren grinned to himself despite his discomfort.

:Let's all hope you're right,: his twin answered soberly.

"Be my eyes and ears, love," Talia had begged Dirk. "They're going to need me—"

"But—" he'd protested.

"Take Rolan; you *know* you can link to him. And when they need me—"

"Not *if*?" He'd sighed. "No, never mind. I link to Rolan and he links to you? Gods, can't you rest for a *moment*?"

"Dare I?"

He'd had no answer to give her. So here he waited, in the lines behind Selenay, waiting for dawn. Praying she didn't kill herself—because if he lost her, now that he'd just found her . . .

When dawn came, Selenay's forces were formed up along the top of the hill, with their backs to the woods. There was a heavy knot of Heralds in Whites at the end of the left flank, hard against the woods to the side. With them was Jeri, wearing some of Elspeth's student Grays; they were hoping Ancar would mistake her for Elspeth and drive for that part of the line. Elspeth herself was back at the Keep, ready to flee at a moment's notice if the tide turned against them. She had agreed to this reluctantly, but saw the sense in it, and she wanted to be certain if everything went wrong that Talia was not left behind. During one of her brief moments of wakefulness, the Queen's Own had soberly asked the Heir to personally be certain that she didn't fall back into Ancar's hands, and Elspeth had promised just as soberly. Although Elspeth had a shrewd notion that Talia meant she should see to it that the Queen's Own received coup de grace, the Heir was determined to bring her along even if it meant carrying the injured Herald herself!

In the pale light of dawn, Selenay's original thousand looked pitiful against Ancar's three thousand.

They were a shade more heavily armored than the Guard; from the way they obeyed their officers' orders, they were as well trained. About five hundred of the three thousand were still mounted; cavalry then, but light cavalry, not heavy. The good news was that their bows were all crossbows—in an open field battle, virtually useless in combat once fired, and lacking the range of a longbow.

Selenay's forces waited, patiently. Ancar would have to come to them.

"He's a good commander, I'll give him that," the Lord Marshal growled, when after an hour of waiting nothing had happened. "He's assessing his chances—and I hope to blazes we look like fools! Wait a minute, something's happening—"

A rider came forward from the ranks with a white parley flag. He rode to the exact middle of the battlefield, and paused.

The Lord Marshal rode forward three paces, his battleharness jingling, and thundered, "Speak, man! Or are you just here to look pretty?"

The rider, a slightly foppish fellow wearing highly ornamented plate with a helmet that bore an outlandish crest, colored angrily and spoke up. "Queen Selenay, your envoys murdered King Alessandar, clearly on your orders. King Ancar has declared a state of war upon Valdemar for your heinous act. Your forces are outnumbered—will you surrender yourself now to Ancar's justice?"

An angry muttering went up along the line, as Selenay grimaced. "I wondered what sort of tale he'd concoct," she murmured to Kyril, then called to the rider: "And just what can I expect from Ancar's justice?"

"You must abdicate and give over your daughter Elspeth in marriage to Ancar. The Heralds of Valdemar must be disbanded and outlawed. Ancar will rule Valdemar jointly with Elspeth; you will be imprisoned in a place of Ancar's choosing for as long as you live."

"Which will be about ten minutes once Ancar has me in his hands," Selenay said loud enough for the envoy to hear. Then she stood up in her stirrups, removed her helm so that the sun shone fully on her golden hair, and called aloud, "What do you say, my people? Shall I surrender?"

The resounding "No!" that met her question rang across the hilltop and caused the envoy's horse to start and shy.

"Now hear *me*—" she said, in a voice so clear and carrying that there was no doubt that every one of Ancar's men could hear it. "Ancar murdered his own father, and my envoy as well. He consorts with evil magicians, and dabbles in blood-sacrifice, and I'd sooner set a blade across Elspeth's throat than have her spend so much as five minutes in his company! Let him beware the vengeance of the gods for his false accusations—and the only way he'll rule Valdemar is when every one of her citizens is dead in her defense!"

The envoy turned his horse back to his own lines, the cheering that followed Selenay's words seeming to push him along before it like a leaf before the wind.

"Well, now we're for it," Selenay said to her commanders, settling her sword a little more comfortably at her side. She replaced her helm, and patted her Companion's neck. "Now we see if our plans work, even at three-to-two."

"And," Kyril replied, "if a Firestarter's the equal of Ancar's mages."

* * *

"Why are they just sitting there?" Griffon asked, his expression perplexed. "Why aren't they charging?"

He was far back behind the first and second lines, with the bowmen. His Gift was far too precious to risk him anywhere near the front, but he chafed at his enforced idleness.

They found out in the next few moments as fog seemed to begin rising from the earth at a point between their lines and Ancar's. The fog was a sickly yellow, and the breeze blowing across the battle field did not disturb it at all. Then it seemed to writhe and curdle; there was an eerie green glow all about it. The breeze brought a whiff of a sulfurous stench, the whole battlefield seemed to shift sideways for an instant, and Griffon's stomach lurched—and in place of the fog was a clutch of demonic monsters.

They were easily seven feet tall, with dark pits in their skulls in place of eyes, in the depths of which a dim red fire seemed to flicker. Their mouths were fanged; their leathery yellow hides, the color of rancid butter, seemed armor enough. They each carried a double-bladed axe in one hand, a knife nearly the length of a sword in the other. There were nearly a hundred of them. A fearful murmuring arose from the ranks of Selenay's forces—a few arrows flew in the direction of the things, but those that connected merely bounced off. As they opened their fanged mouths to roar and began advancing on the center of Selenay's lines, her own troops fell back a step or two involuntarily.

Then, without warning, one of the demon-warriors stopped dead in its tracks, and let out a howl that caused men to clap their hands to their ears; then it burst into flame.

It howled again, and began staggering in circles, a walking pyre. Selenay's troops cheered again; then the cheering died, for the rest of the demons were still coming, oblivious to the fate of the burning one, which had fallen to the ground, still afire.

A second and a third ignited—and still they kept coming. They moved fairly slowly, but it was evident that they would reach Selenay's lines in a few moments.

And so they did—and the slaughter they caused was hideous. The demons waded into the line of fighters as a man might wade into a pack of yipping curs. They swung their heavy axes with deceptive slowness—and sheared through armor and the flesh beneath as if the armor were paper and the flesh as soft as melted cheese. There was no deflecting the blows of those vicious axes; a man in the way of one of them went down with his shield split, and his skull split as well. Incredibly, fighters pressed to replace those that had fallen, but their bravery was useless. The axes continued to swing, and the replacements joined their fellows, either in death or in mangled agony. The Guard swarmed to make a protective wall around Selenay and her commanders, but the demons were inexorably cutting through them. There was blood everywhere—some of it yellow, but precious little compared to the amount of red, human blood flowing. Men cried out in fear or in pain, the monsters roared, and under all was the screech of blade-edge meeting armor and the stink of demon-flesh burning.

Griffon, standing far behind the lines, brow furrowed with concentration, was focusing on yet another of the demons. As it, too, went up in flames, he looked for a new target in despair. It seemed that he alone could kill these monsters—but there were so many of them!

"Herald—" He tried to ignore the insistent voice in his ear, but the man would not go away. He turned impatiently, to see that his persistant companion was the Councilor, Bard Hyron. Hyron was enough of a trained bowman to have warranted a place back here, alongside Griffon.

"Herald—the tales say these things are dependent on their sorcerer. If you kill him, they'll vanish!"

"What if the tales are wrong?"

"You won't have lost anything," the Bard pointed out. "Look—the mage must be in that knot of people back by the standard; just to the left of the center and the rear of Ancar's lines."

"Get me a Farseer!" Before Griffon had finished speaking, the man was off, running faster than Griffon would have guessed he could.

The Bard was back in an instant—too long for Griffon, who watched, sickened, as the demons carved down another swath of the Guard.

"I'm looking, Grif—" It was Griffon's red-haired year-mate, Davan, who came stumbling up in the Bard's wake—stumbling because he had one hand pressed to his forehead, trying to "See" as he ran. "I've— bloody *hell*! I *know* he's there, but they're blocking me! *Damn* you, you bastards—"

Davan went to his knees, face twisted and unrecognizable with the effort of fighting the blockage the mages were putting on him.

"Come *on*, Davan—" Griffon glanced up, and swallowed bile and fear. The demons were continuing to advance. He concentrated, and sent the nearest up in flames, but another took its place.

Hyron froze for a moment, then ran off again. Griffon hardly noticed; he was doing what he could—and it wasn't enough.

Pounding hooves and a flash of white that Griffon saw out of the corner of his eye signaled the arrival of another Herald. Distracted, Griffon turned to see who it was.

Dirk—and not Ahrodie, but *Rolan*!

Dirk slid off the stallion's bare back, and took Davan by the shoulder, shaking him. "Break it off, little brother—that isn't going to get you anywhere," he shouted over the noise of battle. "You two—don't argue. Link with us—"

Griffon did not even bother to think, much less argue. He linked in with Dirk, as he had so often done as a student—

To find himself, not in a four-way linkage, but a *five*. Dirk was linked to Rolan—who in his turn was linked to—Talia?

Yes, it *was* Talia.

Dirk's ability at Mindspeech was limited, but urgency made it clear and strong. :*Davan, follow Her. Mage used death to raise power—pain, despair—She can track it to him. Grif, follow Davan—I hold here.*:

Davan caught that; they all remembered how Talia had used Ylsa's dying to lead Kris' Farsight to where her body lay. The thread of Talia's sending was faint, but unmistakable. Davan caught and followed it, and Griffon, linked in as closely as he dared, was hot on his "heels."

:*Yes—yes, I've got him! I See him! He's dressed in a bright sky-blue velvet robe—Grif, strike now, through me!*:

Clear in Davan's mind, Griffon saw a wizened man in a robe of vivid blue just a little to one side of the knot of people around Ancar's standard. And that was all he needed.

With hatred and anger he hadn't known he could feel, born of the horror he felt watching his fellows being slaughtered, he *reached*—

And found himself blocked, as he'd never been before.

He strove against the wall blocking him, fighting his way through it with every ounce of energy he possessed, fueled by his rage—

He felt it yield just the tiniest amount, and dragged up new reserves of energy—from where, he neither knew nor cared.

There was an explosion in Ancar's lines. And a tower of flame rose next to Ancar's standard—

And the demons vanished.

Griffon's eyes rolled up into his head, he fainted dead away, and Davan went with him; Hyron and Dirk caught them as they fell.

When the demon-warriors vanished, Selenay's forces let out a cheer of relief. Selenay cheered with them, but wondered if they were being a bit premature.

When no other arcane attacks manifested, *then* she truly felt like cheering. There must have been only the one mage, and somehow the Heralds had been able to defeat him.

"Griffon and Davan found the mage and burned him," Kyril said at Selenay's glance of inquiry. "They both collapsed, after. Griffon's still passed out, but it doesn't look as if he'll be needed again in a hurry."

No, it didn't; for now Ancar's regular troops were charging Selenay's line. The bowmen showered them with arrows—no few of which found their marks. Ancar's own crossbowmen had long since expended their own bolts—uselessly, it might be added—and had switched to charging with the rest, swords in hand. Selenay's Guardsfolk braced themselves for the shock, for now the first step of their battle plan was about to take place.

When Ancar's line hit Selenay's with a clangor of metal on metal and cries of battle-rage and pain, most of their force was concentrated on the middle, where Selenay's standard was. She waited, ignoring the sight and sound of her people killing and being killed, for several long moments—for *she,* not the Lord Marshal, was the field commander. Her Gift of Foresight was not a strong one, but it was an invaluable one, for it operated best on the battlefield. It would not tell her what was to happen, but given that there were plans already made, it *would* tell her when the exact instant occurred that those plans should be set into motion.

She waited, listening for that insistent inner prompting. Then— "Tell the left to pull in," she said to Kyril.

He Mindsent, with a frown of concentration, and almost instantly the troops on the lefthand side of the standard began making their way toward the center.

As she'd hoped, Ancar sent his cavalry to the left, with foot following—supposing that he could encircle their line at that point, or even capture the supposed Heir.

"Wheel—" she told Kyril. And relayed by the Heralds with each group, the entire force pivoted on the center, with the leftmost end being on the very edge of the swamp, where some of Ancar's cavalry were even now discovering the two and three feet of water and mud.

She waited another long moment, until all of Ancar's forces were between her line and the woods on the left.

Then—"Now, Kyril! Call them in!"

And pouring from the woods came the troops that had hidden there all night—fresh, angry, and out for blood; the defectors from Alessandar's army, and the Heralds that were their link to the command post. The defectors looked a little odd, for each of them had spent a few moments of his hours in waiting cutting away the sleeves of his uniform tunic so that the sleeves of the white, padded gambeson showed. There could now be no mistaking them on the battlefield for Ancar's troopers.

Caught between two forces, with a morass in front of them, even Ancar's seasoned veterans began to panic.

After that, it was a rout.

Griffon was the first to reach the Keep, half-blind with reaction-headache. He had stayed only long enough to assure himself that the victory was indeed Selenay's, then pulled himself onto his Companion's back and sought the Healers.

"We did it; we pulled it off," he told Elspeth, downing a swallow of headache-potion with a grimace. "Those extra troops from Hardorn turned the tide. By now what's left of Ancar's army is probably being chased across the border with its tail between its legs."

"What about Ancar himself?"

"Never got into the thick of battle; probably he's gotten away. And before you ask, I don't know if Hulda was with him, but I'd guess not. From what I've been able to pick up from you and Talia, I'd say she isn't one to put herself at any kind of risk. She's probably safely back at the capital, consolidating things for her 'little dear.'"

"What about—"

"Elspeth, my head is about ready to break open. I think I know why Lavan called the Firestorm down on himself—it probably felt better than his reaction-headache! I'm going to go pass out for a while. Thank Talia for me. We couldn't have done it without her. And you stay ready; they'll be bringing battle casualties back any minute now. The Healers will need every hand they can get, and there'll be plenty of fellows eager for the privilege of having the Heir listening to their boasts while they're being patched up."

So it proved . . . and Elspeth learned firsthand of the aftermath of battle. She grew a great deal older in the next few hours. And never again would she think of war as "glorious."

* * *

Selenay remained on the Border, as fresh troops came to help with mopping-up, but Elspeth, the Councilors, the wounded, and most of the Heralds (including Talia and Dirk) returned to the capital.

Just before the Councilors left, Selenay called them all together.

"I *must* remain here," she said, feeling gray with exhaustion. "Elspeth has full powers of regency; in my absence she heads the Council—with full vote."

Lord Gartheser looked as if he was about to protest, then subsided, sullenly. The Councilors who had been Orthallen's advocates—with the exception of Hyron—were angry and unhappy and would be Elspeth's first problem.

"You have no choice in this, my Councilors," Selenay told them, fixing her eyes on Gartheser in particular. "In war the Monarch has right of decree, as you well know. And should there be any trouble . . ."

She paused significantly.

"Be certain that I shall hear of it—and act."

Elspeth called a Council meeting as soon as they were all settled, but sent messages that it would be held in Talia's quarters.

With the more aged or slothful of the Councilors grumbling and panting their way up the stairs to the top story, the meeting convened.

Talia was by no means well; she was healed enough to manage an hour or two undrugged, but no more than that. She was propped up on her little couch, positioned just under her window. She wore bandages everywhere except her head and neck; her ruined feet were encased in odd bootlike contraptions. She was nearly as white as the uniform she wore. Elspeth sat next to her, with one eye on her at all times.

Lord Gartheser (predictably) was the first to speak. "What has been going on here?" he snapped angrily. "What's all this nonsense about Orthallen being a traitor? I—"

"It is not nonsense, my lord," Talia interrupted him quietly. "I heard it from his co-conspirators, and his own actions when confronted merely with their names proves his guilt."

Simply, and without elaboration, she told the whole story of what she and Kris had learned about Ancar, of the massacre at the banquet, of Kris' death, and her confrontations with Hulda and Ancar.

When she paused, obviously tired, Elspeth took up the tale, relating what Talia had told them after Dirk had brought her back, and the scene with Orthallen.

Lord Gartheser sat silently through it all, mouth agape, growing paler by the moment.

"So you can see, Councilors," Elspeth finished, "why my very first act as regent *must* be to ascertain your loyalty under Truth Spell. Kyril, would you be willing to administer to your fellow Councilors? I have only one question to put to all of us—where and with whom do your first loyalties lie?"

"Certainly, Elspeth," Kyril replied, nodding his gray head toward her obediently. "And Elcarth can administer the test to me."

"But—I—" Gartheser was sweating profusely.

"You have some objection, Gartheser?" Lady Cathan asked with honeyed sweetness.

"I—uh—"

"If you prefer not to take the test, you could resign your position—"

Lord Gartheser looked from face to face, hoping for a reprieve, and found none. "I—Lady Elspeth, I fear the—the stress of my position is too much for me. With your leave, I should prefer to resign it."

"Very well, Gartheser," Elspeth said calmly. "Does anyone else object? No? Then, my lord, you may leave us. I would suggest you retire to your estates for the quiet, peaceful life you have so richly earned. I do not think, given the stress you have been through, that it would be wise to entertain many visitors."

She watched Gartheser rise and stumble out the door with an impassive expression not even Selenay could have matched.

"Kyril," she said when he was gone, "you may begin with me."

"And after Elspeth, I should like to be tested," Hyron said, shamefacedly, "being as I was one of Orthallen's stronger supporters."

"If you wish. Kyril?"

The testing took a very short time; not surprisingly, all passed.

"Next, we have two Council seats to fill, speaker for the North, and speaker for the Central districts. Any suggestions?"

"For the Central, I would suggest Lord Jelthan," said Lady Kester. "He's young, he's got some good ideas, but he's been lord of his holdings for nearly fourteen years—his father died young."

"Anyone else? No? And the North?"

No one spoke, until Talia's whisper broke the silence. "If no one has any other notions, I suggest Mayor Loschal of Trevendale. He's quite able, he knows the problems of the North intimately, he has no private axe to grind that I am aware of, and he has enough years to balance Lord Jelthan's youth."

"Any other suggestions? So be it—Kyril, see to it, will you? Now, the other matter facing us is Hardorn and Ancar. We are going to have to increase the size of the Guard; that means a tax increase—"

"Why? We beat them, right soundly!"

"There's no need—"

"You're starting at shadows—"

"I know for a fact your mother gave you no such orders—"

"Quiet!" Kyril thundered out over the bedlam. When they stared at him dumbfounded, he continued, "Herald Talia wishes to speak, and she can't be heard over your babbling."

"Elspeth is right," Talia whispered wearily. "I know Ancar better than any of you. He'll be back at us, again and again, until one of our lands lacks its leader. And I tell you, this kingdom is in more danger now than we were before the battle we just won! *Now* he knows some of what we can do, and what kind of strength we can raise at short notice. The next time he comes for us, it will be with a force *he* deems overwhelming; we must be ready to meet that force."

"And that means a larger Guard; taxes to support it—"

"And your help, Councilors. Bard Hyron, the help of your Circle especially," Talia continued.

"My Circle? Why?"

"Because, as you ably demonstrated with Griffon, the Bardic Circle is the only source of information we have on old magic."

"Surely you overestimate these mages—" Lady Wyrist began.

"Look here and tell me I overestimate!" Again Talia pulled gown and bandage from her shoulder to display the handprint-brand, still livid and raw-looking. "I will bear this mark until the day I die, and this was just a *parlor-trick* for Hulda!" Lady Wyrist paled and turned her head away. "Ask the widows and children and widowers of those slain by demons if I overestimate the danger! I tell you now that what Ancar brought with him is likely to be one of his lesser mages—he would not risk the greater in battle. And Hyron, your Circle alone preserves the tradition of what we can expect and how we can defend against it. If, indeed, we can."

"We can," Hyron said thoughtfully. "It's in some of the chronicles from Vanyel's time—when the Gifts were superseding the mage-crafts. It may be that you Heralds and your Companions are all that *will* be able to guard us from Ancar's magicians."

"Sounds like a rare good reason to have them by us, if you ask me," said Lady Kester wryly.

"And we'll need you and your Circle for your traditional reason as well," Elspeth said, smiling at Hyron. "Especially if we're not to end up conscripting for the Guard."

"Rousing patriotic fervor and spreading tales of what's happened and what we can expect? Aye, Lady Elspeth, as always, the Circle is yours to command."

"And keeping the spirits of our people high."

"Ever in your service—"

Elspeth took a quick glance at Talia, as she lay back on her pillows, face pinched and drained. "If there's no more business at hand?"

"None that can't wait," said Lord Gildas.

"Then I think we'd best dismiss, and let the Healers see to Talia."

As the Councilors filed out, Skif slipped in, Healer Devan and Healer Rynee with him.

"Little sister, Dirk's waiting downstairs—" Skif began.

Talia's face crumpled, and she began to cry. "Please—not now—I'm so tired. . . ."

"Listen to me—listen—" He caught one of her hands in his own and knelt beside her couch. "I know what's happening to you, I understand! I've seen you trying not to wince away when he touches you. I've talked him into going home to tell his parents about you; I'm going with him. By the time we get back, you'll be fine again, I know you will. Now gather your courage and give him a wonderful good-bye to keep him going, eh?"

She shuddered; he wiped her tears, and she relaxed. "Is that why you brought Rynee?"

He chuckled. "You've got it. She'll give you a little mental pain-block, as it were. Let her work while I fetch Dirk."

She was able to do all Skif had asked and more, but when the two of them left, she crumbled again.

"Rynee, am I ever going to be able to—be *whole* again? I love him, I need him—but whenever he touches me, I see Ancar and Ancar's guards—"

"Hush, now, hush," Rynee soothed her as if Talia were twelve years her junior instead of four her senior.

"It was fine at first, but after the battle it started to build every time a man touched me, and it was worse than that when the man was *him*! Rynee, I can't bear it, I can't bear it!"

"Talia, dear friend, be easy. Yes, you'll be fine, just like Skif said. It's just a matter of Healing, inside instead of out. Now sleep."

"Will she Heal?" Devan looked at Rynee somberly, as Talia dropped into Healing-trance.

"She will," Rynee replied serenely. "And it'll be mostly her own doing. You'll see."

"I pray you're right."

"I *know* I am."

CHAPTER 12

$\longleftarrow \!\!\!\! \prec \;\; \succ \!\!\!\! \longrightarrow$

SKIF TOOK THE tower stairs at a run, though for all the sound he made, no one would ever have known there was anyone on the stairs at all. He'd been back from the North for several hours now, and he was more than impatient. "You can't see Talia yet," they'd told him. "She's with the Healers every morning, and they've left orders that they're never to be disturbed." Well, all right, but that didn't make a fellow any less twitchy, not when he was worried about her. He'd determined to get up to her room as soon as he'd finished lunch; he'd all but bolted his food and nearly choked as a consequence.

He'd evidently misjudged the timing by a bit, for as he approached the half-open door at the top of the stairs, he'd heard voices inside. He shrank back into a shadow on the landing, and peeked around the corner. From where he was hidden he could see inside the room quite easily. There were two Healers there, both easily identifiable by their Greens, one on either side of a lounge that held someone in Herald's Whites—Talia, without a doubt.

He winced inside, for her face was distorted by pain and her eyes streamed tears, although she did not utter so much as a single moan.

"Enough," said the Healer on her right; and Skif recognized Devan. "That's absolutely all for today, Talia."

Her face relaxed somewhat, and the woman on her left gave her a look of caring sympathy and a handkerchief to dry her tears with.

"You really don't need to be enduring all this, you know," Devan said, a bit crossly. "If you'd let us Heal you at the normal rate it could all be done quite painlessly."

"Dear Devan, I don't have time, and you know that perfectly well," Talia replied softly.

"Then you ought to at least let us work under painblock! And I still don't understand *why* you don't think you have time!"

"But if you worked under painblocks, I wouldn't be able to help—and if I can't help, neither can Rolan. In that case, it would take six of you to do what one does now." Her voice actually held a touch of amusement.

"She's got you there, Devan," the woman Healer—Myrim, the Healer's representative on the Council—pointed out wryly.

He snorted with disgust. "Heralds! I don't know why we put up with you! If you're not out killing yourselves, you're trying to get us to speed-Heal you so that you can go back out and get yourselves ruined that much sooner!"

"Well, old friend, if you'll recall—the first time you ever saw me, I was your patient. There'd already been an attempt to rid the world of me, and I was only a student. You could hardly expect this tabbycat to change color after such an auspicious beginning, could you?"

The Healer reached out and touched her cheek in a spontaneous gesture of affection. "It's just that it hurts me to have to put you through such agony, dearling."

She caught the hand and held it, smiling at him. The smile transformed her from a simply pretty woman (swollen and red-rimmed eyes notwithstanding) to a lovely one. "Take heart, old friend. There are not many more days of this to come; then whatever Healing is left will all be bone-Healing—and you can't speed that." She laughed. "As for why I don't have time, well, I can't tell you, because I don't know myself. I only know it's true, just as true as the fact that Rolan's eyes are blue. Besides, I know you. I'm a cooperative patient; unlike Keren and Dirk, I do exactly what I'm told. Since you can't complain of that, you have to find *something* to be annoyed about!"

Myrim chuckled, as did Healer Devan. "Oh, you know him far too well, milady," she said, standing and stretching. "And we will see you on the morrow."

They left the room and passed Skif without ever noticing that he was there.

But Talia seemed to sense that someone was there. "Whoever's outside, please come in," she called out. "It can't be comfortable on that cold, dark landing."

Skif chuckled, and pushed the door open all the way, to see Talia regarding him with her head tilted to one side and an expectant look on her face. "I never could fool you, could I?"

"Skif!" she exclaimed with delight, and held out both arms to him. "I hadn't expected you back this soon!"

"Oh, you know me—a box of soap and a spare uniform, and I'm ready to go." He embraced her very carefully, and kissed her forehead, before sitting on the floor next to her couch. "And where Skif is— seeing as we went to the same destination—can Dirk be far behind?"

"*You* tell *me*." He was pleased to see her eyes light with carefully contained joy.

"Well, he's not. Far behind, that is. He planned to stay one day longer, but if I'm any judge, he'll have made that up on the road. I wouldn't be surprised to see him here this afternoon. Dear heart, I'm glad to see you want him again."

Her eyes glowed, and she smiled. "I didn't fool you either, did I?"

"Not a bit. That's why I came up with the notion of sending him home to tell his family in person. I could see all that old fear of men— and worse—building up in you every time he touched you, and you trying not to show it so that you wouldn't hurt him."

"Oh, Skif—what ever did I do to deserve you? You were right; it was horrible, I felt like I was at war with myself."

"Dearling, I served a Border Sector, remember? *And* my old home neighborhood was a pretty rough place. You weren't the first woman I've seen that was suffering the aftereffects of rape and abuse. I know what the reaction is. I take it you're—"

"Fine. Better than ever; and half-mad with wanting to see him again."

"That's the best news I've had for a long time. Well, don't you want to know how it all went?"

"I'm consumed with curiosity because if I know Dirk, he probably sent his family a two-line note—'I'm getting married. I'll be there in a week,'—and no further explanation whatsoever."

Skif laughed, and admitted that that was just about what Dirk *had* written, word for word. "And a fine turmoil it sent them into, I can tell you! Especially coming on top of the rest of it—well, let me take it from the beginning."

He settled himself a bit more comfortably. "We got to the farm just about a week after we left here, and it was hard riding all the way. Dirk didn't want to spend any more time traveling than he had to; well, I can't say as I much blame him. When we got there, the entire clan was out waiting for us, since they'd had the children playing lookout ever since his message. Holy Stars, what a mob! You're going to like them, heartsister, they're all as mad as he is. They got us separated almost at once; the younglings plying me with food and drink while Dirk's mother and father dragged him off for a family conference. I could tell that he'd had them fair worried, especially after the last time—that bitch Naril and the way she played with him—"

"I know all about that. I don't blame them for being worried."

"It didn't help much that he was still a bit thin and worn-looking, I'm sure. They weren't easy to convince that everything was all right, because they had him incommunicado for several hours, at least an hour past supper, and we got there just at lunch. The poor youngsters were at their wit's end, trying to find something to distract me with!" Skif's lips pursed in a mischievous smile. "And I'm afraid I didn't help much. I wasn't cooperating at all. Well, they all finally emerged; Father looked satisfied, but Mother still had doubts in her eyes. They fed us all, then it was *my* turn to come under fire. Let me tell you, Dirk's mother is a lovely lady, and she ought to be put in charge of questioning witnesses; the Truth Spell would become entirely superfluous! By the time she was done with me, she knew everything I've ever known about you, including a lot of things I'd forgotten. We were up practically all night, talking; one of the best conversations I've ever had. I didn't mind in the least, she's such a dear. It was worth every yawn to see the worry going out of her eyes, the more I told her."

Talia sighed, and Skif could feel her relief and gratitude as she wordlessly squeezed his hand. "I can't tell you how glad I was that you insisted on going with him. You're a good friend to both of us."

"Hm—you'll be even gladder, I think—none of them are going to be able to be here for the wedding. That's what I meant by 'coming on top of all the rest of it.'"

"What's happened?" she asked anxiously.

"His third sister is having a real problem with this child she's bearing. She can't travel, obviously, her older sisters don't want to leave her. Needless to say, her mother, as Healer as well as parent, feels obligated to stay. And Dirk's father's joint problem is so bad he can't even take long wagon journeys anymore, never mind riding. I did my best to assure them that you wouldn't feel slighted or insulted if they didn't come, given the circumstances."

"I'd never forgive myself if they *had* come, and something had gone wrong at home while they were here."

"Well, that's what I told them. By the next day, we were all good friends, and I was part of the family. Then I had the hardest task I've ever faced. They asked me about Kris."

He looked at his hands, his voice fogged a little with tears. "I—they loved him, little sister. He was like another son to them. I've never had to tell anyone how their son died before."

He felt her hand lightly on his shoulder, and looked up. The sadness that never quite left her face was plain in her eyes. A single tear slid slowly down her cheek, and she did not trouble to wipe it away. He reached up, and brushed it away with gentle fingers.

"I miss him," she said simply. "I miss him every day. If it weren't for what I felt when he—left—it would be unbearable. At least—I know he must be happy. I have that. They don't even have that much comfort."

"I'm glad I got Dirk to go home for that reason, too," Skif replied quietly. "Kris was something special to him—more than a friend, more than anyone else could ever be, I think. When he finally let himself grieve, he needed his family around him . . ."

He took both of her hands in his own and they sat in silence for long moments, mourning their loss.

"Well," he coughed a little, "I wish you had the leisure to wait on this until you were entirely well again."

"I know. So do I." Talia sighed. "But as soon as I can use my feet again, I *have* to return to duty; in fact, Selenay wrote me herself yesterday that if it weren't so damnably painful for me to move, she'd have me on duty now."

"I know, too. Well, it can't be helped. Listen—I have got to tell you what that tribe is like—" Skif launched into a series of affectionate descriptions of the various members of Dirk's family, and had the pleasure of seeing some of the sorrow leave her eyes.

"So that's the last of them," he concluded. Then he noticed a basket of sewing beside her—and none of the garments were her own! "What's all this?" he asked, holding up an enormous shirt with both sleeves pulling out.

Talia blushed a charming crimson. "I can't go anywhere except this couch or my bed. I'm tired of reading, I can't handle my harp very long without hurting myself, and I can't stand having nothing to do. I suppose it goes back to my farmgirl days, when I wasn't even allowed to read without having a task in my hands. So since my embroidery is bad enough to make a cat laugh, I made Elspeth hunt out all of Dirk's clothing, and I've been mending it. I can't keep him from looking rumpled, but at least I can keep him from looking like a rag-bag!"

Before Skif could tease her further, the sound of a familiar footstep—taking the tower stairs three at a time—caused her to direct all her attention to the open door, her visitor momentarily forgotten.

There was no mistaking it—it could only be Dirk. Skif bounced to his feet and took himself out of the way before Dirk reached the door, not wanting to intrude on their greeting. Every time Dirk had spoken of Talia when he'd been with his family, he'd practically glowed. It had been that, at least in part, that had convinced them that all was well. Well, if Skif had thought he'd glowed when he only spoke of Talia, he was incandescent when he saw her waiting for him, with both her hands stretched yearningly out toward him. A quick glance at her proved that she was equally radiant.

Dirk was across the room in a few steps and went to one knee beside her, taking both her hands in his and kissing them gently. What would have been a hopelessly melodramatic scene for anyone else seemed natural for them. Talia drew his hands toward her and laid her cheek against them, and the expression on her face made Skif hold his breath and freeze absolutely still lest he break the mood.

"Has it been very bad, my love?" Dirk asked, so softly Skif could barely make out the words.

"I don't know—while you were gone, all I could think of was how I wished you were here; and now you're here, I'm too busy being glad you're with me," she replied teasingly.

"Why then I must needs find a way to shrink thee, and carry thee in my pocket always," he said tenderly, falling into the speech-mode of his childhood.

Talia freed one hand from his and laid it softly along his cheek. "Would not having me in thy pocket soon make thee tired of my company?"

"Not so long as it spares thee any pain at all. Oh, have a care to thyself, little bird!" he murmured. "Thou hast my soul in thy keeping, and without thee, I would be nothing but an empty, dead shell!"

His tone was jesting, but the light in his eyes said that he spoke nothing less than the truth.

"Oh, beloved, then we are surely lost beyond redemption," she whispered, "for in truth I find myself in the like case. Thou hast mine in trade for thine."

Their joy in each other seemed to brighten the very air around them.

Skif soon realized, however, that it is only possible to go without breathing for a limited amount of time. On the other hand, he couldn't bear the notion that his interference would break the mood of the two before him.

"Dearest," Talia said, with laughter in her voice, "my brotherling Skif is trying to decide between disturbing us and fainting from lack of air—"

Dirk chuckled, and turned his head slightly so that he could see Skif out of the corner of his eye. "Thought I hadn't noticed you were there, did you? Come out of your corner, and stop pretending you're here to pick pockets!"

To Skif's intense relief, the mood had *not* broken. Perhaps the glow had been dimmed a little, but if so, it had been a deliberate action on their part, to make it easier for him. As he took a chair and pulled it nearer to the couch, Dirk removed the pillows behind Talia and took their place. Now she was leaning on his chest and shoulder instead, one of his arms protectively circling her. The vague shadow of anxiety was gone from his face, and the pain that had faintly echoed in her eyes was gone as well. There was a "rightness" about them that defied analysis.

No sooner were they all settled again when more footsteps could be heard running up the stairs. Elspeth came bursting into the room, her arms full of glorious scarlet silk.

"Talia, the dresses are done! Has—" She stopped short at the sight of Dirk, and gave a whoop of joy. She threw the dress at Skif (who caught it gingerly), and danced around to grab both of Dirk's ears and plant an enthusiastic kiss squarely on his mouth.

"Well!" he said, when he could finally speak. "If that's how I'm going to get greeted on my return, I'm going to go away more often!"

"Oh, horse manure," Elspeth giggled, then rescued Skif from the folds of the dress, and planted an equally enthusiastic kiss on his mouth. "I'm just glad to see you for Talia's sake. She's been drooping like a wilted lily since you left!"

"Elspeth!" Talia protested.

"I'm *just* as glad to see Skif. More—he can help me. Or hadn't you heard, oh, cloud-scraper? You get to help me with putting this wedding together. Talia can't, and Dirk hasn't been here."

"And besides that, Dirk has no idea of what is supposed to go on at weddings," Dirk said ruefully. "If you told me I was supposed to suspend myself by my knees from a treelimb, I'd probably believe you."

"Oooh—what a wonderful opportunity!" Elspeth sparkled with mischief. "Maybe I'll do that. No, I'd better not. Talia might tell you to beat me."

"I'd do worse than have Dirk beat you," Talia twinkled back. "I'd tell Alberich that I thought you were shirking your practices."

"You *are* a beast, aren't you? Are you safe to hug, dearling?"

"As of this morning, quite safe."

With that assurance, Elspeth bent over the Heralds and hugged Talia with warmth and enthusiasm, then tweaked Dirk's nose with an impudent grin.

"I have been wanting to do that for *eons*," she said, snatching a pillow from the pile that Dirk had displaced and seating herself on the floor at Talia's feet.

"The hug, or the nose?" Dirk asked.

"Both—but the hug more." She turned to Skif. "You wouldn't know, since you were gone, too—but you hardly knew where you could touch her, at first. Poor Dirk, practically all he could touch were her fingertips before he left!"

"Oh, I found a *few* other places," Dirk chuckled, and Talia blushed furiously. "So tell me, what new and wonderful plans for this fiasco have you managed to crush since I've been gone?"

"You'll adore this one—and it's new today. The Lord Marshal thought it would be a grand idea to load Talia up on a flower-bedecked platform and carry her to the priest on the shoulders of half the Heralds in the Kingdom. You know, like the image of the Goddess in a Midsummer pageant."

"Oh, *no!*" Talia plainly was torn between laughter and embarrassment.

"Oh, *yes!* And once I'd managed to convince him that poor Talia would probably die of mortification if anyone even suggested it, the Lord Patriarch came storming in, demanding to know why the thing wasn't being held in the High Temple!"

"Lord of Lights!"

"After I'd told him that since the Companions had a big part in the rescue, they were being invited, too, he agreed that the High Temple probably wasn't the best site."

"I can just see Dantris helping himself to the Goddess' lilies out of sheer mischief," Dirk muttered.

"Dantris? Bright Havens, love, Rolan and Ahrodie would probably decide to watch from the choir loft and leave hoofmarks all over the hardwood floor!" Talia replied. "And to think that all I ever wanted was a private pledging with a few friends."

"Then you shouldn't have been Chosen Queen's Own," Elspeth

told her sweetly. "You're a figure of national importance, so you can't begrudge people their fun any more than I can."

"And I suppose it's too late to back out now."

"Out of the wedding, or being Queen's Own?" Dirk chuckled.

"Guess."

"I'd rather not. I might not like the answer."

"Look," Elspeth interjected, "since Skif is right here now, why don't I drag him off and tell him what I've gotten set up so far? That way we won't be interrupted."

"Good idea," Dirk approved.

Elspeth gathered up her dress and drew Skif with her into the bedroom, shutting the door after them.

"I really don't need any help in getting these things organized, but let's pretend I do, all right? And let's take lots of time about it," Elspeth said in a low voice. "Being Heir has *some* advantages. As long as it's me that's up here, nobody is going to come bursting in on them the way they do when the Healers aren't with her. You'd think people would give them a *little* time alone! But even though he's just gotten back, they won't."

"But—why?"

"Why are people always up here? A lot of reasons. The Lord Marshal always manages to think up something more about Ancar he'd like to know. Kyril and Hyron are always asking about Hulda. Only the gods know what her powers could mean. Even her friends, Lady bless 'em, are always coming in to 'make sure that she's all right.' Havens, I'm as bad as they are! Here, as long as you're here, you can help me—I want to show this off." She hid behind the wardrobe door for a moment, emerging in the scarlet dress. "Lace me up, would you? Then there's the emergencies, though gods be thanked we haven't had any really bad ones, like the backlash of a Herald getting killed." Her face clouded. "Except for poor Nessa. Well, Talia fixed that quickly enough, once she was well enough to handle it."

"Gods, does everyone in the world pop in and out of here?"

"Sometimes it seems that way. You know, I don't think anyone ever really realized how *many* lives she's touched until we thought we'd lost her. That dress, for instance—have you ever seen anything like that fabric in your life?"

"Never." Skif admired the gown, with an eye trained by thieving to evaluate it; it was of scarlet silk, and patterned through the scarlet of the main fabric were threads of pure gold and deep vermilion. It was incredible stuff.

"Neither have I—and I have seen a *lot* of Court gowns. It came by special messenger, after Dirk had them keep watch for the trader who smuggled in the argonel and the arrows to her, then got the message out to Rolan. Dirk was hoping he could find him and thank him, and let him know she was all right. Well, he managed to get back across the Border before Ancar closed his side, and he got Dirk's message and sent this in reply. The note that went with it said that among his people the bride always wore scarlet, and while he knew that this would not be the case among us, he hoped his 'little gift' could be put to good use. 'Little gift!' Mother said that the last time she saw anything like this it was priced at a rate that would purchase a small town!" Elspeth finished tying up the laces in back. "Talia thought it would be lovely to use it for attendants' dresses. I am not going to argue with her! Mother would never get me anything like this unless they discovered diamonds growing on the trees in Sorrows!" She wiggled sensuously. "Then there was the other truly strange gift. Did she ever tell you about the woman she helped up in Berrybay? The one they called 'Weatherwitch'?"

"A bit."

"Out of the blue came this really *elderly* Herald—I mean, he was *supposed* have retired, that's how old. He came with a message from this Weatherwitch person—the *exactly* perfect day to have the wedding, and you know fall weather. Since we're having it outside, we'd been a good bit worried about that. Talia says Maeven's never wrong, so that's why we're having it then."

She pressed her ear briefly against the door and giggled. "I think it's safe enough to go out now, but I'll bet it wasn't a few minutes ago. Let's go show off."

As far as Skif could tell, neither Talia nor Dirk had moved an inch since they'd left them—although Talia's hair was a trifle mussed, and both of them wore preoccupied and dreaming expressions.

"Well, what do you think?" Elspeth asked, posing dramatically.

"I think it looks wonderful. No one in their right mind is going to be watching me with you and Jeri around," Talia said admiringly.

"Well, Elspeth and I are agreed; we'll take care of the wedding arrangements," Skif said with a proprietary air. "That will free you up a bit more, Dirk—that is, if you don't mind."

"I don't mind at all, and I think it's very good of you," Dirk replied, surprised. "Especially since you know very well that I don't have to be freed up to do anything except spend more time up here."

"That *was* the general idea," Elspeth said mockingly.

"Enough, enough! It's settled then," he laughed, "and much thanks to you both."

"Remember that the next time I do something wrong!" Elspeth giggled back.

She teased Dirk for a few moments longer—then her face clouded with anxiety when she realized that Talia had fallen asleep. She'd been doing that a great deal lately, sometimes right in the middle of a conversation. Elspeth was afraid that this was a sign that she would never be quite well again.

But Dirk and Skif just exchanged amused glances while Dirk settled the sleeping Herald a little more comfortably on his shoulder. Elspeth heaved an audible sigh of relief at this; surely if anyone would know if something were wrong, Dirk would.

Dirk hadn't missed the anxious look or the sigh of relief.

"It's nothing important," he told her; quietly, to avoid waking Talia.

"He's right—honestly!" Skif assured her. "Dirk's mother told us she'll be dropping off like this. It's just a side-effect of speed-Healing. It has something to do with all the energy you're using, and all the strain you're putting on yourself. She says it's the same kind of effect you'd get if you ran twenty or thirty miles, swam a river, and climbed a mountain or two, then stayed up three days straight."

"According to mother," Dirk continued, "it has to do with—fatigue poisons?—I think that's what she called them. When you speed-Heal, they build up faster than the body can get rid of them, and the person you're Healing tends to fall asleep a lot. When they stop the speed-Healing, she'll stop falling asleep all the time."

"Show-off," Skif taunted.

Dirk grinned and shrugged. "See all the useless information you pick up when you're a Healer's offspring?"

Elspeth protested; "Useless, my eye! I thought for sure there was something wrong that nobody wanted to tell me about—like there was when she wouldn't wake up. Nobody ever thinks to tell me *anything* anymore!"

"Well, imp," Dirk retorted, "that's the price you pay for poking your nose into things all the time. People think you already know everything!"

The Border was officially closed, but refugees kept slipping across every night, each of them with a worse tale to tell than the last. Selenay had had a premonition that Ancar wasn't quite through with Valdemar, and had stayed on the Border with a force built mainly of the defectors from Hardorn's army, now fanatically devoted to her. She had been absolutely right.

This time the attack came at night, preceded by a storm Selenay suspected of being mage-caused. There was a feint in the direction of the Border Guardpost, a strong enough feint that it would have convinced most leaders that the attack there was genuine.

But Selenay had Davan—a Farseer—and Alberich—a Foreseer—with her, and knew better. Ancar meant to regain some of his lost soldiers—and plant some traitors in Selenay's new Border Guards. And to do both, he was going to use some of the *other* talents of what was left of his army of thieves and murderers.

But the force of black-clad infiltrators who attempted to penetrate the stockade-enclosed village that housed the defectors and their dependents met with a grave surprise.

They got all the way to the foot of the stockade, when suddenly—

Light! Blinding light burst above their heads, light nearly as bright as day. As they cringed, and looked up through watering eyes, four white-clad figures appeared above them, and out of the darkness at the top of the stockade fence rose hundreds of angry men and women armed with bows, who in no way wished to return to the man who called himself their King. Suspended from the trees by thin wires were burning balls of some unknown substance that flamed with a white ferocity.

"You could have knocked," Griffon called down to them. "We'd have been glad to let you in."

"But perhaps it is that this is no friendly visit—" Alberich dodged as one of those below threw a knife at him in desperation.

"B'God, Alberich, I believe you might be right," Davan dodged a second missile. "Majesty?"

"Take them," Selenay ordered shortly.

A few were taken alive; what they had to tell was interesting. More interesting by far was the assortment of drugs and potions they had intended to use on the village well. Drugs that, according to those Selenay questioned under Truth Spell, would open the minds of those that took them to the influence of Ancar's mages—and Ancar himself.

That told them much about what Ancar was currently able to accomplish. What happened next on Ancar's side of the Border told them more.

He fortified it, created a zone a mile deep in which he allowed neither farm nor dwelling place—then left it. And neither Foreseer nor Farseer could see him doing anything offensive for some time.

So for the moment, Ancar's knife was no longer at Valdemar's throat—and Selenay felt free to come home to resume her Throne, and in time for Talia's wedding.

*   *   *

Companion's Field was the only suitable place within easy reach of the Collegium that could hold all the people expected to attend. The wedding site had to be within easy reach, because Talia's feet were still not healed. The Healers were satisfied that the bones had all set well (after so many sessions of arranging the tiny fragments that nonHealers had begun to wonder if her feet would ever be usable) but they had only begun to knit, and she had been absolutely forbidden to put one ounce of weight on them. That meant that wherever she needed to go, she had to be carried.

The Healers had chosen not to put the kind of plaster casts on her that they had used to hold Keren's broken hip in place. This was mostly because they needed to be able to monitor the Healing they were doing on a much finer level than they had with Keren, but also partially because such casts would have been a considerable burden on a body already heavily taxed and exhausted. Instead they constructed stiff half-boots of glue, wood strips, and hardened leather, all lined with lambswool felt. These had been made in two halves that laced together and could be removed at will. Talia had been much relieved by this solution, needless to say.

"Can you imagine trying to bathe with those plaster things on your feet?" she'd said with a comical expression. "Or trying to find some way of covering them during the wedding? Or finding someone strong enough to carry me and all that damned plaster as well?"

"Not to mention Dirk's displeasure at trying to deal with them afterward—" Elspeth had teased, while Talia blushed.

Elspeth was waiting in Talia's room, watching Keren and Jeri put the final touches on her hair and face. The Heir privately thought that Talia was lovely enough to make anyone's heart break. She was still thin, and very pale from her ordeal, but that only served to make her more attractive, in an odd way. It was rather as if she'd been distilled into the true essence of herself—or tempered and honed like an heirloom blade. They'd taken great pains with her dress of white silk and silver, designing something that draped well when the wearer was being carried and extended past her feet to cover the ugly leather boots. By the same token, nothing would fall far enough to the floor that the person carrying her would be likely to trip over it. Jeri had given her a very simple hairstyle to complement the simplicity of the dress, and her only ornaments were fresh flowers.

" 'Nobody in their right mind is going to look at me with you and

Jeri around,'" Elspeth quoted to Keren under her breath, her eyes sparkling with laughter. "Bright Havens, next to her I look like a half-
fledged red heron!"

"I hope after all this time you women are finally ready," Dirk announced as he came through the door, for once in his life totally immaculate, and resplendent in white velvet.

"Dirk!" Jeri laughed, interposing herself between him and Talia.
"Tradition says you're not supposed to see the bride until you meet
before the priest!"

"Tradition be damned. The only reason I'm letting Skif carry her at
all is because if I try and manage her *and* her ring, I'll drop one of the
two!"

"Oh, all right. I can see you're too stubborn to argue with." She
stepped aside, and at the sight of one another, they seemed to glow
from deep within.

"Two hours I spend on her," Jeri muttered under her breath, obviously amused, "and in two eyeblinks *he* makes everything I did look
insignificant."

Dirk gathered her up carefully, holding her in his arms as if she
weighed next to nothing. "Ready, loveling?" he asked softly.

"I've been ready forever," she replied, never once taking her eyes
from his.

The Field was alive with color; Healer Green, Bard Scarlet, Guard
Blue—the muted grays, pale greens, and red-brown of the students
moving among them, the gilded and bejeweled courtiers catching the
sun. Most prevalent, of course, was Heraldic White, and not just because even more Heralds had managed to appear for this occasion than
had arrived for Elspeth's fealty ceremony. Half of the white figures in
the crowd were Companions, be-flowered and be-ribboned by the
loving hands of their Chosen, and looking for all the world as if it were
they who were being wedded. Even Cymry's foal had a garland—
though he kept trying to eat it.

The ceremony was a simple one, though it was not one that was
often performed—for the wedding of a lifebonded couple was less of a
promising than an affirmation. Despite well-meaning efforts to the
contrary, Skif and Elspeth had managed to keep the pomp and ritual to
an absolute minimum.

Dirk carried his love as far as the priest, handing her very carefully
to Skif, who felt proud and happy enough when he did so to burst.
Elspeth gave him Talia's ring, and he slipped it onto her finger. Skif
and Elspeth both bit their lips to keep from shedding a tear or two at

that moment; partially because she'd moved Kris' friendship ring to the finger next to it, and partially because the wedding ring was still so large for her.

Dirk repeated his vows in a voice that seemed soft, but carried to the edge of the crowd. Then Talia took his ring from Keren, slipped it onto his ring-finger and made her own vows in her clear, sweet voice.

Dirk took her back from Skif—and as he did so, the massed Heralds cheered spontaneously.

Somehow, it seemed totally appropriate.

The wedded couple was enthroned on a pile of cushions brought by every hand in the Collegium, with Talia arranged so that she could see everything without having to strain herself. Elcarth waited until most of the well-wishers had cleared away, and Talia and Dirk were pretty much alone before strolling over to them.

He shook his head at the sight. "I hope you two realize this display of yours is fevering the imaginations of an entire generation of Bards," he said with mock-severity. "I hesitate to think of all the truly awful creations we'll have to suffer through for the next year from the students alone—and every full Bard is going to be determined that *he* will be the writer of the next 'Sun and Shadow.'"

"Oh, gods," Dirk groaned. "I never thought of that. D'you suppose I could give her back?"

Talia eyed him speculatively. "We *could* always have a horrible fight here and now." She hefted a wine bottle, appraising its weight. "This would make a lovely dent in his skull—not to mention the truly spectacular effect it will have when the bottle breaks and the red wine splashes all over that spotless white velvet." She considered it and him for a long moment, then sighed. "No, it just won't do. I might get some of the wine on me. And if I knock him cold, how will I get back to my room?"

"And if I give her away, who will I sleep with tonight?" Dirk added, as Talia giggled. "Sorry, Elcarth. You're just going to have to suffer. What can we do for you?"

"Actually, there is something. I wanted to let you both know what the Circle has decided about Dirk's assignments."

Talia stiffened a little, but otherwise gave no sign that she was dreading what Elcarth's next words might contain.

"First of all—I am retiring as Dean. I intend to stay on as Historian, but to handle both positions is a little more than I can manage these days. I'm a lot older than I look, I'm afraid, and I'm beginning to feel the years. Teren is replacing me. Dirk, *you* are replacing Teren as Orientation instructor, as well as working with training students in their Gifts."

Talia was stunned; she'd expected to learn that he was being given a new partner, or that he would be assigned Sector duty at the least. She had partially resigned herself to the idea, telling herself that having him part of the time was a distinct improvement over not having him at all.

"Elcarth—you can't be serious—" Dirk protested. "I'm no kind of a scholar, you know that! If the Circle is trying to do us a favor by giving us preferential treatment . . ."

"Then we'd rather you didn't," Talia finished for him.

"My dear children! It is *not* preferential treatment that you are getting. Dirk, you will still be expected to take on the kinds of special jobs you used to, make no mistake about it. The only thing we're really pulling you off is riding the problem Sectors. We've picked you to replace Teren for the same reason we picked him to replace Werda as Orientation instructor; your ability to handle children. Both of you are able to take confused, frightened children and give them warmth, reassurance, and the certain knowledge that they are in a place where they belong and have friends. Dirk, you have demonstrated that over and over in training Gifts—the way you brought Griffon along, giving him confidence without once making him feel that his Gift was a frightening or dangerous one, was nothing short of masterful—and look at the result! He trusted you so completely that he linked with you without asking the why or wherefore; he trusted you enough to follow your directions exactly, and now Griffon is the unsung hero of the Battle of Demons. That kind of ability in a teacher is much rarer than scholasticism, and it's one we need. So let's hear no more about 'preferential treatment,' shall we?"

Dirk sighed with relief, and his arm tightened around Talia. She thanked Elcarth with her shining eyes; no words were necessary.

"That isn't *quite* all. You'll also be working with Kyril—Dirk on a regular basis, Talia as time permits. This is the first we've ever heard of the Companions augmenting anyone's abilities purposefully except in chronicles so old we can't winnow fable from truth; we'd like to know if it's something that any Herald can take advantage of, or if it's something peculiar to you two and Elspeth, or even if it's peculiar to your Companions. Before Kyril's through with you, you may wish yourself back in the field again!"

They laughed a little ruefully; Kyril drove himself mercilessly in the cause of investigating Heraldic Gifts, and would expect no less from them.

"Last of all, I bring your wedding gift from the Circle; the next two weeks are yours to do with as you like. We can all get along without either of you for that long. Talia still has to have her sessions with the Healers, of course, but barring that—well, if you should choose to vanish on a few overnight trips, no one will come looking for you. After all, Talia, you may not be able to walk, but you can certainly ride! Just make sure you schedule everything with your Healers. The last thing I need or want is to have Devan after my head! That man can be positively vicious!"

Talia laughed, and promised; she could tell by the speculative glint in Dirk's eyes that he already had a destination or two in mind. They traded a few more pleasantries with Elcarth, then the Historian—Dean no longer, and that would take some getting used to—took himself off.

Dirk shook his head. "I never, ever pictured myself as a teacher," he said quietly. "That was always Kr—"

He choked off the end of the name.

"That was what Kris wanted," Talia finished, watching him. "You've been avoiding speaking about him, love. Why?"

"Fear," he replied frankly. "Fear that I'd hurt you—fear I'd be hurt myself. I—I still don't really know how you felt about each other—"

"All you ever had to do was ask," she said softly, and drew him into rapport with gentle mental fingers.

After a moment he raised his eyes to hers and smiled. "And you said emotions don't speak clearly. So that's how it was?"

She nodded. "No more, no less. He tried to tell you, but you weren't hearing."

"I wasn't, was I?" He sighed. "Gods—I miss him. I miss him so damn much. . . ."

"We lost more than a friend when we lost him," she said, hesitating over the words. "I think—I think we lost a part of ourselves."

He was silent for a long moment. "Talia, what happened after he died? You said some very strange things when you answered my call and came back to us."

She shook her head slightly, her brow wrinkled in thought. "Love, I'm not sure. It's not very clear, and it's all mixed up with pain and fever and drug-dreams. All I can tell you for certain is that I *wanted* to die, and I *should* have died—but something kept me from dying."

"Or someone."

"Or someone," she agreed. "Maybe it *was* Kris. That's who my memories say it was."

"I have a lot to thank him for, and not just that," he said thoughtfully.

"Hm?"

"You learned from him about loving before those beasts hurt you."

"It helped," she said, after a long moment of thought.

"Loveling, are you ready to go through with this?" he asked after a pause. "Are you sure?"

For answer she kissed him with rapport still strung between them. When they came up for air he chuckled, much more relaxed.

"Hedonist," he said.

"At least," she agreed, wrinkling her nose at him, then sobered again. "Yes, there are scars—but you have them, too. The wounds are healed—I'm not the only Healer of minds, you know—just the only one that's a Herald as well. Rynee—she's very good, as good as I am. Besides, I refuse to let what happened ruin what's between us—and really, all they did was hurt my body, they didn't touch *me*. What happened to you was worse—Naril raped your soul."

"That's healed, too," he said quietly.

"Then leave it in the dead past. No one goes through life without picking up a scar or two." She nestled closer to him as someone else came to offer their congratulations.

Then suddenly sat up. "Gods!"

"What?" Dirk asked, anxious until he saw that there was no sign of pain on her face. "What is it?"

"Back on my internship—that business with Maeven Weatherwitch—she ForeSaw something for me, and I couldn't even guess what she meant, then. *Now* I know! She said that I would see the Havens but that love and duty would bar me from them—and—"

She faltered.

"And?" he prompted, gently.

"That—my greatest joy would be preceded by my greatest grief. Oh, gods—if only I'd known—if only I'd *guessed*—"

"You could never have anticipated what happened," Dirk replied with such force that she shook off her anguish to stare at him. "*No one* could. Don't ever blame yourself. Don't you think that with all the ForeSeers among the Heralds if there had been any way of preventing what happened it would have been done?"

She sighed, and relaxed again. "You're right . . ." she said, slowly. "You're right."

*   *   *

The celebrating continued on well past dusk, until at last, by ones and twos, the wedding guests began to drift away. Some were heading for other gatherings—like the one Talia and Dirk knew their fellow Heralds *must* be having somewhere. Some had more private affairs in mind. Finally Talia and Dirk were left alone, a state with which they were not at all displeased.

She rested contentedly on his shoulder, both of his arms lightly around her, and watched the stars blossoming overhead.

"It's getting chilly," she said at last.

"Are you cold?"

"A little."

"Well," he chuckled, "they've certainly made it easy for us to depart unnoticed."

"I'm fairly certain that was on purpose. All that cheering was embarrassing enough, without chivaree, too."

"It could have been worse. Think of the flower-bedecked platform! Think of Companions in the High Temple! Think of the life-sized sugar replicas of both of us!"

"I'd rather not!" She laughed.

"Ready to go?"

"Yes," she said, putting her arms around his neck so that he could lift her.

He took her up the stairs to her rooms—now *their* rooms—this time taking them one at a time, and slowly, so as not to jar her.

To their mutual surprise, they found Elspeth seated on the top step.

"What on earth are you doing here?" he asked.

"Guarding your threshold, oh, magnificent one. It was the students' idea. We took it turn and turn about since you left this morning. Except for during the ceremony itself that is—we left the staircase booby-trapped then. Not that we're suspicious of anyone, mind, but we did want to make certain no one could get in to play any little tricks while you were gone. Some people have very rotten ideas about what's funny. Anyway, that's *our* wedding present." With that, she skipped down the stairs without waiting for thanks.

" 'The caring heart,' " Talia said softly. "She'll be a good Queen, one day."

Dirk nudged the door open with his foot, placed Talia carefully on her couch inside, then turned to close it and throw the latch.

"Not that *I'm* suspicious of anyone," he said with a gleam in his eye, "but a certain earlier performance of yours makes me wish to be certain that we're undisturbed."

"Not *quite* yet," she said with a smile. "First I've got a bride-gift for you."

"A what?"

"One *good* custom of my people. The bride always has a gift for her husband. It's over there—on the hearth."

"But—" For a moment he was speechless. "Talia, that's My Lady. She's *your* harp, I couldn't take her!"

"Look again."

He did—and realized that there was a second harp hidden in the shadows. He pulled both of them out into the light and scrutinized them closely.

"I can't tell them apart," he admitted at last.

"Well, I can, but I've had My Lady for years, I know every line of her grain. No one else can, though. They're twins, made by the same hand, from the same wood; they're even the same age. No—" She held up a warning hand. "Don't ask me where or how I found it. That's *my* secret. But in return for this one, you'll have to promise to teach me to play My Lady as well as she deserves to be played."

"Willingly—gladly. We can play duets—like—"

"Like you and Kris used to play," she finished for him when he could not. "Love—I think it's time for one last gift—" and she touched his mind, sharing with him the incredulous joy that had marked Kris' passing.

"Gods—oh, gods, that helps . . . you must know how much that helps," he managed after a moment. "Now if only—I wish I could know for certain that he knows about us—about now."

He lifted her from the couch to move to the bedroom.

"If I were to have one wish granted, that would be mine, too," she replied, her cheek resting against the velvet of his tunic. "He told me once that it was his own dearest wish to see the two people he loved most find happiness with each other—"

She would have said more, but a familiar perfume wreathed around her, and she gasped.

"What's wrong? Did you hurt something?" Dirk asked anxiously.

"There—on the bed—"

Lying on the coverlet, in the middle and heart-high, was a spray of the little flowers known as Maiden's Hope. Dirk set her down on the bed and she picked it up with trembling hands.

"Did you put this here?" she asked in a voice that shook.

"No."

"And no one else has been here since we left—" In hushed tones she continued: "When Kris gave me this ring, it was around a Midsummer bouquet of those flowers. I'd never smelled anything like them before—and he promised he'd find some for my wedding garland if he had to grow them himself—but I've never seen them anywhere around here—"

"There's more to it than that, little bird," Dirk said, taking the flowers from her and regarding them with wondering eyes. "This flower *only* blooms for the week before and after Midsummer. We're well into fall. They can't be grown in hothouses. People have tried. To find even one bloom, much less as many as this, would take a miracle. No human could do it."

They looked from the flowers to each other—and slowly began to smile; smiles that, for the first time in weeks, had no underlying hint of sadness.

Dirk took her into his arms, with the flowers held between them. "We've had our wish—shall we give him his?"

She carefully reached behind her, and inserted the blossoms into the vase on her nightstand.

"Yes," she breathed, turning back to him, and beginning to touch him with her rapport even as she touched her lips to his. "I think we should."

APPENDIX

Songs of Valdemar

Her Father's Eyes

Lyrics: Mercedes Lackey   Music: Kristoph Klover

(Selenay: *Arrows of the Queen*)

How tenuous the boundary between love and hate—
How easy to mistake the first, and learn the truth too late—
How hard to bear what brings to mind mistakes that we
    despise—
And when I look into her face, I see her father's eyes.

He tried to steal away my throne—he tried to rule my life—
And I am not made to forgive, a cowed and coward wife!
My love became my enemy who sought his Queen's demise—
And when I look into her face, I see her father's eyes.

Poor child, we battled over her as two dogs with a bone—
I should not see his treachery in temper-tantrums thrown—
I should not see betrayal where there's naught but childish
    lies—
But when I look into her face, I see her father's eyes.

Now how am I to deal with this rebellion in my soul?
I cannot treat her fairly when my own heart is not whole.

I truly wish to love her—but I'm not so strong, nor wise—
For when I look into her face, I see her father's eyes—
Only—her father's eyes.

First Love

Lyrics: Mercedes Lackey   Music: Frank Hayes

(Jadus: *Arrows of the Queen*)

Was it so long ago now that we met, you and I?
Both held fast in a passion that we could not deny?
If my hands gave you life, then your voice woke my heart—
From such simple beginnings, how such wonder may start!

Chorus:
Through my long, empty nights, through my cold, lonely days,
How you comfort and cheer me, delight and amaze—
And your soft silver voice could charm life into stone—
My sweet mistress of music, My Lady, my own.

With your sweet song to guide me you have taught me to care
How to open my soul to both love and despair
Though you're wood and bright silver, and not warm flesh and
    bone
I think no one here doubts you've a soul of your own.

And I know my own journey will too soon reach its end—
I must leave you with one I am proud to call friend.
How she opened my life when she opened my door!
Give her comfort, my dear one, when I am no more.

Holderkin Sheep-Song

Lyrics: Mercedes Lackey   Music: Ernie Mansfield

(Talia: *Arrows of the Queen*)

Silly sheep
Go to sleep.

We will watch around you keep
Though the night be dark and deep
Nothing past us dares to creep
Go to sleep.

Wooly heads
Have no dreads
Though we'd rather seek out beds
And our eyes are dull as leads
And we long for hearths and Steads
Have no dreads.

Do not fear
We are here
Though this watch is lone and drear
Lacking in all warmth and cheer
Till the morn again draws near
We are here.

In the night
Stars shine bright
And the moon is at her height
Lending us her little light
Nothing comes to give you fright
Stars shine bright.

With the day
We'll away
Leaving you to greet the day
Other shepherds watch you play
Keep you safe from all that prey
We'll away.
Silly sheep
Go to sleep.
We will watch around you keep
Go to sleep.
Go to sleep.

It Was a Dark and Stormy Night

Lyrics: Mercedes Lackey   Music: Leslie Fish

(Talia: *Arrows of the Queen*)

It was a dark and stormy night—or so the Heralds say—
And lightning striking constantly transformed the night to day
The thunder roared the castle round—or thusly runs the tale—
And rising from the Northeast Tower there came a fearful wail.

It was no beast nor banshee that, the castle folk knew well,
Nor prisoner in agony, nor demon trapped by spell,
No ghost that moaned in penance, nor a soul in mortal fright—
'Twas just the Countess "singing"—for she practiced every night.

The Countess was convinced that she should have been born a
    Bard
And thus she made the lives of those within her power hard.
For they must listen to her sing, and smile at what they heard,
And swear she had a golden voice that rivaled any bird.

The Countess was convinced that she had wedded 'neath her
    state
And so the worst lot fell upon her meek and mild mate.
Not only must the Count each night endure her every song
But suffer silent her abuse, be blamed for every wrong.

It was a dark and stormy night—or so the Bards aver—
And so perhaps that was the reason why there was no stir
When suddenly the "music" ceased; so when dawn raised his
    head
Within the Tower servants found the Countess stiff and dead.

The Heralds came at once to judge if there had been foul play.
They questioned all most carefully to hear what they would say.
And one fact most astounding to them quickly came to light—
That *every* moment of the Count was vouched for on that night.

The castle folk by ones and twos came forward on their own
To swear the Count had never once that night been all alone.

So though the Tower had been locked tight, with two keys to
the door,
One his, one hers; the Count of guilt was plain absolved for
sure.

At length the Heralds then pronounced her death as "suicide."
And all within the district voiced themselves quite satisfied.
It was a verdict, after all, that none wished to refute—
Though no one could imagine why she'd try to eat her
lute.

Musings

Lyrics: Mercedes Lackey   Music: Mercedes Lackey

(Selenay: *Arrows of the Queen*)

How did you grow so wise, so young?
Tell me, Herald, tell me.
How did you grow so wise, so young, Queen's Own?
Where did you learn the words to say
That take my pain and guilt away
And give me strength again today
To sit upon my throne?

How could you be so brave, so young?
Tell me, Herald, tell me.
How could you be so brave, so young, Queen's Own?
How do you overcome your fear?
To know my path was never clear
While knowing Death walks ever near
Would chill me to the bone.

How can you be so kind, so young?
Tell me, Herald, tell me.
How can you be so kind, so young, Queen's Own?
To see the best, and not the worst—
To soothe an anger, pain, or thirst—
To always think of others first
And never self alone.

* * *

Where did you learn to love so young?
Tell me, Herald, tell me.
Where did you learn to love so young, Queen's Own?
How did you teach your heart to care—
To touch in ways I would not dare?
Oh, where did you find the courage? Where?
Ah, Herald—how you've grown!

Philosophy

Lyrics: Mercedes Lackey   Music: Kristoph Klover

(Skif: *Arrows of the Queen*)

What's the use of living if you never learn to laugh?
Look at me, I grew up down among the riff and raff
But you won't catch me glooming 'round without a hint of
    smile
And when I have to do a thing, I do it right, with style!

Chorus:
'Cause if you're gonna be the one to take that tightrope walk,
And if you're gonna be the one to make the gossips talk,
If it's your job to be the one who always takes the chance,
And if you have to cross thin ice—then cross it in a dance!

Now take the time when I was "borrowing" a thing or two—
The owner of the house walked in—well, what was I to do?
I bowed and said, "Don't stir yourself," before he raised a
    shout,
"Thanks for your hospitality, I'll find my own way out!"

I'd just come up a chimney, I was black from head to toe—
Climbed to the yard to find a watchman—wouldn't you just
    know!
But in the dark he took me for a demon, I would bet,
'Cause when I howled and went for him—I think he's running
    yet!

* * *

Take my Companion—did you know I thought to steal her
    too?
This pretty horse out in the street, no owner in my view—
I grabbed her reins and hopped aboard, I thought I was home
    free,
Until I looked into her eyes—and now the joke's on me!

'Cause now *I've* got to be the one to take that tightrope walk
And now *I've* got to be the one who'll make the gossips talk,
And it's my job to be the one who always takes the chance—
But when I have to cross thin ice, I'll cross it in a dance!

Laws

Lyrics: Mercedes Lackey   Music: Leslie Fish

(Skif: *Arrows of the Queen*)

The Law of the Streetwise is "grab all you can
For there's nothing that's true—nothing lasts."
The Law of the Dodger is "learn all the dirt—
The most pious of priests have their pasts."
The Law of the Grifter is "cheat the fool first
Or the one who'll be cheated is you."
But the Law of the Herald is "give all you can
For some day you will need a gift too."

The Law of the Liar is "there is no truth
It is all shades of meaning and greed."
The Law of the Hopeless is "never believe
For all faith is a hollowed-out reed."
The Law of the Empty is "there's nothing more,
Life is nothing but shadow and air."
But the Law of the Herald is "Seek out and find."
And the Law of the Heralds is "Care."

The Law of the Hunted is "guard your own back,
For the enemy strikes from behind."
The Law of the Greedy is "trust no one else,
Hide and hoard anything that you find."

The Law of the Hater is "crush and destroy,"
And the Law of the Bigot is "kill."
But the Law of the Herald is "faith, hope and trust,"
And the strength of the Herald is will.

All these Laws I have learned from the first to the
last
From the ones who would teach me they're true—
And full many the ones who taught anger and fear,
But the ones who taught hope—they were few.
And I ask myself, "Which is the Law I must take,
Fitting truth as a hand fits a glove?"
Then I chose, and I never looked back from that day,
For the Law of the Heralds is "Love."

The Face Within

Lyrics: Mercedes Lackey   Music: Kristoph Klover and Larry Warner

(Dirk and Kris: *Arrow's Flight*)

The Weaponsmaster has no heart; his hide is iron-cold
His soul within that hide is steel; or so I have been told.
His only care is for your skill, his only love, his own.
And where another has a heart, he has a marble stone.

That's what the common wisdom holds, but common is not
    true.
For there is often truth behind what's in the common
    view.
And so it is the Herald's task that hidden truth to win
To see behind the face without and find the face within.
He goads his students into rage, he drives them into pain;
He mocks them and he does not care that tears may fall like
    rain.
He works them when they're weary, and rebukes them when
    they fail—
Cuts them to ribbons with his tongue, as they stand meek and
    pale—

*   *   *

And will our enemies be fair, or come on us behind?
And will they stay their tongues or in their words a weapon
    find?
Or wait till we are rested before making their attacks?
Or will they rather beat us down and then go for our backs?

But he has no compassion, does not care for man nor beast—
And when a student's gone, he does not notice in the least—
And no one calls this man their love, and no one calls him
    friend
And none can judge him by his face, or what he may intend.

But I have seen him speak the word that brings hope from de-
    spair—
Or drop the one-word compliment that makes a student care—
And I have seen his sorrow when he hears the Death Bell cry—
His soul-deep agony of doubt that nothing can deny—

For on his shoulders rests the job of fitting us for war
With nothing to give him the clue of what to train us for.
And if he fails it is not he that pays, but you and I—
And so he dies a little when he hears the Death Bell cry.

And now you know the face within hid by the face without
The pain that he must harbor, all the guilt and all the doubt.
The Weaponsmaster has a heart; so grant his stony mask
For you and I aren't strong enough to bear that kind of task.

Arrow's Flight

Lyrics: Mercedes Lackey   Music: Paul Espinoza

(Talia: *Arrow's Flight*)

Finding your center—not hard for a child—
But I am a woman now, patterned and grown.
Thrown out of balance, my Gift has run wild;
Never have I felt so lost and alone.
Now all the questions that I did not ask
Come back to haunt me by day and by night.

Finding your center—so simple a task—
And one that I fear I shall never set right.

Chorus:
Where has my balance gone, what did I know
That I have forgotten in Time's ebb and flow?
Wrong or right, dark or light, I cannot see—
For I've lost the heart of the creature called "me."

Doubt shatters certainty, fosters despair;
Guilt harbors weakness and fear makes me blind—
Fear of the secrets that I dare not share—
Lost in the spiral maze of my own mind.
Knowing the cost to us all if I fail—
Feeling that failure breathe cold at my back—
All I thought strong now revealed as so frail
That I could not weather one spiteful attack.

An arrow in flight must be sent with control—
But all my control was illusion at best.
Instinct alone cannot captain a soul—
Direction must be learned and not merely guessed.
Seeking with purpose, not flailing about—
Trusting in others as they trust in me—
Starting again from the shadows of doubt
Gods, how I fear what I yet know must be!

Chorus 2:
Finding my center, and with it, control;
Disciplined knowledge must now be my goal.
Knowing my limits, but judging what's right—
Till nothing can hinder the arrow in flight.

Fundamentals

Lyrics: Mercedes Lackey   Music: Kristoph Klover

(Kris: *Arrow's Flight*)

Ground and center; we begin
Feel the shape inside your skin

Feel the earth and feel the air—
Ground and center; "how" and "where."

Ground and center—don't just frown,
Find the leaks and lock them down.
Baby-games you never learned
Bring you pain you never earned.

Ground and center; *do* it, child
If you'd tame that Talent wild—
Girl, you learned it in your youth—
Life's not fair, and that's the truth.

Ground and center, once again;
You're not finished—*I'll* say when.
Ground and center in your sleep
Ground and center 'till you weep.

Ground and center; that's the way—
You might get somewhere, someday.
Yes, I know I'm being cruel
And you're as stubborn as a mule!

Ground and center, feel the flow
Can you tell which way to go?
Instinct's not enough, my friend—
Make it *reflex* in the end.

Ground and center; hold it tight—
Dammit, greenie, *that's not right!*
(Every tear you shed hurts me,
But that's the way it has to be.)

Ground and center; good, at last!
Once again; grab hard, hold fast.
Half asleep or half awake—
Both of us know what's at stake.

Ground and center; now it's sure;
What you have *now* will endure.
Forgive me what I had to do—
Healing hurts—you know that's true.

*   *   *

Ground and center; lover, friend—
You won't break, but now you bend.
Costly lesson, high the price—
But you won't have to learn it twice!

Otherlove

Lyrics: Mercedes Lackey   Music: Leslie Fish

(Talia: *Arrow's Flight*)

I need you as a friend, dear one,
I love you as a brother;
And my body lies beside you
While my heart yearns for another.
I wonder if you understand—
Beneath your careless guise
I seem to sense uneasiness
When looking in your eyes.

I need your help, my friend, and I
Had sworn to stand alone;
How foolish were the vows I made
My present plight has shown.
But don't mistake my need for love
However strong it seems—
For while I lie beside you
Someone else is in my dreams.

I wish that I could know your thoughts;
I only sense your pain—
Unease behind the smile you wear—
A haunted, sad refrain.
I would not be the cause of grief—
I've often told you so—
Yet there's a place within my heart
Where you, love, cannot go.

After Midnight

Lyrics: Mercedes Lackey   Music: Leslie Fish

(Kris: *Arrow's Flight*)

In the dead, dark hours after midnight
When the world seems to stop in its place,
You can see a little more clearly,
You can look your life in the face;
You can see the things that you have to—
Speak the words too true for the day.
In the dead, dark hours after midnight,
Little friend, will you listen—and stay?

In the time when I never knew you
I could view the world as my own—
I was God's own gift to his creatures,
And I wore an armor of stone.
I was wise and faithful and noble—
I was pompous, pious and cold.
I was cruel when I never meant it—
Far too cool to touch or to hold.

It was you who broke through my armor;
It was you who broke through the wall,
With your pain and your desperation—
How could I not answer your call?
How could I have guessed you would touch me,
And in ways I could not control?
How could I have known I would need you—
Or have guessed you'd see to my soul?

For as I taught you, so you taught me,
Taught me how to love and to care—
For your own love melted my armor,
Taught me how to feel and to dare.
When I looked tonight, I discovered
I could not again stand apart—
In the dead, dark hours after midnight,
I discovered I owe you my heart.

Sun and Shadow: Meetings

Lyrics: Mercedes Lackey   Music: Leslie Fish

(Kris: *Arrow's Flight*)

(When the "long version" of "Sun and Shadow" is sung, this is
    sung as a kind of prologue)

She dances in the shadows; like a shadow is her hair.
Her eyes hold midnight captive, like a phantom, fell and fair.
While the woodlarks sing the measures that her flying feet re-
    trace
She dances in the shadows like a dream of darkling grace.

He sings in summer sunlight to the cloudless summer skies;
His head is crowned with sunlight and the heavens match his
    eyes.
All the wildwood seems to listen to the singer's gladsome voice
He sings in summer sunlight and all those who hear rejoice.

She dances in the shadows, for a doom upon her lies;
That if once the sunlight touches her the Shadowdancer dies.
And on his line is this curse laid—that once the day is sped
In sleep like death he lies until again the night has fled.

One evening in the twilight that is neither day nor night,
The time part bred of shadow, and partly born of light,
A trembling Shadowdancer heard the voice of love and doom
That sang a song of sunlight through the gathering evening
    gloom.

A spell it cast upon her, and she followed in its wake
To where Sunsinger sang it, all unheeding, by her lake.
She saw the one that she must love until the day she died—
Bitter tears for bitter loving then Shadowdancer cried.

One evening in the twilight e'er his curse could work its will,
Sunsinger sang of sunlight by a lake serene and still—
When out among the shadow stepped a woman, fey and fair—
A woman sweet as twilight, with the shadows in her hair.

*   *   *

He saw her, and he loved her, and he knew his love was vain
For he was born of sunlight and must be the shadow's bane.
So e'er the curse could claim him, then, he shed one bitter tear
For he knew his only love must also be his only fear.

So now they meet at twilight, though they only meet to part.
Sad meetings, sadder partings, and the breaking of each heart.
Why blame them, if they pray for time or death to bring a
    cure?
For the sake of bitter loving, nonetheless they will endure.

Sun and Shadow

Lyrics: Mercedes Lackey   Music: Paul Espinoza

(Talia and Kris: *Arrow's Flight*)

"What has touched me, reaching deep
Piercing my ensorceled sleep?
Darkling lady, do you weep?
Am I the cause of your grieving?
Why do tears of balm and bane
Bathe my heart with bitter rain?
What is this longing? Why this pain?
What is this spell you are weaving?"

"Sunlight Singer, Morning's peer—
How I long for what I fear!
Not by my will are you here
How I wish I could free you!
Gladly in your arms I'd lie
But I dare not come you nigh
For if you touch me I shall die—
If I were wise I would flee you."

"Shadowdancer, dark and fell,
Lady that I love too well—
Won't you free me from this spell
That you have cast around me?

Star-eyed maid beyond compare,
Mist of twilight in your hair—
Why must you be so sweet and fair?
How is it that you have bound me?"

"In your eyes your soul lies bare
Hope is mingled with despair;
Sunborn lover do I dare
Trust my heart to your keeping?
Sunrise means that I must flee—
Moonrise steals your soul from me;
Nothing behind but agony,
Nothing before us but weeping."

"Sun and Shadow, dark and light;
Child of day and child of night,
Who can set our tale aright?
Is there no future but sorrow?
Will some power hear our plea—
Take the curse from you and me—
Grant us death, or set us free?
Dare we to hope for tomorrow?"

The Healer's Dilemma

Lyrics: Mercedes Lackey   Music: Bill Roper

(Devan: *Arrow's Fall*)

My child, the child of my heart, though never of my name,
Who shares my Gift; whose eyes, though young, are mine—the
    very same
Who shares my every thought, whose skillful hands I taught so
    well
Now hear the hardest lesson I shall ever have to tell.

Young Healer, I have taught you all I know of wounds and
    pain—
Of illnesses, and all the herbs of blessing and of bane—
Of all the usage of your Gift; all that I could impart—

And how you learned, young Healer, brought rejoicing to my
  heart.

But there is yet one lessoning I cannot give to you
For you must find your own way there—judge what is sound
  and true
This lesson is the cruelest ever Healer had to teach—
It is—what you must do when there are those you cannot
  reach.

However great your Gift there will be times when you will fail
There will be those you cannot help, your skill cannot prevail.
When you fight Death, and lose to Him, or what may yet be
  worse
You win—to find the wreck He left regards you with a curse.

And worst of all, and harder still, the times when it's a friend
Who looks to you to bring him peace and make his torment
  end—
What will you do, young Healer, when there's nothing you can
  do?
I can give only counsel, for the rest is up to you.

This only will I counsel you; that if you build a shell
Of armor close about you, then you close yourself in Hell.
And if your heart should harden, then your Gift will fade and
  die
And all that you have lived and learned will then become a lie.

My child, your Healing hands are guided by your Healing
  heart
And that is all the wisdom all my learning can impart.
You take this pain upon you as you challenge life unknown—
And there can be no answer here but one—and that's your
  own.

Herald's Lament

Lyrics: Mercedes Lackey   Music: C. J. Cherryh

(Dirk: *Arrow's Fall*)

A hand to aid along the road—
A laugh to lighten any load—
A place to bring a burdened heart
And heal the ache of sorrow's dart—
Who'd willing share in joy or tears
And help to ease the darkest fears
Or my soul like his own defend—
And all because he was my friend.

No grave could hold so free a soul.
I see him in the frisking foal—
I hear him laughing on the breeze
That stirs the very tops of trees.
He soars with falcons on the wing—
He is the song that nightbirds sing.
Death never dared him captive keep.
He lies not there. He does not sleep.

But—there is silence at my side
That haunts the place he used to ride.
And my Companion can't allay
The loss I have sustained this day.
How bleak the future now has grown
Since I must face it all alone.
My road is weary, dark and steep—
And it is for myself I weep.

For Talia

Lyrics: Mercedes Lackey   Music: Larry Warner and Kristoph Klover

(Dirk: *Arrow's Fall*)

The lady that I cherish is enamored of a fool—
A fool who lacks the wit to speak his mind,

A fool who often wears a mask indifferent and cool,
A fool who's often selfish, dense, and blind.

The lady that I cherish is enamored of a fool—
A fool too often wrapped in other cares,
Forgetting that his singlemindedness is wrong and cruel
To lock her out who gladly trouble shares.

The lady that I cherish is enamored of a fool
Who sometimes does not value what he holds
Until his loneliness confirms 'twere time his heart should rule
And the comfort of her love around him folds.

But though he must have hurt her without ever meaning to
Her temper never breaks and never frays,
And she forgives whatever careless thing that he may do
And loves him still despite his thoughtless ways.

She only smiles and says that there is nothing to forgive—
And I thank God she does so, for you see
I fear without her love and care this poor fool could not live—
The fool she loves and cherishes is me.

Kerowyn's Ride

Lyrics: Mercedes Lackey   Music: Leslie Fish

(This is a fairly common song in Valdemar,
although it originated several lands to the south.)

Kerowyn, Kerowyn, where are you going,
Dressed in men's clothing, a sword by your side,
Your face pale as death, and your eyes full of fury,
Kerowyn, Kerowyn, where do you ride?

Last night in the darkness foul raiders attacked us—
Our hall lies in ruins below—
They've stolen our treasure, and the bride of my brother
And to her side now I must go
To her aid now I must go.

* * *

Kerowyn, Kerowyn, where is your father?
Where is your brother? This fight should be theirs.
It is not seemly that maids should be warriors—
Your pride is your folly; go tend women's cares.

This is far more than a matter of honor
And more than a matter of pride—
She's only a child, all alone, all unaided
Though foolish and reckless beside,
Still now to her aid I must ride.

Grandmother, sorceress, I need a weapon—
I'm one against many—and I am afraid—
For the bastards have bought them a fell wizard's powers—
I can't hope to help her without magic aid.

Kerowyn, granddaughter, into your keeping
I now give the sword I once wore
"Need" is her name, yes, and great are her powers—
She'll serve you as many before—
Though her name be not found in men's lore.

Grandmother, grandmother, now you confuse me—
Was this a testing I got at your hand?
Whence comes this weapon of steel and of magic
And why do you put her now at my command?

Kerowyn, not for the weak or the coward
Is the path of the warrior maid.
Yes my child, you've been tested—now ride with my blessing
And trust in yourself and your blade.
Ride now, and go unafraid!

Threes

Lyrics: Mercedes Lackey   Music: Leslie Fish

> (Again: a similar song from the same region as
> "Kerowyn's Ride" that migrated northward.)

Deep into the stony hills, miles from town or hold
A troupe of guards comes riding, with a lady and her gold
She rides bemused among them, shrouded in her cloak of fur
Companioned by a maiden and a toothless, aged cur.
Three things see no end, a flower blighted ere it bloomed,
A message that miscarries and a journey that is doomed.

One among the guardsmen has a shifting, restless eye
And as they ride, he scans the hills that rise against the sky
He wears a sword and bracelet worth more than he can afford
And hidden in his baggage is a heavy, secret hoard.
Of three things be wary, of a feather on a cat
The shepherd eating mutton, and the guardsman that is fat.

Little does the lady care what all the guardsmen know—
That bandits ambush caravans that on these traderoads go.
In spite of tricks and clever traps and all that men can do
The brigands seem to always sense which trains are false or
    true.
Three things are most perilous—the shape that walks behind,
The ice that will not hold you and the spy you cannot find.

From ambush bandits screaming charge the packtrain and its
    prize
And all but four within the train are taken by surprise
And all but four are cut down as a woodsman fells a log;
The guardsman and the lady and the maiden and the dog.
Three things hold a secret—lady riding in a dream,
The dog that sounds no warning, and the maid who does not
    scream.

Then off the lady pulls her cloak, in armor she is clad—
Her sword is out and ready, and her eyes are fierce and glad.
The maiden makes a gesture, and the dog's a cur no more—

A wolf, sword-maid and sorceress now face the bandit corps.
Three things never anger, or you will not live for long,
A wolf with cubs, a man with power, and a woman's sense of
   wrong.

The lady and her sister by a single trader lone
Were hired out to try to lay a trap all of their own
And no one knew their plan except the two who rode that day
For what you do not know you cannot ever give away!
Three things is it better, far, that only two should know—
Where treasure hides, who shares your bed, and how to catch
   your foe!

The bandits growl a challenge, and the lady only grins
The sorceress bows mockingly, and then the fight begins!
When it ends there are but four left standing from that horde—
The witch, the wolf, the traitor and the woman with the
   sword!
Three things never trust in; the maiden sworn as pure,
The vows a king has given, and the ambush that is "sure."

They strip the traitor naked and then whip him on his way
Into the barren hillsides, like the folk he used to slay—
And what of all the maidens that this filth despoiled, then slew?
Why, as revenge, the sorceress makes him a woman too!
Three things trust above all else—the horse on which you ride,
The beast that guards your sleeping, and your sister at your side.